W9-AWB-542

THE
BELGARIAD
VOLUME TWO

By David and Leigh Eddings
Published by The Random House Publishing Group:

THE BELGARIAD

Book One: *Pawn of Prophecy*
Book Two: *Queen of Sorcery*
Book Three: *Magician's Gambit*
Book Four: *Castle of Wizardry*
Book Five: *Enchanters' End Game*

THE MALLOREON

Book One: *Guardians of the West*
Book Two: *King of the Murgos*
Book Three: *Demon Lord of Karanda*
Book Four: *Sorceress of Darshiva*
Book Five: *The Seeress of Kell*

BELGARATH THE SORCERER

POLGARA THE SORCERESS

THE RIVAN CODEX

THE ELENIUM

Book One: *The Diamond Throne*
Book Two: *The Ruby Knight*
Book Three: *The Sapphire Rose*

THE TAMULI

Book One: *Domes of Fire*
Book Two: *The Shining Ones*
Book Three: *The Hidden City*

THE REDEMPTION OF ALTHALUS

REGINA'S SONG

THE
BELGARIAD

VOLUME TWO

DAVID
EDDINGS

DEL REY

BALLANTINE BOOKS
NEW YORK

A Del Rey® Book
Published by The Random House Publishing Group

Copyright © 1984 by David Eddings
Preface copyright © 2002 by David Eddings

All rights reserved.

Published in the United States by Del Rey Books, an imprint of The Random House Publishing Group, a division of Random House, Inc., New York, and simultaneously in Canada
by Random House of Canada Limited, Toronto.

This work was originally published as two separate volumes by Ballantine Books as *Castle of
Wizardry* and *Enchanters' End Game* in 1984.

Del Rey is a registered trademark and the Del Rey colophon is a trademark of Random
House, Inc.

www.delreybooks.com

Library of Congress Control Number is available upon request from the publisher.

ISBN 0-345-45631-9

Maps by Shelly Shapiro
Cover design by David Stevenson
Cover illustration by Larry Schwinger

Manufactured in the United States of America

First Edition: September 2002

18 17 16 15 14 13

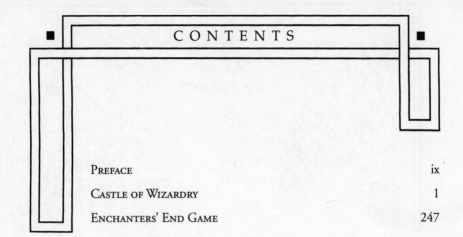

CONTENTS

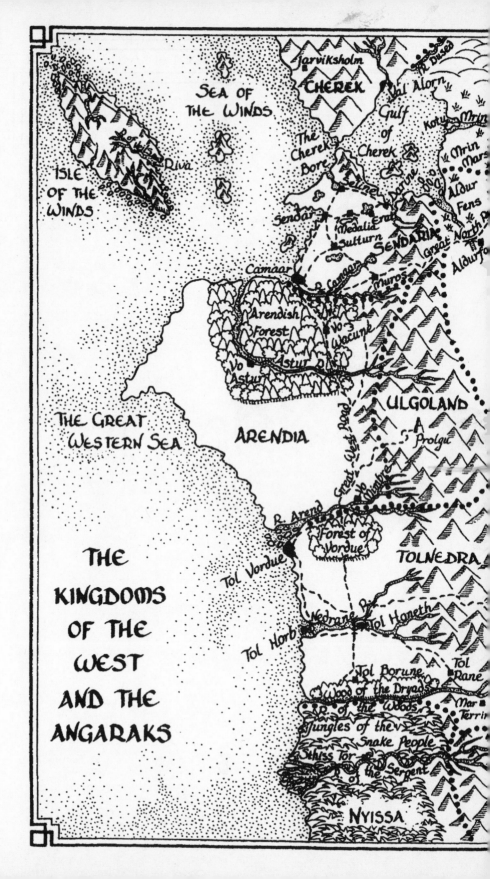

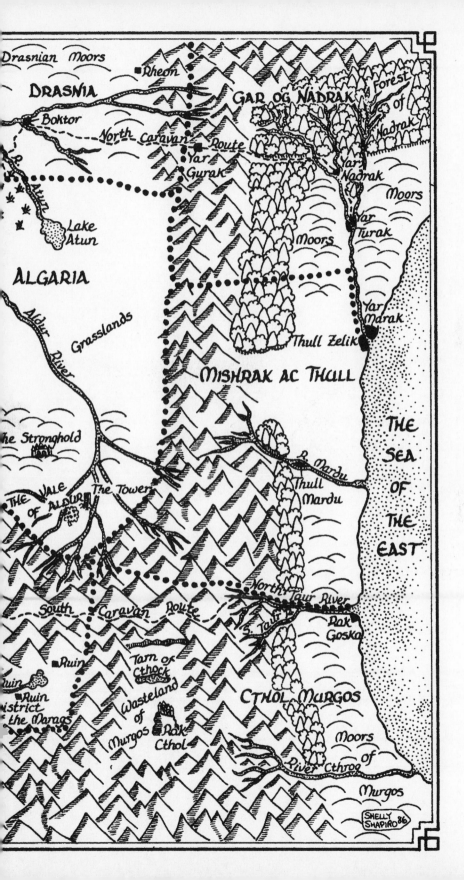

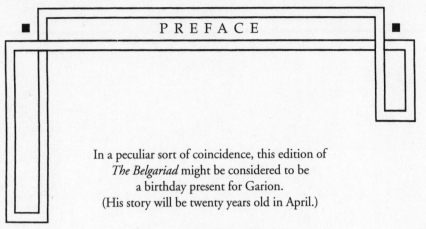

PREFACE

In a peculiar sort of coincidence, this edition of
The Belgariad might be considered to be
a birthday present for Garion.
(His story will be twenty years old in April.)

Many Happy Returns, Kid.

As we previously mentioned (in *The Rivan Codex*,) *The Belgariad* grew out of a map (or a doodle, to be more precise). I'd been working on a piece of literary tripe that even bored me, and I found myself sketching out a map of a place that existed only in my fevered imagination as a form of relaxation. (Sometimes referred to as "goofing off.") Geography is interesting, but it needs people to flesh it out, and people need all the assorted "ologies" to explain why they're doing all those peculiar things to each other.

My area of concentration as a college student had been contemporary American fiction, (Hemingway, Faulkner, Steinbeck, etc.) and I'd noticed that high fantasy lacked the gritty realism of *The Grapes of Wrath* or *For Whom the Bell Tolls*, so in a sense, our fantasies have been an experiment in form—"Realistic Fantasy," perhaps (or Fantastic Realism, take your pick). Evidently we did *something* right, since Garion is still wandering around out there charming the socks off readers all over the world in English (or translations into seventeen other languages).

The story itself is fairly elemental—Good vs. Evil, Nice Guys vs. Nasty Guys, (or Them vs. Us). It has the usual "Quest," the Magic (or Holy) Thingamajig, the Mighty Sorcerer, the Innocent Hero, and the Not Quite So Innocent Heroine— along with a widely varied group of Mighty Warriors with assorted character faults. It wanders around for five books until it finally climaxes with the traditional duel between "Our Hero" and the "Bad Guy." (Would it spoil anything for you if I tell you that our side wins?)

Looking back at this story, I should confess that many of the crucial incidents seem to have popped out of nowhere during the writing. I hardly think that "Divine Inspiration" played any part in that. "Wifely Inspiration" was significant, and so was "Editorial Inspiration," (although Lester Del Rey and I argued extensively during the writing—until Judy-Lynn Del Rey told me to quit picking on him). I suppose I could credit a subconscious game plan for the eventual success, but I lean strongly in the direction of "Dumb Luck."

Anyway, however it got here, it seems to be doing what it was supposed to do. Now I'll shut up, and let you read it for yourself.

Enjoy.
David Eddings

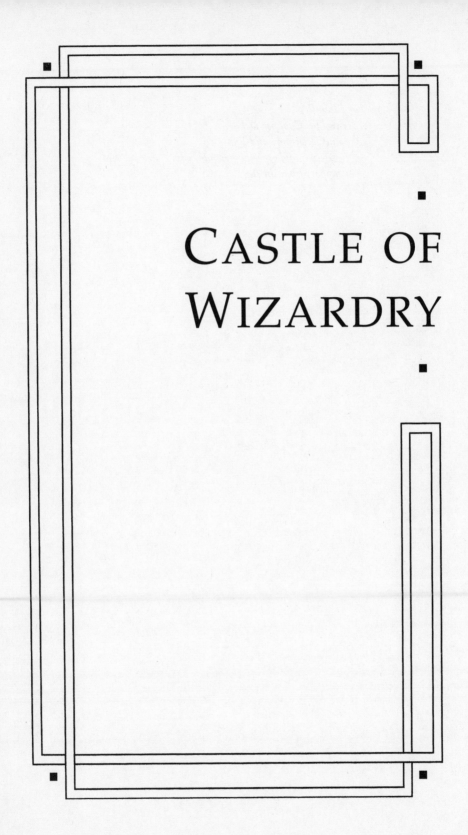

CASTLE OF
WIZARDRY

For Bibbidie,
    and for Chopper Jack
    and for Jimmy and Eddie
    —close and special friends who have given
    support from the start.

Being an account of how Riva Iron-grip became Guardian of the Orb of Aldur and of the evil wrought by Nyissa.
—BASED UPON *THE BOOK OF ALORN* AND
LATER ACCOUNTS

Now a time came when Cherek and his three sons went with Belgarath the Sorcerer into Mallorea. Together they sought to reclaim the Orb of Aldur, which had been stolen by the maimed God Torak. And when they came to the place in the iron tower of Torak where the orb was hidden, only Riva Iron-grip, youngest of the sons, dared seize the great jewel and bear it forth. For Riva alone was free of evil intent within his soul.

And when they were come again to the West, Belgarath gave unto Riva and his descendants eternal guardianship of the Orb, saying: "So long as the Orb rests with you and your line, so long shall the West be safe."

Then Riva took the Orb and sailed with his people to the Isle of the Winds. There, upon the one place where ships might land, Riva caused to be built a Citadel and a walled city around it, which men named *Riva*. It was a fortress city, built for war.

Within the Citadel was built a great hall, with a throne carved of black rock set against the wall. And men called this throne room the Hall of the Rivan King.

Then a deep sleep fell upon Riva, and Belar, Bear-God of the Alorns, appeared to him in a dream, saying: "Behold, Guardian of the Orb, I will cause two stars to fall from the sky. And thou shalt take up the two stars and place them in a fire and forge them. One shalt thou forge into a blade, the other into a hilt, and together they shall be a sword to guard the Orb of my brother Aldur."

When Riva awoke, he saw two stars fall and he sought and found them in the high mountains. And he did with them as Belar had instructed. But when it was done, the blade and hilt could not be joined. Then Riva cried out, "Behold, I have marred the work, for the sword will not become one."

A fox, which had sat nearby to watch him, said to Riva, "The work is not marred, Riva. Take the hilt and place the Orb upon it as a pommel stone." And when Riva did as the fox instructed, the Orb became one with the hilt. But blade and hilt were still unjoined. Again the fox counseled him. "Take the blade in your left hand and the hilt in the right and join them."

"They will not join. It is not possible," Riva said.

"Wise are you, indeed," the fox said, "to know what is not possible before you have made the attempt."

Then Riva was ashamed. He set blade and hilt together, and the blade passed into the hilt as a stick slides into water. The sword was joined forever.

The fox laughed and said, "Take the sword and smite the rock which stands before you."

Riva feared for the blade, lest the blow shatter it, but he smote the rock. The rock broke in two, and water gushed forth in a river and flowed down to the city below. And far to the east in the darkness of Mallorea, maimed Torak started up from his bed as a chill coursed through his heart.

Again the fox laughed. Then it ran away, but stopped to look back. Riva saw that it was a fox no longer, but the great silver wolf form of Belgarath.

Riva had the sword placed upon the face of the black rock wall that stood at the back of his throne with its blade downward so that the Orb at its pommel stood at the highest point. And the sword cleaved itself to the rock. None but Riva could take it down.

As the years passed, men saw that the Orb burned with a cold fire when Riva sat upon the throne; and when he took down the sword and raised it, it became a great tongue of blue flame.

In the early spring of the year after the sword was forged, a small boat came across the dark waters of the Sea of the Winds, moving without oars or sails. Alone within the boat was the fairest maid in all the world. Her name was Beldaran, beloved daughter of Belgarath, and she had come to be a wife to Riva. And Riva's heart melted with love for her, as had been ordained from the beginning of time.

In the year that followed the wedding of Beldaran to Riva, a son was born to them upon Erastide. And upon the right hand of this son of Riva was the mark of the Orb. Straightaway, Riva carried his infant manchild to the Hall of the Rivan King and placed the tiny hand upon the Orb. The Orb knew the child and glowed with love for him. Ever afterward, the hand of each descendant of Riva bore the mark of the Orb that it might know him and not destroy him when he touched it, for only one of Riva's line could touch the Orb in safety. With each touch of infant hand upon the Orb the bond between Riva's line and the Orb grew stronger. And with each joining, the brilliance of the Orb increased.

Thus it was in the city of Riva for a thousand years. Sometimes strangers sailed into the Sea of Winds, seeking trade, but the ships of Cherek, bound to defend the Isle of the Winds, fell upon the strangers and destroyed them. But in time, the Alorn Kings met and determined in council that these strangers were not the servants of Torak, but bowed instead to the God Nedra. Then they agreed to let the ships sail the Sea of the Winds unmolested. "For," the Rivan King told his fellow monarchs, "a time may come when the sons of Nedra will join with us in our struggle against the Angaraks of Torak One-Eye. Let us not offend Nedra by sinking the ships of his children." The ruler of Riva spoke wisely, and the Alorn Kings agreed, knowing that the world was changing.

Then treaties were signed with the sons of Nedra, who took a childish delight in signing scraps of parchment. But when they sailed into the harbor at Riva, with their ships bearing full loads of gaudy trinkets upon which they placed high value, the Rivan King laughed at their folly and closed the gates of the city to them.

The sons of Nedra importuned their king, whom they called Emperor, to force the city gates so that they might hawk their wares in the streets, and the Emperor sent his army to the Isle. Now to permit these strangers from the kingdom they called Tolnedra passage upon the Sea was one thing, but to let them land an army at the gates of Riva without challenge was quite another. The Rivan King ordered that the strand before the city be cleared and the harbor be swept clean of the ships of Tolnedra. And it was done.

Great was the wrath of the Emperor of Tolnedra. He assembled his armies to cross the Sea of the Winds and do war. Then the peace-loving Alorns held council to try reason upon this rash Emperor. And they sent out a message to advise him that, should he persist, they would rise up and destroy Emperor and kingdom and sweep the wreckage thereof into the sea. And the Emperor gave heed to this quiet remonstrance and abandoned his desperate adventure.

As years passed and the Rivan King realized that these merchants from Tolnedra were harmless, he allowed them to build a village upon the strand before his city and there to display their useless goods. Their desperation to sell or trade came to amuse him, and he asked his people to buy some few items from them—though no purpose could be found for the goods thus purchased.

Then, four thousand and two years from the day when Accursed Torak raised the stolen Orb and cracked open the world, other strange people came to the village which the sons of Nedra had built outside the walls of Riva. And it was learned of these strangers that they were the sons of the God Issa. They called themselves Ny-Issans, and they claimed that their ruler was a woman, which seemed unnatural to all who heard. The name of this queen was Salmissra.

They came in dissembling guise, saying that they brought rich gifts from their queen for the Rivan King and his family. Hearing this, Gorek the Wise, aged king in the line of Riva, grew curious to know more of these children of Issa and their queen. With his wife, his two sons and their wives, and all his royal grandchildren, he went from out the fortress and the city to visit the pavilion of the Nyissans, to greet them courteously, and to receive from them the valueless gifts sent by the harlot of Sthiss Tor. With smiles of greeting, the Rivan King and his family were welcomed into the pavilion of the strangers.

Then the foul and accursed sons of Issa struck at all who were the fruit and the seed of the line of Riva. And venom was anointed upon their weapons, so that the merest scratch was death.

Mighty even in age, Gorek struggled with the assassins—not to save himself, for he felt death in his veins from the first blow—but to save at least one of his grandsons that his line might continue. Alas, all were doomed, save only one child who fled and cast himself into the sea. When Gorek saw this, he covered his head with his cloak, groaned, and fell dying beneath the knives of Nyissa.

When word of this reached Brand, Warder of the Citadel, his wrath was dreadful. The traitorous assassins were overcome, and Brand questioned each in turn in ways that made brave men tremble. And the truth was wrung from them. Gorek and his family had been foully murdered at the instructions of Salmissra, Snake Queen of the Nyissans.

Of the child who had cast himself into the sea there was no trace. One assassin claimed that he had seen a snowy owl swoop down and bear the child away, but he was not believed, though even the severest urging would not make him change his story.

Then all Aloria made dreadful war upon the sons of Issa and tore down their cities and put all they could find to the sword. And in her final hour, Salmissra confessed that the evil deed had been done at the urging of Torak One-Eye and his servant Zedar.

Thus there was no longer a Rivan King and Guardian of the Orb, though Brand and those of the same name who followed reluctantly took up rule of Riva. Rumor, ever vagrant, persisted in the years that followed, saying that the seed of Riva still lay hidden in some remote land. But gray-cloaked Rivans scoured the world in search of him and never found him.

The sword remained as Riva had placed it, and the Orb was still affixed to its pommel, though now the jewel was ever dull and seeming without life. And men began to feel that so long as the Orb was there, the West was safe, even though there was no Rivan King. Nor did there seem aught of danger that the Orb could ever be removed, since any man who touched it would be instantly and utterly consumed, were he not truly of the line of Riva.

But now that his minions had removed the Rivan King and Guardian of the Orb, Torak One-Eye again dared begin plans for the conquest of the West. And after many years, he led forth an enormous army of Angaraks to destroy all who opposed him. His hordes raved through Algaria and down through Arendia, to the city of Vo Mimbre.

Now Belgarath and his daughter Polgara the Sorceress came to the one who was Brand and Warder of Riva to advise and counsel with him. With them, Brand led his army to Vo Mimbre. And in the bloody battle before that city, Brand drew upon the power of the Orb to overcome Torak. Zedar spirited the body of his master away and hid it, but not all the disciple's skill could again awaken his God. And again men of the West felt safe, protected by the Orb and Aldur.

Now there came rumors of a prophecy that a Rivan King, true seed of the line of Riva, should again appear and sit upon the throne in the Hall of the Rivan King. And in later years, some claimed that each daughter of an Emperor of Tolnedra appeared on her sixteenth birthday to be the bride of the new king, should he appear. But few regarded such tales. Time passed into centuries, and still the West was safe. The Orb remained, quiet and dark upon the pommel of the sword. And somewhere fearful Torak was said to sleep until the return of the Rivan King—which came to mean never.

And thus the account should be ended. But no true account can ever end. And nothing can ever be safe or sure so long as cunning men plot to steal or destroy.

Again, long centuries passed. And then new rumors came, this time to disturb those in the highest places of power. And it was whispered that somehow the Orb had been stolen. Then Belgarath and Polgara were seen to be moving through the lands of the West again. This time they took with them a young man named Garion who named Belgarath his grandfather and called Polgara his aunt. And as they moved through the kingdoms, they gathered upon them a strange company.

To the Alorn Kings who gathered in council, Belgarath revealed that it was the Apostate Zedar who had somehow contrived to steal the Orb from the sword and who was even then fleeing with it to the East, presumably to use it to awaken sleeping Torak. And it was there Belgarath must go with his company to rescue it.

Then Belgarath discovered that Zedar had found a boy of total innocence who could safely touch the Orb. But now the way led to the grim and dangerous head-quarters of the Grolim priests of Torak, where the magician Ctuchik had seized the Orb and the boy from Zedar.

In time this quest of Belgarath and his company to regain the Orb would come to be known as the *Belgariad*. But the end thereof lay entangled within the Prophecy. And even to the Prophecy was the ultimate conclusion unknown.

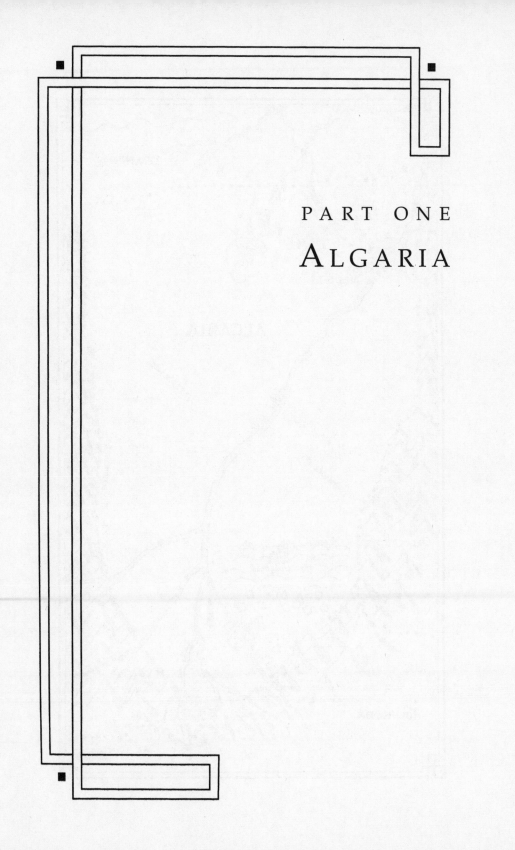

PART ONE

ALGARIA

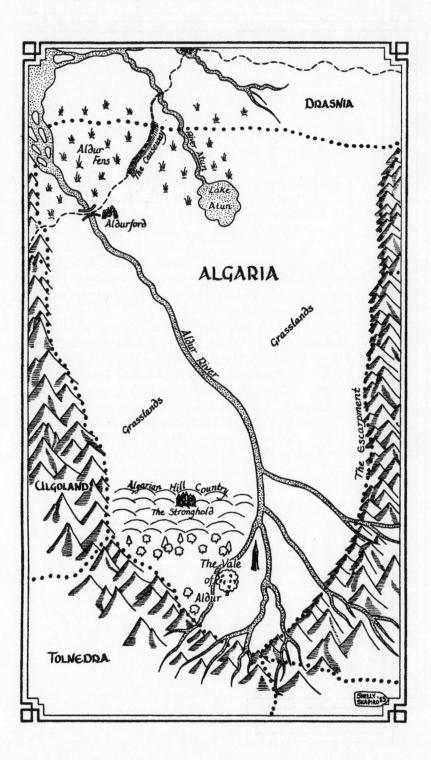

C tuchik was dead—and more than dead—and the earth itself heaved and groaned in the aftershock of his destruction. Garion and the others fled down through the dim galleries that honeycombed the swaying basalt pinnacle, with the rocks grinding and cracking about them and fragments shattering away from the ceilings and raining down on them in the darkness. Even as he ran, Garion's mind jerked and veered, his thoughts tumbling over each other chaotically, stunned out of all coherence by the enormity of what had just happened. Flight was a desperate need, and he fled without thought or even awareness, his running steps as mechanical as his heartbeat.

His ears seemed full of a swelling, exultant song that rang and soared in the vaults of his mind, erasing thought and filling him with stupefied wonder. Through all his confusion, however, he was sharply conscious of the trusting touch of the small hand he held in his. The little boy they had found in Ctuchik's grim turret ran beside him with the Orb of Aldur clasped tightly to his little chest. Garion knew that it was the Orb that filled his mind with song. It had whispered to him as they had mounted the steps of the turret, and its song had soared as he had entered the room where it had lain. It was the song of the Orb that obliterated all thought shock or the thunderous detonation that had destroyed Ctuchik and tumbled Belgarath across the floor like a rag doll or the deep sullen boom of the earthquake that had followed.

Garion struggled with it as he ran, trying desperately to pull his wits into some kind of order, but the song intruded on his every effort, scattering his mind so that chance impression and random memory fluttered and scurried this way and that and left him to flee without design or direction.

The dank reek of the slave pens lying just beneath the disintegrating city of Rak Cthol came sharply through the shadowy galleries. As if suddenly awakened by that single stimulus, a flood of memories of other smells crashed in on Garion's consciousness—the warm smell of fresh-baked bread in Aunt Pol's kitchen back at Faldor's farm, the salt smell of the sea when they had reached Darine on the north coast of Sendaria on the first leg of their quest for the Orb, the stink of the swamps and jungles of Nyissa, the stomach-turning smell of the burning bodies of the sacrificed slaves in the Temple of Torak which even now shattered and fell in upon itself among the collapsing walls of Rak Cthol. But, oddly, the smell that came sharpest to his confused memory was the sun-warmed scent of Princess Ce'Nedra's hair.

"Garion!" Aunt Pol's voice came sharply to him in the near dark through which they ran. "Watch where you're going!" And he struggled to pull his mind back from its wandering even as he stumbled over a pile of broken rock where a large stretch of ceiling had fallen to the floor.

The terrified wails of the imprisoned slaves locked in clammy cells rose all around them now, joining in a weird counterharmony with the rumble and boom of earthquake. Other sounds came from the darkness as well—confused shouts in harshly accented Murgo voices, the lurching stagger of running feet, the clanging of an unlatched iron cell door swinging wildly as the huge rock pinnacle swayed and shuddered and heaved in the surging roll. Dust billowed through the dark caves, a thick, choking rock dust that stung their eyes and made them all cough almost continually as they clambered over the broken rubble.

Garion carefully lifted the trusting little boy over the pile of shattered rock, and the child looked into his face, calm and smiling despite the chaos of noise and stink all around them in the oppressive dimness. He started to set the child down again, but changed his mind. It would be easier and safer to carry the boy. He turned to go on along the passageway, but he recoiled sharply as his foot came down on something soft. He peered at the floor, then felt his stomach suddenly heave with revulsion as he saw that he had stepped on a lifeless human hand protruding from the rockfall.

They ran on through the heaving darkness with the black Murgo robes which had disguised them flapping around their legs and the dust still thick in the air about them.

"Stop!" Relg, the Ulgo zealot, raised his hand and stood with his head cocked to one side, listening intently.

"Not here!" Barak told him, still lumbering forward with the dazed Belgarath in his arms. "Move, Relg!"

"Be still!" Relg ordered. "I'm trying to listen." Then he shook his head. "Go back!" he barked, turning quickly and pushing at them. "Run!"

"There are Murgos back there!" Barak objected.

"Run!" Relg repeated. "The side of the mountain's breaking away!"

Even as they turned, a new and dreadful creaking roar surrounded them. Screeching in protest, the rock ripped apart with a long, hideous tearing. A sudden flood of light filled the gallery along which they fled as a great crack opened in the side of the basalt peak, widening ponderously as a vast chunk of the mountainside toppled slowly outward to fall to the floor of the wasteland thousands of feet below. The red glow of the new-risen sun was blinding as the dark world of the caves was violently opened, and the great wound in the side of the peak revealed a dozen or more dark openings both above and beneath, where caves suddenly ran out into nothingness.

"There!" a shout came from overhead. Garion jerked his head around. Perhaps fifty feet above and out along the sharp angle of the face, a half dozen black-robed Murgos, swords drawn, stood in a cave mouth with the dust billowing about them. One was pointing excitedly at the fleeing fugitives. And then the peak heaved again, and another great slab of rock sheared away, carrying the shrieking Murgos into the abyss beneath.

"Run!" Relg shouted again, and they all pounded along at his heels, back into the darkness of the shuddering passageway.

"Stop a minute," Barak gasped, plowing to a sudden halt after they had retreated several hundred yards. "Let me get my breath." He lowered Belgarath to the floor, his huge chest heaving.

"Can I help thee, my Lord?" Mandorallen offered quickly.

"No," Barak panted. "I can manage all right, I'm just a little winded." The big man peered around. "What happened back there? What set all this off?"

"Belgarath and Ctuchik had a bit of a disagreement," Silk told him with sardonic understatement. "It got a little out of hand toward the end."

"What happened to Ctuchik?" Barak asked, still gasping for breath. "I didn't see anybody else when Mandorallen and I broke into that room."

"He destroyed himself," Polgara replied, kneeling to examine Belgarath's face.

"We saw no body, my Lady," Mandorallen noted, peering into the darkness with his great broadsword in his hand.

"There wasn't that much left of him," Silk said.

"Are we safe here?" Polgara asked Relg.

The Ulgo set the side of his head against the wall of the passageway, listening intently. Then he nodded. "For the moment," he replied.

"Let's stop here for a while then. I want to have a look at my father. Make me some light."

Relg fumbled in the pouches at his belt and mixed the two substances that gave off that faint Ulgo light.

Silk looked curiously at Polgara. "What really happened?" he asked her. "Did Belgarath do that to Ctuchik?"

She shook her head, her hands lightly touching her father's chest. "Ctuchik tried to unmake the Orb for some reason," she said. "Something happened to frighten him so much that he forgot the first rule."

A momentary flicker of memory came to Garion as he set the little boy down on his feet—that brief glimpse of Ctuchik's mind just before the Grolim had spoken the fatal "Be Not" that had exploded him into nothingness. Once again he caught that single image that had risen in the High Priest's mind—the image of himself holding the Orb in his hand—and he felt the blind, unreasoning panic the image had caused Ctuchik. Why? Why would that have frightened the Grolim into that deadly mistake? "What happened to him, Aunt Pol?" he asked. For some reason he had to know.

"He no longer exists," she replied. "Even the substance that formed him is gone."

"That's not what I meant," Garion started to object, but Barak was already speaking.

"Did he destroy the Orb?" the big man asked with a kind of weak sickness in his voice.

"Nothing can destroy the Orb," she told him calmly.

"Where is it then?"

The little boy pulled his hand free from Garion's and went confidently to the big Cherek. "Errand?" he asked, holding out the round, gray stone in his hand.

Barak recoiled from the offered stone. "Belar!" he swore, quickly putting his hands behind his back. "Make him stop waving it around like that, Polgara. Doesn't he know how dangerous it is?"

"I doubt it."

"How's Belgarath?" Silk asked.

"His heart's still strong," Polgara replied. "He's exhausted, though. The fight nearly killed him."

With a long, echoing shudder the quaking subsided, and the silence seemed very loud. "Is it over?" Durnik asked, looking around nervously.

"Probably not," Relg replied, his voice hushed in the sudden quiet. "An earthquake usually goes on for quite some time."

Barak was peering curiously at the little boy. "Where did he come from?" he asked, his rumbling voice also subdued.

"He was in the turret with Ctuchik," Polgara told him. "He's the child Zedar raised to steal the Orb."

"He doesn't look all that much like a thief."

"He isn't precisely." She looked gravely at the blond-headed waif. "Somebody's going to have to keep an eye on him," she observed. "There's something very peculiar about him. After we get down, I'll look into it, but I've got too much on my mind for that at the moment."

"Could it be the Orb?" Silk asked curiously. "I've heard that it has strange effects on people."

"Perhaps that's it." But she didn't sound very convinced. "Keep him with you, Garion, and don't let him lose the Orb."

"Why me?" He said it without thinking.

She gave him a level gaze.

"All right, Aunt Pol." He knew there was no point in arguing with her.

"What was that?" Barak asked, holding up his hand for silence.

Somewhere off in the darkness there was the murmur of voices—harsh, guttural voices.

"Murgos!" Silk whispered sharply, his hand going to his dagger.

"How many?" Barak asked Aunt Pol.

"Five," she replied. "No—six. One's lagging behind."

"Are any of them Grolims?"

She shook her head.

"Let's go, Mandorallen," the big Cherek muttered, grimly drawing his sword.

The knight nodded, shifting his own broadsword in his hands.

"Wait here," Barak whispered to the rest of them. "We shouldn't be long." And then he and Mandorallen moved off into the darkness, their black Murgo robes blending into the shadows.

The others waited, their ears straining to catch any sound. Once again that strange song began to intrude itself upon Garion's awareness, and once again his thoughts scattered before its compulsion. Somewhere a long, hissing slither of dislodged pebbles rattled down a slope, and that sound raised a confused welter of memory in him. He seemed to hear the ring of Durnik's hammer on the anvil at Faldor's farm, and then the plodding step of the horses and the creak of the wagons in which they had carried turnips to Darine back when this had all begun. As clearly as if he were there, he heard again the squealing rush of the boar he had killed in the snowy woods outside Val Alorn, and then the aching song of the Arendish serf-boy's flute that had soared to the sky from the stump-dotted field where Asharak the Murgo had watched with hate and fear on his scarred face.

Garion shook his head, trying to clear his thoughts, but the song drew him back into that bemused reverie. Sharply, he heard the awful, hissing crackle of Asharak burning beneath the vast, ancient trees in the Wood of the Dryads and heard the Grolim's desperate plea, "Master, have mercy." Then there were the screams in Salmissra's palace as Barak, transformed into that dreadful bear shape, clawed and ripped his way toward the throne room with Aunt Pol in her icy fury striding at his side.

And then the voice that had always been in his mind was there again. *"Stop fighting with it."*

"What is it?" Garion demanded, trying to focus his thoughts.

"It's the Orb."

"What's it doing?"

"It wants to know you. This is its way of finding things out."

"Can't it wait? We don't really have time just now."

"You can try to explain that, if you'd like." The voice sounded amused. *"It might listen, but I doubt it. It's been waiting for you for a very long time."*

"Why me?"

"Don't you ever get tired of saying that?"

"Is it doing the same thing to the others?"

"To a lesser degree. You might as well relax. One way or another, it's going to get what it wants."

There was a sudden ring of steel against steel somewhere off in the dark passageways and a startled cry. Then Garion heard the crunch of blows, and someone groaned. After that, there was silence.

A few moments later they heard the scuff of footsteps, and Barak and Mandorallen returned. "We couldn't find that one who was coming along behind the rest of them," Barak reported. "Is Belgarath showing any signs of coming around yet?"

Polgara shook her head. "He's still completely dazed," she replied.

"I'll carry him then. We'd better go. It's a long way back down, and these caves are going to be full of Murgos before long."

"In a moment," she said. "Relg, do you know where we are?"

"Roughly."

"Take us back to the place where we left the slave woman," she instructed in a tone that tolerated no objection.

Relg's face went hard, but he said nothing.

Barak bent and picked up the unconscious Belgarath. Garion held out his arms, and the little boy obediently came to him, the Orb still held protectively against his chest. The child seemed peculiarly light, and Garion carried him with almost no effort. Relg lifted his faintly glowing wooden bowl to illuminate their path, and they started out again, twisting, turning, following a zigzag course that went deeper and deeper into the gloomy caves. The darkness of the peak above them seemed to bear down on Garion's shoulders with a greater and greater weight the farther they went. The song in his mind swelled again, and the faint light Relg carried sent his thoughts roving once more. Now that he understood what was happening, it seemed to go more easily. The song opened his mind, and the Orb leeched out every thought and memory, passing through his life with a light, flickering touch. It had a peculiar kind of curiosity, lingering often on things Garion did not think were all that important and barely touching matters that had seemed so dreadfully urgent when they had occurred. It traced out in detail each step they had taken in their long journey to Rak Cthol. It passed with them to the crystal chamber in the mountains above Maragor where Garion had touched the stillborn colt and given life in that oddly necessary act of atonement that had somehow made up for the burning of Asharak. It went down with them into the Vale where Garion had turned over the large white rock in his first conscious attempt to use the Will and the Word objectively. It scarcely noticed the dreadful fight with Grul the Eldrak nor the visit to the caves of Ulgo, but seemed to have a great curiosity about the shield of imagining which Garion and Aunt Pol had erected to conceal their movements from the searching minds of the Grolims as they had approached Rak Cthol. It ignored the death of Brill and the sickening ceremonies in the Temple of Torak, but lingered instead on the conversation between Belgarath and Ctuchik in the Grolim High Priest's hanging turret. And then, most peculiarly, it went back to sift through every one of Garion's memories of Princess Ce'Nedra— of the way the sun caught her coppery hair, of the lithe grace of her movements, of her scent, of each unconscious gesture, of the flicker and play of emotion across her tiny, exquisite face. It lingered on her in a way that Garion eventually found unsettling. At the same time he found himself a bit surprised that so much of what the princess had said and done had stuck so firmly in his memory.

"Garion," Aunt Pol said, "what *is* the matter with you? I told you to hold on to the child. Pay attention. This isn't the time for daydreaming."

"I wasn't. I was—" How could he explain it?

"You were what?"

"Nothing."

They moved on, and there were periodic tremors as the earth settled uneasily. The huge basalt pinnacle swayed and groaned each time the earth shuddered and convulsed under its base; and at each new quiver, they stopped, almost fearing to breathe.

"How far down have we come?" Silk asked, looking around nervously.

"A thousand feet perhaps," Relg replied.

"That's all? We'll be penned up in here for a week at this rate."

Relg shrugged his heavy shoulders. "It will take as long as it takes," he said in his harsh voice as they moved on.

There were Murgos in the next gallery, and another nasty little fight in the darkness. Mandorallen was limping when he came back.

"Why didn't you wait for me?" Barak demanded crossly.

Mandorallen shrugged. "They were but three, my Lord."

"There's just no point in trying to talk to you, do you know that?" Barak sounded disgusted.

"Are you all right?" Polgara asked the knight.

"A mere scratch, my Lady," Mandorallen replied indifferently. "It is of no moment."

The rock floor of the gallery shuddered and heaved again, and the booming noise echoed up through the caves. They all stood frozen, but the uneasy movement of the earth subsided after a few moments.

They moved steadily downward through the passageways and caves. The aftershocks of the earthquake that had shattered Rak Cthol and sent Ctuchik's turret crashing to the floor of the wasteland of Murgos continued at intervals. At one point, hours later it seemed, a party of Murgos, perhaps a dozen strong, passed through a gallery not far ahead, their torches casting flickering shadows on the walls and their harsh voices echoing. After a brief, whispered conference, Barak and Mandorallen let them go by unmolested and unaware of the terrible violence lurking in the shadows not twenty yards away. After they were out of earshot, Relg uncovered his light again and selected yet another passageway. They moved on, descending, twisting, zigzagging their way down through the caves toward the foot of the pinnacle and the dubious safety of the wasteland which lay outside.

While the song of the Orb did not diminish in any way, Garion was at least able to think as he followed Silk along the twisting passageways with the little boy in his arms. He thought that perhaps it was because he had grown at least partially accustomed to it—or maybe its attention was concentrated on one of the others.

They had done it; that was the amazing thing. Despite all the odds against them, they had retrieved the Orb. The search that had so abruptly interrupted his quiet life at Faldor's farm was over, but it had changed him in so many ways that the boy who had crept out through the gate at Faldor's farm in the middle of a windswept autumn night no longer even existed. Garion could feel the power he had discovered within himself even now and he knew that power was there for a reason. There had been hints along the way—vague, half-spoken, sometimes only implied—that the return of the Orb to its proper place was only a beginning of something much larger and much more serious. Garion was absolutely certain that this was not the end of it.

"It's about time," the dry voice in his mind said.

"What's that supposed to mean?"

"Why do I have to explain this every single time?"

"Explain what?"

"That I know what you're thinking. It's not as if we were completely separate, you know."

"All right, then. Where do we go from here?"

"To Riva."

"And after that?"

"We'll see."

"You aren't going to tell me?"

"No. Not yet. You haven't come nearly as far as you think you have. There's still a very long way to go."

"If you aren't going to tell me anything, why don't you just leave me alone?"

"I just wanted to advise you not to make any long-term plans. The recovery of the Orb was only a step—an important one—but only a beginning."

And then, as if mention of it somehow reminded the Orb of Garion's presence, its song returned in full force, and Garion's concentration dissolved.

Not much later, Relg stopped, lifting the faint light aloft.

"What's the trouble?" Barak demanded, lowering Belgarath to the floor again.

"The ceiling fell in," Relg replied, pointing at the rubble choking the passageway ahead. "We can't get through." He looked at Aunt Pol. "I'm sorry," he said, and Garion felt that he really meant it. "That woman we left down here is on the other side of the cave-in."

"Find another way," she told him shortly.

"There isn't any. This was the only passageway leading to the pool where we found her."

"We'll have to clear it then."

Relg shook his head gravely. "We'd just bring more of it down on top of us. It probably fell in on her as well—at least we can hope so."

"Isn't that just a bit contemptible, Relg?" Silk asked pointedly.

The Ulgo turned to regard the little man. "She has water there and sufficient air to breathe. If the cave-in didn't kill her, she could live for weeks before she starves to death." There was a peculiar, quiet regret in Relg's voice.

Silk stared at him for a moment. "Sorry, Relg," he said finally. "I misunderstood."

"People who live in caves have no desire to see anyone trapped like that."

Polgara, however, was considering the rubble-blocked passageway. "We have to get her out of there," she declared.

"Relg could be right, you know," Barak pointed out. "For all we know, she's buried under half the mountain."

She shook her head. "No," she disagreed. "Taiba's still alive, and we can't leave without her. She's as important to all of this as any one of us." She turned back to Relg. "You'll have to go get her," she told him firmly.

Relg's large, dark eyes widened. "You can't ask that," he protested.

"There's no alternative."

"You can do it, Relg," Durnik encouraged the zealot. "You can go through the rock and bring her out the same way you carried Silk out of that pit where Taur Urgas had him."

Relg had begun to tremble violently. "I can't!" his voice was choked. "I'd have to touch her—put my hands on her. It's sin."

"This is most uncharitable of thee, Relg," Mandorallen told him. "There is no sin in giving aid to the weak and helpless. Consideration for the unfortunate is a paramount responsibility of all decent men, and no force in all the world can corrupt the pure spirit. If compassion doth not move thee to fly to her aid, then mayest thou not perhaps regard her rescue a test of thy purity?"

"You don't understand," Relg told him in an anguished voice. He turned back to Polgara. "Don't make me do this, I beg you."

"You must," she replied quietly. "I'm sorry, Relg, but there's no other way."

A dozen emotions played across the fanatic's face as he shrank under Aunt Pol's unrelenting gaze. Then with a strangled cry, he turned and put his hand to the solid rockface at the side of the passageway. With a dreadful concentration, he pushed his fingers into the rock, demonstrating once more his uncanny ability to slip his very substance through seemingly unyielding stone.

Silk quickly turned his back. "I can't stand to watch that," the little man choked. And then Relg was gone, submerged in the rock.

"Why does he make so much fuss about touching people?" Barak demanded.

But Garion knew why. His enforced companionship with the ranting zealot during the ride across Algaria had given him a sharp insight into the workings of Relg's mind. The harsh-voiced denunciations of the sins of others served primarily to conceal Relg's own weakness. Garion had listened for hours at a time to hysterical and sometimes incoherent confessions about the lustful thoughts that raged through the fanatic's mind almost continually. Taiba, the lush-bodied Marag slave woman, would represent for Relg the ultimate temptation, and he would fear her more than death itself.

In silence they waited. Somewhere a slow drip of water measured the passing seconds. The earth shuddered from time to time as the last uneasy shocks of earthquake trembled beneath their feet. The minutes dragged on in the dim cavern.

And then there was a flicker of movement, and Relg emerged from the rock wall carrying the half-naked Taiba. Her arms were desperately clasped about his neck, and her face was buried in his shoulder. She was whimpering in terror and trembling uncontrollably.

Relg's face was twisted into an agony. Tears of anguish streamed openly from his eyes, and his teeth were clenched as if he were in the grip of intolerable pain. His arms, however, cradled the terrified slave woman protectively, almost gently, and even when they were free of the rock, he held her closely against him as if he intended to hold her thus forever.

CHAPTER TWO

It was noon by the time they reached the foot of the basalt tower and the large cave where they had left the horses. Silk went to the cave mouth to stand watch as Barak carefully lowered Belgarath to the floor. "He's heavier than he looks," the big man grunted, wiping the sweat from his face. "Shouldn't he be starting to come around?"

"It may be days before he's fully conscious," Polgara replied. "Just cover him and let him sleep."

"How's he going to ride?"

"I'll take care of that."

"Nobody's going to be riding anywhere for a while," Silk announced from the narrow mouth of the cave. "The Murgos are swarming around out there like hornets."

"We'll wait until dark," Polgara decided. "We all need some rest anyway." She pushed back the hood of her Murgo robe and went to one of the packs they had piled against the cave wall when they had entered the night before. "I'll see about something to eat, then you'd all better sleep."

Taiba, the slave woman, wrapped once again in Garion's cloak, had been watching Relg almost continually. Her large, violet eyes glowed with gratitude mingled with a faint puzzlement. "You saved my life," she said to him in a rich, throaty voice. She leaned slightly toward him as she spoke. It was an unconscious gesture, Garion was certain, but it was distinctly noticeable. "Thank you," she added, her hand moving to rest lightly on the zealot's arm.

Relg cringed back from her. "Don't touch me," he gasped.

She stared at him in amazement, her hand still half-extended.

"You must *never* put your hands on me," he told her. "Never."

Taiba's look was incredulous. Her life had been spent almost entirely in darkness, and she had never learned to keep her emotions from showing on her face. Amazement gave way to humiliation, and her expression settled then into a kind of stiff, sullen pout as she turned quickly away from the man who had just so harshly rejected her. The cloak slipped from her shoulders as she turned, and the few rags she had for clothing scarcely concealed her nakedness. Despite her tangled hair and the dirty smudges on her limbs, there was a lush, inviting ripeness about her. Relg stared at her and he began to tremble. Then he quickly turned, moved as far away from her as possible, and dropped to his knees, praying desperately and pressing his face against the rocky floor of the cave.

"Is he all right?" Taiba asked quickly.

"He's got some problems," Barak replied. "You'll get used to it."

"Taiba," Polgara said. "Come over here." She looked critically at the woman's scanty clothing. "We're going to have to get something together for you to wear. It's very cold outside. There are other reasons too, it appears."

"I'll see what I can find in the packs," Durnik offered. "We'll need something for the boy too, I think. That smock of his doesn't look any too warm." He looked over at the child, who was curiously examining the horses.

"You won't need to bother about me," Taiba told them. "There's nothing out there for me. As soon as you leave, I'm going back to Rak Cthol."

"What are you talking about?" Polgara asked her sharply.

"I still have something to settle with Ctuchik," Taiba replied, fingering her rusty knife.

Silk laughed from the cave mouth. "We took care of that for you. Rak Cthol's falling to pieces up there, and there isn't enough left of Ctuchik to make a smudge on the floor."

"Dead?" she gasped. "How?"

"You wouldn't believe it," Silk told her.

"Did he suffer?" She said it with a terrible eagerness.

"More than you could ever imagine," Polgara replied.

Taiba drew in a long, shuddering breath, and then she began to cry. Aunt Pol opened her arms and took the sobbing woman into them, comforting her even as she had comforted Garion so often when he was small.

Garion sank wearily to the floor, resting his back against the rocky wall of the cave. Waves of exhaustion washed over him, and a great lassitude drained him of all consciously directed thought. Once again the Orb sang to him, but lulling now. Its curiosity about him apparently was satisfied, and its song seemed to be there only to maintain the contact between them. Garion was too tired even to be curious about why the stone took such pleasure in his company.

The little boy turned from his curious examination of the horses and went to where Taiba sat with one of Aunt Pol's arms about her shoulders. He looked puzzled, and reached out with one hand to touch his fingers to her tear-streaked face.

"What does he want?" Taiba asked.

"He's probably never seen tears before," Aunt Pol replied.

Taiba stared at the child's serious little face, then suddenly laughed through her tears and gave him a quick embrace.

The little boy smiled then. "Errand?" he asked, offering her the Orb.

"Don't take it, Taiba," Polgara told her very quietly. "Don't even touch it."

Taiba looked at the smiling child and shook her head.

The little boy sighed, then came across the cave, sat down beside Garion, and nestled against him.

Barak had gone a short distance back up the passageway they had followed; now he returned, his face grim. "I can hear Murgos moving around up there," the big man reported. "You can't tell how far away they are with all the echoes in these caves, but it sounds as if they're exploring every cave and passageway."

"Let us find some defensible spot then, my Lord, and give them reason to look for us elsewhere," Mandorallen suggested gaily.

"Interesting notion," Barak replied, "but I'm afraid it wouldn't work. Sooner or later they're going to find us."

"I'll take care of it," Relg said quietly, breaking off his praying and getting to his feet. The ritual formulas had not helped him, and his eyes were haunted.

"I'll go with you," Barak offered.

Relg shook his head. "You'd just be in my way," he said shortly, already moving toward the passage leading back into the mountain.

"What's come over him?" Barak asked, puzzled.

"I think our friend's having a religious crisis," Silk observed from the mouth of the cave where he kept watch.

"Another one?"

"It gives him something to occupy his spare moments," Silk replied lightly.

"Come and eat," Aunt Pol told them, laying slices of bread and cheese on top of one of the packs. "Then I want to have a look at the cut on your leg, Mandorallen."

After they had eaten and Polgara had bandaged Mandorallen's knee, she dressed Taiba in a peculiar assortment of clothes Durnik had taken from the packs. Then she turned her attention to the little boy. He returned her grave look with one just as serious, then reached out and touched the white lock at her brow with curious fingers. With a start of remembrance, Garion recalled how many times he had touched that lock with the selfsame gesture, and the memory of it raised a momentary irrational surge of jealousy, which he quickly suppressed.

The little boy smiled with sudden delight. "Errand," he said firmly, offering the Orb to Aunt Pol.

She shook her head. "No, child," she told him. "I'm afraid I'm not the one." She dressed him in clothing that had to be rolled up and taken in with bits of twine in various places, then sat down with her back against the wall of the cave and held out her arms to him. Obediently he climbed into her lap, put one arm about her neck and kissed her. Then he nestled his face down against her, sighed and immediately fell asleep. She looked down at him with a strange expression on her face— a peculiar mixture of wonder and tenderness—and Garion fought down another wave of jealousy.

There was a grinding rumble in the caves above them.

"What's that?" Durnik asked, looking around with apprehension.

"Relg, I'd imagine," Silk told him. "He seems to be taking steps to head off the Murgos."

"I hope he doesn't get carried away," Durnik said nervously, glancing at the rock ceiling.

"How long's it going to take to get to the Vale?" Barak asked.

"A couple of weeks, probably," Silk replied. "A lot's going to depend on the terrain and how quickly the Grolims can organize a search for us. If we can get enough of a head start to put down a good false trail, we can send them all running off to the west toward the Tolnedran border, and we can move toward the Vale without needing to waste all that time dodging and hiding." The little man grinned. "The notion of deceiving the whole Murgo nation appeals to me," he added.

"You don't have to get *too* creative," Barak told him. "Hettar's going to be waiting for us in the Vale—along with King Cho-Hag and half the clans of Algaria. They'll be awfully disappointed if we don't bring them at least a *few* Murgos."

"Life's full of little disappointments," Silk told him sardonically. "As I remember it, the eastern edge of the Vale is very steep and rough. It'll take a couple of days at least to make it down, and I don't think we'll want to try it with all of Murgodom snapping at our heels."

It was midafternoon when Relg returned. His exertions seemed to have quieted some of the turmoil in his mind but there was still a haunted look in his eyes, and he deliberately avoided Taiba's violet-eyed gaze. "I pulled down the ceilings of all the galleries leading to this cave," he reported shortly. "We're safe now."

Polgara, who had seemed asleep, opened her eyes. "Get some rest," she told him.

He nodded and went immediately to his blankets.

They rested in the cave through the remainder of the day, taking turns on watch at the narrow opening. The wasteland of black sand and wind-scoured rock lying out beyond the tumbled scree at the base of the pinnacle was alive with Murgo horsemen scurrying this way and that in a frenzied, disorganized search.

"They don't seem to know what they're doing," Garion observed quietly to Silk as the two of them watched. The sun was just sinking into a bank of cloud on the western horizon, staining the sky fiery red, and the stiff wind brought a dusty chill with it as it seeped into the cave opening.

"I imagine that things are a bit scrambled up in Rak Cthol," Silk replied. "No one's in charge anymore, and that confuses Murgos. They tend to go all to pieces when there's nobody around to give them orders."

"Isn't that going to make it hard for us to get out of here?" Garion asked. "What I mean is that they're not going anyplace. They're just milling around. How are we going to get through them?"

Silk shrugged. "We'll just pull up our hoods and mill around with the rest of them." He pulled the coarse cloth of the Murgo robe he wore closer about him to ward off the chill and turned to look back into the cave. "The sun's going down," he reported.

"Let's wait until it's completely dark," Polgara replied. She was carefully bundling the little boy up in one of Garion's old tunics.

"Once we get out a ways, I'll drop a few odds and ends," Silk said. "Murgos can be a little dense sometimes, and we wouldn't want them to miss our trail." He turned to look back out at the sunset. "It's going to be a cold night," he remarked to no one in particular.

"Garion," Aunt Pol said, rising to her feet, "you and Durnik stay close to Taiba. She's never ridden before, and she might need some help at first."

"What about the little boy?" Durnik asked.

"He'll ride with me."

"And Belgarath?" Mandorallen inquired, glancing over at the still-sleeping old sorcerer.

"When the time comes, we'll just put him on his horse," Polgara replied. "I can keep him in his saddle—as long as we don't make any sudden changes in direction. Is it getting any darker?"

"We'd better wait for a little longer," Silk answered. "There's still quite a bit of light out there."

They waited. The evening sky began to turn purple, and the first stars came out, glittering cold and very far away. Torches began to appear among the searching Murgos. "Shall we go?" Silk suggested, rising to his feet.

They led their horses quietly out of the cave and down across the scree to the sand. There they stopped for several moments while a group of Murgos carrying torches galloped by several hundred yards out. "Don't get separated," Silk told them as they mounted.

"How far is it to the edge of the wasteland?" Barak asked the little man, grunting as he climbed up onto his horse.

"Two days' hard riding," Silk replied. "Or nights in this case. We'll probably want to take cover when the sun's out. We don't look all *that* much like Murgos."

"Let's get started," Polgara told him.

They moved out at a walk, going slowly until Taiba became more sure of herself and Belgarath showed that he could stay in his saddle even though he could not yet communicate with anyone. Then they nudged their horses into a canter that covered a great deal of ground without exhausting the horses.

As they crossed the first ridge, they rode directly into a large group of Murgos carrying torches.

"Who's there?" Silk demanded sharply, his voice harsh with the characteristic accents of Murgo speech. "Identify yourselves."

"We're from Rak Cthol," one of the Murgos answered respectfully.

"I know that, blockhead," Silk barked. "I asked your identity."

"Third Phalanx," the Murgo said stiffly.

"That's better. Put out those torches. How do you expect to see anything beyond ten feet with them flaring in your eyes?"

The torches were immediately extinguished.

"Move your search to the north," Silk commanded. "The Ninth Phalanx is covering this sector."

"But—"

"Are you going to argue with me?"

"No, but—"

"Move! Now!"

The Murgos wheeled their horses about and galloped off into the darkness.

"Clever," Barak said admiringly.

Silk shrugged. "Pretty elementary," he replied. "People are grateful for a bit of direction when they're confused. Let's move along, shall we?"

There were other encounters during the long, cold, moonless night as they rode west. They were inescapable, in view of the hordes of Murgos scouring the wasteland in search of them, but Silk handled each such meeting smoothly, and the night passed without significant incident.

Toward morning the little man began artfully dropping various articles to mark their trail. "A bit overdone, perhaps," he said critically, looking at an old shoe he had just tossed into the hoof-churned sand behind them.

"What are you talking about?" Barak asked him.

"Our trail," Silk replied. "We want them to follow us, remember? They're supposed to think we're headed toward Tolnedra."

"So?"

"I was just suggesting that this is a bit crude."

"You worry too much about things like that."

"It's a question of style, my dear Barak," Silk replied loftily. "Sloppy work tends to be habit-forming."

As the first steel-gray light of dawn began to creep across the wintry sky, they took shelter among the boulders of one of the ridges that laced the floor of the wasteland. Durnik, Barak and Mandorallen stretched the canvas of their tents tautly over a narrow ravine on the west side of the ridge and sprinkled sand on top of it to disguise their makeshift shelter.

"It's probably best not to build a fire," Durnik said to Polgara as they led their horses in under the canvas, "what with the smoke and all."

She nodded her agreement. "We could all use a hot meal," she said, "but I suppose we'll have to wait."

They ate a cold breakfast of bread and cheese and began to settle in, hoping to sleep out the day so that they could ride on the next night.

"I could definitely use a bath," Silk said, brushing sand out of his hair.

The little boy looked at him, frowning slightly. Then he walked over and offered him the Orb. "Errand?" he asked.

Silk carefully put his hands behind his back and shook his head. "Is that the only word he knows?" he asked Polgara.

"It seems to be," she replied.

"I don't quite get the connection," Silk said. "What does he mean by it?"

"He's probably been told that he has an errand to run," she explained, "to steal the Orb. I imagine that Zedar's been telling him that over and over since he was a baby, and the word stuck in his mind."

"It's a bit disconcerting." Silk was still holding his hands behind his back. "It seems oddly appropriate sometimes."

"He doesn't appear to think the way we do," she told him. "The only purpose he has in life is to give the Orb to someone—anyone, it would seem." She frowned thoughtfully. "Durnik, why don't you see if you can make him some kind of pouch to carry it in, and we'll fasten it to his waist. Maybe if he doesn't have it right there in his hand all the time, he won't think about it so much."

"Of course, Mistress Pol," Durnik agreed. "I should have thought of that myself." He went to one of the packs and took out an old, burn-scarred leather apron and fashioned a pouch out of a wide piece of leather he cut from it. "Boy," he said when he had finished, "come here."

The little boy was curiously examining a small, very dry bush at the upper end of the ravine and gave no indication that he knew the smith was calling him.

"You—Errand!" Durnik said.

The little boy looked around quickly and smiled as he went to Durnik.

"Why did you call him that?" Silk asked curiously.

Durnik shrugged. "He seems to be fond of the word and he answers to it. It'll do for a name until we can find something more suitable, I suppose."

"Errand?" the child asked, offering the Orb to Durnik.

Durnik smiled at him, bent over and held the mouth of the pouch open. "Put it in here, Errand," he instructed, "and we'll tie it up all nice and safe so you won't lose it."

The little boy delightedly deposited the Orb in the leather pouch. "Errand," he declared firmly.

"I suppose so," Durnik agreed. He pulled the drawstring tight and then tied the pouch to the bit of rope the boy wore as a belt. "There we are, Errand. All safe and secure now."

Errand examined the pouch carefully, tugging at it a few times as if to be sure it was tightly tied. Then he gave a happy little laugh, put his arms about Durnik's neck and kissed his cheek.

"He's a good lad," Durnik said, looking a trifle embarrassed.

"He's totally innocent," Aunt Pol told him from where she was examining the sleeping Belgarath. "He has no idea of the difference between good and evil, so everything in the world seems good to him."

"I wonder what it's like to see the world that way," Taiba mused, gently touching the child's smiling face. "No sorrow; no fear; no pain—just to love everything you see because you believe that everything is good."

Relg, however, had looked up sharply. The troubled expression that had hovered on his face since he had rescued the trapped slave woman fell away to be replaced by that look of fanatic zeal that it had always worn before. "Monstrous!" he gasped.

Taiba turned on him, her eyes hardening. "What's so monstrous about happiness?" she demanded, putting her arm about the boy.

"We aren't here to be happy," he replied, carefully avoiding her eyes.

"Why are we here then?" she challenged.

"To serve our God and to avoid sin." He still refused to look at her, and his tone seemed a trifle less certain.

"Well, I don't have a God," she retorted, "and the child probably doesn't either, so if it's all the same to you, he and I will just concentrate on trying to be happy—and if a bit of sin gets involved in it, so what?"

"Have you no shame?" His voice was choked.

"I am what I am," she replied, "and I won't apologize, since I didn't have very much to say about it."

"Boy," Relg snapped at the child, "come away from her at once."

Taiba straightened, her face hardening even more, and she faced him defiantly. "What do you think you're going to do?" she demanded.

"I will fight sin wherever I find it," he declared.

"Sin, sin, sin!" she flared. "Is that all you ever think about?"

"It's my constant care. I guard against it every moment."

She laughed. "How tedious. Can't you think of anything better to do? Oh, I forgot," she added mockingly. "There's all that praying too, isn't there? All that bawling at your God about how vile you are. I think you must bore this UL of yours tremendously sometimes, do you know that?"

Enraged, Relg raised his fist. "Don't *ever* speak UL's name again!"

"Will you hit me if I do? It doesn't matter that much. People have been hitting me all my life. Go ahead, Relg. Why don't you hit me?" She lifted her smudged face to him.

Relg's hand fell.

Sensing her advantage, Taiba put her hands to the throat of the rough gray dress Polgara had given her. "I can stop you, Relg," she told him. She began unfastening the dress. "Watch me. You look at me all the time anyway—I've seen you with your hot eyes on me. You call me names and say that I'm wicked, but still you watch. Look then. Don't try to hide it." She continued to unfasten the front of the dress. "If you're free of sin, my body shouldn't bother you at all."

Relg's eyes were bulging now.

"My body doesn't bother me, but it bothers you very much, doesn't it? But is the wickedness in my mind or yours? I can sink you in sin any time I want to. All I have to do is this." And she pulled open the front of her dress.

Relg spun about, making strangled noises.

"Don't you want to look, Relg?" she mocked him as he fled.

"You have a formidable weapon there, Taiba," Silk congratulated her.

"It was the only weapon I had in the slave pens," she told him. "I learned to use it when I had to." She carefully rebuttoned her dress and turned back to Errand as if nothing had happened.

"What's all the shouting?" Belgarath mumbled, rousing slightly, and they all turned quickly to him.

"Relg and Taiba were having a little theological discussion," Silk replied lightly. "The finer points were very interesting. How are you?"

But the old man had already drifted back into sleep.

"At least he's starting to come around," Durnik noted.

"It'll be several days before he's fully recovered," Polgara told him, putting her hand to Belgarath's forehead. "He's still terribly weak."

Garion slept for most of the day, wrapped in his blankets and lying on the stony ground. When the chill and a particularly uncomfortable rock under his hip finally woke him, it was late afternoon. Silk sat guard near the mouth of the ravine, staring out at the black sand and the grayish salt flats, but the rest were all asleep. As he walked quietly down to where the little man sat, Garion noticed that Aunt Pol slept with Errand in her arms, and he pushed away a momentary surge of jealousy. Taiba murmured something as he passed, but a quick glance told him that she was not awake. She was lying not far from Relg; in her sleep, her hand seemed to be reaching out toward the slumbering Ulgo.

Silk's sharp little face was alert and he showed no signs of weariness. "Good morning," he murmured, "or whatever."

"Don't you ever get tired?" Garion asked him, speaking quietly so that his voice would not disturb the others.

"I slept a bit," Silk told him.

Durnik came out from under the canvas roof to join them, yawning and rubbing at his eyes. "I'll relieve you now," he said to Silk. "Did you see anything?" He squinted out toward the lowering sun.

Silk shrugged. "Some Murgos. They were a couple of miles off to the south. I don't think anyone's found our trail yet. We might have to make it a little more obvious for them."

Garion felt a peculiar, oppressive sort of weight on the back of his neck. He glanced around uncomfortably. Then, with no warning, there was a sudden sharp stab that seemed to go straight into his mind. He gasped and tensed his will, pushing the attack away.

"What's wrong?" Silk asked sharply.

"A Grolim," Garion snarled, clenching his will as he prepared to fight.

"Garion!" It was Aunt Pol, and her voice sounded urgent. He turned and darted back in under the canvas with Silk and Durnik on his heels.

She had risen to her feet and was standing with her arms protectively about Errand.

"That was a Grolim, wasn't it?" Garion demanded, his voice sounding a bit shrill.

"It was more than one," she replied tensely. "The Hierarchs control the Grolims now that Ctuchik's dead. They've joined their wills to try to kill Errand."

The others, awakened by her sharp cry, were stumbling to their feet and reaching for weapons.

"Why are they after the boy?" Silk asked.

"They know that he's the only one who can touch the Orb. They think that if he dies, we won't be able to get it out of Cthol Murgos."

"What do we do?" Garion asked her, looking around helplessly.

"I'm going to have to concentrate on protecting the child," she told him. "Step back, Garion."

"What?"

"Get back away from me." She bent and drew a circle in the sand, enclosing herself and the little boy in it. "Listen to me, all of you," she said. "Until we're out of this, none of you come any closer to me than this. I don't want any of you getting hurt." She drew herself up, and the white lock in her hair seemed to blaze.

"Wait," Garion exclaimed.

"I don't dare. They could attack again at any moment. It's going to be up to you to protect your grandfather and the others."

"Me?"

"You're the only one who can do it. You have the power. Use it." She raised her hand.

"How many of them are there that I have to fight off?" Garion demanded, but he already felt the sudden surge and the peculiar roaring sound in his mind as Aunt Pol's will thrust out. The air about her seemed to shimmer, distorting like heat waves on a summer afternoon. Garion could actually feel the barrier encircling her. "Aunt Pol?" he said to her. Then he raised his voice and shouted, "Aunt Pol!"

She shook her head and pointed at her ear. She seemed to say something, but no sound penetrated the shimmering shield she had erected.

"How many?" Garion mouthed the words exaggeratedly.

She held up both hands with one thumb folded in.

"Nine?" he mouthed again.

She nodded and then drew her cloak in around the little boy.

"Well, Garion?" Silk asked then, his eyes penetrating. "What do we do now?"

"Why are you asking me?"

"You heard her. Belgarath's still in a daze, and she's busy. You're in charge now."

"*Me?*"

"What do we do?" Silk pressed. "You've got to learn to make decisions."

"I don't know." Garion floundered helplessly.

"Never admit that," Silk told him. "Act as if you know—even if you don't."

"We—uh—we'll wait until it gets dark, I guess—then we'll keep going the same way we have been."

"There." Silk grinned. "See how easy it is?"

CHAPTER THREE

There was the faintest sliver of a moon low over the horizon as they started out across the black sand of the wasteland in the biting chill. Garion felt distinctly uncomfortable in the role Silk had thrust upon him. He knew that there had been no need for it, since they all knew where they were going and what they had to do. If any kind of leadership had actually been required, Silk himself was the logical one to provide it; but instead, the little man had placed the burden squarely on Garion's shoulders and now seemed to be watching intently to see how he would handle it.

There was no time for leadership or even discussion when, shortly after midnight, they ran into a party of Murgos. There were six of them, and they came galloping over a low ridge to the south and blundered directly into the middle of Garion's party. Barak and Mandorallen reacted with that instant violence of trained warriors, their swords whistling out of their sheaths to crunch with steely ringing sounds into the mail-shirted bodies of the startled Murgos. Even as Garion struggled to draw his own sword, he saw one of the black-robed intruders tumble limply out of his saddle, while another, howling with pain and surprise, toppled slowly backward, clutching at his chest. There was a confusion of shouts and shrill screams from terrified horses as the men fought in the darkness. One frightened Murgo wheeled his mount to flee, but Garion, without even thinking, pulled his horse in front of him, sword raised to strike. The desperate Murgo made a frantic swing with his own weapon, but Garion easily parried the badly aimed swipe and flicked his blade lightly, whiplike, across the Murgo's shoulder. There was a satisfying crunch as the sharp edge bit into the Murgo's mail shirt. Garion deftly parried another clumsy swing and whipped his blade again, slashing the Murgo across the face. All the instruction he had received from his friends seemed to click together into a single, unified style that was part Cherek, part Arendish, part Algar, and was distinctly Garion's own. This style baffled the frightened Murgo, and his efforts became more desperate. But each time he swung, Garion easily parried and instantly countered with those light, flicking slashes that inevitably drew blood. Garion felt a wild, surging exultation boiling in his veins as he fought, and there was a fiery taste in his mouth.

Then Relg darted in out of the shadows, jerked the Murgo off balance, and drove his hook-pointed knife up under the man's ribs. The Murgo doubled over sharply, shuddered, then fell dead from his saddle.

"What did you do that for?" Garion demanded without thinking. "That was *my* Murgo."

Barak, surveying the carnage, laughed, his sudden mirth startling in the darkness. "He's turning savage on us, isn't he?"

"His skill is noteworthy, however," Mandorallen replied approvingly.

Garion's spirits soared. He looked around eagerly for someone else to fight, but the Murgos were all dead. "Were they alone?" he demanded, somewhat out of breath. "I mean, were there any others coming along behind them? Maybe we should go look."

"We *do* want them to find our trail, after all," Silk reminded him. "It's up to you of course, Garion, but if we exterminate all the Murgos in the area, there won't be anyone left to report our direction back to Rak Cthol, will there?"

"Oh," Garion said, feeling a little sheepish, "I forgot about that."

"You have to keep the grand plan in view, Garion, and not lose sight of it during these little side adventures."

"Maybe I got carried away."

"A good leader can't afford to do that."

"All right." Garion began to feel embarrassed.

"I just wanted to be sure you understood, that's all."

Garion didn't answer, but he began to see what it was about Silk that irritated Belgarath so much. Leadership was enough of a burden without these continual sly comments from the weasel-faced little man to complicate things.

"Are you all right?" Taiba was saying to Relg with a strange note of concern in her voice. The Ulgo was still on his knees beside the body of the Murgo he had killed.

"Leave me alone," he told her harshly.

"Don't be stupid. Are you hurt? Let me see."

"Don't touch me!" He cringed away from her outstretched hand. "Belgarion, make her get away from me."

Garion groaned inwardly. "What's the trouble now?" he asked.

"I killed this man," Relg replied. "There are certain things I have to do—certain prayers—purification. She's interfering."

Garion resisted an impulse to swear. "Please, Taiba," he said as calmly as he could, "just leave him alone."

"I just wanted to see if he was all right," Taiba answered a bit petulantly. "I wasn't hurting him." She had an odd look on her face that Garion could not begin to understand. As she stared at the kneeling Ulgo, a curious little smile flickered across her lips. Without warning, she reached her hand out toward him again.

Relg shrank back. "No!" he gasped. Taiba chuckled, a throaty, wicked little sound, and walked away, humming softly to herself.

After Relg had performed his ritual of purification over the dead Murgo's body, they remounted and rode on. The sliver of moon stood high overhead in the chill sky, casting a pale light down on the black sands, and Garion looked about constantly as he rode, trying to pick out any possible dangers lurking ahead. He glanced frequently at Aunt Pol, wishing that she were not so completely cut off from him, but she seemed to be totally absorbed in maintaining her shield of will. She rode with Errand pulled closely against her, and her eyes were distant, unfathomable. Garion looked hopefully at Belgarath, but the old man, though he looked up from his doze at times, seemed largely unaware of his surroundings. Garion sighed, and his eyes resumed their nervous scrutiny of the trail ahead. They rode on through the tag-end of night in the biting chill with the faint moonlight about them and the stars glittering like points of ice in the sky above.

Suddenly Garion heard a roaring in his mind—a sound that had a peculiar echo to it—and the shield of force surrounding Aunt Pol shimmered with an ugly orange glow. He jerked his will in sharply and gestured with a single word. He had no idea what word he used, but it seemed to work. Like a horse blundering into a covey of feeding birds, his will scattered the concerted attack on Aunt Pol and Errand. There had been more than one mind involved in the attack—he sensed that—but it seemed to make no difference. He caught a momentary flicker of chagrin and even fear as the joined wills of Aunt Pol's attackers broke and fled from him.

"Not bad," the voice in his mind observed. *"A little clumsy, perhaps, but not bad at all."*

"It's the first time I ever did it," Garion replied. *"I'll get better with more practice."*

"Don't get overconfident," the voice advised dryly, and then it was gone.

He was growing stronger, there was no doubt about that. The ease with which he had dispersed the combined wills of that group of Grolims Aunt Pol had called the Hierarchs amazed him. He faintly began to understand what Aunt Pol and Belgarath meant in their use of the word "talent." There seemed to be some kind of capacity, a limit beyond which most sorcerers could not go. Garion realized with a certain surprise that he was already stronger than men who had been practicing this art for centuries, and that he was only beginning to touch the edges of his talent. The thought of what he might eventually be able to do was more than a little frightening.

It did, however, make him feel somewhat more secure. He straightened in his saddle and rode a bit more confidently. Perhaps leadership wasn't so bad after all. It took some getting used to, but once you knew what you were doing, it didn't seem all that hard.

The next attack came as the eastern horizon had begun to grow pale behind them. Aunt Pol, her horse, and the little boy all seemed to vanish as absolute blackness engulfed them. Garion struck back instantly and he added a contemptuous little twist to it—a stinging slap at the joined minds that had mounted the attack. He felt a glow of self-satisfaction at the surprise and pain in the minds as they flinched back from his quick counterblow. There was a glimpse—just a momentary one—of nine very old men in black robes seated around a table in a room somewhere. One of the walls of the room had a large crack in it, and part of the ceiling had collapsed as a result of the earthquake that had convulsed Rak Cthol. Eight of the evil old men looked surprised and frightened; the ninth one had fainted. The darkness surrounding Aunt Pol disappeared.

"What are they doing?" Silk asked him.

"They're trying to break through Aunt Pol's shield," Garion replied. "I gave them something to think about." He felt a little smug about it.

Silk looked at him, his eyes narrowed shrewdly. "Don't overdo things, Garion," he advised.

"Somebody had to do something," Garion protested.

"That's usually the way it works out. All I'm saying is that you shouldn't lose your perspective."

The broken wall of peaks that marked the western edge of the wasteland was clearly visible as the light began to creep up the eastern sky. "How far would you say it is?" Garion asked Durnik.

The smith squinted at the mountains ahead. "Two or three leagues at least," he judged. "Distances are deceiving in this kind of light."

"Well?" Barak asked. "Do we take cover for the day here or do we make a run for it?"

Garion thought about that. "Are we going to change direction as soon as we get to the mountains?" he asked Mandorallen.

" 'Twould seem better mayhap to continue our present course for some little distance first," the knight replied thoughtfully. "A natural boundary such as that which lies ahead might attract more than passing scrutiny."

"That's a good point," Silk agreed.

Garion scratched at his cheek, noticing that his whiskers had begun to sprout again. "Maybe we should stop here then," he suggested. "We could start out again when the sun goes down, get up into the mountains a way and then rest. When the sun comes up tomorrow morning, we can change our route. That way, we'll have light enough to see any tracks we leave and cover them up."

"Seems like a good plan," Barak approved.

"Let's do it that way then," Garion decided.

They sought out another ridge and another ravine, and once again concealed it with their tent canvas. Although he was tired, Garion was reluctant to lose himself in sleep. Not only did the cares of leadership press heavily on him, but he also felt apprehensive about the possibility of an attack by the Hierarchs coming while he was asleep. As the others began to unroll their blankets, he walked about rather aimlessly, stopping to look at Aunt Pol, who sat with her back against a large rock, holding the sleeping Errand and looking as distant as the moon behind her shimmering shield. Garion sighed and went on down to the mouth of the ravine where Durnik was attending to the horses. It had occurred to him that all their lives depended on the well-being of their mounts, and that gave him something else to worry about.

"How are they?" he asked Durnik as he approached.

"They're bearing up fairly well," Durnik replied. "They've come a long way, though, and it's beginning to show on some of them."

"Is there anything we can do for them?"

"A week's rest in a good pasture, perhaps," Durnik answered with a wry smile.

Garion laughed. "I think we could all use a week's rest in a good pasture."

"You've really grown, Garion," Durnik observed as he lifted another horse's hind hoof to examine it for cuts or bruises.

Garion glanced at his arm and saw that his wrist stuck an inch or two out of his sleeve. "Most of my clothes still fit—pretty much," he replied.

"That's not the way I meant," Durnik hesitated. "What's it like, Garion? Being able to do things the way you do?"

"It scares me, Durnik," Garion admitted quietly. "I didn't really want any of this, but it didn't give me any choice."

"You mustn't let it frighten you, you know," Durnik said, carefully lowering the horse's hoof. "If it's part of you, it's part of you—just like being tall or having blond hair."

"It's not really like that, Durnik. Being tall or having blond hair doesn't hurt anybody. This can."

Durnik looked out at the long shadows of the ridge stretching away from the newly risen sun. "You just have to learn to be careful with it, that's all. When I was about your age, I found out that I was much stronger than the other young men in our village—probably because I worked in the smithy. I didn't want to hurt anybody, so I wouldn't wrestle with my friends. One of them thought I was a coward because of that and he pushed me around for about six months until I finally lost my temper."

"Did you fight him?"

Durnik nodded. "It wasn't really much of a contest. After it was over, he realized that I wasn't a coward after all. We even got to be good friends again—after his bones all healed up and he got used to the missing teeth."

Garion grinned at him, and Durnik smiled back a bit ruefully. "I was ashamed of myself afterward, of course."

Garion felt very close to this plain, solid man. Durnik was his oldest friend—somebody he could always count on.

"What I'm trying to say, Garion," Durnik continued seriously, "is that you can't go through life being afraid of what you are. If you do that, sooner or later somebody'll come along who'll misunderstand, and you'll have to do something to show him that it's not *him* that you're afraid of. When it goes that far, it's usually much worse for you—and for him, too."

"The way it was with Asharak?"

Durnik nodded. "It's always best in the long run to be what you are. It isn't proper to behave as if you were more, but it isn't good to behave as if you were less, either. Do you understand what I'm trying to say?"

"The whole problem seems to be finding out just exactly *what* you really are," Garion observed.

Durnik smiled again. "That's the part that gets most of us in trouble at times," he agreed. Suddenly the smile fell away from his face and he gasped. Then he fell writhing to the ground, clutching at his stomach.

"Durnik!" Garion cried, "What's wrong?"

But Durnik could not answer. His face was ashen and contorted with agony as he twisted in the dirt.

Garion felt a strange, alien pressure and he understood instantly. Thwarted in their attempts to kill Errand, the Hierarchs were directing their attacks at the others in the hope of forcing Aunt Pol to drop her shield. A terrible rage boiled up in him. His blood seemed to burn, and a fierce cry came to his lips.

"Calmly." It was the voice within his mind again.

"What do I do?"

"Get out into the sunlight."

Garion did not understand that, but he ran out past the horses into the pale morning light.

"Put yourself into your shadow."

He looked down at the shadow stretching out on the ground in front of him and obeyed the voice. He wasn't sure exactly how he did it, but he poured his will and his awareness into the shadow.

"Now, follow the trail of their thought back to them. Quickly."

Garion felt himself suddenly flying. Enclosed in his shadow, he touched the still-writhing Durnik once like a sniffing hound, picked up the direction of the concerted thought that had felled his friend, and then flashed through the air back over the miles of wasteland toward the wreckage of Rak Cthol. He had, it seemed, no weight, and there was an odd purplish cast to everything he saw.

He felt his immensity as he entered the room with the cracked wall where the nine black-robed old men sat, trying with the concerted power of their minds to kill Durnik. Their eyes were all focused on a huge ruby, nearly the size of a man's head, which lay flickering in the center of the table around which they sat. The slanting rays of the morning sun had distorted and enlarged Garion's shadow, and he filled one corner of the room, bending slightly so that he could fit under the ceiling. "Stop!" he roared at the evil old men. "Leave Durnik alone!"

They flinched back from his sudden apparition, and he could feel the thought they were directing at Durnik through the stone on the table falter and begin to fall apart. He took a threatening step and saw them cringe away from him in the purple light that half clouded his vision.

Then one of the old men—very thin and with a long dirty beard and completely hairless scalp—seemed to recover from his momentary fright. "Stand firm!" he snapped at the others. "Keep the thought on the Sendar!"

"Leave him alone!" Garion shouted at them.

"Who says so?" the thin old man drawled insultingly.

"I do."

"And just who are you?"

"I am Belgarion. Leave my friends alone."

The old man laughed, and his laugh was as chilling as Ctuchik's had been. "Actually, you're only Belgarion's shadow," he corrected. "We know the trick of the shadow. You can talk and bluster and threaten, but that's all you can do. You're just a powerless shade, Belgarion."

"Leave us alone!"

"And what will you do if we don't?" The old man's face was filled with contemptuous amusement.

"Is he right?" Garion demanded of the voice within his mind.

"Perhaps—perhaps not," the voice replied. *"A few men have been able to go beyond the limitation. You won't know unless you try."*

Despite his dreadful anger, Garion did not want to kill any of them. "Ice!" he said, focusing on the idea of cold and lashing out with his will. It felt odd—almost tenuous, as if it had no substance behind it, and the roaring was hollow and puny-sounding.

The bald old man sneered and waggled his beard insultingly.

Garion ground his insubstantial teeth and drew himself in with dreadful concentration. "Burn!" he said then, driving his will. There was a flicker and then a sudden flash. The force of Garion's will burst forth, directed not at the bald man himself, but rather at his whiskers.

The Hierarch jumped up and stumbled back with a hoarse exclamation, trying desperately to beat the flames out of his beard.

The concerted thought of the Hierarchs shattered as the rest of them scrambled to their feet in terrified astonishment. Grimly, Garion gathered his swelling will and began to lay about him with his immensely long arms. He tumbled the Hierarchs across the rough stone floor and slammed them into walls. Squealing with fright, they scurried this way and that, trying to escape, but he methodically reached out and grasped them one by one to administer his chastisement. With a peculiar kind of detachment, he even stuffed one of them headfirst into the crack in the wall, pushing quite firmly until only a pair of wriggling feet were sticking out.

Then, when it was done, he turned back to the bald Hierarch, who had managed finally to beat the last of the fire out of his beard. "It's impossible—impossible," the Hierarch protested, his face stunned. "How did you do it?"

"I told you—I am Belgarion. I can do things you can't even imagine."

"The jewel," the voice told him. *"They're using the jewel to focus their attacks. Destroy it."*

"How?"

"It can only hold so much. Look."

Garion suddenly found that he could actually see into the interior of the still-flickering ruby on the table. He saw the minute stress lines within its crystalline structure, and then he understood. He turned his will on it and poured all his anger into it. The stone blazed with light and began to pulsate as the force within it swelled. Then, with a sharp detonation, the stone exploded into fragments.

"No!" the bald Hierarch wailed. "You idiot! That stone was irreplaceable."

"Listen to me, old man," Garion said in an awful voice, "you *will* leave us alone. You will *not* pursue us, or try to injure any of us anymore." He reached out with his shadowy hand and slid it directly into the bald man's chest. He could feel the heart flutter like a terrified bird and the lungs falter as the Hierarch's breath stopped and he gaped with horror at the arm sticking out of his chest. Garion slowly opened his fingers very wide. "Do you understand me?" he demanded.

The Hierarch gurgled and tried to take hold of the arm, but his fingers found nothing to grasp.

"Do you understand me?" Garion repeated and suddenly clenched his fist.

The Hierarch screamed.

"Are you going to leave us alone?"

"Please, Belgarion! No more! I'm dying!"

"Are you going to leave us alone?" Garion demanded again.

"Yes, yes—anything, but please stop! I beg you! I'll do anything. Please!"

Garion unclenched his fist and drew his hand out of the Hierarch's heaving chest. He held it up, clawlike, directly in front of the old man's face. "Look at this and remember it," he said in a dreadfully quiet voice. "Next time I'll reach into your chest and pull your heart out."

The Hierarch shrank back, his eyes filled with horror as he stared at the awful hand. "I promise you," he stammered. "I promise."

"Your life depends on it," Garion told him, then turned and flashed back across the empty miles toward his friends. Quite suddenly he was standing at the mouth of the ravine staring down at his shadow slowly re-forming on the ground before him. The purple haze was gone; strangely enough, he didn't even feel tired.

Durnik drew in a shuddering breath and struggled to rise.

Garion turned quickly and ran back to his friend. "Are you all right?" he asked, taking hold of the smith's arm.

"It was like a knife twisting inside me," Durnik replied in a shaking voice. "What was it?"

"The Grolim Hierarchs were trying to kill you," Garion told him. Durnik looked around, his eyes frightened.

"Don't worry, Durnik. They won't do it again." Garion helped him to his feet and together they went back into the ravine.

Aunt Pol was looking directly at him as he approached her. Her eyes were penetrating. "You're growing up very fast," she said to him.

"I had to do something," he replied. "What happened to your shield?"

"It doesn't seem to be necessary any more."

"Not bad," Belgarath said. The old man was sitting up. He looked weak and drawn, but his eyes were alert. "Some of it was a bit exotic; but on the whole, it wasn't bad at all. The business with the hand was just a little overdone, though."

"I wanted to be sure he understood that I meant what I was saying." Garion felt a tremendous wave of relief at his grandfather's return to consciousness.

"I think you convinced him," Belgarath said dryly. "Is there anything to eat somewhere nearby?" he asked Aunt Pol.

"Are you all right now, Grandfather?" Garion asked him.

"Aside from being as weak as a fresh-hatched baby chick and as hungry as a she-wolf with nine puppies, I'm just fine," Belgarath replied. "I could *really* use something to eat, Polgara."

"I'll see what I can find, Father," she told him, turning to the packs.

"I don't know that you need to bother cooking it," he added.

The little boy had been looking curiously at Garion, his wide, blue eyes serious and slightly puzzled. Quite suddenly he laughed; smiling, he looked into Garion's face. "Belgarion," he said.

CHAPTER FOUR

"No regrets?" Silk asked Garion that evening as they rode toward the sharply rising peaks outlined against the glittering stars ahead.

"Regrets about what?"

"Giving up command." Silk had been watching him curiously ever since the setting sun had signaled the resumption of their journey.

"No," Garion replied, not quite sure what the little man meant. "Why should there be?"

"It's a very important thing for a man to learn about himself, Garion," Silk told him seriously. "Power can be very sweet for some men, and you never know how a man's going to handle it until you give him the chance to try."

"I don't know why you went to all the trouble. It's not too likely that I'm going to be put in charge of things very often."

"You never know, Garion. You never know."

They rode on across the barren black sands of the wasteland toward the mountains looming ahead. The quarter moon rose behind them, and its light was cold and white. Near the edge of the wasteland there were a few scrubby thorn-bushes huddling low to the sand and silvered with frost. It was an hour or so before midnight when they finally reached rocky ground, and the hooves of their horses clattered sharply as they climbed up out of the sandy waste. When they topped the first ridge, they stopped to look back. The dark expanse of the wasteland behind them was dotted with the watch fires of the Murgos, and far back along their trail they saw moving torches.

"I was starting to worry about that," Silk said to Belgarath, "but it looks as if they found our trail after all."

"Let's hope they don't lose it again," the old man replied.

"Not too likely, really. I made it pretty obvious."

"Murgos can be a bit undependable sometimes." Belgarath seemed to have recovered almost completely, but Garion noted a weary slump to his shoulders and was glad that they did not plan to ride all night.

The mountains into which they rode were as arid and rocky as the ones lying to the north had been. There were looming cliffs and patches of alkali on the ground and a bitingly cold wind that seemed to wail endlessly through the rocks and to tug at the coarse-woven Murgo robes that disguised them. They pushed on until they were well into the mountains; then, several hours before dawn, they stopped to rest and to wait for the sun to rise.

When the first faint light appeared on the eastern horizon, Silk rode out and located a rocky gap passing to the northwest between two ocherous cliff faces. As soon as he returned, they saddled their horses again and moved out at a trot.

"We can get rid of these now, I think," Belgarath said, pulling off his Murgo robe.

"I'll take them," Silk suggested as he reined in. "The gap's just ahead there." He pointed. "I'll catch up in a couple of hours."

"Where are you going?" Barak asked him.

"I'll leave a few miles more of false trail," Silk replied. "Then I'll double back and make sure that you haven't left any tracks. It won't take long."

"You want some company?" the big man offered.

Silk shook his head. "I can move faster alone."

"Be careful."

Silk grinned. "I'm always careful." He took the Murgo garments from them and rode off to the west.

The gap into which they rode appeared to be the bed of a stream that had dried up thousands of years before. The water had cut down through the rock, revealing layer upon layer of red, brown, and yellow stone lying in bands, one atop the other. The sound of their horses' hooves was very loud as they clattered along between the cliffs, and the wind whistled as it poured through the cut.

Taiba drew her horse in beside Garion's. She was shivering and she had the cloak he had given her pulled tightly about her shoulders. "Is it always this cold?" she asked, her large, violet eyes very wide.

"In the wintertime," he replied. "I imagine it's pretty hot here in the summer."

"The slave pens were always the same," she told him. "We never knew what season it was."

The twisting streambed made a sharp bend to the right, and they rode into the light of the newly risen sun. Taiba gasped.

"What's wrong?" Garion asked her quickly.

"The light," she cried, covering her face with her hands. "It's like fire in my eyes."

Relg, who rode directly in front of them, was also shielding his eyes. He looked back over his shoulder at the Marag woman. "Here," he said. He took one of the veils he usually bound across his eyes when they were in direct sunlight and handed it back to her. "Cover your face with this until we're back into the shadows again." His voice was peculiarly neutral.

"Thank you," Taiba said, binding the cloth across her eyes. "I didn't know that the sun could be so bright."

"You'll get used to it," Relg told her. "It just takes some time. Try to protect your eyes for the first few days." He seemed about to turn and ride on, then he looked at her curiously. "Haven't you ever seen the sun before?" he asked her.

"No," she replied. "Other slaves told me about it, though. The Murgos don't use women on their work gangs, so I was never taken out of the pens. It was always dark down there."

"It must have been terrible." Garion shuddered.

She shrugged. "The dark wasn't so bad. It was the light we were afraid of. Light meant that the Murgos were coming with torches to take someone to the Temple to be sacrificed."

The trail they followed turned again, and they rode out of the bright glare of sunlight. "Thank you," Taiba said to Relg, removing the veil from her eyes and holding it out to him.

"Keep it," he told her. "You'll probably need it again." His voice seemed oddly subdued, and his eyes had a strange gentleness in them. As he looked at her, the haunted expression crept back over his face.

Since they had left Rak Cthol, Garion had covertly watched these two. He knew that Relg, despite all his efforts, could not take his eyes off the Marag woman he had been forced to rescue from her living entombment in the caves. Although Relg still ranted about sin continually, his words no longer carried the weight of absolute conviction; indeed quite often, they seemed to be little more than a mechanical repetition of a set of formulas. Occasionally, Garion had noted, even those formulas had faltered when Taiba's deep violet eyes had turned to regard the Ulgo's face. For her part, Taiba was quite obviously puzzled. Relg's rejection of her simple gratitude had humiliated her, and her resentment had been hot and immediate. His constant scrutiny, however, spoke to her with a meaning altogether different from the words coming from his lips. His eyes told her one thing, but his mouth said something else. She was baffled by him, not knowing whether to respond to his look or his words.

"You've lived your whole life in the dark, then?" Relg asked her curiously.

"Most of it," she replied. "I saw my mother's face once—the day the Murgos came and took her to the Temple. I was alone after that. Being alone is the worst of it. You can bear the dark if you aren't alone."

"How old were you when they took your mother away?"

"I don't really know. I must have been almost a woman, though, because not long after that the Murgos gave me to a slave who had pleased them. There were a lot of slaves in the pens who did anything the Murgos wanted, and they were rewarded with extra food—or with women. I cried at first; but in time I learned to accept it. At least I wasn't alone anymore."

Relg's face hardened, and Taiba saw the expression. "What should I have done?" she asked him. "When you're a slave, your body doesn't belong to you. They can sell you or give you to anybody they want to, and there's nothing you can do about it."

"There must have been *something*."

"Such as what? I didn't have any kind of weapon to fight with—or to kill myself with—and you can't strangle yourself." She looked at Garion. "Did you know that? Some of the slaves tried it, but all you do is fall into unconsciousness, and then you start to breathe again. Isn't that curious?"

"Did you try to fight?" It seemed terribly important to Relg for some reason.

"What would have been the point? The slave they gave me to was stronger than I. He'd have just hit me until I did what he wanted."

"You should have fought," Relg declared adamantly. "A little pain is better than sin, and giving up like that is sin."

"Is it? If somebody forces you to do something and there's no possible way to avoid it, is it really sin?"

Relg started to answer, but her eyes, looking directly into his face, seemed to stop up his tongue. He faltered, unable to face that gaze. Abruptly he turned his mount and rode back toward the pack animals.

"Why does he fight with himself so much?" Taiba asked.

"He's completely devoted to his God," Garion explained. "He's afraid of anything that might take away some of what he feels he owes to UL."

"Is this UL of his really that jealous?"

"No, I don't think so, but Relg does."

Taiba pursed her lips into a sensual pout and looked back over her shoulder at the retreating zealot. "You know," she said, "I think he's actually afraid of me." She laughed then, that same low, wicked little laugh, and lifted her arms to run her fingers through the glory of her midnight hair. "No one's ever been afraid of me before—not ever. I think I rather like it. Will you excuse me?" She turned her horse without waiting for a reply and quite deliberately rode back after the fleeing Relg.

Garion thought about it as he rode on through the narrow, twisting canyon. He realized that there was a strength in Taiba that none of them had suspected, and he finally concluded that Relg was in for a very bad time.

He trotted on ahead to speak to Aunt Pol about it as she rode with her arms about Errand.

"It's really none of your business, Garion," she told him. "Relg and Taiba can work out their problems without any help from you."

"I was just curious, that's all. Relg's tearing himself apart, and Taiba's all confused about him. What's *really* going on between them, Aunt Pol?"

"Something very necessary," she replied.

"You could say that about nearly everything that happens, Aunt Pol." It was almost an accusation. "You could even say that the way Ce'Nedra and I quarrel all the time is necessary too, couldn't you?"

She looked slightly amused. "It's not exactly the same thing, Garion," she answered, "but there's a certain necessity about that too."

"That's ridiculous," he scoffed.

"Is it really? Then why do you suppose the two of you go out of your way so much to aggravate each other?"

He had no answer for that, but the entire notion worried him. At the same time the very mention of Ce'Nedra's name suddenly brought her sharply into his mind, and he realized that he actually missed her. He rode along in silence beside Aunt Pol for a while, feeling melancholy. Finally he sighed.

"And why so great a sigh?"

"It's all over, isn't it?"

"What's that?"

"This whole thing. I mean—we've recovered the Orb. That's what this was all about, wasn't it?"

"There's more to it than that, Garion—much more—and we're not out of Cthol Murgos yet, are we?"

"You're not really worried about that, are you?" But then, as if her question had suddenly uncovered some lingering doubts in his own mind, he stared at her in sudden apprehension. "What would happen if we didn't?" he blurted. "If we didn't make it out, I mean. What would happen to the West if we didn't get the Orb back to Riva?"

"Things would become unpleasant."

"There'd be a war, wouldn't there? And the Angaraks would win, and there'd be Grolims everywhere with their knives and their altars." The thought of Grolims marching up to the gates of Faldor's farm outraged him.

"Don't go borrowing trouble, Garion. Let's worry about one thing at a time, shall we?"

"But what if—"

"Garion," she said with a pained look, "don't belabor the 'what ifs,' please. If you start that, you'll just worry everybody to death."

"*You* say 'what if' to Grandfather all the time," he accused.

"That's different," she replied.

They rode hard for the next several days through a series of passes with the dry, bitter chill pressing at them like some great weight. Silk rode back often to look for any signs of pursuit, but their ruse seemed to have fooled the Murgos. Finally, about noon on a cold, sunless day when the wind was kicking up dust clouds along the horizon, they reached the broad, arid valley through which the south caravan route wound. They took cover behind a low hill while Silk rode on ahead to take a quick look.

"Thinkest thou that Taur Urgas hath joined in the search for us?" Mandorallen, dressed again in his armor, asked Belgarath.

"It's hard to say for sure," the old sorcerer replied. "He's a very unpredictable man."

"There's a Murgo patrol headed east on the caravan route," Silk reported when he returned. "It'll be another half hour or so until they're out of sight."

Belgarath nodded.

"Do you think we'll be safe once we cross over into Mishrak ac Thull?" Durnik asked.

"We can't count on it," Belgarath replied. "Gethel, the king of the Thulls, is afraid of Taur Urgas, so he wouldn't make any kind of fuss about a border violation if Taur Urgas decided to follow us."

They waited until the Murgos had crossed a low ridge to the east and then moved out again.

For the next two days they rode steadily to the northwest. The terrain grew less rocky after they crossed into the land of the Thulls, and they saw the telltale dust clouds far behind them that spoke of mounted Murgo search parties. It was late in the afternoon of a murky day when they finally reached the top of the eastern escarpment.

Barak glanced back over his shoulder at the dust clouds behind them, then pulled his horse in beside Belgarath's. "Just how rough is the ground leading down into the Vale?" he asked.

"It's not the easiest trail in the world."

"Those Murgos are less than a day behind us, Belgarath. If we have to pick our way down, they'll be on top of us before we make it."

Belgarath pursed his lips, squinting at the dust clouds on the southern horizon. "Perhaps you're right," he said. "Maybe we'd better think this through." He raised his hand to call a halt. "It's time to make a couple of decisions," he told the rest of them. "The Murgos are a little closer than we really want them to be. It takes two to three days to make the descent into the Vale, and there are places where one definitely doesn't want to be rushed."

"We could always go on to that ravine we followed coming up," Silk suggested. "It only takes a half day to go down that way."

"But Lord Hettar and the Algar clans of King Cho-Hag await us in the Vale," Mandorallen objected. "Were we to go on, would we not lead the Murgos down into undefended country?"

"Have we got any choice?" Silk asked him.

"We could light fires along the way," Barak suggested. "Hettar will know what they mean."

"So would the Murgos," Silk said. "They'd ride all night and be right behind us every step of the way down."

Belgarath scratched sourly at his short white beard. "I think we're going to have to abandon the original plan," he decided. "We have to take the shortest way down, and that means the ravine, I'm afraid. We'll be on our own once we get down, but that can't be helped."

"Surely King Cho-Hag will have scouts posted along the foot of the escarpment," Durnik said, his plain face worried.

"We can *hope* so," Barak replied.

"All right," Belgarath said firmly, "we'll use the ravine. I don't altogether like the idea, but our options seem to have been narrowed a bit. Let's ride."

It was late afternoon when they reached the shallow gully at the top of the steep notch leading down to the plain below. Belgarath glanced once down the precipitous cut and shook his head. "Not in the dark," he decided. "Can you see any signs of the Algars?" he asked Barak, who was staring out at the plain below.

"I'm afraid not," the red-bearded man answered. "Do you want to light a fire to signal them?"

"No," the old man replied. "Let's not announce our intentions."

"I *will* need a small fire, though," Aunt Pol told him. "We all need a hot meal."

"I don't know if that's wise, Polgara," Belgarath objected.

"We'll have a hard day tomorrow, Father," she said firmly. "Durnik knows how to build a small fire and keep it hidden."

"Have it your own way, Pol," the old man said in a resigned tone of voice.

"Naturally, Father."

It was cold that night, and they kept their fire small and well sheltered. As the first light of dawn began to stain the cloudy sky to the east, they rose and prepared to descend the rocky cut toward the plain below.

"I'll strike the tents," Durnik said.

"Just knock them down," Belgarath told him. He turned and nudged one of the packs thoughtfully with his foot. "We'll take only what we absolutely have to have," he decided. "We're not going to have the time to waste on these."

"You're not going to leave them?" Durnik sounded shocked.

"They'll just be in the way, and the horses will be able to move faster without them."

"But—all of our belongings!" Durnik protested.

Silk also looked a bit chagrined. He quickly spread out a blanket and began rummaging through the packs, his quick hands bringing out innumerable small, valuable items and piling them in a heap on the blanket.

"Where did you get all those?" Barak asked him.

"Here and there," Silk replied evasively.

"You stole them, didn't you?"

"Some of them," Silk admitted. "We've been on the road for a long time, Barak."

"Do you really plan to carry all of that down the ravine?" Barak asked, curiously eyeing Silk's treasures.

Silk looked at the heap, mentally weighing it. Then he sighed with profound regret. "No," he said, "I guess not." He stood up and scattered the heap with his foot. "It's all very pretty though, isn't it? Now I guess I'll have to start all over again." He grinned then. "It's the stealing that's fun, anyway. Let's go down." And he started toward the top of the steeply descending streambed that angled sharply down toward the base of the escarpment.

The unburdened horses were able to move much more rapidly, and they all passed quite easily over spots Garion remembered painfully from the upward climb weeks before. By noon they were more than halfway down.

Then Polgara stopped and raised her face. "Father," she said calmly, "they've found the top of the ravine."

"How many of them?"

"It's an advance patrol—no more than twenty."

Far above them they heard a sharp clash of rock against rock, and then, after a moment, another. "I was afraid of that," Belgarath said sourly.

"What?" Garion asked.

"They're rolling rocks down on us." The old man grimly hitched up his belt. "All right, the rest of you go on ahead. Get down as fast as you can."

"Are you strong enough, Father?" Aunt Pol asked, sounding concerned. "You still haven't really recovered, you know."

"We're about to find out," the old man replied, his face set. "Move—all of you." He said it in a tone that cut off any possible argument.

As they all began scrambling down over the steep rocks, Garion lagged farther and farther behind. Finally, as Durnik led the last packhorse over a jumble of broken stone and around a bend, Garion stopped entirely and stood listening. He could hear the clatter and slide of hooves on the rocks below and, from above, the clash and bounce of a large stone tumbling over the ravine, coming closer and closer. Then there was a familiar surge and roaring sound. A rock, somewhat larger than a man's head, went whistling over him, angling sharply up out of the cut to fall harmlessly far out on the tumbled debris at the floor of the escarpment. Carefully Garion began climbing back up the ravine, pausing often to listen.

Belgarath was sweating as Garion came into sight around a bend in the ravine a goodly way above and ducked back out of the old man's sight. Another rock, somewhat larger than the first, came bounding and crashing down the narrow ravine, bouncing off the walls and leaping into the air each time it struck the rocky streambed. About twenty yards above Belgarath, it struck solidly and spun into the air. The old man gestured irritably, grunting with the effort, and the rock sailed out in a long arc, clearing the walls of the ravine and falling out of sight.

Garion quickly crossed the streambed and went down several yards more, staying close against the rocky wall and peering back to be sure he was concealed from his grandfather.

When the next rock came bouncing and clashing down toward them, Garion gathered his will. He'd have to time it perfectly, he knew, and he peered around a corner, watching the old man intently. When Belgarath raised his hand, Garion pushed his own will in to join his grandfather's, hoping to slip a bit of unnoticed help to him.

Belgarath watched the rock go whirling far out over the plain below, then he turned and looked sternly down the ravine. "All right, Garion," he said crisply, "step out where I can see you."

Somewhat sheepishly Garion went out into the center of the streambed and stood looking up at his grandfather.

"Why is it that you can never do what you're told to do?" the old man demanded.

"I just thought I could help, that's all."

"Did I ask for help? Do I look like an invalid?"

"There's another rock coming."

"Don't change the subject. I think you're getting above yourself, young man."

"Grandfather!" Garion said urgently, staring at the large rock bounding down the ravine directly for the old man's back. He threw his will under the rock and hurled it out of the ravine.

Belgarath looked up at the stone soaring over his head. "Tacky, Garion," he said disapprovingly, "very tacky. You don't have to throw them all the way to Prolgu, you know. Stop trying to show off."

"I got excited," Garion apologized. "I pushed a little too hard."

The old man grunted. "All right," he said a bit ungraciously, "as long as you're here anyway—but stick to your own rocks. I can manage mine, and you throw me off balance when you come blundering in like that."

"I just need a little practice, that's all."

"You need some instruction in etiquette, too," Belgarath told him, coming on down to where Garion stood. "You don't just jump in with help until you're asked. That's very bad form, Garion."

"Another rock coming," Garion informed him politely. "Do you want to get it or shall I?"

"Don't get snippy, young man," Belgarath told him, then turned and flipped the approaching rock out of the ravine.

They moved on down together, taking turns on the rocks the Murgos were rolling down the ravine. Garion discovered that it grew easier each time he did it, but Belgarath was drenched with sweat by the time they neared the bottom. Garion considered trying once again to slip his grandfather a bit of assistance, but the old sorcerer glared at him so fiercely as he started to gather in his will that he quickly abandoned the idea.

"I wondered where you'd gone," Aunt Pol said to Garion as the two clambered out over the rocks at the mouth of the ravine to rejoin the rest of the party. She looked closely at Belgarath. "Are you all right?" she asked.

"I'm just fine," he snapped. "I had all this assistance—unsolicited, of course." He glared at Garion again.

"When we get a bit of time, we're going to have to give him some lessons in controlling the noise," she observed. "He sounds like a thunderclap."

"That's not all he has to learn to control." For some reason the old man was behaving as if he'd just been dreadfully insulted.

"What now?" Barak asked. "Do you want to light signal fires and wait here for Hettar and Cho-Hag?"

"This isn't a good place, Barak," Silk pointed out. "Half of Murgodom's going to come pouring down that ravine very shortly."

"The passage is not wide, Prince Kheldar," Mandorallen observed. "My Lord Barak and I can hold it for a week or more if need be."

"You're backsliding again, Mandorallen," Barak told him.

"Besides, they'd just roll rocks down on you," Silk said. "And they're going to be dropping boulders off the edge up there before long. We're probably going to have to get out on the plain a ways to avoid that sort of thing."

Durnik was staring thoughtfully at the mouth of the ravine. "We need to send something up there to slow them down, though," he mused. "I don't think we want them right behind us."

"It's a little hard to make rocks roll uphill," Barak said.

"I wasn't thinking of rocks," Durnik replied. "We'll need something much lighter."

"Like what?" Silk asked the smith.

"Smoke would be good," Durnik answered. "The ravine should draw just like a chimney. If we build a fire and fill the whole thing with smoke, nobody's going to come down until the fire goes out."

Silk grinned broadly. "Durnik," he said, "you're a treasure."

CHAPTER FIVE

There were bushes, scrub and bramble for the most part, growing here and there along the base of the cliff, and they quickly fanned out with their swords to gather enough to build a large, smoky fire. "You'd better hurry," Belgarath called to them as they worked. "There are a dozen Murgos or more already halfway down the ravine."

Durnik, who had been gathering dry sticks and splintered bits of log, ran back to the mouth of the ravine, knelt and began striking sparks from his flint into the tinder he always carried. In a few moments he had a small fire going, the orange flames licking up around the weathered gray sticks. Carefully he added larger pieces until his fire was a respectable blaze. Then he began piling thornbushes and brambles atop it, critically watching the direction of the smoke. The bushes hissed and smoldered fitfully at first, and a great cloud of smoke wafted this way and that for a moment, then began to pour steadily up the ravine. Durnik nodded with satisfaction. "Just like a chimney," he observed. From far up the cut came shouts of alarm and a great deal of coughing and choking.

"How long can a man breathe smoke before he chokes to death?" Silk asked.

"Not very long," Durnik replied.

"I didn't think so." The little man looked happily at the smoking blaze. "Good fire," he said, holding his hands out to the warmth.

"The smoke's going to delay them, but I think it's time to move on out," Belgarath said, squinting at the cloud-obscured ball of the sun hanging low over the horizon to the west. "We'll move on up the face of the escarpment and then make a run for it. We'll want to surprise them a bit, to give us time to get out of range before they start throwing rocks down on us."

"Is there any sign of Hettar out there?" Barak asked, peering out at the grassland.

"We haven't seen any yet," Durnik replied.

"You do know that we're going to lead half of Cthol Murgos out onto the plain?" Barak pointed out to Belgarath.

"That can't be helped. For right now, we've got to get out of here. If Taur Urgas is up there, he's going to send people after us, even if he has to throw them off the cliff personally. Let's go."

They followed the face of the cliff for a mile or more until they found a spot where the rockfall did not extend so far out onto the plain. "This'll do," Belgarath decided. "As soon as we get to level ground, we ride hard straight out. An arrow shot off the top of that cliff will carry a long way. Is everybody ready?" He looked around at them. "Let's move, then."

They led their horses down the short, steep slope of rock to the grassy plain below, mounted quickly and set off at a dead run.

"Arrow!" Silk said sharply, looking up and back over his shoulder.

Garion, without thinking, slashed with his will at the tiny speck arching down toward them. In the same instant he felt a peculiar double surge coming from either side of him. The arrow broke into several pieces in midair.

"If you two don't mind!" Belgarath said irritably to Garion and Aunt Pol, half reining in his horse.

"I just didn't want you to tire yourself, Father," Aunt Pol replied coolly. "I'm sure Garion feels the same way."

"Couldn't we discuss it later?" Silk suggested, looking apprehensively back at the towering escarpment.

They plunged on, the long, brown grass whipping at the legs of their horses. Other arrows began to fall, dropping farther and farther behind them as they rode. By the time they were a half mile out from the sheer face, the arrows were sheeting down from the top of the cliff in a whistling black rain.

"Persistent, aren't they?" Silk observed.

"It's a racial trait," Barak replied. "Murgos are stubborn to the point of idiocy."

"Keep going," Belgarath told them. "It's just a question of time until they bring up a catapult."

"They're throwing ropes down the face of the cliff," Durnik reported, peering back at the escarpment. "As soon as a few of them get to the bottom, they'll pull the fire clear of the ravine and start bringing horses down."

"At least it slowed them down a bit," Belgarath said.

Twilight, hardly more than a gradual darkening of the cloudy murk that had obscured the sky for several days, began to creep across the Algarian plain. They rode on.

Garion glanced back several times as he rode and noticed moving pinpoints of light along the base of the cliff. "Some of them have reached the bottom, Grandfather," he called to the old man, who was pounding along in the lead. "I can see their torches."

"It was bound to happen," the sorcerer replied.

It was nearly midnight by the time they reached the Aldur River, lying black and oily-looking between its frosty banks.

"Does anybody have any idea how we're going to find that ford in the dark?" Durnik asked.

"I'll find it," Relg told him. "It isn't all that dark for me. Wait here."

"That could give us a certain advantage," Silk noted. "We'll be able to ford the river, but the Murgos will flounder around on this side in the dark for half the night. We'll be leagues ahead of them before they get across."

"That was one of the things I was sort of counting on," Belgarath replied smugly.

It was a half an hour before Relg returned. "It isn't far," he told them.

They remounted and rode through the chill darkness, following the curve of the river bank until they heard the unmistakable gurgle and wash of water running over stones. "That's it just ahead," Relg said.

"It's still going to be dangerous fording in the dark," Barak pointed out.

"It isn't that dark," Relg said. "Just follow me." He rode confidently a hundred yards farther upriver, then turned and nudged his horse into the shallow rippling water.

Garion felt his horse flinch from the icy chill as he rode out into the river, following closely behind Belgarath. Behind him he heard Durnik coaxing the now-unburdened pack animals into the water.

The river was not deep, but it was very wide—almost a half mile—and in the process of fording, they were all soaked to the knees.

"The rest of the night promises to be moderately unpleasant," Silk observed, shaking one sodden foot.

"At least you've got the river between you and Taur Urgas," Barak reminded him.

"That does brighten things up a bit," Silk admitted.

They had not gone a half mile, however, before Mandorallen's charger went down with a squeal of agony. The knight, with a great clatter, tumbled in the grass as he was pitched out of the saddle. His great horse floundered with threshing legs, trying futilely to rise.

"What's the matter with him?" Barak demanded sharply.

Behind him, with another squeal, one of the packhorses collapsed.

"What is it?" Garion asked Durnik, his voice shrill.

"It's the cold," Durnik answered, swinging down from his saddle. "We've ridden them to exhaustion, and then we made them wade across the river. The chill's settled into their muscles."

"What do we do?"

"We have to rub them down—all of them—with wool."

"We don't have time for that," Silk objected.

"It's that or walk," Durnik declared, pulling off his stout wool cloak and beginning to rub vigorously at his horse's legs with it.

"Maybe we should build a fire," Garion suggested, also dismounting and beginning to rub down his horse's shivering legs.

"There isn't anything around here to burn," Durnik told him. "This is all open grassland."

"And a fire would set up a beacon for every Murgo within ten miles," Barak added, massaging the legs of his gray horse.

They all worked as rapidly as possible, but the sky to the east had begun to pale with the first hints of dawn before Mandorallen's horse was on its feet again and the rest of their mounts were able to move.

"They won't be able to run," Durnik declared somberly. "We shouldn't even ride them."

"Durnik," Silk protested, "Taur Urgas is right behind us."

"They won't last a league if we try to make them run," the smith said stubbornly. "There's nothing left in them."

They rode away from the river at a walk. Even at that pace, Garion could feel the trembling of his horse under him. They all looked back frequently, watching the dark-shrouded plain beyond the river as the sky grew gradually lighter. When they reached the top of the first low hills, the deep shadow which had obscured the grasslands behind them faded and they were able to see movement. Then, as the light grew stronger, they saw an army of Murgos swarming toward the river. In the midst of them were the flapping black banners of Taur Urgas himself.

The Murgos came on in waves until they reached the far bank of the river. Then their mounted scouts ranged out until they located the ford. The bulk of the army Taur Urgas had brought down to the plain was still on foot, but clusters of horses were being driven up from the rear as rapidly as they could be brought down the narrow cut leading from the top of the escarpment.

As the first units began splashing across the ford, Silk turned to Belgarath. "Now what?" the little man asked in a worried voice.

"We'd better get off the top of this hill," the old man replied. "I don't think they've seen us yet, but it's just a question of time, I'm afraid."

They rode down into a little swale just beyond the hill. The overcast which had obscured the sky for the past week or more had begun to blow off, and broad patches of pale, icy blue had begun to appear, though the sun had not yet come up.

"My guess is that he's going to hold the bulk of his army on the far side," Belgarath told them after they had all dismounted. "He'll bring them on across as their horses catch up. As soon as they get to this side, they're going to spread out to look for us."

"That's the way I'd do it," Barak agreed.

"Somebody ought to keep an eye on them," Durnik suggested. He started back up the hill on foot. "I'll let you know if they start doing anything unusual."

Belgarath seemed lost in thought. He paced up and down, his hands clasped together behind his back and an angry look on his face. "This isn't working out the way I'd expected," he said finally. "I hadn't counted on the horses playing out on us."

"Is there any place we can hide?" Barak asked.

Belgarath shook his head. "This is all grassland," he replied. "There aren't any rocks or caves or trees, and it's going to be impossible to cover our tracks." He kicked at the tall grass. "This isn't turning out too well," he admitted glumly. "We're all alone out here on exhausted horses." He chewed thoughtfully at his lower lip. "The nearest help is in the Vale. I think we'd better turn south and make for it. We're fairly close."

"*How* close?" Silk asked.

"Ten leagues or so."

"That's going to take all day, Belgarath. I don't think we've got that long."

"We might have to tamper with the weather a bit," Belgarath conceded. "I don't like doing that, but I might not have any choice."

There was a distant low rumble somewhere off to the north. The little boy looked up and smiled at Aunt Pol. "Errand?" he asked.

"Yes, dear," she replied absently.

"Can you pick up any traces of Algars in the vicinity, Pol?" Belgarath asked her.

She shook her head. "I think I'm too close to the Orb, Father. I keep getting an echo that blots things out more than a mile or so away."

"It always has been noisy," he grunted sourly.

"Talk to it, Father," she suggested. "Maybe it'll listen to you."

He gave her a long, hard look—a look she returned quite calmly. "I can do without that, miss," he told her finally in a crisp voice.

There was another low rumble, from the south this time.

"Thunder?" Silk said, looking a bit puzzled. "Isn't this an odd time of year for it?"

"This plain breeds peculiar weather," Belgarath said. "There isn't anything between here and Drasnia but eight hundred leagues of grass."

"Do we try for the Vale then?" Barak asked.

"It looks as if we'll have to," the old man replied.

Durnik came back down the hill. "They're coming across the river," he reported, "but they aren't spreading out yet. It looks as if they want to get more men across before they start looking for us."

"How hard can we push the horses without hurting them?" Silk asked him.

"Not very," Durnik replied. "It'd be better to save them until we absolutely have to use up whatever they've got left. If we walk and lead them for an hour or so, we might be able to get a canter out of them—for short periods of time."

"Let's go along the back side of the crest," Belgarath said, picking up the reins of his horse. "We'll stay pretty much out of sight that way, but I want to keep an eye on Taur Urgas." He led them at an angle back up out of the swale.

The clouds had broken even more now, and the tatters raced in the endless winds that swept the vast grassland. To the east, the sky was turning a pale pink. Although the Algarian plain did not have that bitter, arid chill that had cut at them in the uplands of Cthol Murgos and Mishrak ac Thull, it was still very cold. Garion shivered, drew his cloak in tight about him, and kept walking, trailing his weary horse behind him.

There was another brief rumble, and the little boy, perched in the saddle of Aunt Pol's horse laughed. "Errand," he announced.

"I wish he'd stop that," Silk said irritably.

They glanced from time to time over the crest of the long hill as they walked. Below, in the broad valley of the Aldur River, the Murgos of Taur Urgas were fording in larger and larger groups. It appeared that fully half his army had reached the west bank by now, and the red-and-black standard of the king of the Murgos stood planted defiantly on Algarian soil.

"If he brings too many more men down the escarpment, it's going to take something pretty significant to dislodge him," Barak rumbled, scowling down at the Murgos.

"I know," Belgarath replied, "and that's the one thing I've wanted to avoid. We aren't ready for a war just yet."

The sun, huge and red, ponderously moved up from behind the eastern escarpment, turning the sky around it rosy. In the still-shadowed valley below them, the Murgos continued to splash across the river in the steely morning light.

"Methinks he will await the sun before he begins the search for us," Mandorallen observed.

"And that's not very far off," Barak agreed, glancing at the slowly moving band of sunlight just touching the hill along which they moved. "We've probably got half an hour at the most. I think it's getting to the point where we're going to have to gamble on the horses. Maybe if we switch mounts every mile or so, we can get some more distance out of them."

The rumble that came then could not possibly have been thunder. The ground shook with it, and it rolled on and on endlessly from both the north and south.

And then, pouring over the crests of the hills surrounding the valley of the Aldur like some vast tide suddenly released by the bursting of a mighty dam, came the clans of the Algars. Down they plunged upon the startled Murgos thickly clustered along the banks of the river, and their great war cry shook the very heavens as they fell like wolves upon the divided army of Taur Urgas.

A lone horseman veered out of the great charge of the clans and came pounding up the hillside toward Garion and his friends. As the warrior drew closer, Garion could see his long scalp lock flowing behind him and his drawn saber catching the first rays of the morning sun. It was Hettar. A vast surge of relief swept over Garion. They were safe.

"Where have you been?" Barak demanded in a great voice as the hawk-faced Algar rode closer.

"Watching," Hettar replied calmly as he reined in. "We wanted to let the Murgos get out a ways from the escarpment so we could cut them off. My father sent me to see how you all are."

"How considerate," Silk observed sardonically. "Did it ever occur to you to let us know you were out there?"

Hettar shrugged. "We could see that you were all right." He looked critically at their exhausted mounts. "You didn't take very good care of them," he said accusingly.

"We were a bit pressed," Durnik apologized.

"Did you get the Orb?" the tall man asked Belgarath, glancing hungrily down toward the river where a vast battle had been joined.

"It took a bit, but we got it," the old sorcerer replied.

"Good." Hettar turned his horse, and his lean face had a fierce look on it. "I'll tell Cho-Hag. Will you excuse me?" Then he stopped as if remembering something. "Oh," he said to Barak, "congratulations, by the way."

"For what?" the big man asked, looking puzzled.

"The birth of your son."

"What?" Barak sounded stunned. "How?"

"In the usual way, I'd imagine," Hettar replied.

"I mean how did you find out?"

"Anheg sent word to us."

"When was he born?"

"A couple months ago." Hettar looked nervously down at the battle which was raging on both sides of the river and in the middle of the ford as well. "I really have to go," he said. "If I don't hurry, there won't be any Murgos left." And he drove his heels into his horse's flanks and plunged down the hill.

"He hasn't changed a bit," Silk noted.

Barak was standing with a somewhat foolish grin on his big, red-bearded face.

"Congratulations, my Lord," Mandorallen said to him, clasping his hand.

Barak's grin grew broader.

It quickly became obvious that the situation of the encircled Murgos below was hopeless. With his army cut in two by the river, Taur Urgas was unable to mount even an orderly retreat. The forces he had brought across the river were quickly swarmed under by King Cho-Hag's superior numbers, and the few survivors of that short, ugly mêlée plunged back into the river, protectively drawn up around the red-and-black banner of the Murgo king. Even in the ford, however, the Algar warriors pressed him. Some distance upriver Garion could see horsemen plunging into the icy water to be carried down by the current to the shallows of the ford in an effort to cut off escape. Much of the fight in the river was obscured by the sheets of spray kicked up by struggling horses, but the bodies floating downstream testified to the savagery of the clash.

Briefly, for no more than a moment, the red and black banner of Taur Urgas was confronted by the burgundy-and-white horse-banner of King Cho-Hag, and then the two were swept apart.

"That could have been an interesting meeting," Silk noted. "Cho-Hag and Taur Urgas have hated each other for years."

Once the king of the Murgos regained the east bank, he rallied what forces he could, turned, and fled back across the open grassland toward the escarpment with Algar clansmen hotly pursuing him. For the bulk of his army, however, there was no escape. Since their horses had not yet descended the narrow ravine from the top of the escarpment, they were forced to fight on foot. The Algars swept down upon them in waves, sabers flashing in the morning sun. Faintly, Garion could hear the screams. Sickened finally, he turned away, unable to watch the slaughter any longer.

The little boy, who was standing close beside Aunt Pol with his hand in hers, looked at Garion gravely. "Errand," he said with a sad conviction.

By midmorning the battle was over. The last of the Murgos on the far bank of the river had been destroyed, and Taur Urgas had fled with the tattered remnants of his army back up the ravine. "Good fight," Barak observed professionally, looking down at the bodies littering both banks of the river and bobbing limply in the shallows downstream from the ford.

"The tactics of thine Algar cousins were masterly," Mandorallen agreed. "Taur Urgas will take some time to recover from this morning's chastisement."

"I'd give a great deal to see the look on his face just now." Silk laughed. "He's probably frothing at the mouth."

King Cho-Hag, dressed in steel-plated black leather and with his horse-banner streaming triumphantly in the bright morning sun, came galloping up the hill toward them, closely surrounded by the members of his personal guard. "Interesting morning," he said with typical Algar understatement as he reined in. "Thanks for bringing us so many Murgos."

"He's as bad as Hettar," Silk observed to Barak.

The king of the Algars grinned openly as he slowly dismounted. His weak legs seemed almost to buckle as he carefully put his weight on them, and he held on to his saddle for support. "How did things go in Rak Cthol?" he asked.

"It wound up being rather noisy," Belgarath replied.

"Did you find Ctuchik in good health?"

"Moderately. We corrected that, however. The whole affair set off an earthquake. Most of Rak Cthol slid off its mountaintop, I'm afraid."

Cho-Hag grinned again. "What a shame."

"Where's Hettar?" Barak asked.

"Chasing Murgos, I imagine," Cho-Hag replied. "Their rearguard got cut off, and they're out there trying to find someplace to hide."

"There aren't very many hiding places on this plain, are there?" Barak asked.

"Almost none at all," the Algar king agreed pleasantly.

A dozen or so Algar wagons crested a nearby hill, rolling toward them through the tall, brown grass. They were square-boxed conveyances, looking not unlike houses on wheels. They had roofs, narrow windows, and steps at the rear leading up to the doorway on the back of each wagon. It looked, Garion thought, almost like a moving city as they approached.

"I imagine Hettar's going to be a while," Cho-Hag noted. "Why don't we have a bit of lunch? I'd like to get word to Anheg and Rhodar about what's happened here as soon as possible, but I'm sure you'll want to pass a few things along as well. We can talk while we eat."

Several of the wagons were drawn up close together and their sides were let down and joined to form a spacious, low-ceilinged dining hall. Braziers provided warmth, and candles illuminated the interior of the quickly assembled hall, supplementing the bright winter sunlight streaming in through the windows.

They dined on roasted meat and mellow ale. Garion soon found that he was wearing far too many clothes. It seemed that he had not been warm in months, and the glowing braziers shimmered out a welcome heat. Although he was tired and very dirty, he felt warm and safe, and he soon found himself nodding over his plate, almost drowsing as Belgarath recounted the story of their escape to the Algar king.

Gradually, however, as the old man spoke, something alerted Garion. There was, it seemed, a trace too much vivacity in his grandfather's voice, and Belgarath's words sometimes seemed almost to tumble over each other. His blue eyes were very bright, but seemed occasionally a bit unfocused.

"So Zedar got away," Cho-Hag was saying. "That's the only thing that mars the whole affair."

"Zedar's no problem," Belgarath replied, smiling in a slightly dazed way.

His voice seemed strange, uncertain, and King Cho-Hag looked at the old man curiously. "You've had a busy year, Belgarath," he said.

"A good one, though." The sorcerer smiled again and lifted his ale cup. His hand was trembling violently, and he stared at it in astonishment.

"Aunt Pol!" Garion called urgently.

"Are you all right, Father?"

"Fine, Pol, perfectly fine." He smiled vaguely at her, his unfocused eyes blinking owlishly. He rose suddenly to his feet and began to move toward her, but his steps were lurching, almost staggering. And then his eyes rolled back in his head and he fell to the floor like a pole-axed cow.

"Father!" Aunt Pol exclaimed, leaping to his side.

Garion, moving almost as fast as his aunt, knelt on the other side of the unconscious old man. "What's wrong with him?" he demanded.

But Aunt Pol did not answer. Her hands were at Belgarath's wrist and brow, feeling for his pulse. She peeled back one of his eyelids and stared intently into his blank, unseeing eyes. "Durnik!" she snapped. "Get my herb-bag—quickly!"

The smith bolted for the door.

King Cho-Hag had half risen, his face deathly pale. "He isn't—"

"No," she answered tensely. "He's alive, but only barely."

"Is something attacking him?" Silk was on his feet, looking around wildly, his hand unconsciously on his dagger.

"No. It's nothing like that." Aunt Pol's hands had moved to the old man's chest. "I should have known," she berated herself. "The stubborn, proud old fool! I should have been watching him."

"Please, Aunt Pol," Garion begged desperately, "what's wrong with him?"

"He never really recovered from his fight with Ctuchik," she replied. "He's been forcing himself, drawing on his will. Then those rocks in the ravine—but he wouldn't quit. Now he's burned up all his vital energy and will. He barely has enough strength left to keep breathing."

Garion had lifted his grandfather's head and cradled it on his lap.

"Help me, Garion!"

He knew instinctively what she wanted. He gathered his will and held out his hand to her. She grasped it quickly, and he felt the force surge out of him.

Her eyes were very wide as she intently watched the old man's face. "Again!" And once more she pulled the quickly gathered will out of him.

"What are we doing?" Garion's voice was shrill.

"Trying to replace some of what he's lost. Maybe—" She glanced toward the door. "Hurry, Durnik!" she shouted.

Durnik rushed back into the wagon.

"Open the bag," she instructed, "and give me that black jar—the one that's sealed with lead—and a pair of iron tongs."

"Should I open the jar, Mistress Pol?" the smith asked.

"No. Just break the seal—carefully. And give me a glove—leather, if you can find one."

Wordlessly, Silk pulled a leather gauntlet from under his belt and handed it to her. She pulled it on, opened the black jar, and reached inside with the tongs. With great care, she removed a single dark, oily-looking green leaf. She held it very carefully in the tongs. "Pry his mouth open, Garion," she ordered.

Garion wedged his fingers between Belgarath's clenched teeth and carefully pried the old man's jaws apart. Aunt Pol pulled down her father's lower lip, reached inside his mouth with the shiny leaf, and lightly brushed his tongue with it, once and once only.

Belgarath jumped violently, and his feet suddenly scraped on the floor. His muscles heaved, and his arms began to flail about.

"Hold him down," Aunt Pol commanded. She pulled back sharply and held the leaf out of the way while Mandorallen and Barak jumped in to hold down Belgarath's convulsing body. "Give me a bowl," she ordered. "A wooden one."

Durnik handed her one, and she deposited the leaf and the tongs in it. Then, with great care, she took off the gauntlet and laid it atop the leaf. "Take this," she told the smith. "Don't touch any part of the glove."

"What do you want me to do with it, Mistress Pol?"

"Take it out and burn it—bowl and all—and don't let anyone get into the smoke from it."

"Is it *that* dangerous?" Silk asked.

"It's even worse, but those are the only precautions we can take out here."

Durnik swallowed very hard and left the wagon, holding the bowl as if it were a live snake.

Polgara took a small mortar and pestle and began grinding certain herbs from her bag into a fine powder as she watched Belgarath intently. "How far is it to the Stronghold, Cho-Hag?" she asked the Algar king.

"A man on a good horse could make it in half a day," he replied.

"How long by wagon—a wagon driven carefully to avoid bouncing?"

"Two days."

She frowned, still mixing the herbs in the mortar. "All right, there's no help for it, I guess. Please send Hettar to Queen Silar. Have him tell her that I'm going to need a warm, well-lighted chamber with a good bed and no drafts. Durnik, I want you to drive the wagon. Don't hit any bumps—even if it means losing an hour."

The smith nodded.

"He's going to be all right, isn't he?" Barak asked, his voice strained and his face shocked by Belgarath's sudden collapse.

"It's really too early to say," she replied. "He's been on the point of collapse for days maybe. But he wouldn't let himself go. I think he's past this crisis, but there may be others." She laid one hand on her father's chest. "Put him in bed—carefully. Then I want a screen of some kind around the bed—blankets will do. We have to keep him very quiet and out of drafts. No loud noises."

They all stared at her as the significance of her extreme precautions struck them.

"Move, gentlemen," she told them firmly. "His life may depend on a certain speed."

CHAPTER SIX

The wagon seemed barely to crawl. The high, thin cloud had swept in again to hide the sun, and a kind of leaden chill descended on the featureless plain of southern Algaria. Garion rode inside the wagon, thick-headed and numb with exhaustion, watching with dreadful concern as Aunt Pol hovered over the unconscious Belgarath. Sleep was out of the question. Another crisis could arise at any time and he had to be ready to leap to her aid, joining his will and the power of his amulet with hers. Errand, his small face grave, sat quietly in a chair at the far side of the wagon, his hands firmly clasped around the pouch Durnik had made for him. The sound of the Orb still hung in Garion's ears, muted but continual. He had grown almost accustomed to the song in the weeks since they had left Rak Cthol; but at quiet moments or when he was tired, it always seemed to return with renewed strength. It was somehow a comforting sound.

Aunt Pol leaned forward to touch Belgarath's chest.

"What's wrong?" Garion asked in a sharp whisper.

"Nothing's wrong, Garion," she replied calmly. "Please don't keep saying that every time I so much as move. If something's wrong, I'll tell you."

"I'm sorry—I'm just worried, that's all."

She turned to give him a steady look. "Why don't you take Errand and go up and ride on top of the wagon with Silk and Durnik?"

"What if you need me?"

"I'll call you, dear."

"I'd really rather stay, Aunt Pol."

"I'd really rather you didn't. I'll call if I need you."

"But—"

"Now, Garion."

Garion knew better than to argue. He took Errand out the back door of the wagon and up the steps to the top.

"How is he?" Silk asked.

"How should I know? All I know is that she chased me out." Garion's reply was a bit surly.

"That might be a good sign, you know."

"Maybe." Garion looked around. Off to the west there was a range of low hills. Rearing above them stood a vast pile of rock.

"The Algar Stronghold," Durnik told Garion, pointing.

"Are we that close?"

"That's still a good day's ride."

"How high is it?" Garion asked.

"Four or five hundred feet at least," Silk told him. "The Algars have been building at it for several thousand years. It gives them something to do after the calving season."

Barak rode up. "How's Belgarath?" he asked as he approached.

"I think he might be improving just a little," Garion answered. "I don't know for sure, though."

"That's something, anyway." The big man pointed toward a gully just ahead. "You'd better go around that," he told Durnik. "King Cho-Hag says that the ground gets a bit rough through there."

Durnik nodded and changed the wagon's direction.

Throughout the day, the Stronghold of the Algars loomed higher and higher against the western horizon. It was a vast, towering fortress rearing out of the dun-colored hills.

"A monument to an idea that got out of hand," Silk observed as he lounged idly atop the wagon.

"I don't quite follow that," Durnik said.

"Algars are nomads," the little man explained. "They live in wagons like this one and follow their herds. The Stronghold gives Murgo raiders something to attack. That's its only real purpose. Very practical, really. It's much easier than looking for them all over these plains. The Murgos always come here, and it's a convenient place to wipe them out."

"Don't the Murgos realize that?" Durnik looked a bit skeptical.

"Quite possibly, but they come here anyway because they can't resist the place. They simply can't accept the fact that nobody really lives here." Silk grinned his ferretlike little grin. "You know how stubborn Murgos are. Anyway, over the years the Algar clans have developed a sort of competition. Every year they try to outdo one another in hauling rock, and the Stronghold keeps growing higher and higher."

"Did Kal Torak *really* lay siege to it for eight years?" Garion asked him.

Silk nodded. "They say that his army was like a sea of Angaraks dashing itself to pieces against the walls of the Stronghold. They might still be here, but they ran out of food. That's always been the problem with large armies. Any fool can raise an army, but you start running into trouble around suppertime."

As they approached the man-made mountain, the gates opened and a party emerged to greet them. In the lead on a white palfrey rode Queen Silar with Hettar close behind. At a certain point they stopped and sat waiting.

Garion lifted a small trapdoor in the roof of the wagon. "We're here, Aunt Pol," he reported in a hushed voice.

"Good," she replied.

"How's Grandfather?"

"He's sleeping. His breathing seems a bit stronger. Go ask Cho-Hag to take us inside immediately. I want to get Father into a warm bed as soon as possible."

"Yes, Aunt Pol." Garion lowered the trapdoor and then went down the steps at the rear of the slowly moving wagon. He untied his horse, mounted and rode to the front of the column where the Algar queen was quietly greeting her husband.

"Excuse me," he said respectfully, swinging down from his horse, "but Aunt Pol wants to get Belgarath inside at once."

"How is he?" Hettar asked.

"Aunt Pol says that his breathing's getting stronger, but she's still worried."

From the rear of the group that had emerged from the Stronghold, there was a flurry of small hooves. The colt that had been born in the hills above Maragor burst into view and came charging directly at them. Garion immediately found himself swarmed under by the colt's exuberant greetings. The small horse nuzzled him and butted at him with its head, then pranced away only to gallop back again. When Garion put his hand on the animal's neck to calm him, the colt quivered with joy at his touch.

"He's been waiting for you," Hettar said to Garion. "He seems to have known you were coming."

The wagon drew up and stopped. The door opened, and Aunt Pol looked out.

"Everything's ready, Polgara," Queen Silar told her.

"Thank you, Silar."

"Is he recovering at all?"

"He seems better, but it's very hard to say for sure at this point."

Errand, who had been watching from the top of the wagon, suddenly clambered down the steps at the rear, hopped to the ground, and ran out along the legs of the horses.

"Catch him, Garion," Aunt Pol said. "I think he'd better ride in here with me until we get inside the Stronghold."

As Garion started after the little boy, the colt scampered away, and Errand, laughing with delight, ran after him. "Errand!" Garion called sharply. The colt, however, had turned in midgallop and suddenly bore down on the child, his hooves flailing wildly. Errand, showing no signs of alarm, stood smiling directly in its path. Startled, the little horse stiffened his legs and skidded to a stop. Errand laughed and held out his hand. The colt's eyes were wide as he sniffed curiously at the hand, and then the boy touched the small animal's face.

Again within the vaults of his mind Garion seemed to hear that strange, bell-like note, and the dry voice murmured, *"Done,"* with a peculiar sort of satisfaction.

"What's that supposed to mean?" Garion asked silently, but there was no answer. He shrugged and picked Errand up to avoid any chance collision between horse and child. The colt stood staring at the two of them, its eyes wide as if in amazement; when Garion turned to carry Errand back to the wagon, it trotted alongside, sniffing and even nuzzling at the child. Garion wordlessly handed Errand up to Aunt Pol and looked her full in the face. She said nothing as she took the child, but her expression told him plainly that something very important had just happened.

As he turned to remount his horse, he felt that someone was watching him, and he turned quickly toward the group of riders that had accompanied Queen Silar from the Stronghold. Just behind the queen was a tall girl mounted on a roan horse. She had long, dark brown hair, and the eyes she had fixed on Garion were gray, calm, and very serious. Her horse pranced nervously, and she calmed him with a quiet word and a gentle touch, then turned to gaze openly at Garion again. He had the peculiar feeling that he ought to know her.

The wagon creaked as Durnik shook the reins to start the team, and they all followed King Cho-Hag and Queen Silar through a narrow gate into the Stronghold. Garion saw immediately that there were no buildings inside the towering fortress. Instead there was a maze of stone walls perhaps twenty feet high twisting this way and that without any apparent plan.

"But where is thy city, your Majesty?" Mandorallen asked in perplexity.

"Inside the walls themselves," King Cho-Hag replied. "They're thick enough and high enough to give us all the room we could possibly need."

"What purpose hath all this, then?"

"It's just a trap." The king shrugged. "We permit attackers to break through the gates, and then we deal with them in here. We want to go this way." He led them along a narrow alleyway.

They dismounted in a courtyard beside the vast wall. Barak and Hettar unhooked the latches and swung the side of the wagon down. Barak tugged thoughtfully at his beard as he looked at the sleeping Belgarath. "It would probably disturb him less if we just took him inside bed and all," he suggested.

"Right," Hettar agreed, and the two of them climbed up into the wagon to lift out the sorcerer's bed.

"Just don't bounce him around," Polgara cautioned. "And don't drop him."

"We've got him, Polgara," Barak assured her. "I know you might not believe it, but we're almost as concerned about him as you are."

With the two big men carrying the bed, they passed through an arched doorway into a wide, torch-lighted corridor and up a flight of stairs, then along another hallway to another flight. "Is it much farther?" Barak asked. Sweat was running down his face into his beard. "This bed isn't getting any lighter, you know."

"Just up here," the Algar Queen told him.

"I hope he appreciates all this when he wakes up," Barak grumbled.

The room to which they carried Belgarath was large and airy. A glowing brazier stood in each corner and a broad window overlooked the maze inside the walls of the Stronghold. A canopied bed stood against one wall and a large wooden tub against the other.

"This will be just fine," Polgara said approvingly. "Thank you, Silar."

"We love him too, Polgara," Queen Silar replied quietly.

Polgara drew the drapes, darkening the room. Then she turned back the covers, and Belgarath was transferred to the canopied bed so smoothly that he did not even stir.

"He *looks* a little better," Silk said.

"He needs sleep, rest and quiet more than anything right now," Polgara told him, her eyes intent on the old man's sleeping face.

"We'll leave you with him, Polgara," Queen Silar said. She turned to the rest of them. "Why don't we all go down to the main hall? Supper's nearly ready, but in the meantime I'll have some ale brought in."

Barak's eyes brightened noticeably, and he started toward the door.

"Barak," Polgara called to him, "aren't you and Hettar forgetting something?" She looked pointedly at the bed they had used for a stretcher.

Barak sighed. He and Hettar picked up the bed again.

"I'll send some supper up for you, Polgara," the queen said.

"Thank you, Silar." Aunt Pol turned to Garion, her eyes grave. "Stay for a few moments, dear," she asked, and he remained as the others all quietly left.

"Close the door, Garion," she said, pulling a chair up beside the sleeping old man's bed.

He shut the door and crossed the room back to her. "Is he really getting better, Aunt Pol?"

She nodded. "I think we're past the immediate danger. He seems stronger physically. But it's not his physical body I'm worried about—it's his mind. That's why I wanted to talk to you alone."

Garion felt a sudden cold grip of fear. "His mind?"

"Keep your voice down, dear," she told him quietly. "This has to be kept strictly between us." Her eyes were still on Belgarath's face. "An episode like this can have very serious effects, and there's no way to know how he'll be when he recovers. He could be very seriously weakened."

"Weakened? How?"

"His will could be greatly reduced—to that of any other old man. He drained it to the utter limit, and he might have gone so far that he'll never regain his powers."

"You mean he wouldn't be a sorcerer anymore?"

"Don't repeat the obvious, Garion," she said wearily. "If that happens, it's going to be up to you and me to conceal it from everybody. Your grandfather's power is the one thing that has held the Angaraks in check for all these years. If something has happened to that power, then you and I will have to make it *look* as if he's the same as he always was. We'll have to conceal the truth even from him, if that's possible."

"What can we do without him?"

"We'd go on, Garion," she replied quietly, looking directly into his eyes. "Our task is too important for us to falter because a man falls by the wayside—even if that man happens to be your grandfather. We're racing against time in all this. We absolutely must fulfill the Prophecy and get the Orb back to Riva by Erastide, and there are people who must be gathered up to go with us."

"Who?"

"Princess Ce'Nedra, for one."

"Ce'Nedra?" Garion had never really forgotten the little princess, but he failed to see why Aunt Pol was making such an issue of her going with them to Riva.

"In time you'll understand, dear. All of this is part of a series of events that must occur in proper sequence and at the proper time. In most situations, the present is determined by the past. This series of events is different, however. In this case, what's happening in the present is determined by the future. If we don't get it exactly the way it's supposed to be, the ending will be different, and I don't think any of us would like that at all."

"What do you want me to do?" he asked, placing himself unquestioningly in her hands.

She smiled gratefully at him. "Thank you, Garion," she said simply. "When you rejoin the others, they're going to ask you how father's coming along, and I want you to put on your best face and tell them that he's doing fine."

"You want me to lie to them." It was not even a question.

"No place in the world is safe from spies, Garion. You know that as well as I, and no matter what happens, we can't let any hint that Father might not recover fully get back to the Angaraks. If necessary, you'll lie until your tongue turns black. The whole fate of the West could depend on how well you do it."

He stared at her.

"It's possible that all this is totally unnecessary," she reassured him. "He may be exactly the same as always after he's had a week or two of rest, but we've got to be ready to move smoothly, just in case he's not."

"Can't we do something?"

"We're doing all we can. Go back to the others now, Garion—and smile. Smile until your jaw aches if you have to."

There was a faint sound in the corner of the room, and they both turned sharply. Errand, his blue eyes very serious, stood watching them.

"Take him with you," Aunt Pol said. "See that he eats and keep an eye on him."

Garion nodded and beckoned to the child. Errand smiled his trusting smile and crossed the room. He reached out and patted the unconscious Belgarath's hand, then turned to follow Garion from the room.

The tall, brown-haired girl who had accompanied Queen Silar out through the gates of the Stronghold was waiting for him in the corridor outside. Her skin, Garion noticed, was very pale, almost translucent, and her gray eyes were direct. "Is the Eternal Man really any better?" she asked.

"Much better," Garion replied with all the confidence he could muster. "He'll be out of bed in no time at all."

"He seems so weak," she said. "So old and frail."

"Frail? Belgarath?" Garion forced a laugh. "He's made out of old iron and horseshoe nails."

"He *is* seven thousand years old, after all."

"That doesn't mean anything to him. He stopped paying attention to the years a long time ago."

"You're Garion, aren't you?" she asked. "Queen Silar told us about you when she returned from Val Alorn last year. For some reason I thought you were younger."

"I was then," Garion replied. "I've aged a bit this last year."

"My name is Adara," the tall girl introduced herself. "Queen Silar asked me to show you the way to the main hall. Supper should be ready soon."

Garion inclined his head politely. In spite of the worry gnawing at him, he could not shake off the peculiar feeling that he ought to know this quiet, beautiful girl. Errand reached out and took the girl's hand, and the three of them passed hand in hand down the torchlit corridor.

King Cho-Hag's main hall was on a lower floor. It was a long, narrow room where chairs and padded benches sat in little clusters around braziers filled with glowing coals. Barak, holding a large ale tankard in one huge fist, was describing with some embellishment their descent from the top of the escarpment.

"We didn't really have any choice, you see," the big man was saying. "Taur Urgas had been frothing on our heels for several days, and we had to take the shortest way down."

Hettar nodded. "Plans sometimes have a way of changing when the unexpected crops up," he agreed. "That's why we put men to watching every known pass down from the top of the escarpment."

"I still think you might have let us know you were there." Barak sounded a little injured.

Hettar grinned wolfishly. "We couldn't really take the chance, Barak," he explained. "The Murgos might have seen us, and we didn't want to frighten them off. It would have been a shame if they'd gotten away, wouldn't it?"

"Is that all you ever think about?"

Hettar considered the question for a moment. "Pretty much, yes," he admitted.

Supper was announced then, and they all moved to the long table at the far end of the hall. The general conversation at the table made it unnecessary for Garion to lie directly to anyone about the frightening possibility Aunt Pol had raised, and after supper he sat beside Adara and lapsed into a kind of sleepy haze, only half listening to the talk.

There was a stir at the door, and a guard entered. "The priest of Belar!" he announced in a loud voice, and a tall man in a white robe strode into the room, followed by four men dressed in shaggy furs. The four walked with a peculiar shuffling gait, and Garion instantly recognized them as Bear-cultists, indistinguishable from the Cherek members of the same group he had seen in Val Alorn.

"Your Majesty," the man in the white robe boomed.

"Hail, Cho-Hag," the cultists intoned in unison, "Chief of the Clan-Chiefs of the Algars and guardian of the southern reaches of Aloria."

King Cho-Hag inclined his head briefly. "What is it, Elvar?" he asked the priest.

"I have come to congratulate your Majesty upon the occasion of your great victory over the forces of the Dark God," the priest replied.

"You are most kind, Elvar," Cho-Hag answered politely.

"Moreover," Elvar continued, "it has come to my attention that a holy object has come into the Stronghold of the Algars. I presume that your Majesty will wish to place it in the hands of the priesthood for safekeeping."

Garion, alarmed at the priest's suggestion, half rose from his seat, but stopped, not knowing how to voice his objection. Errand, however, with a confident smile, was already walking toward Elvar. The knots Durnik had so carefully tied were undone, and the child took the Orb out of the pouch at his waist and offered it to the startled priest. "Errand?" he said.

Elvar's eyes bulged and he recoiled from the Orb, lifting his hands above his head to avoid touching it.

"Go ahead, Elvar," Polgara's voice came mockingly from the doorway. "Let him who is without ill intent in the silence of his soul stretch forth his hand and take the Orb."

"Lady Polgara," the priest stammered. "We thought—that is—I—"

"He seems to have some reservations," Silk suggested dryly. "Perhaps he has some lingering and deep-seated doubts about his own purity. That's a serious failing in a priest, I'd say."

Elvar looked at the little man helplessly, his hands still held aloft.

"You should never ask for something you're not prepared to accept, Elvar," Polgara suggested.

"Lady Polgara," Elvar blurted, "we thought that you'd be so busy caring for your father that—" He faltered.

"—That you could take possession of the Orb before I knew about it? Think again, Elvar. I won't allow the Orb to fall into the hands of the Bear-cult." She smiled rather sweetly at him. "Unless *you* happen to be the one destined to wield it, of course. My father and I would both be overjoyed to hand the burden over to someone else. Why don't we find out? All you have to do is reach out your hand and take the Orb."

Elvar's face blanched, and he backed away from Errand fearfully.

"I believe that will be all, Elvar," King Cho-Hag said firmly.

The priest looked about helplessly, then turned and quickly left the hall with his cultists close behind him.

"Make him put it away, Durnik," Polgara told the smith. "And see if you can do something about the knots."

"I could seal them up with lead," Durnik mused. "Maybe that would keep him from getting it open."

"It might be worth a try." Then she looked around. "I thought you might all like to know that my father's awake," she told them. "The old fool appears to be stronger than we thought."

Garion, immediately alert, looked at her sharply, trying to detect some hint that she might not be telling them everything, but her calm face was totally unreadable.

Barak, laughing loudly with relief, slapped Hettar on the back. "I *told* you he'd be all right," he exclaimed delightedly. The others in the room were already crowding around Polgara, asking for details.

"He's awake," she told them. "That's about all I can say at the moment—except that he's his usual charming self. He's already complaining about lumps in the bed and demanding strong ale."

"I'll send some at once," Queen Silar said.

"No, Silar," Polgara replied firmly. "He gets broth, not ale."

"He won't like that much," Silk suggested.

"Isn't that a shame?" She smiled. She half turned, as if about to go back to the sickroom, then stopped and looked rather quizzically at Garion who sat, relieved, but still apprehensive about Belgarath's true condition, beside Adara. "I see that you've met your cousin," she observed.

"*Who?*"

"Don't sit there with your mouth open, Garion," she advised him. "It makes you look like an idiot. Adara's the youngest daughter of your mother's sister. Haven't I ever told you about her?"

It all came crashing in on him. "Aunt Pol!" he protested. "How could you forget something that important?"

But Adara, obviously as startled by the announcement as he had been, gave a low cry, put her arms about his neck and kissed him warmly. "Dear cousin!" she exclaimed.

Garion flushed, then went pale, then flushed again. He stared first at Aunt Pol, then at his cousin, unable to speak or even to think coherently.

CHAPTER SEVEN

In the days that followed, while the others rested and Aunt Pol nursed Belgarath back to health, Garion and his cousin spent every waking moment together. From the time he had been a very small child he had believed that Aunt Pol was his only family. Later, he had discovered that Mister Wolf—Belgarath— was also a relative, though infinitely far removed. But Adara was different. She was nearly his own age, for one thing, and she seemed immediately to fill that void that had always been there. She became at once all those sisters and cousins and younger aunts that others seemed to have but that he did not.

She showed him the Algar Stronghold from top to bottom. As they wandered together down long, empty corridors, they frequently held each other's hands. Most of the time, however, they talked. They sat together in out-of-the-way places with their heads close together, talking, laughing, exchanging confidences and opening their hearts to each other. Garion discovered a hunger for talk in himself that he had not suspected. The circumstances of the past year had made him reticent, and now all that flood of words broke loose. Because he loved his tall, beautiful cousin, he told her things he would not have told any other living soul.

Adara responded to his affection with a love of her own that seemed as deep, and she listened to his outpourings with an attention that made him reveal himself even more.

"Can you really do that?" she asked when, one bright winter afternoon, they sat together in an embrasure high up in the fortress wall with a window behind them overlooking the vast sea of winter-brown grass stretching to the horizon. "Are you really a sorcerer?"

"I'm afraid so," he replied.

"Afraid?"

"There are some pretty awful things involved in it, Adara. At first I didn't want to believe it, but things kept happening because I wanted them to happen. It finally reached the point where I couldn't doubt it anymore."

"Show me," she urged him.

He looked around a bit nervously. "I don't really think I should," he apologized. "It makes a certain kind of noise, you see, and Aunt Pol can hear it. For some reason I don't think she'd approve if I just did it to show off."

"You're not afraid of her, are you?"

"It's not exactly that. I just don't want her to be disappointed in me." He considered that. "Let me see if I can explain. We had an awful argument once—in Nyissa. I said some things I didn't really mean, and she told me exactly what she'd gone through for me." He looked somberly out of the window, remembering Aunt Pol's words on the steamy deck of Greldik's ship. "She's devoted a thousand years to me, Adara—to my family actually, but finally all because of me. She's given up every single thing that's ever been important to her for me. Can you imagine the kind of obligation that puts on me? I'll do anything she wants me to, and I'd cut off my arm before I'd ever hurt her again."

"You love her very much, don't you, Garion?"

"It goes beyond that. I don't think there's even been a word invented yet to describe what exists between us."

Wordlessly Adara took his hand, her eyes warm with a wondering affection.

Later that afternoon, Garion went alone to the room where Aunt Pol was caring for her recalcitrant patient. After the first few days of bed rest, Belgarath had steadily grown more testy about his enforced confinement. Traces of that irritability lingered on his face even as he dozed, propped up by many pillows in his canopied bed. Aunt Pol, wearing her familiar gray dress, sat nearby, her needle busy as she altered one of Garion's old tunics for Errand. The little boy, sitting not far away, watched her with that serious expression that always seemed to make him look older than he really was.

"How is he?" Garion asked softly, looking at his sleeping grandfather.

"Improving," Aunt Pol replied, setting aside the tunic. "His temper's getting worse, and that's always a good sign."

"Are there any hints that he might be getting back his—? Well, you know." Garion gestured vaguely.

"No," she replied. "Nothing yet. It's probably too early."

"Will you two stop that whispering?" Belgarath demanded without opening his eyes. "How can I possibly sleep with all that going on?"

"You were the one who said he didn't want to sleep," Polgara reminded him.

"That was before," he snapped, his eyes popping open. He looked at Garion. "Where have you been?" he demanded.

"Garion's been getting acquainted with his cousin Adara," Aunt Pol explained.

"He *could* stop by to visit me once in a while," the old man complained.

"There's not much entertainment in listening to you snore, Father."

"I do *not* snore, Polgara."

"Whatever you say, Father," she agreed placidly.

"Don't patronize me, Pol!"

"Of course not, Father. Now, how would you like a nice hot cup of broth?"

"I would *not* like a nice hot cup of broth. I want meat—rare, red meat—and a cup of strong ale."

"But you won't get meat and ale, Father. You'll get what I decide to give you—and right now it's broth and milk."

"*Milk?*"

"Would you prefer gruel?"

The old man glared indignantly at her, and Garion quietly left the room.

After that, Belgarath's recovery was steady. A few days later he was out of bed, though Polgara raised some apparently strenuous objections. Garion knew them both well enough to see directly to the core of his aunt's behavior. Prolonged bed rest had never been her favorite form of therapy. She had always wanted her patients ambulatory as soon as possible. By *seeming* to want to coddle her irascible father, she had quite literally forced him out of bed. Even beyond that, the precisely calibrated restrictions she imposed on his movements were deliberately designed to anger him, to goad his mind to activity—never anything more than he could handle at any given time, but always just enough to force his mental recovery to keep pace with his physical recuperation. Her careful manipulation of the old man's convalescence stepped beyond the mere practice of medicine into the realm of art.

When Belgarath first appeared in King Cho-Hag's hall, he looked shockingly weak. He seemed actually to totter as he leaned heavily on Aunt Pol's arm, but a bit later when the conversation began to interest him, there were hints that this apparent fragility was not wholly genuine. The old man was not above a bit of self-dramatization once in a while, and he soon demonstrated that no matter how skillfully Aunt Pol played, he could play too. It was marvelous to watch the two of them subtly maneuvering around each other in their elaborate little game.

The final question, however, still remained unanswered. Belgarath's physical and mental recovery now seemed certain, but his ability to bring his will to bear had not yet been tested. That test, Garion knew, would have to wait.

Quite early one morning, perhaps a week after they had arrived at the Stronghold, Adara tapped on the door of Garion's room; even as he came awake, he knew it was she. "Yes?" he said through the door, quickly pulling on his shirt and hose.

"Would you like to ride today, Garion?" she asked. "The sun's out, and it's a little warmer."

"Of course," he agreed immediately, sitting to pull on the Algar boots Hettar had given him. "Let me get dressed. I'll just be a minute."

"There's no great hurry," she told him. "I'll have a horse saddled for you and get some food from the kitchen. You should probably tell Lady Polgara where you're going, though. I'll meet you in the west stables."

"I won't be long," he promised.

Aunt Pol was seated in the great hall with Belgarath and King Cho-Hag, while Queen Silar sat nearby, her fingers flickering through warp and woof on a large loom upon which she was weaving. The click of her shuttle was a peculiarly drowsy sort of sound.

"Travel's going to be difficult in midwinter," King Cho-Hag was saying. "It'll be savage in the mountains of Ulgo."

"I think there's a way we can avoid all that," Belgarath replied lazily. He was lounging deeply in a large chair. "We'll go back to Prolgu the way we came, but I need to talk to Relg. Do you suppose you could send for him?"

Cho-Hag nodded and gestured to a serving man. He spoke briefly to him as Belgarath negligently hung one leg over the arm of his chair and settled in even deeper. The old man was wearing a soft, gray woolen tunic; although it was early, he held a tankard of ale.

"Don't you think you're overdoing that a bit?" Aunt Pol asked him, looking pointedly at the tankard.

"I have to regain my strength, Pol," he explained innocently, "and strong ale restores the blood. You seem to forget that I'm still practically an invalid."

"I wonder how much of your invalidism's coming out of Cho-Hag's ale-barrel," she commented. "You looked terrible when you came down this morning."

"I'm feeling much better now, though." He smiled, taking another drink.

"I'm sure you are. Yes, Garion?"

"Adara wants me to go riding with her," Garion said. "I—that is, she—thought I should tell you where I was going."

Queen Silar smiled gently at him. "You've stolen away my favorite lady in waiting, Garion," she told him.

"I'm sorry," Garion quickly replied. "If you need her, we won't go."

"I was only teasing you." The queen laughed. "Go ahead and enjoy your ride."

Relg came into the hall just then, and not far behind him, Taiba. The Marag woman, once she had bathed and been given decent clothes to wear, had surprised them all. She was no longer the hopeless, dirty slave woman they had found in the caves beneath Rak Cthol. Her figure was full and her skin very pale. She moved with a kind of unconscious grace, and King Cho-Hag's clansmen looked after her as she passed, their lips pursed speculatively. She seemed to know she was being watched, and, far from being offended by the fact, it seemed rather to please her and to increase her self-confidence. Her violet eyes glowed, and she smiled often now. She was, however, never very far from Relg. At first Garion had believed that she was deliberately placing herself where the Ulgo would have to look at her out of a perverse enjoyment of the discomfort it caused him, but now he was not so sure. She no longer even seemed to think about it, but followed Relg wherever he went, seldom speaking, but always there.

"You sent for me, Belgarath?" Relg asked. Some of the harshness had gone out of his voice, but his eyes still looked peculiarly haunted.

"Ah, Relg," Belgarath said expansively. "There's a good fellow. Come, sit down. Take a cup of ale."

"Water, thank you," Relg replied firmly.

"As you wish." Belgarath shrugged. "I was wondering, do you by any chance know a route through the caves of Ulgo that reaches from Prolgu to the southern edge of the land of the Sendars?"

"That's a very long way," Relg told him.

"Not nearly as long as it would be if we rode over the mountains," Belgarath pointed out. "There's no snow in the caves, and no monsters. Is there such a way?"

"There is," Relg admitted.

"And would you be willing to guide us?" the old man pressed.

"If I must," Relg agreed with some reluctance.

"I think you must, Relg," Belgarath told him.

Relg sighed. "I'd hoped that I could return home now that our journey's al-most over," he said regretfully.

Belgarath laughed. "Actually, our journey's only just started, Relg. We have a long way to go yet."

Taiba smiled a slow, pleased little smile at that.

Garion felt a small hand slip into his, and he smiled down at Errand, who had just come into the hall. "Is it all right, Aunt Pol?" he asked. "If I go riding, I mean?"

"Of course, dear," she replied. "Just be careful. Don't try to show off for Adara. I don't want you falling off a horse and breaking anything."

Errand let go of Garion's hand and walked over to where Relg stood. The knots on the pouch that Durnik had so carefully sealed with lead were undone again, and the little boy took the Orb out and offered it to Relg. "Errand?" he said.

"Why don't you take it, Relg?" Taiba asked the startled man. "No one in the world questions *your* purity."

Relg stepped back and shook his head. "The Orb is the holy object of another religion," he declared. "It is from Aldur, not UL, so it wouldn't be proper for me to touch it."

Taiba smiled knowingly, her violet eyes intent on the zealot's face.

"Errand," Aunt Pol said, "come here."

Obediently he went to her. She took hold of the pouch at his belt and held it open. "Put it away," she told him.

Errand sighed and deposited the Orb in the pouch.

"How *does* he manage to keep getting this open?" she said half to herself as she examined the strings of the pouch.

Garion and Adara rode out from the Stronghold into the rolling hills to the west. The sky was a deep blue, and the sunlight was very bright. Although the morning was crisp, it was not nearly as cold as it had been for the past week or so. The grass beneath their horses' hooves was brown and lifeless, lying dormant under the win-ter sky. They rode together without speaking for an hour or so, and finally they stopped and dismounted on the sunny south side of a hill where there was shelter from the stiff breeze. They sat together looking out at the featureless miles of the Algarian plain.

"How much can actually be done with sorcery, Garion?" she asked after a long silence.

He shrugged. "It depends on who's doing it. Some people are very powerful; others can hardly do anything at all."

"Could you—" She hesitated. "Could you make this bush bloom?" She went on quickly, and he knew that was not the question she had originally intended to ask. "Right now, I mean, in the middle of wintertime," she added.

Garion looked at the dry, scrubby bit of gorse, putting the sequence of what he'd have to do together. "I suppose I could," he replied, "but if I did that in the wrong season, the bush wouldn't have any defense against the cold, and it would die."

"It's only a bush, Garion."

"Why kill it?"

She avoided his eyes. "Could you make something happen for me, Garion?" she asked. "Some small thing. I need something to believe in very much just now."

"I can try, I guess." He did not understand her suddenly somber mood. "How about something like this?" He picked up a twig and turned it over in his hands, looking carefully at it. Then he wrapped several strands of dry grass around it and studied it again until he had what he wanted to do firmly in his mind. When he released his will on it, he did not do it all at once, so the change was gradual. Adara's eyes widened as the sorry-looking clump of twig and dry grass was transmuted before her.

It really wasn't much of a flower. It was a kind of pale lavender color, and it was distinctly lopsided. It was quite small, and its petals were not very firmly attached. Its fragrance, however, was sweet with all the promise of summer. Garion felt very strange as he wordlessly handed the flower to his cousin. The sound of it had not been that rushing noise he'd always associated with sorcery, but rather was very much like the bell tone he'd heard in the glowing cave when he'd given life to the colt. And when he had begun to focus his will, he had not drawn anything from his surroundings. It had all come from within him, and there had been a deep and peculiar joy in it.

"It's lovely," Adara said, holding the little flower gently in her cupped hands and inhaling its fragrance. Her dark hair fell across her cheek, hiding her face from him. Then she lifted her chin, and Garion saw that her eyes were filled with tears. "It seems to help," she said, "for a little while, anyway."

"What's wrong, Adara?"

She did not answer, but looked out across the dun-brown plain. "Who's Ce'Nedra?" she asked suddenly. "I've heard the others mention her."

"Ce'Nedra? She's an Imperial Princess—the daughter of Ran Borune of Tolnedra."

"What's she like?"

"Very small—she's part Dryad—and she has red hair and green eyes and a bad temper. She's a spoiled little brat, and she doesn't like me very much."

"But you could change that, couldn't you?" Adara laughed and wiped at the tears.

"I'm not sure I follow you."

"All you'd have to do is—" She made a vague kind of gesture.

"Oh." He caught her meaning. "No, we can't do very much with other people's thoughts and feelings. What I mean is—well, there's nothing to get hold of. I wouldn't even know where to start."

Adara looked at him for a moment, then she buried her face in her hands and began to cry.

"What's the matter?" he asked, alarmed.

"Nothing," she said. "It's not important."

"It *is* important. Why are you crying?"

"I'd hoped—when I first heard that you were a sorcerer—and then when you made this flower, I thought you could do anything. I thought that maybe you might be able to do something for me."

"I'll do anything you ask, Adara. You know that."

"But you can't, Garion. You just said so yourself."

"What was it that you wanted me to do?"

"I thought that perhaps you might be able to make somebody fall in love with me. Isn't that a foolish idea?"

"Who?"

She looked at him with a quiet dignity, her eyes still full of tears. "It doesn't really matter, does it? You can't do anything about it, and neither can I. It was just a foolish notion, and I know better now. Why don't we just forget that I ever said anything?" She rose to her feet. "Let's go back now. It's not nearly as nice a day as I'd thought, and I'm starting to get cold."

They remounted and rode in silence back toward the looming walls of the Stronghold. They did not speak anymore. Adara did not wish to talk, and Garion did not know what to say.

Behind them, forgotten, lay the flower he had created. Protected by the slope and faintly warmed by the winter sun, the flower that had never existed before swelled with silent, vegetative ecstasy and bore its fruit. A tiny seed pod at its heart opened, scattering infinitesimal seeds that sifted down to the frozen earth through the stalks of winter grass, and there they lay, awaiting spring.

CHAPTER EIGHT

The Ulgo girls had pale skin, white-blond hair and huge, dark eyes. Princess Ce'Nedra sat in the midst of them like a single red rose in a garden of lilies. They watched her every move with a sort of gentle astonishment as if overwhelmed by this vibrant little stranger who had quite suddenly become the center of their lives. It was not merely her coloring, though that was astonishing enough. Ulgos by nature were a serious, reserved people, seldom given to laughter or outward displays of emotion. Ce'Nedra, however, lived as always on the extreme outside of her skin. They watched, enthralled, the flicker and play of mood and emotion across her exquisite little face. They blushed and giggled nervously at her outrageous and often wicked little jokes. She drew them into confidences, and each of the dozen or so who had become her constant companions had at one time or another opened her heart to the little princess.

There were bad days, of course, days when Ce'Nedra was out of sorts, impatient, willful, and when she drove the gentle-eyed Ulgo girls from her with savage vituperation, sending them fleeing in tears from her unexplained tantrums. Later, though they all resolved after such stormy outbursts never to go near her again, they would hesitantly return to find her smiling and laughing as if nothing at all had happened.

It was a difficult time for the princess. She had not fully realized the implications of her unhesitating acquiescence to the command of UL when he had told her to remain behind in the caves while the others journeyed to Rak Cthol. For her entire life, Ce'Nedra had been at the center of events, but here she was, shunted into the background, forced to endure the tedious passage of hours spent doing nothing but waiting. She was not emotionally constructed for waiting, and the outbursts that scattered her companions like startled doves were at least in part generated by her enforced inactivity.

The wild swings of her moods were particularly trying for the Gorim. The frail, ancient holy man had lived for centuries a life of quiet contemplation, and Ce'Nedra had exploded into the middle of that quiet like a comet. Though sometimes tried to the very limits of his patience, he endured the fits of bad temper, the storms of weeping, the unexplained outbursts—and just as patiently her sudden exuberant displays of affection when she would throw her arms about his neck and cover his startled face with kisses.

On those days when Ce'Nedra's mood was congenial, she gathered her companions among the columns on the shore of the Gorim's island to talk, laugh, and play the little games she had invented, and the dim silent cavern was filled with the babble and laughter of adolescent girls. When her mood was pensive, she and the Gorim sometimes took short walks to view the strange splendors of this subterranean world of cave and gallery and cavern beneath the abandoned city of Prolgu. To the unpracticed eye, it might have appeared that the princess was so involved in her own emotional pyrotechnics that she was oblivious to anything around her, but such was not the case. Her complex little mind was quite capable of observing, analyzing, and questioning, even in the very midst of an outburst. To the Gorim's surprise, he found her mind quick and retentive. When he told her the stories of his people, she questioned him closely, moving always to the meaning that lay behind the stories.

The princess made many discoveries during those talks. She discovered that the core of Ulgo life was religion, and that the moral and theme of all their stories was the duty of absolute submission to the will of UL. A Tolnedran might quibble or even try to strike bargains with his God. Nedra expected it, and seemed to enjoy the play of offer and counteroffer as much as did his people. The Ulgo mind, however, was incapable of such casual familiarity. "We were nothing," the Gorim explained. "Less than nothing. We had no place and no God, but wandered outcast in the world until UL consented to become our God. Some of the zealots have even gone so far as to suggest that if one single Ulgo displeases our God, he will withdraw himself from us. I don't pretend to know the mind of UL entirely, but I don't think he's quite that unreasonable. Still, he didn't really want to be our God in the first place, so it's best probably not to offend him."

"He loves *you*," Ce'Nedra pointed out quickly. "Anyone could see that in his face when he came to us that time."

The Gorim looked doubtful. "I *hope* I haven't disappointed him too much."

"Don't be silly," the princess said airily. "Of course he loves you. Everyone in the whole world loves you." Impulsively, as if to prove her point, she kissed his pale cheek fondly.

The Gorim smiled at her. "Dear child," he observed, "your own heart is so open that you automatically assume that everyone loves those whom you love. It's not always that way, I'm afraid. There are a good number of people in our caves who aren't all that fond of me."

"Nonsense," she said. "Just because you argue with someone doesn't mean that you don't love him. I love my father very much, but we fight all the time. We enjoy fighting with each other." Ce'Nedra knew that she was safe using such terms as "silly" and "nonsense" with the Gorim. She had by now so utterly charmed him that she was quite sure she could get away with almost anything.

Although it might have been difficult to persuade anyone around her that such was the case, there *had* been a few distinct but subtle changes in Ce'Nedra's behavior. Impulsive though she might seem to these serious, reserved people, she now gave at least a moment's thought—however brief—before acting or speaking. She had on occasion embarrassed herself here in the caves, and embarrassment was the one thing Ce'Nedra absolutely could not bear. Gradually, imperceptibly, she learned the value of marginal self-control, and sometimes she almost appeared ladylike.

She had also had time to consider the problem of Garion. His absence during the long weeks had been particularly and inexplicably painful for her. It was as if she had misplaced something—something very valuable—and its loss left an aching kind of vacancy. Her emotions had always been such a jumble that she had never fully come to grips with them. Usually they changed so rapidly that she never had time to examine one before another took its place. This yearning sense of something missing, however, had persisted for so long that she finally had to face it.

It could not be love. That was impossible. Love for a peasant scullion—no matter how nice he was—was quite out of the question! She was, after all, an Imperial Princess, and her duty was crystal clear. If there had been even the faintest suspicion in her mind that her feelings had moved beyond casual friendship, she would have an absolute obligation to break off any further contact. Ce'Nedra did not *want* to send Garion away and never see him again. The very thought of doing so made her lip tremble. So, quite obviously, what she felt was not—could not—be love. She felt much better once she had worked that out. The possibility had been worrying her, but now that logic had proved beyond all doubt that she was safe, she was able to relax. It was a great comfort to have logic on her side.

That left only the waiting, the seemingly endless, unendurable waiting for her friends. Where *were* they? When were they coming back? What were they doing out there that could take so long? The longer she waited, the more frequently her newfound self-control deserted her, and her pale-skinned companions learned to watch apprehensively for those minute danger signs that announced imminent eruption.

Then finally the Gorim told her that word had reached him that her friends were returning, and the little princess went absolutely wild with anticipation. Her preparations were lengthy and elaborate. She would greet them properly of course. No little-girl enthusiasm this time. Instead, she would be demure, reserved, imperial and altogether grown-up. Naturally, she would have to look the part.

She fretted for hours before selecting the perfect gown, a floor-length Ulgo dress of glistening white. Ulgo gowns, however, were perhaps a trifle too modest for Ce'Nedra's taste. While she wished to appear reserved, she did not want to be that reserved. Thoughtfully, she removed the sleeves from the gown and made a few modifications to the neckline. Some elaborate cross-tying at bodice and waist with a slender gold sash accentuated things a bit. Critically she examined the results of her efforts and found them to her liking.

Then there was the problem of her hair. The loose, tumbled style she had always worn would never do. It needed to be up, piled in a soft mass of curls atop her head and then cascading elegantly down over one shoulder to add that splash of color across the pristine whiteness of her bodice that would set things off just right. She worked on it until her arms ached from being raised over her head for so long. When she was finished, she studied the entire effect of gown and hair and demurely regal expression. It wasn't bad, she congratulated herself. Garion's eyes would fall out when he saw her. The little princess exulted.

When the day finally arrived, Ce'Nedra, who had scarcely slept, sat nervously with the Gorim in his now-familiar study. He was reading from a long scroll, rolling the top with one hand while he unrolled the bottom with another. As he read, the princess fidgeted, nibbling absently on a lock.

"You seem restless today, child," he observed.

"It's just that I haven't seen him—them—for so long," she explained quickly. "Are you sure I look all right?" She had only asked the question six or eight times that morning already.

"You're lovely, child," he assured her once again.

She beamed at him.

A servingman came into the Gorim's study. "Your guests have arrived, Holy One," he said with a respectful bow.

Ce'Nedra's heart began to pound.

"Shall we go greet them, child?" the Gorim suggested, laying aside his scroll and rising to his feet.

Ce'Nedra resisted her impulse to spring from her chair and run out of the room. With an iron grip she controlled herself. Instead, she walked at the Gorim's side, silently repeating to herself, "Dignity. Reserve. Imperially demure."

Her friends were travel-stained and weary-looking as they entered the Gorim's cavern, and there were strangers with them Ce'Nedra did not recognize. Her eyes however, sought out only one face.

He looked older than she remembered him. His face, which had always been so serious, had a gravity to it now that had not been there before. Things had obviously happened to him while he had been gone—important things—and the princess felt a little pang at having been excluded from such momentous events in his life.

And then her heart froze. Who was that great gangling girl at his side? And why was he being so deferential to the big cow? Ce'Nedra's jaws clenched as she glared across the calm waters of the lake at the perfidious young man. She had *known* it would happen. The minute she had let him out of her sight, he had run headlong into the arms of the first girl who happened by. How *dared* he? *How dared he!*

As the group on the far side of the lake began to come across the causeway, Ce'Nedra's heart sank. The tall girl was lovely. Her dark hair was lustrous, and her features were perfect. Desperately, Ce'Nedra looked for some flaw, some blemish.

And the way the girl moved! She actually seemed to flow with a grace that nearly brought tears of despair to Ce'Nedra's eyes.

The greetings and introductions seemed hardly more than some incoherent babble to the suffering princess. Absently she curtsied to the king of the Algars and his lovely queen. Politely she greeted the lushly beautiful woman—Taiba, her name was—whom Lady Polgara introduced to her. The moment she was dreading was approaching, and there was no way she could forestall it.

"And this is Adara," Lady Polgara said, indicating the lovely creature at Garion's side. Ce'Nedra wanted to cry. It wasn't fair! Even the girl's name was beautiful. Why couldn't it have been something ugly?

"Adara," Lady Polgara continued, her eyes intently on Ce'Nedra's face, "this is her Imperial Highness, the Princess Ce'Nedra."

Adara curtsied with a grace that was like a knife in Ce'Nedra's heart. "I've so wanted to meet your Highness," the tall girl said. Her voice was vibrant, musical.

"Charmed, I'm sure," Ce'Nedra replied with a lofty superiority. Though every nerve within her screamed with the need to lash out at this detested rival, she held herself rigid and silent. Any outburst, even the faintest trace of dismay showing in her expression or her voice would make this Adara's victory complete. Ce'Nedra was too much a princess—too much a *woman*—to permit that ultimate defeat. Though her pain was as real as if she were in the hands of a torturer, she stood erect, enclosed in all the imperial majesty she could muster. Silently she began to repeat all of her titles over and over to herself, steeling herself with them, reminding herself grimly just who she was. An Imperial Princess did not cry. The daughter of Ran Borune did not snivel. The flower of Tolnedra would *never* grieve because some clumsy scullery boy had chosen to love somebody else.

"Forgive me, Lady Polgara," she said, pressing a trembling hand to her forehead, "but I suddenly seem to have the most dreadful headache. Would you excuse me, please?" Without waiting for an answer, she turned to walk slowly toward the Gorim's house. She paused only once, just as she passed Garion. "I hope you'll be very happy," she lied to him.

He looked baffled.

It had gone too far. It had been absolutely necessary to conceal her emotions from Adara, but this was Garion, and she had to let him know exactly how she felt. "I *despise* you, Garion," she whispered at him with a terrible intensity, "and I don't ever want to lay eyes on you again."

He blinked.

"I don't think you can even begin to imagine how much I *loathe* the very sight of you," she added. And with that she continued on into the Gorim's house, her back straight and her head unbowed.

Once she was inside, she fled to her room, threw herself on the bed, and wept in brokenhearted anguish.

She heard a light step near the doorway, and then the Lady Polgara was there. "All right, Ce'Nedra," she said, "what's this all about?" She sat down on the edge of the bed and put one hand on the shoulder of the sobbing little princess.

"Oh, Lady Polgara," Ce'Nedra wailed, suddenly throwing herself into Polgara's arms. "I-I've l-lost him. He-he's in love with h-h-her."

"Who's that, dear?" Polgara asked her calmly.

"Garion. He's in love with that Adara, and he doesn't even know I'm alive any m-m-more."

"You silly little goose," Polgara chided her gently.

"He *does* love her, doesn't he?" Ce'Nedra demanded.

"Of course he does, dear."

"I knew it," Ce'Nedra wailed, collapsing into a fresh storm of weeping.

"It's only natural for him to love her," Polgara continued. "She's his cousin, after all."

"His cousin?" Ce'Nedra's tear-streaked face came up suddenly.

"The daughter of his mother's sister," Polgara explained. "You did know that Garion's mother was an Algar, didn't you?"

Ce'Nedra shook her head mutely.

"Is that what all this is about?"

Ce'Nedra nodded. Her weeping had suddenly stopped.

Lady Polgara took a handkerchief from her sleeve and offered it to the tiny girl. "Blow your nose, dear," she instructed. "Don't sniff like that. It's very unbecoming."

Ce'Nedra blew her nose.

"And so you've finally admitted it to yourself," Polgara observed. "I was wondering how long it was going to take you."

"Admitted what?"

Polgara gave her a long, steady look, and Ce'Nedra flushed slowly, lowering her eyes. "That's better," Polgara said. "You mustn't try to hide things from me, Ce'Nedra. It doesn't do any good, you know, and it only makes things more difficult for you."

Ce'Nedra's eyes had widened as the full impact of her tacit admission struck her. "It's not possible," she gasped in absolute horror. "It can't happen."

"As my father's so fond of saying, just about anything is possible," Polgara told her.

"What am I going to do?"

"First you ought to go wash your face," Polgara told her. "Some girls can cry without making themselves ugly, but you don't have the right coloring for it. You're an absolute fright. I'd advise you never to cry in public if you can help it."

"That's not what I meant," Ce'Nedra said. "What am I going to do about Garion?"

"I don't know that you really need to do anything, dear. Things will straighten themselves out eventually."

"But I'm a princess, and he's—well, he's just Garion. This sort of thing isn't permitted."

"Everything will probably turn out all right," Lady Polgara assured her. "Trust me, Ce'Nedra. I've been handling matters like this for a very long time. Now go wash your face."

"I made a terrible fool of myself out there, didn't I?" Ce'Nedra said.

"It's nothing that can't be fixed," Polgara said calmly. "We can pass it off as something brought on by the excitement of seeing your friends again after so long. You *are* glad to see us, aren't you?"

"Oh, Lady Polgara," Ce'Nedra said, embracing her and laughing and crying at the same time.

After the ravages of Ce'Nedra's crying fit had been repaired, they rejoined the others in the Gorim's familiar study.

"Are you recovered, my child?" the Gorim asked her gently, concern written all over his dear old face.

"Just a touch of nerves, Holy One," Lady Polgara reassured him. "Our princess, as you've probably noticed, is somewhat high-strung."

"I'm so sorry that I ran off like that," Ce'Nedra apologized to Adara. "It was silly of me."

"Your Highness could never be silly," Adara told her.

Ce'Nedra lifted her chin. "Oh yes I can," she declared. "I've got as much right to make a fool of myself in public as anyone else."

Adara laughed, and the entire incident was smoothed over.

There was still, however, a problem. Ce'Nedra had, she realized, gone perhaps a bit too far in her impulsive declaration of undying hatred for Garion. His expression was confused, even a trifle hurt. Ce'Nedra decided somewhat loftily to ignore the injury she had inflicted upon him. *She* had suffered through that dreadful scene on the shore of the Gorim's island, and it seemed only fair that *he* should suffer a little as well—not too much, of course, but a little anyway. He did, after all, have it coming. She allowed him a suitable period of anguish—at least she hoped it was anguish—then spoke to him warmly, even fondly, as if those spiteful words had never passed her lips. His expression became even more baffled, and then she turned the full force of her most winsome smile on him, noting with great satisfaction its devastating effect. After that she ignored him.

While Belgarath and Lady Polgara were recounting the events of their journey to Rak Cthol, the princess sat demurely beside Adara on a bench, half listening, but for the most part turning the amazing discovery of the past hour over and over in her mind. Suddenly, she felt eyes on her, and she looked up quickly. The little blond boy Lady Polgara called Errand was watching her, his small face very serious. There was something about his eyes. With a sudden and absolute certainty, she knew that the child was looking directly into her heart. He smiled at her then; without knowing why, she felt a sudden overwhelming surge of joy at his smile. He walked toward her, still smiling, and his little hand dipped into the pouch at his waist. He took out a round, gray stone and offered it to her. "Errand?" he said. For an instant Ce'Nedra seemed to see a faint blue flicker deep within the stone.

"Don't touch it, Ce'Nedra," Lady Polgara told her in a tone that made Ce'Nedra's hand freeze in the very act of reaching for the stone.

"Durnik!" Lady Polgara said to the smith with an odd note of complaint in her voice.

"Mistress Pol," he said helplessly, "I don't know what else to do. No matter how I seal it up, he always manages to get it open."

"Make him put it away," she told him with just a hint of exasperation.

Durnik went to the little boy, knelt and took hold of the pouch. Without a word he held it open, and the child dropped the stone into it. Durnik tied the pouch shut, pulling the knots as tight as he could. When he had finished, the little boy put his arms affectionately around the smith's neck. Durnik looked a bit embarrassed and was about to lead the child away, but Errand pulled his hand free and climbed instead into Ce'Nedra's lap. Quite seriously he kissed her, then nestled down in her arms and promptly fell asleep.

Feelings moved in Ce'Nedra that she had never felt before. Without knowing why, she was happier than she had ever been in her life. She held the child close against her, her arms protectively about him and her cheek laid snugly against his pale blond curls. She felt an impulse to rock him and perhaps to croon a very soft lullaby to him.

"We'll have to hurry," Belgarath was saying to the Gorim. "Even with Relg's help, it'll take a week or more to reach the Sendarian border. Then we'll have to cross the whole country, and the snow in Sendaria can pile up in a hurry this time of year. To make things even worse, this is the season for storms in the Sea of the Winds, and it's a long way over open water from Sendar to Riva."

The word "Riva" jerked Ce'Nedra out of her reverie. From the very moment that she and Jeebers had crept from the Imperial Palace at Tol Honeth, one single thought had dominated her thinking. She was *not* going to Riva. Though she might have seemed on occasion to have surrendered on that point, her acquiescence had always been a subterfuge. Now, however, she would have to take a stand. The reasons for her adamant refusal to obey the provisions of the Accords of Vo Mimbre were no longer entirely clear to her. So much had happened that she was not even the same person, but one thing was absolutely certain no matter who she was. She was *not* going to Riva. It was a matter of principle.

"I'm sure that once we reach Sendaria, I'll be able to make my way to an Imperial garrison," she said as casually as if the matter had already been decided.

"And why would you want to do that, dear?" Lady Polgara asked her.

"As I said earlier, I'm not going to Riva," Ce'Nedra replied. "The legionnaires will be able to make arrangements to return me to Tol Honeth."

"Perhaps you *should* visit your father," Polgara said quite calmly.

"You mean you're just going to let me go?"

"I didn't say that. I'm sure we'll be able to find a ship bound for Tol Honeth sometime in the late spring or early summer. Rivan commerce with the Empire is extensive."

"I don't think you fully understand me, Lady Polgara. I said that I'm *not* going to go to Riva—under any circumstances."

"I heard you, Ce'Nedra. You're wrong, however. You *are* going to Riva. You have an appointment there, remember?"

"I *won't* go!" Ce'Nedra's voice went up an octave or two.

"Yes, you will." Polgara's voice was deceptively calm, but there was a hint of steel in it.

"I absolutely refuse," the princess declared. She was about to say more, but a small finger gently brushed her lips. The sleepy child in her arms raised his hand to touch her mouth. She moved her head irritably. "I've told you all before that I will not submit to—" The child touched her lips again. His eyes were drowsy as he looked up at her, but his gaze was calm and reassuring. Ce'Nedra forgot what she had been saying. "I am not going to the Isle of the Winds," she concluded rather lamely, "and that's final." The trouble was that it didn't sound all that final.

"It seems that we've had this discussion once or twice before," Polgara observed.

"You have no right to—" Ce'Nedra's words trailed off again as her thoughts went astray once more. The child's eyes were so blue—so very blue. She found herself unable to look away from them and seemed to be sinking into that incredible color. She shook her head. It was so completely unlike her to keep losing track of an argument this way. She tried to concentrate. "I refuse to be publicly humiliated," she declared. "I will *not* stand in the Hall of the Rivan King like a beggar while all the Alorns snicker up their sleeves at me." That was better. Her momentary distraction seemed to be fading. Inadvertantly she glanced down at the child and it all went out the window again. "I don't even have the right kind of dress," she added plaintively. Now what had made her say that?

Polgara said nothing, but her eyes seemed very wise as she watched the princess flounder. Ce'Nedra stumbled along, her objections growing less and less relevant. Even as she argued, she realized that there was no real reason for her not going to Riva. Her refusal seemed frivolous—even childish. Why on earth had she made such a fuss about it? The little boy in her arms smiled encouragingly at her, and, unable to help herself, she smiled back at him, her defenses crumbling. She made one last try. "It's only some silly old formality anyway, Lady Polgara," she said. "There won't be anyone waiting for me in the Hall of the Rivan King—there never has been. The Rivan line is extinct." She tore her eyes away from the child's face. "Do I really *have* to go?"

Lady Polgara nodded gravely.

Ce'Nedra heaved a great sigh. All this bickering seemed so unnecessary. What was the point of making such an issue of a simple trip? It was not as if there was any danger involved. If it would make people happy, why be stubborn about it? "Oh, all right," she surrendered. "If it's so important to everyone, I suppose I can go to Riva." For some reason, saying it made her feel much better. The child in her arms smiled again, gently patted her cheek and went back to sleep. Lost in a sudden inexplicable happiness, the princess nestled her cheek against his curls again and began to rock back and forth gently, crooning very softly.

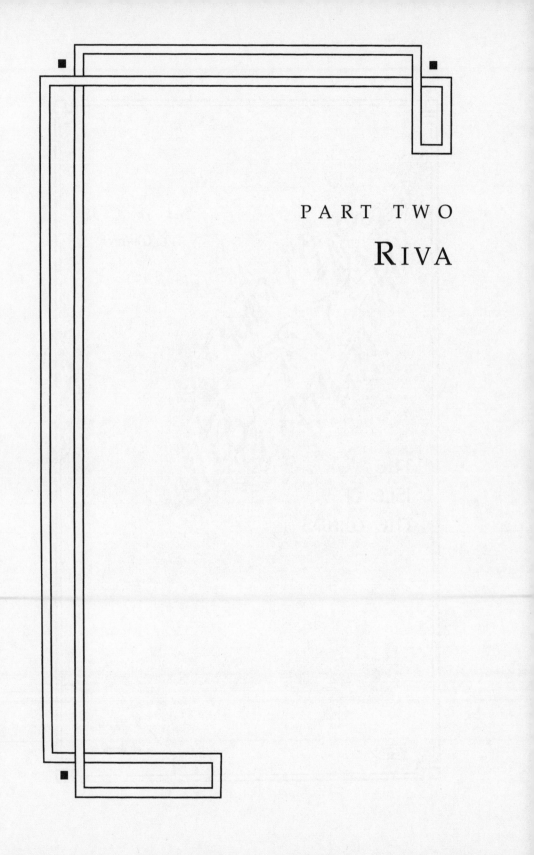

PART TWO

RIVA

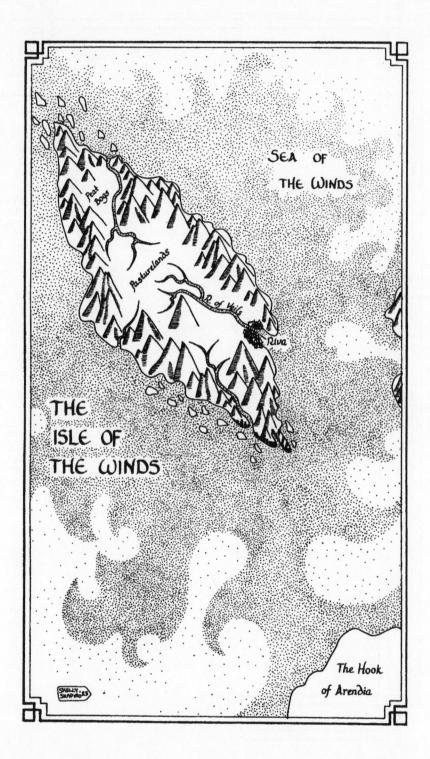

SEA OF
THE WINDS

Peat
Bogs

Pasturelands

R. of Vild

Riva

THE
ISLE OF
THE WINDS

The Hook
of Arendia

SHELLY
SHAPIRO 83

Once more Relg led them through the dark, silent world of the caves, and once more Garion hated every moment of it. It seemed an eternity ago that they had left Prolgu, where Ce'Nedra's farewells to the frail old Gorim had been long and tearful. The princess rather baffled Garion, and he gave himself over to some speculation about her as he stumbled along in the musty-smelling darkness. Something had happened at Prolgu. In some very subtle ways, Ce'Nedra was different—and the differences made Garion jumpy for some reason.

When at last, after uncountable days in the dark, twisting galleries, they emerged once again into the world of light and air, it was through an irregular, brush-choked opening in the wall of a steep ravine. It was snowing heavily outside, with large flakes settling softly down through the windless air.

"Are you sure this is Sendaria?" Barak asked Relg as he bulled his way through the obstructing brush at the cave mouth.

Relg shrugged, once more binding a veil across his face to protect his eyes from the light. "We're no longer in Ulgo."

"There are a lot of places that aren't in Ulgo, Relg," Barak reminded him sourly.

"It sort of looks like Sendaria," King Cho-Hag observed, leaning over in his saddle to stare out of the cave at the softly falling snow. "Can anybody make a guess at the time of day?"

"It's really very hard to say when it's snowing this hard, Father," Hettar told him. "The horses think it's about noon, but their idea of time is a bit imprecise."

"Wonderful," Silk noted sardonically. "We don't know where we are or what time it is. Things are getting off to a splendid start."

"It's not really that important, Silk," Belgarath said wearily. "All we have to do is go north. We're bound to run into the Great North Road eventually."

"Fine," Silk replied. "But which way is north?"

Garion looked closely at his grandfather as the old man squeezed out into the snowy ravine. The old man's face was etched with lines of weariness, and the hollows under his eyes were dark again. Despite the two weeks or more of convalescence at the Stronghold and Aunt Pol's considered opinion that he was fit to travel, Belgarath had obviously not yet fully recovered from his collapse.

As they emerged from the cave, they pulled on their heavy cloaks and tightened the cinches on their saddles in preparation to move out.

"Uninviting sort of place, isn't it?" Ce'Nedra observed to Adara, looking around critically.

"This is mountain country," Garion told her, quickly coming to the defense of his homeland. "It's no worse than the mountains of eastern Tolnedra."

"I didn't say it was, Garion," she replied in an infuriating way.

They rode for several hours until they heard the sound of axes somewhere off in the forest. "Woodcutters," Durnik surmised. "I'll go talk with them and get directions." He rode off in the direction of the sound. When he returned, he had a slightly disgusted look on his face. "We've been going south," he told them.

"Naturally," Silk said sardonically. "Did you find out what time it is?"

"Late afternoon," Durnik told him. "The woodcutters say that if we turn west, we'll strike a road that runs northwesterly. It'll bring us to the Great North Road about twenty leagues on this side of Muros."

"Let's see if we can find this road before dark, then," Belgarath said.

It took them several days to ride down out of the mountains and several more before they had passed through the sparsely inhabited stretches of eastern Sendaria to the more thickly populated plains around Lake Sulturn. It snowed intermittently the entire time, and the heavily traveled roads of south-central Sendaria were slushy and lay like ugly brown scars across the snowy hills. Their party was large, and they usually had to split up among several inns in the neat, snow-covered villages at which they stopped. Princess Ce'Nedra quite frequently used the word "quaint" to describe both the villages and the accommodations, and Garion found her fondness for the word just a trifle offensive.

The kingdom through which they traveled was not the same Sendaria he had left more than a year before. Garion saw quiet evidence of mobilization in almost every village along the way. Groups of country militia drilled in the brown slush in village squares; old swords and bent pikes, long forgotten in dusty attics or damp cellars, had been located and scraped free of rust in preparation for the war everyone knew was coming. The efforts of these peaceful farmers and villagers to look warlike were often ludicrous. Their homemade uniforms were in every possible shade of red or blue or green, and their bright-colored banners obviously showed that treasured petticoats had been sacrificed to the cause. The faces of these simple folk, however, were serious. Though young men strutted in their uniforms for the benefit of village girls, and older men tried to look like veterans, the atmosphere in each village was grave. Sendaria stood quietly on the brink of war.

At Sulturn, Aunt Pol, who had been looking thoughtfully at each village through which they passed, apparently reached a decision. "Father," she said to Belgarath as they rode into town, "you and Cho-Hag and the rest go straight on to Sendar. Durnik, Garion, and I need to make a little side trip."

"Where are you going?"

"To Faldor's farm."

"Faldor's? What for?"

"We all left things behind, Father. You hustled us out of there so fast that we barely had time to pack." Her tone and expression were so matter-of-fact that Garion immediately suspected subterfuge, and Belgarath's briefly raised eyebrow indicated that he also was fairly certain that she was not telling him everything.

"We're starting to trim this a bit close, Pol," the old man pointed out.

"There's still plenty of time, Father," she replied. "It's not really all that far out of our way. We'll only be a few days behind you."

"Is it really that important, Pol?"

"Yes, Father. I think it is. Keep an eye on Errand for me, won't you? I don't think he really needs to go with us."

"All right, Pol."

A silvery peal of laughter burst from the lips of the Princess Ce'Nedra, who was watching the stumbling efforts of a group of militiamen to execute a right turn without tripping over their own weapons. Aunt Pol's expression did not change as she turned her gaze on the giggling jewel of the Empire. "I think we'll take that one with us, however," she added.

Ce'Nedra protested bitterly when she was advised that she would not be traveling directly to the comforts of King Fulrach's palace at Sendar, but her objections had no impact on Aunt Pol.

"Doesn't she *ever* listen to *anybody*?" the little princess grumbled to Garion as they rode along behind Aunt Pol and Durnik on the road to Medalia.

"She always listens," Garion replied.

"But she never changes her mind, does she?"

"Not very often—but she *does* listen."

Aunt Pol glanced over her shoulder at them. "Pull up your hood, Ce'Nedra," she instructed. "It's starting to snow again, and I don't want you riding with a wet head."

The princess drew in a quick breath as if preparing to retort.

"I wouldn't," Garion advised her softly.

"But—"

"She's not in the mood for discussion just now."

Ce'Nedra glared at him, but pulled up her hood in silence.

It was still snowing lightly when they reached Medalia that evening. Ce'Nedra's reaction to the lodgings offered at the inn was predictable. There was, Garion had noted, a certain natural rhythm to her outbursts. She never began at the top of her voice, but rather worked her way up to it with an impressively swelling crescendo. She had just reached the point of launching herself into full voice when she was suddenly brought up short.

"What an absolutely charming display of good breeding," Aunt Pol observed calmly to Durnik. "All of Garion's old friends will be terribly impressed by this sort of thing, don't you think?"

Durnik looked away, hiding a smile. "I'm sure of it, Mistress Pol."

Ce'Nedra's mouth was still open, but her tirade had been cut off instantly. Garion was amazed at her sudden silence. "I *was* being a bit silly, wasn't I?" she said after a moment. Her tone was reasonable—almost sweet-natured.

"Yes, dear—just a bit," Aunt Pol agreed.

It was perhaps noon of the following day when they turned off the main road leading to Erat into the country lane that led to Faldor's farm. Since that morning, Garion's excitement had risen to almost intolerable heights. Every milepost, every bush and tree was familiar to him now. And over there—wasn't that old Cralto riding an unsaddled horse on some errand for Faldor? Finally, at the sight of a tall, familiar figure clearing brush and twigs from a drainage ditch, he was no longer able to restrain himself. He drove his heels into his horse's flanks, smoothly jumped a fence and galloped across the snowy field toward the solitary worker.

"Rundorig!" he shouted, hauling his horse to a stop and flinging himself from his saddle.

"Your Honor?" Rundorig replied, blinking with astonishment.

"Rundorig, it's me—Garion. Don't you recognize me?"

"Garion?" Rundorig blinked several more times, peering intently into Garion's face. The light dawned slowly in his eyes like a sunrise on a murky day. "Why, I believe you're right," he marveled. "You *are* Garion, aren't you?"

"Of course I am, Rundorig," Garion exclaimed, reaching out to take his friend's hand.

But Rundorig shoved both hands behind him and stepped back. "Your clothing, Garion! Have a care. I'm all over mud."

"I don't care about my clothes, Rundorig. You're my friend."

The tall lad shook his head stubbornly. "You mustn't get mud on them. They're too splendid. Plenty of time to shake hands after I clean up." He stared curiously at Garion. "Where did you get such fine things? And a sword? You'd better not let Faldor see you wearing a sword. You know he doesn't approve of that sort of thing."

Somehow things were not going the way they were supposed to be going. "How's Doroon?" Garion asked, "and Zubrette?"

"Doroon moved away last summer," Rundorig replied after a moment's struggle to remember. "I think his mother remarried—anyway, they're on a farm down on the other side of Winold. And Zubrette—well, Zubrette and I started walking out together not too long after you left." The tall young man suddenly blushed and looked down in embarrassed confusion. "There's a sort of an understanding between us, Garion," he blurted.

"How splendid, Rundorig!" Garion exclaimed quickly to cover the little dagger cut of disappointment.

Rundorig, however, had already taken the next step. "I know that you and she were always fond of each other," he said, his long face miserably unhappy. "I'll have a talk with her." He looked up, tears standing in his eyes. "It wouldn't have gone so far, Garion, except that none of us thought that you were ever coming back."

"I haven't really, Rundorig," Garion quickly assured his friend. "We only came by to visit and to pick up some things we left behind. Then we'll be off again."

"Have you come for Zubrette, too?" Rundorig asked in a numb, stricken sort of voice that tore at Garion's heart.

"Rundorig," he said it very calmly, "I don't even have a home anymore. One night I sleep in a palace; the next night in the mud beside the road. Would either one of us want that kind of life for Zubrette?"

"I think she'd go with you if you asked her to, though," Rundorig said. "I think she'd endure anything to be with you."

"But we won't let her, will we? So far as we're concerned, the understanding between the two of you is official."

"I could never lie to her, Garion," the tall boy objected.

"*I* could," Garion said bluntly. "Particularly if it'll keep her from living out her life as a homeless vagabond. All you have to do is keep your mouth shut and let me do the talking." He grinned suddenly. "Just as in the old days."

A slow smile crept shyly across Rundorig's face.

The gate of the farm stood open, and good, honest Faldor, beaming and rubbing his hands with delight, was bustling around Aunt Pol, Durnik, and Ce'Nedra. The tall, thin farmer seemed as lean as always, and his long jaw appeared to have grown even longer in the year and more since they had left. There was a bit more gray at his temples, but his heart had not changed.

Princess Ce'Nedra stood demurely to one side of the little group, and Garion carefully scanned her face for danger signs. If anyone could disrupt the plan he had in mind, it would most likely be Ce'Nedra; but, try though he might, he could not read her face.

Then Zubrette descended the stairs from the gallery that encircled the interior of the courtyard. Her dress was a country dress, but her hair was still golden, and she was even more beautiful than before. A thousand memories flooded over Garion all at once, together with an actual pain at what he had to do. They had grown up together, and the ties between them were so deep that no outsider could ever fully understand what passed between them in a single glance. And it was with a glance that Garion lied to her. Zubrette's eyes were filled with love, and her soft lips were slightly parted as if almost ready to answer the question she was sure he would ask, even before he gave it voice. Garion's look, however, feigned friendship, affection even, but no love. Incredulity flickered across her face and then a slow flush. The pain Garion felt as he watched the hope die in her blue eyes was as sharp as a knife. Even worse, he was forced to retain his pose of indifference while she wistfully absorbed every feature of his face as if storing up those memories which would have to last her a lifetime. Then she turned and, pleading some errand, she walked away from them. Garion knew that she would avoid him thereafter and that he had seen her for the last time in his life.

It had been the right thing to do, but it had very nearly broken Garion's heart. He exchanged a quick glance with Rundorig that said all that needed saying, then he sadly watched the departure of the girl he had always thought that one day he might marry. When she turned a corner and disappeared, he sighed rather bitterly, turned back and found Ce'Nedra's eyes on him. Her look plainly told him that she understood precisely what he had just done and how much it had cost him. There was sympathy in that look—and a peculiar questioning.

Despite Faldor's urgings, Polgara immediately rejected the role of honored guest. It was as if her fingers itched to touch all the familiar things in the kitchen once more. No sooner had she entered than her cloak went on a peg, an apron went about her waist, and her hands fell to work. Her polite suggestions remained so for almost a full minute and a half before they became commands, and then everything was back to normal again. Faldor and Durnik, their hands clasped behind their backs, strolled about the courtyard, looking into storage sheds, talking about the weather and other matters, and Garion stood in the kitchen doorway with Princess Ce'Nedra.

"Will you show me the farm, Garion?" she asked very quietly.

"If you wish."

"Does Lady Polgara really like to cook that much?" She looked across the warm kitchen to where Aunt Pol, humming happily to herself, was rolling out a pie crust.

"I think so," Garion answered. "Her kitchen's an orderly kind of place, and she likes order. Food goes in one end and supper comes out the other." He looked around at the low-beamed room with all the polished pots and pans hanging on the wall. His life seemed to have come full circle. "I grew up in this room," he said quietly. "There are worse places to grow up, I suppose."

Ce'Nedra's tiny hand crept into his. There was a kind of tentativeness in her touch—almost as if she were not entirely certain how the gesture would be received. There was something peculiar and rather comforting about holding her hand. It was a very small hand; sometimes Garion found himself forgetting just how diminutive Ce'Nedra really was. At the moment she seemed very tiny and very vulnerable, and Garion felt protective for some reason. He wondered if it would be appropriate to put his arm about her shoulder.

Together they wandered about the farmstead, looking into barns and stables and hen roosts. Finally they reached the hayloft that had always been Garion's favorite hiding place. "I used to come here when I knew that Aunt Pol had work for me to do," he confessed with a rueful little laugh.

"Didn't you want to work?" Ce'Nedra asked him. "Everybody here seems to be busy every single moment."

"I don't mind working," Garion told her. "It's just that some of the things she wanted me to do were pretty distasteful."

"Like scrubbing pots?" she asked, her eyes twinkling.

"That's not one of my favorites—no."

They sat together on the soft, fragrant hay in the loft. Ce'Nedra, her fingers now locked firmly in Garion's, absently traced designs on the back of his hand with her other forefinger. "You were very brave this afternoon, Garion," she told him seriously.

"Brave?"

"You gave up something that's always been very special and very important to you."

"Oh," he said. "You mean Zubrette. I think it was for the best, really. Rundorig loves her, and he can take care of her in ways that I probably won't be able to."

"I'm not sure I understand."

"Zubrette needs a lot of special attention. She's clever and pretty, but she's not really very brave. She used to run away from trouble a lot. She needs someone to watch over her and keep her warm and safe—somebody who can devote his entire life to her. I don't think I'll be able to do that."

"If you'd stayed here at the farm, though, you'd have married her, wouldn't you?"

"Probably," he admitted, "but I didn't stay at the farm."

"Didn't it hurt—giving her up like that?"

Garion sighed. "Yes," he said, "it did, sort of, but it was best for all of us, I think. I get a feeling that I'm going to spend a lot of my life traveling about, and Zubrette's really not the sort of person you can ask to sleep on the ground."

"You people never hesitated to ask *me* to sleep on the ground," Ce'Nedra pointed out a trifle indignantly.

Garion looked at her. "We didn't, did we? I guess I never thought about that before. Maybe it's because you're braver."

The following morning after extended farewells and many promises to return, the four of them set out for Sendar.

"Well, Garion?" Aunt Pol said as they rode across the hill that put Faldor's farm irrevocably behind them.

"Well what?"

She gave him a long, silent look.

He sighed. There was really not much point in trying to hide things from her. "I won't be able to go back there, will I?"

"No, dear."

"I guess I always thought that when this was all finished, maybe we could go back to the farm—but we won't, will we?"

"No, Garion, we won't. You had to see it again to realize it, though. It was the only way to get rid of the little bits and pieces of it you've been trailing behind you all these months. I'm not saying that Faldor's is a bad place, you understand. It's just that it's not right for certain people."

"We made the trip all the way up there just so I could find that out?"

"It *is* fairly important, Garion—of course I enjoyed visiting with Faldor, too—and there were a few special things I left in the kitchen—things I've had for a very long time and that I'd rather not lose."

A sudden thought had occurred to Garion, however. "What about Ce'Nedra? Why did you insist that she come along?"

Aunt Pol glanced back once at the little princess, who was riding some yards behind them with her eyes lost in thought. "It didn't hurt her, and she saw some things there that were important for her to see."

"I'm fairly sure that I'll never understand that."

"No, dear," she agreed, "probably not."

It snowed fitfully for the next day and a half as they rode along the road that crossed the white central plain toward the capital at Sendar. Though it was not particularly cold, the sky remained overcast and periodic flurries swept in on them as they rode west. Near the coastline, the wind picked up noticeably, and the occasional glimpses of the sea were disquieting. Great waves ran before the wind, their tops ripped to frothy tatters.

At King Fulrach's palace, they found Belgarath in a foul humor. It was little more than a week until Erastide, and the old man stood glaring out a window at the stormy sea as if it were all some kind of vast, personal insult. "So nice you could join us," he said sarcastically to Aunt Pol when she and Garion entered the room where he brooded.

"Be civil, Father," she replied calmly, removing her blue cloak and laying it across a chair.

"Do you see what it's doing out there, Pol?" He jabbed an angry finger toward the window.

"Yes, Father," she said, not even looking. Instead, she peered intently at his face. "You aren't getting enough rest," she accused him.

"How can I rest with all that going on?" He waved at the window again.

"You're just going to agitate yourself, Father, and that's bad for you. Try to keep your composure."

"We have to be in Riva by Erastide, Pol."

"Yes, Father, I know. Have you been taking your tonic?"

"There's just no talking with her." The old man appealed directly to Garion. "You can see that, can't you?"

"You don't really expect me to answer a question like that, do you, Grandfather? Not right here in front of her?"

Belgarath scowled at him. "Turncoat," he muttered spitefully.

The old man's concern, however, was unfounded. Four days before Erastide, Captain Greldik's familiar ship sailed into the harbor out of a seething sleet storm. Her masts and bulwarks were coated with ice, and her mainsail was ripped down the center.

When the bearded sailor arrived at the palace, he was escorted to the room where Belgarath waited with Captain—now Colonel—Brendig, the sober baronet who had arrested them all in Camaar so many months before. Brendig's rise had been very rapid, and he was now, along with the Earl of Seline, among King Fulrach's most trusted advisors.

"Anheg sent me," Greldik reported laconically to Belgarath. "He's waiting at Riva with Rhodar and Brand. They were wondering what was keeping you."

"I can't find any ship captain willing to venture out of the harbor during this storm," Belgarath replied angrily.

"Well, I'm here now," Greldik told him. "I've got to patch my sail, but that won't take too long. We can leave in the morning. Is there anything to drink around here?"

"How's the weather out there?" Belgarath asked.

"A little choppy," Greldik admitted with an indifferent shrug. He glanced through a window at the twelve-foot waves crashing green and foamy against the icy stone wharves in the harbor below. "Once you get out past the breakwater it isn't too bad."

"We'll leave in the morning then," Belgarath decided. "You'll have twenty or so passengers. Have you got room?"

"We'll make room," Greldik said. "I hope you're not planning to take horses this time. It took me a week to get my bilges clean after the last trip."

"Just one," Belgarath replied. "A colt that seems to have become attached to Garion. He won't make that much mess. Do you need anything?"

"I could still use that drink," Greldik replied hopefully.

The following morning the queen of Sendaria went into hysterics. When she learned that *she* was going to accompany the party to Riva, Queen Layla went all to pieces. King Fulrach's plump little wife had an absolute horror of sea travel—even in the calmest weather. She could not so much as look at a ship without trembling.

When Polgara informed her that she *had* to go with them to Riva, Queen Layla promptly collapsed.

"Everything will be all right, Layla," Polgara kept repeating over and over again, trying to calm the agitated little queen. "I won't let anything happen to you."

"We'll all drown like rats," Queen Layla wailed in stark terror. "Like rats! Oh, my poor orphaned children."

"Now stop that at once!" Polgara told her.

"The sea monsters will eat us all up," the queen added morbidly, "crunching all our bones with their horrid teeth."

"There aren't any monsters in the Sea of the Winds, Layla," Polgara said patiently. "We *have* to go. We *must* be in Riva on Erastide."

"Couldn't you tell them that I'm sick—that I'm dying?" Queen Layla pleaded. "If it would help, I *will* die. Honestly, Polgara, I'll die right here and now on this very spot. Only, please, don't make me get on that awful ship. *Please.*"

"You're being silly, Layla," Polgara chided her firmly. "You have no choice in the matter—none of us do. You and Fulrach and Seline and Brendig all have to go to Riva with the rest of us. That decision was made long before any of you were born. Now stop all this foolishness and start packing."

"I *can't!*" the queen sobbed, flinging herself into a chair.

Polgara looked at the panic-stricken queen with a kind of understanding sympathy, but when she spoke there was no trace of it in her voice. "Get up, Layla," she commanded briskly. "Get on your feet and pack your clothes. You *are* going to Riva. You'll go even if I have to drag you down to the ship and tie you to the mast until we get there."

"You *wouldn't!*" Queen Layla gasped, shocked out of her hysteria as instantly as if she had just been doused with a pail full of cold water. "You wouldn't do that to me, Polgara."

"Wouldn't I?" Polgara replied. "I think you'd better start packing, Layla."

The queen weakly struggled to her feet. "I'll be seasick every inch of the way," she promised.

"You can if it makes you happy, dear," Polgara said sweetly, patting the plump little queen gently on the cheek.

CHAPTER TEN

They were two days at sea from Sendar to Riva, running before a quartering wind with their patched sail booming and the driving spray that froze to everything it touched. The cabin belowdecks was crowded, and Garion spent most of his time topside, trying to stay out of the wind and out from under the sailors' feet at the same time. Inevitably, he moved finally to the sheltered spot in the prow, sat with his back against the bulwark and his blue hooded cloak tight about him, and gave himself over to some serious thinking. The ship rocked and pitched in the heavy swells and frequently slammed head-on into monstrous black waves, shooting spray in all directions. The sea around them was flecked with whitecaps, and the sky was a threatening, dirty gray.

Garion's thoughts were almost as gloomy as the weather. His life for the past fifteen months had been so caught up in the pursuit of the Orb that he had not had time to look toward the future. Now the quest was almost over, and he began to wonder what would happen once the Orb had been restored to the Hall of the Rivan King. There would no longer be any reason for his companions to remain together. Barak would return to Val Alorn; Silk would certainly find some other part of the world more interesting; Hettar and Mandorallen and Relg would return home; and even Ce'Nedra, once she had gone through the ceremony of presenting herself in the throne room, would be called back to Tol Honeth. The adventure was almost over, and they would all pick up their lives again. They would promise to get together someday and probably be quite sincere about it; but Garion knew that once they parted, he would never see them all together again.

He wondered also about his own life. The visit to Faldor's farm had forever closed that door to him, even if it had ever really been open. The bits and pieces of information he had been gathering for the past year and more told him quite plainly that he was not going to be in a position to make his own decisions for quite some time.

"I don't suppose you'd consider telling me what I'm supposed to do next?" He didn't really expect any kind of satisfactory answer from that other awareness.

"It's a bit premature," the dry voice in his mind replied.

"We'll be in Riva tomorrow," Garion pointed out. *"As soon as we put the Orb back where it belongs, this part of the adventure will be all finished. Don't you think that a hint or two might be in order along about now?"*

"I wouldn't want to spoil anything for you."

"You know, sometimes I think you keep secrets just because you know that it irritates people."

"What an interesting idea."

The conversation got absolutely nowhere after that.

It was about noon on the day before Erastide when Greldik's ice-coated ship tacked heavily into the sheltered harbor of the city of Riva on the east coast of the Isle of the Winds. A jutting promontory of wind-lashed rock protected the harbor basin and the city itself. Riva, Garion saw immediately, was a fortress. The wharves were backed by a high, thick city wall, and the narrow, snow-choked gravel strand stretching out to either side of the wharves was also cut off from access to the city. A cluster of makeshift buildings and low, varicolored tents stood on the strand, huddled against the city wall and half-buried in snow. Garion thought he recognized Tolnedrans and a few Drasnian merchants moving quickly through the little enclave in the raw wind.

The city itself rose sharply up the steep slope upon which it was built, each succeeding row of gray stone houses towering over the ones below. The windows facing out toward the harbor were all very narrow and very high up in the buildings, and Garion could see the tactical advantage of such construction. The terraced city was a series of successive barriers. Breaching the gates would accomplish virtually nothing. Each terrace would be as impregnable as the main wall. Surmounting the entire city and brooding down at it rose the final fortress, its towers and battlements as gray as everything else in the bleak city of the Rivans. The blue and white swordbanners of Riva stood out stiffly in the wind above the fortress, outlined sharply against the dark gray clouds scudding across the winter sky.

King Anheg of Cherek, clad in fur, and Brand, the Rivan Warder, wearing his gray cloak, stood on the wharf before the city gates waiting for them as Greldik's sailors rowed the ship smartly up to the wharf. Beside them, his reddish-gold hair spread smoothly out over his green-cloaked shoulders, stood Lelldorin of Wildantor. The young Asturian was grinning broadly. Garion took one incredulous look at his friend; then, with a shout of joy, he jumped to the top of the rail and leaped across to the stone wharf. He and Lelldorin caught each other in a rough bear hug, laughing and pounding each other on the shoulders with their fists.

"Are you all right?" Garion demanded. "I mean, did you completely recover and everything?"

"I'm as sound as ever," Lelldorin assured him with a laugh.

Garion looked at his friend's face dubiously. "You'd say that even if you were bleeding to death, Lelldorin."

"No, I'm really fine," the Asturian protested. "The young sister of Baron Oltorain leeched the Algroth poison from my veins with poultices and vile-tasting potions and restored me to health with her art. She's a marvelous girl." His eyes glowed as he spoke of her.

"What are you doing here in Riva?" Garion demanded.

"Lady Polgara's message reached me last week," Lelldorin explained. "I was still at Baron Oltorain's castle." He coughed a bit uncomfortably. "For one reason or another, I had kept putting off my departure. Anyway, when her instruction to travel to Riva with all possible haste reached me, I left at once. Surely you knew about the message."

"This is the first I'd heard of it," Garion replied, looking over to where Aunt Pol, followed by Queen Silar and Queen Layla, was stepping down from the ship to the wharf.

"Where's Rhodar?" Cho-Hag was asking King Anheg.

"He stayed up at the Citadel." Anheg shrugged. "There isn't really that much point to his hauling that paunch of his up and down the steps to the harbor any more than he has to."

"How is he?" King Fulrach asked.

"I think he's lost some weight," Anheg replied. "The approach of fatherhood seems to have had some impact on his appetite."

"When's the child due?" Queen Layla asked curiously.

"I really couldn't say, Layla," the king of Cherek told her. "I have trouble keeping track of things like that. Porenn had to stay at Boktor, though. I guess she's too far along to travel. Islena's here, though."

"I need to talk with you, Garion," Lelldorin said nervously.

"Of course." Garion led his friend several yards down the snowy pier away from the turmoil of disembarking.

"I'm afraid that the Lady Polgara's going to be cross with me, Garion," Lelldorin said quietly.

"Why cross?" Garion said it suspiciously.

"Well—" Lelldorin hesitated. "A few things went wrong along the way—sort of."

"What exactly are we talking about when we say 'went wrong—sort of'?"

"I was at Baron Oltorain's castle," Lelldorin began.

"I got that part."

"Ariana—the Lady Ariana, that is, Baron Oltorain's sister—"

"The blond Mimbrate girl who nursed you back to health?"

"You remember her," Lelldorin sounded very pleased about that. "Do you remember how lovely she is? How—"

"I think we're getting away from the point, Lelldorin," Garion said firmly. "We were talking about why Aunt Pol's going to be cross with you."

"I'm getting to it, Garion. Well—to put it briefly—Ariana and I had become—well—friends."

"I see."

"Nothing improper, you understand," Lelldorin said quickly. "But our friendship was such that—well—we didn't want to be separated." The young Asturian's face appealed to his friend for understanding. "Actually," he went on, "it was a bit more than 'didn't want to.' Ariana told me that she'd die if I left her behind."

"Possibly she was exaggerating," Garion suggested.

"How could I risk it, though?" Lelldorin protested. "Women are much more delicate than we are—besides, Ariana's a physician. She'd know if she'd die, wouldn't she?"

"I'm sure she would." Garion sighed. "Why don't you just plunge on with the story, Lelldorin? I think I'm ready for the worst now."

"It's not that I really meant any harm," Lelldorin said plaintively.

"Of course not."

"Anyway, Ariana and I left the castle very late one evening. I knew the knight on guard at the drawbridge, so I hit him over the head because I didn't want to hurt him."

Garion blinked.

"I knew that he'd be honor-bound to try to stop us," Lelldorin explained. "I didn't want to have to kill him, so I hit him over the head."

"I suppose that makes sense," Garion said dubiously.

"Ariana's almost positive that he won't die."

"Die?"

"I hit him just a little too hard, I think."

The others had all disembarked and were preparing to follow Brand and King Anheg up the steep, snow-covered stairs toward the upper levels of the city.

"So that's why you think Aunt Pol might be cross with you," Garion said as he and Lelldorin fell in at the rear of the group.

"Well, that's not exactly the whole story, Garion," Lelldorin admitted. "A few other things happened, too."

"Such as what?"

"Well—they chased us—a little—and I had to kill a few of their horses."

"I see."

"I specifically aimed my arrows at the horses and not at the men. It wasn't my fault that Baron Oltorain couldn't get his foot clear of the stirrup, was it?"

"How badly was he hurt?" Garion was almost resigned by now.

"Nothing serious at all—at least I don't think so. A broken leg perhaps—the one he broke before when Sir Mandorallen unhorsed him."

"Go on," Garion told him.

"The priest *did* have it coming, though," Lelldorin declared hotly.

"What priest?"

"The priest of Chaldan at that little chapel who wouldn't marry us because Ariana couldn't give him a document proving that she had her family's consent. He was very insulting."

"Did you break anything?"

"A few of his teeth is about all—and I stopped hitting him as soon as he agreed to perform the ceremony."

"And so you're married? Congratulations. I'm sure you'll both be very happy— just as soon as they let you out of prison."

Lelldorin drew himself up. "It's a marriage in name only, Garion. I would never take advantage of it—you know me better than that. We reasoned that Ariana's reputation might suffer if it became known that we were traveling alone like that. The marriage was just for the sake of appearances."

As Lelldorin described his disastrous journey through Arendia, Garion glanced curiously at the city of Riva. There was a kind of unrelieved bleakness about its snow-covered streets. The buildings were all very tall and were of a uniform gray color. The few evergreen boughs, wreaths, and brightly hued buntings hung in celebration of the Erastide season seemed somehow to accentuate the stiff grimness of the city. There were, however, some very interesting smells coming from kitchens where Erastide feasts simmered and roasted under the watchful eyes of the women of Riva.

"That was all of it, then?" Garion asked his friend. "You stole Baron Oltorain's sister, married her without his consent, broke his leg and assaulted several of his people—and a priest. That was everything that happened?"

"Well—not exactly." Lelldorin's face was a bit pained.

"There's *more*?"

"I didn't really *mean* to hurt Torasin."

"Your cousin?"

Lelldorin nodded moodily. "Ariana and I took refuge at my Uncle Reldegin's house, and Torasin made some remarks about Ariana—she *is* a Mimbrate after all, and Torasin's very prejudiced. My remonstrances were quite temperate, I thought— all things considered—but after I knocked him down the stairs, nothing would satisfy him but a duel."

"You killed him?" Garion asked in a shocked voice.

"Of course I didn't kill him. All I did was run him through the leg—just a lit-tle bit."

"How can you run somebody through just a little bit, Lelldorin?" Garion de-manded of his friend in exasperation.

"You're disappointed in me, aren't you, Garion?" The young Asturian seemed almost on the verge of tears.

Garion rolled his eyes skyward and gave up. "No, Lelldorin, I'm not disappointed—a little startled perhaps—but not really disappointed. Was there anything else you can remember?—anything you might have left out?"

"Well, I hear that I've sort of been declared an outlaw in Arendia."

"Sort of?"

"The crown's put a price on my head," Lelldorin admitted, "or so I understand."

Garion began to laugh helplessly.

"A true friend wouldn't laugh at my misfortunes," the young man complained, looking injured.

"You managed to get into that much trouble in just a week?"

"None of it was really my fault, Garion. Things just got out of hand, that's all. Do you think Lady Polgara's going to be angry?"

"I'll talk to her," Garion assured his impulsive young friend. "Maybe if she and Mandorallen appeal to King Korodullin, they can get him to take the price off your head."

"Is it true that you and Sir Mandorallen destroyed the Murgo Nachak and all his henchmen in the throne room at Vo Mimbre?" Lelldorin asked suddenly.

"I think the story might have gotten a bit garbled," Garion replied. "I de-nounced Nachak, and Mandorallen offered to fight him to prove that what I said was true. Nachak's men attacked Mandorallen then, and Barak and Hettar joined in. Hettar's the one who actually killed Nachak. We *did* manage to keep your name—and Torasin's—out of it."

"You're a true friend, Garion."

"Here?" Barak was saying. "What's she doing here?"

"She came with Islena and me," King Anheg replied.

"Did she—?"

Anheg nodded. "Your son's with her—and your daughters. His birth seems to have mellowed her a bit."

"What does he look like?" Barak asked eagerly.

"He's a great, red-haired brute of a boy." Anheg laughed. "And when he gets hungry, you can hear him yell for a mile."

Barak grinned rather foolishly.

When they reached the top of the stairs and came out in the shallow square before the great hall, two rosy-cheeked little girls in green cloaks were waiting im-patiently for them. They both had long, reddish-blond braids and seemed to be only slightly older than Errand. "Poppa," the youngest of the two squealed, run-ning to Barak. The huge man caught her up in his arms and kissed her soundly. The second girl, a year or so older than her sister, joined them with a show of dig-nity but was also swept up in her father's embrace.

"My daughters," Barak introduced the girls to the rest of the party. "This is

Gundred." He poked his great red beard into the face of the eldest girl, and she giggled as his whiskers tickled her face. "And this is little Terzie." He smiled fondly at the youngest.

"We have a little brother, Poppa," the elder girl informed him gravely.

"What an amazing thing," Barak replied, feigning a great show of astonishment.

"You knew about it already!" Gundred accused him. "We wanted to be the ones to tell you." She pouted.

"His name's Unrak, and he's got red hair—just the same as you have," Terzie announced, "but he doesn't have a beard yet."

"I expect that will come in time," Barak assured her.

"He yells a lot," Gundred reported, "and he hasn't got any teeth."

Then the broad gateway to the Rivan Citadel swung open and Queen Islena, wearing a dark red cloak, emerged from within, accompanied by a lovely blond Arendish girl and by Merel, Barak's wife. Merel was dressed all in green and she was carrying a blanket-wrapped bundle in her arms. Her expression was one of pride.

"Hail Barak, Earl of Trellheim and husband," she said with great formality. "Thus have I fulfilled my ultimate duty." She extended the bundle. "Behold your son Unrak, Trellheim's heir."

With a strange expression, Barak gently set his daughters down, approached his wife, and took the bundle from her. Very gently, his great fingers trembling, he turned back the blanket to gaze for the first time at his son's face. Garion could see only that the baby had bright red hair, much the same color as Barak's.

"Hail, Unrak, heir to Trellheim and my son," Barak greeted the infant in his rumbling voice. Then he kissed the child in his hands. The baby boy giggled and cooed as his father's great beard tickled his face. His two tiny hands reached up and clutched at the beard, and he burrowed his face into it like a puppy.

"He's got a good strong grip," Barak commented to his wife, wincing as the infant tugged at his beard.

Merel's eyes seemed almost startled, and her expression was unreadable.

"This is my son Unrak," Barak announced to the rest of them, holding the baby up so that they could see him. "It may be a bit early to tell, but he shows some promise."

Barak's wife had drawn herself up with pride. "I have done well then, my Lord?"

"Beyond all my expectations, Merel," he told her. Then, holding the baby in one arm, he caught her in the other and kissed her exuberantly. She seemed even more startled than before.

"Let's go inside," the brutish-looking King Anheg suggested. "It's very cold out here, and I'm a sentimental man. I'd rather not have tears freezing in my beard."

The Arendish girl joined Lelldorin and Garion as they entered the fortress.

"And this is my Ariana," Lelldorin told Garion with an expression of total adoration on his face.

For a moment—for just a moment—Garion had some hope for his impossible friend. Lady Ariana was a slim, practical-looking Mimbrate girl, whose medical studies had given her face a certain seriousness. The look she directed at Lelldorin, however, immediately dispelled any hope. Garion shuddered inwardly at the total lack of anything resembling reason in the gaze these two exchanged. Ariana would not restrain Lelldorin as he crashed headlong into disaster after disaster; she would encourage him; she would cheer him on.

"My Lord hath awaited thy coming most eagerly," she said to Garion as they followed the others along a broad stone corridor. The very slight stress she put on "My Lord" indicated that while Lelldorin might think that their marriage was one in name only, *she* did not.

"We're very good friends," Garion told her. He looked around, a bit embarrassed by the way these two kept staring into each other's eyes. "Is this the Hall of the Rivan King, then?" he asked.

" 'Tis generally called so," Ariana replied. "The Rivans themselves speak with more precision, however. Lord Olban, youngest son of the Rivan Warder, hath most graciously shown us throughout the fortress, and he doth speak of this as the Citadel. The Hall of the Rivan King is the throne room itself."

"Ah," Garion said, "I see." He looked away quickly, not wanting to see the way all thought vanished from her eyes when they returned to their contemplation of Lelldorin's face.

King Rhodar of Drasnia, wearing his customary red robe, was sitting in the large, low-beamed dining room where a fire crackled in a cavelike fireplace and a multitude of candles gave off a warm, golden light. Rhodar vastly filled a chair at the head of a long table with the ruins of his lunch spread before him. His crown was hung negligently on the back of his chair, and his round, red face was gleaming with perspiration. "Finally!" he said with a grunt. He waddled ponderously to greet them. He fondly embraced Polgara, kissed Queen Silar and Queen Layla, and took the hands of King Cho-Hag and King Fulrach in his own. "It's been a long time," he said to them. Then he turned to Belgarath. "What took you so long?" he asked.

"We had a long way to go, Rhodar," the old sorcerer replied, pulling off his cloak and backing up to the broad-arched fireplace. "You don't go from here to Rak Cthol in a week, you know."

"I hear that you and Ctuchik finally had it out," the king said.

Silk laughed sardonically. "It was a splendid little get-together, Uncle."

"I'm sorry I missed it." King Rhodar looked inquiringly at Ce'Nedra and Adara, his expression openly admiring. "Ladies," he said to them bowing politely, "if someone will introduce us, I'll be more than happy to bestow a few royal kisses."

"If Porenn catches you kissing pretty girls, she'll carve out your tripes, Rhodar." King Anheg laughed crudely.

As Aunt Pol made the introductions, Garion drew back a few paces to consider the havoc Lelldorin had caused in one short week. It was going to take months to unravel it, and there was no guarantee that it would not happen again—indeed, that it would not happen every time the young man got loose.

"What's the matter with your friend?" It was the Princess Ce'Nedra, and she was tugging on Garion's sleeve.

"What do you mean, what's the matter with him?"

"You mean he's always like that?"

"Lelldorin—" Garion hesitated. "Well, Lelldorin's very enthusiastic about things, and sometimes he speaks or acts without stopping to think." Loyalty made him want to put the best face on it.

"Garion." Ce'Nedra's gaze was very direct. "I know Arends, and he's the most Arendish Arend I've ever met. He's so Arendish that he's almost incapacitated."

Garion quickly came to the defense of his friend. "He's not *that* bad."

"Really? And Lady Ariana. She's a lovely girl, a skilled physician—and utterly devoid of anything remotely resembling thought."

"They're in love," Garion said, as if that explained everything.

"What's that got to do with it?"

"Love does things to people," Garion told her. "It seems to knock holes in their judgment or something."

"What a fascinating observation," Ce'Nedra replied. "Do go on."

Garion was too preoccupied with the problem to catch the dangerous lilt in her voice. "As soon as somebody falls in love, all the wits seem to dribble out of the bottom of his head," he continued moodily.

"What a *colorful* way to put it," Ce'Nedra said.

Garion even missed *that* warning. "It's almost as if it were some kind of disease," he added.

"Do you know something, Garion?" the princess said in a conversational, almost casual tone of voice. "Sometimes you make me positively sick." And she turned and walked away, leaving him staring after her in openmouthed astonishment.

"What did I say?" he called after her, but she ignored him.

After they had all dined, King Rhodar turned to Belgarath. "Do you suppose we might have a look at the Orb?" he asked.

"Tomorrow," the old man answered. "We'll reveal it when it's returned to its proper place in the Hall of the Rivan King at midday."

"We've all seen it before, Belgarath," King Anheg asserted. "What's the harm in our having a look now?"

Belgarath shook his head stubbornly. "There are reasons, Anheg," he said. "I think it may surprise you tomorrow, and I wouldn't want to spoil it for anyone."

"Stop him, Durnik," Polgara said as Errand slipped from his seat and walked around the table toward King Rhodar, his hand fumbling with the strings of the pouch at his waist.

"Oh no, little fellow," Durnik said, catching the boy from behind and lifting him up into his arms.

"What a beautiful child," Queen Islena observed. "Who is he?"

"That's our thief," Belgarath replied. "Zedar found him someplace and raised him as a total innocent. At the moment, he seems to be the only one in the world who can touch the Orb."

"Is that it in the pouch?" Anheg asked.

Belgarath nodded. "He's caused us all some anxiety along the way. He keeps trying to give it to people. If he decides to offer you something, I don't really advise taking it."

"I wouldn't dream of it," Anheg agreed.

As was usually the case, once Errand's attention had been diverted, he immediately seemed to forget about the Orb. His gaze focused on the infant Barak was holding; as soon as Durnik set him down, he went over to look at the baby. Unrak returned the look and some kind of peculiar recognition seemed to pass between them. Then Errand gently kissed the child in Barak's arms, and Unrak, smiling, took hold of the strange little boy's finger. Gundred and Terzie gathered close, and Barak's great face rose from the garden of children clustered about him. Garion could clearly see the tears glistening in his friend's eyes as he looked at his wife Merel. The look she returned him was strangely tender; for the first time Garion could remember, she smiled at her husband.

CHAPTER ELEVEN

That night a sudden, savage storm howled down from the northwest to claw at the unyielding rock of the Isle of the Winds. Great waves crashed and thundered against the cliffs, and a shrieking gale howled among the ancient battlements of Iron-grip's Citadel. The firm-set rock of the fortress seemed almost to shudder as the seething storm lashed again and again at the walls.

Garion slept fitfully. There was not only the shriek and bellow of wind and the rattle of sleet against close-shuttered windows to contend with, nor the gusting drafts that blew suddenly down every corridor to set unlatched doors banging, but there were also those peculiar moments of oppressive silence that were almost as bad as the noise. Strange dreams stalked his sleep that night. Some great, momentous, and unexplained event was about to take place, and there were all manner of peculiar things that he had to do in preparation for it. He did not know why he had to do them, and no one would tell him if he were doing them right or not. There seemed to be some kind of dreadful hurry, and people kept rushing him from one thing to the next without ever giving him time to make sure that anything was really finished.

Even the storm seemed to be mixed up in it—like some howling enemy trying with noise and wind and crashing waves to break the absolute concentration necessary to complete each task.

"Are you ready?" It was Aunt Pol, and she was placing a long-handled kitchen kettle on his head like a helmet and handing him a pot-lid shield and a wooden stick sword.

"What am I supposed to do?" he demanded of her.

"You know," she replied. "Hurry. It's getting late."

"No, Aunt Pol, I don't—really."

"Of course you do. Now stop wasting time."

He looked around, feeling very confused and apprehensive. Not far away,

Rundorig stood with that same rather foolish look on his face that had always been there. Rundorig also had a kettle on his head, a pot-lid shield, and a wooden sword. Apparently he and Rundorig were supposed to do this together. Garion smiled at his friend, and Rundorig grinned back.

"That's right," Aunt Pol said encouragingly. "Now kill him. Hurry, Garion. You have to be finished by suppertime."

He spun around to stare at her. Kill Rundorig? But when he looked back, it was not Rundorig. Instead the face that looked at him from beneath the kettle was maimed and hideous.

"No, no," Barak said impatiently. "Don't hold it like that. Grip it in both hands and keep it pointed at his chest. Keep the point low so that when he charges he doesn't knock the spear aside with his tusks. Now do it again. Try to get it right this time. Hurry, Garion. We don't have all day, you know." The big man nudged the dead boar with his foot, and the boar got up and began to paw at the snow. Barak gave Garion a quick look. "Are you ready?" he demanded.

Then he was standing on a strange, colorless plain, and there seemed to be statues all around him. No. Not statues—figures. King Anheg was there—or a figure that looked like him—and King Korodullin, and Queen Islena, and there was the Earl of Jarvik, and over there was Nachak, the Murgo ambassador at Vo Mimbre.

"*Which piece do you want to move?*" It was the dry voice in his mind.

"*I don't know the rules,*" Garion objected.

"*That doesn't matter. You have to move. It's your turn.*"

When Garion turned back, one of the figures was rushing at him. It wore a cowled robe, and its eyes bulged with madness. Without thinking, Garion raised his hand to ward off the figure's attack.

"*Is that the move you want to make?*" the voice asked him.

"*I don't know.*"

"*It's too late to change it now. You've already touched him. From now on, you have to make your own moves.*"

"*Is that one of the rules?*"

"*That's the way it is. Are you ready?*"

There was the smell of loam and of ancient oak trees. "You really must learn to control your tongue, Polgara," Asharak the Murgo said with a bland smile, slapping Aunt Pol sharply across the face.

"*It's your move again,*" the dry voice said. "*There's only one that you can make.*"

"*Do I have to do it? Isn't there anything else I can do?*"

"*It's the only move there is. You'd better hurry.*"

With a deep sigh of regret, Garion reached out and set fire to Asharak with the palm of his hand.

A SUDDEN, GUSTING draft banged open the door of the room Garion shared with Lelldorin, and the two of them sat bolt upright in their beds.

"I'll latch it again," Lelldorin said, throwing back the covers and stumbling across the chilly stones of the floor.

"How long's it going to keep blowing like this?" Garion asked peevishly. "How's anyone supposed to sleep with all this noise?"

Lelldorin closed the door again, and Garion heard him fumbling around in the darkness. There was a scraping click and a sudden bright spark. The spark went out, and Lelldorin tried again. This time it caught in the tinder. The young Asturian blew on it, and it grew brighter, than flared into a small finger of flame.

"Have you got any idea what time it is?" Garion asked as his friend lighted the candle.

"Some hours before dawn, I imagine," Lelldorin replied.

Garion groaned. "It feels like this night's already been about ten years long."

"We can talk for a while," Lelldorin suggested. "Maybe the storm will die down toward dawn."

"Talking's better than lying here in the dark, jumping at every sound," Garion agreed, sitting up and pulling his blanket around his shoulders.

"Things have happened to you since we saw each other last, haven't they, Garion?" Lelldorin asked, climbing back into his own bed.

"A lot of things," Garion told him, "not all of them good, either."

"You've changed a great deal," Lelldorin noted.

"I've *been* changed. There's a difference. Most of it wasn't my idea. You've changed, too, you know."

"Me?" Lelldorin laughed ruefully. "I'm afraid not, my friend. The mess I've made of things in the past week is proof that I haven't changed at all."

"That *will* take a bit of straightening out, won't it?" Garion agreed. "The funny part about it all is that there *is* a perverse sort of logic about the whole thing. There wasn't one single thing you did that was actually insane. It's just when you put them all together that it starts to look like a catastrophe."

Lelldorin sighed. "And now my poor Ariana and I are doomed to perpetual exile."

"I think we'll be able to fix it," Garion assured him. "Your uncle will forgive you, and Torasin probably will, too. He likes you too much to stay angry for long. Baron Oltorain is probably very put out with you, but he's a Mimbrate Arend. He'll forgive anything if it's done for love. We might have to wait until his leg heals up again, though. That was the part that was a real blunder, Lelldorin. You shouldn't have broken his leg."

"Next time I'll try to avoid that," Lelldorin promised quickly.

"Next time?"

They both laughed then and talked on as their candle flickered in the vagrant drafts stirred by the raging storm. After an hour or so, the worst of the gale seemed to pass, and the two of them found their eyes growing heavy once more.

"Why don't we try to sleep again?" Garion suggested.

"I'll blow out the candle," Lelldorin agreed. He got up out of bed and stepped to the table. "Are you ready?" he asked Garion.

GARION SLEPT AGAIN almost immediately, and almost immediately heard a sibilant whisper in his ear and felt a dry, cold touch. "Are you ready?" the whispering voice hissed, and he turned to look with uncomprehending eyes at the face of Queen Salmissra, a face that shifted back and forth from woman to snake to something midway between.

Then he stood beneath the shimmering dome of the cave of the Gods and moved without thought to touch the unblemished, walnut-colored shoulder of the stillborn colt, thrusting his hand into the absolute silence of death itself.

"Are you ready?" Belgarath asked quite calmly.

"I think so."

"All right. Put your will against it and push."

"It's awfully heavy, Grandfather."

"You don't have to pick it up, Garion. Just push it. It'll roll over if you do it right. Hurry up. We have a great deal more to do."

Garion began to gather his will.

And then he sat on a hillside with his cousin Adara. In his hand he held a dead twig and a few wisps of dry grass.

"Are you ready?" the voice in his mind asked him.

"Is this going to mean anything?" Garion asked. *"I mean, will it make any difference?"*

"That depends on you and how well you do it."

"That's not a very good answer."

"It wasn't a very good question. If you're ready, turn the twig into a flower."

Garion did that and looked critically at the result. *"It's not a very good flower, is it?"* he apologized.

"It'll have to do," the voice told him.

"Let me try it again."

"What are you going to do with this one?"

"I'll just—" Garion raised his hand to obliterate the defective bloom he had just created.

"That's forbidden, you know," the voice reminded him.

"I made it, didn't I?"

"That has nothing to do with it. You can't unmake it. It'll be fine. Come along now. We have to hurry."

"I'm not ready yet."

"That's too bad. We can't wait any longer."

AND THEN GARION woke up. He felt oddly light-headed, as if his troubled sleep had done him more harm than good. Lelldorin was still deep in slumber, and Garion found his clothes in the dark, pulled them on and quietly left the room. The strange dream nagged at his mind as he wandered in the dimly lighted corridors of Iron-grip's Citadel. He still felt that pressing urgency and the peculiar sense that everyone was waiting impatiently for him to do something.

He found a windswept courtyard where snow had piled up in the corners and the stones were black and shiny with ice. Dawn was just breaking, and the battlements surrounding the courtyard were etched sharply against a sky filled with scudding cloud.

Beyond the courtyard lay the stables—warm, smelling of fragrant hay and of horses. Durnik had already found his way there. As was so frequently the case, the smith was uncomfortable in the presence of nobility, and he sought the company of animals instead. "Couldn't you sleep either?" he asked as Garion entered the stable.

Garion shrugged. "For some reason sleep just made things worse. I feel as if my head's stuffed full of straw."

"Joyous Erastide, Garion," Durnik said then.

"That's right. It is, isn't it?" In all the rush, the holiday seemed to have crept up on him. "Joyous Erastide, Durnik."

The colt, who had been sleeping in a back stall, nickered softly as he caught Garion's scent, and Garion and Durnik went back to where the small animal stood.

"Joyous Erastide, horse," Garion greeted him a bit whimsically. The colt nuzzled at him. "Do you think that the storm's blown over completely?" Garion asked Durnik as he rubbed the colt's ears. "Or is there more on the way?"

"It has the smell of being over," Durnik answered. "Weather could smell differently here on this island, though."

Garion nodded his agreement, patted the colt's neck and turned toward the door. "I suppose I'd better go find Aunt Pol," he said. "She was saying something last night about wanting to check my clothes. If I make her look for me, she'll probably make me wish I hadn't."

"Age is bringing you wisdom, I see." Durnik grinned at him. "If anyone wants me, I'll be here."

Garion put his hand briefly on Durnik's shoulder and then left the stable to go looking for Aunt Pol.

He found her in the company of women in the apartment that appeared to have been set aside for her personal use centuries before. Adara was there and Taiba, Queen Layla and Ariana, the Mimbrate girl; in the center of the room stood Princess Ce'Nedra.

"You're up early," Aunt Pol observed, her needle flickering as she made some minute modification to Ce'Nedra's creamy gown.

"I had trouble sleeping," he told her, looking at the princess with a certain puzzlement. She looked different somehow.

"Don't stare at me, Garion," she told him rather primly.

"What have you done to your hair?" he asked her.

Ce'Nedra's flaming hair had been elaborately arranged, caught at brow and temples by a gold coronet in the form of a band of twined oak leaves. There was some rather intricate braiding involved at the back and then the coppery mass flowed smoothly down over one of her tiny shoulders. "Do you like it?" she asked him.

"That's not the way you usually wear it," he noted.

"We're all aware of that, Garion," she replied loftily. Then she turned and looked rather critically at her reflection in the mirror. "I'm still not convinced about the braiding, Lady Polgara," she fretted. "Tolnedran ladies don't braid their hair. This makes me look like an Alorn."

"Not entirely, Ce'Nedra," Adara murmured.

"You know what I mean, Adara—all those buxom blondes with their braids and their milkmaid complexions."

"Isn't it a little early to be getting ready?" Garion asked. "Grandfather said that we weren't going to take the Orb to the throne room until noon."

"That's not really that far off, Garion," Aunt Pol told him, biting a thread and stepping back to look critically at Ce'Nedra's dress. "What do you think, Layla?"

"She looks just like a princess, Pol," Queen Layla gushed.

"She *is* a princess, Layla," Aunt Pol reminded the plump little queen. Then she turned to Garion. "Get some breakfast and have someone show you the way to the baths," she instructed. "They're in the cellars under the west wing. After you've bathed, you'll need a shave. Try not to cut yourself. I don't want you bleeding all over your good clothes."

"Do I have to wear all that?"

She gave him a look that immediately answered that question—as well as several others he might have asked.

"I'll go find Silk," he agreed quickly. "He'll know where the baths are."

"Do that," she told him quite firmly. "And don't get lost. When the time comes, I want you to be ready."

Garion nodded and left. Her words had somehow strangely echoed the words of his dream, and he wondered about that as he went looking for Silk.

The little man was lounging in the company of the others in a large, torch-lit room in the west wing. The kings were there, with Brand, Belgarath and Garion's other friends. They were breakfasting on cakes and hot spiced wine.

"Where did you go this morning?" Lelldorin asked him. "You were gone when I woke up."

"I couldn't sleep anymore," Garion replied.

"Why didn't you wake me?"

"Why should you lose sleep just because I'm having a restless night?" Garion could see that they were deep in a discussion, and he sat down quietly to wait for the opportunity to speak to Silk.

"I think we've managed to aggravate Taur Urgas pretty thoroughly in the past couple of months," Barak was saying. The big man was sprawled deep in a high-backed chair with his face sunk in the shadows from the flaring torch behind him. "First Relg steals Silk right out from under his nose, then Belgarath destroys Ctuchik and knocks down Rak Cthol in the process of taking back the Orb, and finally Cho-Hag and Hettar exterminate a sizable piece of his army when he tries to follow us. The king of the Murgos has had a bad year." The big man's chuckle rumbled out of the shadows. For a moment—a fleeting instant—Garion seemed to see a different shape sprawled there. Some trick of the flickering light and dancing shadows made it appear momentarily that a great, shaggy bear sat in Barak's place. Then it was gone. Garion rubbed at his eyes and tried to shake off the half-bemused reverie that had dogged him all morning.

"I still don't quite follow what you mean about Relg going into the rock to rescue Prince Kheldar." King Fulrach frowned. "Do you mean that he can burrow through?"

"I don't think you'd understand unless you saw it, Fulrach," Belgarath told him. "Show him, Relg."

The Ulgo zealot looked at the old man, then walked over to the stone wall beside the large window. Silk instantly turned his back, shuddering. "I still can't stand to watch that," he declared to Garion.

"Aunt Pol said I was supposed to ask you the way to the baths," Garion said quietly. "She wants me to get cleaned up and shaved, and then I guess I'm supposed to put on my best clothes."

"I'll go with you," Silk offered. "I'm sure that all these gentlemen are going to be fascinated by Relg's demonstration, and they'll want him to repeat it. What's he doing?"

"He stuck his arm through the wall and he's wiggling his fingers at them from outside the window," Garion reported.

Silk glanced once over his shoulder, then shuddered again and quickly averted his eyes. "That makes my blood cold," he said with revulsion. "Let's go bathe."

"I'll go along," Lelldorin said, and the three of them quietly left the room.

The baths were in a cavernous cellar beneath the west wing of the Citadel. There were hot springs deep in the rock, and they bubbled up to fill the tiled chambers with steam and a faintly sulfurous smell. There were but few torches and only one attendant who wordlessly handed them towels and then went off into the steam to manage the valves that adjusted the water temperature.

"The big pool there gets hotter the closer you go toward the far end," Silk told Garion and Lelldorin as they all disrobed. "Some people say you should go in until it's as hot as you can stand it, but I prefer just to pick a comfortable temperature and soak." He splashed down into the water.

"Are you sure we'll be alone here?" Garion asked nervously. "I don't think I'd care to have a group of ladies come trooping in while I'm trying to bathe."

"The women's baths are separate," Silk assured him. "The Rivans are very proper about that sort of things. They aren't nearly as advanced as the Tolnedrans yet."

"Are you *really* sure that bathing in the wintertime is healthy?" Lelldorin asked, eyeing the steaming water suspiciously.

Garion plunged into the pool and moved quickly out of the tepid water at the near end toward the hotter area. The steam rose more thickly as he waded out into the pool, and the pair of torches set in rings on the back wall receded into a kind of ruddy glow. The tiled walls echoed back the sounds of their voices and splashing with a peculiar, cavernlike hollowness. The steam eddied up out of the water, and he found himself suddenly shut off by it, separated from his friends in the hazy dimness. The hot water relaxed him, and he seemed almost to want to float, half-aware, and let it soak out all memory—all the past and all the future. Dreamily he lay back, and then, not knowing why, he allowed himself to sink beneath the dark, steaming water. How long he floated, his eyes closed and all sense suspended, he could not have said, but finally his face rose to the surface and he stood up, the water streaming out of his hair and down across his shoulders. He felt strangely purified by his immersion. And then the sun broke through the tattered cloud outside for a moment, and a single shaft of sunlight streamed down through a small grilled window to fall fully upon Garion. The sudden light was diffused by the steam and seemed to flicker with an opalescent fire.

"*Hail, Belgarion,*" the voice in his mind said to him. "*I greet thee on this Erastide.*" There was no hint of the usual amusement in the voice, and the formality seemed strange, significant.

"*Thank you,*" Garion replied gravely, and they did not speak again.

The steam rose and eddied about him as he waded back toward the cooler reaches of the pool where Silk and Lelldorin, both sunk to their necks in warm water, were talking quietly together.

About half an hour before noon, Garion, in response to a summons from Aunt Pol, walked down a long stone corridor toward a room a few steps from the huge, carved doors that gave entrance into the Hall of the Rivan King. He was wearing his best doublet and hose, and his soft leather half-boots had been brushed until they glowed. Aunt Pol wore a deep blue robe, cowled and belted at the waist. For once Belgarath, also blue-robed, did not look rumpled or spotted. The old man's face was very serious; as he and Aunt Pol spoke together, there was no hint of the banter that usually marked their conversation. Seated quietly in the corner of the little room, Errand, dressed all in white linen, gravely watched.

"You look very nice, Garion," Aunt Pol said, reaching out to smooth his sandy hair back from his forehead.

"Shouldn't we go inside?" Garion asked. He had seen others, gray-clad Rivans and the more brightly garbed visitors entering the hall.

"We will, Garion," she replied. "All in good time." She turned to Belgarath. "How long?" she asked.

"Another quarter hour or so," he replied.

"Is everything ready?"

"Ask Garion," the old man told her. "I've taken care of everything I can. The rest is up to him."

Aunt Pol turned to Garion then, her eyes very serious and the white lock at her brow gleaming silver in the darkness of her hair. "Well, Garion," she asked, "are you ready?"

He looked at her, baffled. "I had the oddest dream last night," he said. "Everyone kept asking me that same question. What does it mean, Aunt Pol? Am I ready for what?"

"That'll become clearer in a bit," Belgarath told him. "Take out your amulet. You'll wear it on the outside of your clothes today."

"I thought it was supposed to be out of sight."

"Today's different," the old man replied. "As a matter of fact, today's unlike any day I've ever seen—and I've seen a lot of them."

"Because it's Erastide?"

"That's part of it." Belgarath reached inside his robe and drew out his own silver medallion. He glanced at it briefly. "It's getting a little worn," he noted. Then he smiled. "—but then, so am I, I suppose."

Aunt Pol drew out her own amulet. She and Belgarath each reached out to take Garion's hands and then to join their own.

"It's been a long time coming, Polgara," Belgarath said.

"Yes it has, Father," Aunt Pol agreed.

"Any regrets?"

"I can live with them, old wolf."

"Let's go in then."

Garion started toward the door.

"Not you, Garion," Aunt Pol told him. "You'll wait here with Errand. You two will come in later."

"You'll send somebody for us?" he asked her. "What I mean is, how will we know when we're supposed to come in?"

"You'll know," Belgarath told him. And then they left him alone with Errand.

"They didn't give us very complete instructions, did they?" Garion said to the child. "I hope we don't make any mistakes."

Errand smiled confidently, reached out and put his small hand in Garion's. At his touch, the song of the Orb filled Garion's mind again, sponging away his worries and doubts. He could not have said how long he stood holding the child's hand and immersed in that song.

"It's come at last, Belgarion." The voice seemed to come from outside somehow, no longer confined within Garion's mind, and the look on Errand's face made it quite clear that he also could hear the words.

"Is this what I'm supposed to do?" Garion asked.

"It's part of it."

"What are they doing in there?" Garion looked rather curiously toward the door.

"They're getting the people in the Hall ready for what's going to happen."

"Will they be ready?"

"Will you?" There was a pause. "Are you ready, Belgarion?"

"Yes," Garion replied. "Whatever it is, I think I'm ready for it."

"Let's go then."

"You'll tell me what to do?"

"If it's necessary."

With his hand still holding Errand's, Garion walked toward the door. He raised his other hand to push it open, but it swung inexplicably open ahead of him before he touched it.

There were two guards at the huge, carved door a few steps down the hall, but they seemed frozen into immobility as Garion and Errand approached. Once again Garion raised his hand, and the immense doors to the Hall of the Rivan King swung silently open in response to his hand alone.

The Hall of the Rivan King was a huge, vaulted throne room with massive and ornately carved wooden buttresses supporting the ceiling beams. The walls were festooned with banners and green boughs, and hundreds of candles burned in iron sconces. Three great stone firepits were set at intervals in the floor; instead of logs, blocks of peat glowed in the pits, radiating an even, fragrant warmth. The Hall was crowded, but there was a broad avenue of blue carpet leading from the doors to the throne. Garion's eyes, however, scarcely noted the crowd. His thoughts seemed suspended by the song of the Orb, which now filled his mind completely. Bemused, freed of all thought or fear or hint of self-consciousness, he walked with Errand close beside him toward the front of the Hall where Aunt Pol and Belgarath stood, one on each side of the throne.

The throne of the Rivan King had been chiseled from a single basalt block. Its back and arms were all one height, and there was a massiveness about it that made it seem more permanent than the mountains themselves. It sat solidly against the wall and, hanging point downward above it, was a great sword.

Somewhere in the Citadel, a bell had begun to peal, and the sound of it mingled with the song of the Orb as Garion and Errand moved down the long, carpeted pathway toward the front of the hall. As they passed each sconce, the candles inexplicably dropped to the merest pinpoint. There was no draft, no flickering, as, one by one, the candles dimmed and the Hall filled with deepening shadow.

When they reached the front of the Hall, Belgarath, his face a mystery, looked gravely at them for a moment, then looked out at the throng assembled in the Hall of the Rivan King. "Behold the Orb of Aldur," he announced in a solemn voice.

Errand released Garion's hand, tugged open the pouch, and reached inside. As he turned to face the darkened Hall, Errand drew the round gray stone out of the pouch and lifted it with both hands, displaying it for all to see.

The song of the Orb was overpowering; joining with it, there was a kind of vast, shimmering sound. The sound seemed to soar, rising, ringing higher and higher as Garion stood beside the child, looking at the faces of the assemblage. Within the stone Errand held aloft there seemed to be a pinpoint of intense blue light. The light grew brighter as the shimmering sound rose higher. The faces before him were all familiar, Garion could see. Barak was there and Lelldorin, Hettar, Durnik, Silk, and Mandorallen. Seated in a royal box beside the Tolnedran ambassador, with Adara and Ariana directly behind her, was Ce'Nedra, looking every inch an Imperial Princess. But, mingled somehow with the familiar faces were others—strange, stark faces, each so caught up in a single overriding identity that they seemed almost masklike. Mingled with Barak was the Dreadful Bear, and Hettar bore with him the sense of thousands upon thousands of horses. With Silk stood the figure of the Guide and with Relg that of the Blind Man. Lelldorin was the Archer and Mandorallen the Knight Protector. Seeming to hover in the air above Taiba was the sorrowing form of the Mother of the Race That Died, and her sorrow was like the sorrow of Mara. And Ce'Nedra was no longer a princess but now a queen—the one Ctuchik had called the Queen of the World. Strangest of all, Durnik, good solid Durnik, stood with his two lives plainly evident on his face. In the searing blue light of the Orb and with the strange sound shimmering in his ears, Garion looked in wonder at his friends, realizing with amazement that he was seeing for the first time what Belgarath and Aunt Pol had seen all along.

From behind him he heard Aunt Pol speak, her voice calm and very gentle. "Your task is completed, Errand. You may now give up the Orb."

The little boy crowed with delight, turned, and presented the glowing Orb to Garion. Uncomprehending, Garion stared at the fiery stone. He could not take it. It was death to touch the Orb.

"Reach forth thy hand, Belgarion, and receive thy birthright from the child who hath borne it unto thee." It was the familiar voice, and yet at the same time it was not. When *this* voice spoke, there was no possibility of refusal. Garion's hand stretched out without his even being aware that it was moving.

"Errand!" the child declared, firmly depositing the Orb in Garion's outstretched hand. Garion felt the peculiar, seething touch of it against the mark on his palm. It was alive! He could feel the life in it, even as he stared in blank incomprehension at the living fire he held in his naked hand.

"Return the Orb to the pommel of the sword of the Rivan King," the voice instructed, and Garion turned with instant, unthinking obedience. He stepped up onto the seat of the basalt throne and then onto the wide ledge formed by its back

and arms. He stretched up, taking hold of the huge sword hilt to steady himself, and placed the Orb on the great sword's pommel. There was a faint but clearly audible click as the Orb and the sword became one, and Garion could feel the living force of the Orb surging down through the hilt he gripped in one hand. The great blade began to glow, and the shimmering sound rose yet another octave. Then the huge weapon quite suddenly came free from the wall to which it had been attached for so many centuries. The throng in the hall gasped. As the sword began to drop free, Garion caught hold of the hilt with both hands, half turning as he did so, striving to keep the great blade from falling to the floor.

What pulled him off balance was the fact that it had no apparent weight. The sword was so huge that he should not have been able to hold it, much less lift it; but as he braced himself with his feet widespread and his shoulders pressed back against the wall, the point of the sword rose easily until the great blade stood upright before him. He stared at it in amazement, feeling a strange throbbing between the hands he had clasped about the hilt. The Orb flared and began to pulsate. Then, as the shimmering sound soared into a mighty crescendo of jubilation, the sword of the Rivan King burst into a great tongue of searing blue flame. Without knowing why, Garion lifted the flaming sword over his head with both hands, staring up at it in wonder.

"Let Aloria rejoice!" Belgarath called out in a voice like thunder, "for the Rivan King has returned! All hail Belgarion, King of Riva and Overlord of the West!"

And yet in the midst of the turmoil that followed and even with the shimmering chorus of what seemed a million million voices raised in an exultation echoing from one end of the universe to the other, there was a sullen clang of iron as if the rust-scoured door of some dark tomb had suddenly burst open, and the sound of that clanging chilled Garion's heart. A voice echoed hollowly from the tomb, and it did not join the universal rejoicing. Ripped from its centuries of slumber, the voice in the tomb awoke raging and crying out for blood.

Stunned past all thought, Garion stood with his flaming sword aloft as, with a steely rustle, the assembled Alorns unsheathed their swords to raise them in salute.

"Hail Belgarion, my King," Brand, the Rivan Warder, boomed, sinking to one knee and lifting his sword. His four sons knelt behind him, their swords also lifted. "Hail Belgarion, King of Riva!" they cried.

"Hail Belgarion!" The great shout shook the Hall of the Rivan King, and a forest of upraised swords glittered in the fiery blue light of the flaming blade in Garion's hands. Somewhere within the Citadel, a bell began to peal. As the news raced through the breathless city below, other bells caught the sound, and their iron rejoicing echoed back from the rocky crags to announce to the icy waters of the sea the return of the Rivan King.

One in the Hall, however, did not rejoice. In the instant that the kindling of the sword had irrevocably announced Garion's identity, Princess Ce'Nedra had started to her feet, her face deathly pale and her eyes wide with absolute consternation. She had instantly grasped something that eluded him—something so unsettling that it drained the color from her face and brought her to her feet to stare at him with an expression of total dismay. Then there suddenly burst from the lips of the Imperial Princess Ce'Nedra a wail of outrage and protest.

With a voice that rang in the rafters she cried out, *"OH NO!"*

■ CHAPTER TWELVE ■

The worst part of it all was that people kept bowing to him. Garion had not the slightest idea of how he should respond. Should he bow back? Should he nod slightly in acknowledgment? Or perhaps might it not be better just to ignore the whole business and act as if he hadn't seen it, or something? But what was he supposed to do when someone called him, "Your Majesty"?

The events of the previous day were still a confused blur in his mind. He seemed to remember being presented to the people of the city—standing on the battlements of Iron-grip's Citadel with a great, cheering throng below and the huge sword that somehow seemed weightless still blazing in his hands. Stupendous as they were, however, the overt events of the day were unimportant when compared to things which were taking place on a different level of reality. Enormous forces had focused on the moment of the revelation of the Rivan King, and Garion was still numb as a result of things he had seen and perceived in that blinding instant when he had at last discovered who he was.

There had been endless congratulations and a great many preparations for his coronation, but all of that blurred in his mind. Had his life depended upon it, he could not have given a rational, coherent account of the day's events.

Today promised to be even worse, if that were possible. He had not slept well. For one thing, the great bed in the royal apartments to which he had been escorted the previous evening was definitely uncomfortable. It had great round posts rising from each corner and it was canopied and curtained in purple velvet. It seemed much too large for him and it was noticeably on the soft side. For the past year and more he had done most of his sleeping on the ground, and the down-filled mattress on the royal bed was too yielding to be comfortable. There was, moreover, the sure and certain knowledge that as soon as he arose, he was going to be the absolute center of attention.

On the whole, he decided, it might just be simpler to stay in bed. The more he thought about that, the better it sounded. The door to the royal bedchamber, however, was not locked. Sometime not long after sunrise it swung open, and Garion could hear someone moving around. Curious, he peeked through the purple drapery enclosing his bed. A sober-looking servant was busily opening the drapes at the window and stirring up the fire. Garion's attention, however, moved immediately to the large, covered silver tray sitting on the table by the fireplace. His nose recognized sausage and warm, fresh-baked bread—and butter—there was definitely butter involved somewhere on that tray. His stomach began to speak to him in a loud voice.

The servant glanced around the room to make sure everything was in order, then came to the bed with a no-nonsense expression. Garion burrowed quickly back under the covers.

"Breakfast, your Majesty," the servant announced firmly, drawing the curtains open and tying them back.

Garion sighed. Quite obviously, decisions about staying in bed were not his to make. "Thank you," he replied.

"Does your Majesty require anything else?" the servant asked solicitously, holding open a robe for Garion to put on.

"Uh—no—not right now, thank you," Garion answered, climbing out of the royal bed and down the three carpeted steps leading up to it. The servant helped him into the robe, then bowed and quietly left the room. Garion went to the table, seated himself, lifted the cover from the tray, and assaulted breakfast vigorously.

When he had finished eating, he sat for a time in a large, blue-upholstered armchair looking out the window at the snowy crags looming above the city. The storm that had raked the coast for days had blown off—at least for the moment; the winter sun was bright, and the morning sky very blue. The young Rivan King stared for a time out his window, lost in thought.

Something nagged at the back of his memory—something he had heard once but had since forgotten. It seemed that there was something he ought to remember that involved Princess Ce'Nedra. The tiny girl had fled from the Hall of the Rivan King almost immediately after the sword had so flamboyantly announced his identity the previous day. He was fairly sure that it was all mixed together. Whatever it was that he was trying to recall had been directly involved in her flight. With some people it might be better to let things quiet down before clearing the air, but Garion knew that this was not the proper way to deal with Ce'Nedra. Things should never be allowed to fester in her mind. That only made matters worse. He sighed and began to dress.

As he walked purposefully through the corridors, he met with startled looks and hasty bows. He soon realized that the events of the preceding day had forever robbed him of his anonymity. Someone—Garion could never catch a glimpse of his face—even went so far as to follow him, probably in the hope of performing some service. Whoever it was kept a discreet distance behind, but Garion caught occasional glimpses of him far back along the corridor—a gray-cloaked man who moved on strangely noiseless feet. Garion did not like being followed, whatever the reason, but he resisted the urge to turn around and tell the man to go away.

The Princess Ce'Nedra had been given several rooms just down the hall from Aunt Pol's apartments, and Garion steeled himself as he raised his hand to rap on the door.

"Your Majesty," Ce'Nedra's maid greeted him with a startled curtsy.

"Would you please ask her Highness if I might have a word with her?" Garion asked.

"Certainly, your Majesty," the girl replied and darted into the next chamber.

There was a brief murmur of voices and then Ce'Nedra swept into the room.

She wore a plain gown, and her face was as pale as it had been the previous day. "Your Majesty," she greeted him in an icy voice, and then she curtsied, a stiff little curtsy that spoke whole volumes.

"Something's bothering you," Garion said bluntly. "Would you like to get it out in the open?"

"Whatever your Majesty wishes," she replied.

"Do we have to do this?"

"I can't imagine what your Majesty is talking about."

"Don't you think we know each other well enough to be honest?"

"Of course. I suppose I'd better accustom myself to obeying your Majesty immediately."

"What's that supposed to mean?"

"Don't pretend that you don't know," she flared.

"Ce'Nedra, I haven't the faintest idea what you're talking about."

She looked at him suspiciously, then her eyes softened just a bit. "Perhaps you don't at that," she murmured. "Have you ever read the Accords of Vo Mimbre?"

"You taught me how to read yourself," he reminded her, "about six or eight months ago. You know every book I've read. You gave me most of them yourself."

"That's true, isn't it?" she said. "Wait just a moment. I'll be right back." She went briefly into the adjoining room and returned with a rolled parchment. "I'll read it to you," she told him. "Some of the words are a little difficult."

"I'm not *that* stupid," he objected.

But she had already begun to read. " '—And when it shall come to pass that the Rivan King returns, he shall have Lordship and Dominion, and swear we all fealty to him as Overlord of the Kingdoms of the West. And he shall have an Imperial Princess of Tolnedra to wife, and—' "

"Wait a minute," Garion interrupted her with a strangled note in his voice.

"Was there something you didn't understand? It all seems quite clear to me."

"What was that last part again?"

"—'he shall have an Imperial Princess of Tolnedra to wife, and—' "

"Are there any other princesses in Tolnedra?"

"Not that I know of."

"Then that means—" He gaped at her.

"Precisely." She said it like a steel trap suddenly snapping shut.

"Is that why you ran out of the Hall yesterday?"

"I did *not* run."

"You don't want to marry me." It was almost an accusation.

"I didn't say that."

"Then you *do* want to marry me?"

"I didn't say that either—but it doesn't really matter, does it? We don't have any choice at all—neither one of us."

"Is that what's bothering you?"

Her look was lofty. "Of course not. I've always known that my husband would be selected for me."

"What's the problem, then?"

"I'm an Imperial Princess, Garion."

"I know that."

"I'm not accustomed to being anyone's inferior."

"Inferior? To who—whom?"

"The Accords state that you are the Overlord of the West."

"What does that mean?"

"It means, your Majesty, that you outrank me."

"Is that all that's got you so upset?"

Her look was like a drawn dagger. "With your Majesty's permission, I believe I'd like to withdraw." And without waiting for an answer, she swept from the room.

Garion stared after her. This was going too far. He considered going immediately to Aunt Pol to protest, but the more he thought about it, the more convinced he became that she would be totally unsympathetic. Too many little things began to click together all at once. Aunt Pol was not merely a party to this absurd notion; she had actively done everything in her power to make absolutely sure that there was no escape for him. He needed someone to talk to—someone devious enough and unscrupulous enough to think a way out of this. He left Ce'Nedra's sitting room and went looking for Silk.

The little man was not in his room, and the servant who was making up the bed kept bowing as he stammered out his apologies at not having the slightest notion of where Silk might be. Garion left quickly.

Since the apartment Barak shared with his wife and children was only a few steps down the corridor, Garion went there, trying not to look back at the gray-cloaked attendant he knew was still following him. "Barak," he said, knocking on the big Cherek's door, "it's me, Garion. May I come in?"

The Lady Merel opened the door immediately and curtsied respectfully.

"Please, don't do that," Garion begged her.

"What's the trouble, Garion?" Barak asked from the green-covered chair where he sat, bouncing his infant son on his knee.

"I'm looking for Silk," Garion replied, entering the large, comfortable room that was littered with clothes and children's toys.

"You're a little wild around the eyes," the big man noted. "Is something wrong?"

"I've just had some very unsettling news," Garion told him, shuddering. "I need to talk to Silk. Maybe he can come up with an answer for me."

"Would you like some breakfast?" Lady Merel suggested.

"I've already eaten, thank you," Garion replied. He looked at her a bit more closely. She had undone the rather severe braids she customarily wore, and her blond hair framed her face softly. She wore her usual green gown, but her carriage seemed not to have the rigidity it had always had. Barak, Garion noted, had also lost a bit of the grim defensiveness that had always been there previously when he was in the presence of his wife.

Barak's two daughters entered the room then, one on each side of Errand. They all sat down in the corner and began playing an elaborate little game that seemed to involve a great deal of giggling.

"I think my daughters have decided to steal him," Barak grinned. "Quite suddenly I'm up to my ears in wife and children, and the funny part about it is that I don't seem to mind it at all."

Merel threw him a quick, almost shy smile. Then she looked over at the laughing children. "The girls absolutely adore him," she said, and then turned back to Garion. "Have you ever noticed that you can't look directly into his eyes for more than a moment or so? He seems to be looking right into your heart."

Garion nodded. "I think it might have something to do with the way he trusts everybody," he suggested. He turned back to Barak. "Do you have any idea where I might find Silk?"

Barak laughed. "Walk up and down the halls and listen for the rattle of dice. The little thief's been gambling ever since we got here. Durnik might know. He's been hiding out in the stables. Royalty makes him nervous."

"It does the same thing to me," Garion said.

"But you *are* royalty, Garion," Merel reminded him.

"That makes me even more nervous," he replied.

There was a series of back hallways that led to the stables, and Garion decided to follow that route rather than pass through the more stately corridors where he might encounter members of the nobility. These narrower passageways were used for the most part by servants going to and from the kitchen, and Garion reasoned that most of the minor household staff would probably not recognize him yet. As he walked quickly along one of the passageways with his head down to avoid any chance recognition, he caught another glimpse behind him of the man who had dogged his steps ever since he had left the royal apartments. Irritated finally to the point where he no longer cared about concealing his identity, Garion turned to confront his pursuer. "I know you're there," he declared. "Come out where I can see you." He waited, tapping his foot impatiently.

The hallway behind him remained empty and silent.

"Come out here at once," Garion repeated, his voice taking on an unaccustomed note of command. But there was no movement, no sound. Garion thought for a moment of retracing his steps to catch this persistent attendant in the act of creeping along behind him, but just then a servant carrying a tray of dirty dishes came along from the direction Garion had just come.

"Did you see anybody back there?" Garion asked him.

"Back where?" the servant said, obviously not recognizing his king.

"Back along the hall."

The servant shook his head. "I haven't seen anyone since I left the apartments of the King of Drasnia," he replied. "Would you believe that this is his third breakfast? I've never seen anybody eat so much." He looked curiously at Garion. "You shouldn't be back here, you know," he warned. "If the head cook catches you, he'll thrash you. He doesn't like anybody in this hall who doesn't have business here."

"I'm just on my way to the stables," Garion told him.

"I'd move right along, then. The head cook's got a vicious temper."

"I'll keep that in mind," Garion assured him.

Lelldorin was coming out of the stable, and he gave Garion a startled look as the two of them approached each other in the snowy courtyard. "How did you manage to escape from all the officials?" he asked. Then, as if remembering, he bowed.

"Please don't do that, Lelldorin," Garion told him.

"The situation *is* a bit awkward, isn't it?" Lelldorin agreed.

"We'll behave toward each other the same as we've always behaved," Garion said firmly. "At least until they tell us we can't. Have you any idea where Silk might be?"

"I saw him earlier this morning," Lelldorin replied. "He said he was going to visit the baths. He looked a bit unwell. I think he celebrated last night."

"Let's go find him," Garion suggested. "I've got to talk to him."

They found Silk sitting in a tiled stone room thick with steam. The little man had a towel about his waist and he was sweating profusely.

"Are you sure this is good for you?" Garion asked, waving his hand in front of his face to clear an eddying cloud of steam.

"Nothing would really be good for me this morning, Garion," Silk replied sadly. He put his elbows on his knees and sank his face miserably into his hands.

"Are you sick?"

"Horribly."

"If you knew it was going to make you feel this way, why did you drink so much last night?"

"It seemed like a good idea at the time—at least I think it did. I seem to have lost track of several hours." An attendant brought the suffering man a foaming tankard, and Silk drank deeply.

"Is that really wise?" Lelldorin asked him.

"Probably not," Silk admitted with a shudder, "but it's the best I could come up with on short notice." He shuddered again. "I feel absolutely wretched," he declared. "Was there anything in particular you wanted?"

"I've got a problem," Garion blurted. He looked quickly at Lelldorin. "I'd rather this didn't go beyond the three of us," he said.

"You have my oath on it," Lelldorin responded instantly.

"Thank you, Lelldorin." It was easier to accept the oath than to try to explain why it wasn't really necessary. "I've just read the Accords of Vo Mimbre," he told them. "Actually, I had them read to me. Did you know that I'm supposed to marry Ce'Nedra?"

"I hadn't actually put that part together yet," Silk admitted, "but the Accords do mention something about it, don't they?"

"Congratulations, Garion!" Lelldorin exclaimed, suddenly clapping his friend on the shoulder. "She's a beautiful girl."

Garion ignored that. "Can you think of some way I can get out of it?" he demanded of Silk.

"Garion, right now I can't really think of anything except how awful I feel. My first hunch though, is that there isn't any way out for you. Every kingdom in the west is signatory to the Accords—and then I think the Prophecy's involved too."

"I'd forgotten about that," Garion admitted glumly.

"I'm sure they'll give you time to get used to the idea," Lelldorin said.

"But how much time will they give Ce'Nedra? I talked to her this morning, and she's not happy about the idea at all."

"She doesn't actually dislike you," Silk told him.

"That's not what the problem is. She seems to think that I outrank her, and that's what's got her upset."

Silk began to laugh weakly.

"A real friend wouldn't laugh," Garion accused him.

"Is rank really that important to your princess?" Lelldorin asked.

"Probably not much more important than her right arm," Garion replied sourly. "I think she reminds herself that she's an Imperial Princess six or eight times every hour. She makes a pretty big issue about it. Now I come along from out of nowhere, and suddenly I outrank her. It's the sort of thing that's going to set her teeth on edge—permanently, I expect." He stopped and looked rather closely at Silk. "Do you think there's any chance of your getting well today?"

"What have you got in mind?"

"Do you know your way around Riva at all?"

"Naturally."

"I was sort of thinking that I ought to go down into the city—not with trumpets blowing and all that—but just dressed like somebody ordinary. I don't know anything at all about the Rivans, and now—" He faltered with it.

"And now you're their king," Lelldorin finished for him.

"It's probably not a bad idea," Silk agreed. "Though I can't really say for sure. My brain isn't working too well just now. It'll have to be today, of course. Your coronation's scheduled for tomorrow, and your movements are likely to be restricted after they've put the crown on your head."

Garion didn't want to think about that.

"I hope the two of you don't mind if I take a little while to pull myself together first, though," Silk added, drinking from the tankard again. "Actually it doesn't really matter if you mind or not. It's a question of necessity."

It took the rat-faced little man only about an hour to recuperate. His remedies were brutally direct. He soaked up hot steam and cold ale in approximately equal amounts, then emerged from the steamroom to plunge directly into a pool of icy water. He was blue and shaking when he came out, but the worst of his indisposition seemed to be gone. He carefully selected nondescript clothes for the three of them, then led the way out of the Citadel by way of a side gate. As they left, Garion glanced back several times, but he seemed to have shaken off the persistent attendant who had been following him all morning.

As they wandered down into the city, Garion was struck again by the bleak severity of the place. The outsides of the houses were uniformly gray and totally lacking any form of exterior decoration. They were solid, square, and absolutely colorless. The gray cloak which was the outstanding feature of the Rivan national costume gave the people in the narrow streets an appearance of that same grimness. Garion quailed a bit at the thought of spending the rest of his life in so uninviting a place.

They walked down a long street in pale winter sunshine with the salt smell of the harbor strong in their nostrils and passed a house from which came the sound of children singing. Their voices were very clear and merged together in subtle harmonies. Garion was astonished at the complexity of the children's song.

"A national pastime," Silk said. "Rivans are very much involved in music. I suppose it helps relieve the boredom. I'd hate to offend your Majesty, but your kingdom's a tedious sort of place." He looked around. "I have an old friend who lives not far from here. Why don't we pay him a visit?"

He led them down a long stairway to the street below. Not far up that street a large building stood solidly on the downhill side. Silk strode up to the door and knocked. After a moment, a Rivan in a burn-spotted leather smock answered. "Radek, old friend," he said with a certain surprise. "I haven't seen you in years."

"Torgan." Silk grinned at him. "I thought I'd stop by and see how you were doing."

"Come in, come in," Torgan said, opening the door wider.

"You've expanded things a bit, I see," Silk noticed, looking around.

"The market's been good to me," Torgan replied modestly. "The perfume makers in Tol Borune are buying just about any kind of bottle they can get." The Rivan was a solid-looking man with iron-gray hair and strangely rounded and rosy cheeks. He glanced curiously at Garion and frowned slightly as if trying to remember something. Garion turned to examine a row of delicate little glass bottles standing neatly on a nearby table, trying to keep his face turned away.

"You're concentrating on bottle making then?" Silk asked.

"Oh, we still try to turn out a few good pieces," Torgan replied a bit ruefully. "I've got an apprentice who's an absolute genius. I have to let him spend a certain amount of time on his own work. I'm afraid that if I kept him blowing bottles all day, he'd leave me." The glassmaker opened a cabinet and carefully took out a small velvet-wrapped bundle. "This is a piece of his work," he said, folding back the cloth.

It was a crystal wren, wings half-spread, and it was perched on a leafy twig with buds at its tip. The entire piece was so detailed that even the individual feathers were clearly visible. "Amazing," Silk gasped, examining the glass bird. "This is exquisite, Torgan. How did he get the colors so perfect?"

"I have no idea," Torgan admitted. "He doesn't even measure when he mixes, and the colors always come out exactly right. As I said, he's a genius." He carefully rewrapped the crystal bird and placed it back in the cabinet.

There were living quarters behind the workshop, and the rooms were filled with warmth and affection and vibrant colors. Brightly colored cushions were everywhere, and paintings hung on the walls in every room. Torgan's apprentices seemed to be not so much workers as members of his family, and his eldest daughter played for them as they concentrated on the molten glass, her fingers touching the strings of her harp in cascading waterfalls of music.

"It's so unlike the outside," Lelldorin observed, his face puzzled.

"What's that?" Silk asked him.

"The outside is so grim—so stiff and gray—but once you come inside the building, it's all warmth and color."

Torgan smiled. "It's something outsiders don't expect," he agreed. "Our houses are very much like ourselves. Out of necessity, the outside is bleak. The city of Riva was built to defend the Orb, and every house is part of the overall fortifications. We can't change the outside, but inside we have art and poetry and music. We ourselves wear the gray cloak. It's a useful garment—woven from the wool of goats—light, warm, nearly waterproof—but it won't accept dye, so it's always gray. But even though we're gray on the outside, that doesn't mean that we have no love of beauty."

The more Garion thought about that, the more he began to understand these bleak-appearing islanders. The stiff reserve of the gray-cloaked Rivans was a face they presented to the world. Behind that face, however, was an altogether different kind of people.

The apprentices for the most part were blowing the delicate little bottles that were the major item in the trade with the perfume makers of Tol Borune. One apprentice, however, worked alone, fashioning a glass ship cresting a crystal wave. He was a sandy-haired young man with an intent expression. When he looked up from his work and saw Garion, his eyes widened, but he lowered his head quickly to his work again.

Back at the front of the shop as they were preparing to leave, Garion asked to look once more at the delicate glass bird perched on its gleaming twig. The piece was so beautiful that it made his heart ache.

"Does it please your Majesty?" It was the young apprentice, who had quietly entered from the workroom. He spoke softly. "I was in the square yesterday when Brand introduced you to the people," he explained. "I recognized you as soon as I saw you."

"What's your name?" Garion asked curiously.

"Joran, your Majesty," the apprentice replied.

"Do you suppose we could skip the 'Majesties'?" Garion said rather plaintively. "I'm not really comfortable with that sort of thing yet. The whole business came as a complete surprise to me."

Joran grinned at him. "There are all kinds of rumors in the city. They say you were raised by Belgarath the Sorcerer in his tower in the Vale of Aldur."

"Actually I was raised in Sendaria by my Aunt Pol, Belgarath's daughter."

"Polgara the Sorceress?" Joran looked impressed. "Is she as beautiful as men say she is?"

"I've always thought so."

"Can she really turn herself into a dragon?"

"I suppose she could if she wanted to," Garion admitted, "but she prefers the shape of an owl. She loves birds for some reason—and birds go wild at the sight of her. They talk to her all the time."

"What an amazing thing," Joran marveled. "I'd give anything to be able to meet her." He pursed his lips thoughtfully, hesitating a moment. "Do you think she'd like this little thing?" he blurted finally, touching the crystal wren.

"Like it?" Garion said. "She'd love it."

"Would you give it to her for me?"

"Joran!" Garion was startled at the idea. "I couldn't take it. It's too valuable, and I don't have any money to pay you for it."

Joran smiled shyly. "It's only glass," he pointed out, "and glass is only melted sand—and sand's the cheapest thing in the world. If you think she'd like it, I'd really like for her to have it. Would you take it to her for me—please? Tell her it's a gift from Joran the glassmaker."

"I will, Joran," Garion promised, impulsively clasping the young man's hand. "I'll be proud to carry it to her for you."

"I'll wrap it," Joran said then. "It's not good for glass to go out in the cold from a warm room." He reached for the piece of velvet, then stopped. "I'm not being entirely honest with you," he admitted, looking a bit guilty. "The wren's a very good piece, and if the nobles up at the Citadel see it, they might want me to make other things for them. I need a few commissions if I'm ever going to open my own shop, and—" He glanced once at Torgan's daughter, his heart in his eyes.

"—And you can't get married until you've established your own business?" Garion suggested.

"Your Majesty will be a very wise king," Joran said gravely.

"If I can get past all the blunders I'll make during the first few weeks," Garion added ruefully.

Later that afternoon he delivered the crystal bird to Aunt Pol in her private apartment.

"What's this?" she asked, taking the cloth-wrapped object.

"It's a present for you from a young glassmaker I met down in the city," Garion replied. "He insisted that I give it to you. His name's Joran. Be careful. I think it's kind of fragile."

Aunt Pol gently unwrapped the crystal piece. Her eyes slowly widened as she stared at the exquisitely wrought bird. "Oh, Garion," she murmured, "it's the most beautiful thing I've ever seen."

"He's awfully good," Garion told her. "He works for a glassmaker called Torgan, and Torgan says he's a genius. He wants to meet you."

"And I want to meet him," she breathed, her eyes lost in the glowing detail of the glass figure. Then she carefully set the crystal wren down on a table. Her hands were trembling and her glorious eyes were full of tears.

"What's wrong, Aunt Pol?" Garion asked her, slightly alarmed.

"Nothing, Garion," she replied. "Nothing at all."

"Why are you crying then?"

"You'd never understand, dear," she told him. Then she put her arms around him and pulled him to her in an almost fierce embrace.

THE CORONATION TOOK place at noon the following day. The Hall of the Rivan King was full to overflowing with nobles and royalty, and the city below was alive with the sound of bells.

Garion could never actually remember very much of his coronation. He did remember that the ermine-bordered cape was hot and that the plain gold crown the Rivan Deacon placed on his head was very heavy. What stood out most in his mind was the way the Orb of Aldur filled the entire Hall with an intense blue light that grew brighter and brighter as he approached the throne and overwhelmed his ears with that strange, exultant song he always seemed to hear whenever he came near it. The song of the Orb was so loud that he scarcely heard the great cheer that greeted him as he turned, robed and crowned, to face the throng in the Hall of the Rivan King.

He did, however, hear one voice very clearly.

"Hail, Belgarion," the voice in his mind said quietly to him.

CHAPTER THIRTEEN

King Belgarion sat somewhat disconsolately on his throne in the Hall of the Rivan King, listening to the endless, droning voice of Valgon, the Tolnedran ambassador. It had not been an easy time for Garion. There were so many things he did not know how to do. For one thing, he was totally incapable of giving orders; for another, he discovered that he had absolutely no time to himself and that he had not the faintest idea of how to dismiss the servants who continually hovered near him. He was followed wherever he went, and he had even given up trying to catch the overzealous bodyguard or valet or messenger who was always in the passageways behind him.

His friends seemed uncomfortable in his presence and they persisted in calling him "your Majesty" no matter how many times he asked them not to. He didn't feel any different, and his mirror told him that he didn't look any different, but everyone behaved as if he had changed somehow. The look of relief that passed over their faces each time he left injured him, and he retreated into a kind of protective shell, nursing his loneliness in silence.

Aunt Pol stood continually at his side now, but there was a difference there as well. Before, he had always been an adjunct to her, but now it was the other way around, and that seemed profoundly unnatural.

"The proposal, if your Majesty will forgive my saying so, is most generous," Valgon observed, concluding his reading of the latest treaty offered by Ran Borune. The Tolnedran ambassador was a sardonic man with an aquiline nose and an aristocratic bearing. He was a Honethite, a member of that family which had founded the Empire and from which three Imperial dynasties had sprung, and he had a scarcely concealed contempt for all Alorns. Valgon was a continual thorn in Garion's side. Hardly a day passed that some new treaty or trade agreement did not arrive from the Emperor. Garion had quickly perceived that the Tolnedrans were desperately nervous about the fact that they did not have his signature on a single piece of parchment, and they were proceeding on the theory that if they kept shoving documents in front of a man, eventually he would sign something just to get them to leave him alone.

Garion's counterstrategy was very simple; he refused to sign anything.

"It's exactly the same as the one they offered last week," Aunt Pol's voice observed in the silence of his mind. *"All they did was switch the clauses around and change a few words. Tell him no."*

Garion looked at the smug ambassador with something very close to active dislike. "Totally out of the question," he replied shortly.

Valgon began to protest, but Garion cut him short. "It's identical to last week's proposal, Valgon, and we both know it. The answer was no then, and it's still no. I will *not* give Tolnedra preferred status in trade with Riva; I will *not* agree to ask Ran Borune's permission before I sign any agreement with any other nation; and I most certainly will *not* agree to any modification of the terms of the Accords of Vo Mimbre. Please ask Ran Borune not to pester me anymore until he's ready to talk sense."

"Your Majesty!" Valgon sounded shocked. "One does not speak so to the Emperor of Tolnedra."

"I'll speak any way I please," Garion told him. "You have my—*our* permission to leave."

"Your Majesty—"

"You're dismissed, Valgon," Garion cut him off.

The ambassador drew himself up, bowed coldly, and stalked from the Hall.

"Not bad," King Anheg drawled from the partially concealed embrasure where he and the other kings generally gathered. The presence of these royal onlookers made Garion perpetually uneasy. He knew they were watching his every move, judging, evaluating his decisions, his manner, his words. He knew he was bound to make mistakes during these first few months, and he'd have greatly preferred to make them without an audience, but how could he tell a group of sovereign kings that he would prefer not to be the absolute center of their attention?

"A trifle blunt, though, wouldn't you say?" King Fulrach suggested.

"He'll learn to be more diplomatic in time," King Rhodar predicted. "I expect that Ran Borune will find this directness refreshing—just as soon as he recovers from the fit of apoplexy our Belgarion's reply is going to give him."

The assembled kings and nobles all laughed at King Rhodar's sally, and Garion tried without success to keep from blushing. "Do they have to do that?" he whispered furiously to Aunt Pol. "Every time I so much as hiccup, I get all this commentary."

"Don't be surly, dear," she replied calmly. "It *was* a trifle impolite, though. Are you really sure you want to take that tone with your future father-in-law?"

That was something of which Garion most definitely did not wish to be reminded. The Princess Ce'Nedra had still not forgiven him for his sudden elevation, and Garion was having grave doubts about the whole notion of marrying her. Much as he liked her—and he *did* like her—he regretfully concluded that Ce'Nedra would not make him a good wife. She was clever and spoiled, and she had a streak of stubbornness in her nature as wide as an oxcart. Garion was fairly certain that she would take a perverse delight in making his life as miserable as she possibly could. As he sat on his throne listening to the jocular comments of the Alorn Kings, he began to wish that he had never heard of the Orb.

As always, the thought of the jewel made him glance up to where it glowed on the pommel of the massive sword hanging above the throne. There was something so irritatingly smug about the way it glowed each time he sat on the throne. It always seemed to be congratulating itself—as if he, Belgarion of Riva, were somehow its own private creation. Garion did not understand the Orb. There was an awareness about it; he knew that. His mind had tentatively touched that awareness and then had carefully retreated. Garion had been touched on occasion by the minds of Gods, but the consciousness of the Orb was altogether different. There was a power in it he could not even begin to comprehend. More than that, its attachment to him seemed quite irrational. Garion knew himself, and he was painfully aware that he was not that lovable. But each time he came near it, it would begin to glow insufferably, and his mind would fill with that strange, soaring song he had first heard in Ctuchik's turret. The song of the Orb was a kind of compelling invitation. Garion knew that if he should take it up, its will would join with his, and there would be nothing that between them they could not do. Torak had raised the Orb and had cracked the world with it. Garion knew that if he chose, *he* could raise the Orb and mend that crack. More alarming was the fact that as soon as the notion occurred to him, the Orb began to provide him with precise instructions on how to go about it.

"Pay attention, Garion," Aunt Pol's voice said to him.

The business of the morning, however, was very nearly completed. There were a few other petitions and a peculiar note of congratulation that had arrived that morning from Nyissa. The tone of the note was tentatively conciliatory, and it appeared over the signature of Sadi the eunuch. Garion decided that he wanted to think things through rather carefully before he drafted a reply. The memory of what had happened in Salmissra's throne room still bothered him, and he was not entirely sure he wanted to normalize relations with the snake-people just yet.

Then, since there was no further court business, he excused himself and left the Hall. His ermine-trimmed robe was very hot, and the crown was beginning to give him a headache. He most definitely wanted to return to his apartment and change clothes.

The guards at the side door to the Hall bowed respectfully as he passed them and drew up into formation to accompany him. "I'm not really going anyplace," Garion told the sergeant in charge. "Just back to my rooms, and I know the way. Why don't you and your men go have some lunch?"

"Your Majesty is very kind," the sergeant replied. "Will you need us later?"

"I'm not sure. I'll send somebody to let you know."

The sergeant bowed again, and Garion went on along the dimly lighted corridor. He had found this passageway about two days after his coronation. It was relatively unused and it was the most direct route from the royal apartment to the throne room. Garion liked it because he could follow it to and from the great Hall with a minimum of pomp and ceremony. There were only a few doors, and the candles on the walls were spaced far enough apart to keep the light subdued. The dimness seemed comforting for some reason, almost as if it restored in some measure his anonymity.

He walked along, lost in thought. There were so many things to worry about. The impending war between the West and the Angarak kingdoms was uppermost in his mind. He, as Overlord of the West, would be expected to lead the West; and Kal Torak, awakened from his slumber, would come against him with the multitudes of Angarak. How could he possibly face so terrible an adversary? The very name of Torak chilled him, and what did he know about armies and battles? Inevitably, he would blunder, and Torak would smash all the forces of the West with one mailed fist.

Not even sorcery could help him. His own power was still too untried to risk a confrontation with Torak. Aunt Pol would do her best to aid him, of course, but without Belgarath they had little hope of success; and Belgarath had still not given any indication that his collapse had not permanently impaired his abilities.

Garion did not want to think about that anymore, but his other problems were nearly as bad. Very soon he was going to have to come to grips with Ce'Nedra's adamant refusal to make peace. If she would only be reasonable, Garion was sure that the marginal difference in their rank would not make all that much difference. He liked Ce'Nedra. He was even prepared to admit that his feelings for her went quite a bit deeper than that. She could—usually when she wanted something—be absolutely adorable. If they could just get past this one minor problem, things might turn out rather well. That possibility brightened his thoughts considerably. Musing about it, he continued on down the corridor.

He had gone only a few more yards when he heard that furtive step behind him again. He sighed, wishing that his ever-present attendant would find some other amusement. Then he shrugged and, deep in thought about the Nyissan question, he continued on along the corridor.

The warning was quite sharp and came at the last instant. *"Look out!"* the voice in his mind barked at him. Not knowing exactly why, not even actually thinking about it, Garion reacted instantly, diving headlong to the floor. His crown went rolling as, with a great shower of sparks, a thrown dagger clashed into the stone wall and went bouncing and skittering along the flagstones. Garion swore, rolled quickly and came to his feet with his own dagger in his hand. Outraged and infuriated by this sudden attack, he ran back along the corridor, his ermine-trimmed robe flapping and tangling cumbersomely around his legs.

He caught only one or two momentary glimpses of his gray-cloaked attacker as he ran after the knife thrower. The assassin dodged into a recessed doorway some yards down the corridor, and Garion heard a heavy door slam behind the fleeing man. When he reached the door and wrenched it open, his dagger still in his fist, he found only another long, dim passageway. There was no one in sight.

His hands were shaking, but it was more from anger than from fright. He briefly considered calling the guards, but almost immediately dismissed that idea. To continue following the assailant was, the more he thought about it, even more unwise. He had no weapon but his dagger, and the possibility of meeting someone armed with a sword occurred to him. There might even be more than one involved in this business, and these dimly lighted and deserted corridors were most certainly not a good place for confrontations.

As he started to close the door, something caught his eye. A small scrap of gray wool lay on the floor just at the edge of the door frame. Garion bent, picked it up and carried it over to one of the candles hanging along the wall. The bit of wool was no more than two fingers wide and seemed to have been torn from the corner of a gray Rivan cloak. In his haste to escape, the assassin had, Garion surmised, inadvertently slammed the door on his own cape, and then had ripped off this fragment in his flight. Garion's eyes narrowed and he turned and hurried back up the corridor, stooping once to retrieve his crown and again to pick up his assailant's dagger. He looked around once. The hallway was empty and somehow threatening. If the unknown knife thrower were to return with three or four companions, things could turn unpleasant. All things considered, it might be best to get back to his own apartments as quickly as possible—and to lock his door. Since there was no one around to witness any lack of dignity, Garion lifted the skirts of his royal robe and bolted like a rabbit for safety.

He reached his own door, jerked it open and jumped inside, closing and locking it behind him. He stood with his ear against the door, listening for any sounds of pursuit.

"Is something wrong, your Majesty?"

Garion almost jumped out of his skin. He whirled to confront his valet, whose eyes widened as he saw the daggers in the king's hands. "Uh—nothing" he replied quickly, trying to cover his confusion. "Help me out of this thing." He struggled with the fastenings of his robe. His hands seemed to be full of daggers and crowns. With a negligent flip he tossed his crown into a nearby chair, sheathed his own dagger and then carefully laid the other knife and the scrap of wool cloth on the polished table.

The valet helped him to remove the robe and then carefully folded it over his arm. "Would your Majesty like to have me get rid of these for you?" he asked, looking a bit distastefully at the dagger and the bit of wool on the table.

"No," Garion told him firmly. Then a thought occurred to him. "Do you know where my sword is?" he asked.

"Your Majesty's sword hangs in the throne room," the valet replied.

"Not that one," Garion said. "The other one. The one I was wearing when I first came here."

"I suppose I could find it," the valet answered a bit dubiously.

"Do that," Garion said. "I think I'd like to have it where I can get my hands on it. And please see if you can find Lelldorin of Wildantor for me. I need to talk to him."

"At once, your Majesty." The valet bowed and quietly left the room.

Garion took up the dagger and the scrap of cloth and examined both rather closely. The dagger was just a commonplace knife, heavy, sturdily made and with a wirebound hilt. It bore no ornaments or identifying marks of any kind. Its tip was slightly bent, the result of its contact with the stone wall. Whoever had thrown it had thrown very hard. Garion developed a definitely uncomfortable sensation between his shoulder blades. The dagger would probably not be very useful. There were undoubtedly a hundred like it in the Citadel. The wool scrap, on the other hand, might prove to be very valuable. Somewhere in this fortress, there was a man with the corner of his cloak torn off. The torn cloak and this little piece of cloth would very likely match rather closely.

About a half an hour later Lelldorin arrived. "You sent for me, Garion?" he asked.

"Sit down, Lelldorin," Garion told his friend, then pointedly waited until the valet left the room. "I think I've got a little bit of a problem," he said then, sprawling deeper in the chair by the table. "I wondered if I might ask your help."

"You know you don't have to ask, Garion," the earnest young Asturian told him.

"This has to be just between the two of us," Garion cautioned. "I don't want anyone else to know."

"My word of honor on it," Lelldorin replied instantly.

Garion slid the dagger across the table to his friend. "A little while ago when I was on my way back here, somebody threw this at me."

Lelldorin gasped and his eyes went wide. "Treason?" he gasped.

"Either that or something personal," Garion replied. "I don't know what it's all about."

"You must alert your guards," Lelldorin declared, jumping to his feet.

"No," Garion answered firmly. "If I do that, they'll lock me up entirely. I don't have very much freedom left at all, and I don't want to lose it."

"Did you see him at all?" Lelldorin asked, sitting down again and examining the dagger.

"Just his back. He was wearing one of those gray cloaks."

"All Rivans wear gray cloaks, Garion."

"We do have something to work with, though." Garion took the scrap of wool out from under his tunic. "After he threw the knife, he ran through a door and slammed it shut behind him. He caught his cloak in the door and this got ripped off."

Lelldorin examined the bit of cloth. "It looks like a corner," he noted.

"That's what I think, too," Garion agreed. "If we both keep our eyes open, we might just happen to see somebody with the corner of his cloak missing. Then, if we can get our hands on his cloak, we might be able to see if this piece matches."

Lelldorin nodded his agreement, his face hardening. "When we find him, though, *I* want to deal with him. A king isn't supposed to become personally involved in that sort of thing."

"I might decide to suspend the rules," Garion said grimly. "I don't like having knives thrown at me. But let's find out who it is first."

"I'll start at once," Lelldorin said, rising quickly. "I'll examine every corner of every cloak in Riva if I have to. We'll find this traitor, Garion. I promise you."

Garion felt better after that, but it was still a wary young king who, in the company of a detachment of guards, went late that afternoon to the private apartments of the Rivan Warder. He looked about constantly as he walked, and his hand was never far from the hilt of the sword at his waist.

He found Brand seated before a large harp. The Warder's big hands seemed to caress the strings of the instrument, bringing forth a plaintively rippling melody. The big, grim man's face was soft and reflective as he played, and Garion found that the music was even more beautiful because it was so unexpected.

"You play very well, my Lord," he said respectfully as the last notes of the song lingered in the strings.

"I play often, your Majesty," Brand replied. "Sometimes as I play I can even forget that my wife is no longer with me." He rose from the chair in front of the harp and squared his shoulders, all softness going out of his face. "How may I serve you, King Belgarion?"

Garion cleared his throat a trifle nervously. "I'm probably not going to say this very well," he admitted, "but please take it the way I mean it and not the way it might come out."

"Certainly, your Majesty."

"I didn't ask for all this, you know," Garion began with a vague gesture that took in the entire Citadel. "The crown, I mean, and being king—all of it. I was really pretty happy the way I was."

"Yes, your Majesty?"

"What I'm trying to get at is—well—you were the ruler here in Riva until I came along."

Brand nodded soberly.

"I didn't really want to be king," Garion rushed on, "and I certainly didn't want to push you out of your position."

Brand looked at him, and then he slowly smiled. "I'd wondered why you seemed so uneasy whenever I came into the room, your Majesty. Is that what's been making you uncomfortable?"

Mutely, Garion nodded.

"You don't really know us yet, Belgarion," Brand told him. "You've only been here for a little more than a month. We're a peculiar sort of people. For over three thousand years we've been protecting the Orb—ever since Iron-grip came to this island. That's why we exist, and I think that one of the things we've lost along the way is that sense of self other men seem to feel is so important. Do you know why I'm called Brand?"

"I never really thought about it," Garion admitted.

"I do have another name, of course," Brand said, "but I'm not supposed ever to mention it. Each Warder has been called Brand so that there could never be any sense of personal glory in the office. We serve the Orb; that's our only purpose. To be quite honest with you, I'm really rather glad you came when you did. It was getting close to the time when I was supposed to choose my successor—with the help of the Orb, of course. But I didn't have the faintest idea who I was supposed to choose. Your arrival has relieved me of that task."

"We can be friends, then?"

"I think we already are, Belgarion," Brand replied gravely. "We both serve the same master, and that always brings men closer together."

Garion hesitated. "Am I doing all right?" he blurted.

Brand considered that. "Some of the things you've done weren't exactly the way I might have done them, but that's to be expected. Rhodar and Anheg don't always do things the same way either. Each of us has his own particular manner."

"They make fun of me, don't they—Anheg, Rhodar, and the others. I hear all the clever remarks every time I make a decision."

"I wouldn't worry too much about that, Belgarion. They're Alorns, and Alorns don't take kings very seriously. They make fun of each other too, you know. You could almost say that as long as they're joking, everything is all right. If they suddenly become very serious and formal, then you'll know that you're in trouble."

"I suppose I hadn't thought of it that way," Garion admitted.

"You'll get used to it in time," Brand assured him.

Garion felt much better after his conversation with Brand. In the company of his guards he started back toward the royal apartments; but partway there, he changed his mind and went looking for Aunt Pol instead. When he entered her rooms, his cousin Adara was sitting quietly with her, watching as Aunt Pol carefully mended one of Garion's old tunics. The girl rose and curtsied formally.

"Please, Adara," he said in a pained voice, "don't do that when we're alone. I see enough of it out there." He gestured in the direction of the more public parts of the building.

"Whatever your Majesty wishes," she replied.

"And don't call me that. I'm still just Garion."

She looked gravely at him with her calm, beautiful eyes. "No, Cousin," she disagreed, "you'll never be 'just Garion' anymore."

He sighed as the truth of that struck his heart.

"If you'll excuse me," she said then, "I must go attend Queen Silar. She's a bit unwell, and she says it comforts her to have me near."

"It comforts all of us when you're near," Garion told her without even thinking about it.

She smiled at him fondly.

"There might be some hope for him after all," Aunt Pol observed, her needle busy.

Adara looked at Garion. "He's never really been that bad, Lady Polgara," she said. She inclined her head toward them both and quietly left the room.

Garion wandered around for a few moments and then flung himself into a chair. A great deal had happened that day, and he felt suddenly at odds with the whole world.

Aunt Pol continued to sew.

"Why are you doing that?" Garion demanded finally. "I'll never wear that old thing again."

"It needs fixing, dear," she told him placidly.

"There are a hundred people around who could do it for you."

"I prefer to do it myself."

"Put it down and talk to me."

She set the tunic aside and looked at him inquiringly. "And what did your Majesty wish to discuss?" she inquired.

"Aunt Pol!" Garion's voice was stricken. "Not you too."

"Don't give orders then, dear," she recommended, picking up the tunic again.

Garion watched her at her sewing for a few moments, not really knowing what to say. A strange thought occurred to him. "Why *are* you doing that, Aunt Pol?" he asked, really curious this time. "Probably nobody'll ever use it again, so you're just wasting time on it."

"It's my time, dear," she reminded him. She looked up from her sewing, her eyes unreadable. Then, without explanation she held up the tunic with one hand and ran the forefinger of her other hand carefully up the rip. Garion felt a very light surge, and the sound was only a whisper. The rip mended itself before his eyes, rewoven as if it had never existed. "Now you can see how completely useless mending it really is," she told him.

"Why do you do it then?"

"Because I like to sew, dear," she replied. With a sharp little jerk she ripped the tunic again. Then she picked up her needle and patiently began repairing the rip. "Sewing keeps the hands and eyes busy, but leaves the mind free for other things. It's very relaxing."

"Sometimes you're awfully complicated, Aunt Pol."

"Yes, dear. I know."

Garion paced about for a bit, then suddenly knelt beside her chair and, pushing her sewing aside, he put his head into her lap. "Oh, Aunt Pol," he said, very close to tears.

"What's the matter, dear?" she asked, carefully smoothing his hair.

"I'm so *lonely*."

"Is *that* all?"

He lifted his head and stared at her incredulously. He had not expected that.

"Everyone's lonely, dear," she explained, drawing him close to her. "We touch other people only briefly, then we're alone again. You'll get used to it in time."

"Nobody will talk to me now—not the way they did before. They're always bowing and saying 'Your Majesty' to me."

"You *are* the king, after all," she replied.

"But I don't want to be."

"That's too bad. It's the destiny of your family, so there's not a thing you can do about it. Did anyone ever tell you about Prince Gared?"

"I don't think so. Who was he?"

"He was the only survivor when the Nyissan assassins killed King Gorek and his family. He escaped by throwing himself into the sea."

"How old was he?"

"Six. He was a very brave child. Everyone thought that he had drowned and that his body had been washed out to sea. Your grandfather and I encouraged that belief. For thirteen hundred years we've hidden Prince Gared's descendants. For generations they've lived out their lives in quiet obscurity for the single purpose of bringing *you* to the throne—and now you say that you don't want to be king?"

"I don't know any of those people," he said sullenly. He knew he was behaving badly, but he couldn't seem to help himself.

"Would it help if you did know them—some of them, anyway?"

The question baffled him.

"Perhaps it might," she decided. She laid her sewing aside and stood up, drawing him to his feet. "Come with me," she told him and led him to the tall window that looked out over the city below. There was a small balcony outside; in one corner where a rain gutter had cracked, there had built up during the fall and winter a sheet of shiny black ice, curving down over the railing and spreading out on the balcony floor.

Aunt Pol unlatched the window and it swung open, admitting a blast of icy air that made the candles dance. "Look directly into the ice, Garion," she told him, pointing at the glittering blackness. "Look deep into it."

He did as she told him and felt the force of her mind at work.

Something was in the ice—shapeless at first but emerging slowly and becoming more and more visible. It was, he saw finally, the figure of a pale blond woman, quite lovely and with a warm smile on her lips. She seemed young, and her eyes were directly on Garion's face. "My baby," a voice seemed to whisper to him. "My little Garion."

Garion began to tremble violently. "Mother?" he gasped.

"So tall now," the whisper continued. "Almost a man."

"And already a king, Ildera," Aunt Pol told the phantom in a gentle voice.

"Then he *was* the chosen one," the ghost of Garion's mother exulted. "I knew it. I could feel it when I carried him under my heart."

A second shape had begun to appear beside the first. It was a tall young man with dark hair but a strangely familiar face. Garion clearly saw its resemblance to his own. "Hail Belgarion, my son," the second shape said to him.

"Father," Garion replied, not knowing what else to say.

"Our blessings, Garion," the second ghost said as the two figures started to fade.

"I avenged you, Father," Garion called after them. It seemed important that they know that. He was never sure, however, if they had heard him.

Aunt Pol was leaning against the window frame with a look of exhaustion on her face.

"Are you all right?" Garion asked her, concerned.

"It's a very difficult thing to do, dear," she told him, passing a weary hand over her face.

But there was yet another flicker within the depths of the ice, and the familiar shape of the blue wolf appeared—the one who had joined Belgarath in the fight with Grul the Eldrak in the mountains of Ulgo. The wolf sat looking at them for a moment, then flickered briefly into the shape of a snowy owl and finally became a tawny-haired woman with golden eyes. Her face was so like Aunt Pol's that Garion could not help glancing quickly back and forth to compare them.

"You left it open, Polgara," the golden-eyed woman said gently. Her voice was as warm and soft as a summer evening.

"Yes, Mother," Aunt Pol replied. "I'll close it in a moment."

"It's all right, Polgara," the wolf-woman told her daughter. "It gave me the chance to meet him." She looked directly into Garion's face. "A touch or two is still there," she observed. "A bit about the eyes and in the shape of the jaw. Does he know?"

"Not everything, Mother," Aunt Pol answered.

"Perhaps it's as well," Poledra noted.

Once again another figure emerged out of the dark depths of the ice. The second woman had hair like sunlight, and her face was even more like Aunt Pol's than Poledra's. "Polgara, my dear sister," she said.

"Beldaran," Aunt Pol responded in a voice overwhelmed with love.

"And Belgarion," Garion's ultimate grandmother said, "the final flower of my love and Riva's."

"Our blessings also, Belgarion," Poledra declared. "Farewell for now, but know that we love thee." And then the two were gone.

"Does that help?" Aunt Pol asked him, her voice deep with emotion and her eyes filled with tears.

Garion was too stunned by what he had just seen and heard to answer. Dumbly, he nodded.

"I'm glad the effort wasn't wasted then," she said. "Please close the window, dear. It's letting the winter in."

CHAPTER FOURTEEN

It was the first day of spring, and King Belgarion of Riva was terribly nervous. He had watched the approach of Princess Ce'Nedra's sixteenth birthday with a steadily mounting anxiety and, now that the day had finally arrived, he hovered on the very edge of panic. The deep blue brocade doublet over which a half dozen tailors had labored for weeks still did not seem to feel just right. Somehow it was a bit tight across the shoulders, and the stiff collar scratched his neck. Moreover, his gold crown seemed unusually heavy on this particular day, and, as he fidgeted, his throne seemed even more uncomfortable than usual.

The Hall of the Rivan King had been decorated extensively for the occasion, but even the banners and garlands of pale spring flowers could not mask the ominous starkness of the great throne room. The assembled notables, however, chatted and laughed among themselves as if nothing significant were taking place. Garion felt rather bitter about their heartless lack of concern in the face of what was about to happen to him.

Aunt Pol stood at the left side of his throne, garbed in a new silver gown and with a silver circlet about her hair. Belgarath lounged indolently on the right, wearing a new green doublet which had already become rumpled.

"Don't squirm so much, dear," Aunt Pol told Garion calmly.

"That's easy enough for *you* to say," Garion retorted in an accusing tone.

"Try not to think about it," Belgarath advised. "It'll all be over in a little while."

Then Brand, his face seeming even more bleak than usual, entered the Hall from the side door and came to the dais. "There's a Nyissan at the gate of the Citadel, your Majesty," he said quietly. "He says that he's an emissary of Queen Salmissra and that he's here to witness the ceremony."

"Isn't that impossible?" Garion asked Aunt Pol, startled by the Warder's surprising announcement.

"Not entirely," she replied. "More likely, though, it's a diplomatic fiction. I'd imagine that the Nyissans would prefer to keep Salmissra's condition a secret."

"What do I do?" Garion asked.

Belgarath shrugged. "Let him in."

"In here?" Brand's voice was shocked. "A Nyissan in the throne room? Belgarath, you're not serious."

"Garion is Overlord of the West, Brand," the old man replied, "and that includes Nyissa. I don't imagine that the snake-people will be much use to us at any time, but let's be polite, at least."

Brand's face went stiff with disapproval. "What is your Majesty's decision?" he asked Garion directly.

"Well—" Garion hesitated. "Let him come in, I guess."

"Don't vacillate, Garion," Aunt Pol told him firmly.

"I'm sorry," Garion said quickly.

"And don't apologize," she added. "Kings don't apologize."

He looked at her helplessly. Then he turned back to Brand. "Tell the emissary from Nyissa to join us," he said, though his tone was placating.

"By the way, Brand," Belgarath suggested, "I wouldn't let anyone get too excited about this. The Nyissan has ambassadorial status, and it'd be a serious breach of protocol if he died unexpectedly."

Brand bowed rather stiffly, turned, and left the Hall.

"Was that really necessary, Father?" Aunt Pol asked.

"Old grudges die hard, Pol," Belgarath replied. "Sometimes it's best to get everything right out in front so that there aren't any misunderstandings later."

When the emissary of the Snake Queen entered the Hall, Garion started with surprise. It was Sadi, the chief eunuch in Salmissra's palace. The thin man with the dead-looking eyes and shaved head wore the customary iridescent blue-green Nyissan robe, and he bowed sinuously as he approached the throne. "Greetings to his Majesty, Belgarion of Riva, from Eternal Salmissra, Queen of the Snake-People," he intoned in his peculiarly contralto voice.

"Welcome, Sadi," Garion replied formally.

"My queen sends her regards on this happy day," Sadi continued.

"She didn't really, did she?" Garion asked a bit pointedly.

"Not precisely, your Majesty," Sadi admitted without the least trace of embarrassment. "I'm sure she would have, however, if we'd been able to make her understand what was happening."

"How is she?" Garion remembered the dreadful transformation Salmissra had undergone.

"Difficult," Sadi answered blandly. "Of course that's nothing new. Fortunately she sleeps for a week or two after she's been fed. She moulted last month, and it made her dreadfully short-tempered." He rolled his eyes ceilingward. "It was ghastly," he murmured. "She bit three servants before it was over. They all died immediately, of course."

"She's venomous?" Garion was a bit startled at that.

"She's always been venomous, your Majesty."

"That's not the way I mean."

"Forgive my little joke," Sadi apologized. "Judging from the reactions of people she's bitten, I'd guess that she's at least ten times more deadly than a common cobra."

"Is she terribly unhappy?" Garion felt a strange pity for the hideously altered queen.

"That's really rather hard to say, your Majesty," Sadi replied clinically. "It's difficult to tell what a snake's really feeling, you understand. By the time she'd learned to communicate her wishes to us, she seemed to have become reconciled to her new form. We feed her and keep her clean. As long as she has her mirror and someone to bite when she's feeling peevish, she seems quite content."

"She still looks at herself in the mirror? I wouldn't think she'd want to now."

"Our race has a somewhat different view of the serpent, your Majesty," Sadi explained. "We find it a rather attractive creature, and our queen is a splendid-looking snake, after all. Her new skin is quite lovely, and she seems very proud of it." He turned and bowed deeply to Aunt Pol. "Lady Polgara," he greeted her.

"Sadi," she acknowledged with a brief nod.

"May I convey to you the heartfelt thanks of her Majesty's government?"

One of Aunt Pol's eyebrows rose inquiringly.

"The government, my Lady—not the queen herself. Your—ah—intervention, shall we say, has simplified things in the palace enormously. We no longer have to worry about Salmissra's whims and peculiar appetites. We rule by committee and we hardly ever find it necessary to poison each other anymore. No one's tried to poison me for months. It's all very smooth and civilized in Sthiss Tor now." He glanced briefly at Garion. "May I also offer my congratulations on your success with his Majesty? He seems to have matured considerably. He was really very callow when last we met."

"Whatever happened to Issus?" Garion asked him, ignoring that particular observation.

Sadi shrugged. "Issus? Oh, he's still about, scratching out a living as a paid assassin, probably. I imagine that one day we'll find him floating facedown in the river. It's the sort of end one expects for someone like that."

There was a sudden blare of trumpets from just beyond the great doors at the back of the Hall. Garion started nervously, and his mouth quite suddenly went dry.

The heavy doors swung open, and a double file of Tolnedran legionnaires marched in, their breastplates burnished until they shone like mirrors, and the tall crimson plumes on their helmets waving as they marched. The inclusion of the legionnaires in the ceremony had infuriated Brand. The Rivan Warder had stalked about in icy silence for days after he had discovered that Garion had granted ambassador Valgon's request for a proper escort for Princess Ce'Nedra. Brand did not like Tolnedrans, and he had been looking forward to witnessing the pride of the Empire humbled by Ce'Nedra's forlorn and solitary entrance into the Hall. The presence of the legionnaires spoiled that, of course, and Brand's disappointment and disapproval had been painfully obvious. As much as Garion wanted to stay on Brand's good side, however, he did not intend to start off the official relationship between his bride-to-be and himself by publicly humiliating her. Garion was quite ready to acknowledge his lack of education, but he was not prepared to admit to being *that* stupid.

When Ce'Nedra entered, her hand resting lightly on Valgon's arm, she was every inch an Imperial Princess. Garion could only gape at her. Although the Accords of Vo Mimbre required that she present herself in her wedding gown, Garion was totally unprepared for such Imperial magnificence. Her gown was of gold and white brocade covered with seed pearls, and its train swept the floor behind her.

Her flaming hair was intricately curled and cascaded over her left shoulder like a deep crimson waterfall. Her circlet of tinted gold held in place a short veil that did not so much conceal her face as soften it into luminousness. She was tiny and perfect, exquisite beyond belief, but her eyes were like little green agates.

She and Valgon moved at a stately pace down between the ranks of her tall, burnished legionnaires; when they reached the front of the hall, they stopped.

Brand, sober-faced and imposing, took his staff of office from Bralon, his eldest son, and rapped sharply on the stone floor with its butt three times. "Her Imperial Highness Ce'Nedra of the Tolnedran Empire," he announced in a deep, booming voice. "Will your Majesty grant her audience?"

"I will receive the princess," Garion declared, straightening a bit on his throne.

"The Princess Ce'Nedra may approach the throne," Brand proclaimed. Though his words were ritual formality, they had obviously been chosen with great care to make it absolutely clear that Imperial Tolnedra came to the Hall of the Rivan King as a suppliant. Ce'Nedra's eyes flashed fire, and Garion groaned inwardly. The little princess, however, glided to the appointed spot before the dais and curtsied regally. There was no submission in that gesture.

"The Princess has permission to speak," Brand boomed. For a brief, irrational moment Garion wanted to strangle him.

Ce'Nedra drew herself up, her face as cold as a winter sea. "Thus I, Ce'Nedra, daughter to Ran Borune XXIII and Princess of Imperial Tolnedra, present myself as required by treaty and law in the presence of his Majesty, Belgarion of Riva," she declared. "And thus has the Tolnedran Empire once more demonstrated her willingness to fulfill her obligations as set forth in the Accords of Vo Mimbre. Let other kingdoms witness Tolnedra's meticulous response and follow her example in meeting their obligations. I declare before these witnesses that I am an unmarried virgin of a suitable age. Will his Majesty consent to take me to wife?"

Garion's reply had been carefully thought out. The quiet inner voice had suggested a way to head off years of marital discord. He rose to his feet and said, "I, Belgarion, King of Riva, hereby consent to take the Imperial Princess Ce'Nedra to be my wife and queen. I declare, moreover, that she will rule jointly by my side in Riva and wheresoever else the authority of our throne may extend."

The gasp that rippled through the Hall was clearly audible, and Brand's face went absolutely white. The look Ce'Nedra gave Garion was quizzical, and her eyes softened slightly. "Your majesty is too kind," she responded with a graceful little curtsy. Some of the edge had gone out of her voice, and she threw a quick sidelong glance at the spluttering Brand. "Have I your Majesty's permission to withdraw?" she asked sweetly.

"As your Highness wishes," Garion replied, sinking back down onto his throne. He was perspiring heavily.

The princess curtsied again with a mischievous little twinkle in her eyes, then turned and left the Hall with her legionnaires drawn up in close order about her.

As the great doors boomed shut behind her, an angry buzz ran through the crowd. The word "outrageous" seemed to be the most frequently repeated.

"This is unheard of, your Majesty," Brand protested.

"Not entirely," Garion replied defensively. "The throne of Arendia is held jointly by King Korodullin and Queen Mayaserana." He looked to Mandorallen, gleaming in his armor, with a mute appeal in his eyes.

"His Majesty speaks truly, my Lord Brand," Mandorallen declared. "I assure thee that our kingdom suffers not from the lack of singularity upon the throne."

"That's Arendia," Brand objected. "This is Riva. The situations are entirely different. No Alorn kingdom has ever been ruled by a woman."

"It might not hurt to examine the possible advantages of the situation," King Rhodar suggested. "My own queen, for example, plays a somewhat more significant role in Drasnian affairs than custom strictly allows."

With great difficulty Brand regained at least some of his composure. "May I withdraw, your Majesty?" he asked, his face still livid.

"If you wish," Garion answered quietly. It wasn't going well. Brand's conservatism was the one stumbling block he hadn't considered.

"It's an interesting notion, dear," Aunt Pol said quietly to him, "but don't you think it might have been better to consult with someone before you made it a public declaration?"

"Won't it help to cement relations with the Tolnedrans?"

"Quite possibly," she admitted. "I'm not saying that it's a bad idea, Garion; I just think it might have been better to warn a few people first. What *are* you laughing at?" she demanded of Belgarath, who was leaning against the throne convulsed with mirth.

"The Bear-cult's going to have collective apoplexy," he chortled.

Her eyes widened slightly. "Oh, dear," she said. "I'd forgotten about them."

"They aren't going to like it very much, are they?" Garion concluded. "Particularly since Ce'Nedra's a Tolnedran."

"I think you can count on them to go up in flames," the old sorcerer replied, still laughing.

IN THE DAYS that followed, the usually bleak halls of the Citadel were filled with color as official visitors and representatives teemed through them, chatting, gossiping, and conducting business in out-of-the-way corners. The rich and varied gifts they had brought to celebrate the occasion filled several tables lining one of the walls in the great throne room. Garion, however, was unable to visit or to examine the gifts. He spent his days in a room with his advisors and with the Tolnedran ambassador and his staff as the details of the official betrothal document were hammered out.

Valgon had seized on Garion's break with tradition and was trying to wring the last measure of advantage from it, while Brand was desperately trying to add clauses and stipulations to rigidly circumscribe Ce'Nedra's authority. As the two haggled back and forth, Garion found himself more and more frequently staring out the window. The sky over Riva was an intense blue, and puffy white clouds ran before the wind. The bleak crags of the island were touched with the first green blush of spring. Faintly, carried by the wind, the high, clear voice of a shepherdess singing to her flock wafted through the open window. There was a pure, unschooled quality to her voice, and she sang with no hint of self-consciousness, as if there were not a human ear within a hundred leagues. Garion sighed as the last notes of her song died away and then returned his attention to the tedious negotiations.

His attention, however, was divided in those early days of spring. Since he was unable to pursue the search for the man with the torn cloak himself, he was forced to rely on Lelldorin to press the investigation. Lelldorin was not always entirely reliable, and the search for the would-be assassin seemed to fire the enthusiastic young Asturian's imagination. He crept about the Citadel with dark, sidelong glances, and reported his lack of findings in conspiratorial whispers. Turning things over to Lelldorin might have been a mistake, but there had been no real choice in the matter. Any of Garion's other friends would have immediately raised a general outcry, and the entire affair would have been irrevocably out in the open. Garion did not want that. He was not prepared to make any decisions about the assassin until he found out who had thrown the knife and why. Too many other things could have been involved. Only Lelldorin could be relied upon for absolute secrecy, even though there was some danger in turning him loose in the Citadel with a license to track someone down. Lelldorin had a way of turning simple things into catastrophes, and Garion worried almost as much about that as he did about the possibility of another knife hurtling out of the shadows toward his unprotected back.

Among the visitors present for the betrothal ceremonies was Ce'Nedra's cousin Xera, who was present as the personal representative of Queen Xantha. Though shy at first, the Dryad soon lost her reserve—particularly when she found herself the center of the attention of a cluster of smitten young noblemen.

The gift of Queen Xantha to the royal couple was, Garion thought, somewhat peculiar. Wrapped in plain leaves, Xera presented them with two sprouted acorns. Ce'Nedra, however, seemed delighted. She insisted upon planting the two seeds immediately and rushed down to the small private garden adjoining the royal apartments.

"It's very nice, I suppose," Garion commented dubiously as he stood watching his princess on her knees in the damp loam of the garden, busily preparing the earth to receive Queen Xantha's gift.

Ce'Nedra looked at him sharply. "I don't believe your Majesty understands the significance of the gift," she said in the hatefully formal tone she had assumed with him.

"Stop that," Garion told her crossly. "I still have a name, after all—and I'm almost positive you haven't forgotten it."

"If your Majesty insists," she replied loftily.

"My Majesty does. What's so significant about a couple of nuts?"

She looked at him almost pityingly. "You wouldn't understand."

"Not if you won't take the trouble to explain it to me."

"Very well." She sounded irritatingly superior. "The one acorn is from my very own tree. The other is from Queen Xantha's."

"So?"

"See how impossibly dense he is," the princess said to her cousin.

"He's not a Dryad, Ce'Nedra," Xera replied calmly.

"Obviously."

Xera turned to Garion. "The acorns are not really from my mother," she explained. "They're gifts from the trees themselves."

"Why didn't you tell me that in the first place?" Garion demanded of Ce'Nedra. She sniffed and returned to her digging.

"While they're still just young shoots, Ce'Nedra will bind them together," Xera went on. "The shoots will intertwine as they grow, embracing each other and forming a single tree. It's the Dryad symbol for marriage. The two will become one—just as you and Ce'Nedra will."

"That remains to be seen," Ce'Nedra sniffed, troweling busily in the dirt.

Garion sighed. "I hope the trees are patient."

"Trees are very patient, Garion," Xera replied. She made a little gesture that Ce'Nedra could not see, and Garion followed her to the other end of the garden.

"She does love you, you know," Xera told him quietly. "She won't admit it, of course, but she loves you. I know her well enough to see that."

"Why's she acting the way she is, then?"

"She doesn't like being forced into things, that's all."

"I'm not the one who's forcing her. Why take it out on me?"

"Can you think of anyone else she can take it out on?"

Garion hadn't thought of that. He left the garden quietly. Xera's words gave him some hope that one of his problems, at least, might eventually be resolved. Ce'Nedra would pout and storm for a while, and then—after she had made him suffer enough—she would relent. Perhaps it might speed things along if he suffered a bit more obviously.

The other problems had not changed significantly. He was still going to have to lead an army against Kal Torak; Belgarath had still given no sign that his power was intact; and someone in the Citadel was still, so far as Garion knew, sharpening another knife for him. He sighed and went back to his own rooms where he could worry in private.

Somewhat later he received word that Aunt Pol wanted to see him in her private apartment. He went immediately and found her seated by the fire, sewing as usual. Belgarath, dressed in his shabby old clothes, sat in one of the deep, comfortable chairs on the other side of the fire with his feet up and a tankard in his hand.

"You wanted to see me, Aunt Pol?" Garion inquired as he entered.

"Yes, dear," she replied. "Sit down." She looked at him somewhat critically. "He still doesn't look much like a king, does he, Father?"

"Give him time, Pol," the old man told her. "He hasn't been at it for very long."

"You both knew all along, didn't you?" Garion accused them. "Who I was, I mean."

"Naturally," Aunt Pol answered in that maddening way of hers.

"Well, if you'd wanted me to behave like a king, you should have told me about it. That way I'd have had some time to get used to the idea."

"It seems to me we discussed this once before," Belgarath mentioned, "a long time ago. If you'll stop and think a bit, I'm sure you'll be able to see why we had to keep it a secret."

"Maybe." Garion said it a bit doubtfully. "All this has happened too fast, though. I hadn't even got used to being a sorcerer yet, and now I have to be a king, too. It's all got me off balance."

"You're adaptable, Garion," Aunt Pol told him, her needle flickering.

"You'd better give him the amulet, Pol," Belgarath mentioned. "The princess should be here soon."

"I was just about to, Father," she replied, laying aside her sewing.

"What's this?" Garion asked.

"The princess has a gift for you," Aunt Pol said. "A ring. It's a bit ostentatious, but act suitably pleased."

"Shouldn't I have something to give her in return?"

"I've already taken care of that, dear." She took a small velvet box from the table beside her chair. "You'll give her this." She handed the box to Garion.

Inside the box lay a silver amulet, a bit smaller than Garion's own. Represented on its face in minute and exquisite detail was the likeness of that huge tree which stood in solitary splendor in the center of the Vale of Aldur. There was a crown woven into the branches. Garion held the amulet in his right hand, trying to determine if it had some of the same kind of force about it that he knew was in the one he wore. There was something there, but it didn't feel at all the same.

"It doesn't seem to be like ours," he concluded.

"It isn't," Belgarath replied. "Not exactly, anyway. Ce'Nedra's not a sorceress, so she wouldn't be able to use one like yours."

"You said 'not exactly.' It does have some kind of power, then?"

"It will give her certain insights," the old man answered, "if she's patient enough to learn how to use it."

"Exactly what are we talking about when we use the word 'insight'?"

"An ability to see and hear things she wouldn't otherwise be able to see or hear," Belgarath specified.

"Is there anything else I should know about it before she gets here?"

"Just tell her that it's a family heirloom," Aunt Pol suggested. "It belonged to my sister, Beldaran."

"You should keep it, Aunt Pol," Garion objected. "I can get something else for the princess."

"No, dear. Beldaran wants her to have it."

Garion found Aunt Pol's habit of speaking of people long dead in the present tense a trifle disconcerting, so he didn't pursue the matter.

There was a light tap on the door.

"Come in, Ce'Nedra," Aunt Pol answered.

The little princess was wearing a rather plain green gown open at the throat, and her expression was somewhat subdued. "Come over by the fire," Aunt Pol told her. "The evenings are still a bit chilly this time of year."

"Is it always this cold and damp in Riva?" Ce'Nedra asked, coming to the fire.

"We're a long ways north of Tol Honeth," Garion pointed out.

"I'm aware of that," she said with that little edge in her voice.

"I always thought it was customary to wait until *after* the wedding to start bickering," Belgarath observed slyly. "Have the rules changed?"

"Just practicing, Belgarath," Ce'Nedra replied impishly. "Just practicing for later on."

The old man laughed. "You can be a charming little girl when you put your mind to it," he said.

Ce'Nedra bowed mockingly. Then she turned to Garion. "It's customary for a Tolnedran girl to give her betrothed a gift of a certain value," she informed him. She held up a heavy, ornate ring set with several glowing stones. "This ring belonged to Ran Horb II, the greatest of all Tolnedran Emperors. Wearing it *might* help you to be a better king."

Garion sighed. It was going to be one of those meetings. "I'll be honored to wear the ring," he replied as inoffensively as possible, "and I'd like for you to wear this." He handed her the velvet box. "It belonged to the wife of Riva Iron-grip, Aunt Pol's sister."

Ce'Nedra took the box and opened it. "Why, Garion," she exclaimed, "it's lovely." She held the amulet in her hand, turning it to catch the firelight. "The tree looks so real that you can almost smell the leaves."

"Thank you," Belgarath replied modestly.

"*You* made it?" The princess sounded startled.

The old man nodded. "When Polgara and Beldaran were children, we lived in the Vale. There weren't very many silversmiths there, so I had to make their amulets myself. Aldur helped me with some of the finer details."

"This is a priceless gift, Garion." The tiny girl actually glowed, and Garion began to have some hope for the future. "Help me with it," she commanded, handing him the two ends of the chain and turning with one hand holding aside the mass of her deep red hair.

"Do you accept the gift, Ce'Nedra?" Aunt Pol asked her, giving the question a peculiar emphasis.

"Of course I do," the princess replied.

"Without reservation and of your own free will?" Aunt Pol pressed, her eyes intent.

"I accept the gift, Lady Polgara," Ce'Nedra replied. "Fasten it for me, Garion. Be sure it's secure. I wouldn't want it to come undone."

"I don't think you'll need to worry too much about that," Belgarath told her.

Garion's fingers trembled slightly as he fastened the curious clasp. His fingertips tingled peculiarly as the two ends locked together with a faintly audible click.

"Hold the amulet in your hand, Garion," Aunt Pol instructed him. Ce'Nedra lifted her chin and Garion took the medallion in his right hand. Then Aunt Pol and Belgarath closed their hands over his. Something peculiar seemed to pass through their hands and into the talisman at Ce'Nedra's throat.

"Now you are sealed to us, Ce'Nedra," Aunt Pol told the princess quietly, "with a tie that can never be broken."

Ce'Nedra looked at her with a puzzled expression, and then her eyes slowly widened and a dreadful suspicion began to grow in them. "Take it off," she told Garion sharply.

"He can't do that," Belgarath informed her, sitting back down and picking up his tankard again.

Ce'Nedra was tugging at the chain, pulling with both hands.

"You'll just scratch your neck, dear," Aunt Pol warned gently. "The chain won't break; it can't be cut; and it won't come off over your head. You'll never have to worry about losing it."

"*You* did this," the princess stormed at Garion.

"Did what?"

"Put this slave chain on me. It wasn't enough that I had to bow to you; now you've put me in chains as well."

"I didn't know," he protested.

"Liar!" she screamed at him. Then she turned and fled the room, sobbing bitterly.

CHAPTER FIFTEEN

Garion was in a sour mood. The prospect of another day of ceremony and tedious conferences was totally unbearable, and he had risen early to escape from the royal bedchamber before the insufferably polite appointment secretary with his endless lists could arrive to nail down the entire day. Garion privately detested the inoffensive fellow, even though he knew the man was only doing his job. A king's time had to be organized and scheduled, and it was the appointment secretary's task to take care of that. And so, each morning after breakfast, there came that respectful tapping at the door, and the appointment secretary would enter, bow, and then proceed to arrange the young king's day, minute by minute. Garion was morbidly convinced that somewhere, probably hidden away and closely guarded, was the ultimate master list that laid out the schedule for the rest of his life—including his royal funeral.

But this day dawned too gloriously for thoughts of stuffy formality and heavy conference. The sun had come boiling up out of the Sea of the Winds, touching the snowfields atop the craggy peaks with a blushing pink, and the morning shadows in the deep valleys above the city were a misty blue. The smell of spring pushed urgently in from the little garden outside his window, and Garion knew he must escape, if only for an hour or so. He dressed quickly in tunic, hose, and soft Rivan boots, rather carefully selecting clothes as unroyal as his wardrobe offered. Pausing only long enough to belt on his sword, he crept out of the royal apartments. He even considered not taking along his guards, but prudently decided against that.

They were at a standstill in the search for the man who had tried to kill him in that dim hallway, but both Lelldorin and Garion had discovered that the outer garments of any number of Rivans needed repair. The gray cloak was not a ceremonial garment, but rather was something thrown on for warmth. It was a sturdy, utilitarian covering, and quite a number of such robes had been allowed to fall into a condition of shocking disrepair. Moreover, now that spring was here, men would soon stop wearing them, and the only clue to the attacker's identity would be locked away in a closet somewhere.

Garion brooded about that as he wandered moodily through the silent corridors of the Citadel with two mailed guards following at a respectful distance. The attempt, he reasoned, had not come from a Grolim. Aunt Pol's peculiar ability to recognize the mind of a Grolim would have alerted her instantly. In all probability the attacker had not been a foreigner of any kind. There were too few foreigners on the island to make that very likely. It had to be a Rivan, but why would a Rivan want to kill the king who had just returned after thirteen hundred years?

He sighed with perplexity over the problem and let his mind drift off to other matters. He wished that he were only Garion again; he wished that more than anything. He wished that it might be possible for him to awaken in some out-of-the-way inn somewhere and start out in the silver light of daybreak to ride alone to the top of the next hill to see what lay beyond. He sighed again. He was a public person now, and such freedom was denied him. He was coldly certain that he was never going to have a moment to himself again.

As he passed an open doorway, he suddenly heard a familiar voice. "Sin creeps into our minds the moment we let our thoughts stray," Relg was saying. Garion stopped, motioning his guards to silence.

"Must everything be a sin?" Taiba asked. Inevitably they were together. They had been together almost continually from the moment Relg had rescued Taiba from her living entombment in the cave beneath Rak Cthol. Garion was almost certain that neither of them was actually conscious of that fact. Moreover, he had seen evidence of discomfort, not only on Taiba's face, but on Relg's as well, whenever they were apart. Something beyond the control of either of them drew them together.

"The world is filled with sin," Relg declared. "We must guard against it constantly. We must stand jealous guard over our purity against all forms of temptation."

"That would be very tiresome." Taiba sounded faintly amused.

"I thought you wanted instruction," Relg accused her. "If you just came here to mock me, I'll leave right now."

"Oh, sit down, Relg," she told him. "We'll never get anywhere with this if you take offense at everything I say."

"Have you no idea at all about the meaning of religion?" he asked after a moment. He actually sounded curious about it.

"In the slave pens, the word religion meant death. It meant having your heart cut out."

"That was a Grolim perversion. Didn't you have a religion of your own?"

"The slaves came from all over the world, and they prayed to many Gods—usually for death."

"What about your own people? Who is your God?"

"I was told that his name is Mara. We don't pray to him though—not since he abandoned us."

"It's not man's place to accuse the Gods," Relg told her sternly. "Man's duty is to glorify his God and pray to him—even if the prayers aren't answered."

"And what about the God's duty to man?" she asked pointedly. "Can a God not be negligent as well as a man? Wouldn't you consider a God negligent if he allowed his children to be enslaved and butchered—or if he allowed his daughters to be given as a reward to other slaves when they pleased their masters—as I was?"

Relg struggled with that painful question.

"I think you've led a very sheltered life, Relg," she told the zealot. "I think you have a very limited idea of human suffering—of the kinds of things men can do to other men—and women—apparently with the full permission of the Gods."

"You should have killed yourself," he said stubbornly.

"Whatever for?"

"To avoid corruption, naturally."

"You *are* an innocent, aren't you? I didn't kill myself because I wasn't ready to die. Even in the slave pens, life can be sweet, Relg, and death is bitter. What you call corruption is only a small thing—and not even always unpleasant."

"Sinful woman!" he gasped.

"You worry too much about that, Relg," she advised him. "Cruelty is a sin; lack of compassion is a sin. But that other little thing? I hardly think so. I begin to wonder about you. Could it be that this UL of yours is not quite so stern and unforgiving as you seem to believe? Does he really want all these prayers and rituals and grovelings? Or are they your way to hide from your God? Do you think that praying in a loud voice and pounding your head on the ground will keep him from seeing into your heart?"

Relg was making strangled noises.

"If our Gods really loved us, they'd want our lives filled with joy," she continued relentlessly. "But you hate joy for some reason—probably because you're afraid of it. Joy is not sin, Relg; joy is a kind of love, and I think the Gods approve of it—even if you don't."

"You're hopelessly depraved."

"Perhaps so," she admitted casually, "but at least I look life right in the face. I'm not afraid of it, and I don't try to hide from it."

"Why are you doing this?" he demanded of her in an almost tragic voice. "Why must you forever follow me and mock me with your eyes?"

"I don't really know," she replied, sounding almost puzzled. "You're not really that attractive. Since we left Rak Cthol, I've seen dozens of men who interested me much more. At first it was because I knew that I made you nervous and because you were afraid of me. I rather enjoyed that, but lately there's more to it than that. It doesn't make any sense, of course. You're what you are, and I'm what I am, but for some reason I want to be with you." She paused. "Tell me, Relg—and don't try to lie about it—would you *really* want me to go away and never see you again?"

There was a long and painful silence. "May UL forgive me!" Relg groaned finally.

"I'm sure he will, Relg," she assured him gently.

Garion moved quietly on down the corridor away from the open door. Something he had not understood before had begun to become quite clear. *"You're doing this, aren't you?"* he asked silently.

"Naturally," the dry voice in his mind replied.

"But why those two?"

"*Because it's necessary, Belgarion. I don't do things out of whim. We're all compelled by necessity—even I. Actually, what's going on between Relg and Taiba doesn't remotely concern you.*"

Garion was a little stung by that. "*I thought—well—*"

"*You assumed that you were my only care—that you were the absolute center of the universe? You're not, of course. There are other things almost equally important, and Relg and Taiba are centrally involved in one of those things. Your participation in that particular matter is peripheral at the most.*"

"*They're going to be desperately unhappy if you force them together,*" Garion accused.

"*That doesn't matter in the slightest. Their being together is necessary. You're wrong, though. It'll take them a while to get used to it, but once they do, they're both going to be very happy. Obedience to Necessity does have its rewards, after all.*"

Garion struggled with that idea for a while, then finally gave up. His own problems intruded once more on his thoughts. Inevitably, as he always did when he was troubled, he went looking for Aunt Pol. He found her sitting before the cozy fire in her apartment, sipping a cup of fragrant tea and watching through the window as the rosy morning sunlight set the snowfields above the city ablaze. "You're up early," she observed as he entered.

"I wanted to talk to you," he told her, "and the only way I ever get the chance to do what I want is to leave my room before the man with my schedule for the day shows up." He flung himself into a chair. "They never give me a minute to myself."

"You're an important person now, dear."

"That wasn't *my* idea." He stared moodily out the window. "Grandfather's all right now, isn't he?" he asked suddenly.

"What gave you that idea?"

"Well—the other day, when we gave Ce'Nedra the amulet—didn't he—sort of—?"

"Most of that came from you, dear," she replied.

"I felt something else."

"That could have been just me. It was a pretty subtle thing, and even I couldn't be sure if he had any part in it."

"There has to be some way we can find out."

"There's only one way, Garion, and that's for him to do something."

"All right, let's go off with him someplace and have him try—something sort of small, maybe."

"And how would we explain that to him?"

"You mean he doesn't know?" Garion sat up quickly.

"He might, but I rather doubt it."

"You didn't tell him?"

"Of course not. If he has any doubts whatsoever about his ability, he'll fail, and if he fails once, that'll be the end of it."

"I don't understand."

"A very important part of it is *knowing* that it's going to work. If you aren't absolutely sure, then it won't. That's why we can't tell him."

Garion thought about it. "I suppose that makes sense, but isn't it sort of dangerous? I mean, what if something really urgent comes up, and he tries to do something about it, and we all of a sudden find out that he can't?"

"You and I would have to deal with it then, dear."

"You seem awfully calm about it."

"Getting excited doesn't really help very much, Garion."

The door burst open, and Queen Layla, her hair awry and her crown slipping precariously over one ear, stormed in. "I won't have it, Polgara," she declared angrily. "I absolutely won't have it. You've got to talk to him. Oh, excuse me, your Majesty," the plump little queen added, noticing Garion. "I didn't see you." She curtsied gracefully.

"Your Highness," Garion replied, getting up hurriedly and bowing in return.

"Who did you wish me to speak with, Layla?" Aunt Pol asked.

"Anheg. He insists that my poor husband sit up and drink with him every night. Fulrach's so sick this morning that he can barely lift his head off the pillow. That great bully of a Cherek is ruining my husband's health."

"Anheg likes your husband, Layla. It's his way of showing his friendship."

"Can't they be friends without drinking so much?"

"I'll talk to him, dear," Aunt Pol promised.

Mollified somewhat, Queen Layla departed, curtsying again to Garion.

Garion was about to return to the subject of Belgarath's infirmity when Aunt Pol's maid came in to announce Lady Merel.

Barak's wife entered the room with a somber expression. "Your Majesty," she greeted Garion perfunctorily.

Garion rose again to bow and politely respond. He was getting rather tired of it.

"I need to talk with you, Polgara," Merel declared.

"Of course," Aunt Pol replied. "Would you excuse us, Garion?"

"I'll wait in the next room," he offered. He crossed to the door, but did not close it all the way. Once again his curiosity overcame his good manners.

"They all keep throwing it in my face," Merel blurted almost before he was out of the room.

"What's that?"

"Well—" Merel hesitated, then spoke quite firmly. "My lord and I were not always on the best of terms," she admitted.

"That's widely known, Merel," Aunt Pol told her diplomatically.

"That's the whole problem," Merel complained. "They all keep laughing behind their hands and waiting for me to go back to being the way I was before." A note of steel crept into her voice. "Well, it's not going to happen," she declared, "so they can laugh all they want to."

"I'm glad to hear that, Merel," Aunt Pol replied.

"Oh, Polgara," Merel said with a helpless little laugh, "he looks so much like a great shaggy bear, but he's so gentle inside. Why couldn't I have seen that before? All those years wasted."

"You had to grow up, Merel," Aunt Pol told her. "It takes some people longer, that's all."

After Lady Merel had left, Garion came back in and looked quizzically at Aunt Pol. "Has it always been like that?" he asked her. "What I mean is—do people always come to you when they've got problems?"

"It happens now and then," she replied. "People seem to think that I'm very wise. Usually they already know what they have to do, so I listen to them and agree with them and give them a bit of harmless support. It makes them happy. I set aside a certain amount of time each morning for these visits. They know that I'm here if they feel the need for someone to talk to. Would you care for some tea?"

He shook his head. "Isn't it an awful burden—all these other people's problems, I mean?"

"It's not really that heavy, Garion," she answered. "Their problems are usually rather small and domestic. It's rather pleasant to deal with things that aren't quite so earthshaking. Besides, I don't mind visitors—whatever their reasons for coming."

The next visitor, however, was Queen Islena, and her problem was more serious. Garion withdrew again when the maid announced that the Queen of Cherek wished to speak privately with the Lady Polgara; but, as before, his curiosity compelled him to listen at the door of the adjoining chamber.

"I've tried everything I can think of, Polgara," Islena declared, "but Grodeg won't let me go."

"The High Priest of Belar?"

"He knows everything, naturally," Islena confirmed. "All his underlings reported my every indiscretion to him. He threatens to tell Anheg if I try to sever my connection with the Bear-cult. How could I have been so stupid? He's got his hand around my throat."

"Just how indiscreet have you been, Islena?" Aunt Pol asked the queen pointedly.

"I went to some of their rituals," Islena confessed. "I put a few cult members in positions in the palace. I passed some information along to Grodeg."

"Which rituals, Islena?"

"Not *those*, Polgara," Islena replied in a shocked voice. "I'd never stoop to that."

"So all you really did was attend a few harmless gatherings where people dress up in bearskins and let a few cultists into the palace—where there were probably a dozen or more already anyway—and pass on a bit of harmless palace gossip?—It *was* harmless, wasn't it?"

"I didn't pass on any state secrets, Polgara, if that's what you mean," the queen said stiffly.

"Then Grodeg doesn't really have any hold over you, Islena."

"What should I do, Polgara?" the queen asked in an anguished voice.

"Go to Anheg. Tell him everything."

"I can't."

"You must. Otherwise Grodeg will force you into something worse. Actually, the situation could be turned to Anheg's advantage. Tell me exactly how much you know about what the cult's doing."

"They've begun creating chapters among the peasants, for one thing."

"They've never done that before," Aunt Pol mused. "The cult's always been re-stricted to the nobility and the priesthood."

"I can't be sure," Islena told her, "but I think they're preparing for something major—some kind of confrontation."

"I'll mention it to my father," Aunt Pol replied. "I think he'll want to take steps. As long as the cult was the plaything of the priesthood and the minor nobil-ity, it wasn't really all that important, but rousing the peasantry is quite another thing."

"I've heard a few other things as well," Islena continued. "I think they're try-ing to penetrate Rhodar's intelligence service. If they can get a few people in the right places in Boktor, they'll have access to most of the state secrets in the West."

"I see." Aunt Pol's voice was as cold as ice.

"I heard Grodeg talking once," Islena said in a tone of distaste. "It was before he found out that I didn't want anything more to do with him. He'd been reading the auguries and the signs in the heavens, and he was talking about the return of the Rivan King. The cult takes the term 'Overlord of the West' quite seriously. I honestly believe that their ultimate goal is to elevate Belgarion to the status of Em-peror of all the West—Aloria, Sendaria, Arendia, Tolnedra—and Nyissa."

"That's not how the term was meant to be interpreted," Aunt Pol objected.

"I know," Islena replied, "but Grodeg wants to twist it until it comes out that way. He's a total fanatic, and he wants to convert all the people of the West to Belar—by the sword, if necessary."

"That idiot!" Aunt Pol raged. "He'd start a general war in the West if he tried that—and even set the Gods to wrangling. What is there about Alorns that makes them continually want to expand to the south? Those boundaries were established by the Gods themselves. I think it's time for someone to put his foot down on Grodeg's neck—firmly. Go to Anheg immediately. Tell him everything and then tell him that I want to see him. I imagine that my father's going to want to discuss the matter with him as well."

"Anheg's going to be furious with me, Polgara," Islena faltered.

"I don't think so," Aunt Pol assured her. "As soon as he realizes that you've ex-posed Grodeg's plan, he'll probably be rather grateful. Let him think that you went along with Grodeg simply to get more information. That's a perfectly respectable motive—and it's the sort of thing a good wife would do."

"I hadn't thought of that," Islena said, already sounding more sure of herself. "It would have been a brave thing to do, wouldn't it?"

"Absolutely heroic, Islena," Aunt Pol replied. "Now go to Anheg."

"I will, Polgara." There was the sound of quick, determined steps, and then a door closed.

"Garion, come back in here." Aunt Pol's voice was firm.

He opened the door.

"You were listening?" It wasn't really a question.

"Well—"

"We're going to have to have a talk about that," she told him. "But it doesn't really matter this time. Go find your grandfather and tell him that I want to see him immediately. I don't care what he's doing. Bring him to me now."

"But how do we know he can do anything?" Garion demanded. "I mean, if he's lost his power—"

"There are many kinds of power, Garion. Sorcery's only one of them. Now go fetch him at once."

"Yes, Aunt Pol," Garion replied, already moving toward the door.

CHAPTER SIXTEEN

The High Priest of Belar was an imposing-looking man nearly seven feet tall. He had a long gray beard and burning eyes sunk deep in their sockets beneath bristling black eyebrows. He arrived from Val Alorn the following week after the seemingly endless negotiations had finally produced the official betrothal document. Accompanying him as a kind of retinue were two dozen hard-faced warriors dressed in bear skins.

"Bear-cultists," Barak observed sourly to Garion and Silk as the three of them stood atop the wall of the Citadel, watching the High Priest and his men mounting the steps from the harbor in the bright spring sunshine.

"I didn't say anything about bringing soldiers with him," Garion objected indignantly.

"I imagine he took it upon himself," Silk replied. "Grodeg's very good at taking things upon himself."

"I wonder how he'd like it if I threw him into a dungeon," Garion said hotly. "Do I have a dungeon?"

"We could improvise one, I suppose." Barak grinned at him. "Some nice damp cellar someplace. You might have to import some rats, though. The island's reputed to be free of them."

"You're making fun of me," Garion accused his friend, flushing slightly.

"Now you know I wouldn't do that, Garion," Barak replied, pulling at his beard.

"I'd talk with Belgarath before I had Grodeg clapped in irons, though," Silk suggested. "The political implications might go a bit further than you intend. Whatever you do, don't let Grodeg talk you into letting him leave any of his men behind. He's been trying to get a foothold on the Isle of the Winds for twenty years now. Not even Brand has had the nerve to let him go that far."

"Brand?"

"Isn't it obvious? I wouldn't want to say that Brand's a Cult member, but his sympathies certainly lie in that direction."

Garion was shocked at that, and a little sick. "What do you think I ought to do?" he asked.

"Don't try to play politics with these people," Barak replied. "Grodeg's here to conduct the official betrothal ceremony. Just let it go at that."

"He'll try to talk to me, though," Garion fretted. "He's going to try to make me lead an invasion into the southern kingdoms so that he can convert the Arends and Tolnedrans and Nyissans to the worship of Belar."

"Where did you hear that?" Silk asked curiously.

"I'd rather not say," Garion evaded.

"Does Belgarath know?"

Garion nodded. "Aunt Pol told him."

Silk chewed thoughtfully on a fingernail. "Just be stupid," he said finally.

"What?"

"Pretend to be a simple country bumpkin with no idea of what's going on. Grodeg's going to do everything he can to get you alone so he can wring concessions out of you. Just keep smiling and nodding foolishly, and every time he makes a proposal, send for Belgarath. Let him think that you can't make a single decision on your own."

"Won't that make me seem—well—?"

"Do you really care what he thinks?"

"Well, not really, I guess, but—"

"It'll drive him crazy," Barak pointed out with a wicked grin. "He'll think that you're a complete idiot—a ripe plum ready for picking. But he'll realize that if he wants you, he'll have to fight Belgarath to get you. He'll be tearing out his beard in frustration before he leaves." He turned and looked admiringly at Silk. "That's really a terrible thing to do to a man like Grodeg, you know."

Silk smirked. "Isn't it though?"

The three of them stood grinning at each other and finally burst into laughter.

The official betrothal ceremony was conducted the following day. There had been a great deal of haggling about who should enter the Hall of the Rivan King first, but that difficulty had been overcome by Belgarath's suggestion that Garion and Ce'Nedra could enter arm in arm. "This is all in preparation for a wedding, after all," he had pointed out. "We might as well start off with a semblance at least of friendship."

Garion was very nervous as the hour approached. His princess had been smoldering since the incident with the amulet, and he was almost certain that there was going to be trouble. But to his surprise, Ce'Nedra was radiant as the two of them waited alone together in a small antechamber while the official guests gathered in the Hall. Garion fidgeted a great deal and walked up and down, nervously adjusting his clothing, but Ce'Nedra sat rather demurely, patiently awaiting the trumpet fanfare which was to announce their entrance.

"Garion," she said after a while.

"Yes?"

"Do you remember that time we bathed together in the Wood of the Dryads?"

"We did *not* bathe together," Garion replied quickly, blushing to the roots of his hair.

"Well, very nearly." She brushed his distinction aside. "Do you realize that Lady Polgara kept throwing us together like that all the time we were traveling? She knew that all this was going to happen, didn't she?"

"Yes," Garion admitted.

"So she kept shoving us at each other, hoping something might happen between us."

Garion thought about that. "You're probably right," he concluded. "She likes to arrange people's lives for them."

Ce'Nedra sighed. "Look at all the opportunities we missed," she said somewhat regretfully.

"*Ce'Nedra!*" Garion gasped, shocked at her suggestion.

She giggled a bit wickedly. Then she sighed again. "Now it's all going to be dreadfully official—and probably not nearly as much fun."

Garion's face was flaming by now.

"Anyway," she continued, "that time we bathed together—do you remember that I asked you if you'd like to kiss me?"

Garion nodded, not trusting himself to speak.

"I never got that kiss, you know," she said archly, standing up and crossing the small room to him, "and I think I'd like it now." She took hold of the front of his doublet firmly with both little hands. "You owe me a kiss, Belgarion of Riva, and a Tolnedran always collects what people owe her." The look she directed up through her lashes at him smoldered dangerously.

Just outside, the trumpets blared out an extended fanfare.

"We're supposed to go in now," Garion sputtered a bit desperately.

"Let them wait," she murmured, her arms sliding up around his neck.

Garion tried for a quick, perfunctory kiss, but his princess had other ideas. Her little arms were surprisingly strong, and her fingers locked in his hair. The kiss was lingering, and Garion's knees began to tremble.

"There," Ce'Nedra breathed when she finally released him.

"We'd better go in," Garion suggested as the trumpets blared again.

"In a moment. Did you muss me?" She turned around so that he could inspect her.

"No," he replied. "Everything still seems to be in order."

She shook her head rather disapprovingly. "Try to do a little better next time," she told him. "Otherwise I might start to think that you're not taking me seriously."

"I'm never going to understand you, Ce'Nedra."

"I know," she said with a mysterious little smile. Then she patted his cheek gently. "And I'm going to do everything I can to keep it that way. Shall we go in? We really shouldn't keep our guests waiting, you know."

"That's what I said in the first place."

"We were busy then," she declared with a certain grand indifference. "Just a moment." She carefully smoothed his hair. "There. That's better. Now give me your arm."

Garion extended his arm, and his princess laid her hand on it. Then he opened the door to the third chorus from the trumpets. They entered the Hall, and an excited buzz ran through the crowd assembled there. Taking his cue from Ce'Nedra, Garion moved at a stately pace, his face sober and regal-looking.

"Not quite so grim," she whispered. "Smile just a little—and nod occasionally. It's the thing to do."

"If you say so," he replied. "I really don't know too much about this sort of thing."

"You'll be just fine," she assured him.

Smiling and nodding to the spectators, the royal couple passed through the Hall to the chair that had been placed near the front for the princess. Garion held the chair for her, then bowed and mounted the dais to his throne. As always happened, the Orb of Aldur began to glow as soon as he sat down. This time, however, it seemed to have a faint pink cast to it.

The official betrothal ceremony began with a rolling invocation delivered in a thunderous voice by the High Priest of Belar. Grodeg took full advantage of the dramatics of the situation.

"Tiresome old windbag, isn't he?" Belgarath murmured from his accustomed place at the right of the throne.

"What were you and Ce'Nedra doing in there?" Aunt Pol asked Garion.

"Nothing," Garion replied, blushing furiously.

"Really? And it took you all that time? How extraordinary."

Grodeg had begun reading the first clauses of the betrothal agreement. To Garion they sounded like pure gibberish. At various points Grodeg stopped his reading to look sternly at Garion. "Does His Majesty, Belgarion of Riva, agree to this?" he demanded each time.

"I do," Garion replied.

"Does Her Highness Ce'Nedra of the Tolnedran Empire agree to this?" Grodeg asked the princess.

Ce'Nedra responded in a clear voice, "I do."

"How are you two getting along?" Belgarath asked, ignoring the droning voice of the clergyman.

"Who knows?" Garion answered helplessly. "I can't tell from one minute to the next what she's going to do."

"That's the way it's supposed to be," Aunt Pol told him.

"I don't suppose you'd consider explaining that."

"No, dear," she replied with a smile as mysterious as Ce'Nedra's had been.

"I didn't really think so," he grumbled.

Garion thought about Ce'Nedra's rather open invitation to muss her during the interminable reading of the document which was firmly nailing down the remainder of his life, and the more he thought about it, the more he found the notion of a bit of polite mussing attractive. He rather hoped that the princess would linger after the ceremony and that they might go someplace private to discuss it. Following Grodeg's pompous benediction, however, Ce'Nedra was immediately surrounded by all the younger girls in the court and swept away for some private celebration of their own. From all the giggling and wicked little glances cast in his direction, he concluded that the conversation at their little get-together was going to be very frank, probably naughty, and that the less he knew about it the better.

As Silk and Barak had predicted, the High Priest of Belar tried several times to speak to Garion privately. Each time, however, Garion put on a great show of ingenuousness and sent immediately for Belgarath. Grodeg left the island with his entire retinue the following day. To add a final insult to the whole matter, Garion insisted that he and Belgarath accompany the fuming ecclesiast to his ship to see him off—and to be certain that no Bear-cultist might inadvertently be left behind.

"Whose idea was all of this?" Belgarath inquired as he and Garion climbed the steps back to the Citadel.

"Silk and I worked it out," Garion replied smugly.

"I might have known."

"I thought things went quite well," Garion congratulated himself.

"You've made yourself a dangerous enemy, you know."

"We can handle him."

"You're getting to be very free with that 'we,' Garion," Belgarath said disapprovingly.

"We're all in this together, aren't we, Grandfather?"

Belgarath looked at him helplessly for a moment and then began to laugh.

In the days that followed Grodeg's departure, however, there was little occasion for laughter. Once the official ceremonies were over, the Alorn Kings, King Fulrach, and various advisers and generals got down to business. Their subject was war.

"The most recent reports I have from Cthol Murgos indicate that Taur Urgas is preparing to move the southern Murgos up from Rak Hagga as soon as the weather breaks on the eastern coast," King Rhodar advised them.

"And the Nadraks?" King Anheg asked.

"They appear to be mobilizing, but there's always a question about the Nadraks. They play their own game, so it takes a lot of Grolims to whip them into line. The Thulls just obey orders."

"The Thulls don't really concern anyone," Brand observed. "The key to the whole situation is how many Malloreans are going to be able to take the field against us."

"There's a staging area for them being set up at Thull Zelik," Rhodar reported, "but they're also waiting for the weather to break in the Sea of the East."

King Anheg frowned thoughtfully. "Malloreans are bad sailors," he mused. "They won't move until summer, and they'll hug the north coast all the way to Thull Zelik. We need to get a fleet into the Sea of the East as soon as possible. If we can sink enough of their ships and drown enough of their soldiers, we might be able to keep them out of the war entirely. I think we should strike in force into Gar og Nadrak. Once we get into the forests, my men can build ships. We'll sail down the River Cordu and out into the Sea of the East."

"Thy plan hath merit, your Majesty," Mandorallen approved, studying the large map hanging on the wall. "The Nadraks are fewest in number and farthest removed from the hordes of southern Cthol Murgos."

King Rhodar shook his head stubbornly. "I know you want to get to the sea as quickly as possible, Anheg," he objected, "but you're committing me to a campaign in the Nadrak forest. I need open country to maneuver in. If we strike at the Thulls, we can cut directly across to the upper reaches of the River Mardu, and you can sail on down to the sea that way."

"There aren't that many trees in Mishrak ac Thull," Anheg protested.

"Why build ships out of green lumber if you don't have to?" Rhodar asked. "Why not sail up the Aldur and then portage across?"

"You want my men to portage ships up the eastern escarpment? Rhodar, be serious."

"We have engineers, Anheg. They can devise ways to lift your ships to the top of the escarpment."

Garion did not want to intrude his inexperience on the conference, but the question came out before he had time to think about it. "Have we decided where the final battle's going to be?" he asked.

"Which final battle was that, Garion?" Rhodar asked politely.

"When we meet them head-on—like Vo Mimbre."

"There won't be a Vo Mimbre in this war," Anheg told him. "Not if we can help it."

"Vo Mimbre was a mistake, Garion," Belgarath said quietly. "We all knew it, but there wasn't anything we could do about it."

"We won, didn't we?"

"That was pure luck, and you can't plan a campaign on the hope that you might get lucky. Nobody wanted the battle at Vo Mimbre—we didn't, and Kal Torak didn't, but nobody had any choice in the matter. We had to commit to battle before the second Angarak column arrived in the West. Kal Torak had been holding the southern Murgos and eastern Malloreans in reserve near Rak Hagga, and they started to march when he turned west from the siege of the Stronghold. If they'd been able to join forces with Kal Torak, there wouldn't have been enough men in all the West to meet them, so we had to fight. Vo Mimbre was the least objectionable battlefield."

"Why didn't Kal Torak just wait until they arrived?" Garion asked.

"You can't stop an army in unfriendly territory, King Belgarion," Colonel Brendig explained. "You have to keep moving, or the local populace destroys all the food and starts coming out at night to cut up your people. You can lose half your army that way."

"Kal Torak didn't want the meeting at Vo Mimbre any more than we did," Belgarath went on. "The column from Rak Hagga got caught in a spring blizzard in the mountains and bogged down for weeks. They finally had to turn back, and Torak was forced to fight at Vo Mimbre without any advantage of numbers, and nobody in his right mind goes into battle that way."

"Thy force should be larger by a quarter than thine adversary's," Mandorallen agreed, "else the outcome must be in doubt."

"By a third," Barak corrected in a rumbling voice. "By half if you can arrange it."

"Then all we're going to do is spread out all over the eastern half of the continent and fight a whole series of little battles?" Garion demanded incredulously. "That could take years—decades. It could go on for a century."

"If it has to," Belgarath told him bluntly. "What did you expect, Garion? A short little ride in the sunshine, a nice easy fight, and then home before winter? I'm afraid it won't be like that. You'd better get used to wearing armor and a sword, because you'll probably be dressed that way for most of the rest of your life. This is likely to be a very long war."

Garion's illusions were crumbling rapidly.

The door to the council room opened, then, and Olban, Brand's youngest son, entered and spoke with his father. The weather had turned blustery, and a spring storm was raking the island. Olban's gray Rivan cloak was dripping as he entered.

Dismayed by the prospect of year after year of campaigning in the East, Garion distractedly stared at the puddle forming around Olban's feet as the young man talked quietly with Brand. Then, out of habit, he lifted his eyes slightly to look at the hem of Olban's cloak. There was a small tear on the left corner of the cloak, and a scrap of cloth seemed to be missing.

Garion stared at the telltale rip for a moment without realizing exactly what it was he saw. Then he went suddenly cold. With a slight start, he jerked his eyes up to look at Olban's face. Brand's youngest son was perhaps Garion's own age, a bit shorter, but more muscular. His hair was pale blond, and his young face was serious, reflecting already the customary Rivan gravity. He seemed to be trying to avoid Garion's eyes, but showed no other sign of nervousness. Once, however, he looked inadvertantly at the young king and seemed to flinch slightly as guilt rose clearly into his eyes. Garion had found the man who had tried to kill him.

The conference continued after that, but Garion did not hear any more of it. What was he to do? Had Olban acted alone, or were others involved? Had Brand himself been a part of it? It was so difficult to know what a Rivan was thinking. He trusted Brand, but the big Warder's connection with the Bear-cult gave a certain ambiguity to his loyalties. Could Grodeg be behind all this? Or perhaps a Grolim? Garion remembered the Earl of Jarvik, whose soul had been purchased by Asharak and who had mounted rebellion in Val Alorn. Had Olban fallen perhaps under the spell of the bloodred gold of Angarak as Jarvik had? But Riva was an island, the one place in the world where no Grolim could ever come. Garion discounted the possibility of bribery. In the first place, it was not in the Rivan character. In the second, Olban had not likely ever been in a situation to come into contact with a Grolim. Rather grimly, Garion decided on a course of action.

Lelldorin, of course, had to be kept out of it. The hot-headed young Asturian was incapable of the kind of delicate discretion that seemed to be called for. Lelldorin would reach for his sword, and the whole business would disintegrate rather rapidly after that.

When the conference broke up for the day late that afternoon, Garion went looking for Olban. He did not take a guard with him, but he did wear his sword.

As chance had it, it was in a dim corridor not unlike the one where the assassination attempt had taken place that the young king finally ran Brand's youngest son down. Olban was coming along the passageway in one direction, and Garion was going the other. Olban's face paled slightly when he saw his king, and he bowed deeply to hide his expression. Garion nodded as if intending to pass without speaking, but turned after the two of them had gone by each other. "Olban," he said quietly.

Brand's son turned, a look of dread on his face.

"I noticed that the corner of your cloak is torn," Garion said in an almost neutral tone. "When you take it to have it mended, this might help." He took the scrap of cloth out from under his doublet and offered it to the pale-faced young Rivan.

Olban stared wide-eyed at him, not moving.

"And as long as we're at it," Garion continued, "you might as well take this, too. I think you dropped it somewhere." He reached inside his doublet again and took out the dagger with its bent point.

Olban started to tremble violently, then he suddenly dropped to his knees. "Please, your Majesty," he begged, "let me kill myself. If my father finds out what I've done, it will break his heart."

"Why did you try to kill me, Olban?" Garion asked.

"For love of my father," Brand's son confessed, tears welling up in his eyes. "He was ruler here in Riva until you came. Your arrival degraded him. I couldn't bear that. Please, your Majesty, don't have me dragged to the scaffold like a common criminal. Give me the dagger and I'll bury it in my heart right here. Spare my father this last humiliation."

"Don't talk nonsense," Garion told him, "and get up. You look silly down there on your knees."

"Your Majesty—" Olban began to protest.

"Oh, be still," Garion told him irritably. "Let me think for a moment." Dimly he began to see the glimmer of an idea. "All right," he said finally, "this is what we're going to do. You're going to take this knife and this wool scrap down to the harbor and throw them into the sea, and then you're going to go on about your life as if this had never happened."

"Your Majesty—"

"I'm not finished. Neither you nor I will ever speak of this again. I don't want any hysterical public confessions, and I absolutely forbid you to kill yourself. Do you understand me, Olban?"

Dumbly the young man nodded.

"I need your father's help too much to have this come out or for him to be distracted by personal tragedy. This did not happen, and that's an end of it. Take these and get out of my sight." He shoved the knife and the wool scrap into Olban's hands. He was suddenly infuriated. The weeks of looking nervously over his shoulder had all been so unnecessary—so useless. "Oh, one other thing, Olban," he added as the stricken young Rivan turned to leave. "Don't throw any more knives at me. If you want to fight, let me know, and we'll go someplace private and cut each other to ribbons, if that's what you want."

Olban fled sobbing.

"*Very well done, Belgarion,*" the dry voice complimented him.

"Oh, shut up," Garion said.

He slept very little that night. He had a few doubts about the wisdom of the course he had taken with Olban; but on the whole, he was satisfied that what he had done had been right. Olban's act had been no more than an impulsive attempt to erase what he believed to be his father's degradation. There had been no plot involved in it. Olban might resent Garion's magnanimous gesture, but he would not throw any more daggers at his king's back. What disturbed Garion's sleep the most during that restless night was Belgarath's bleak appraisal of the war upon which they were about to embark. He slept briefly on toward dawn and awoke from a dreadful nightmare with icy sweat standing out on his forehead. He had just seen himself, old and weary, leading a pitifully small army of ragged, gray-haired men into a battle they could not possibly win.

"There's an alternative, of course—if you've recovered enough from your bout of peevishness to listen," the voice in his mind advised him as he sat bolt upright and trembling in his bed.

"What?" Garion answered aloud. "Oh, that—I'm sorry I spoke that way. I was irritated, that's all."

"In many ways you're like Belgarath—remarkably so. This irritability seems to be hereditary."

"It's only natural, I suppose," Garion conceded. "You said there was an alternative. An alternative to what?"

"To this war that's giving you nightmares. Get dressed. I want to show you something."

Garion climbed out of his bed and hastily jerked on his clothing. "Where are we going?" he asked, still speaking aloud.

"It isn't far."

The room to which the other awareness directed him was musty and showed little evidence of use. The books and scrolls lining the shelves along its walls were dust-covered, and cobwebs draped the corners. Garion's lone candle cast looming shadows that seemed to dance along the walls.

"On the top shelf," the voice told him. *"The scroll wrapped in yellow linen. Take it down."*

Garion climbed up on a chair and took down the scroll. "What is this?" he asked.

"The Mrin Codex. Take off the cover and start unrolling it. I'll tell you when to stop."

It took Garion a moment or two to get the knack of unrolling the bottom of the scroll with one hand and rolling up the top with the other.

"There," the voice said. *"That's the passage. Read it."*

Garion struggled over the words. The script was spidery, and he still did not read very well. "It doesn't make any sense," he complained.

"The man who wrote it down was insane," the voice apologized, *"and he was an imbecile besides, but he was all I had to work with. Try it again—out loud."*

Garion read: "Behold, it shall come to pass that in a certain moment, that which must be and that which must not be shall meet, and in that meeting shall be decided all that has gone before and all that will come after. Then will the Child of Light and the Child of Dark face each other in the broken tomb, and the stars will shudder and grow dim." Garion's voice trailed off. "It still doesn't make any sense," he objected.

"It's a bit obscure," the voice admitted. *"As I said, the man who wrote it was insane. I put the ideas there, but he used his own words to express them."*

"Who is the Child of Light?" Garion asked.

"You are—for the moment at least. It changes."

"Me?"

"Of course."

"Then who's this Child of Dark I'm supposed to meet?"

"Torak."

"Torak!"

"I should have thought that would be obvious by now. I told you once about the two possible destinies coming together finally. You and Torak—the Child of Light and the Child of Dark—embody those destinies."

"But Torak's asleep."

"Not anymore. When you first put your hand on the Orb, the touch signaled his awakening. Even now he stirs on the edge of awareness, and his hand fumbles for the hilt of Cthrek-Goru, his black sword."

Garion went very cold. "Are you trying to say that I'm supposed to fight Torak? *Alone?*"

"It's going to happen, Belgarion. The universe itself rushes toward it. You can gather an army if you want, but your army—or Torak's—won't mean anything. As the Codex says, everything will be decided when you finally meet him. In the end, you'll face each other alone. That's what I meant by an alternative."

"What you're trying to say is that I'm just supposed to go off alone and find him and fight him?" Garion demanded incredulously.

"Approximately, yes."

"I won't do it."

"That's up to you."

Garion struggled with it. "If I take an army, I'll just get a lot of people killed, and it won't make any difference in the end anyway."

"Not the least bit. In the end it will just be you, Torak, Cthrek-Goru, and the sword of the Rivan King."

"Don't I have any choice at all?"

"None whatsoever."

"Do I have to go alone?" Garion asked plaintively.

"It doesn't say that."

"Could I take one or two people with me?"

"That's your decision, Belgarion. Just don't forget to take your sword."

He thought about it for the rest of the day. In the end his choice was obvious. As evening settled over the gray city of Riva, he sent for Belgarath and Silk. There were some problems involved, he knew, but there was no one else he could rely on. Even if his power were diminished, Belgarath's wisdom made Garion not even want to consider the undertaking without him. And Silk, of course, was just as essential. Garion reasoned that his own increasing talent for sorcery could see them through any difficulties if Belgarath should falter, and Silk could probably find ways to avoid most of the serious confrontations. Garion was confident that the three of them would be able to cope with whatever arose—until they found Torak. He didn't want to think about what might happen then.

When the two of them arrived, the young king was staring out the window with haunted eyes.

"You sent for us?" Silk asked.

"I have to make a journey," Garion replied in a scarcely audible voice.

"What's bothering you?" Belgarath said. "You look a bit sick."

"I just found out what it is that I'm supposed to do, Grandfather."

"Who told you?"

"*He* did."

Belgarath pursed his lips. "A bit premature, perhaps," he suggested. "I was going to wait a while longer, but I have to assume he knows what he's doing."

"Who is this we're talking about?" Silk asked.

"Garion has a periodic visitor," the old man answered. "A rather special visitor."

"That's a singularly unenlightening response, old friend."

"Are you sure you really want to know?"

"Yes," Silk replied, "I think I do. I get the feeling that I'm going to be involved in it."

"You're aware of the Prophecy?"

"Naturally."

"It appears that the Prophecy is a bit more than a statement about the future. It seems to be able to take a hand in things from time to time. It speaks to Garion on occasion."

Silk's eyes narrowed as he thought about that. "All right," he said finally.

"You don't seem surprised."

The rat-faced little man laughed. "Belgarath, nothing about this whole thing surprises me anymore."

Belgarath turned back to Garion. "Exactly what did he tell you?"

"He showed me the Mrin Codex. Have you ever read it?"

"From end to end and backward and forward—even from side to side a couple of times. Which part did he show you?"

"The part about the meeting of the Child of Light and the Child of Dark."

"Oh," Belgarath said. "I was afraid it might have been that part. Did he explain it?"

Dumbly, Garion nodded.

"Well," the old man said with a penetrating look, "now you know the worst. What are you going to do about it?"

"He gave me a couple of alternatives," Garion said. "I can wait until we get an army together, and we can go off and fight back and forth with the Angaraks for generations. That's one way, isn't it?"

Belgarath nodded.

"Of course that will get millions of people killed for nothing, won't it?"

The old man nodded again.

Garion drew in a deep breath. "Or," he continued, "I can go off by myself and find Torak—wherever he is—and try to kill him."

Silk whistled, his eyes widening.

"He said that I didn't have to go alone," Garion added hopefully. "I asked him about that."

"Thanks," Belgarath said dryly.

Silk sprawled in a nearby chair, rubbing thoughtfully at his pointed nose. He looked at Belgarath. "You know that Polgara would skin the both of us inch by inch if we let him go off alone, don't you?"

Belgarath grunted.

"Where did you say Torak is?"

"Cthol Mishrak—in Mallorea."

"I've never been there."

"I have—a few times. It's not a very attractive place."

"Maybe time has improved it."

"That's not very likely."

Silk shrugged. "Maybe we ought to go with him—show him the way, that sort of thing. It's time I left Riva anyway. Some ugly rumors are starting to go around about me."

"It *is* rather a good time of year for traveling," Belgarath admitted, giving Garion a sly, sidelong glance.

Garion felt better already. He knew from their bantering tone that they had already made up their minds. He would not have to go in search of Torak alone. For now that was enough: there'd be time for worrying later. "All right," he said, "what do we do?"

"We creep out of Riva very quietly," Belgarath replied. "There's nothing to be gained by getting into any long discussions with your Aunt Pol about this."

"The wisdom of ages," Silk agreed fervently. "When do we start?" His ferret eyes were very bright.

"The sooner the better." Belgarath shrugged. "Did you have any plans for tonight?"

"Nothing I can't postpone."

"All right then. We'll wait until everyone goes to bed, and then we'll pick up Garion's sword and get started."

"Which way do we go?" Garion asked him.

"Sendaria first," Belgarath replied, "and then across Drasnia to Gar og Nadrak. Then north to the archipelago that leads to Mallorea. It's a long way to Cthol Mishrak and the tomb of the one-eyed God."

"And then?"

"Then, Garion, we settle this once and for all."

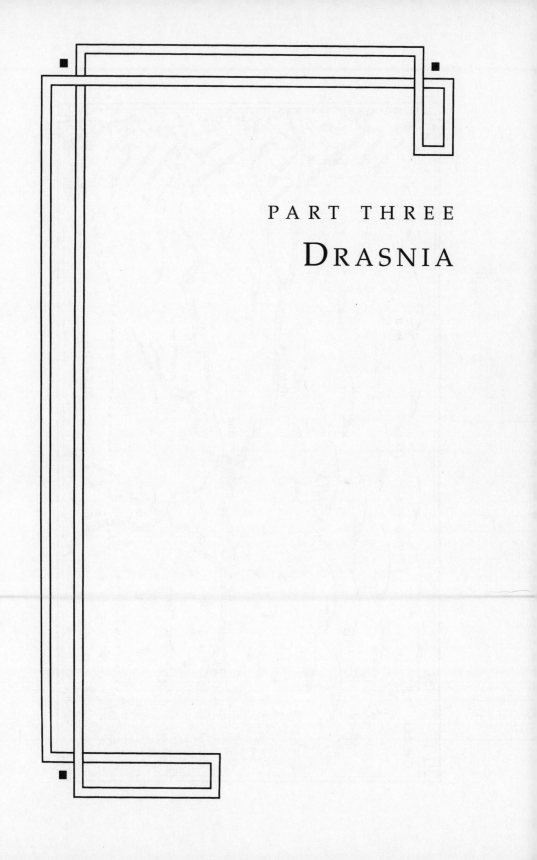

PART THREE

DRASNIA

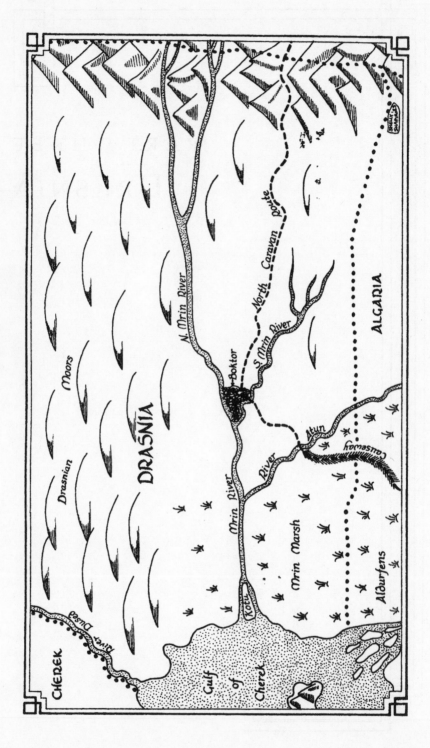

"Dear Aunt Pol," Garion's note began, "I know this is going to make you angry, but there's no other way. I've seen the Mrin Codex, and now I know what I have to do. The—" He broke off, frowning. "How do you spell 'Prophecy'?" he asked.

Belgarath spelled it out for him. "Don't drag it out too much, Garion," the old man advised. "Nothing you say is going to make her happy about this, so stick to the point."

"Don't you think I ought to explain why we're doing this?" Garion fretted.

"She's read the Codex, Garion," Belgarath replied. "She'll know why without your explanation."

"I really ought to leave a note for Ce'Nedra, too," Garion considered.

"Polgara can tell her what she needs to know," Belgarath said. "We have things to do and we can't afford to spend the whole night on correspondence."

"I've never written a letter before," Garion remarked. "It's not nearly as easy as it looks."

"Just say what you have to say and then stop," the old man advised. "Don't labor at it so much."

The door opened and Silk came back in. He was dressed in the nondescript clothing he had worn on the road, and he carried two bundles. "I think these should fit you," he said, handing one of the bundles to Belgarath and the other to Garion.

"Did you get the money?" the old man asked him.

"I borrowed some from Barak."

"That's surprising," Belgarath replied. "He isn't notorious for generosity."

"I didn't tell him I was borrowing it," the little man returned with a broad wink. "I thought it would save time if I didn't have to go into long explanations."

One of Belgarath's eyebrows shot up.

"We *are* in a hurry, aren't we?" Silk asked with an innocent expression. "And Barak can be tedious when it comes to money."

"Spare me the excuses," Belgarath told him. He turned back to Garion. "Have you finished with that yet?"

"What do you think?" Garion asked, handing him the note.

The old man glanced at it. "Good enough," he said. "Now sign it and we'll put it where somebody'll find it sometime tomorrow."

"Late tomorrow," Silk suggested. "I'd like to be well out of Polgara's range when she finds out that we've left."

Garion signed the note, folded it and wrote, "For Lady Polgara," across the outside.

"We'll leave it on the throne," Belgarath said. "Let's change clothes and go get the sword."

"Isn't the sword going to be a bit bulky?" Silk asked after Garion and Belgarath had changed.

"There's a scabbard for it in one of the antechambers," Belgarath answered, opening the door carefully and peering out into the silent hall. "He'll have to wear it slung across his back."

"That glow is going to be a bit ostentatious," Silk said.

"We'll cover the Orb," Belgarath replied. "Let's go."

The three of them slipped out into the dimly lighted corridor and crept through the midnight stillness toward the throne room. Once, a sleepy servant going toward the kitchen almost surprised them, but an empty chamber provided them with a temporary hiding place until he had passed. Then they moved on.

"Is it locked?" Silk whispered when they reached the door to the Hall of the Rivan King.

Garion took hold of the large handle and twisted, wincing as the latch clacked loudly in the midnight stillness. He pushed, and the door creaked as it swung open.

"You ought to have somebody take care of that," Silk muttered.

The Orb of Aldur began to glow faintly as soon as the three of them entered the Hall.

"It seems to recognize you," Silk observed to Garion.

When Garion took down the sword, the Orb flared, filling the Hall of the Rivan King with its deep blue radiance. Garion looked around nervously, fearful that someone passing might see the light and come in to investigate. "Stop that," he irrationally admonished the stone. With a startled flicker, the glow of the Orb subsided back into a faint, pulsating light, and the triumphant song of the Orb stilled to a murmur.

Belgarath looked quizzically at his grandson, but said nothing. He led them to an antechamber and removed a long, plain scabbard from a case standing against the wall. The belt attached to the scabbard had seen a certain amount of use. The old man buckled it in place for Garion, passing it over the young man's right shoulder and down across his chest so that the scabbard, attached to the belt in two places, rode diagonally down his back. There was also a knitted tube in the case, almost like a narrow sock. "Slide this over the hilt," Belgarath instructed.

Garion covered the hilt of his great sword with the tube and then took hold of the blade itself and carefully inserted the tip into the top of the scabbard. It was awkward, and neither Silk nor Belgarath offered to help him. All three of them knew why. The sword slid home and, since it seemed to have no weight, it was not too uncomfortable. The crosspiece of the hilt, however, stood out just at the top of his head and tended to poke him if he moved too quickly.

"It wasn't really meant to be worn," Belgarath told him. "We had to improvise."

Once again, the three of them passed through the dimly lighted corridors of the sleeping palace and emerged through a side door. Silk slipped on ahead, moving as soundlessly as a cat and keeping to the shadows. Belgarath and Garion waited. An open window perhaps twenty feet overhead faced out into the courtyard. As they stood together beneath it, a faint light appeared, and the voice that spoke down to them was very soft. "Errand?" it said.

"Yes," Garion replied without thinking. "Everything's all right. Go back to bed."

"Belgarion," the child said with a strange kind of satisfaction. Then he added, "Good-bye," in a somewhat more wistful tone, and he was gone.

"Let's hope he doesn't run straight to Polgara," Belgarath muttered.

"I think we can trust him, Grandfather. He knew we were leaving and he just wanted to say good-bye."

"Would you like to explain how you know that?"

"I don't know." Garion shrugged. "I just do."

Silk whistled from the courtyard gate, and Belgarath and Garion followed him down into the quiet streets of the city.

It was still early spring, and the night was cool but not chilly. There was a fragrance in the air, washing down over the city from the high meadows in the mountains behind Riva and mingling with peat smoke and the salty tang of the sea. The stars overhead were bright, and the newly risen moon, looking swollen as it rode low over the horizon, cast a glittering golden path across the breast of the Sea of the Winds. Garion felt that excitement he always experienced when starting out at night. He had been cooped up too long, and each step that took him farther and farther from the dull round of appointments and ceremonies filled him with an almost intoxicating anticipation.

"It's good to be on the road again," Belgarath murmured, as if reading his thoughts.

"Is it always like this?" Garion whispered back. "I mean, even after all the years that you've been doing it?"

"Always," Belgarath replied. "Why do you think I prefer the life of a vagabond?"

They moved on down through the dark streets to the city gate and out through a small sally port to the wharves jutting into the moon-dappled waters of the harbor.

Captain Greldik was a bit drunk when they reached his ship. The vagrant seaman had ridden out the winter in the safety of the harbor at Riva. His ship had been hauled out on the strand, her bottom scraped and her seams recaulked. Her mainmast, which had creaked rather alarmingly on the voyage from Sendaria, had been reinforced and fitted with new sails. Then Greldik and his crew had spent much of their time carousing. The effects of three months of steady dissipation showed on his face when they woke him. His eyes were bleary, and there were dark-stained pouches under them. His bearded face looked puffy and unwell.

"Maybe tomorrow," he grunted when Belgarath told him of their urgent need to leave the island. "Or the next day. The next day would be better, I think."

Belgarath spoke more firmly.

"My sailors couldn't possibly man the oars," Greldik objected. "They'll be throwing up all over the deck, and it takes a week to clean up a mess like that."

Belgarath delivered a blistering ultimatum, and Greldik sullenly climbed out of his rumpled bunk. He lurched toward the crew's quarters, pausing only long enough to be noisily sick over the rail, and then he descended into the forward hold, where with kicks and curses he roused his men.

The moon was high and dawn only a few hours off when Greldik's ship slid quietly out of the harbor and met the long, rolling swells of the Sea of the Winds. When the sun came up they were far out at sea.

The weather held fair, even though the winds were not favorable, and in two days' time Greldik dropped Garion, Silk and Belgarath off on a deserted beach just north of the mouth of the Seline River on the northwest coast of Sendaria.

"I don't know that I'd be in all that big a hurry to go back to Riva," Belgarath told Greldik as he stepped out of the small boat onto the sand of the beach. He handed the bearded Cherek a small pouch of jingling coins. "I'm sure you and your crew can find a bit of diversion somewhere."

"It's always nice in Camaar this time of year," Greldik mused, bouncing the pouch thoughtfully in his hand, "and I know a young widow there who's always been very friendly."

"You ought to pay her a visit," Belgarath suggested. "You've been away for quite some time, and she's sure to have been terribly lonely for you."

"I think maybe I will," Greldik said, his eyes suddenly bright. "Have a good trip." He motioned to his men, and they began rowing the small boat back toward the lean ship standing a few hundred yards offshore.

"What was that all about?" Garion asked.

"I'd like to get a bit of distance between us and Polgara before she gets her hands on Greldik," the old man replied. "I don't particularly want her chasing us." He looked around. "Let's see if we can find somebody with a boat to row us upriver to Seline. We should be able to buy horses and supplies there."

A fisherman, who immediately saw that turning ferryboatman would provide a more certain profit than trusting his luck on the banks off the northwest coast, agreed to take them upriver. By the time the sun was setting, they had arrived in the city of Seline. They spent the night in a comfortable inn and went the following morning to the central market. Silk negotiated the purchase of horses, haggling down to the last penny, bargaining more out of habit, Garion thought, than out of any real necessity. Then they bought supplies for the trip. By midmorning, they were pounding along the road that led toward Darine, some forty leagues distant.

The fields of northern Sendaria had begun to sprout that first green blush that lay on damp earth like a faint jade mist and more than anything announced spring. A few fleecy clouds scampered across the blue of the sky, and, though the wind was gusty, the sun warmed the air. The road opened before them, stretching across the verdant fields; and though their mission was deadly serious, Garion almost wanted to shout out of pure exuberance.

In two more days they reached Darine. "Do you want to take ship here?" Silk asked Belgarath as they crested the hill up which they had come so many months before with their three wagonloads of turnips. "We could be in Kotu inside a week."

Belgarath scratched at his beard, looking out at the expanse of the Gulf of Cherek, glittering in the afternoon sun. "I don't think so," he decided. He pointed at several lean Cherek warboats patrolling just outside Sendarian territorial waters.

"The Chereks are always moving around out there," Silk replied. "It might have nothing whatsoever to do with us."

"Polgara's very persistent," Belgarath said. "She can't leave Riva herself as long as so many things are afoot there, but she can send people out to look for us. Let's avoid any possible trouble if we can. We'll go along the north coast and then on up through the fens to Boktor."

Silk gave him a look of profound distaste. "It'll take a lot longer," he objected.

"We aren't in all that great a hurry," Belgarath remarked blandly. "The Alorns are beginning to mass their armies, but they still need more time, and it's going to take a while to get the Arends all moving in the same direction."

"What's that got to do with it?" Silk asked him.

"I have plans for those armies, and I'd like to start them moving before we cross into Gar og Nadrak if possible—and certainly before we get to Mallorea. We can afford the time it'll take to avoid any unpleasantness with the people Polgara's sent out to find us."

And so they detoured around Darine and took the narrow, rocky road that led along the cliffs where the waves crashed and boomed and foamed, beating themselves to fragments against the great rocks of the north coast.

The mountains of eastern Sendaria ran down into the Gulf of Cherek along that forbidding shore, and the road, which twisted and climbed and dropped steeply again, was not good. Silk grumbled every mile of the way.

Garion, however, had other worries. The decision he had made after reading the Mrin Codex had seemed quite logical at the time, but logic was scant comfort now. He was deliberately riding toward Mallorea to face Torak in a duel. The more he thought about it, the more insane it seemed. How could he possibly hope to defeat a God? He brooded about that as they rode eastward along the rocky coast, and his mood became as unpleasant as Silk's.

After about a week, the cliffs became lower, and the land more gently rolling. From the top of the last of the eastern foothills, they looked out and saw what appeared to be a vast, flat plain, dark-green and very damp-looking. "Well, there they are," Silk sourly informed Belgarath.

"What's got you so bad-tempered?" the old man asked him.

"One of the main reasons I left Drasnia in the first place was to avoid the possibility of ever being obliged to go anywhere near the fens," Silk replied crisply. "Now you propose to drag me lengthwise through the whole soggy, stinking expanse of them. I'm bitterly disappointed in you, old friend, and it's altogether possible that I'll never forgive you for this."

Garion was frowning at the marshland spread out below. "That wouldn't be Drasnia, would it?" he asked. "I thought that Drasnia was farther north."

"It's Algaria, actually," Belgarath told him. "The beginning of Aldurfens. Up beyond the mouths of the Aldur River is the Drasnian border. They call it Mrin marsh up there, but it's all the same swamp. It goes on for another thirty leagues or so beyond Kotu at the mouth of the Mrin River."

"Most people just call it the fens and let it go at that," Silk observed. "Most people have sense enough to stay out of it," he added pointedly.

"Quit complaining so much," Belgarath told him bluntly. "There are fishermen along this coast. We'll buy a boat."

Silk's eyes brightened. "We can go up along the coast then," he suggested.

"That wouldn't be very prudent," Belgarath disagreed, "Not with Anheg's fleet scouring the Gulf of Cherek looking for us."

"You don't know that they're looking for us," Silk said quickly.

"I know Polgara," Belgarath answered.

"I feel that this trip is definitely growing sour on us," Silk grumbled.

The fishermen along the marshy coast were a peculiar mixture of Algars and Drasnians, close-mouthed and wary of strangers. Their villages were built on pilings driven deep into the marshy earth, and there lingered about them that peculiar odor of long-dead fish that hovers over fishing villages wherever one finds them. It took some time to find a man with a boat he was willing to sell and even longer to persuade him that three horses and a few silver coins beside was a fair price for it.

"It leaks," Silk declared, pointing at the inch or so of water that had collected in the bottom of the boat as they poled away from the reeking village.

"All boats leak, Silk," Belgarath replied calmly. "It's the nature of boats to leak. Bail it out."

"It'll just fill up again."

"Then you can bail it out again. Try not to let it get too far ahead of you."

The fens stretched on interminably, a wilderness of cattails and rushes and dark, slow-moving water. There were channels and streams and quite frequently small lakes where the going was much easier. The air was humid and, in the evenings, thick with gnats and mosquitoes. Frogs sang of love all night, greeting spring with intoxicated fervor—little chirping frogs and great, booming, bull-voiced frogs as big as dinner plates. Fish leaped in the ponds and lakes, and beaver and muskrats nested on soggy islands.

They poled their way through the confused maze of channels marking the mouths of the Aldur and continued northeasterly in the slowly warming northern spring. After a week or more, they crossed the indeterminate border and left Algaria behind.

A false channel put them aground once, and they were obliged to climb out to heave and push their boat off a mudbank by main strength. When they were afloat again, Silk sat disconsolately on the gunwale regarding his ruined boots that were dripping thick mud into the water. When he spoke, his voice was filled with profound disgust. "Delightful," he said. "How wonderful to be home again in dear old mucky Drasnia."

CHAPTER EIGHTEEN

Although it was all one vast swampland, it seemed to Garion that the fens here in Drasnia were subtly different from those farther south. The channels were narrower, for one thing, and they twisted and turned more frequently. After a couple of days poling, he developed a growing conviction that they were lost. "Are you sure you know where we're going?" he demanded of Silk.

"I haven't the vaguest idea," Silk replied candidly.

"You keep saying that you know the way everywhere," Garion accused him.

"There isn't any certain way here in the fens, Garion," Silk told him. "All you can do is keep going against the current and hope for the best."

"There's got to be a route," Garion objected. "Why don't they put up markers or something?"

"It wouldn't do any good. Look." The little man put his pole against a solid-looking hummock rising out of the water beside the boat and pushed. The hummock moved sluggishly away. Garion stared at it in amazement.

"It's floating vegetation," Belgarath explained, stopping his poling to wipe the sweat from his face. "Seeds fall on it, and it grows grass just like solid earth—except that it isn't solid. It floats wherever the wind and current push it. That's why there aren't any permanent channels and there's no definite route."

"It's not always just wind and current," Silk added darkly. He glanced out at the lowering sun. "We'd better find something solid to tie up to for the night," he suggested.

"How about that one?" Belgarath replied, pointing at a brushy hummock that was somewhat higher than those surrounding it.

They poled their way to the clump of ground rising out of the surrounding water, and Silk kicked at it experimentally a few times. "It seems to be stationary," he confirmed. He stepped out of the boat and climbed to the top, frequently stamping his feet. The ground responded with a satisfactorily solid sound. "There's a dry spot up here," he reported, "and a pile of driftwood on the other side. We can sleep on solid ground for a change, and maybe even have a hot meal."

They pulled the boat far up onto the sloping side, and Silk took some rather exotic-seeming precautions to make certain that it was securely tied.

"Isn't that sort of unnecessary?" Garion asked him.

"It isn't much of a boat," Silk replied, "but it's the only one we've got. Let's not take chances with it."

They got a fire going and erected their single tent as the sun slowly settled in a cloudbank to the west, painting the marsh in a ruddy glow. Silk dug out a few pans and began to work on supper.

"It's too hot," Garion advised critically as the rat-faced little man prepared to lay strips of bacon in a smoking iron pan.

"Do you want to do this?"

"I was just warning you, that's all."

"I don't have your advantages, Garion," Silk replied tartly. "I didn't grow up in Polgara's kitchen the way you did. I just make do the best I can."

"You don't have to get grumpy about it," Garion said. "I just thought you'd like to know that the pan's too hot."

"I think I can manage without any more advice."

"Suit yourself—but you're going to burn the bacon."

Silk gave him an irritated look and started slapping bacon slices into the pan. The slices sizzled and smoked, and their edges turned black almost immediately.

"I told you so," Garion murmured.

"Belgarath," Silk complained, "make him leave me alone."

"Come away, Garion," the old man said. "He can burn supper without any help."

"Thanks," Silk responded sarcastically.

Supper was not an absolute disaster. After they had eaten, they sat watching as the fire burned down and purple evening crept across the fens. The frogs took up their vast chorus among the reeds, and birds perched on the bending stalks of cattails, clucking and murmuring sleepily. There were faint splashes and rippling sounds in the brown water about them and occasional eruptions of bubbles as swamp gas gurgled to the surface. Silk sighed bitterly. "I hate this place," he said. "I absolutely hate it."

That night Garion had a nightmare. It was not the first he had suffered since they had left Riva; and as he sat up, sweat-drenched and trembling, he was positive it would not be the last. It was not a new nightmare, but rather was one which had periodically haunted his sleep since boyhood. Unlike an ordinary bad dream, this one did not involve being chased or threatened, but consisted rather of a single image—the image of a hideously maimed face. Although he had never actually seen the owner of the face, he knew exactly whose face it was, and now he knew why it inhabited his darkest dreams.

The next day dawned cloudy with a threat of approaching rain. As Belgarath stirred up the fire and Silk rummaged through his pack for something suitable for breakfast, Garion stood looking out at the swamp around him. A flight of geese swept by overhead in a ragged V, their wings whistling and their muted cries drifting, lonely and remote. A fish jumped not far from the edge of the hummock, and Garion watched the ripples widening out toward the far shore. He looked for quite some time at that shore before he realized exactly what it was he was seeing. Concerned, then a bit alarmed, he began to peer first this way and then that.

"Grandfather!" he cried. "Look!"

"At what?"

"It's all changed. There aren't any channels anymore. We're in the middle of a big pond, and there isn't any way out of it." He spun around, desperately trying to see some exit, but the edges of the pond in which they sat were totally unbroken. There were no channels leading out of it, and the brown water was absolutely still, showing no evidence of current.

Then in the center of the pond, without making so much as a ripple, a round, furred head emerged from the water. The animal's eyes were very large and bright;

it had no external ears, and its little nose was as black as a button. It made a peculiar chirping noise, and another head emerged out of the water a few feet away.

"Fenlings!" Silk gasped, drawing his short sword with a steely rustle.

"Oh, put that away," Belgarath told him disgustedly. "They aren't going to hurt you."

"They've trapped us, haven't they?"

"What do they want?" Garion asked.

"Breakfast, obviously," Silk answered, still holding his sword.

"Don't be stupid, Silk," Belgarath told him. "Why would they want to eat a raw Drasnian when there's a whole swampful of fish available? Put the sword away."

The first fenling which had poked its head up out of the water lifted one of its webbed forefeet and made a peremptory gesture. The webbed foot was strangely handlike.

"They seem to want us to follow them," Belgarath said calmly.

"And you're going to do it?" Silk was aghast. "Are you mad?"

"Do we have any choice?"

Without further discussion, Belgarath began taking down the tent.

"Are they monsters, Grandfather?" Garion asked worriedly as he helped. "Like Algroths or Trolls?"

"No, they're just animals—like seals or beaver. They're curious and intelligent and very playful."

"But they play very nasty games," Silk added.

After they had stowed all their packs into the boat, they pushed it down the bank into the water. The fenlings watched them curiously with no particular threat or malice in their gaze, but rather a kind of firm determination on their furry little faces. The solid-looking edge of the pond opened then to reveal the channel that had been concealed during the night. The strangely rounded head of the fenling who had gestured to them moved on ahead, leading the way and glancing back often to be certain they were following. Several others trailed after the boat, their large eyes alert.

It began to rain, a few drops at first, and then a steady drizzle that veiled the endless expanse of reed and cattail stretching out on all sides of them.

"Where do you think they're taking us?" Silk asked, stopping his poling to wipe the rain out of his face. One of the fenlings behind the boat chattered angrily at him until he dug his pole into the muddy bottom of the channel again.

"We'll just have to wait and see," Belgarath replied.

The channel continued to open before them, and they poled steadily along, following the round-headed fenling who had first appeared.

"Are those trees up ahead?" Silk asked, peering into the misty drizzle.

"It appears so," Belgarath answered. "I suspect that's where we're going."

The large cluster of trees slowly emerged from the mist. As they drew closer, Garion could see a gentle rise of ground swelling up out of the reeds and water. The grove which crowned the island appeared to be mostly willows with long, trailing branches.

The fenling who had been leading them swam on ahead. When it reached the island, it emerged half out of the water and gave a strange, whistling cry. A moment or so later, a hooded figure stepped out of the trees and moved slowly down to the bank. Garion did not know what to expect, but he was more than a little startled when the brown-cloaked figure on the shore pushed back the hood to reveal a woman's face that, though very old, still bore the luminous traces of what had once been an extraordinary beauty.

"Hail, Belgarath," she greeted the old sorcerer in an oddly neutral voice.

"Hello, Vordai," he replied conversationally. "It's been quite a while, hasn't it?"

The little creatures that had guided them to the island waded out of the water to gather around the brown-cloaked woman. They chirped and chattered to her, and she looked at them fondly, touching their wet fur with gentle fingers. They were medium-sized animals with short hind legs and little rounded bellies and they walked upright with a peculiar quick shuffle, their forepaws held delicately in front of their furry chests.

"Come inside out of the rain, Belgarath," the woman said. "Bring your friends." She turned and walked up a path leading into the willow grove with her fenlings scampering along beside her.

"What do we do?" Garion whispered.

"We go inside," Belgarath replied, stepping out of the boat onto the island.

Garion was not sure what to expect as he and Silk followed the old man up the path toward the dripping willows, but he was totally unprepared for the neat, thatch-roofed cottage with its small adjoining garden. The house was built of weathered logs, tightly chinked with moss, and a wispy tendril of smoke drifted from its chimney.

At the doorway, the woman in brown carefully wiped her feet on a rush mat and shook the rain out of her cloak. Then she opened the door and went inside without looking back.

Silk's expression was dubious as he stopped outside the cottage. "Are you sure this is a good idea, Belgarath?" he asked quietly. "I've heard stories about Vordai."

"It's the only way to find out what she wants," Belgarath told him, "and I'm fairly sure we aren't going any farther until we talk with her. Let's go in. Be sure to wipe your feet."

The interior of Vordai's cottage was scrupulously neat. The ceilings were low and heavily beamed. The wooden floor was scrubbed to whiteness, and a table and chairs sat before an arched fireplace where a pot hung in the flames from an iron arm. There were wildflowers in a vase on the table and curtains at the window overlooking the garden.

"Why don't you introduce your friends to me, Belgarath?" the woman suggested, hanging her cloak on a peg. She smoothed the front of her plain brown dress.

"As you wish, Vordai," the old man replied politely. "This is Prince Kheldar, your countryman. And this is King Belgarion of Riva."

"Noble guests," the woman observed in that strangely neutral voice. "Welcome to the house of Vordai."

"Forgive me, madam," Silk said in his most courtly manner, "but your reputation seems to be grossly inaccurate."

"Vordai, the witch of the fens?" she asked, looking amused. "Do they still call me that?"

He smiled in return. "Their descriptions are misleading, to say the least."

"The hag of the swamps." She mimicked the speech of a credulous peasant. "Drowner of travelers and queen of the fenlings." There was a bitter twist to her lips.

"That's more or less what they say," he told her. "I always believed you were a myth conjured up to frighten unruly children."

"Vordai will get you and gobble you up!" She laughed, but there was no humor in her laughter. "I've been hearing that for generations. Take off your cloaks, gentlemen. Sit down and make yourselves comfortable. You'll be staying for a while."

One of the fenlings—the one who had led them to the island, Garion thought—chattered at her in a piping little voice, glancing nervously at the pot hanging in the fire.

"Yes," she answered quite calmly, "I know that it's boiling, Tupik. It has to boil or it won't cook." She turned back to her guests. "Breakfast will be ready in a bit," she told them. "Tupik tells me you haven't eaten yet."

"You can communicate with them?" Silk sounded surprised.

"Isn't that obvious, Prince Kheldar? Here, let me hang your cloaks by the fire to dry." She stopped and regarded Garion gravely. "So great a sword for one so young," she noted, looking at the great hilt rising above his shoulder. "Stand it in the corner, King Belgarion. There's no one to fight here."

Garion inclined his head politely, unbuckled the sword belt and handed her his cloak.

Another, somewhat smaller fenling darted out of a corner with a piece of cloth and began busily wiping up the water that had dripped from their cloaks, chattering disapprovingly all the while.

"You'll have to forgive Poppi." Vordai smiled. "She's obsessed with tidiness. I sometimes think that if I left her alone she'd sweep holes in the floor."

"They're changing, Vordai," Belgarath said gravely, seating himself at the table.

"I know," she replied, going to the fireplace to stir the bubbling pot. "I've watched them over the years. They're not the same as they were when I came here."

"It was a mistake to tamper with them," he told her.

"So you've said before—you and Polgara both. How is she, by the way?"

"Probably raging by now. We slipped out of the Citadel at Riva without telling her we were leaving, and that sort of thing irritates her."

"Polgara was born irritable."

"We agree on that point anyway."

"Breakfast's ready." She lifted the pot with a curved iron hook and set it on the table. Poppi scampered over to a cupboard standing against the far wall and brought back a stack of wooden bowls, then returned for spoons. Her large eyes were very bright, and she chittered seriously at the three visitors.

"She's telling you not to drop crumbs on her clean floor," Vordai advised them, removing a steaming loaf of bread from an oven built into the side of the fireplace. "Crumbs infuriate her."

"We'll be careful," Belgarath promised.

It was a peculiar sort of breakfast, Garion thought. The stew that came steaming from the pot was thick, with strange vegetables floating in it, and large chunks of fish. It was delicately seasoned, however, and he found it delicious. By the time he had finished eating, he rather reluctantly concluded that Vordai might even be as good a cook as Aunt Pol.

"Excellent, Vordai," Belgarath complimented her, finally pushing his bowl away. "Now suppose we get down to business. Why did you have us brought here?"

"To talk, Belgarath," she replied. "I don't get much company, and conversation's a good way to pass a rainy morning. Why have you come into the fens?"

"The Prophecy moves on, Vordai—even if sometimes we don't. The Rivan King has returned, and Torak stirs in his sleep."

"Ah," she said without much real interest.

"The Orb of Aldur stands on the pommel of Belgarion's sword. The day is not far off when the Child of Light and the Child of Dark must meet. We go toward that meeting, and all mankind awaits the outcome."

"Except me, Belgarath." She gave him a penetrating look. "The fate of mankind is a matter of only the mildest curiosity to me. I was excluded from mankind three hundred years ago, you'll remember."

"Those people are all long dead, Vordai."

"Their descendants are no different. Could I walk into any village in this part of Drasnia and tell the good villagers who I am without being stoned or burned?"

"Villagers are the same the world over, madam," Silk put in. "Provincial, stupid, and superstitious. Not all men are like that."

"All men are the same, Prince Kheldar," she disagreed. "When I was young, I tried to involve myself in the affairs of my village. I only wanted to help, but very soon not a cow died or a baby took colic without my being blamed for it. They stoned me finally and tried to drag me back to the village to burn me at the stake. They had quite a celebration planned. I managed to escape, though, and I took refuge here in the fens. After that I had very little interest in the affairs of men."

"You probably shouldn't have displayed your talents quite so openly," Belgarath told her. "People prefer not to believe in that sort of thing. There's a whole catalogue of nasty little emotions curdling in the human spirit, and anything the least bit out of the ordinary raises the possibility of retribution."

"My village learned that it was more than a possibility," she replied with a certain grim satisfaction.

"What happened?" Garion asked curiously.

"It started raining," Vordai told him with an odd smile.

"Is that all?"

"It was enough. It rained on that village for five years, King Belgarion—just on the village. A hundred yards beyond the last house everything was normal, but in the village there was rain. They tried to move twice, but the rain followed them.

Finally they gave up and left the area. For all I know, some of their descendants are still wandering."

"You're not serious," Silk scoffed.

"Quite serious." She gave him an amused look. "Your credulity appears selective, Prince Kheldar. Here you are, going about the world in the company of Belgarath the Sorcerer. I'm sure you believe in his power; but you can't bring yourself to accept the idea of the power of the witch of the fens."

Silk stared at her.

"I really am a witch, Prince Kheldar. I could demonstrate if you wish, but I don't think you'd like it very much. People seldom do."

"That isn't really necessary, Vordai," Belgarath said. "What is it that you want exactly?"

"I was coming to that, Belgarath," she replied. "After I escaped into the fens, I discovered my little friends here." She affectionately stroked the side of Poppi's furry little face, and Poppi nuzzled at her hand ecstatically. "They were afraid of me at first, but they finally grew less shy. They began bringing me fish—and flowers—as tokens of friendship, and I needed friends very badly at that time. I altered them a bit out of gratitude."

"You shouldn't have, you know," the old man said rather sadly.

She shrugged. "Should and shouldn't have very little meaning to me anymore."

"Not even the Gods would do what you did."

"The Gods have other amusements." She looked directly at him then. "I've been waiting for you, Belgarath—for years now. I knew that sooner or later you'd come back into the fens. This meeting you spoke of is very important to you, isn't it?"

"It's the most important event in the history of the world."

"That depends on your point of view, I suppose. You need my help, though."

"I think we can manage, Vordai."

"Perhaps, but how do you expect to get out of the fens?"

He looked at her sharply.

"I can open the way for you to the dry ground at the edge of the swamp, or I can see to it that you wander around in these marshes forever—in which case this meeting you're concerned about will never happen, will it? That puts me in a very interesting situation, wouldn't you say?"

Belgarath's eyes narrowed.

"I discovered that when men deal with each other, there's usually an exchange of some kind," she added with a strange little smile. "Something for something; nothing for nothing. It seems to be a sensible arrangement."

"Exactly what did you have in mind?"

"The fenlings are my friends," she replied. "In a very special way, my children. But men look upon them as animals with pelts worth the taking. They trap them, Belgarath, and they kill them for their fur. The fine ladies in Boktor and Kotu dress themselves in the skins of my children and give no thought to the grief it causes me. They call my children animals and they come into the fens to hunt them."

"They *are* animals, Vordai," he told her gently.

"Not any more." Almost without seeming to think, Vordai put her arm about Poppi's shoulders. "It may be that you were right when you said that I shouldn't have tampered with them, but it's too late now to change it back." She sighed. "I'm a witch, Belgarath," she continued, "not a sorceress. My life has a beginning and an end, and it's approaching its end, I think. I won't live forever, as you and Polgara have. I've lived several hundred years already and I'm growing very tired of life. As long as I'm alive, I can keep men from coming into the fens; but once I'm gone, my children will have no protection."

"And you want me to take them into my care?"

"No, Belgarath. You're too busy; and sometimes you forget promises you don't care to remember. I want you to do the one thing that will make it forever impossible for men to think of the fenlings as animals."

His eyes widened as what she was suggesting dawned on him.

"I want you to give my children the power of speech, Belgarath," Vordai said. "I can't do it. My witchcraft doesn't reach that far. Only a sorcerer can make it possible for them to talk."

"Vordai!"

"That's my price, Belgarath," she told him. "That's what my help will cost you. Take it or leave it."

CHAPTER NINETEEN

They slept that night in Vordai's cottage, though Garion slept very little. The ultimatum of the witch of the fens troubled him profoundly. He knew that tampering with nature had far-reaching effects, and to go as far as Vordai wished might forever erase the dividing line between men and animals. The philosophical and theological implications of that step were staggering. There were, moreover, other worries. It was entirely possible that Belgarath could not do what Vordai demanded of him. Garion was almost positive that his grandfather had not attempted to use his will since his collapse months before, and now Vordai had set him an almost impossible task.

What would happen to Belgarath if he tried and failed? What would that do to him? Would the doubts then take over and rob him of any possibility of ever regaining his power? Desperately Garion tried to think of a way to warn his grandfather without arousing those fatal doubts.

But they absolutely had to get out of the fens. However reluctantly Garion had made the decision to meet Torak, he now knew that it was the only possible choice open to him. The meeting, however, could not be delayed indefinitely. If it were put off too long, events would move on, and the world would be plunged into the war they were all so desperately trying to head off. Vordai's threat to trap them all here in the fens unless Belgarath paid her price threatened not only them, but the entire world. In a very real sense, she held the fate of all mankind in her un-caring hands. Try though he might, Garion could not think of any way to avoid the test of Belgarath's will. Though he would reluctantly have done what Vordai wished himself, he did not even know where to begin. If it could be done at all, his grandfather was the only one who could do it—if his illness had not destroyed his power.

When dawn crept through the misty fens, Belgarath arose and sat before the fire, brooding into the crackling flames with a somber face.

"Well?" Vordai asked him. "Have you decided?"

"It's wrong, Vordai," he told her. "Nature cries out against it."

"I'm much closer to nature than you are, Belgarath," she replied. "Witches live more intimately with her than sorcerers do. I can feel the turning of the seasons in my blood, and the earth is alive under my feet. I hear no outcry. Nature loves all her creatures, and she would grieve over the obliteration of my fenlings almost as much as I. But that's really beside the point, isn't it? Even though the very rocks shrieked out against it, I would not relent."

Silk exchanged a quick look with Garion, and the little man's sharp face seemed as troubled as Belgarath's.

"Are the fenlings really beasts?" Vordai continued. She pointed to where Poppi still slept, her delicate forepaws open like little hands. Tupik, moving stealthily, crept back into the house, carrying a handful of dew-drenched swamp flowers. With precise care, he placed them about the slumbering Poppi and gently laid the last one in her open hand. Then, with an oddly patient expression, he sat on his haunches to watch her awakening.

Poppi stirred, stretched, and yawned. She brought the flower to her little black nose and sniffed at it, looking affectionately at the expectant Tupik. She made a happy little chirping sound, and then she and Tupik scampered off together for a morning swim in the cool water of the swamp.

"It's a courting ritual," Vordai explained. "Tupik wants Poppi to be his mate, and as long as she continues to accept his gifts, he knows that she's still fond of him. It will go on for quite some time, and then they'll swim off into the swamp together for a week or so. When they come back, they'll be mates for life. Is that really so different from the way young humans behave?"

Her question profoundly disturbed Garion for some reason he could not quite put his finger on.

"Look there," Vordai told them, pointing through the window at a group of young fenlings, scarcely more than babies, at play. They had fashioned a ball out of moss and were rapidly passing it around in a circle, their large eyes intent on their game. "Couldn't a human child join that group and not feel the slightest bit out of place?" Vordai pressed.

Not far beyond the game, a mature female fenling cradled her sleeping baby, rocking gently with her cheek against the little one's face. "Isn't motherhood uni-versal?" Vordai asked. "In what way do my children differ from humans?—except that they're perhaps more decent, more honest and loving with each other?"

Belgarath sighed. "All right, Vordai," he said, "you've made your point. I'll grant that the fenlings are probably nicer creatures than men. I don't know that speech will improve them, but if that's what you want—" He shrugged.

"You'll do it then?"

"I know it's wrong, but I'll try to do what you ask. I really don't have much choice, do I?"

"No," she replied, "you don't. Will you need anything? I have all the customary implements and compounds."

He shook his head. "Sorcery doesn't work that way. Witchcraft involves the summoning of spirits, but sorcery comes all from within. Someday, if we have the leisure, I'll explain the difference to you." He stood up. "I don't suppose you'd care to change your mind about this?"

Her face hardened. "No, Belgarath," she replied.

He sighed again. "All right, Vordai. I'll be back in a bit." He turned quietly and walked out into the mist-shrouded morning.

In the silence that followed his departure, Garion closely watched Vordai for some hint that her determination might not be as iron-hard as it seemed. It had occurred to him that if she were not blindly adamant, he might be able to explain the situation and persuade her to relent. The witch of the fens paced nervously about the room, picking things up absently and setting them down again. She seemed unable to concentrate her attention on any one thing for more than a moment.

"This may ruin him, you know," Garion told her quietly. Bluntness perhaps might sway her where other attempts at persuasion had failed.

"What are you talking about?" she demanded sharply.

"He was very ill last winter," Garion replied. "He and Ctuchik fought each other for possession of the Orb. Ctuchik was destroyed, but Belgarath nearly died too. It's quite possible that his power was destroyed by his illness."

Silk's gasp was clearly audible. "Why didn't you tell us?" he exclaimed.

"Aunt Pol said that we didn't dare," Garion said. "We couldn't take any chance of word of it getting back to the Angaraks. Belgarath's power is the one thing that's held them in check all these years. If he's lost it and they find out, they'll feel free to invade the West."

"Does *he* know?" Vordai asked quickly.

"I don't think so. Neither one of us said anything to him about it. We couldn't let him think for a moment that anything might be wrong. If he has one single doubt, it won't work for him. That's the main thing about sorcery. You have to believe that what you want to happen is going to. Otherwise, nothing happens at all—and each time you fail, it gets worse."

"What did you mean when you said that this might ruin him?" Vordai's face looked stricken, and Garion began to have some hope.

"He may still have his power—or some of it," he explained. "But not enough to do what you've asked of him. It takes a tremendous effort to do even simple things, and what you've asked him to do is very difficult. It could be too much for him; but once he starts, he won't be able to stop. And the effort may drain his will and his life energy until he cannot ever recover—or until he dies."

"Why didn't you tell me?" Vordai demanded, her face anguished.

"I couldn't—not without his hearing me, too."

She turned quickly toward the door. "Belgarath!" she cried. "Wait!" She spun back to Garion. "Go after him! Stop him!"

That was what Garion had been waiting for. He jumped to his feet and ran to the door. As he swung it open and was about to call out across the rainy yard, he felt a strange oppression as if something were almost happening—almost, but not quite. The shout froze on his lips.

"Go on, Garion," Silk urged him.

"I can't," Garion groaned. "He's already begun to pull in his will. He wouldn't even hear me."

"Can you help him?"

"I don't even know exactly what he's trying to do, Silk," Garion replied helplessly. "If I went blundering in there now, all I'd do is make things worse."

They stared at him in consternation.

Garion felt a strange echoing surge. It was not at all what he expected, and so he was totally unprepared for it. His grandfather was not trying to move anything or change anything, but instead he was calling out—reaching across some vast distance with the voice of his mind. The words were not at all distinct, but the one word, "Master," did come through once quite distinctly. Belgarath was trying to reach Aldur.

Garion held his breath.

Then, from infinitely far away, Aldur's voice replied. They spoke together quietly for several moments, and all the while Garion could feel the force of Belgarath's will, infused and magnified by the will of Aldur, growing stronger and stronger.

"What's happening?" Silk's voice was almost frightened.

"He's talking with Aldur. I can't hear what they're saying."

"Will Aldur help him?" Vordai asked.

"I don't know. I don't know if Aldur can use his will here anymore. There's some kind of limitation—something that he and the other Gods agreed to."

Then the strange conversation ended, and Garion felt Belgarath's will mounting, gathering itself. "He's begun," Garion said in a half-whisper.

"His power's still there?" Silk asked.

Garion nodded.

"As strong as ever?"

"I don't know. There's no way to measure it."

The tension of it grew until it was almost intolerable. What Belgarath was doing was at once very subtle and very profound. There was no rushing surge or hollow echo this time. Instead, Garion felt an odd, tingling whisper as the old man's will was unleashed with agonizing slowness. The whisper seemed to be saying something over and over—something Garion could almost understand, but which tantalizingly eluded him.

Outside, the young fenlings stopped their game. The ball dropped unnoticed as the players all stood, listening intently. Poppi and Tupik, returning hand in hand from their swim, froze in their tracks and stood with their heads cocked as Belgarath's whisper spoke gently to them, reaching down into their thoughts, murmuring, explaining, teaching. Then their eyes widened as if in sudden understanding.

Belgarath emerged finally from the misty willows, his step heavy, weary. He walked slowly toward the house, stopping just outside to look intently at the stunned faces of the fenlings gathered in the dooryard. He nodded then and came back inside. His shoulders were slumped with exhaustion, and his white-bearded face seemed drained.

"Are you all right?" Vordai asked him, her tone no longer neutral.

He nodded and sank into a chair by the table. "It's done," he said shortly.

Vordai looked at him, and her eyes narrowed suspiciously.

"No tricks, Vordai," he said. "And I'm too tired to try to lie to you. I've paid your price. If it's all right with you, we'll leave right after breakfast. We still have a long way to go."

"I'll need more than just your word, Belgarath. I don't really trust you—or any human, for that matter. I want proof that you've paid."

But there was a strange new voice from the doorway. Poppi, her furry little face contorted with the effort, was struggling with something. "M-m-m-m-," she stammered. Her mouth twisted, and she tried again. "M-m-m-m-." It seemed to be the hardest thing she had ever tried to do. She took a deep breath and tried once more. "M-m-m-mo-therr," Poppi said.

With a low cry, Vordai rushed to the little creature, knelt, and embraced her.

"Mother," Poppi said again. It was clearer this time.

From outside the cottage there came a growing babble of small, squeaky voices, all repeating, "Mother, mother, mother." The excited fenlings converged on the cottage, their voices swelling as more and more of them emerged from the swamps.

Vordai wept.

"You'll have to teach them, of course," Belgarath said wearily. "I gave them the ability, but they don't know very many words yet."

Vordai looked at him with tears streaming down her face. "Thank you, Belgarath," she said in a faltering voice.

The old man shrugged. "Something for something," he replied. "Wasn't that the bargain?"

It was Tupik who led them from the fens. The little creature's chirping to his fellows, however, now had words mixed in with it—faltering, often badly mispronounced, but words nonetheless.

Garion thought for a long time before he spoke, wrestling with an idea as he pushed on his pole. "Grandfather," he said finally.

"Yes, Garion," the old man replied from where he rested in the stern of their boat.

"You knew all along, didn't you?"

"Knew what?"

"That it was possible that you couldn't make things happen anymore?"

Belgarath stared at him. "Where did you get that idea?" he asked.

"Aunt Pol said that after you got sick last winter, you might have lost all your power."

"She said *what*?"

"She said that—"

"I heard you." The old man was frowning, his face creased with thought. "That possibility never even occurred to me," he admitted. Suddenly he blinked and his eyes opened very wide. "You know, she might have been right. The illness *could* have had that sort of effect. What an amazing thing."

"You didn't feel any—well—weaker?"

"What? No, of course not." Belgarath was still frowning, turning the idea over in his mind. "What an amazing thing," he repeated, and then he suddenly laughed.

"I don't see what's so funny."

"Is that what's been bothering you and your aunt for all these months? The two of you have been tiptoeing around me as if I were made out of thin glass."

"We were afraid the Angaraks might find out, and we didn't dare say anything to you because—"

"Because you were afraid it might make me doubt my abilities?"

Garion nodded.

"Maybe in the long run it wasn't a bad idea at that. I certainly didn't need any doubts plaguing me this morning."

"Was it terribly difficult?"

"Moderately so, yes. I wouldn't want to have to try that sort of thing every day."

"But you didn't really have to do it, did you?"

"Do what?"

"Show the fenlings how to talk. If you've still got your power, then between the two of us, you and I could have opened a channel straight through to the edge of the swamp—no matter what Vordai or the fenlings could have done to try to stop us."

"I wondered how long it was going to be before that occurred to you," the old man replied blandly.

Garion gave him an irritated look. "All right," he said, "why did you do it then, since you didn't have to?"

"That question's rather impolite, Garion," Belgarath chided. "There are certain courtesies customarily observed. It's not considered good manners to ask another sorcerer why he did something."

Garion gave his grandfather an even harder look. "You're evading the question," he said bluntly. "Let's agree that I don't have very good manners, and then you can go ahead and answer anyway."

Belgarath appeared slightly injured. "It's not my fault that you and your aunt were so worried. You don't really have any reason to be so cross with me." He paused, then looked at Garion. "You're absolutely going to insist?" he asked.

"Yes, I think I really am. Why did you do it?"

Belgarath sighed. "Vordai's been alone for most of her life, you know," he replied, "and life's been very hard to her. Somehow I've always thought that she de-served better. Maybe this makes up for it—a little bit."

"Did Aldur agree with you?" Garion pressed. "I heard his voice when the two of you were talking."

"Eavesdropping is really a bad habit, Garion."

"I've got lots of bad habits, Grandfather."

"I don't know why you're taking this tone with me, boy," the old man complained. "All right, since you're going to be this way about it, I did, as a matter of fact, have to talk rather fast to get my Master to agree."

"You did all of this because you felt sorry for her?"

"That's not exactly the right term, Garion. Let's just say that I have certain feelings about justice."

"If you knew you were going to do it anyway, why did you argue with her?"

Belgarath shrugged. "I wanted to be sure that she really wanted it. Besides, it's not a good idea to let people get the idea that you'll do anything they ask just because you might feel that they have a certain claim on you."

Silk was staring at the old man in amazement. "Compassion, Belgarath?" he demanded incredulously. "From *you*? If word of this ever gets out, your reputation's going to be ruined."

Belgarath looked suddenly painfully embarrassed. "I don't know that we need to spread it around all that much, Silk," he said. "People don't really have to know about this, do they?"

Garion felt as if a door had suddenly opened. Silk, he realized, was right. He had never precisely thought of it that way, but Belgarath *did* have a certain reputation for ruthlessness. Most men felt that there was a kind of implacableness about the Eternal Man—a willingness to sacrifice anything in his single-minded drive toward a goal so obscure that no one else could ever fully understand it. But with this single act of compassion, he had revealed another, softer side of his nature. Belgarath the Sorcerer was capable of human emotion and feeling, after all. The thought of how those feelings had been wounded by all the horrors and pain he had seen and endured in seven thousand years came crashing in on Garion, and he found himself staring at his grandfather with a profound new respect.

The edge of the fens was marked by a solid-looking dike that stretched off into the misty distance in either direction.

"The causeway," Silk told Garion, pointing at the dike. "It's part of the Tolnedran highway system."

"Bel-grath," Tupik said, his head popping up out of the water beside the boat, "thank-you."

"Oh, I rather think you'd have learned to talk eventually anyway, Tupik," the old man replied. "You were very close to it, you know."

"May-be, may-be-not," Tupik disagreed. "Want-to-talk and talk dif-ferent. Not-same."

"Soon you'll learn to lie," Silk told him sardonically, "and then you'll be as good as any man alive."

"Why learn to talk if only to lie?" Tupik asked, puzzled.

"It'll come to you in time."

Tupik frowned slightly, and then his head slipped under the water. He came up one more time some distance away from the boat. "Good-bye," he called to them. "Tupik thanks you—for Mother." Then, without a ripple, he disappeared.

"What a strange little creature." Belgarath smiled.

With a startled exclamation, Silk frantically dug into his pocket. Something a pale green color leaped from his hand to plop into the water.

"What's the matter?" Garion asked him.

Silk shuddered. "The little monster put a frog in my pocket."

"Perhaps it was meant as a gift," Belgarath suggested.

"A frog?"

"Then again perhaps it wasn't." Belgarath grinned. "It's a little primitive perhaps, but it might just be the beginnings of a sense of humor."

There was a Tolnedran hostel a few miles up the great causeway that ran north and south through the eastern edge of the fens. They reached it in the late afternoon and purchased horses at a price that made Silk wince. The following morning they moved out at a canter in the direction of Boktor.

The strange interlude in the fens had given Garion a great deal to think about. He began to perceive that compassion was a kind of love—broader and more encompassing than the somewhat narrow idea he had previously had of that emotion. The word love seemed, as he thought more deeply about it, to include a great number of things that at first glance did not seem to have anything whatsoever to do with it. As his understanding of this grew, a peculiar notion took hold of his imagination. His grandfather, the man they called Eternal, had probably in his seven thousand years developed a capacity for love beyond the ability of other men even remotely to guess at. In spite of that gruff, irritable exterior, Belgarath's entire life had been an expression of that transcendent love. As they rode, Garion glanced often at the strange old man, and the image of the remote, all-powerful sorcerer towering above the rest of humanity gradually faded; he began to see the real man behind that image—a complicated man to be sure, but a very human one.

Two days later in clearing weather, they reached Boktor.

CHAPTER TWENTY

There was an open quality about Boktor that Garion noticed immediately as they rode through its broad streets. The houses were not for the most part over two stories high, and they were not jammed up against each other as they were in other cities he had seen. The avenues were wide and straight, and there was a minimum of litter in them.

He commented on that as they rode along a spacious, tree-lined boulevard.

"Boktor's a new city," Silk explained, "at least relatively."

"I thought that it's been here since the time of Dras Bullneck."

"Oh, it has," Silk replied, "but the old city was destroyed by the Angaraks when they invaded, five hundred years ago."

"I'd forgotten that," Garion admitted.

"After Vo Mimbre, when the time came to rebuild, it was decided to take advantage of the chance to start over," Silk continued. He looked about rather distastefully. "I don't really like Boktor," he said. "There aren't enough alleys and back streets. It's almost impossible to move around without being seen." He turned to Belgarath. "That reminds me of something, by the way. It probably wouldn't be a bad idea to avoid the central marketplace. I'm rather well known here, and there's no point in letting the whole city know we've arrived."

"Do you think we'll be able to slip through unnoticed?" Garion asked him.

"In Boktor?" Silk laughed. "Of course not. We've already been identified a half dozen times. Spying is a major industry here. Porenn knew we were coming before we'd even entered the city." He glanced up at a second floor window, and his fingers flickered a quick rebuke in the gestures of the Drasnian secret language. The curtain at the window gave a guilty little twitch. "Just too clumsy," he observed with profound disapproval. "Must be a first-year student at the academy."

"Probably nervous about seeing a celebrity," Belgarath suggested. "You are, after all, something of a legend, Silk."

"There's still no excuse for sloppy work," Silk said. "If I had time, I'd stop by the academy and have a talk with the headmaster about it." He sighed. "The quality of student work has definitely gone downhill since they discontinued the use of the whipping post."

"The what?" Garion exclaimed.

"In my day, a student who was seen by the person he was assigned to watch was flogged," Silk told him. "Flogging's a very effective teaching technique, Garion."

Just ahead of them a door to a large house opened, and a dozen uniformed pikemen marched out into the street, halted and turned to face them. The officer in charge came forward and bowed politely. "Prince Kheldar," he greeted Silk, "Her Highness wonders if you'd be so good as to stop by the palace."

"You see," Silk said to Garion. "I told you she knew we were here." He turned to the officer. "Just out of curiosity, Captain, what would you do if I told you that we didn't feel like being so good as to stop by the palace?"

"I'd probably have to insist," the captain replied.

"I rather thought you might feel that way about it."

"Are we under arrest?" Garion asked nervously.

"Not precisely, your Majesty," the captain answered. "Queen Porenn most definitely wishes to speak with you, however." He bowed then to Belgarath. "Ancient One," he greeted the old man respectfully. "I think that if we went around to the side entrance, we'd attract less attention." And he turned and gave his men the order to march.

"He knows who we are," Garion muttered to Silk.

"Naturally," Silk said.

"How are we going to get out of this? Won't Queen Porenn just ship us all back to Riva?"

"We'll talk to her," Belgarath said. "Porenn's got good sense. I'm sure we can explain this to her."

"Unless Polgara's been issuing ultimatums," Silk added. "She does that when she gets angry, I've noticed."

"We'll see."

Queen Porenn was even more radiantly lovely than ever. Her slimness made it obvious that the birth of her first child had already occurred. Motherhood had brought a glow to her face and a look of completion to her eyes. She greeted them fondly as they entered the palace and led them immediately to her private quarters. The little queen's rooms were somehow lacy and feminine with ruffles on the furniture and soft, pink curtains at the windows. "Where have you been?" she asked them as soon as they were alone. "Polgara's frantic."

Belgarath shrugged. "She'll recover. What's happening in Riva?"

"They're directing the search for you, naturally," Porenn replied. "How did you manage to get this far? Every road's been blocked."

"We were ahead of everybody, Auntie dearest." Silk grinned impudently at her. "By the time they started blocking roads, we'd already gone through."

"I've asked you not to call me that, Kheldar," she admonished him.

"Forgive me, your Highness," he said with a bow, though still grinning mockingly.

"You're impossible," she told him.

"Of course I am," he answered. "It's part of my charm."

The queen sighed. "What am I going to do with all of you now?"

"You're going to let us continue our journey," Belgarath replied calmly. "We'll argue about it, of course, but in the end that's the way it'll turn out."

She stared at him.

"You did ask, after all. I'm sure you feel better now that you know."

"You're as bad or worse than Kheldar," she accused.

"I've had more practice."

"It's quite out of the question," she told him firmly. "I have strict orders from Polgara to send you all back to Riva."

Belgarath shrugged.

"You'll go?" She seemed surprised.

"No," he replied, "we won't. You said that Polgara gave you strict orders to send us back. All right, then, *I* give you strict orders not to. Now where does that leave us?"

"That's cruel, Belgarath."

"Times are hard."

"Before we get down to serious squabbling, do you suppose we might have a look at the heir to the throne?" Silk asked. His question was artful. No new mother could resist the opportunity to show off her infant, and Queen Porenn had already turned toward the cradle standing in the corner of the room before she realized that she was being cleverly manipulated. "You're bad, Kheldar," she said reprovingly, but she nonetheless pulled back the satin coverlet to reveal the baby that had become the absolute center of her life.

The Crown Prince of Drasnia was very seriously attempting to put one of his toes in his mouth. With a happy little cry, Porenn caught him up in her arms and hugged him. Then she turned him and held him out for them to see. "Isn't he beautiful?" she demanded.

"Hail, Cousin," Silk greeted the baby gravely. "Your timely arrival has ensured that I will be spared the ultimate indignity."

"What's that supposed to mean?" Porenn asked him suspiciously.

"Only that his little pink Highness has permanently removed any possibility of my ever ascending the throne," Silk replied. "I'd be a very bad king, Porenn. Drasnia would suffer almost as much as I would if that disaster ever took place. Our Garion here is already a better king by accident than I could ever be."

"Oh dear." Porenn flushed slightly. "That completely slipped my mind." She curtsied somewhat awkwardly, her baby still in her arms. "Your Majesty," she greeted Garion formally.

"Your Highness," Garion answered with the bow Aunt Pol had made him practice for hours.

Porenn laughed her silvery little laugh. "That all seems so inappropriate." She put one hand to the back of Garion's neck, drew his head down and kissed him warmly. The baby in her other arm cooed. "Dear Garion," she said. "You've grown so tall."

There wasn't much he could say to that.

The queen studied his face for a moment. "Many things have happened to you," she observed shrewdly. "You're not the same boy I knew in Val Alorn."

"He's making progress," Belgarath agreed, settling himself into a chair. "How many spies are listening to us at the moment, Porenn?"

"Two that I know of," she replied, returning her baby to his cradle.

Silk laughed. "And how many spies are spying on the spies?"

"Several, I'd imagine," Porenn told him. "If I tried to unravel all the spying that goes on here, I'd never get anything done."

"I'll assume that they're all discreet," Belgarath said with a meaningful glance around at the walls and draperies.

"Of course they are," Porenn declared, sounding slightly offended. "We do have standards, you know. Amateurs are never allowed to spy inside the palace."

"All right, let's get down to business, then. Is it really going to be necessary for us to go through some long, involved argument about whether or not you're going to try to send us back to Riva?"

She sighed and then gave a helpless little laugh. "I suppose not," she surrendered. "You are going to have to give me an excuse to give to Polgara, though."

"Just tell her that we're acting on the instructions contained in the Mrin Codex."

"Are there instructions in the Mrin Codex?" She sounded surprised.

"There might be," he replied. "Most of it's such unmitigated gibberish that no one can be absolutely sure one way or the other."

"Are you asking me to try to deceive her?"

"No, I'm asking you to let her think that I deceived you—there's a difference."

"A very subtle one, Belgarath."

"It'll be all right," he assured her. "She's always ready to believe the worst about me. Anyway, the three of us are on our way to Gar og Nadrak. Get word to

Polgara that we're going to need a diversion of sorts. Tell her that I said to stop wasting time looking for us and to mass an army somewhere in the south—make a lot of noise. I want the Angaraks all to be so busy watching her that they don't have time to look for us."

"What on earth are you going to do in Gar og Nadrak?" Porenn asked curiously.

Belgarath looked suggestively at the walls behind which the official spies—as well as a few unofficial ones—lurked. "Polgara will know what we're doing. What's the current situation along the Nadrak border?"

"Tense," she replied. "It's not hostile yet, but it's a long way from cordial. The Nadraks don't really want to go to war. If it weren't for the Grolims, I honestly think we could persuade them to stay neutral. They'd much rather kill Murgos than Drasnians."

Belgarath nodded. "Pass the word on to your husband that I'd like him to keep a fairly tight rein on Anheg," he continued. "Anheg's brilliant, but he's a trifle erratic at times. Rhodar's steadier. Tell him that what I want in the south is a diversion, not a general war. Alorns sometimes get overenthusiastic."

"I'll get word to him," Porenn promised. "When will you start?"

"Let's leave that a bit tentative." The old man glanced once again at the walls of the queen's room.

"You'll stay the night, at least," she insisted.

"How could we possibly refuse?" Silk asked mockingly.

Queen Porenn looked at him for a long moment. Then she sighed. "I guess I should tell you, Kheldar," she said very quietly. "Your mother's here."

Silk's face blanched. "Here? In the palace?"

The queen nodded. "She's in the west wing. I've given her that apartment near the garden she loves so much."

Silk's hands had begun to tremble visibly, and his face was still ashen. "How long has she been here?" he asked in a strained voice.

"Several weeks. She came before the baby was born."

"How is she?"

"The same." The little blond queen's voice was hushed with sadness. "You'll have to see her, you know."

Silk drew in a deep breath and squared his shoulders. His face, however, was still stricken. "There's no avoiding it, I guess," he said, almost to himself. "I might as well get it over with. You'll excuse me?"

"Of course."

He turned and left the room, his face somber.

"Doesn't he like his mother?" Garion asked.

"He loves her very much," the queen replied. "That's why it's so terribly difficult for him. She's blind—fortunately."

"Fortunately?"

"There was a pestilence in western Drasnia about twenty years ago," Porenn explained. "It was a horrible disease, and it left dreadful scars on the faces of the survivors. Prince Kheldar's mother had been one of the most beautiful women in Drasnia. We've concealed the truth from her. She doesn't realize how disfigured her face is—at least we hope she doesn't. The meetings between Kheldar and his mother are heartbreaking. There's no hint in his voice of what he sees, but his eyes—" She broke off. "Sometimes I think that's why he stays away from Drasnia," she added. Then she straightened. "I'll ring for supper," she said, "and something to drink. Kheldar usually needs that after he's visited with his mother."

It was an hour or more before Silk returned, and he immediately started drinking. He drank grimly like a man bent on reducing himself to unconsciousness as quickly as possible.

It was an uncomfortable evening for Garion. Queen Porenn cared for her infant son even while keeping a watchful eye on Silk. Belgarath sat silently in a chair, and Silk kept drinking. Finally, pretending a weariness he did not feel, Garion went to bed.

He had not realized how much he had depended on Silk in the year and a half he had known him. The rat-faced little Drasnian's sardonic humor and towering self-reliance had always been something to cling to. To be sure, Silk had his quirks and peculiarities. He was a high-strung, complex little man, but his unfailing sense of humor and his mental agility had seen them all through some very unpleasant situations. Now, however, all traces of humor and wit were gone, and the little man seemed on the verge of total collapse.

The dreadful confrontation toward which they rode seemed all the more perilous now for some reason. Although Silk might not have been able to help him when he finally faced Torak, Garion had counted on his friend to assist him through the terrible days leading up to the meeting. Now even that slight comfort seemed to have been taken away. Unable to sleep, he tossed and turned for hours; finally, well past midnight, he rose, pulled his cloak about him and padded on stockinged feet to see if his friend had made it to bed.

Silk had not. He still sat in the same chair. His tankard, unnoticed, had spilled, and he sat with his elbows in a puddle of ale and his face in his hands. Not far away, her face unreadable, sat the weary little blond queen of Drasnia. As Garion watched from the doorway, a muffled sound came from between Silk's hands. With a gentle, almost tender expression, Queen Porenn rose, came around the table and put her arms about his head, drawing him to her. With a despairing cry Silk clung to her, weeping openly like a hurt child.

Queen Porenn looked across the little man's shaking head at Garion. Her face quite clearly revealed that she was aware of Silk's feelings for her. Her look was one of helpless compassion for this man of whom she was fond—but not in the way he wished—and combined with that was a deep sympathy for the suffering his visit with his mother had caused him.

Silently Garion and the Queen of Drasnia stood looking at each other. Speech was unnecessary; they both understood. When at last Porenn did speak, her tone was curiously matter-of-fact. "I think you can put him to bed now," she said. "Once he's able to cry, the worst is usually over."

THE NEXT MORNING they left the palace and joined an eastbound caravan. The Drasnian moors beyond Boktor were desolate. The North Caravan Route wound through low, rolling hills covered with sparse vegetation and scanty grass. Although it was the middle of spring, there seemed to be a sere quality to the moors, as if the seasons only lightly touched them; the wind, sweeping down from the polar ice, still had the smell of winter in it.

Silk rode in silence, his eyes on the ground, though whether from grief or from the aftereffects of the ale he had drunk, Garion could not guess. Belgarath was also quiet, and the three of them rode with only the sound of the harness bells of a Drasnian merchant's mules for companionship.

About noon, Silk shook himself and looked around, his eyes finally alert, though still a bit bloodshot. "Did anybody think to bring something to drink?" he asked.

"Didn't you get enough last night?" Belgarath replied.

"That was for entertainment. What I need now is something therapeutic."

"Water?" Garion suggested.

"I'm thirsty, Garion, not dirty."

"Here." Belgarath handed the suffering man a wineskin. "But don't overdo it."

"Trust me," Silk said, taking a long drink. He shuddered and made a face. "Where did you buy this?" he inquired. "It tastes like somebody's been boiling old shoes in it."

"You don't have to drink it."

"I'm afraid I do." Silk took another drink, then restoppered the wineskin and handed it back. He looked sourly around at the moors. "Hasn't changed much," he observed. "Drasnia has very little to recommend it, I'm afraid. It's either too wet or too dry." He shivered in the chilly wind. "Are either of you aware of the fact that there's nothing between us and the pole to break the wind but an occasional stray reindeer?"

Garion began to relax. Silk's sallies and comments grew broader and more outrageous as they rode through the afternoon. By the time the caravan stopped for the night, he seemed to be almost his old self again.

CHAPTER TWENTY-ONE

The caravan wound its slow way through the dreary moors of eastern Drasnia with the sound of mule bells trailing mournfully behind it. Sparse patches of heath, which had but lately begun to bloom with tiny, pink flowers, dotted the low, rolling hills. The sky had turned cloudy, and the wind, seemingly perpetual, blew steadily out of the north.

Garion found his mood growing as sad and bleak as the moors around him. There was one inescapable fact which he no longer could hide from himself. Each mile, each step, brought him closer to Mallorea and closer to his meeting with Torak. Even the whispered song of the Orb, murmuring continually in his ears from the pommel of the great sword strapped to his back, could not reassure him. Torak was a God—invincible, immortal; and Garion, not even yet full-grown, was quite deliberately trekking to Mallorea to seek him out and to fight him to the death. Death was a word Garion tried very hard not to think about. It had been a possibility once or twice during their long pursuit of Zedar and the Orb; but now it seemed a certainty. He would meet Torak alone. Mandorallen or Barak or Hettar could not come to his aid with their superior skill at swordsmanship; Belgarath or Aunt Pol could not intercede for him with sorcery; Silk would not be able to devise some clever ruse to allow him to escape. Titanic and enraged, the Dark God would rush upon him, eager for blood. Garion began to fear sleep, for sleep brought nightmares which would not go away and which haunted his days, making each worse than the last.

He was afraid. The fear grew worse with each passing day until the sour taste of it was always in his mouth. More than anything, he wanted to run, but he knew that he could not. Indeed, he did not even know any place where he *could* run. There was no place in all the world for him to hide. The Gods themselves would seek him out if he tried and sternly drive him to that awful meeting which had been fated to take place since the beginning of time. And so it was that, sick with fear, Garion rode to meet his fate.

Belgarath, who was not always asleep when he seemed to doze in his saddle, watched, shrewdly waiting until Garion's fear had reached its peak before he spoke. Then, one cloudy morning when the lead-gray sky was as dreary as the moors around them, he pulled his horse in beside Garion's. "Do you want to talk about it?" he asked calmly.

"What's the point, Grandfather?"

"It might help."

"Nothing's going to help. He's going to kill me."

"If I thought it was that inevitable, I wouldn't have let you start on this journey."

"How can I possibly fight with a God?"

"Bravely," was the unhelpful reply. "You've been brave at some pretty inappropriate times in the past. I don't imagine you've changed all that much."

"I'm so afraid, Grandfather," Garion confessed, his voice anguished. "I think I know how Mandorallen felt now. The fear's so awful that I can't live with it."

"You're stronger than you think you are. You can live with it if you have to."

Garion brooded about that. It didn't seem to help much. "What's he like?" he asked, suddenly filled with a morbid curiosity.

"Who?"

"Torak."

"Arrogant. I never cared much for him."

"Is he like Ctuchik was—or Asharak?"

"No. They tried to be like *him*. They didn't succeed, of course, but they tried. If it's any help to you, Torak's probably as much afraid of you as you are of him. He knows who you are. When you meet him, he isn't going to see a Sendarian scullery boy named Garion; he's going to see Belgarion, the Rivan King, and he's going to see Riva's sword thirsting for his blood. He's also going to see the Orb of Aldur. And *that* will probably frighten him more than anything."

"When was the first time you met him?" Garion suddenly wanted the old man to talk—to tell stories as he had so long ago. Stories somehow always helped.

He could lose himself in a story, and for a little while it might make things bearable.

Belgarath scratched at his short, white beard. "Let's see," he mused. "I think the first time was in the Vale—it was a very long time ago. The others had gathered there—Belzedar, Beldin, all the rest—and each of us was involved in his own studies. Our Master had withdrawn into his tower with the Orb, and sometimes months would pass during which we didn't see him.

"Then one day a stranger came to us. He seemed to be about the same height as I, but he walked as if he were a thousand feet tall. His hair was black and his skin was very pale, and he had, as I remember, greenish-colored eyes. His face was beautiful to the point of being pretty, and his hair looked as if he spent a lot of time combing it. He appeared to be the kind of person who always has a mirror in his pocket."

"Did he say anything?" Garion asked.

"Oh, yes," Belgarath replied. "He came up to us and said, 'I would speak with my brother, thy Master,' and I *definitely* didn't care for his tone. He spoke as if we were servants—it's a failing he's always had. Still, my Master had—after a great deal of trouble—taught me at least a few manners. 'I shall tell my Master you have come,' I told him as politely as I could manage.

" 'That is not needful, Belgarath,' he told me in that irritatingly superior tone of his. 'My brother knows I am here.' "

"How did he know your name, Grandfather?"

Belgarath shrugged. "I never found that out. I assume that my Master had communicated with him—and the other Gods—from time to time and told them about us. At any rate, I led this over-pretty visitor to my Master's tower. I didn't bother to speak to him along the way. When we got there, he looked me straight in the face and said, 'A bit of advice for thee, Belgarath, by way of thanks for thy service. Seek not to rise above thyself. It is not *thy* place to approve or disapprove of *me*. For thy sake I hope that when next we meet thou wilt remember this and behave in a manner more seemly.'

" 'Thank you for the advice,' I told him—a bit tartly, I'll admit. 'Will you require anything else?'

" 'Thou art pert, Belgarath,' he said to me. 'Perhaps one day I shall give myself leisure to instruct thee in proper behavior.' And then he went into the tower. As you can see, Torak and I got off on the wrong foot right at the very beginning. I didn't care for his attitude, and he didn't care for mine."

"What happened then?" Garion's curiosity had begun to quiet the fear somewhat.

"You know the story," Belgarath replied. "Torak went up into the tower and spoke with Aldur. One thing led to another and finally Torak struck my Master and stole the Orb." The old man's face was bleak. "The next time I saw him, he wasn't nearly so pretty," he continued with a certain grim satisfaction. "That was after the Orb had burned him and he'd taken to wearing a steel mask to hide the ruins of his face."

Silk had drawn closer and was riding with them, fascinated by the story. "What did you all do then? After Torak stole the Orb, I mean?" he asked.

"Our Master sent us to warn the other Gods," Belgarath replied. "I was supposed to find Belar—he was in the north someplace, carousing with his Alorns. Belar was a young God at that time, and he enjoyed the diversions of the young. Alorn girls used to dream about being visited by him, and he tried to make as many dreams come true as he possibly could—or so I've been told."

"I've never heard *that* about him." Silk seemed startled.

"Perhaps it's only gossip," Belgarath admitted.

"Did you find him?" Garion asked.

"It took me quite a while. The shape of the land was different then. What's now Algaria stretched all the way to the east—thousands of leagues of open grassland. At first I took the shape of an eagle, but that didn't work out too well."

"It seems quite suitable," Silk observed.

"Heights make me giddy," the old man replied, "and my eyes were continually getting distracted by things on the ground. I kept having this overpowering urge to swoop down and kill things. The character of the forms we assume begins to dominate our thinking after a while, and although the eagle is quite splendid-looking, he's really a very stupid bird. Finally I gave that idea up and chose the form of the wolf instead. It worked out much better. About the only distraction I encountered was a young she-wolf who was feeling frolicsome." There was a slight tightening about his eyes as he said it, and his voice had a peculiar catch in it.

"Belgarath!" Silk actually sounded shocked.

"Don't be so quick to jump to conclusions, Silk. I considered the morality of the situation. I realized that being a father is probably all well and good, but that a litter of puppies might prove embarrassing later on. I resisted her advances, even though she persisted in following me all the way to the north where the Bear-God dwelt with his Alorns." He broke off and looked out at the gray-green moors, his face unreadable. Garion knew that there was something the old man wasn't saying—something important.

"Anyway," Belgarath continued, "Belar accompanied us back to the Vale where the other Gods had gathered, and they held a council and decided that they'd have to make war on Torak and his Angaraks. That was the start of it all. The world has never been the same since."

"What happened to the wolf?" Garion asked, trying to pin down his grandfather's peculiar evasion.

"She stayed with me," Belgarath replied calmly. "She used to sit for days on end in my tower watching me. She had a curious turn of mind, and her comments were frequently a trifle disconcerting."

"Comments?" Silk asked. "She could talk?"

"In the manner of the wolf, you understand. I'd learned how they speak during our journey together. It's really a rather concise and often quite beautiful language. Wolves can be eloquent—even poetic—once you get used to having them speak to you without words."

"How long did she stay with you?" Garion asked.

"Quite a long time," Belgarath replied. "I remember that I asked her about that once. She answered with another question. It was an irritating habit of hers.

She just said, "What is time to a wolf?' I made a few calculations and found out that she'd been with me for just over a thousand years. I was a bit amazed by that, but she seemed indifferent to the fact. 'Wolves live as long as they choose to live,' was all she said. Then one day I had to change my form for some reason or other— I forget exactly why. She saw me do it, and that was the end of any peace for me. She just said, 'So *that's* how you do it,' and promptly changed herself into a snowy owl. She seemed to take a great delight in startling me, and I never knew what shape I'd see when I turned around. She was fondest of the owl, though. A few years after that she left me. I was rather surprised to find that I missed her. We'd been together for a very long time." He broke off and once again he looked away.

"Did you ever see her again?" Garion wanted to know.

Belgarath nodded. "She saw to that—though I didn't know it at the time. I was running an errand for my Master somewhere to the north of the Vale and I came across a small, neatly thatched cottage in a grove of trees by a small river. A woman named Poledra lived in the cottage—a woman with tawny hair and curiously golden eyes. We grew to know each other, and eventually we were married. She was Polgara's mother—and Beldaran's."

"You were saying that you met the wolf again," Garion reminded him.

"You don't listen too well, Garion," the old man said, looking directly at his grandson. There was a deep and ancient injury in his eyes—a hurt so great that Garion knew it would be there for as long as the old man lived.

"You don't mean—?"

"It took me a while to accept it myself, actually. Poledra was very patient and very determined. When she found out that I couldn't accept her as a mate in the form of a wolf, she simply found a different shape. She got what she wanted in the end." He sighed.

"Aunt Pol's mother was a *wolf*?" Garion was stunned.

"No, Garion," Belgarath replied calmly, "she was a woman—a very lovely woman. The change of shape is absolute."

"But—but she started out as a wolf?"

"So?"

"But—" The whole notion was somehow shocking.

"Don't let your prejudices run away with you," Belgarath told him.

Garion struggled with the idea. It seemed monstrous somehow. "I'm sorry," he said finally. "It's unnatural, no matter what you say."

"Garion," the old man reminded him with a pained look, "just about everything we do is unnatural. Moving rocks with your mind isn't the most natural thing in the world, if you stop and think about it."

"But this is different," Garion protested. "Grandfather, you married a wolf— and the wolf had children. How could you do that?"

Belgarath sighed and shook his head. "You're a very stubborn boy, Garion," he observed. "It seems that you're never going to understand until you've been through the experience. Let's go over behind that hill, and I'll show you how it's done. There's no point in upsetting the rest of the caravan."

"Mind if I come along?" Silk asked, his nose twitching with curiosity.

"Might not be a bad idea," Belgarath agreed. "You can hold the horses. Horses tend to panic in the presence of wolves."

They rode away from the caravan track under the leaden sky and circled around behind a low, heath-covered hill. "This should do," Belgarath decided, reining in and dismounting in a shallow swale just behind the hill. The swale was covered with new grass, green with spring.

"The whole trick is to create the image of the animal in your mind," Belgarath explained, "down to the last detail. Then you direct your will inward—upon yourself—and then change, fitting yourself into the image."

Garion frowned, not understanding.

"It's going to take too long if I have to explain it in words," Belgarath said. "Here—watch—and watch with your mind as well as your eyes."

Unbidden, the shape of the great gray wolf he had seen on occasion before came into Garion's mind. He could clearly see the gray-shot muzzle and the silver ruff. Then he felt the surge and heard the hollow roaring sound in his mind. For an instant, the image of the wolf curiously mingled with an image of Belgarath himself—as if the two were trying to both occupy the same space. Then Belgarath was gone and only the wolf remained.

Silk whistled, then took a firmer grip on the reins of their startled horses.

Belgarath changed back again to an ordinary-looking old man in a rust-brown tunic and gray, hooded cloak. "Do you understand?" he asked Garion.

"I think so," Garion replied, a bit dubiously.

"Try it. I'll lead you through it one step at a time."

Garion started to put a wolf together in his mind.

"Don't forget the toenails," Belgarath told him. "They may not look like much, but they're very important."

Garion put the toenails in.

"Tail's too short."

Garion fixed that.

"That's about right. Now fit yourself into it."

Garion put his will to it. "Change," he said.

It seemed almost as if his body had grown somehow fluid, shifting, altering, flowing into the image of the wolf that he had in his mind. When the surge was gone, he sat on his haunches panting. He felt very strange.

"Stand up and let's have a look at you," Belgarath told him.

Garion rose and stood on all four paws. His tail felt extremely peculiar.

"You made the hind legs a bit too long," Belgarath noted critically.

Garion started to object that it was the first time he'd ever done it, but his voice came out in a peculiar series of whines and yelps.

"Stop that," Belgarath growled. "You sound like a puppy. Change back."

Garion did that.

"Where do your clothes go?" Silk asked curiously.

"They're with us," Belgarath replied, "but at the same time they're not. It's kind of hard to explain, actually. Beldin tried to work out exactly where the clothes were once. He seems to think he's got the answer, but I never understood the whole theory. Beldin's quite a bit more intelligent than I am, and his explanations are sometimes a bit exotic. At any rate, when we return to our original shape, our clothing is always just as it was."

"Even Garion's sword?" Silk asked. "And the Orb?"

The old man nodded.

"Isn't it sort of dangerous having it floating around out there—unattached, so to speak?"

"It isn't really unattached. It's still there—but at the same time it's not."

"I'll take your word for it," Silk conceded dubiously.

"Try it again, Garion," Belgarath suggested.

Garion switched back and forth several times until his wolf-shape satisfied his grandfather.

"Stay with the horses," the old man told Silk. "We'll be back in a little bit." He flickered and shimmered into the great gray wolf. "Let's run for a bit," he said to Garion. The meaning of what he said was conveyed directly from his mind to Garion's, aided only slightly by expressions and positions of his head and ears and a few brief barking sounds. Garion suddenly understood why the bond of the pack was so strong in wolves. Quite literally, they inhabited each others' minds. What one saw, they all saw; and what one felt, they all felt.

"Where do we run to?" Garion asked, not really surprised at how easily the speech of wolves came to him.

"No place in particular. I just need to stretch out a few kinks." And the gray wolf bounded away with astonishing speed.

The tail was a definite problem at first. Garion kept forgetting that it was there, and its swishing back and forth kept jerking him off balance. By the time he got the hang of it, the old wolf was far out ahead of him on the gray-green moors. After a while, however, Garion found himself literally flying across the ground. His paws scarcely seemed to touch the earth as he bunched and stretched his body in great bounds. He marveled at the economy of the running gait of the wolf. He ran not with his legs alone, but with his entire body. He became quite certain that, if need be, he could run for days without tiring.

The rolling moors were different somehow. What had seemed as desolate and empty as the dead sky overhead was suddenly teeming with life. There were mice and burrowing squirrels; in scrubby brown thickets, rabbits, petrified with fright, watched him as he loped by with his toenails digging into the springy turf. Silently he exulted in the strength and freedom of his new body. He was the lord of the plain, and all creatures gave way to him.

And then he was not alone. Another wolf ran beside him—a strangely insubstantial-looking wolf that seemed to have a bluish, flickering light playing about her. "And how far will you run?" she asked him in the manner of wolves.

"We can stop if you'd like," Garion replied politely, dropping back into a lope and then a trot.

"It's easier to talk if one isn't running," she agreed. She stopped and dropped to her haunches.

Garion also stopped. "You're Poledra, aren't you?" He asked it very directly, not yet accustomed to the subtleties of the language of wolves.

"Wolves have no need of names," she sniffed. "*He* used to worry about that, too." It was not exactly like the voice that had been in his mind since his child-hood. He didn't actually hear her, but instead he seemed to know exactly what she wanted to say to him.

"Grandfather, you mean?"

"Who else? Men seem to have a need to classify things and put names on them. I think they overlook some very important things that way."

"How is it that you're here? Aren't you—well—?"

"Dead, you mean? Don't be afraid of the word. It's only a word, after all. I suppose I am, though. It doesn't really feel all that much different."

"Doesn't somebody have to do something to bring you back?" he asked. "Like what Aunt Pol did that time when we were fighting with Grul in the mountains of Ulgo?"

"It's not entirely necessary. I can be summoned that way, but I can manage it myself if I have to." She looked at him quizzically. "You're really confused by all this, aren't you?"

"All of what?"

"Everything. Who you are; who we are; what you have to do."

"A little," he admitted.

"Let me see if I can explain it. Take him for instance. I never really saw him as a man, you know. There's something decidedly wolfish about him. I always rather thought that his being born in man-shape had been a mistake of some kind. Maybe it was because of what he had to do. The shape doesn't really matter, though."

"It doesn't?"

"Did you really think it did?" She almost seemed to laugh. "Here. Let me show you. Let's change." She shimmered into air and was standing before him then in the form of a tawny-haired woman with golden eyes. Her gown was very plain and brown.

Garion shrugged himself back into his natural form.

"Am I really any different, Belgarion?" she asked him. "Am I not who I am, whether as wolf or owl or woman?"

And then he understood. "May I call you Grandmother?" he asked her, a bit embarrassed.

"If it makes you happy," she replied. "It's a bit inaccurate, though."

"I know," he said, "but I feel a little more comfortable with it."

"Have you finally accepted who you are?"

"I don't have much choice, do I?"

"But you're afraid of it and what you have to do, is that it?"

He nodded mutely.

"You're not going to be alone, you know."

He looked at her sharply. "I thought the Codex said—"

"The Codex doesn't really say everything that's involved," she told him. "Your meeting with Torak will be the coming together of two enormous, opposing forces. The two of you are really just the representatives of those forces. There'll be so much power involved in your meeting that you and Torak will be almost incidental to what's really happening."

"Why couldn't somebody else do it then?" he asked quickly. "Somebody better suited to it?"

"I said *almost* incidental," she said firmly. "It has to be you, and it's always been Torak. You are the channels through which the forces will collide. When it happens, I think you'll be surprised at how easy it all is."

"Am I going to win?"

"I don't know. The universe itself doesn't know. That's why you have to meet him. If we knew how it would turn out, the meeting wouldn't be necessary." She looked around. "Belgarath's coming back. I'll have to leave you now."

"Why?"

"My presence pains him—more than you could ever know."

"Because—?" He broke off, not knowing how to say it.

"We were closer than others and we were together for a very long time. Sometimes I wish that he could understand that we haven't really been separated, but perhaps it's too early."

"It's been three thousand years, Grandmother."

"What is time to a wolf?" she asked cryptically. "The mating of wolves is permanent, and the grief caused by separation is also permanent. Perhaps someday—" Her voice trailed off wistfully, and then she sighed. "As soon as I leave, change back again. Belgarath will want you to hunt with him. It's sort of a formality. You'll understand when you're back in the shape of a wolf."

Garion nodded and began to form the image of the wolf in his mind.

"One other thing, Belgarion."

"Yes, Grandmother?"

"I do love you, you know."

"I love you too, Grandmother."

And then she was gone. Garion sighed and changed himself back into a wolf. And then he went out from that place to join Belgarath in the hunt.

PART FOUR

THE RIVAN QUEEN

The Princess Ce'Nedra was in a thoughtful, even pensive mood. Much as she had enjoyed the turmoil her periodic outbursts of temper had caused, she rather regretfully concluded that it was probably time to put them aside and make peace with Garion. They were going to be married, after all, and there was no real point in upsetting him any more than absolutely necessary. Her tantrums had established the fact that, although he might outrank her, she would not enter the marriage as his inferior, and that was really all she had wanted anyway. On the whole, the prospect of being married to Garion was not nearly as unpleasant as she pretended. She did love him after all, and now that he understood exactly how things were going to stand between them, everything was likely to be quite satisfactory. She decided to find him that very day and make peace with him.

The largest part of her attention that spring morning had been taken up by a book on protocol and a chart she was carefully drawing up. As Imperial Princess of Tolnedra *and* Queen of Riva, she would, of course, absolutely outrank every grand duchess of every house in the Empire. She was also fairly sure that she outranked Queen Islena of Cherek and Queen Silar of Algaria. Mayaserana's status as co-ruler of Arendia raised some problems, however. It was entirely possible that she and Mayaserana were equals. Ce'Nedra made a note on a scrap of parchment reminding herself to have Ambassador Valgon direct an inquiry to the chief of protocol in Tol Honeth concerning the matter. She felt a nice little glow as she surveyed the chart. With the exception of Lady Polgara and the motherly little Queen Layla of Sendaria, to whom everyone deferred because she was such a dear, Ce'Nedra concluded that she would in fact outrank or at least equal every noble lady in the West.

Suddenly there was a shattering thunderclap so violent that it shook the very walls of the Citadel. Startled, Ce'Nedra glanced at the window. It was a bright, sunny morning. How could there be thunder? Another rending crash ripped the silence, and there was a frightened babble in the halls. Impatiently, the princess picked up a small silver bell and rang for her maid.

"Go see what's happening," she instructed the girl and returned to her study of the chart she had drawn. But there was another thunderous crash and even more shouting and confusion in the corridor outside. It was impossible! How could she concentrate with all that noise going on? Irritably she rose and went to the door.

People were running—actually fleeing. Just down the hall Queen Layla of Sendaria bolted from the door of Lady Polgara's private apartment, her eyes wide with terror and her crown very nearly falling off.

"What *is* the matter, your Majesty?" Ce'Nedra demanded of the little queen.

"It's Polgara!" Queen Layla gasped, stumbling in her haste to escape. "She's destroying everything in sight!"

"Lady Polgara?"

Another deafening crash sent the little queen reeling, and she clung to Ce'Nedra in terror. "Please, Ce'Nedra. Find out what's wrong. Make her stop before she shakes down the entire fortress."

"Me?"

"She'll listen to you. She loves you. Make her stop."

Without pausing to consider the possible danger, Ce'Nedra went quickly to Lady Polgara's door and glanced inside. The apartment was a total shambles. Furniture was overturned; wall hangings had been ripped down; the windows were shattered and the air was full of smoke. Ce'Nedra had thrown enough tantrums in her own life to appreciate artistry when she saw it, but the disaster inside Polgara's apartment was so absolute that it went beyond art into the realms of natural catastrophe. Lady Polgara herself stood, wild-eyed and disheveled in the center of the room, cursing incoherently in a dozen languages at once. In one hand she held a crumpled sheet of parchment; her other hand was raised like a claw before her, half clenched about an incandescent mass of blazing energy that she seemed to have summoned out of air itself and which she now fed with her own fury. The princess stood in awe as Polgara began a fresh tirade. The dreadful cursing began in a low contralto and rose in an awful crescendo into the upper registers and beyond. As she reached the limits of her voice, she began slashing the air with the blazing mass in her hand, punctuating each curse with a crackling burst of raw energy that sizzled from between her fingers like a bolt of lightning to shatter whatever her eyes fell upon. With a series of vile oaths, she detonated six teacups in a row into shards, then quite methodically she went back down the line, exploding the saucers upon which they had sat. Almost as an afterthought, she blew the table into splinters.

Ce'Nedra heard a strangled gasp directly behind her. King Anheg, the blood drained from his face, looked once through the door, then turned and ran.

"Lady Polgara," Ce'Nedra remonstrated to the sorceress, trying not so much to reason with her as to minimize the destruction.

Polgara shattered four priceless vases standing on the mantelpiece with four precisely separate explosions. Outside the window, the bright spring morning vanished as if the sun had suddenly been extinguished, and there was a sullen rumble of thunder that Ce'Nedra prayed devoutly was natural.

"Whatever is the matter?" the princess asked, hoping to draw the enraged sorceress into explanation rather than more curses. It was the curses that had to be headed off. Polgara seemed to have a deep-seated need to emphasize her oaths with explosions.

Polgara, however, did not reply. Instead she merely threw the parchment at Ce'Nedra, turned, and blew a marble statue into fine white gravel. Wild-eyed, she wheeled about, looking for something else to break, but there was very little left in the smoking room that she had not already reduced to rubble.

"No!" Ce'Nedra cried out sharply as the raging woman's eyes fell on the exquisite crystal wren Garion had given her. The princess knew that Polgara valued the glass bird more than anything else she possessed, and she leaped forward to protect the delicate piece.

"Get it," Polgara snarled at her from between clenched teeth. "Take it out of my sight." Her eyes burned with a terrible need to destroy something else. She spun and hurled the incandescent ball of fire she had wielded out through the shattered window. The explosion, when it burst in the suddenly murky air outside, was ghastly. With her fists clenched tightly at her sides, she raised her distorted face and began to curse again. From roiling black clouds that had suddenly appeared out of nowhere, shattering bolts of lightning began to rain down on the island. No longer satisfied with localized destruction, Polgara expanded her rage to rake the Isle and the Sea of the Winds with sizzling fire and earsplitting thunder. Then, with a dreadful intensity, she raised one fist and suddenly opened it. The downpour of rain she called was beyond belief. Her glittering eyes narrowed, and she raised her other fist. The rain instantly turned to hail—great, jagged chunks of ice that crashed and splintered against the rocks to fill the air with flying fragments and thick steam.

Ce'Nedra caught up the wren, stooped to grab the rumpled piece of parchment from the floor, and then she fled.

King Anheg poked his frightened face from around a corner. "Can't you stop her?" he demanded in a shaking voice.

"Nothing can stop her, your Majesty."

"Anheg! Get in here!" Polgara's voice rang above the thunder and the crashing deluge of hail that shook the Citadel.

"Oh, Belar," King Anheg muttered devoutly, casting his eyes skyward even as he hurried toward Polgara's door.

"Get word to Val Alorn immediately!" she commanded him. "My father, Silk, and Garion slipped out of the Citadel last night. Get your fleet out and bring them back! I don't care if you have to take the world apart stone by stone. Find them and bring them back!"

"Polgara, I—" The King of Cherek faltered.

"Don't stand there gaping like an idiot! *Move!*"

Carefully, almost with a studied calm, the Princess Ce'Nedra handed the glass wren to her frightened maid. "Put this someplace safe," she said. Then she turned and went back to the center of the storm. "What was that you just said?" she asked Polgara in a level voice.

"My idiot father, Garion, and that disgusting thief decided last night to go off on their own," Polgara replied in an icy voice made even more terrible by the superhuman control that held it in.

"They did what?" Ce'Nedra asked flatly.

"They left. They sneaked away during the night."

"Then you must go after them."

"I can't, Ce'Nedra." Polgara spoke as if explaining something to a child. "Someone has to stay here. There are too many things here that could go wrong. He knows that. He did it deliberately. He's trapped me here."

"Garion?"

"No, you silly girl! My father!" And Polgara began cursing again, each oath punctuated with a crash of thunder.

Ce'Nedra, however, scarcely heard her. She looked around. There was really nothing left to break in here. "You'll excuse me, I hope," she said. Then she turned, went back to her own rooms, and began breaking everything she could lay her hands on, screeching all the while like a Camaar fishwife.

Their separate rages lasted for several hours, and they rather carefully avoided each other during this period. Some emotions needed to be shared, but insane fury was not one of those. Eventually, Ce'Nedra felt she had exhausted the possibilities of her extended outburst, and she settled into the icy calm of one who has been mortally insulted. No matter what face his illiterate note put on the matter, it would be at the very most a week before the entire world knew that Garion had jilted her. The flight of her reluctant bridegroom would become a universal joke. It was absolutely intolerable!

She would meet the world, however, with a lifted chin and an imperious gaze. However she might weep and storm and rage in private, the face she presented to the world would betray no hint of how deeply she had been injured. All that was left for her was her pride, and she would never abandon that.

The Lady Polgara, however, seemed to feel no need for such imperial reserve. Once her initial fury had subsided to the degree that she allowed her private thunderstorm to pass, a few hardy souls assumed that the worst of it was over. The Earl of Trellheim went to her in an attempt to mollify her. He left her apartment moments later at a run with her crackling vituperation sizzling in the air about his ears. Barak was pale and shaken when he reported back to the others. "Don't go near her," he advised in a frightened voice. "Do whatever she says as quickly as you can, and stay absolutely out of her sight."

"Isn't she calming down at all?" King Rhodar asked.

"She's finished breaking the furniture," Barak replied. "I think she's getting ready to start on people."

Thereafter, each time Polgara emerged from her apartment, the warning spread instantly, and the halls of Iron-grip's Citadel emptied. Her commands, delivered usually by her maid, were all variations of the initial orders she had given King Anheg. They were to find the vagrant trio and bring them back to face her.

In the days that followed, Princess Ce'Nedra's first rage settled into a sort of peevishness that made people avoid her almost as much as they avoided Polgara—all but gentle Adara, who endured the tiny girl's outbursts with a calm patience. The two of them spent most of their time sitting in the garden adjoining the royal apartments where Ce'Nedra could give vent to her emotions without fear of being overheard.

It was five days after Garion and the others had left before Ce'Nedra discovered the full implications of their departure.

The day was warm—spring came eventually even to a bleak place like Riva—and the small bit of lawn in the center of the garden was a lush green. Pink, blue, and flaming red flowers nodded in their beds as bright yellow bees industriously carried kisses from blossom to blossom. Ce'Nedra, however, did not want to think about kisses. Dressed in her favorite pale green Dryad tunic, she bit rather savagely at an unoffending lock of hair and spoke to the patient Adara at length about the inconstancy of men.

It was about midafternoon when Queen Layla of Sendaria found them there. "Oh, there you are," the plump little queen bubbled at them. As always, her crown was a little awry. "We've been looking all over for you."

"Why?" was Ce'Nedra's somewhat ungracious reply.

Queen Layla stopped and looked critically at the princess. "My," she said, "aren't we cross today? Just what is your problem, Ce'Nedra? You've barely been civil for days now."

Ce'Nedra caught Adara's warning look to the queen, and that irritated her all the more. Her response was chilly. "I'm finding the experience of being jilted to be just a bit annoying, your Highness," she said.

Queen Layla's sunny face hardened. "Would you excuse us, Adara?" she asked.

"Of course, your Highness," Adara replied, rising quickly. "I'll be inside, Ce'Nedra," she said and went gracefully out of the garden.

Queen Layla waited until the girl was out of earshot, then sat down on a marble bench. "Come here, Ce'Nedra," she said firmly.

The princess looked at the motherly little woman, a bit startled by the iron in her voice. Obediently she went to the bench and sat.

"You really should stop interpreting everything that happens in the world as a personal insult, you know," Layla told her. "That's a very unbecoming habit. What Garion, Belgarath, and Kheldar did has absolutely nothing to do with you." She looked sternly at Ce'Nedra. "Do you know anything at all about the Prophecy?"

"I've heard about it," Ce'Nedra sulked. "Tolnedrans don't really believe in that sort of thing."

"Perhaps that's the problem," Layla said. "I want you to listen very carefully, Ce'Nedra. You may not believe, but you *will* understand." The queen thought for a moment. "The Prophecy clearly states that when the Rivan King returns, Torak will awaken."

"Torak? That's nonsense. Torak's dead."

"Don't interrupt, dear," Layla told her. "You traveled with them for all that time and you still don't understand? For a little girl who seems so bright, you're remarkably dense."

Ce'Nedra flushed at that.

"Torak is a God, Ce'Nedra," Layla continued. "He's asleep, not dead. He did not die at Vo Mimbre, much as some people might like to think he did. The instant that Garion touched the Orb, Torak began to stir. Haven't you ever wondered why Polgara insisted that Errand carry the Orb back from Rak Cthol? Garion could have carried it just as easily, you know."

Ce'Nedra hadn't thought of that.

"But if Garion had touched it—still on Angarak soil and without his sword—Torak might very well have jumped up and gone after him immediately, and Garion would have been killed."

"Killed?" Ce'Nedra gasped.

"Of course, dear. That's what this is all about. The Prophecy says that Torak and the Rivan King will eventually meet, and that in their meeting shall be decided the fate of mankind."

"Garion?" Ce'Nedra exclaimed, stunned and disbelieving. "Surely you're not serious?"

"I've never been more serious in my life, child. Garion has to fight Torak—to the death—to decide the fate of the world. Now do you understand? That's why Belgarath and Kheldar and Garion left Riva so suddenly. They're on their way to Mallorea so that Garion can fight Torak. He could have taken an army with him, but he knew that would only cause needless deaths. That's why the three of them went alone. Now don't you think it's time that you grew up just a little bit?"

Ce'Nedra was greatly subdued after her conversation with Queen Layla. For perhaps the first time in her life, she began to think more about someone else than she did about herself. She worried constantly about Garion, and at night she had dreadful nightmares about the hideous things that could happen to him.

To make matters worse, there seemed to be a persistent buzzing in her ears that was at times quite maddening. It was rather like the sound of voices coming from a long way off—voices that verged just on the edge of being understandable, but never quite were. The buzzing sound, coupled with her anxiety about Garion, made her moody and frequently short-tempered. Even Adara began to avoid her.

The irritating sound in her ears continued for several days before she discovered, quite by accident, the significance of it. The weather on the Isle of the Winds was never really very good, and spring was a particularly unpredictable time of year. A series of storms, following one after another in dreary progression, lashed at the rocky coast, and nasty little rain squalls swept the city and the island. One somber, rainy morning the princess sat in her chambers looking glumly out the window at the soggy garden. The fire which crackled on her hearth did little to warm her mood. After a while she sighed and, for want of anything better to do, she sat at her dressing table and began to brush her hair.

The silver flicker at her throat distracted her eye momentarily as she looked at herself in the mirror. It was the medallion Garion had given her just after her birthday. She had by now grown accustomed to its being there, though the fact that she could not take it off still caused her periodic fits of anger. Without actually thinking about it, she stopped brushing and touched the amulet with her fingertips.

"—but we can't do a thing until the Arends and the Tolnedrans are fully mobilized." It was the voice of King Rhodar of Drasnia. Ce'Nedra started and turned quickly, wondering why the portly monarch had entered her room. As soon as she removed her fingers from the silver amulet, the voice stopped. Ce'Nedra looked around, puzzled. She frowned and touched the amulet again. "No, no," another voice said, "you don't add the spices until after it starts to boil." Ce'Nedra again removed her fingertips from the talisman at her throat, and that voice too stopped abruptly. Fascinated, she touched it for the third time. "You make up the bed, and I'll straighten up. We'll have to hurry. The Queen of Cherek might come back at any minute."

Wonderingly, the princess touched the amulet again and again, and her ears ranged randomly through the Citadel.

"The fire's too hot. This iron will scorch anything it touches."

Then she heard a snatch of whispered conversation. "What if somebody comes?" It was a girl's voice.

"Nobody's going to come." The young man's voice which replied had a peculiar wheedling quality. "We're all safe and cozy here, and I really do love you."

Ce'Nedra quickly jerked her fingers from the amulet, blushing furiously.

At first there was no direction to it; but as the princess experimented, she gradually learned to focus this peculiar phenomenon. After a couple of hours of intense concentration, she found that she could skim rapidly through all the talking that was going on in a given quarter of the Citadel until she found a conversation that interested her. In the process she learned many secrets, some very interesting, and some not very nice. She knew that she should feel guilty about her surreptitious eavesdropping, but for some reason she did not.

"Thy reasoning is sound, your Majesty." It was Mandorallen's voice. "King Korodullin is committed to the cause, though it will take some weeks for his call to arms to gather the forces of Arendia. Our major concern must be the position the Emperor will take in the affair. Without the legions, our situation is perilous."

"Ran Borune has no choice in the matter," King Anheg declared. "He's bound by the provisions of the Accords of Vo Mimbre."

Brand, the Rivan Warder, cleared his throat. "I don't think it's that simple, your Majesty," he said quietly in his deep voice. "The Accords state that the Kingdoms of the West must respond to a call from the Rivan King, and Belgarion is not here to issue that call."

"We're acting in his behalf," King Cho-Hag asserted.

"The problem lies in convincing Ran Borune of that," Rhodar pointed out. "I know the Tolnedrans. They'll have whole battalions of legal experts working on the Accords. Unless Belgarion himself meets Ran Borune face to face and issues his command in person, the Emperor will take the position that he's not legally bound to join us. The Rivan King is the only one who can issue a call to war."

Ce'Nedra let her fingertips drop from the amulet at her throat. An idea was beginning to take shape in her mind. It was an exciting idea, but she was not at all certain that she could bring it off. Alorns, she knew, were stubborn and reluctant to accept any new ideas. She quickly laid aside her hairbrush and went to a small chest standing against the wall near the window. She opened the chest and began rummaging through it. After a moment she found the tightly rolled parchment she had been seeking. She unrolled it and read through it quickly until she found the passage she wanted. She read it carefully several times. It seemed to say what she wanted it to say.

She considered the idea throughout the rest of the day. The possibility that anyone might succeed in catching up with Garion and stopping him was remote, to say the very least. Belgarath and Prince Kheldar were too skilled at evasion to allow themselves to be easily caught. Chasing them was simply a waste of time. Since Polgara was not yet rational enough to see things in this light, it fell to Ce'Nedra to take immediate steps to minimize Garion's danger once he had entered the lands of the Angaraks. All she had to do now was convince the Alorn Kings that she was the logical one to take those steps.

It was still raining the next morning, and she rose early to make her preparations.

She must, of course, look positively regal. Her choice of an emerald velvet gown and matching cape was artful. She knew that she was stunning in green, and her circlet of gold oak leaves was enough like a crown to convey the right suggestion. She was glad she had waited until morning. Men were easier to deal with in the morning, she had discovered. They would fight her at first, and she wanted the idea implanted in their minds before they were fully awake. As she gave herself a last-minute check in the tall mirror in her dressing room, she gathered her determination and marshaled all her arguments. The slightest objection must be met instantly. Carefully she put herself in an imperial frame of mind and, taking the rolled parchment, she moved toward the door.

The council chamber in which the Alorn Kings usually gathered was a large room high up in one of the massive towers of the Citadel. There were heavy beams on the ceiling, a deep maroon carpet on the floor, and a fireplace at the far end big enough to stand in. Maroon drapes flanked the windows where tatters of rain slashed across the solid stones of the tower. The walls of the chamber were covered with maps, and the large table was littered with parchments and ale cups. King Anheg, in his blue robe and dented crown, sprawled in the nearest chair, as shaggy and brutish-looking as always. King Rhodar was vast in his crimson mantle, but the other kings and generals wore rather plain clothing.

Ce'Nedra entered the chamber without knocking and stared regally at the somewhat confused men who struggled to their feet in acknowledgment of her presence.

"Your Highness," King Rhodar began with a portly bow. "You honor us. Was there—"

"Your Majesty," she responded with a little curtsy, "and gentlemen, I find that I need your advice in a matter of state."

"We are all at your immediate disposal, your Highness," King Rhodar replied with a sly little twinkle in his eyes.

"In the absence of King Belgarion, it appears that I must act in his stead," Ce'Nedra announced, "and I need your advice on how to proceed. I wish the transfer of power into my hands to go as smoothly as possible."

They all stared at her disbelievingly.

King Rhodar recovered his wits first. "An interesting proposal, your Highness," he murmured politely. "We have, however, made other arrangements. There's a long-standing precedent in the matter. We thank your Highness for her gracious offer nonetheless."

"It was not precisely an offer, your Majesty," Ce'Nedra told him, "and any previous precedents have been superceded."

King Anheg was spluttering, but Rhodar was already moving along smoothly. Ce'Nedra realized that the rotund Drasnian king was likely to be her most serious adversary—or her most effective ally. "We'd all be fascinated to examine the instrument vesting your Highness with royal authority," he said. "I presume that the parchment you carry is relevant?"

"It is indeed, your Majesty," Ce'Nedra declared. "The document quite clearly lists my responsibilities."

"May I?" Rhodar asked, extending his hand.

Ce'Nedra handed him the parchment and he carefully unrolled it. "Uh—your Highness. This is your betrothal agreement. Perhaps you meant to bring a different document."

"The pertinent material is contained in the fourth paragraph, your Majesty."

Rhodar quickly read the paragraph, frowning slightly.

"What does it say, Rhodar?" King Anheg asked impatiently.

"Interesting," Rhodar murmured, scratching his ear.

"Rhodar," Anheg complained, "what does it *say*?"

King Rhodar cleared his throat and began to read aloud. " 'It is agreed that King Belgarion and his Queen shall rule jointly, and that in his absence shall she assume fully the duties and authority of the Rivan Throne.' "

"Let me see that," Anheg demanded, snatching the parchment from Rhodar.

"It doesn't mean anything," Brand declared. "She isn't his queen yet. She won't be until after the wedding."

"That's only a formality, my Lord Warder," Ce'Nedra told him.

"A rather important one, I'd say," he retorted.

"The precedent is well established," she said coolly. "When a king dies, the next in line assumes the duties of the crown, doesn't he, even though there hasn't been a formal coronation?"

"That's different," Brand growled.

"I fail to see the difference, my Lord. I have been designated Belgarion's co-ruler. In his absence or an emergency, I am obliged to take command. It is my right and my responsibility. The formalities may have to wait, but I *am* the Rivan Queen. This is King Belgarion's will and intent. Will you defy your king?"

"There's something to what she says, my Lord Warder," the Earl of Seline mused. "The document is quite clear."

"But look at this," Anheg said triumphantly. "In paragraph two it says that should the wedding not take place, all gifts are to be returned. The wedding has not taken place."

"I'm not sure that power is a gift, Anheg," King Fulrach suggested. "You can't give it and then take it back."

"There's no way she could rule," Anheg declared stubbornly. "She doesn't know the first thing about Alorns."

"Neither did Garion," King Cho-Hag murmured in his quiet voice. "She can learn the same way he did."

Ce'Nedra had been rather carefully assessing their mood. Most of them seemed willing at least to consider her idea. Only the two conservatives, Brand and Anheg, were actually resisting. It seemed the time now for a dignified withdrawal coupled with a disarming offer. "I will leave you gentlemen to discuss the matter," she declared somewhat loftily. "I would like you to know, however, that I realize the gravity of the situation confronting the West." She deliberately put on a winsome, little-girl face. "I'm only a young girl," she confessed, "unused to the intricacies of strategy and tactics. I could never make any decisions in that area without the fullest advice from you gentlemen."

She curtsied then to King Rhodar, choosing him deliberately. "Your Majesty," she said, "I shall await your decision."

He bowed in response, a bit floridly. "Your Majesty," he replied with a sly wink.

Ce'Nedra retired and literally flew down the corridors to her own quarters. Breathlessly she closed the door behind her and touched the talisman at her throat with trembling fingertips. She sorted quickly through random conversation until she found the one she wanted.

"—refuse to be a party to an absurdity," Anheg was saying.

"Anheg, my friend," King Fulrach of Sendaria said with surprising firmness, "you are my dear brother king, but you do have a few blind spots. Wouldn't it be more statesmanlike to consider the advantages and disadvantages of the situation dispassionately?"

"The Alorns will never follow her," Anheg declared. "That's a major disadvantage right there."

"The Alorns will follow us, though," King Cho-Hag said quietly. "She's only going to be a figurehead, after all—a symbol of unity."

"I suspect that Cho-Hag's hit the exact point we should examine most closely," King Rhodar urged. "My apologies, Baron Mandorallen, but the Arends are totally disunited. Asturia and Mimbre are hovering on the verge of reopening hostilities, and a call from King Korodullin could very possibly be ignored in northern Arendia—in which case the Mimbrate knights would almost be compelled to stay home to defend against possible Asturian uprisings. We have to have someone who can make them forget their squabbles and join with us. We need the Asturian bowmen and the Mimbrate knights."

"I must sadly concur, your Majesty," Mandorallen agreed. "My poor Arendia must needs be united in one cause from the outside. We are not wise enough to unify ourselves."

"Ce'Nedra can serve us there as well as Garion could have done," Barak reasoned. "I don't think anybody expected him to be a general. All we were going to do was put a crown on him and let him ride at the head of the army—and Arends get all gushy and romantic about pretty girls. That betrothal document makes her claim at least semi-legitimate. All we'd have to do is act as if *we* accepted her and talk very fast. Add the prospect of a nice little war someplace, and the Arends will unite behind us, I think."

"The main point to consider, though," King Rhodar emphasized, "is the impact she's going to have in Tolnedra. Ran Borune dotes on her, and he might agree to lend her his legions—at least some of them—which he'd never do if we were the ones asking it of him. He'll see the political advantage of having her in command almost immediately. We need those legions. I personally don't like Tolnedrans, but the legions are the finest fighting force in the world. I'll bend my knee to Ce'Nedra if I have to in order to get them. Let her play queen if she wants to."

Ce'Nedra smiled. Things were going even better than she had expected. All in all, she was quite pleased with herself as she sat down at her dressing table and began to brush her hair, humming softly all the while.

CHAPTER TWENTY-THREE

Delban the armorer was a gruff, bald man with broad shoulders, huge callused hands and a grizzled beard. He was a craftsman, an artist, and he had absolutely no respect for anyone. Ce'Nedra found him to be impossible.

"I don't make armor for women," was his initial response to her inquiry when she, accompanied by Durnik the smith, entered his workshop. He had then turned his back on her and begun pounding noisily on a sheet of glowing steel. It took the better part of an hour to convince him even to consider the idea. The heat shimmered out from his glowing forge, and the redbrick walls seemed to reflect the heat and intensify it. Ce'Nedra found herself perspiring heavily. She had made some sketches of what she thought might be a suitable design for her armor. All in all, she thought it would look rather nice, but Delban laughed raucously when he saw them.

"What's so amusing?" she demanded.

"You'd be like a turtle in something like that," he replied. "You wouldn't be able to move."

"The drawings are only intended to give you a general idea," she told him, trying to keep a grip on her temper.

"Why don't you be a good girl and take these to a dressmaker?" he suggested. "I work in steel, not brocade or satin. Armor like this would be useless and so uncomfortable that you wouldn't be able to wear it."

"Then modify it," she grated from between clenched teeth.

He glanced at her design again, then deliberately crumpled her drawings in his fist and threw them into the corner. "Foolishness," he grunted.

Ce'Nedra resisted the urge to scream. She retrieved the drawings. "What's the matter with them?" she persisted.

"Too much here." He stabbed a thick finger at the shoulder represented on the drawing. "You wouldn't be able to lift your arm. And here." He pointed at the armhole on the breastplate she had drawn. "If I make it that tight, your arms would stick straight out. You wouldn't even be able to scratch your nose. As long as we're at it, where did you get the whole notion in the first place? Do you want a mail shirt or a breastplate? You can't have both."

"Why not?"

"The weight. You wouldn't be able to carry it."

"Make it lighter then. Can't you do that?"

"I can make it like cobwebs if you want, but what good would it be if I did? You could cut through it with a paring knife."

Ce'Nedra drew in a deep breath. "Master armorer," she said to him in a level voice, "look at me. In all the world do you think there's a single warrior small enough for me to fight?"

He considered her tiny form, scratching his bald head and looking down at her with pursed lips. "You *are* a bit undergrown," he admitted. "If you aren't going to fight, why do you need armor?"

"It's not actually going to be armor," she explained to him rather impatiently, "but I need to look like I'm wearing armor. It's sort of in the nature of a costume." She saw instantly that her choice of words had been a mistake. Delban's face darkened, and he threw her drawings away again. It took another ten minutes to mollify him. Eventually, after much wheedling and outrageous flattery, she persuaded him to consider the whole notion as something in the nature of an artistic challenge.

"All right," he surrendered finally with a sour look, "take off your clothes."

"*What?*"

"Take your dress off," he repeated. "I need exact measurements."

"Do you realize what you're suggesting?"

"Little girl," he said testily, "I'm a married man. I've got daughters older than you are. You are wearing underclothes, aren't you?"

"Yes, but—"

"That'll satisfy the demands of modesty. Take off the dress."

With a flaming face, Ce'Nedra removed her dress. Durnik the smith, who had watched the entire exchange from the doorway with an open grin on his face, politely turned his back.

"You ought to eat more," Delban told her. "You're as scrawny as a chicken."

"I can do without the comments," she replied tartly. "Get on with this. I'm not going to stand around in my chemise all day."

Delban picked up a piece of stout cord with knots tied in it at regular intervals. He took a great many measurements with the cord, meticulously recording them on a piece of flat board. "All right," he said finally. "That ought to do it. Go ahead and get dressed again."

Ce'Nedra scrambled back into her dress. "How long will it take?" she asked.

"Two or three weeks."

"Impossible. I need it next week."

"Two weeks," he repeated stubbornly.

"Ten days," she countered.

For the first time since she had entered his workshop, the blunt man smiled. "She's used to getting her own way, isn't she?" he observed to Durnik.

"She's a princess," Durnik informed him. "She usually gets what she wants in the end."

"All right, my scrawny little princess." Delban laughed. "Ten days."

Ce'Nedra beamed at him. "I knew you'd see it my way."

Precisely ten days later, the princess, with Durnik once again in tow, returned to Delban's workshop. The mail shirt the craftsman had fashioned was so light that it could almost have been described as delicate. The helmet, hammered from thin steel, was surmounted with a white plume and was encircled with a gold crown. The greaves, which were to protect the fronts of Ce'Nedra's legs, fit to perfection. There was even an embossed shield rimmed with brass and a light sword with an ornate hilt and scabbard.

Ce'Nedra, however, was staring disapprovingly at the breastplate Delban had made for her. It would quite obviously fit—too well. "Didn't you forget something?" she asked him.

He picked the breastplate up in his big hands and examined it. "It's all there," he told her. "Front, back, all the straps to hook them together. What else did you want?"

"Isn't it a trifle—understated?" Ce'Nedra suggested delicately.

"It's made to fit," he replied. "The understatement isn't my fault."

"I want it a little more—" She made a sort of curving gesture with her hands. "What for?"

"Never mind what for. Just do it."

"What do you plan to put in it?"

"That's my business. Just do it the way I told you to."

He tossed a heavy hammer down on his anvil. "Do it yourself," he told her bluntly.

"Durnik," Ce'Nedra appealed to the smith.

"Oh, no, Princess," Durnik refused. "I don't touch another man's tools. That just isn't done."

"Please, Delban," she wheedled.

"It's foolishness," he told her, his face set.

"It's important," she coaxed. "If I wear it like that, I'll look like a little boy. When people see me, they have to know that I'm a woman. It's terribly, terribly important. Couldn't you—well—just a little bit?" She cupped her hands slightly.

Delban gave Durnik a disgusted look. "You had to bring her to my workshop, didn't you?"

"Everybody said you were the best," Durnik replied mildly.

"Just a little bit, Delban?" Ce'Nedra urged.

Delban gave up. "Oh, all right," he growled, picking up his hammer. "Anything to get you out of my shop—but not clear out to here." He made an exaggerated gesture.

"I'll depend on your good taste, Delban." She smiled, patting his cheek with a fond little laugh. "Shall we say tomorrow morning?"

The armor, Ce'Nedra decided the following morning as she inspected herself in the mirror, was perfect. "Well, what do you think, Adara?" she asked her friend.

"It looks very nice, Ce'Nedra," the tall girl replied, although a bit dubiously.

"It's just exactly right," Ce'Nedra said happily, turning so that the blue cape fastened to the shoulder pieces of the breastplate flared and swirled dramatically. The gleaming mail shirt she wore under the breastplate reached to her knees and wrists. The greaves covering her calves and the armguards reaching to her elbows were inlaid with brass; Delban had steadfastly refused the notion of gold. The armor did chafe a bit through the thick linen undershirt she wore, Ce'Nedra privately admitted, but she was prepared to accept that. She brandished her sword, studying the effect in her mirror.

"You're holding it wrong, Ce'Nedra," Adara suggested politely.

"Show me," Ce'Nedra said, handing over her sword.

Adara took the weapon and gripped it firmly, its point low. She looked extremely competent.

"Where did you ever learn to do that?" Ce'Nedra asked her.

"We're given instruction," Adara replied, handing back the sword. "It's traditional."

"Help me on with my shield."

Between them, they managed to gird the princess in all her warlike equipment.

"How ever do you keep it from getting tangled up in your legs?" Ce'Nedra demanded, fumbling with the long scabbard at her waist.

"Hold on to the hilt," Adara told her. "Do you want me to go along?"

Ce'Nedra thought about that as she smoothed her hair and settled her plumed helmet more firmly in place. "I guess not," she decided rather reluctantly. "I think I'll have to face them alone. Do I really look all right?"

"You'll be fine," Adara assured her.

A sudden thought struck the princess. "What if they laugh?" she demanded in a frightened voice.

"You could draw your sword on them, I suppose," Adara replied gravely.

"Are you making fun of me, Adara?"

"Of course not, Princess," Adara answered with an absolutely straight face.

When Ce'Nedra reached the door to the council chamber, she drew in a deep breath and entered, once again without knocking. Knocking would have been inappropriate, suggesting somehow that she had doubts about her right to be there.

"Well, gentlemen?" she said to the assembled kings and generals as she stepped to the center of the room where they could all see her.

King Rhodar rose politely. "Your Majesty," he greeted her, bowing. "We were curious about your absence. The reason is now abundantly clear."

"Do you approve?" she could not help asking. She turned so they could all see her armor.

King Rhodar looked at her, his eyes speculative. "It *is* impressive, don't you think?" he said to the others. "Just the right touches in the right places. The Arends will flock to her, and the Tolnedrans—well, we'll have to see about the Tolnedrans."

King Anheg looked like a man having a serious struggle with himself. "Why do I feel that I'm being pushed into something?" he complained. "The very notion of this makes my blood cold, but I can't think of any rational arguments against it." He critically scrutinized Ce'Nedra. "She doesn't really look all that bad, does she?" he conceded grudgingly. "It's absolutely unnatural, of course, but the armor does add something. This might even work."

"I'm so glad I meet with your Majesty's approval," Ce'Nedra almost gushed at him. She tried to curtsy, but her armor made that impossible. She gave a helpless little laugh and fluttered her eyelashes at the brutish-looking King of Cherek.

"Don't do that, Ce'Nedra," he told her irritably. "I'm having enough trouble with this as it is." He almost glared at her. "All right," he said finally, "as long as we all understand that she's not going to make any decisions, I'll go along with the idea. I don't like it much, but that's beside the point, I suppose." He stood up and bowed to her. "Your Majesty," he said, looking as if the words nearly choked him.

Ce'Nedra beamed at him and instinctively tried to respond to his bow.

"Don't bow, Ce'Nedra," he advised her with a pained look. "The Overlord of the West doesn't bow to anyone." He turned in exasperation to the King of Drasnia. "That isn't going to work, Rhodar. What are we going to call her? The Overlady of the West? We'll be the laughing stock of the twelve kingdoms if we do."

"We call her the Rivan Queen, my dear Anheg," King Rhodar replied urbanely. "And we break the head of any man who refuses to bow to her."

"You can count on that." Anheg scowled. "If I bow to her, everybody's going to bow to her."

"I'm glad that's all been settled," a familiar voice came from a dim corner of the council chamber.

"Lady Polgara," Ce'Nedra gasped with a certain confusion. "I didn't realize you were here."

"That's fairly obvious," Polgara replied. "You *have* been busy, haven't you, dear?"

"I—" Ce'Nedra faltered.

Polgara carefully set down her teacup and moved into the light. Her face was serious, but there was a faintly amused twinkle in her eyes as she examined the armor-clad princess. "Very interesting," was all she said.

Ce'Nedra was crushed.

"Gentlemen," Polgara said to the council, "I'm sure you still have much to discuss. In the meantime, her Majesty and I need to have a little discussion of our own. I'm sure you'll excuse us." She moved toward the door. "Come along, Ce'Nedra," she said without so much as a backward glance.

Trembling, the princess followed her from the room.

Polgara said nothing until the door to her own chambers had closed behind them. Then she turned and looked gravely at the princess in her armor. "I've heard about what you've been up to, Ce'Nedra. Would you care to explain?"

"They were all arguing so much," Ce'Nedra began lamely. "They needed somebody to unite them."

"And you decided to take that upon yourself?"

"Well—"

"How did you know they were arguing?"

Ce'Nedra flushed guiltily.

"I see," Polgara murmured. "You've discovered how to use my sister's amulet. How clever of you."

"Let me do it, Lady Polgara!" Ce'Nedra pleaded suddenly. "Let me lead them; I know I can do it. Let me prove that I'm fit to be Garion's queen."

Polgara gazed at her thoughtfully. "You're growing up very rapidly, Ce'Nedra," she said finally.

"You'll let me do it?"

"We'll talk about it. Take off your helmet and shield, dear, and stand your sword over in the corner. I'll make us a nice cup of tea, and you can tell me exactly what you've got in mind. I'd rather not have any surprises, once we get started in this."

"You're going with us?" For some reason that startled Ce'Nedra.

"Of course I am," Polgara told her. She smiled then. "Possibly I can keep at least you out of trouble. I seem not to have had much success with Garion." She stopped and looked rather pointedly at Ce'Nedra's breastplate. "Isn't that a trifle overdone, dear?"

Ce'Nedra blushed. "I thought it would be more—well—" She floundered with it defensively.

"Ce'Nedra," Polgara told her, "you don't have to be so self-conscious. You're still a young girl, after all. Give it some time. Things will improve."

"I'm so flat," the princess wailed, almost in despair about it. A thought occurred to her. "Do you suppose you could—well—" She made a sort of a gesture.

"No, dear," Polgara said firmly. "That wouldn't be a good idea. It would do some very strange things to certain necessary balances within you, and those are not the sort of things to be tampered with. Just be patient. If nothing else, a few children will fill you out."

"Oh, Lady Polgara," Ce'Nedra said with a helpless little laugh, "you seem to know everything. You're like the mother I never had." Impulsively she threw her arms about Polgara's neck.

Polgara wrinkled her nose. "Ce'Nedra," she suggested, "why don't you take off your armor? You smell like an iron pot."

Ce'Nedra began to laugh.

In the days that followed, a number of people left Riva on important missions. Barak sailed north to Val Alorn to attend the outfitting of the Cherek fleet. Mandorallen left for Vo Mimbre to report to King Korodullin. The fiery young Lelldorin, who had received a pardon at Garion's request, took ship to return to Asturia to make certain preparations there. Hettar, Relg, and Colonel Brendig departed for Camaar, where they would separate and each would return home to oversee the final stages of the mobilization. Events, which always moved at their own pace, began to stir and quicken as the West moved inexorably toward war.

CHAPTER TWENTY-FOUR

Princess Ce'Nedra soon discovered that Alorns were a surprisingly emotional people. She was forced from the outset to abandon the stereotypical Tolnedran view of this northern race as brutish savages, ravening on the extreme edges of civilization. She found them instead to be an extraordinarily complex people often capable of an extreme range of highly subtle emotions.

There was nothing subtle, however, about the apoplectic fury of King Anheg of Cherek when he came bursting into the council chamber a few days later with his eyes bulging and his face aflame. "Do you have any idea what you've done?" he bellowed at Ce'Nedra.

"Done to what, your Majesty?" she replied calmly.

"To Cherek!" he shouted, his dented crown sliding down over one ear. "This little game you've been playing gave my wife the brilliant idea that she's going to run my country while I'm gone."

"She's your wife, King Anheg," Ce'Nedra pointed out coolly. "It's only proper that she should mind the kingdom in your absence."

"*Mind?*" he almost screamed. "Islena doesn't have a mind. There's nothing between her ears but empty air."

"Why did you marry her then?"

"It certainly wasn't for her mind."

"She might surprise you, Anheg," King Rhodar suggested with an amused look on his face.

"The only thing that'd surprise me would be to find anything left when I get back," Anheg retorted, collapsing in a chair. "And there's nothing I can do to stop her. No matter what I say, she'll assume the throne as soon as I leave. It's going to be a disaster. Women have no business in politics. They're too weak-brained for it."

"I'm afraid that suggestion won't endear you very much in this particular company, Anheg." King Rhodar chuckled, glancing at Polgara. One of her eyebrows had shot up at Anheg's last remark.

"Oh—sorry, Polgara," Anheg muttered, embarrassed. "I didn't mean you, of course. I don't really think of you as a woman."

"I wouldn't pursue it any further, Anheg," King Rhodar advised him. "You've blundered quite enough for one day already."

"That's all right, Rhodar," Polgara said in a frigid tone. "I find the observations of the King of Cherek most interesting."

Anheg winced.

"I really can't understand you, my friend," King Rhodar said to Anheg. "You've given yourself the finest education in the north. You've studied art and poetry and history and philosophy, but on this one subject you're as blind as an illiterate peasant. What disturbs you so much about the idea of a woman with authority?"

"It's—it's unnatural," Anheg blurted. "Women were not meant to rule. The whole idea violates the order of things."

"I'm not certain that we're getting anywhere with this," Polgara observed. "If you gentlemen will excuse us, her Majesty and I still have preparations to make." She rose and led Ce'Nedra from the council chamber.

"He's very excitable, isn't he?" Ce'Nedra said as the two of them passed through the corridors of Iron-grip's Citadel toward Lady Polgara's apartments.

"He tends to be overdramatic at times," Polgara replied. "These outbursts of his aren't always genuine. Sometimes he behaves the way he does because he thinks people expect it of him." She frowned slightly. "He's right about one thing, though. Islena's not qualified to rule. I think we'll have to have a talk with her—and with the other ladies as well." She opened the door to her apartment, and the two of them went inside.

Most of the damage that had resulted from Polgara's vast rage had been repaired, and there remained only a few scorchmarks on the stone walls to testify to the violence of her fury. She seated herself at a table and turned again to the letter which had arrived that morning from Queen Porenn in Drasnia. "I think it's rather obvious that we're not going to be able to catch up with my father and the others now," she observed somewhat regretfully, "but at least there's one thing we won't have to worry about anymore."

"Which one is that?" Ce'Nedra asked, seating herself across the table from Polgara.

"There'd been some question about my father's recovery from that collapse he suffered last winter, but from what Porenn says, he's completely back to normal—although that's not an unmixed blessing." She laid Porenn's letter aside. "I think the time's come for us to have a little talk, Ce'Nedra. You've done a great deal of maneuvering and manipulating in the past few weeks. Now I want to know exactly what's behind it all. Precisely why have you seen fit to ram your new status down everybody's throat?"

Ce'Nedra flushed. "I *am* the Rivan Queen after all, Lady Polgara," she replied stiffly.

"Don't be absurd. You're wearing a fictional crown because Rhodar decided to let you wear it, and because he's convinced Anheg and Brand and Cho-Hag that you're not going to do any damage. Now what's behind all this?" Polgara's look was very direct, and Ce'Nedra squirmed uncomfortably.

"We have to bring in the Arends and my father's legions," she said as if that explained it.

"That's fairly obvious."

"But the Alorn Kings wouldn't be able to do it."

"Why not?"

"Because a committee can't win people's hearts." It was out in the open now, and Ce'Nedra rushed on. "Garion could have done it. The entire West would have risen at the call of the Rivan King, but Garion isn't here, so somebody else has to do it. I've studied history, Lady Polgara. No army led by a committee has ever succeeded. The success of an army depends on the spirit of the soldiers, and the soldiers have to have *one* leader—someone who fires their imagination."

"And you've elected yourself?"

"It doesn't have to be anybody brilliant or anything—not really. It's just got to be somebody visible—and unusual."

"And you think that a woman's going to be unusual enough and visible enough to raise an army—and incidentally to pose enough of a threat to attract the undivided attention of Taur Urgas and 'Zakath, the Mallorean Emperor?"

"Well, it's never been done before." Ce'Nedra felt a little defensive about it.

"A lot of things have never been done before, Ce'Nedra. That's not necessarily the best recommendation—and what convinced you that *I* wasn't qualified?"

Ce'Nedra swallowed hard. "You were so angry," she faltered, "and I wasn't sure how long you were going to stay angry. Somebody had to take charge immediately. Besides—" she hesitated.

"Go on."

"My father doesn't like you," Ce'Nedra blurted. "He'd never order his legions to follow you. I'm the only one who has a chance to convince him that he ought to join us. I'm sorry, Lady Polgara. I don't mean to offend you."

Polgara, however, waved that aside. Her face was thoughtful as she considered

Ce'Nedra's arguments. "It would seem that you *have* given the matter some thought," she concluded. "All right, Ce'Nedra, we'll try it your way—for now. Just don't do anything exotic. Now I think we'd better have a talk with the ladies."

The conference that took place in Polgara's apartments that afternoon concerned matters of state. She waited quietly until the little group had all gathered, and then she spoke to them rather gravely. "Ladies," she began, "in a very short time the Alorns and others will be taking the field on an expedition of some importance."

"You mean war, Pol?" Queen Layla asked in a sinking voice.

"We're going to try to avoid that if it's at all possible," Polgara replied. "At any rate, the departure of your husband and the Alorn Kings will leave affairs at home in your hands—and the same holds true for each of you. I wanted to go over a few things with all of you before we left." She turned to Queen Islena, who was splendidly gowned in red velvet. "Your husband is somewhat less than enthusiastic about any arrangements that will leave you in charge of Cherek, Islena."

Islena sniffed. "Anheg can be tiresome at times."

"Try not to agitate him. Drop a hint or two that you'll allow yourself to be guided by advisers he trusts. It'll set his mind at rest a bit." Polgara looked around at them. "The campaign is not likely to take us so far away that you won't be able to stay in touch with us—not at first, anyway. If anything serious comes up, communicate with your husbands immediately. Deal with the day-to-day matters yourselves. I also think you should all stay in close contact with each other, once your husbands have left—and also with Porenn in Boktor and Mayaserana in Vo Mimbre. You all have your strengths and your weaknesses, but if you're not afraid to seek advice from each other, everything will be all right."

"Possibly we should arrange for some kind of network for communications," Queen Layla mused thoughtfully. "Relays of horses, messengers, fast ships—that sort of thing. The Tolnedrans have done that for centuries."

"I'm sure you'll be able to arrange it, Layla." Polgara smiled at her. "The one thing you all must remember is to pay close attention to anything Porenn tells you. I know she's very young and a bit shy about putting herself forward, but Drasnian intelligence will report directly to her, and she'll be aware of things long before any of the rest of you are. And I want you all to keep a particularly close watch on the Tolnedrans. They like to take advantage of periods of turmoil. Absolutely do not sign anything offered to you by a Tolnedran—no matter how attractive it looks. I trust Ran Borune about as much as I'd trust a fox in a henhouse—no offense intended, Ce'Nedra."

"I know my father too, Lady Polgara," Princess Ce'Nedra replied with a smile.

"Please, ladies," Polgara told them firmly, "no adventures while I'm gone. Just try to keep things running smoothly, and don't be afraid to consult with one another. You'll also want to keep in touch with Xantha. The Dryads have access to a great deal of information about what's going on in the south. If any real emergency arises, get word to me immediately."

"Will you want me to keep the little boy?" Merel asked. "I'll be at Val Alorn with Islena, so he'll be safe with me. My girls are very fond of him, and he seems happy with us."

Polgara thought about it for a moment. "No," she decided finally. "Errand's going to have to go with me. Aside from Garion, he's the only person in the world who can touch the Orb. The Angaraks may realize that and try to take him."

"I'll care for him," Taiba offered in her rich voice. "He knows me, and we're comfortable with each other. It'll give me something to do."

"Surely you are not planning to go along on the campaign, Taiba," Queen Layla objected.

Taiba shrugged. "Why not?" she replied. "I don't have a house to keep or a kingdom to oversee. There are other reasons, too."

They all understood. What existed between Taiba and Relg was so profound that it seemed somehow outside the sphere of normal human attachment, and the Ulgo's absence had caused the strange woman something rather close to physical pain. It was now obvious that she intended to follow him—even into battle if necessary.

Ariana, the blond Mimbrate girl who had accompanied Lelldorin of Wildantor to Riva, cleared her throat in preparation to raising a matter of some delicacy. "The lives of women are circumscribed by proprieties," she noted. "Though battle doth rage about her and rude war turneth all to confusion, a lady must not be unattended in the midst of an army lest her reputation suffer. Lady Adara and I have of late held some conversation concerning this and have concluded that we must accompany Princess Ce'Nedra as her companions. We would do this out of duty even were we not impelled by love."

"Very nicely put, Ariana," Adara murmured without any hint of a smile.

"Oh dear," Queen Layla sighed. "Now I have two more to worry about."

"I think that covers everything, then," Polgara said. "Running a kingdom isn't all that much different from running a house, and you've all had experience at that. Don't change any major policies, and don't sign any treaties. Aside from that, just let yourselves be guided by common sense. I think we can join the gentlemen now. It's getting on toward suppertime, and men tend to grow restless if they aren't fed regularly."

A few days later, Barak returned to Riva, accompanied by a lean-faced Drasnian nobleman. The two of them immediately went to the council chamber to report to the kings. Princess Ce'Nedra considered following them into the conference, but decided against it. Her presence might inhibit the discussion, and she had another way to find out what was going on. She retired quickly to her rooms and touched her fingertips to the amulet at her throat.

"—going fairly well," she heard Barak's voice say after she had finally located the conversation she wished to hear. "The fleet's ready to move out of Val Alorn, and Queen Porenn's got the Drasnian pikemen gathering just south of Boktor. The mobilization's very nearly complete. I think we've got some problems, though. Count Kharel here has just returned from Thull Mardu. All the reports out of northern Cthol Murgos have been channeled to him, so he can give us a fairly clear assessment of the situation there."

King Rhodar cleared his throat. "Kharel's a very senior member of the intelligence service," he said by way of introduction. "I've always found his reports to be extremely accurate."

"Your Majesty is too kind," an unfamiliar voice responded.

"Have the southern Murgos begun their march north?" King Anheg asked.

"It goes a bit farther than that, your Majesty," Kharel replied. "All reports I have indicate that the march is nearly completed. There are somewhat in excess of four million of them encamped in the vicinity of Rak Goska."

"What?" Anheg exclaimed.

"It appears that Taur Urgas began the march sometime last fall," the Drasnian told him.

"In the winter?"

"It seems so, your Majesty."

"I imagine that cost him a few of his men," King Cho-Hag said.

"A hundred thousand or so, your Majesty," Kharel answered, "but human life doesn't mean that much to Taur Urgas."

"This changes everything, Rhodar," Anheg said tersely. "Our advantage has always been the time that march was going to take. We've lost it now."

"Unfortunately there's more, your Majesty," Kharel continued. "The western Malloreans have begun to arrive at Thull Zelik. Their numbers aren't really that significant yet, but they're ferrying in several thousand a day."

"We've got to cut that off as quickly as we can," Anheg growled. "Rhodar, can you get your engineers to the eastern escarpment within a month? I'm going to have to portage a fleet across to the headwaters of the River Mardu. We've got to get ships into the Sea of the East as soon as possible. If we don't head off 'Zakath, his Malloreans will swarm us under."

"I'll send word to Porenn immediately," Rhodar agreed.

"One wonders if the noble count has any good news," the Earl of Seline suggested dryly.

"There is some possibility of division in the enemy ranks, my Lord," Kharel replied. "Taur Urgas is behaving as if he considers himself the only possible choice as overgeneral of the Angarak armies; at the moment, he's got the advantage of numbers on his side. That may change if the Malloreans manage to land a big enough army. There are rumors that 'Zakath would like to dispute the leadership of Taur Urgas, but he's reluctant to try it in the face of four million Murgos."

"Let's try to keep it that way," Rhodar said. "Taur Urgas is insane, and crazy men make mistakes. I've heard about 'Zakath, and I'd rather not face him in the field."

King Cho-Hag spoke wryly. "Even as it stands without the Malloreans, we're going to be taking the field at about a two to one disadvantage—and that's assuming that we can persuade the Arends and Tolnedrans to join us."

"It's a rotten way to start a war, Rhodar," Anheg complained.

"We'll just have to adjust our tactics," Rhodar replied. "We've got to avoid a pitched battle as long as possible to save as many men as we can."

"I thought we weren't even considering a battle," Barak objected, "and Belgarath said that all he wants is a diversion."

"The situation's changed, Barak," King Rhodar declared. "We hadn't counted on the southern Murgos or the Malloreans being in place this soon. We're going to have to do something a bit more significant than stage a few hit-and-run attacks.

The Angaraks have enough men now to be able to ignore minor raids and skirmishes. If we don't make a major thrust—and very soon—they'll spread out all over the eastern half of the continent."

"Belgarath doesn't like it when you change plans on him," Anheg reminded Rhodar.

"Belgarath isn't here, and he doesn't know what's going on. If we don't act rather decisively, he and Belgarion and Kheldar haven't a hope of getting through."

"You're talking about a war we can't win, Rhodar," Anheg said bluntly.

"I know," King Rhodar admitted.

There was a long silence. "So that's the way it is, then," Brand said finally.

"I'm afraid so," Rhodar told them somberly. "There has to be a diversion, or Belgarion and his sword will never get to the meeting with Torak. That's the only thing that really matters, and we'll all have to lay down our lives if necessary to make it happen."

"You're going to get us all killed, Rhodar," Anheg said bluntly, "and all our armies with us."

"If that's what it takes, Anheg," Rhodar answered grimly. "If Belgarion doesn't get to Torak, our lives don't mean anything, anyway. Even if we all have to die to get him there, it's still worth it."

Ce'Nedra's fingertips slid numbly from her amulet as she fell back in her chair. Suddenly she began to weep. "I won't do it," she sobbed. "I can't." She saw before her a multitude—an army of widows and orphans all staring accusingly at her, and she shrank from their eyes. If she perpetrated this horror, the rest of her life would be spent in an agony of self-loathing. Still weeping, she stumbled to her feet, fully intending to rush to the council chamber and declare that she would have nothing further to do with this futile war. But then she stopped as the image of Garion's face rose in her mind—that serious face with the unruly hair she always wanted to straighten. He depended on her. If she shrank from this, the Angaraks would be free to hunt him down. His very life—and with it the future of the world—was in her hands. She had no choice but to continue. If only she did not know that the campaign was doomed! It was the knowledge of the disaster that awaited them that made it all so terrible.

Knowing that it was useless, she began to tug at the chain that held the amulet about her neck. Had it not been for the amulet, she would have remained blissfully ignorant of what lay ahead. Still sobbing, she yanked frantically at the chain, ignoring the sting as it cut into the soft skin of her neck. "I hate you!" she blurted irrationally at the silver amulet with its crowned tree.

But it was useless. The medallion would remain chained about her neck for the rest of her life. Ashen-faced, Ce'Nedra let her hands drop. Even if she were able to remove the amulet, what good would it do? She already knew and she must conceal the knowledge in her heart. If the faintest hint of what she knew showed in her face or her voice, she would fail—and Garion would suffer for her failure. She must steel herself and face the world as if certain of victory.

And so it was that the Rivan Queen drew herself erect and bravely lifted her chin—even though her heart lay like lead in her breast.

CHAPTER TWENTY-FIVE

Barak's new ship was larger by half than most of the other Cherek warboats in the fleet, but she moved before the spring breeze like a gull skimming low over the water. Fleecy white clouds ran across the blue sky, and the surface of the Sea of the Winds sparkled in the sunlight as the great ship heeled over and cut cleanly through the waves. Low on the horizon before them rose the green shoreline of the hook of Arendia. They were two days out from Riva, and the Cherek fleet spread out behind them in a vast crowd of sails, carrying the graycloaked Rivans to join the armies of King Fulrach of Sendaria.

Ce'Nedra nervously paced the deck near the prow, her blue cloak tossing in the wind and her armor gleaming. Despite the dreadful knowledge concealed in her heart, there was an excitement to all of this. The gathering of men, swords, and ships, the running before the wind, the sense of a unified purpose, all combined to make her blood race and to fill her with an exhilaration she had never felt before.

The coast ahead loomed larger—a white sand beach backed by the dark green of the Arendish forest. As they neared the shoreline, an armored knight on a huge roan stallion emerged from the trees and rode down the beach to the edge of the water where foamy breakers crashed on the damp sand. The princess shaded her eyes with one hand and peered intently at the gleaming knight. Then, as he turned with a broad sweep of his arm which told them to continue up the coast, she saw the crest on his shield. Her heart suddenly soared. "Mandorallen!" she cried out in a vibrant trumpet note as she clung to the ropes in the very prow of Barak's ship, with the wind whipping at her hair.

The great knight waved a salute and, spurring his charger, galloped through the seething foam at the edge of the beach, the silver-and-blue pennon at the tip of his lance snapping and streaming over his head. Their ship heeled over as Barak swung the tiller, and, separated by a hundred yards or so of foaming surf, the ship and the rider on the beach kept abreast of each other.

It was a moment Ce'Nedra would remember for all her life—a single image so perfect that it seemed forever frozen in her memory. The great ship flew before the wind, cutting the sparkling blue water, with her white sails booming; the mighty warhorse on the beach plunged through the gleaming foam at the edge of the sand with spray flying out from beneath his great hooves. Locked together in that endless moment, ship and rider raced along in the warm spring sunshine toward a wooded promontory a mile ahead, with Ce'Nedra exulting in the ship's prow and her flaming hair streaming like a banner.

Beyond the promontory lay a sheltered cove, and drawn up on the beach stood the camp of the Sendarian army, row upon orderly row of dun-colored tents. Barak swung his tiller over, and his sails flapped as the ship coasted into the cove with the Cherek fleet close behind.

"Ho, Mandorallen!" Barak bellowed as the anchor ropes sang and great iron anchors plunged down through crystal water toward the sandy bottom.

"My Lord Barak," Mandorallen shouted his reply, "welcome to Arendia. Lord Brendig hath devised a means to speed thy disembarking." He pointed to where a hundred or so Sendarian soldiers were busily poling a series of large rafts into position, lashing them together to form a long floating wharf extending out into the waters of the cove.

Barak laughed. "Trust a Sendar to come up with something practical."

"Can we go ashore now?" King Rhodar asked plaintively as he emerged from the cabin. The king was not a good sailor, and his broad, round face had a pale greenish cast to it. He looked oddly comical in his mail shirt and helmet, and the ravages of seasickness on his face added little to his dignity. Despite his unwarlike exterior, however, the other kings had already begun to defer to his wisdom. Beneath his vast rotundity, Rhodar concealed a genius for tactics and a grasp of overall strategy that made the others turn to him almost automatically and accept his unspoken leadership.

A small fishing boat that had been pressed into service as a ferry drew alongside Barak's ship, almost before the anchors had settled, and the kings and their generals and advisers were transferred to the beach in less than half an hour.

"I think I'm hungry," Rhodar announced the moment he stepped onto solid ground.

Anheg laughed. "I think you were born hungry." The king wore a mail shirt and had a broad sword belt about his waist. His coarse features seemed less out of place somehow, now that he was armed.

"I haven't been able to eat for two days, Anheg." Rhodar groaned. "My poor stomach's beginning to think I've abandoned it."

"Food hath been prepared, your Majesty," Mandorallen assured him. "Our Asturian brothers have provided goodly numbers of the king's deer—doubtless obtained lawfully—though I chose not to investigate that too closely."

Someone standing in the group behind Mandorallen laughed, and Ce'Nedra looked at the handsome young man with reddish-gold hair and the longbow slung over the shoulder of his green doublet. Ce'Nedra had not had much opportunity to become acquainted with Lelldorin of Wildantor while they had been at Riva. She knew him to be Garion's closest friend, however, and she realized the importance of gaining his confidence. It should not be too hard, she decided as she looked at his open, almost innocent face. The gaze he returned was very direct, and one glance into those eyes told the princess that there was a vast sincerity and very little intelligence behind them.

"We've heard from Belgarath," Barak advised Mandorallen and the young Asturian.

"Where are they?" Lelldorin demanded eagerly.

"They were in Boktor," King Rhodar replied, his face still a trifle green from his bout of seasickness. "For reasons of her own, my wife let them pass through. I imagine they're somewhere in Gar og Nadrak by now."

Lelldorin's eyes flashed. "Maybe if I hurry, I can catch up with them," he said eagerly, already starting to look around for his horse.

"It's fifteen hundred leagues, Lelldorin," Barak pointed out politely.

"Oh—" Lelldorin seemed a bit crestfallen. "I suppose you're right. It would be a little difficult to catch them now, wouldn't it?"

Barak nodded gravely.

And then the blond Mimbrate girl, Ariana, stepped forward, her heart in her eyes. "My Lord," she said to Lelldorin, and Ce'Nedra remembered with a start that the two were married—technically at least. "Thine absence hath given me great pain."

Lelldorin's eyes were immediately stricken. "My Ariana." He almost choked. "I swear that I'll never leave you again." He took both her hands in his and gazed adoringly into her eyes. The gaze she returned was just as full of love and just as empty of thought. Ce'Nedra shuddered inwardly at the potential for disaster implicit in the look the two exchanged.

"Does anyone care that I'm starving to death right here on the spot?" Rhodar asked.

The banquet was laid on a long table set up beneath a gaily striped pavilion on the beach not far from the edge of the forest. The table quite literally groaned under its weight of roasted game, and there was enough to eat to satisfy even the enormous appetite of King Rhodar. When they had finished eating, they lingered at the table in conversation.

"Thy son, Lord Hettar, hath advised us that the Algar clans are gathering at the Stronghold, your Majesty," Mandorallen reported to King Cho-Hag.

Cho-Hag nodded.

"And we've had word from the Ulgo—Relg," Colonel Brendig added. "He's gathered a small army of warriors from the caves. They'll wait for us on the Algarian side of the mountains. He said you'd know the place."

Barak grunted. "The Ulgos can be troublesome," he said. "They're afraid of open places, and daylight hurts their eyes, but they can see in the dark like cats. That could be very useful at some point."

"Did Relg send any—personal messages?" Taiba asked Brendig with a little catch in her voice.

Gravely, the Sendar took a folded parchment from inside his tunic and handed it to her. She took it with a rather helpless expression and opened it, turning it this way and that.

"What's the matter, Taiba?" Adara asked quietly.

"He knows I can't read," Taiba protested, holding the note tightly pressed against her.

"I'll read it to you," Adara offered.

"But maybe it's—well—personal," Taiba objected.

"I promise I won't listen," Adara told her without the trace of a smile.

Ce'Nedra covered her own smile with her hand. Adara's penetrating and absolutely straight-faced wit was one of the qualities that most endeared her to the princess. Even as she smiled, however, Ce'Nedra could feel eyes on her, and she knew that she was being examined with great curiosity by the Arends—both Asturian and Mimbrate—who had joined them. Lelldorin in particular seemed unable to take his eyes from her. The handsome young man sat close beside the blond

Mimbrate girl, Ariana, and stared openly at Ce'Nedra even while, unconsciously perhaps, he held Ariana's hand. Ce'Nedra endured his scrutiny with a certain nervousness. To her surprise, she found that she wanted this rather foolish young man's approval.

"Tell me," she said directly to him, "what are the sentiments here in Asturia—concerning our campaign, I mean?"

Lelldorin's eyes clouded. "Unenthusiastic for the most part, your Majesty," he replied. "I'm afraid there's suspicion that this might all be some Mimbrate plot."

"That's absurd," Ce'Nedra declared.

Lelldorin shrugged. "It's the way my countrymen think. And those who don't think it's a plot are looking at the idea that all the Mimbrate knights might join a crusade against the East. That raises certain hopes in some quarters."

Mandorallen sighed. "The same sentiments exist in some parts of Mimbre," he said. "We are a woefully divided kingdom, and old hatreds and suspicions die hard."

Ce'Nedra felt a sudden wave of consternation. She had not counted on this. King Rhodar had made it plain that he absolutely had to have the Arends, and now the idiotic hatred and suspicion between Mimbre and Asturia seemed about to bring the entire plan crashing down around her ears. Helplessly she turned to Polgara.

The sorceress, however, seemed undisturbed by the news that the Arends were reluctant to join the campaign. "Tell me, Lelldorin," she said calmly, "could you gather some of your less suspicious friends in one place—some secure place where they won't be afraid we might want to ambush them?"

"What have you got in mind, Polgara?" King Rhodar asked, his eyes puzzled.

"Someone's going to have to talk to them," Polgara replied. "Someone rather special, I think." She turned back to Lelldorin. "I don't think we'll want a large crowd—not at first, anyway. Forty or fifty ought to be enough—and no one too violently opposed to our cause."

"I'll gather them at once, Lady Polgara," Lelldorin declared, impulsively leaping to his feet.

"It's rather late, Lelldorin," she pointed out, glancing at the sun hovering low over the horizon.

"The sooner I start, the sooner I can gather them," Lelldorin said fervently. "If friendship and the ties of blood have any sway at all, I will not fail." He bowed deeply to Ce'Nedra. "Your Majesty," he said by way of farewell and ran to where his horse was tethered.

Ariana sighed as she looked after the departing young enthusiast.

"Is he always like that?" Ce'Nedra asked her curiously.

The Mimbrate girl nodded. "Always," she admitted. "Thought and deed are simultaneous with him. He hath no understanding of the meaning of the word reflection, I fear. It doth add to his charm, but it is sometimes disconcerting, I must admit."

"I can imagine," Ce'Nedra agreed.

Later, when the princess and Polgara were alone in their tent, Ce'Nedra turned a puzzled look upon Garion's Aunt. "What are we going to do?" she asked.

"Not we, Ce'Nedra—you. You're going to have to talk to them."

"I'm not very good at speaking in public, Lady Polgara," Ce'Nedra confessed, her mouth going dry. "Crowds frighten me, and I get all tongue-tied."

"You'll get over it, dear," Polgara assured her. She looked at the princess with a slightly amused expression. "You're the one who wanted to lead an army, remember? Did you really think that all you were going to have to do was put on your armor, jump into the saddle and shout 'follow me' and then the whole world would fall in behind you?"

"Well—"

"You spent all that time studying history and missed the one thing all great leaders have had in common? You must have been very inattentive, Ce'Nedra."

Ce'Nedra stared at her with slowly dawning horror.

"It doesn't take that much to raise an army, dear. You don't have to be brilliant; you don't have to be a warrior; your cause doesn't even have to be great and noble. All you have to do is be eloquent."

"I can't do that, Lady Polgara."

"You should have thought of that before, Ce'Nedra. It's too late to go back now. Rhodar will command the army and see to it that all the details are taken care of, but *you're* the one who'll have to make them want to follow you."

"I wouldn't have the faintest idea what to say to them," Ce'Nedra protested.

"It'll come to you, dear. You do believe in what we're doing, don't you?"

"Of course, but—"

"You decided to do this, Ce'Nedra. You decided it all by yourself. And as long as you've come this far, you might as well go all the way."

"Please, Lady Polgara," Ce'Nedra begged. "Speaking in public makes me sick to my stomach. I'll throw up."

"That happens now and then," Polgara observed calmly. "Just try not to do it in front of everybody."

Three days later, the princess, Polgara, and the Alorn Kings journeyed to the ruined city of Vo Astur deep in the silences of the Arendish forest. Ce'Nedra rode through the sunny woods in a state hovering on the verge of panic. In spite of all her arguments, Polgara had remained adamant. Tears had not budged her; even hysterics had failed. The princess was morbidly convinced that, even if she were to die, Polgara would prop her up in front of the waiting throng and make her go through the agony of addressing them. Feeling absolutely helpless, she rode to meet her fate.

Like Vo Wacune, Vo Astur had been laid waste during the dark centuries of the Arendish civil war. Its tumbled stones were green with moss and they lay in the shade of vast trees that seemed to mourn the honor, pride, and sorrow of Asturia. Lelldorin was waiting, and with him were perhaps fifty richly dressed young noblemen, their eyes filled with curiosity faintly tinged with suspicion.

"It's as many as I could bring together in a short time, Lady Polgara," Lelldorin apologized after they had dismounted. "There are others in the region, but they're convinced that our campaign is some kind of Mimbrate treachery."

"These will do nicely, Lelldorin," Polgara replied. "They'll spread the word about what happens here." She looked around at the mossy, sun-dappled ruins. "I think that spot over there will be fine." She pointed at a broken bit of one of the walls. "Come with me, Ce'Nedra."

The princess, dressed in her armor, hung her helmet and shield on the saddle of the white horse King Cho-Hag had brought for her from Algaria and led the patient animal as she tremblingly followed the sorceress.

"We want them to be able to see you as well as hear you," Polgara instructed, "so climb up on that piece of wall and speak from there. The spot where you'll be standing is in the shade now, but the sun's moving around so that it'll be fully on you as you finish your speech. I think that'll be a nice touch."

Ce'Nedra quailed as she saw how far the sun had to go. "I think I'm going to be sick," she said in a quivering little voice.

"Maybe later, Ce'Nedra. You don't have time just now." Polgara turned to Lelldorin. "I think you can introduce her Majesty now," she told him.

Lelldorin stepped up onto the wall and held up his hand for silence. "Countrymen," he announced in a loud voice, "last Erastide an event took place which shook our world to its foundations. For a thousand years and more we have awaited that moment. My countrymen, the Rivan King has returned!"

The throng stirred at his announcement, and an excited buzz rippled through it.

Lelldorin, always extravagant, warmed to his subject. He told them of the flaming sword that had announced Garion's true identity and of the oaths of fealty sworn to Belgarion of Riva by the Alorn Kings. Ce'Nedra, almost fainting with nervousness, scarcely heard him. She tried to run over her speech in her mind, but it all kept getting jumbled. Then, in near panic, she heard him say, "Countrymen, I present to you her Imperial Highness, Princess Ce'Nedra—the Rivan Queen." And all eyes turned expectantly to her.

Trembling in every limb, she mounted the broken wall and looked at the faces before her. All her preparations, all the rehearsed phrases, evaporated from her mind, and she stood, white-faced and shaking, without the faintest idea of how to begin. The silence was dreadful.

As chance had it, one of the young Asturians in the very front had tasted perhaps more wine that morning than was good for him. "I think her Majesty has forgotten her speech," he snickered loudly to one of his companions.

Ce'Nedra's reaction was instantaneous. "And I think the gentleman has forgotten his manners," she flared, not even stopping to think. Incivility infuriated her.

"I don't think I'm going to listen to this," the tipsy young man declared in a tone filled with exaggerated boredom. "It's just a waste of time. I'm not a Rivan and neither are any of the rest of you. What could a foreign queen possibly say that would be of any interest to Asturian patriots?" And he started to turn away.

"Is the patriotic Asturian gentleman so wine-soaked that he's forgotten that there's more to the world than this forest?" Ce'Nedra retorted hotly. "Or perhaps he's so unschooled that he doesn't know what's happening out there." She leveled a threatening finger at him. "Hear me, patriot," she said in a ringing voice. "You may think that I'm just here to make some pretty little speech, but what I've come to say to you is the most important thing you'll ever hear. You can listen, or you can turn your back and walk away—and a year from now when there is no Asturia and when your homes are smoking in ruins and the Grolims are herding your families to the altar of Torak with its fire and its bloody knives, you can look back on this day and curse yourself for not listening."

And then as if her anger with this one rude young man had suddenly burst a dam within her, Ce'Nedra began to speak. She spoke to them directly, not with the studied phrases she had rehearsed, but with words that came from her heart. The longer she spoke, the more impassioned she became. She pleaded; she cajoled— and finally she commanded. She would never remember exactly what she said, but she would never forget how she felt as she said it. All the passion and fire that had filled the stormy outbursts and tantrums of her girlhood came into full play. She spoke fervently with no thought of herself, but rather with an all-consuming belief in what she said. In the end she won them over.

As the sun fell full upon her, her armor gleamed and her hair seemed to leap into flame. "Belgarion, King of Riva and Overlord of the West, calls you to war!" she declared to them. "I am Ce'Nedra, his queen, and I stand before you as a living banner. Who among you will answer Belgarion's call and follow me?"

It was the young man who had laughed at her whose sword leaped first into his hand. Raising it in salute, he shouted, "I will follow!" As if his declaration were a signal, half a hundred swords flashed in the sunlight as they were raised in salute and pledge, and half a hundred voices echoed his shout. "I will follow!"

With a broad sweep of her arm, Ce'Nedra drew her own sword and lifted it. "Follow, then!" she sang to them. "We ride to meet the fell hordes of Angarak. Let the world tremble at our coming!" With three quick steps, she reached her horse and literally threw herself into the saddle. She wheeled her prancing mount and galloped from the ruins, her sword aloft and her flaming hair streaming. The Asturians as one man rushed to their horses to follow.

As she plunged into the forest, the princess glanced back once at the brave, foolish young men galloping behind her, their faces exalted. She had won, but how many of these unthinking Asturians would she lead back when the war was done? How many would die in the wastes of the East? Her eyes suddenly filled with tears; but, dashing those tears away with one hand, the Rivan Queen galloped on, leading the Asturians back to join her army.

CHAPTER TWENTY-SIX

The Alorn Kings praised Ce'Nedra extravagantly, and hard-bitten warriors looked at her with open admiration. She lapped up their adulation and purred like a happy kitten. The only thing that kept her triumph from being complete was Polgara's strange silence. Ce'Nedra was a little hurt by that. The speech had not been perfect, perhaps, but it had won Lelldorin's friends completely, and surely success made up for any minor flaws.

Then, when Polgara sent for her that evening, Ce'Nedra thought she understood. The sorceress wished to congratulate her in private. Humming happily to herself, the princess went along the beach to Polgara's tent with the sound of waves on the white sand in her ears.

Polgara sat at her dressing table, alone except for the sleepy child, Errand. The candlelight played softly over her deep blue robe and the perfection of her features as she brushed her long, dark hair. "Come in, Ce'Nedra," she said. "Sit down. We have a great deal to discuss."

"Were you surprised, Lady Polgara?" The princess could no longer contain herself. "You were, weren't you? I even surprised myself."

Polgara looked at her gravely. "You mustn't allow yourself to become so excited, Ce'Nedra. You have to learn to conserve your strength and not squander it by dashing about in hysterical self-congratulation."

Ce'Nedra stared at her. "Don't you think I did well today?" she asked, hurt to the quick.

"It was a very nice speech, Ce'Nedra," Polgara told her in a way that took all the fun out of it.

A strange thought occurred to the princess then. "You knew, didn't you?" she blurted. "You knew all along."

A faint flicker of amusement touched Polgara's lips. "You always seem to forget that I have certain advantages, dear," she replied, "and one of those is that I have a general idea of how things are going to turn out."

"How could you possibly—"

"Certain events don't just happen, Ce'Nedra. Some things have been implicit in this world since the moment it was made. What happened today was one of those things." She reached over and picked up an age-darkened scroll from the table. "Would you like to hear what the Prophecy says about you?"

Ce'Nedra felt a sudden chill.

Polgara ran her eyes down the crackling parchment. "Here it is," she said, lifting the scroll into the candlelight. " 'And the voice of the Bride of Light shall be heard in the kingdoms of the world,' " she read, " 'and her words shall be as a fire in dry grass, that the multitudes shall rise up to go forth under the blaze of her banner.' "

"That doesn't mean anything at all, Lady Polgara," Ce'Nedra objected. "It's absolute gibberish."

"Does it become any clearer when you find out that Garion is the Child of Light?"

"What is that?" Ce'Nedra demanded, staring at the parchment. "Where did you get it?"

"It's the Mrin Codex, dear. My father copied it for me from the original. It's a bit obscure because the Mrin prophet was so hopelessly insane that he couldn't speak coherently. King Dras Bull-neck finally had to keep him chained to a post like a dog."

"King Dras? Lady Polgara, that was over three thousand years ago!"

"About that long, yes," Polgara agreed.

Ce'Nedra began to tremble. "That's impossible!" she blurted.

Polgara smiled. "Sometimes, Ce'Nedra, you sound exactly like Garion. I wonder why young people are so fond of that word."

"But, Lady Polgara, if it hadn't been for that young man who was so insulting, I might not have said anything at all." The princess bit her lip. She had not meant to confess that.

"That's probably why he was so insulting, then. It's quite possible that insulting you at that particular moment was the only reason he was born in the first place. The Prophecy leaves nothing to chance. Do you think you might need him to help you get started next time? I can arrange to have him get drunk again if you do."

"Next time?"

"Of course. Did you think that one speech to a very small audience was going to be the end of it? Really, Ce'Nedra, you have to learn to pay more attention to what's going on. You're going to have to speak in public at least once a day for the next several months."

The princess stared at her in horror. "I *can't*!" she wailed.

"Yes, you can, Ce'Nedra. Your voice will be heard in the land, and your words shall be as a fire in dry grass, and the multitudes of the West shall rise up to follow your banner. Down through all the centuries, I've never known the Mrin Codex to be wrong—not once. The important thing at the moment is for you to get plenty of rest and to eat regularly. I'll prepare your meals myself." She looked rather critically at the tiny girl. "It would help if you were a bit more robust, but I guess we'll have to make do with what we have. Go get your things, Ce'Nedra. From now on, you'll be staying with me. I think I'm going to want to keep an eye on you."

In the weeks that followed, they moved down through the moist, green Arendish forest, and word of their coming spread throughout Asturia. Ce'Nedra was dimly aware that Polgara was carefully controlling the size and composition of the audiences to be addressed. Poor Lelldorin was seldom out of his saddle as he and a carefully selected group of his friends ranged ahead of the advancing army to prepare each gathering.

Ce'Nedra, once she had finally accepted her duty, had assumed that speaking in public would grow easier with practice. Unfortunately, she was wrong. Panic still gripped her before each speech, and quite frequently she was physically sick. Although Polgara assured her that her speeches were getting better, Ce'Nedra complained that they were not getting easier. The drain on her physical and emotional reserves became more and more evident. Like most girls her age, Ce'Nedra could and often did talk endlessly, but her orations were not random talk. They required an enormous control and a tremendous expenditure of emotional energy, and no one could help her.

As the crowds grew larger, however, Polgara did provide some aid in a purely technical matter. "Just speak in a normal tone of voice, Ce'Nedra," she instructed. "Don't exhaust yourself by trying to shout. I'll see to it that everybody can hear you." Aside from that, however, the princess was on her own, and the strain became more and more visible. She rode listlessly at the head of her growing army, seeming sometimes almost to be in a trance.

Her friends watched her and worried.

"I'm not sure how much longer she can keep up this pace," King Fulrach confided to King Rhodar as they rode directly behind the drooping little queen toward the ruins of Vo Wacune, where she was to address yet another gathering. "I think we tend sometimes to forget how small and delicate she is."

"Maybe we'd better consult with Polgara," King Rhodar agreed. "I think the child needs a week's rest."

Ce'Nedra, however, knew that she could not stop. There was a momentum to this, a kind of accelerating rhythm that could not be broken. At first, word of her coming had spread slowly, but now it ran ahead of them, and she knew they must run faster and faster to keep up with it. There was a crucial point at which the curiosity about her must be satisfied or the whole thing would collapse and she'd have to begin all over again.

The crowd at Vo Wacune was the largest she had yet addressed. Half-convinced already, they needed only a single spark to ignite them. Once again sick with unreasoning panic, the Rivan Queen gathered her strength and rose to address them and to set them aflame with her call to war.

When it was over and the young nobles had been gathered into the growing ranks of the army, Ce'Nedra sought a few moments of solitude on the outskirts of the camp to compose herself. This had become a kind of necessary ritual for her. Sometimes she was sick after a speech and sometimes she wept. Sometimes she merely wandered listlessly, not even seeing the trees about her. At Polgara's instruction, Durnik always accompanied her, and Ce'Nedra found the company of this solid, practical man strangely comforting.

They had walked some distance from the ruins. The afternoon was bright and sunny, and birds sang among the trees. Pensively, Ce'Nedra walked, letting the peace of the forest quiet the agitated turmoil within her.

"It's all very well for noblemen, Detton," she heard someone say somewhere on the other side of a thicket, "but what does it have to do with us?"

"You're probably right, Lammer," a second voice agreed with a regretful sigh. "It was very stirring, though, wasn't it?"

"The only thing that ought to stir a serf is the sight of something to eat," the first man declared bitterly. "The little girl can talk all she wants about duty, but my only duty is to my stomach." He stopped abruptly. "Are the leaves of that plant over there fit to eat?" he asked.

"I think they're poisonous, Lammer," Detton replied.

"But you're not sure? I'd hate to pass up something I could eat if there was any chance that it wouldn't kill me."

Ce'Nedra listened to the two serfs with growing horror. Could anybody be reduced to that level? Impulsively, she stepped around the thicket to confront them. Durnik, as always, stayed close by her side.

The two serfs were dressed in mud-spattered rags. They were both men of middle years, and there was no evidence on their faces that either of them had ever known a happy day. The leaner of the two was closely examining a thick-leafed weed, but the other saw Ce'Nedra approaching and started with obvious fright. "Lammer." He gasped. "It's her—the one who spoke today."

Lammer straightened, his gaunt face going pale beneath the dirt that smudged it. "Your Ladyship," he said, grotesquely trying to bow. "We were just on our way back to our villages. We didn't know this part of the forest was yours. We didn't take anything." He held out his empty hands as if to prove his words.

"How long has it been since you've had anything to eat?" she demanded of him.

"I ate some grass this morning, your Ladyship," Lammer replied, "and I had a couple of turnips yesterday. They were a little wormy, but not too bad."

Ce'Nedra's eyes suddenly filled with tears. "Who's done this to you?" she asked him.

Lammer looked a little confused at her question. Finally he shrugged slightly. "The world, I guess, your Ladyship. A certain part of what we raise goes to our lord, and a certain part to his lord. Then there's the part that has to go to the king and the part that has to go to the royal governor. And we're still paying for some wars my lord had a few years ago. After all of that's been paid, there isn't very much left for us."

A horrible thought struck her. "I'm gathering an army for a campaign in the East," she told them.

"Yes, your Ladyship," the other serf, Detton, replied. "We heard your speech today."

"What will that do to you?"

Detton shrugged. "It will mean more taxes, your Ladyship—and some of our sons will be taken for soldiers if our lords decide to join you. Serfs don't really make very good soldiers, but they can always carry baggage. And when the time comes to storm a castle, the nobility seem to want to have a lot of serfs around to help with the dying."

"Then you never feel any patriotism when you go to war?"

"What could patriotism have to do with serfs, my Lady?" Lammer asked her. "Until a month or so ago I didn't even know the name of my country. None of it belongs to me. Why should I have any feelings about it?"

Ce'Nedra could not answer that question. Their lives were so bleak, so hopelessly empty, and her call to war meant only greater hardship and more suffering for them. "What about your families?" she asked. "If Torak wins, the Grolims will come and slaughter your families on his altars."

"I have no family, my Lady," Lammer replied in a dead voice. "My son died several years ago. My lord was fighting a war somewhere, and when they attacked a castle, the people inside poured boiling pitch down on the serfs who were trying to raise a ladder. My wife starved herself to death after she heard about it. The Grolims can't hurt either one of them now, and if they want to kill me, they're welcome to."

"Isn't there anything at all you'd be willing to fight for?"

"Food, I suppose," Lammer said after a moment's thought. "I'm very tired of being hungry."

Ce'Nedra turned to the other serf. "What about you?" she asked him.

"I'd walk into fire for somebody who fed me," Detton replied fervently.

"Come with me," Ce'Nedra commanded them, and she turned and led the way back to the camp and the large, bulky supply wagons that had transported the vast quantities of food from the storehouses of Sendaria. "I want these two men fed," she told a startled cook. "As much as they can eat." Durnik, however, his honest eyes brimming with compassion, had already reached into one of the wagons and taken out a large loaf of bread. He tore it in two and gave half to Lammer and half to Detton.

Lammer stared at the chunk of bread in his hands, trembling violently. "I'll follow you, my Lady," he declared in a quavering voice. "I've eaten my shoes and lived on boiled grass and tree roots." His fists closed about the chunk of bread as if he were afraid someone might take it away from him. "I'll follow you to the end of the world and back for this." And he began to eat, tearing at the bread with his teeth.

Ce'Nedra stared at him, and then she suddenly fled. By the time she reached her tent she was weeping hysterically. Adara and Taiba tried without success to comfort her, and finally they sent for Polgara.

When the sorceress arrived, she took one brief look and asked Taiba and Adara to leave her alone with the sobbing girl. "All right, Ce'Nedra," she said calmly, sitting on the bed and gathering the princess in her arms, "what's this all about?"

"I can't do it any more, Lady Polgara," Ce'Nedra cried. "I just can't."

"It was your idea in the first place," Polgara reminded her.

"I was wrong." Ce'Nedra sobbed. "Wrong, wrong! I should have stayed in Riva."

"No," Polgara disagreed. "You've done something that none of the rest of us could have. You've guaranteed us the Arends. I'm not even sure Garion could have done that."

"But they're all going to die!" Ce'Nedra wailed.

"Where did you get that idea?"

"The Angaraks are going to outnumber us at least two to one. They'll butcher my army."

"Who told you that?"

"I—I listened," Ce'Nedra replied, fumbling with the amulet at her throat. "I heard what Rhodar, Anheg, and the others said when they heard about the southern Murgos."

"I see," Polgara said gravely.

"We're going to throw away our lives. Nothing can save us. And just now I even found a way to bring the serfs into it. Their lives are so miserable that they'll follow me just for the chance to eat regularly. And I'll do it, Lady Polgara. If I think I might need them, I'll deliberately take them from their homes and lead them to their deaths. I can't help myself."

Polgara took a glass from a nearby table and emptied a small glass vial into it. "The war isn't over yet, Ce'Nedra. It hasn't even begun." She swirled the dark amber liquid around in the bottom of the glass. "I've seen hopeless wars won before. If you give in to despair before you begin, you'll have no chance at all. Rhodar's a very clever tactician, you know, and the men in your army are very brave. We won't commit to any battle until we absolutely have to, and if Garion can reach Torak in time—and if he wins—the Angaraks will fall apart, and we won't have to fight them at all. Here." She held out the glass. "Drink this."

Numbly, Ce'Nedra took the glass and drank. The amber liquid was bitter, and it left a strange, fiery aftertaste in her mouth. "It all depends on Garion, then," she said.

"It always has depended on him, dear," Polgara told her.

Ce'Nedra sighed. "I wish—" she began, then faltered to a stop.

"Wish what, dear?"

"Oh, Lady Polgara, I never once told Garion that I love him. I'd give anything to be able to tell him that—just once."

"He knows, Ce'Nedra."

"But it's not the same." Ce'Nedra sighed again. A strange lassitude had begun to creep over her, and she had stopped crying. It was difficult somehow even to remember why she had been weeping. She suddenly felt eyes on her and turned. Errand sat quietly in the corner watching her. His deep blue eyes were filled with sympathy and, oddly, with hope. And then Polgara took the princess in her arms and began rocking slowly back and forth and humming a soothing kind of melody. Without knowing when it happened, Ce'Nedra fell into a deep and dreamless sleep.

The attempt on her life came the following morning. Her army was marching south from Vo Wacune, passing through the sunlit forest along the Great West Road. The princess was riding at the head of the column, talking with Barak and Mandorallen, when an arrow, buzzing spitefully, came out of the trees. It was the buzz that gave Barak an instant of warning. "Look out!" he shouted, suddenly covering Ce'Nedra with his great shield. The arrow shattered against it, and Barak, cursing horribly, drew his sword.

Brand's youngest son, Olban, however, was already plunging at a dead run into the forest. His face had gone deathly pale, and his sword seemed to leap into his hand as he spun his horse. The sound of his galloping mount faded back among the trees. After several moments, there was a dreadful scream.

Shouts of alarm came from the army behind them and a confused babble of voices. Polgara rode forward, her face white. "I'm all right, Lady Polgara," Ce'Nedra assured her quickly. "Barak saved me."

"What happened?" Polgara demanded.

"Someone shot an arrow at her," Barak growled. "If I hadn't heard it buzz, it might have been very bad."

Lelldorin had picked up the shattered arrow shaft and was looking at it closely. "The fletching is loose," he said, rubbing his finger over the feathers. "That's what made it buzz like that."

Olban came riding back out of the forest, his bloody sword still in his hand. "Is the queen safe?" he demanded; for some reason, his voice seemed on the verge of hysteria.

"She's fine," Barak said, looking at him curiously. "Who was it?"

"A Murgo, I think," Olban replied. "He had scars on his cheeks."

"Did you kill him?"

Olban nodded. "Are you sure you're all right, my Queen?" he asked Ce'Nedra. His pale blond hair was tousled, and he seemed very young and very earnest.

"I'm just fine, Olban," she replied. "You were very brave, but you should have waited instead of riding off alone like that. There might have been more than one."

"Then I'd have killed them all," Olban declared fiercely. "I'll destroy anyone who even raises a finger against you." The young man was actually trembling with rage.

"Thy dedication becomes thee, young Olban," Mandorallen told him.

"I think we'd better put out some scouts," Barak suggested to King Rhodar. "At least until we get out of these trees. Korodullin was going to chase all the Murgos out of Arendia, but it looks as if he missed a few."

"Let me lead the scouting parties," Olban begged.

"Your son has a great deal of enthusiasm," Rhodar observed to Brand. "I like that in a young man." He turned back to Olban. "All right," he said. "Take as many men as you need. I don't want any Murgos within five miles of the princess."

"You have my word on it," Olban declared, wheeling his horse and plunging back into the forest.

They rode a bit more cautiously after that, and archers were placed strategically to watch the crowd when Ce'Nedra spoke. Olban rather grimly reported that a few more Murgos had been flushed out of the trees ahead of them, but there were no further incidents.

It was very nearly the first day of summer when they rode out of the forest onto the central Arendish plain. Ce'Nedra by that time had gathered nearly every able-bodied Asturian into her army, and her hosts spread out behind her in a sea of humanity as she led the way out onto the plain. The sky above was very blue as they left the trees behind, and the grass was very green beneath the hooves of their horses.

"And where now, your Majesty?" Mandorallen inquired.

"To Vo Mimbre," Ce'Nedra replied. "I'll speak to the Mimbrate knights, and then we'll go on to Tolnedra."

"I hope your father still loves you, Ce'Nedra," King Rhodar said. "It'll take a lot of love to make Ran Borune forgive you for entering Tolnedra with this army at your back."

"He adores me," Ce'Nedra assured him confidently.

King Rhodar still looked dubious.

The army marched down through the plains of central Arendia toward the capital at Vo Mimbre where King Korodullin had assembled the Mimbrate knights and their retainers. The weather continued fair, and they marched in bright sunshine.

One sunny morning shortly after they had set out, Lady Polgara rode forward and joined Ce'Nedra at the head of the column. "Have you decided how you're going to deal with your father yet?" she asked.

"I'm not sure," the princess confessed. "He's probably going to be extremely difficult."

"The Borunes usually are."

"*I'm* a Borune, Lady Polgara."

"I know." Polgara looked penetratingly at the princess. "You've grown considerably in the past few months, dear," she observed.

"I didn't really have much choice, Lady Polgara. This all came on rather sud-

denly." Ce'Nedra giggled then as a thought suddenly struck her. "Poor Garion."
She laughed.

"Why poor Garion?"

"I was horrid to him, wasn't I?"

"Moderately horrid, yes."

"How were any of you able to stand me?"

"We clenched our teeth frequently."

"Do you think he'd be proud of me—if he knew what I'm doing, I mean?"

"Yes," Polgara told her, "I think he would be."

"I'm going to make it all up to him, you know," Ce'Nedra promised. "I'm going to be the best wife in the world."

"That's nice, dear."

"I won't scold or shout or anything."

"Don't make promises you can't keep, Ce'Nedra," Polgara said wisely.

"Well," the little princess amended, "almost never anyway."

Polgara smiled. "We'll see."

The Mimbrate knights were encamped on the great plain before the city of Vo
Mimbre. Together with their men-at-arms, they comprised a formidable army, glittering in the sunlight.

"Oh dear," Ce'Nedra faltered as she stared down at the vast gathering from
the hilltop where she and the Alorn Kings had ridden to catch the first glimpse of
the city.

"What's the problem?" Rhodar asked her.

"There are so many of them."

"That's the whole idea, isn't it?"

A tall Mimbrate knight with dark hair and beard, wearing a black velvet surcoat over his polished armor, galloped up the hill and reined in some yards before
them. He looked from face to face, then inclined his head in a polite bow. He
turned to Mandorallen. "Greetings to the Bastard of Vo Mandor from Korodullin,
King of Arendia."

"You still haven't gotten that straightened out, have you?" Barak muttered to
Mandorallen.

"I have not had leisure, my Lord," Mandorallen replied. He turned to the
knight. "Hail and well met, Sir Andorig. I pray thee, convey our greetings to his
Majesty and advise him that we come in peace—which he doubtless doth know
already."

"I will, Sir Mandorallen," Andorig responded.

"How's your apple tree doing, Andorig?" Barak asked, grinning openly.

"It doth flourish, my Lord of Trellheim," Andorig answered proudly. "My care
for it hath been most tender, and I have hopes of a bounteous harvest. I am confident that I have not disappointed Holy Belgarath." He turned and clattered back
down the hill, sounding his horn every hundred yards or so.

"What was that all about?" King Anheg asked his red-bearded cousin with a
puzzled frown.

"We've been here before," Barak replied. "Andorig didn't believe us when we told him who Belgarath was. Belgarath made an apple tree grow up out of the stones of the courtyard, and that sort of convinced him."

"I pray thee," Mandorallen said then, his eyes clouded with a sudden pain. "I see the approach of dear friends. I shall return presently." He moved his horse at a canter toward a knight and a lady who were riding out from the city.

"Good man there," Rhodar mused, watching the great knight as he departed. "But why do I get the feeling that when I'm talking to him my words are bouncing off solid bone?"

"Mandorallen is my knight," Ce'Nedra quickly came to the defense of her champion. "He doesn't need to think. I'll do his thinking for him." She stopped suddenly. "Oh dear," she said. "That sounds dreadful, doesn't it?"

King Rhodar laughed. "You're a treasure, Ce'Nedra," he said fondly, "but you do tend to blurt out things on occasion."

"Who are those people?" Ce'Nedra asked, curiously watching as Mandorallen rode to meet the couple who had emerged from the gates of Vo Mimbre.

"That's the Baron of Vo Ebor," Durnik replied quietly, "and his wife, the Baroness Nerina. Mandorallen's in love with her."

"*What?*"

"It's all very proper," Durnik assured her quickly. "I didn't understand it at first myself, but I guess it's the sort of thing that happens here in Arendia. It's a tragedy, of course. All three of them are suffering terribly." The good man sighed.

"Oh dear," Ce'Nedra said, biting her lip. "I didn't know—and I've treated him so badly at times."

"I'm sure he'll forgive you, Princess," Durnik told her. "He has a very great heart."

A short time later, King Korodullin rode out from the city, accompanied by Mandorallen and a score of armored knights. Ce'Nedra had met the young King of Arendia several years before, and she remembered him as a pale, thin young man with a beautiful voice. On this occasion he was dressed in full armor and a crimson surcoat. He raised his visor as he approached. "Your Majesty," he greeted her gravely, "we have awaited thy coming with great anticipation."

"Your Majesty is too kind," Ce'Nedra replied.

"We have marveled at the stories of thy mobilization of our Asturian cousins," the king told her. "Thine oratory must be wonderously persuasive to move them to lay aside their customary enmities."

"The day wears on, your Majesty," King Rhodar observed. "Her Majesty would like to address your knights—with your permission, of course. Once you've heard her, I think you'll understand her value to our cause."

"At once, your Majesty," Korodullin agreed. He turned to one of his men. "Assemble the knights and men-at-arms of Mimbre that the Rivan Queen may disclose her mind to them," he commanded.

The army which had followed Ce'Nedra down through the plains of Arendia had begun to arrive and was flowing down onto the plain before the city in a vast multitude. Drawn up to meet that force stood the glittering Mimbrate knights. The air crackled with suspicion as the two groups eyed each other.

"I think we'd better move right along," King Cho-Hag suggested. "An accidental remark out there could precipitate some unpleasantness we'd all prefer to avoid."

Ce'Nedra had already begun to feel sick to her stomach. The feeling by now, however, was so familiar that it no longer even worried her. A platform had been erected on a spot that stood midway between Ce'Nedra's army and the armored knights of King Korodullin. The princess, accompanied by all her friends and the Mimbrate honor guard, rode down to the platform, where she nervously dismounted.

"Feel free to speak at length, Ce'Nedra," Lady Polgara quietly advised. "Mimbrates dote on ceremony and they're as patient as stones if you give them something formal to watch. It's about two hours until sunset. Try to time the climax of your speech to coincide with that."

Ce'Nedra gasped. "Two *hours*?"

"If you need longer, we can build bonfires," Durnik offered helpfully.

"Two hours ought to be about right," Lady Polgara surmised.

Ce'Nedra quickly began mentally revising her speech. "You'll make sure they can all hear me?" she asked Polgara.

"I'll take care of it, dear."

Ce'Nedra drew in a deep breath. "All right, then," she said, "here we go." And she was helped up onto the platform.

It was not pleasant. It never was, but her weeks of practice in northern Arendia had given her the ability to assess the mood of a crowd and to adjust the pace of her delivery accordingly. As Polgara had suggested, the Mimbrates seemed quite willing to listen interminably. Moreover, standing here on the field at Vo Mimbre gave her words a certain dramatic impact. Torak himself had stood here, and the vast human sea of the Angarak hordes had hurled themselves from here against the unyielding walls of the city gleaming at the edge of the plain. Ce'Nedra spoke, the words rolling from her mouth as she delivered her impassioned address. Every eye was upon her, and every ear was bent to her words. Whatever sorcery Lady Polgara used to make the Rivan Queen's voice audible at the farthest edge of the crowd was clearly working. Ce'Nedra could see the impact of what she was saying rippling through the hosts before her like a breeze touching a field of bending wheat.

And then, as the sun hovered in golden clouds just above the western horizon, the little queen moved into the climactic crescendo of her oration. The words "pride," "honor," "courage," and "duty" sang in the blood of her rapt listeners. Her final question, "Who will follow me?" was delivered just as the setting sun bathed the field with flaming light and was answered with an ear-splitting roar as the Mimbrate knights drew their swords in salute.

Perspiring heavily in her sun-heated armor, Ce'Nedra, as was her custom, drew her own sword in reply, leaped to her horse and led her now enormous army from the field.

"Stupendous!" she heard King Korodullin marvel as he rode behind her.

"Now you see why we follow her," King Anheg told him.

"She's magnificent!" King Korodullin declared. "Truly, my Lords, such eloquence

can only be a gift from the Gods. I had viewed our enterprise with some trepidation—
I confess it—but gladly would I challenge all the hosts of Angarak now. Heaven itself
is with this marvelous child, and we cannot fail."

"I'll feel better after I see how the legions respond to her," King Rhodar observed. "They're a pretty hard-bitten lot, and I think it might take a bit more than
a speech about patriotism to move them."

Ce'Nedra, however, had already begun to work on that. She considered the
problem from every angle as she sat alone in her tent that evening, brushing her
hair. She needed something to stir her countrymen and she instinctively knew
what it must be.

Quite suddenly the silver amulet at her throat gave a strange little quiver,
something it had never done before. Ce'Nedra laid down her brush and touched
her fingertips to the talisman.

"I know you can hear me, Father," she heard Polgara say. A sudden image rose
in Ce'Nedra's mind of Polgara, wrapped in her blue cloak, standing atop a hill with
the night breeze stirring her hair.

"Have you regained your temper yet?" Belgarath's voice sounded wary.

"We'll talk about that some other time. What are you up to?"

"At the moment, I'm up to my ears in drunk Nadraks. We're in a tavern in Yar
Nadrak."

"I might have guessed. Is Garion all right?"

"Of course he is. I'm not going to let anything happen to him, Pol. Where are
you?"

"At Vo Mimbre, we've raised the Arends, and we're going on to Tolnedra in the
morning."

"Ran Borune won't like that much."

"We have a certain advantage. Ce'Nedra's leading the army."

"Ce'Nedra?" Belgarath sounded startled.

"It seems that was what the passage in the Codex meant. She's been preaching
the Arends out of the trees as if she owned them."

"What an amazing thing."

"Did you know that the southern Murgos are already gathered at Rak Goska?"

"I've heard some rumors."

"It changes things, you know."

"Perhaps. Who's in charge of the army?"

"Rhodar."

"Good. Tell him to avoid anything major as long as possible, Pol, but keep the
Angaraks off my back."

"We'll do what we can." She seemed to hesitate for a moment. "Are you all
right, Father?" she asked carefully. The question seemed important for some reason.

"Do you mean am I still in full possession of my faculties?" He sounded
amused. "Garion told me that you were worried about that."

"I told him not to say anything."

"By the time he got around to it, the whole question was pretty much
academic."

"Are you—? I mean can you still—?"

"Everything seems to work the same as always, Pol," he assured her.

"Give my love to Garion."

"Of course. Don't make a habit of this, but keep in touch with me."

"Very well, Father."

The amulet under Ce'Nedra's fingers quivered again. Then Polgara's voice spoke quite firmly. "All right, Ce'Nedra," the sorceress said, "you can stop eavesdropping now."

Guiltily, Ce'Nedra jerked her fingers from the amulet.

The next morning, even before the sun came up, she sent for Barak and Durnik.

"I'm going to need every scrap of Angarak gold in the entire army," she announced to them. "Every single coin. Buy it from the men if you have to, but get me all the red gold you can lay your hands on."

"I don't suppose you'd care to tell us why," Barak said sourly. The big man was surly about being pulled from his bed before daylight.

"I'm a Tolnedran," she informed him, "and I know my countrymen. I think I'm going to need some bait."

■ CHAPTER TWENTY-SEVEN ■

Ran Borune XXIII, Emperor of Tolnedra, was livid with rage. Ce'Nedra noticed with a certain pang that her father had aged considerably in the year that she had been absent and she wished that their meeting might be more cordial than this one promised to be.

The Emperor had drawn up his legions on the plains of northern Tolnedra, and they faced Ce'Nedra's army as it emerged from the forest of Vordue. The sun was warm, and the crimson standards of the legions, rising from what seemed a vast sea of brightly burnished steel, waved imposingly in the summer breeze. The massed legions had taken up positions along the crest of a line of low hills and they looked down at Ce'Nedra's sprawling army with the tactical advantage of terrain in their favor.

King Rhodar quietly pointed this out to the young queen as they dismounted to meet the Emperor. "We definitely don't want to provoke anything here," he advised her. "Try your best to be polite at least."

"I know what I'm doing, your Majesty," she replied airily, removing her helmet and carefully smoothing her hair.

"Ce'Nedra," Rhodar said bluntly, taking her arm in a firm grasp, "you've been playing this on your veins since the first day we landed on the hook of Arendia. You don't know from one minute to the next what you're going to do. I most definitely do *not* propose to attack the Tolnedran legions uphill, so be civil to your father or I'll take you over my knee and spank you. Do you understand me?"

"Rhodar!" Ce'Nedra gasped. "What a terrible thing to say!"

"I mean every word," he told her. "You mind your manners, young lady."

"Of course I will," she promised. She gave him a shy, little-girl look through fluttering eyelashes. "Do you still love me, Rhodar?" she asked in a tiny voice.

He gave her a helpless look, and then she patted his broad cheek. "Everything will be just fine, then," she assured him. "Here comes my father."

"Ce'Nedra," Ran Borune demanded angrily, striding to meet them, "just exactly what do you think you're doing?" The Emperor was dressed in gold-embossed armor, and Ce'Nedra thought he looked rather silly in it.

"Just passing through, Father," she replied as inoffensively as possible. "You've been well, I trust?"

"I was until you violated my borders. Where did you get the army?"

"Here and there, Father." She shrugged. "We really ought to talk, you know—someplace private."

"I don't have anything to say to you," the bald-headed little man declared. "I refuse to talk to you until you get this army off Tolnedran soil."

"Oh, Father," she reprimanded him, "stop being so childish."

"Childish?" The Emperor exploded. *"Childish!"*

"Her Majesty perhaps chose the wrong word," King Rhodar interposed, giving Ce'Nedra a hard look. "As we all know, she tends at times to be a trifle undiplomatic."

"What are you doing here, Rhodar?" Ran Borune demanded. He looked around quickly at the other kings. "Why have the Alorns invaded Tolnedra?"

"We haven't invaded you, Ran Borune," Anheg told him. "If we had, the smoke from burning towns and villages would be rising behind us. You know how we make war."

"What are you doing here, then?"

King Cho-Hag answered in a calm voice. "As her Majesty advised you, we're only passing through on our way to the East."

"And exactly what do you plan to do in the East?"

"That's our business," Anheg told him bluntly.

"Try to be civil," Lady Polgara said to the Cherek king. She turned to the Emperor. "My father and I explained to you what was happening last summer, Ran Borune. Weren't you listening?"

"That was before you stole my daughter," he retorted. "What have you done to her? She was difficult before, but now she's absolutely impossible."

"Children grow up, your Majesty," Polgara replied philosophically. "The queen's point was well taken, however. We do need to talk—preferably in private."

"What queen are we talking about?" the Emperor asked bitingly. "I don't see any queen here."

Ce'Nedra's eyes hardened. "Father," she snapped, "you know what's been happening. Now stop playing games and talk sense. This is very important."

"Your Highness knows me well enough to know that I don't play games," he told her in an icy tone.

"Your *Majesty*," she corrected him.

"Your *Highness*," he insisted.

"Your *Majesty*," she repeated, her voice going up an octave.

"Your *Highness*," he snarled from between clenched teeth.

"Do we really need to squabble like bad-tempered children right in front of the armies?" Polgara asked calmly.

"She's right, you know," Rhodar said to Ran Borune. "We're all beginning to look a bit foolish out here. We ought to try to maintain the fiction of dignity at least."

The Emperor glanced involuntarily over one shoulder at the glittering ranks of his legions drawn up on the hilltops not far away. "Very well," he conceded grudgingly, "but I want it clearly understood that the only thing we're going to talk about is your withdrawal from Tolnedran soil. If you'll follow me, we'll go to my pavilion."

"Which stands right in the middle of your legions," King Anheg added, "Forgive me, Ran Borune, but we're not that stupid. Why don't we go to my pavilion instead?"

"I'm no stupider than you are, Anheg," the Emperor retorted.

"If I may," King Fulrach said mildly. "In the interests of expediency, might we not assume that this spot is more or less neutral?" He turned to Brendig. "Colonel, would you be so good as to have a large tent erected here?"

"At once, your Majesty," the sober-faced Brendig replied.

King Rhodar grinned. "As you can see, the legendary practicality of the Sendars is not a myth."

The Emperor looked a bit sour, but finally seemed to remember his manners. "I haven't seen you in a long time, Fulrach," he said. "I hope Layla's well."

"She sends her regards," the King of Sendaria replied politely.

"You've got good sense, Fulrach," the Emperor burst out. "Why have you lent yourself to this insane adventure?"

"I think that might be one of the things we ought to discuss in private, don't you?" Polgara suggested smoothly.

"How's the squabble over the succession going?" Rhodar asked in the tone of a man making small talk.

"It's still up in the air," Ran Borune responded, also in a neutral manner. "The Honeths seem to be joining forces, though."

"That's unfortunate," Rhodar murmured. "The Honeths have a bad reputation."

Under Colonel Brendig's direction, a squad of Sendarian soldiers were quickly erecting a large, bright-colored pavilion on the green turf not far away.

"Did you deal with Duke Kador, Father?" Ce'Nedra inquired.

"His Grace found his life burdensome," Ran Borune replied with a short laugh. "Someone rather carelessly left some poison lying about in his prison cell, and he sampled it extensively. We gave him a splendid funeral."

Ce'Nedra smiled. "I'm so sorry I missed it."

"The pavilion is ready now," King Fulrach told them. "Shall we go inside?"

They all entered and sat at the table the soldiers had placed inside. Lord Morin, the Emperor's chamberlain, held Ce'Nedra's chair for her.

"How has he been?" Ce'Nedra whispered to the brown-mantled official.

"Not well, Princess," Morin replied. "Your absence grieved him more than he cared to admit."

"Is he eating well—and getting his rest?"

"We try, Highness." Morin shrugged. "But your father's not the easiest person in the world to get along with."

"Do you have his medicine?"

"Naturally, Highness. I never go anywhere without it."

"Suppose we get down to business," Rhodar was saying. "Taur Urgas has sealed his western border, and the southern Murgos have moved into position around Rak Goska. 'Zakath, the Mallorean Emperor, has set up a staging area on the plains outside Thull Zelik to receive his troops as he ferries them in. We're running out of time, Ran Borune."

"I'm negotiating with Taur Urgas," the Emperor replied, "and I'll dispatch a plenipotentiary to 'Zakath immediately. I'm certain this can be settled without a war."

"You can talk to Taur Urgas until your tongue falls out," Anheg snorted, "and 'Zakath probably doesn't even know or care who you are. As soon as they've gathered their forces, they'll march. The war can't be avoided, and I for one am just as happy about that. Let's exterminate the Angaraks once and for all."

"Isn't that just a bit uncivilized, Anheg?" Ran Borune asked him.

"Your Imperial Majesty," King Korodullin said formally, "the King of Cherek speaks hastily perhaps, but there is wisdom in his words. Must we live forever under the threat of invasion from the East? Might it not be best forever to quell them?"

"All of this is very interesting," Ce'Nedra interrupted them coolly. "but it's really beside the point. The actual point at issue here is that the Rivan King has returned, and Tolnedra is required by the provisions of the Accords of Vo Mimbre to submit to his leadership."

"Perhaps," her father replied. "But young Belgarion seems to be absent. Have you misplaced him somewhere? Or is it perhaps that he still had pots to scrub in the scullery at Riva so that you had to leave him behind?"

"That's beneath you, Father," Ce'Nedra said scornfully. "The Overlord of the West requires your service. Are you going to shame the Borunes and Tolnedra by abrogating the Accords?"

"Oh, no, Daughter," he said, holding up one hand. "Tolnedra always meticulously observes every clause of every treaty she's ever signed. The Accords require me to submit to Belgarion, and I'll do precisely that—just as soon as he comes here and tells me what he wants."

"I am acting in his stead," Ce'Nedra announced.

"I don't seem to recall anything that states that the authority is transferable."

"I *am* the Rivan Queen," Ce'Nedra retorted hotly, "and I've been invested with co-rulership by Belgarion himself."

"The wedding must have been very private. I'm a little hurt that I wasn't invited."

"The wedding will take place in due time, Father. In the meantime, I speak for Belgarion and for Riva."

"Speak all you want, girl." He shrugged. "I'm not obliged to listen, however. At the moment, you're only the betrothed of the Rivan King. You are not his wife and therefore not his queen. If we want to be strictly legal about it, until such time as you do marry, you're still under my authority. Perhaps if you apologize and get out of that stupid-looking armor and put on proper clothing, I'll forgive you. Otherwise, I'll be forced to punish you."

"Punish? *Punish!*"

"Don't scream at me, Ce'Nedra," the Emperor said hotly.

"Things seem to be deteriorating rapidly," Barak observed dryly to Anheg.

"I noticed that," Anheg agreed.

"I *am* the Rivan Queen!" Ce'Nedra shouted at her father.

"You're a silly girl!" he shot back.

"That does it, Father," she declared, leaping to her feet. "You will deliver command of your legions to me at once, and then you'll return to Tol Honeth where your servants can wrap you in shawls and feed you gruel, since you're obviously too senile to be of any further use to me."

"*Senile?*" the Emperor roared, also jumping up. "Get out of my sight! Take your stinking Alorn army out of Tolnedra at once, or I'll order my legions to throw you out."

Ce'Nedra, however, was already storming toward the door of the tent.

"You come back here!" he raged at her. "I haven't finished talking to you yet."

"Yes you have, Father," she shouted back. "Now *I'm* going to talk. Barak, I need that sack you have tied to your saddle." She rushed from the tent and climbed onto her horse, spluttering with apparent fury.

"Are you sure you know what you're doing?" Barak asked her as he tied the sack of Angarak coins to her saddle.

"Perfectly," she replied in a calm voice.

Barak's eyes narrowed as he looked at her. "You seem to have regained your temper in a remarkably short time."

"I never lost it, Barak."

"You were acting in there?"

"Obviously. Well, at least partially. It'll take my father an hour or so to regain his composure, and by then it'll be too late. Tell Rhodar and the others to prepare the army to march. The legions will be joining us."

"What makes you think that?"

"I'm going to go fetch them right now." She turned to Mandorallen, who had just emerged from the tent. "Where have you been?" she asked. "Come along. I need an escort."

"Where are we going, pray?" the knight asked.

"You'll see," she told him, and she turned her mount and rode at a trot up the hillside toward the massed legions. Mandorallen exchanged a helpless look with Barak and then clanged into his saddle to follow.

Ce'Nedra, riding ahead, carefully put her fingertips to her amulet. "Lady Polgara," she whispered, "can you hear me?" She wasn't certain that the amulet would work that way, but she had to try. "Lady Polgara," she whispered again, a bit more urgently.

"What are you doing, Ce'Nedra?" Polgara's voice sounded quite clearly in the little queen's ears.

"I'm going to talk to the legions," Ce'Nedra answered. "Can you fix it so they'll hear me?"

"Yes, but the legions won't be much interested in a speech about patriotism."

"I've got a different one," Ce'Nedra assured her.

"Your father's having a fit in here. He's actually foaming at the mouth."

Ce'Nedra sighed regretfully. "I know," she said. "It happens fairly often. Lord Morin has the medicine with him. Please try to keep him from biting his tongue."

"You goaded him into this deliberately, didn't you, Ce'Nedra?"

"I needed time to talk to the legions," the princess replied. "The fit won't really hurt him very much. He's had fits all his life. He'll have a nosebleed and a terrible headache when it's over. Please take care of him, Lady Polgara. I do love him, you know."

"I'll see what I can do, but you and I are going to have a long talk about this, young lady. There are some things you just don't do."

"I didn't have any choice, Lady Polgara. This is for Garion. Please do what you have to do so that the legions can hear me. It's awfully important."

"All right, Ce'Nedra, but don't do anything foolish." Then the voice was gone.

Ce'Nedra quickly scanned the standards drawn up before her, selected the familiar emblem of the Eighty-third Legion, and rode toward it. It was necessary that she place herself in front of men who would recognize her and confirm her identity to the rest of her father's army. The Eighty-third was primarily a ceremonial unit, and by tradition its barracks were inside the Imperial compound at Tol Honeth. It was a select group, still limited to the traditional thousand men, and it served primarily as a palace guard. Ce'Nedra knew every man in the Eighty-third by sight, and most of them by name. Confidently, she approached them.

"Colonel Albor," she courteously greeted the commander of the Eighty-third, a stout man with a florid face and a touch of gray at his temples.

"Your Highness," the colonel replied with a respectful inclination of his head. "We've missed you at the palace."

Ce'Nedra knew that to be a lie. The duty of guarding her person had been one of the common stakes in barracks dice games, with the honor always going to the loser. "I need a small favor, Colonel," she said to him as winsomely as she could.

"If it's in my power, Highness," he answered, hedging a bit.

"I wish to address my father's legions," she explained, "and I want them to know who I am." She smiled at him—warmly, insincerely. Albor was a Horbite, and Ce'Nedra privately detested him. "Since the Eighty-third practically raised me," she continued, "you of all people should recognize me and be able to identify me."

"That's true, your Highness," Albor admitted.

"Do you suppose you could send runners to the other legions to inform them just who I am?"

"At once, your Highness," Albor agreed. He obviously saw nothing dangerous in her request. For a moment Ce'Nedra almost felt sorry for him.

The runners—trotters actually, since members of the Eighty-third were not very athletic—began to circulate through the massed legions. Ce'Nedra chatted the while with Colonel Albor and his officers, though she kept a watchful eye on the tent where her father was recuperating from his seizure and also on the gold-colored canopy beneath which the Tolnedran general staff was assembled. She definitely did not want some curious officer riding over to ask what she was doing.

Finally, when she judged that any further delay might be dangerous, she politely excused herself. She turned her horse and, with Mandorallen close behind her, she rode back out to a spot where she was certain she could be seen.

"Sound your horn, Mandorallen," she told her knight.

"We are some distance from our own forces, your Majesty," he reminded her. "I pray thee, be moderate in thine address. Even I might experience some difficulty in facing the massed legions of all Tolnedra."

She smiled at him. "You know you can trust me, Mandorallen."

"With my life, your Majesty," he replied and lifted his horn to his lips.

As his last ringing notes faded, Ce'Nedra, her stomach churning with the now-familiar nausea, rose in her stirrups to speak. "Legionnaires," she called to them. "I am Princess Ce'Nedra, the daughter of your Emperor." It wasn't perhaps the best beginning in the world, but she had to start somewhere, and this was going to be something in the nature of a performance, rather than an oration, so a bit of awkwardness in places wouldn't hurt anything.

"I have come to set your minds at rest," she continued. "The army massed before you comes in peace. This fair, green field, this sacred Tolnedran soil, shall not be a battleground this day. For today at least, no legionnaire will shed his blood in defense of the Empire."

A ripple of relief passed through the massed legions. No matter how professional soldiers might be, an avoided battle was always good news. Ce'Nedra drew in a deep, quivering breath. It needed just a little twist now, something to lead logically to what she really wanted to say. "Today you will not be called upon to die for your brass half crown." The brass half crown was the legionnaire's standard daily pay. "I cannot, however, speak for tomorrow," she went on. "No one can say when the affairs of Empire will demand that you lay down your lives. It may be tomorrow that the interests of some powerful merchant may need legion blood for protection." She lifted her hands in a rueful little gesture. "But then, that's the way it's always been, hasn't it? The legions die for brass so that others might have gold."

A cynical laugh of agreement greeted that remark. Ce'Nedra had heard enough of the idle talk of her father's soldiers to know that this complaint was at the core of every legionnaire's view of the world. "Blood and gold—our blood and their gold," was very nearly a legion motto. They were almost with her now. The quivering in her stomach subsided a bit, and her voice became stronger.

She told them a story then—a story she'd heard in a half dozen versions since her childhood. It was the story of a good legionnaire who did his duty and saved his money. His wife had suffered through the hardships and separations that went with being married to a legionnaire. When he was mustered out of his legion, they had gone home and bought a little shop, and all the years of sacrifice seemed worthwhile.

"And then one day, his wife became very ill," Ce'Nedra continued her story, "and the physician's fee was very high." She had been carefully untying the sack fastened to her saddle while she spoke. "The physician demanded this much," she said, taking three blood-red Murgo coins from the sack and holding them up for all to see. "And the legionnaire went to a powerful merchant and borrowed the money to pay the physician. But the physician, like most of them, was a fraud, and the legionnaire's money might as well have been thrown away." Quite casually, Ce'Nedra tossed the gold coins into the high grass behind her. "The soldier's good and faithful wife died. And when the legionnaire was bowed down with grief, the powerful merchant came to him and said, 'Where's the money I lent to you?' " She took out three more coins and held them up. " 'Where's that good red gold I gave you to pay the physician?' But the legionnaire had no gold. His hands were empty." Ce'Nedra spread her fingers, letting the gold coins fall to the ground. "And so the merchant took the legionnaire's shop to pay the debt. A rich man grew richer. And what happened to the legionnaire? Well, he still had his sword. He had been a good soldier, so he had kept it bright and sharp. And after his wife's funeral, he took his sword and went out into a field not far from the town and he fell upon it. And that's how the story ends."

She had them now. She could see it in their faces. The story she had told them had been around for a long time, but the gold coins she had so casually tossed away gave it an entirely new emphasis. She took out several of the Angarak coins and looked at them curiously as if seeing them for the first time. "Why do you suppose that all the gold we see these days is red?" she asked them. "I always thought gold was supposed to be yellow. Where does all this red gold come from?"

"From Cthol Murgos," several of them answered her.

"Really?" She looked at the coins with an apparent distaste. "What's Murgo gold doing in Tolnedra?" And she threw the coins away.

The iron discipline of the legions wavered, and they all took an involuntary step forward.

"Of course, I don't suppose an ordinary soldier sees much red gold. Why should a Murgo try to bribe a common soldier when he can bribe the officers—or the powerful men who decide where and when the legions are to go to bleed and die?" She took out another coin and looked at it. "Do you know, I think that every single one of these is from Cthol Murgos," she said, negligently throwing the coin away. "Do you suppose that the Murgos are trying to buy up Tolnedra?"

There was an angry mutter at that.

"There must be a great deal of this red gold lying about in the Angarak kingdoms if that's what they have in mind, wouldn't you say? I've heard stories about that, though. Don't they say that the mines of Cthol Murgos are bottomless and that there are rivers in Gar og Nadrak that look like streams of blood because the gravel over which they flow is pure gold? Why, gold must be as cheap as dirt in the lands of the East." She took out another coin, glanced at it and then tossed it away.

The legions took another involuntary step forward. The officers barked the command to stand fast, but they also looked hungrily toward the tall grass where the princess had been so indifferently throwing the red gold coins.

"It may be that the army I'm leading will be able to find out just how much gold lies on the ground in the lands of the Angaraks," Ce'Nedra confided to them. "The Murgos and the Grolims have been practicing this same kind of deceit in Arendia and Sendaria and the Alorn kingdoms. We're on our way to chastise them for it." She stopped as if an idea had just occurred to her. "There's always room in any army for a few more good soldiers," she mused thoughtfully. "I know that most legionnaires serve out of loyalty to their legions and love for Tolnedra, but there may be a few among you who aren't satisfied with one brass half crown a day. I'm sure such men would be welcome in my army." She took another red coin out of her dwindling supply. "Would you believe that there's *another* Murgo gold piece?" she demanded and let the coin drop from her fingers.

A sound went through the massed legions that was almost a groan.

The princess sighed then. "I forgot something," she said regretfully. "My army's leaving at once, and it takes weeks for a legionnaire to arrange for leave, doesn't it?"

"Who needs leave?" someone shouted.

"You wouldn't actually desert your legions, would you?" she asked them incredulously.

"The princess offers gold!" another man roared. "Let Ran Borune keep his brass!"

Ce'Nedra dipped one last time into the bag and took out the last few coins. "Would you actually follow me?" she asked in her most little-girl voice, "just for this?" And she let the coins trickle out of her hand.

The Emperor's general staff at that point made a fatal mistake. They dispatched a platoon of cavalry to take the princess into custody. Seeing mounted men riding toward the ground Ce'Nedra had so liberally strewn with gold and mistaking their intent, the legions broke. Officers were swarmed under and trampled as Ran Borune's army lunged forward to scramble in the grass for the coins.

"I pray thee, your Majesty," Mandorallen urged, drawing his sword, "let us withdraw to safety."

"In a moment, Sir Mandorallen," Ce'Nedra replied quite calmly. She stared directly at the desperately greedy legionnaires running toward her. "My army marches immediately," she announced. "If the Imperial Legions wish to join us, I welcome them." And with that, she wheeled her horse and galloped back toward her own forces with Mandorallen at her side.

Behind her she heard the heavy tread of thousands of feet. Someone among the massed legions began a chant that soon spread. "Ce-Ne-dra! Ce-Ne-dra!" they shouted, and their heavy steps marked time to that chant.

The Princess Ce'Nedra, her sun-touched hair streaming in the wind behind her, galloped on, leading the mass mutiny of the legions. Even as she rode, Ce'Nedra knew that her every word had been a deception. There would be no more wealth for these legionnaires than there would be glory or easy victory for the Arends she had gathered from the forests of Asturia and the plains of Mimbre. She had raised an army to lead into a hopeless war.

It was for love of Garion, however, and perhaps for even more. If the Prophecy that so controlled their destinies demanded this of her, there was no way she could have refused. Despite all the anguish that lay ahead, she would have done this and more. For the first time Ce'Nedra accepted the fact that she no longer controlled her own destiny. Something infinitely more powerful than she commanded her, and she must obey.

Polgara and Belgarath, with lives spanning eons, could perhaps devote themselves to an idea, a concept; but Ce'Nedra was barely sixteen years old, and she needed something more human to arouse her devotion. At this very moment, somewhere in the forests of Gar og Nadrak, there was a sandy-haired young man with a serious face whose safety—whose very life—depended on every effort she could muster. The princess surrendered finally to love. She swore to herself that she would never fail her Garion. If this army were not enough, she would raise another—at whatever cost.

Ce'Nedra sighed, then squared her shoulders and led the Tolnedran legions across the sunny fields to swell the ranks of her army.

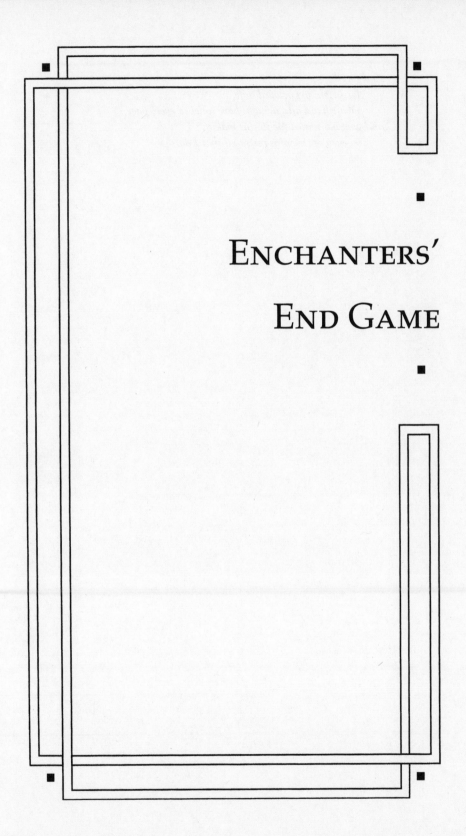

ENCHANTERS'
END GAME

And finally,
    for Leigh, my beloved wife,
       whose hand and thought have touched every page,
and who has joined me in this making
    —even as she joins me in all that I do.

PROLOGUE

Being an account of beginnings—and endings.
—Excerpts from *The Book of Torak**

Hear me, ye Angaraks, for I am Torak, Lord of Lords and King of Kings. Bow before my Name and worship me with prayers and with sacrifices, for I am your God and I have dominion over all the realms of the Angaraks. And great shall be my wrath if ye displease me.

I was before the world was made. I shall be after the mountains crumble into sand, the seas dwindle to stagnant pools, and the world shrivels and is no more. For I was before time and shall be after.

From the timeless reaches of Infinity, I gazed upon the future. And I beheld that there were two Destinies and that they must rush toward each other from the endless corridors of Eternity. Each Destiny was Absolute, and in that final meeting, all that was divided should be made one. In that instant, all that was, all that is, and all that was yet to be should be gathered into one Purpose.

And because of my Vision, I led my six brothers to join hands to make all that is, in fulfillment of the needs of the Destinies. Thus we set the moon and the sun in their courses and we brought forth this world. We covered the world with forests and grasses and made beasts, fowls, and fishes to fill the lands and skies and waters which we had made.

But our Father took no joy in this creation which I had caused to be. He turned his face from our labor to contemplate the Absolute. I went alone into the high places of Korim, which are no more, and I cried out to him to accept what I had made. But he rejected the work I had caused to be and turned from me. Then I hardened my heart against him and went down from that place, fatherless evermore.

Once more I counseled my brothers, and we joined our hands and brought forth man to be the instrument of our will. We created man as many peoples. And to each people, we gave a choice to select among us the one who should be their God. And the peoples chose from us, save only that no people chose Aldur, who was ever contrary and discontented that we would not grant him dominion. Then Aldur withdrew himself from among us and sought to entice our servants away from us with enchantments. But few were they who accepted him.

---

*Editor's Note: This version, said to be from the dread *Book of Torak*, is one of several circulated among the Nadraks. Since only the high Grolims were permitted official copies of the work, it is impossible to establish that this version is authentic, though internal evidence suggests that much of it may be. A true copy of the complete *Book of Torak* is believed to be in the library of King Anheg of Cherek, but this was not available for comparison.

The peoples who were mine called themselves the Angaraks. I was well pleased with them and I led them to the high places of Korim, which are no more, and to them I revealed the nature of the Purpose for which I had caused the world to be.

Then they worshiped me with prayers and offered burnt offerings unto me. And I blessed them, and they prospered and grew numerous. In their gratitude they raised up an altar to me and there made sacrifice to me of their fairest maidens and a portion of their bravest youths. And I was well pleased with them and again I blessed them, so that they prospered above all other men and multiplied exceedingly.

Now the heart of Aldur was filled with envy for the worship that was given to me, and he was driven with despite for me. Then did he conspire against me within the secret places of his soul, and he took up a stone and breathed life into it, that it might thwart my Purpose. And in that stone he sought to gain dominion over me. Thus Cthrag Yaska came to be. And there was eternal enmity sealed within Cthrag Yaska against me. And Aldur sat apart with those whom he called his disciples and plotted how the stone should give him dominion.

I saw that the accursed stone had divided Aldur from me and from his other brothers. And I went to Aldur and remonstrated with him, begging that he lift the wicked enchantment from the stone and take back the life he had breathed into it. This I did that Aldur might no longer be divided from his brothers. Yea, I did even weep and abase myself before him.

But already the evil stone had gained possession over the soul of Aldur, and he had hardened his heart against me. And I saw then that the stone which Aldur had created would forever hold my brother in thralldom. And he spoke slightingly to me and would have driven me forth.

Then for the love I bore him and to save him from the evil course which my Vision revealed, I struck my brother Aldur down and took from him the accursed rock. And I bore Cthrag Yaska away to bend my will upon it and to still the malice within it and quell the wickedness for which it was created. So it was that I took the burden of the thing which Aldur had created upon myself.

Aldur was wroth with me. He went to our brothers and spoke to them falsely against me. And each of them came to me and spoke slightingly to me, commanding that I return to Aldur that which had twisted his soul and which I had taken to free him from the enchantment of it. But I resisted.

Then they girded for war. The sky was blackened with the smoke of their forges as their peoples beat out weapons of iron to spill the blood of my Angaraks upon the ground. When the year turned, their hosts marched forth and onto the lands of the Angaraks. And my brothers loomed tall in the forefront of the hosts.

Now was I greatly loath to lift my hand against them. Yet I could not permit that they should despoil the lands of my people or loose the blood of those who worshiped me. And I knew that from such war between my brothers and me could come only evil. In that struggle, the Destinies I had seen might be sent against each other before it was time, and the universe be shaken apart in that meeting.

And so I chose that which I feared, but which was less evil than the danger I foresaw. I took up the accursed Cthrag Yaska and raised it against the earth itself. And in me lay the Purpose of one Destiny, while the Purpose of the other was affixed within the stone Aldur had created. The weight of all that was or will be was upon us, and the earth could not bear our weight. Then did her mantle rend asunder before me, and the sea rushed in to drown the dry land. Thus were the peoples separated one from the other, that they might not come upon each other and their blood be spilled.

But such was the malice which Aldur had wrought within the stone that it smote me with fire as I raised it to divide the world and prevent evil bloodshed. Even as I spoke the commands unto it, it burst into dreadful fire and smote me. The hand with which I held it was consumed and the eye with which I beheld it was blinded. One half of my face was marred by its burning. And I, who had been the fairest among my brothers, was now abhorrent to the eyes of all, and I must cover my face with a living mask of steel, lest they shun me.

An agony filled me from the evil that was done me, and pain lived within me, which could never be quenched until the foul stone could be freed of its evil and could repent of its malice.

But the dark sea stood between my people and those who would come against them, and my enemies fled in terror of that which I had done. Yea, even my brothers fled from the world which we had made, for they dared no longer come against me. Yet still did they conspire with their followers in spirit form.

Then I bore my people away to the wastelands of Mallorea and there caused them to build a mighty city on a sheltered place. They named it Cthol Mishrak, as a remembrance of the suffering I had undergone for them. And I concealed their city with a cloud that should ever be above it.

Then I had a cask of iron forged, and in it I bound Cthrag Yaska, that the evil stone should never again be free to unleash its power to destroy flesh. For a thousand years and still another thousand years I labored, contending with the stone that I might release the curse of malice which Aldur had laid upon it. Great were the enchantments and words of power which I cast at the obdurate stone, but still its evil fire burned when I came near to it, and I felt its curse lying ever upon the world.

Then Belar, youngest and most rash of my brothers, conspired against me with Aldur, who still bore hatred and jealousy within his soul toward me. And Belar spoke in spirit to his uncouth people, the Alorns, and set them against me. The spirit of Aldur sent Belgarath, the disciple in whom he had most wholly instilled his despite, to join with them. And the foul counsel of Belgarath prevailed upon Cherek, chief of the Alorns, and upon his three sons.

By evil sorcery, they passed the barrier of the sea I had caused to be and they came like thieves in the night to the city of Cthol Mishrak. By stealth and low cunning, they crept through my tower of iron and made their way to the chest that held the evil stone.

The youngest son of Cherek, whom men called Riva Iron-grip, had been so woven about with spells and enchantments that he could take up the accursed stone and not perish. And they fled with it to the west.

With the warriors of my people I pursued them, that the curse of Cthrag Yaska not again be loosed upon the land. But the one called Riva raised the stone and loosed its evil fire upon my people. Thus the thieves escaped, bearing the evil of the stone with them into their lands of the west.

Then I pulled down the mighty city of Cthol Mishrak, that my people must flee from its ruins. And I divided the Angaraks into tribes. The Nadraks I set in the north to guard the ways in which the thieves had come. The Thulls, broad of back for the bearing of burdens, I set in the middle lands. The Murgos, fiercest of my people, I sent to the south. And the most numerous I kept with me in Mallorea, to serve me and multiply against a day when I should have need of an army against the west.

Above all these peoples I set the Grolims and instructed them in enchantments and wizardry, that they be a priesthood to me and watch over the zeal of all others. And them I instructed to keep my altars burning and to be unceasing in their sacrifices to me.

Belgarath, in his wickedness, had sent Riva with the accursed stone to rule an island in the Sea of Winds. And there Belar caused two stars to fall to earth. From these, Riva forged a sword and set Cthrag Yaska into its pommel.

And when Riva gripped that sword, the universe shuddered about me, and I cried out, for my Vision had opened to me, revealing much that had been hidden before. I saw that Belgarath's sorcerous daughter should in time be my bride, and I rejoiced. But I also saw that a Child of Light would descend from Riva's loins, and he would be an instrument of that Destiny which opposed that other Destiny which gave me my Purpose. Then would come a day when I must wake from some long sleep to face the sword of the Child of Light. And upon that day, the two Destinies would clash, with only one victor alive and one Destiny thenceforth. But which was not revealed.

Long I pondered this Vision, but no more was revealed. And a thousand years passed, and even more.

Then I called to me Zedar, a wise and just man who had fled from the malice of Aldur's teachings and had come unto me with an offer of service. And I sent him to the court of the Serpent People who dwelt among swamps in the west. Their God was Issa, but he was ever lazy and he slept, leaving the people who called themselves Ny-Issans to the sole rule of their queen. And to her Zedar did make certain offers, which were pleasing to her. And she sent her assassins as emissaries to the court of Riva's descendants. There did they slay all of that line, save only one child who chose to drown himself in the sea.

Thus did the Vision err, for what Child of Light can be born when none remain to bear him?

And thus have I assured that my Purpose shall be served and that the evil of Aldur and his brothers shall not destroy the world which I caused to be created.

The Kingdoms of the West which have harkened unto the counsel and beguilements of wicked Gods and evil sorcerers will be brought unto the dust. And I will harry those who sought to deny me and confound me and multiply their suffering. And they shall be brought low and they shall fall before me, offering themselves as a sacrifice upon my altars.

And the time shall come when I have Lordship and dominion over all the earth, and all peoples shall be mine.

Hear me, ye peoples, and fear me. Bow down before me and worship me. For I am Torak, forever King of Kings, Lord of Lords, and God alone to this world which I have caused to be.

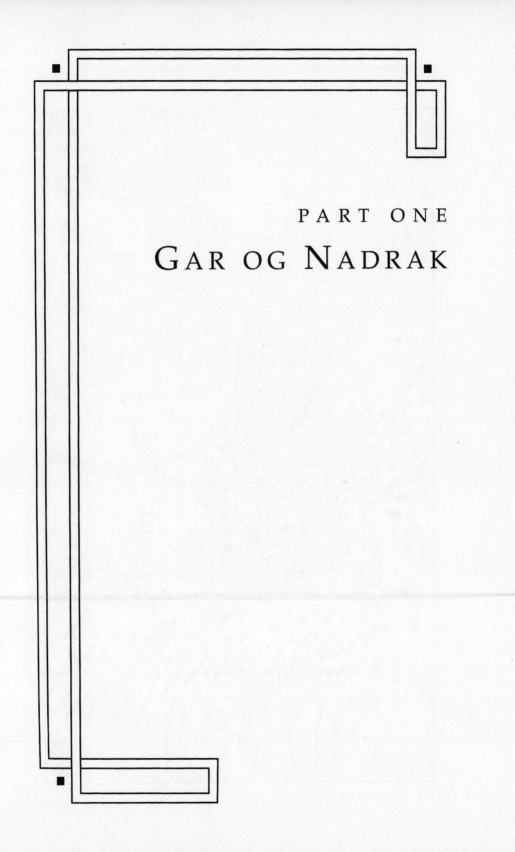

PART ONE

GAR OG NADRAK

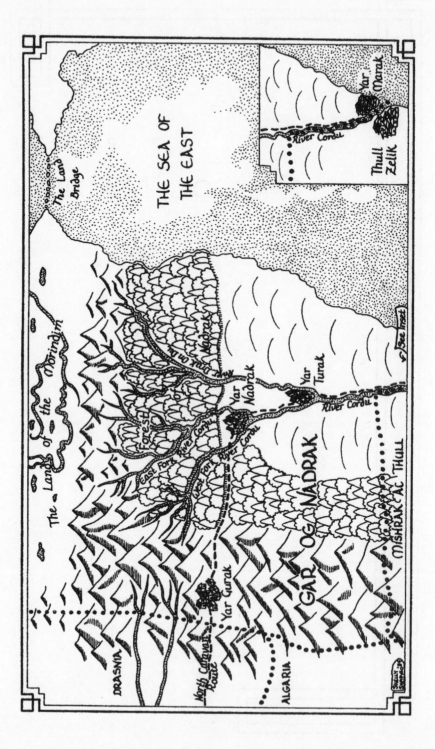

CHAPTER ONE

There was, Garion decided, something definitely mournful about the sound of mule bells. The mule was not a particularly lovable animal to begin with, and there was a subtle difference to his gait that imparted a lugubrious note to a bell hung about his neck. The mules were the property of a Drasnian merchant named Mulger, a lanky, hard-eyed man in a green doublet, who—for a price—had allowed Garion, Silk, and Belgarath to accompany him on his trek into Gar og Nadrak. Mulger's mules were laden with trade goods, and Mulger himself seemed to carry a burden of preconceptions and prejudices almost as heavy as a fully loaded mule pack. Silk and the worthy merchant had disliked each other at first sight, and Silk amused himself by baiting his countryman as they rode eastward across the rolling moors toward the jagged peaks that marked the boundary between Drasnia and the land of the Nadraks. Their discussions, hovering just on the verge of wrangling, grated on Garion's nerves almost as much as the tiresome clanging of the bells on Mulger's mules.

Garion's edginess at this particular time came from a very specific source. He was afraid. There was no point in trying to conceal that fact from himself. The cryptic words of the Mrin Codex had been explained to him in precise detail. He was riding toward a meeting that had been ordained since the beginning of time, and there was absolutely no way he could avoid it. The meeting was the end result of not one, but *two* distinct Prophecies, and even if he could persuade one of them that there had been a mistake someplace, the other would drive him to the confrontation without mercy or the slightest consideration for his personal feelings.

"I think you're missing the point, Ambar," Mulger was saying to Silk with that kind of acid precision some men use when talking to someone they truly despise. "My patriotism or lack of it has nothing to do with the matter. The well-being of Drasnia depends on trade, and if you people in the Foreign Service keep hiding your activities by posing as merchants, it won't be long before an *honest* Drasnian isn't welcome anywhere." Mulger, with that instinct that seemed inborn in all Drasnians, had instantly recognized the fact that Silk was not what he pretended to be.

"Oh, come now, Mulger," Silk replied with an airy condescension, "don't be so naïve. Every kingdom in the world conceals its intelligence activities in exactly the same way. The Tolnedrans do it; the Murgos do it; even the Thulls do it. What do you want me to do—walk around with a sign on my chest reading 'spy'?"

"Frankly, Ambar, I don't care what you do," Mulger retorted, his lean face hardening. "All I can say is that I'm getting very tired of being watched everyplace I go, just because you people can't be trusted."

Silk shrugged with an impudent grin. "It's the way the world is, Mulger. You might as well get used to it, because it's not going to change."

Mulger glared at the rat-faced little man helplessly, then turned abruptly and rode back to keep company with his mules.

"Aren't you pushing it a little?" Belgarath suggested, lifting his head from the apparent doze in which he usually rode. "If you irritate him enough, he'll denounce you to the border guards, and we'll never get into Gar og Nadrak."

"Mulger's not going to say a word, old friend," Silk assured him. "If he does, he'll be held for investigation, too, and there's not a merchant alive who doesn't have a few things concealed in his packs that aren't supposed to be there."

"Why don't you just leave him alone?" Belgarath asked.

"It gives me something to do," Silk replied with a shrug. "Otherwise I'd have to look at the scenery, and eastern Drasnia bores me."

Belgarath grunted sourly, pulled his gray hood up over his head, and settled back into his nap.

Garion returned to his melancholy thoughts. The gorse bushes which covered the rolling moors had a depressing gray-green color to them, and the North Caravan Route wound like a dusty white scar across them. The sky had been overcast for nearly two weeks, though there was no hint of moisture in the clouds. They plodded along through a dreary, shadowless world toward the stark mountains looming on the horizon ahead.

It was the unfairness of it all that upset Garion the most. He had never asked for any of this. He did not *want* to be a sorcerer. He did not *want* to be the Rivan King. He was not even sure that he really *wanted* to marry Princess Ce'Nedra—although he was of two minds about that. The little Imperial Princess could be—usually when she wanted something—absolutely adorable. Most of the time, however, she did not want anything, and her true nature emerged. If he had consciously sought any of this, he could have accepted the duty which lay on him with a certain amount of resignation. He had been given no choice in the matter, though, and he found himself wanting to demand of the uncaring sky, "Why me?"

He rode on beside his dozing grandfather with only the murmuring song of the Orb of Aldur for company, and even that was a source of irritation. The Orb, which stood on the pommel of the great sword strapped to his back, sang to him endlessly with a kind of silly enthusiasm. It might be all very well for the Orb to exult about the impending meeting with Torak, but it was Garion who was going to have to face the Dragon-God of Angarak, and it was Garion who was going to have to do all the bleeding. He felt that the unrelieved cheerfulness of the Orb was—all things considered—in very poor taste, to say the least.

The border between Drasnia and Gar og Nadrak straddled the North Caravan Route in a narrow, rocky gap where two garrisons, one Drasnian and one Nadrak, faced each other across a simple gate that consisted of a single, horizontal pole. By itself, the pole was an insubstantial barrier. Symbolically, however, it was more intimidating than the gates of Vo Mimbre or Tol Honeth. On one side of the gate stood the West; on the other, the East. With a single step, one could move from one world into a totally different one, and Garion wished with all his being that he did not have to take that step.

As Silk had predicted, Mulger said nothing about his suspicions to either the Drasnian pikemen or the leather-clad Nadrak soldiers at the border, and they passed without incident into the mountains of Gar og Nadrak. Once it passed the border, the caravan route climbed steeply up a narrow gorge beside a swiftly tumbling mountain stream. The rock walls of the gorge were sheer, black, and oppressive. The sky overhead narrowed to a dirty gray ribbon, and the clanging mule bells echoed back from the rocks to accompany the rush and pounding gurgle of the stream.

Belgarath awoke and looked around, his eyes alert. He gave Silk a quick, sidelong glance that cautioned the little man to keep his mouth shut, then cleared his throat. "We want to thank you, worthy Mulger, and to wish you good luck in your dealings here."

Mulger looked at the old sorcerer sharply, his eyes questioning.

"We'll be leaving you at the head of this gorge," Belgarath continued smoothly, his face bland. "Our business is off that way." He gestured rather vaguely.

Mulger grunted. "I don't want to know anything about it," he declared.

"You don't, really," Belgarath assured him. "And please don't take Ambar's remarks too seriously. He has a comic turn of mind and he says things he doesn't always mean, because he enjoys irritating people. Once you get to know him, he's not quite so bad."

Mulger gave Silk a long, hard look and let it pass without comment. "Good luck in whatever it is you're doing," he said grudgingly, forced to say it more out of courtesy than out of any genuine good feeling. "You and the young man weren't bad traveling companions."

"We are in your debt, worthy Mulger," Silk added with mocking extravagance. "Your hospitality has been exquisite."

Mulger looked directly at Silk again. "I don't really like you, Ambar," he said bluntly. "Why don't we just let it go at that?"

"I'm crushed." Silk grinned at him.

"Let it lie," Belgarath growled.

"I made every effort to win him over," Silk protested.

Belgarath turned his back on him.

"I really did." Silk appealed to Garion, his eyes brimming with mock sincerity.

"I don't believe you either," Garion told him.

Silk sighed. "Nobody understands me," he complained. Then he laughed and rode on up the gorge, whistling happily to himself.

At the head of the gorge, they left Mulger and struck off to the left of the caravan route through a jumble of rock and stunted trees. At the crest of a stony ridge, they stopped to watch the slow progress of the mules until they were out of sight.

"Where are we headed?" Silk asked, squinting up at the clouds scudding past overhead. "I thought we were going to Yar Gurak."

"We are," Belgarath replied, scratching at his beard, "but we'll circle around and come at the town from the other side. Mulger's opinions make traveling with him just a bit chancy. He might let something slip at the wrong time. Besides,

Garion and I have something to take care of before we get there." The old man looked around. "Over there ought to do," he said, pointing at a shallow green dale, concealed on the far side of the ridge. He led them down into the dale and dismounted.

Silk, leading their single packhorse, pulled up beside a small pool of spring water and tied the horses to a dead snag standing at its edge.

"What is it that we have to do, Grandfather?" Garion asked, sliding out of his saddle.

"That sword of yours is a trifle obvious," the old man told him. "Unless we want to spend the whole trip answering questions, we're going to have to do something about it."

"Are you going to make it invisible?" Silk asked hopefully.

"In a manner of speaking," Belgarath answered. "Open your mind to the Orb, Garion. Just let it talk to you."

Garion frowned. "I don't understand."

"Just relax. The Orb will do the rest. It's very excited about you, so don't pay too much attention to it if it starts making suggestions. It has a severely limited understanding of the real world. Just relax and let your mind sort of drift. I've got to talk to it, and I can only do that through you. It won't listen to anybody else."

Garion leaned back against a tree; in a moment he found his mind filled with all manner of peculiar images. The world he perceived in that imagining was tinged over with a faint blue haze, and everything seemed angular, as if constructed out of the flat planes and sharp edges of a crystal. He caught a vivid picture of himself, flaming sword in hand, riding at great speed with whole hordes of faceless men fleeing out of his path. Belgarath's voice sounded sharply in his mind then. "Stop that." The words, he realized, were not directed at him, but instead at the Orb itself. Then the old man's voice dropped to a murmur, instructing, explaining something. The responses of that other, crystalline awareness seemed a trifle petulant; but eventually there seemed to be an agreement of some kind, and then Garion's mind cleared.

Belgarath was shaking his head with a rueful expression. "It's almost like talking to a child sometimes," he said. "It has no conception of numbers, and it can't even begin to comprehend the meaning of the word danger."

"It's still there," Silk noted, sounding a bit disappointed. "I can still see the sword."

"That's because you know it's there," Belgarath told him. "Other people will overlook it."

"How can you overlook something that big?" Silk objected.

"It's very complicated," Belgarath replied. "The Orb is simply going to encourage people not to see it—or the sword. If they look very closely, they might realize that Garion's carrying *something* on his back, but they won't be curious enough about it to try to find out what it is. As a matter of fact, quite a few people won't even notice Garion himself."

"Are you trying to say that Garion's invisible?"

"No. He's just sort of unremarkable for the time being. Let's move on. Night comes on quickly up in these mountains."

Yar Gurak was perhaps the ugliest town Garion had ever seen. It was strung out on either side of a roiling yellow creek, and muddy, unpaved streets ran up the steep slopes of the cut the stream had gouged out of the hills. The sides of the cut beyond the town had been stripped of all vegetation. There were shafts running back into the hillsides, and great, rooted-out excavations. There were springs among the diggings, and they trickled muddy water down the slopes to pollute the creek. The town had a slapdash quality about it, and all the buildings seemed somewhat temporary. Construction was, for the most part, log and uncut rock, and several of the houses had been finished off with canvas.

The streets teemed with lanky, dark-faced Nadraks, many of whom were obviously drunk. A nasty brawl erupted out of a tavern door as they entered the town, and they were forced to stop while perhaps two dozen Nadraks rolled about in the mud, trying with a fair amount of success to incapacitate or even maim each other.

The sun was going down as they found an inn at the end of a muddy street. It was a large, square building with the main floor constructed of stone, a second story built of logs, and stables attached to the rear. They put up their horses, took a room for the night, and then entered the barnlike common room in search of supper. The benches in the common room were a bit unsteady, and the tabletops were grease-smeared and littered with crumbs and spilled food. Oil lamps hung smoking on chains, and the smell of cooking cabbage was overpowering. A fair number of merchants from various parts of the world sat at their evening meal in the room—wary-eyed men in tight little groups, with walls of suspicion drawn around them.

Belgarath, Silk, and Garion sat down at an unoccupied table and ate the stew brought to them in wooden bowls by a tipsy servingman in a greasy apron. When they had finished, Silk glanced at the open doorway leading into the noisy taproom and then looked inquiringly at Belgarath.

The old man shook his head. "Better not," he said. "Nadraks are a high-strung people, and relations with the West are a little tense just now. There's no point in asking for trouble."

Silk nodded his glum agreement and led the way up the stairs at the back of the inn to the room they had taken for the night. Garion held up their guttering candle and looked dubiously at the log-frame bunks standing against the walls of the room. The bunks had rope springs and mattresses stuffed with straw; they looked lumpy and not very clean. The noise from the taproom below was loud and raucous.

"I don't think we're going to get much sleep tonight," he observed.

"Mining towns aren't like farm villages," Silk pointed out. "Farmers feel the need for decorum—even when they're drunk. Miners tend on the whole to be somewhat rowdier."

Belgarath shrugged. "They'll quiet down in a bit. Most of them will be unconscious long before midnight." He turned to Silk. "As soon as the shops open up in the morning, I want you to get us some different clothing—used, preferably. If we look like gold hunters, nobody's going to pay very much attention to us. Get a pick handle and a couple of rock hammers. We'll tie them to the outside of the pack on our spare horse for show."

"I get the feeling you've done this before."

"From time to time. It's a useful disguise. Gold hunters are crazy to begin with, so people aren't surprised if they show up in strange places." The old man laughed shortly. "I even found gold once—a vein as thick as your arm."

Silk's face grew immediately intent. "Where?"

Belgarath shrugged. "Off that way somewhere," he replied with a vague gesture. "I forget exactly."

"Belgarath," Silk objected with a note of anguish in his voice.

"Don't get sidetracked," Belgarath told him. "Let's get some sleep. I want to be out of here as early as possible tomorrow morning."

The overcast which had lingered for weeks cleared off during the night; when Garion awoke, the new-risen sun streamed golden through the dirty window. Belgarath was seated at the rough table on the far side of the room, studying a parchment map, and Silk had already left.

"I thought for a while that you were going to sleep past noon," the old man said as Garion sat up and stretched.

"I had trouble getting to sleep last night," Garion replied. "It was a little noisy downstairs."

"Nadraks are like that."

A sudden thought occurred to Garion. "What do you think Aunt Pol is doing just now?" he asked.

"Sleeping, probably."

"Not *this* late."

"It's much earlier where she is."

"I don't follow that."

"Riva's fifteen hundred leagues west of here," Belgarath explained. "The sun won't get that far for several hours yet."

Garion blinked. "I hadn't thought of that," he admitted.

"I didn't think you had."

The door opened, and Silk came in, carrying several bundles and wearing an outraged expression. He threw his bundles down and stamped to the window, muttering curses under his breath.

"What's got you so worked up?" Belgarath asked mildly.

"Would you look at this?" Silk waved a piece of parchment at the old man.

"What's the problem?" Belgarath took the parchment and read it.

"That whole business was settled years ago," Silk declared in an irritated voice. "Why are these things still being circulated?"

"The description *is* colorful," Belgarath noted.

"Did you see that?" Silk sounded mortally offended. He turned to Garion. "Do I look like a weasel to you?"

"—an ill-favored, weasel-faced man," Belgarath read, "shifty-eyed and with a long, pointed nose. A notorious cheat at dice."

"Do you *mind*?"

"What's this all about?" Garion asked.

"I had a slight misunderstanding with the authorities some years ago," Silk explained deprecatingly. "Nothing all that serious, actually—but they're *still* circulating that thing." He gestured angrily at the parchment Belgarath was still reading with an amused expression. "They've even gone so far as to offer a *reward*." He considered for a moment. "I'll have to admit that the sum is flattering, though," he added.

"Did you get the things I sent you after?" Belgarath asked.

"Of course."

"Let's change clothes, then, and leave before your unexpected celebrity attracts a crowd."

The worn Nadrak clothing was made mostly of leather—snug black trousers, tight-fitting vests, and short-sleeved linen tunics.

"I didn't bother with the boots," Silk said. "Nadrak boots are pretty uncomfortable—probably since it hasn't occurred to them yet that there's a difference between the right foot and the left." He settled a pointed felt cap at a jaunty angle. "What do you think?" he asked, striking a pose.

"Doesn't look at all like a weasel, does he?" Belgarath asked Garion.

Silk gave him a disgusted look, but said nothing.

They went downstairs, led their horses out of the stables attached to the inn, and mounted. Silk's expression remained sour as they rode out of Yar Gurak. When they reached the top of a hill to the north of town, he slid off his horse, picked up a rock, and threw it rather savagely at the buildings clustered below.

"Make you feel better?" Belgarath asked curiously.

Silk remounted with a disdainful sniff and led the way down the other side of the hill.

CHAPTER TWO

They rode for the next few days through a wilderness of stone and stunted trees. The sun grew warmer each day, and the sky overhead was intensely blue as they pressed deeper and deeper into the snowcapped mountains. There were trails of sorts up here, winding, vagrant tracks meandering between the dazzling white peaks and across the high, pale green meadows where wildflowers nodded in the mountain breeze. The air was spiced with the resinous odor of evergreens, and now and then they saw deer grazing or stopping to watch them with large, startled eyes as they passed.

Belgarath moved confidently in a generally eastward course and he appeared to be alert and watchful. There were no signs of the half doze in which he customarily rode on more clearly defined roads, and he seemed somehow younger up here in the mountains.

They encountered other travelers—leather-clad Nadraks for the most part—although they did see a party of Drasnians laboring up a steep slope and, once, a long way off, what appeared to be a Tolnedran. Their exchanges with these others were brief and wary. The mountains of Gar og Nadrak were at best sketchily policed, and it was necessary for every man who entered them to provide for his own security.

The sole exception to this suspicious taciturnity was a garrulous old gold hunter mounted on a donkey, who appeared out of the blue-tinged shadows under the trees one morning. His tangled hair was white, and his clothing was mismatched, appearing to consist mostly of castoffs he had found beside this trail or that. His tanned, wrinkled face was weathered like a well-cured old hide, and his blue eyes twinkled merrily. He joined them without any greeting or hint of uncertainty as to his welcome and began talking immediately as if taking up a conversation again that had only recently been interrupted.

There was a sort of comic turn to his voice and manner that Garion found immediately engaging.

"Must be ten years or more since I've followed this path," he began, jouncing along on his donkey as he fell in beside Garion. "I don't come down into this part of the mountains very much anymore. The streambeds down here have all been worked over a hundred times at least. Which way are you bound?"

"I'm not really sure," Garion replied cautiously. "I've never been up here before, so I'm just following along."

"You'd find better gravel if you struck out to the north," the man on the donkey advised, "up near Morindland. Of course, you've got to be careful up there, but, like they say, no risk, no profit." He squinted curiously at Garion. "You're not a Nadrak, are you?"

"Sendar," Garion responded shortly.

"Never been to Sendaria," the old gold hunter mused. "Never been anyplace really—except up here." He looked around at the white-topped peaks and deep green forests with a sort of abiding love. "Never really wanted to go anyplace else. I've picked these mountains over from end to end for seventy years now and never made much at it—except for the pleasure of being here. Found a river bar one time, though, that had so much red gold in it that it looked like it was bleeding. Winter caught me up there, and I almost froze to death trying to come out."

"Did you go back the next spring?" Garion couldn't help asking.

"Meant to, but I did a lot of drinking that winter—I had gold enough. Anyway, the drink sort of addled my brains. When I set out the following year, I took along a few kegs for company. That's always a mistake. The drink takes you harder when you get up into the mountains, and you don't always pay attention to things the way you should." He leaned back in his donkey saddle, scratching reflectively at his stomach. "I went out onto the plains north of the mountains—up in Morindland. Seems that I thought at the time that the going might be easier out on flat ground. Well, to make it short, I ran across a band of Morindim and they took me prisoner. I'd been up to my ears in an ale keg for a day or so, and I was far gone when they took me. Lucky, I guess. Morindim are superstitious, and they thought I was possessed. That's probably all that saved my life. They kept me for five or six years, trying to puzzle out the meaning behind my ravings—once I got sober and saw the situation, I took quite a bit of care to do a lot of raving. Eventually they got tired of it and weren't so careful about watching me, so I escaped. By then I'd sort of forgotten exactly where that river was. I look for it now and then when I'm up that way." His speech seemed rambling, but his old blue eyes were very penetrating. "That's a big sword you're carrying, boy. Who do you plan to kill with it?"

The question came so fast that Garion did not even have time to be startled.

"Funny thing about that sword of yours," the shabby old man added shrewdly. "It seems to be going out of its way to make itself inconspicuous." Then he turned to Belgarath, who was looking at him with a level gaze. "You haven't hardly changed at all," he noted.

"And you still talk too much," Belgarath replied.

"I get hungry for talk every few years," the old man on the donkey admitted. "Is your daughter well?"

Belgarath nodded.

"Fine-looking woman, your daughter—bad-tempered, though."

"That hasn't changed noticeably."

"Didn't imagine it had." The old gold hunter chuckled, then hesitated for a moment. "If you don't mind some advice, be careful in case you plan to go down into the low country," he said seriously. "It looks like things might be coming to a boil down there. A lot of strangers in red tunics are roaming about, and there's been smoke coming up from old altars that haven't been used for years. The Grolims are out again, and their knives are all new-sharpened. The Nadraks who come up here keep looking back over their shoulders." He paused, looking directly at Belgarath. "There've been some other signs, too," he added. "The animals are all jumpy—like just before a big storm—and sometimes at night, if you listen close, there's something like thunder way off in the distance—like maybe from as far off as Mallorea. The whole world seems to be uneasy. I've got a hunch that something pretty big's about to happen—maybe the sort of thing *you'd* be involved in. The point is that *they* know you're out here. I wouldn't count too much on being able to slip through without somebody noticing you." He shrugged then, as if washing his hands of the matter. "I just thought you'd like to know."

"Thank you," Belgarath replied.

"Didn't cost me anything to say it." The old man shrugged again. "I think I'll go that way." He pointed off to the north. "Too many strangers coming into the mountains in the last few months. It's starting to get crowded. I've about talked myself out now, so I think I'll go look myself up a bit of privacy." He turned his donkey and trotted off. "Good luck," he threw back over his shoulder by way of farewell and then he disappeared into the blue shadows under the trees.

"You're acquainted with him, I take it," Silk observed to Belgarath.

The old sorcerer nodded. "I met him about thirty years ago. Polgara had come to Gar og Nadrak to find out a few things. After she'd gathered all the information she wanted, she sent word to me, and I came here and bought her from the man who owned her. We started home, but an early snowstorm caught us up here in the mountains. He found us floundering along, and he took us to the cave where he holes up when the snow gets too deep. Quite a comfortable cave really—except that he insists on bringing his donkey inside. He and Pol argued about that all winter, as I recall."

"What's his name?" Silk asked curiously.

Belgarath shrugged. "He never said, and it's not polite to ask."

Garion, however, had choked on the word "bought." A kind of helpless outrage welled up in him. "Somebody *owned* Aunt Pol?" he demanded incredulously.

"It's a Nadrak custom," Silk explained. "In their society, women are considered property. It's not seemly for a woman to go about without an owner."

"She was a *slave*?" Garion's knuckles grew white as he clenched his fists.

"Of course she wasn't a slave," Belgarath told him. "Can you even remotely imagine your aunt submitting to that sort of thing?"

"But you said—"

"I said I bought her from the man who owned her. Their relationship was a formality—nothing more. She needed an owner in order to function here, and he gained a great deal of respect from other men as a result of his ownership of so remarkable a woman." Belgarath made a sour face. "It cost me a fortune to buy her back from him. I sometimes wonder if she was really worth it."

"Grandfather!"

"I'm sure she'd be fascinated by that last observation, old friend," Silk said slyly.

"I don't know that it's necessary to repeat it to her, Silk."

"You never know." Silk laughed. "I might need something from you someday."

"That's disgusting."

"I know." Silk grinned and looked around. "Your friend took quite a bit of trouble to look you up," he suggested. "What was behind it?"

"He wanted to warn me."

"That things were tense in Gar og Nadrak? We knew that already."

"His warning was a great deal more urgent than that."

"He didn't *sound* very urgent."

"That's because you don't know him."

"Grandfather," Garion said suddenly, "how did he manage to see my sword? I thought we'd taken care of that."

"He sees *everything*, Garion. He could glance once at a tree and tell you ten years later exactly how many leaves were on it."

"Is he a sorcerer?"

"Not as far as I know. He's just a strange old man who likes the mountains. He doesn't know what's going on because he doesn't *want* to know. If he really wanted to, he could probably find out everything that's happening in the world."

"He could make a fortune as a spy, then," Silk mused.

"He doesn't want a fortune. Isn't that obvious? Any time he needs money, he just goes back to that river bar he mentioned."

"But he said he'd forgotten how to find it," Garion protested.

Belgarath snorted. "He's never forgotten anything in his life." Then his eyes grew distant. "There are a few people like him in the world—people who have no interest whatsoever in what other people are doing. Maybe that's not such a bad trait. If I had my life to live over, I might not mind doing it his way." He looked around then, his eyes very alert. "Let's take that path over there," he suggested, pointing at a scarcely visible track angling off across an open meadow, littered with bits of log bleached white by sun and weather. "If what he says is true, I think we'll want to avoid any large settlements. That path comes out farther north where there aren't so many people."

Not long afterward the terrain began to slope downward, and the three of them moved along briskly, riding down out of the mountains toward the vastness of the forest of Nadrak. The peaks around them subsided into forested foothills. Once they topped a rise, they were able to look out at the ocean of trees lying below. The forest stretched to the horizon and beyond, dark green beneath a blue sky. A faint breeze was blowing, and the sigh of its passage through the mile upon mile of trees below had a kind of endless sadness to it, a regretful memory of summers past and springs that would never come again.

Some distance up the slope from the forest stood a village, huddled at the side of a vast, open pit that had been gouged, raw and ugly, in the red dirt of the hillside.

"A mine town," Belgarath noted. "Let's nose about a bit and see what's going on."

They rode warily down the hill. As they drew closer, Garion could see that the village had that same temporary kind of appearance he had noticed about Yar Gurak. The buildings were constructed in the same way—unpeeled logs and rough stone—and the low-pitched roofs had large rocks laid on them to keep the shingles from blowing off during the winter blizzards. Nadraks seemed not to be concerned about the external appearance of their structures; once the walls and roofs were completed, they appeared quite content to move in and devote their attentions to other matters, without attending to those final finishing touches which gave a house that look of permanence that a Sendar or Tolnedran would feel absolutely necessary. The entire settlement seemed to reflect an attitude of "good enough" that offended Garion, for some reason.

Some of the miners who lived in the village came out into the dirt streets to watch the strangers ride in. Their black leather clothing was stained red by the earth in which they dug, and their eyes were hard and suspicious. An air of fearful wariness hung over the whole place, seasoned with a touch of defiant bellicosity.

Silk jerked his head toward a large, low building with a crude painting of a cluster of grapes on a sign banging in the breeze by the double doors at the front. A wide, roofed porch surrounded the building, and leather-garbed Nadraks lounged on benches along the porch, watching a dogfight in progress out in the middle of the street.

Belgarath nodded. "But let's go around to the side," he suggested, "in case we have to leave in a hurry."

They dismounted at the side porch, tied their horses to the railing, and went inside.

The interior of the tavern was smoky and dim, since windows seemed to be a rare feature in Nadrak buildings. The tables and benches were rough-hewn, and what light there was came from smoking oil lamps that hung on chains from the rafters. The floor was mud-stained and littered with bits of food. Dogs roamed at will under the tables and benches. The smell of stale beer and unwashed bodies hung heavy in the air, and, though it was only early afternoon, the place was crowded. Many of the men in the large room were already far gone with drink. It was noisy, since the Nadraks lounging at the tables or stumbling about the room seemed all habitually to speak at the top of their voices.

Belgarath pushed his way toward a table in the corner where a solitary man sat bleary-eyed and slack-lipped, staring into his ale cup.

"You don't mind if we share the table, do you?" the old man demanded of him in an abrupt manner, sitting down without awaiting a reply.

"Would it do any good if I did?" the man with the cup asked. He was unshaven, and his eyes were pouchy and bloodshot.

"Not much," Belgarath told him bluntly.

"You're new here, aren't you?" The Nadrak looked at the three of them with only a hint of curiosity, trying with some difficulty to focus his eyes.

"I don't really see that it's any of your business," Belgarath retorted rudely.

"You've got a sour mouth for a man past his prime," the Nadrak suggested, flexing his fingers ominously.

"I came here to drink, not fight," Silk declared in a harsh tone. "I might change my mind later, but right now, I'm thirsty." He reached out and caught the arm of a passing servingman. "Ale," he ordered. "And don't take all day."

"Keep your hands to yourself," the servingman told him. "Are you with him? He pointed at the Nadrak they had joined.

"We're sitting with him, aren't we?"

"You want three cups or four?"

"I want one—for now. Bring the others what they want, too. I'll pay for the first time around."

The servingman grunted sourly and pushed his way off through the crowd, pausing long enough to kick a dog out of his way.

Silk's offer seemed to quiet their Nadrak companion's belligerence. "You've picked a bad time to come to town," he told them. "The whole region's crawling with Mallorean recruiters."

"We've been up in the mountains," Belgarath said. "We'll probably go back in a day or so. Whatever's happening down here doesn't interest us very much."

"You'd better take an interest while you're here—unless you'd like to try army life."

"Is there a war someplace?" Silk asked him.

"Likely to be—or so they say. Someplace down in Mishrak ac Thull."

Silk snorted. "I've never met a Thull worth fighting."

"It's not the Thulls. It's supposed to be the Alorns. They've got a *queen*—if you can imagine such a thing—and she's moving to invade the Thulls."

"A *queen*?" Silk scoffed. "Can't be much of an army, then. Let the Thulls fight her themselves."

"Tell that to the Mallorean recruiters," the Nadrak suggested.

"Did you have to *brew* that ale?" Silk demanded of the servingman, who was returning with four large cups.

"There are other taverns, friend," the servingman replied. "If you don't like this one, go find another. That'll be twelve pennies."

"Three pennies a cup?" Silk exclaimed.

"Times are hard."

Grumbling, Silk paid him.

"Thanks," the Nadrak they were sitting with said, taking one of the cups.

"Don't mention it," Silk said sourly.

"What are the Malloreans doing here?" Belgarath asked.

"Rounding up everyone who can stand up, see lightning, and hear thunder. They do their recruiting with leg irons, so it's a little hard to refuse. They've got Grolims with them too, and the Grolims keep their gutting knives out in plain sight as a sort of a hint about what might happen to anybody who objects too much."

"Maybe you were right when you said we picked a bad time to come down out of the mountains," Silk said.

The Nadrak nodded. "The Grolims say that Torak's stirring in his sleep."

"That's not very good news," Silk replied.

"I think we could all drink to that." The Nadrak lifted his ale cup. "You find anything worth digging for up there in the mountains?"

Silk shook his head. "A few traces is all. We've been working the streambeds for free gold. We don't have the equipment to drive shafts back into the rock."

"You'll never get rich squatting beside a creek and sifting gravel."

"We get by." Silk shrugged. "Someday maybe we'll hit a good pocket and we'll be able to pick up enough to buy some equipment."

"And someday maybe it'll rain beer, too."

Silk laughed.

"You ever thought about taking in another partner?"

Silk squinted at the unshaven Nadrak. "Have you been up there before?" he asked.

The Nadrak nodded. "Often enough to know that I don't like it—but I think I'd like a stint in the army a lot less."

"Let's have another drink and talk about it," Silk suggested.

Garion leaned back, putting his shoulders against the rough log wall. Nadraks didn't seem to be so bad, once you got past the crudity of their nature. They were a blunt-spoken people and a bit sour-faced, but they did not seem to have that icy animosity toward outsiders he had noted among the Murgos.

He let his mind drift back to what the Nadrak had said about a queen. He quickly dismissed the notion that any of the queens staying at Riva might, under any circumstances, have assumed such authority. That left only Aunt Pol. The Nadrak's information could have been garbled a bit; but in Belgarath's absence, Aunt Pol *might* have taken charge of things—although that was not like her, at all. What could possibly have happened back there to force her to go to such extremes?

As the afternoon wore on, more and more of the men in the tavern grew reeling drunk, and occasional fights broke out—although the fights usually consisted of shoving matches, since few in the room were sober enough to aim a good blow. Their companion drank steadily and eventually laid his head down on his arms and began to snore.

"I think we've got just about everything we can use here," Belgarath suggested quietly. "Let's drift on out. From what our friend here says, I don't think it'd be a good idea to sleep in town."

Silk nodded his agreement, and the three of them rose from the table and made their way through the crowd to the side door.

"Did you want to pick up any supplies?" the little man asked.

Belgarath shook his head. "I have a feeling that we want to get out of here as soon as possible."

Silk gave him a quick look, and the three of them untied their horses, mounted and rode back out into the red dirt street. They moved at a walk to avoid arousing suspicion, but Garion could feel a sort of tense urgency to put this raw, mud-smeared village behind them. There was something threatening in the air, and the golden late afternoon sun seemed somehow shadowed, as if by an unseen cloud. As they were passing the last rickety house on the downhill edge of the village, they heard an alarmed shout from somewhere back near the center of town. Garion turned quickly and saw a party of perhaps twenty mounted men in red tunics plunging at a full gallop toward the tavern the three of them had just left. With a practiced skill, the scarlet-clad strangers swung down from their horses and immediately covered all the doors to cut off an escape for those inside.

"Malloreans!" Belgarath snapped. "Make for the trees!" And he drove his heels into his horse's flanks. They galloped across the weedy, stump-cluttered clearing that surrounded the village, toward the edge of the forest and safety, but there was no outcry or pursuit. The tavern appeared to contain enough fish to fill the Mallorean net. From a safe vantage point beneath spreading tree limbs, Garion, Silk, and Belgarath watched as a disconsolate-looking string of Nadraks, chained together at the ankle, were led out of the tavern into the red dust of the street to stand under the watchful eyes of the Mallorean recruiters.

"It looks like our friend has joined the army, after all," Silk observed.

"Better him than us," Belgarath replied. "We might be just a little out of place in the middle of an Angarak horde." He squinted at the ruddy disk of the setting sun. "Let's move out. We've got a few hours before dark. It looks as if military service might be contagious in this vicinity, and I wouldn't want to catch it."

CHAPTER THREE

The forest of Nadrak was unlike the Arendish forest lying far to the south. The differences were subtle, and it took Garion several days to put his finger on them. For one thing, the trails they followed had no sense of permanence about them. They were so infrequently traveled that they were not beaten into the loamy soil of the forest floor. In the Arendish forest, the marks of man were everywhere, but here man was an intruder, merely passing through. Moreover, the forest in Arendia had definite boundaries, but this ocean of trees went on to the farthest edge of the continent, and it had stood so since the beginning of the world.

The forest teemed with life. Tawny deer flickered among the trees, and vast, shaggy bison, with curved black horns shiny as onyx, grazed in clearings. Once a bear, grumbling and muttering irritably, lumbered across the trail in front of them. Rabbits scurried through the undergrowth and partridges exploded into flight from underfoot with a heart-stopping thunder of wings. The ponds and streams abounded with fish, muskrat, otter, and beaver. There were also, they soon discovered, smaller forms of life. The mosquitoes seemed only slightly smaller than sparrows, and there was a nasty little brown fly that bit anything that moved.

The sun rose early and set late, dappling the dark forest floor with golden light. Although it was midsummer now, it was never exactly hot, and the air was rich with that smell of urgent growth common to the lands of the north, where summer was short and winter very long.

Belgarath seemed not to sleep at all once they entered the forest. Each evening, as Silk and Garion wearily rolled themselves in their blankets, the old sorcerer threaded his way back into the shadowy trees and disappeared. Once, several hours past dusk on a night filled with starlight, Garion awoke briefly and heard the loping touch of paws skittering lightly across a leaf-carpeted clearing; even as he drifted back to sleep, he understood. The great silver wolf who was his grandfather roamed the night, scouring the surrounding forest for any hint of pursuit or danger.

The old man's nocturnal roamings were as silent as smoke, but they did not pass unnoticed. Early one morning, before the sun rose and while the trees were still hazy and half-obscured by ground fog, several shadowy shapes drifted among the dark trunks and stopped not far away. Garion, who had just risen and was preparing to stir up the fire, froze half bent over. As he slowly straightened, he could feel eyes on him, and his skin prickled peculiarly. Perhaps ten feet away stood a huge, dark gray wolf. The wolf's expression was serious, and its eyes were as yellow as sunlight. There was an unspoken question in those golden eyes, and Garion realized that he understood that question.

"One wonders why you are doing that?"

"Doing what?" Garion asked politely, responding automatically in the language of wolves.

"Going about in that peculiar form."

"It's necessary to do it."

"Ah." With exquisite courtesy the wolf did not pursue the matter further. "One is curious to know if you don't find it somewhat restricting," he noted however.

"It's not as bad as it looks—once one gets used to it."

The wolf looked unconvinced. He sat down on his haunches. "One has seen the other one several times in the past few darknesses," he said in the manner of wolves, "and one is curious to know why you and he have come into our range."

Garion knew instinctively that his answer to that question was going to be very important. "We are going from one place to another," he replied carefully. "It is not our intention to seek dens or mates in your range or to hunt the creatures that are yours." He could not have explained how he knew what to say.

The wolf seemed satisfied with his response. "One would be pleased if you would present our esteem to the one with fur like frost," he said formally. "One has noted that he is worthy of great respect."

"One would be pleased to give him your words," Garion responded, a bit surprised at how easily the elaborate phrasing came to him.

The wolf lifted his head and sniffed at the air. "It is time for us to hunt," he said. "May you find what you seek."

"May your hunt be successful," Garion returned.

The wolf turned and padded back into the fog, followed by his companions.

"On the whole, you handled that rather well, Garion," Belgarath said from the deep shadows of a nearby thicket.

Garion jumped, a bit startled. "I didn't know you were there," he said.

"You should have," the old man replied, stepping out of the shadows.

"How did he know?" Garion asked. "That I'm a wolf sometimes, I mean?"

"It shows. A wolf is very alert to that sort of thing."

Silk came out from under the tree where he had been sleeping. The little man's step was wary, but his nose twitched with curiosity. "What was that all about?" he asked.

"The wolves wanted to know what we were doing in their territory," Belgarath replied. "They were investigating to see if they were going to have to fight us."

"Fight?" Garion was startled.

"It's customary when a strange wolf enters the hunting range of another pack. Wolves prefer not to fight—it's a waste of energy—but they will, if the situation demands it."

"What happened?" Silk asked. "Why did they just go away like that?"

"Garion convinced them that we were just passing through."

"That was clever of him."

"Why don't you stir up the fire, Garion?" Belgarath suggested. "Let's have some breakfast and move on. It's still a long way to Mallorea, and we don't want to run out of good weather."

Later that same day, they rode down into a valley where a collection of log houses and tents stood beside a fair-sized stream at the edge of a meadow.

"Fur traders," Silk explained to Garion, pointing at the rough settlement. "There are places like this on just about every major stream in this part of the forest." The little man's pointed nose began to twitch, and his eyes grew bright. "A lot of buying and selling goes on in these little towns."

"Never mind," Belgarath told him pointedly. "Try to keep your predatory instincts under control."

"I wasn't even considering anything," Silk protested.

"Really? Aren't you feeling well?"

Silk loftily ignored that.

"Wouldn't it be safer to go around it?" Garion asked as they rode across the broad meadow.

Belgarath shook his head. "I want to know what's going on ahead of us, and the quickest way to find out is to talk to people who've been there. We'll drift in, circulate for an hour or so and then drift on out again. Just keep your ears open. If anyone asks, we're on our way toward the north range to look for gold."

There were differences between the hunters and trappers who roamed the streets of this settlement and the miners they had met in the last village. They were more open for one thing—less surly and distinctly less belligerent. Garion surmised that the enforced solitude of their occupation made them appreciate companionship all the more during their infrequent visits to the fur-trading centers. Although they drank probably as much as the miners, their drinking seemed to lead more often to singing and laughter than to fighting.

A large tavern stood near the center of the village, and they rode slowly along a dirt street toward it. "Side door," Belgarath said tersely as they dismounted in front of the tavern, and they led their horses around the building and tied them at the porch railing.

The interior of the tavern was cleaner, less crowded, and somewhat lighter than the miners' tavern had been, and it smelled of woods and open air instead of damp, musty earth. The three of them sat at a table not far from the door and ordered cups of ale from a polite servingman. The ale was a rich, dark brown, well chilled, and surprisingly inexpensive.

"The fur buyers own the place," Silk explained, wiping foam from his upper lip. "They've discovered that a trapper is easier to bargain with if he's a little drunk, so they make the ale cheap and plentiful."

"I suppose that makes sense," Garion admitted, "but don't the trappers know that?"

"Of course they do."

"Why do they drink before they do business, then?"

Silk shrugged. "They like to drink."

The two trappers seated at the next table were renewing an acquaintanceship that obviously stretched back a dozen years or more. Their beards were both touched with gray, but they spoke lightheartedly in the manner of much younger men.

"You have any trouble with Morindim while you were up there?" one was asking the other.

The second shook his head. "I put pestilence-markers on both ends of the valley where I set out my traps," he replied. "A Morind will go a dozen leagues out of his way to avoid a spot that's got pestilence."

The first nodded his agreement. "That's usually the best way. Gredder always claimed that curse-markers worked better; but as it turned out, he was wrong."

"I haven't seen him in the last few seasons."

"I'd be surprised if you had. The Morindim got him about three years ago. I buried him myself—what was left of him anyway."

"Didn't know that. Spent a winter with him once over on the headwaters of the Cordu. He was a mean-tempered sort of a man. I'm surprised that the Morindim would cross a curse-marker, though."

"As near as I could judge, some magician came along and uncursed his markers. I found a dried weasel foot hung from one of them with three stems of grass tied around each toe."

"That's a potent spell. They must have wanted him pretty badly for a magician to take that much trouble."

"You know how he was. He could irritate people ten leagues away just walking by."

"That's the truth."

"Not anymore, though. His skull's decorating some Morind magician's quest-staff now."

Garion leaned toward his grandfather. "What do they mean when they talk about markers?" he whispered.

"They're warnings," Belgarath replied. "Usually sticks poked into the ground and decorated with bones or feathers. The Morindim can't read, so you can't just put up a signboard for them."

A stooped old trapper, his leather clothing patched and shiny from wear, shuf-fled toward the center of the tavern. His lined, bearded face had a slightly apolo-getic expression on it. Following after him came a young Nadrak woman in a heavy, red felt dress belted about the waist with a glittering chain. There was a leash about her neck, and the old trapper held the end of the tether firmly in his fist. De-spite the leash, the young woman's face had a proud, disdainful look, and she stared at the men in the tavern with barely concealed contempt. When the old trapper reached the center of the room, he cleared his throat to get the attention of the crowd. "I've got a woman I want to sell," he announced loudly.

Without changing expression the woman spat upon him.

"Now you know that's just going to lower your price, Vella," the old man told her in a placating tone of voice.

"You're an idiot, Tashor," she retorted. "No one here can afford me—you know that. Why didn't you do what I told you to and offer me to the fur buyers?"

"The fur buyers aren't interested in women, Vella," Tashor replied in that same mild tone. "The price'll be better here, believe me."

"I wouldn't believe you if you said the sun was going to rise tomorrow, you old fool."

"The woman, as you can see, is quite spirited," Tashor announced rather lamely.

"Is he trying to sell his wife?" Garion demanded, choking on his ale.

"She isn't his wife," Silk corrected. "He owns her, that's all."

Garion clenched his fists and half rose, his face mottled with anger, but Bel-garath's hand closed firmly about his wrist. "Sit down," the old man ordered.

"But—"

"I said sit down, Garion. This is none of your business."

"Unless you want to buy the woman, of course," Silk suggested lightly.

"Is she healthy?" a lean-faced trapper with a scar across one cheek called to Tashor.

"She is," Tashor declared, "and she's got all her teeth, too. Show them your teeth, Vella."

"They aren't looking at my teeth, idiot," she told him, looking directly at the scar-faced trapper with a sultry challenge in her black eyes.

"She's an excellent cook," Tashor continued quickly, "and she knows remedies for rheumatism and ague. She can dress and tan hides and she doesn't eat too much. Her breath doesn't smell too bad—unless she eats onions—and she almost never snores, except when she's drunk."

"If she's such a good woman, why do you want to sell her?" the lean-faced trapper wanted to know.

"I'm getting older," Tashor replied, "and I'd like a little peace and quiet. Vella's exciting to be around, but I've had all the excitement I need. I think I'd like to settle down someplace—maybe raise some chickens or goats." The bent old trapper's voice sounded a trifle plaintive.

"Oh, this is impossible," Vella burst out. "Do I have to do everything myself? Get out of the way, Tashor." Rudely, she pushed the old trapper aside and glared at the crowd, her black eyes flashing. "All right," she announced firmly, "let's get down to business. Tashor wants to sell me. I'm strong and healthy. I can cook, cure hides and skins, tend to common illnesses, bargain closely when I buy supplies, and I can brew good beer." Her eyes narrowed grimly. "I have not gone to any man's bed, and I keep my daggers sharp enough to persuade strangers not to try to force me. I can play the wood flute and I know many old stories. I can make curse-markers and pestilence-markers and dream-markers to frighten off the Morindim and once I killed a bear at thirty paces with a bow."

"Twenty paces," Tashor corrected mildly.

"It was closer to thirty," she insisted.

"Can you dance?" the lean trapper with the scarred face asked.

She looked directly at him. "Only if you're seriously interested in buying me," she replied.

"We can talk about that after I see you dance," he said.

"Can you hold a beat?" she demanded.

"I can."

"Very well." Her hands went to the chain about her waist, and it jingled as she unfastened it. She opened the heavy red dress, stepped out of it, and handed it to Tashor. Then she carefully untied the leash from about her neck and bound a ribbon of red silk about her head to hold back her wealth of lustrous, blue-black hair. Beneath the red felt dress, she wore a filmy rose-colored gown of Mallorean silk that whispered and clung to her as she moved. The silk gown reached to midcalf, and she wore soft leather boots on her feet. Protruding from the top of each boot was the jeweled hilt of a dagger, and a third dagger rode on the leather belt about her waist. Her gown was caught in a tight collar about her throat, but it left her arms bare to the shoulder. She wore a half dozen narrow gold bracelets about each wrist. With a conscious grace, she bent and fastened a string of small bells to each ankle. Then she lifted her smoothly rounded arms until her hands were beside her face. "This is the beat, scar-face," she told the trapper. "Try to hold it." And she began to clap her hands together. The beat was three measured claps followed by four staccato ones. Vella began her dance slowly with a kind of insolent strut. Her gown whispered as she moved, its hem sighing about her lush calves.

The lean trapper took up her beat, his callused hands clapping together loudly in the sudden silence as Vella danced.

Garion began to blush. Vella's movements were subtle and fluid. The bells at her ankles and the bracelets about her wrists played a tinkling counterpoint to the trapper's beat. Her feet seemed almost to flicker in the intricate steps of her dance, and her arms wove patterns in the air. Other, even more interesting, things were going on inside the rose-colored, gossamer gown. Garion swallowed hard and discovered that he had almost stopped breathing.

Vella began to whirl, and her long black hair flared out, almost perfectly matching the flare of her gown. Then she slowed and once again dropped back into that proud, sensual strut that challenged every man in the room.

They cheered when she stopped, and she smiled a slow, mysterious little smile.

"You dance very well," the scar-faced trapper observed in a neutral voice.

"Naturally," she replied. "I do everything very well."

"Are you in love with anyone?" The question was bluntly put.

"No man has won my heart," Vella declared flatly. "I haven't seen a man yet who was worthy of me."

"That may change," the trapper suggested. "One goldmark." It was a firm offer.

"You're not serious," she snorted. "Five goldmarks."

"One and a half," he countered.

"This is just *too* insulting." Vella raised both hands up in the air, and her face took on a tragic expression. "Not a copper less than four."

"Two goldmarks," the trapper offered.

"Unbelievable!" she exclaimed, spreading both arms. "Why don't you just cut my heart out and have done with it? I couldn't consider anything less than three and a half."

"To save time, why don't we just say three?" He said it firmly. "With intention that the arrangement become permanent," he added, almost as an afterthought.

"Permanent?" Vella's eyes widened.

"I like you," he replied. "Well, what do you say?"

"Stand up and let me have a look at you," she ordered him.

Slowly he unwound himself from the chair in which he had lounged. His tall body was as lean as his scarred face, and there was a hard-muscled quality about him. Vella pursed her lips and looked him over. "Not bad, is he?" she murmured to Tashor.

"You could do worse, Vella," her owner answered encouragingly.

"I'll consider your offer of three with intentions," Vella declared. "Have you got a name?"

"Tekk," the tall trapper introduced himself with a slight bow.

"Well then, Tekk," Vella told him, "don't go away. Tashor and I need to talk over your offer." She gave him an almost shy look. "I think I like you, too," she added in a much less challenging tone. Then she took hold of the leash that was still wrapped around Tashor's fist and led him out of the tavern, glancing back over her shoulder once or twice at the lean-faced Tekk.

"That is a *lot* of woman," Silk murmured with a note of profound respect.

Garion found that he was able to breathe again, though his ears still felt very hot. "What did they mean by intention?" he quietly asked Silk.

"Tekk offered an arrangement that usually leads to marriage," Silk explained.

That baffled Garion. "I don't understand at all," he confessed.

"Just because someone owns her doesn't give him any special rights to her person," Silk told him, "and those daggers of hers enforce that. One does *not* approach a Nadrak woman unless one's tired of living. *She* makes that decision. The wedding customarily takes place after the birth of her first child."

"Why was she so interested in the price?"

"Because she gets half," Silk shrugged.

"She gets half of the money every time she's sold?" Garion was incredulous.

"Of course. It'd hardly be fair otherwise, would it?"

The servingman who was bringing them three more cups of ale had stopped and was staring openly at Silk.

"Is something wrong, friend?" Silk asked him mildly.

The servingman lowered his eyes quickly. "Sorry," he mumbled. "I just thought—you reminded me of somebody, that's all. Now that I see you closer, I realize that I was mistaken." He put down the cups quickly, turned, and left without picking up the coins Silk had laid on the table.

"I think we'd better leave," Silk said quietly.

"What's the matter?" Garion asked him.

"He knows who I am—and there's that reward notice that's being circulated."

"Maybe you're right," Belgarath agreed, rising to his feet.

"He's talking with those men over there," Garion said, watching the servingman, who was in urgent conversation with a group of hunters on the far side of the room and was casting frequent looks in their direction.

"We've got about a half a minute to get outside," Silk said tensely. "Let's go."

The three of them moved quickly toward the door.

"You there!" someone behind them shouted. "Wait a minute!"

"Run!" Belgarath barked, and they bolted outside and hurled themselves into their saddles just as a half dozen leather-garbed men burst out through the tavern door.

The shout, "Stop those men!" went largely unheeded as they galloped off down the street. Trappers and hunters as a breed were seldom inclined to mix themselves in other men's affairs, and Garion, Silk, and Belgarath had passed through the village and were splashing across a ford before any kind of pursuit could be organized.

Silk was swearing as they entered the forest on the far side of the river, spitting out oaths like melon seeds. His profanity was colorful and wide-ranging, reflecting on the birth, parentage, and uncleanly habits of not only those pursuing them, but of those responsible for circulating the reward notice as well.

Belgarath reined in sharply, raising his hand as he did. Silk and Garion hauled their horses to a stop. Silk continued to swear.

"Do you suppose you could cut short your eloquence for a moment?" Belgarath asked him. "I'm trying to listen."

Silk muttered a few more choice oaths, then clamped his teeth shut. There were confused shouts far behind them and a certain amount of splashing.

"They're crossing the stream," Belgarath noted. "It looks as if they plan to take the business seriously. Seriously enough to chase us, at any rate."

"Won't they give up when it gets dark?" Garion asked.

"These are Nadrak hunters," Silk said, sounding profoundly disgusted. "They'll follow us for days—just for the enjoyment of the hunt."

"There's not much we can do about that now," Belgarath grunted. "Let's see if we can outrun them." And he thumped his heels to his horse.

It was midafternoon as they rode at a gallop through the sunlit forest. The undergrowth was scanty, and the tall, straight trunks of fir and pine rose like great columns toward the blue sky overhead. It was a good day for a ride, but not a good day for being chased. No day was good for that.

They topped a rise and stopped again to listen. "They seem to be falling behind," Garion noted hopefully.

"That's just the drunk ones," Silk disagreed sourly. "The ones who are serious about all this are probably much closer. You don't shout when you're hunting. See—look back there." He pointed.

Garion looked. There was a pale flicker back among the trees. A man on a white horse was riding in their direction, leaning far over in his saddle and looking intently at the ground as he rode.

"If he's any kind of tracker at all, it'll take us a week to shake him off," Silk said disgustedly.

Somewhere, far off among the trees to their right, a wolf howled.

"Let's keep going," Belgarath told them.

They galloped on then, plunging down the far side of the rise, threading their way among the trees. The thud of their horses' hoofs was a muffled drumming on the thick loam of the forest floor, and clots of half-decayed debris spattered out behind them as they fled.

"We're leaving a trail as wide as a house," Silk shouted to Belgarath.

"That can't be helped for now," the old man replied. "We need some more distance before we start playing games with the tracks."

Another howl drifted mournfully through the forest, from the left this time. It seemed a bit closer than the first had been.

They rode on for another quarter of an hour and then they suddenly heard a great babble of confusion to the rear. Men were shouting with alarm, and horses squealed in panic. Garion could also hear savage growls. At Belgarath's signal, they slowed their horses to listen. The terrified squeals of horses rang sharply through the trees, punctuated by their riders' curses and frightened shouts. A chorus of howls rose from all around. The forest seemed suddenly full of wolves. The pursuit behind them disintegrated as the horses of the Nadrak reward hunters bolted with screams of sheer panic in all directions.

With a certain grim satisfaction, Belgarath listened to the fading sounds behind them. Then, his tongue lolling from his mouth, a huge, dark-furred wolf trotted out of the woods about thirty yards away, stopped, and dropped to his haunches, his yellow eyes gazing intently at them.

"Keep a tight grip on your reins," Belgarath instructed quietly, stroking the neck of his suddenly wild-eyed mount.

The wolf did not say anything, but merely sat and watched.

Belgarath returned that steady gaze quite calmly, then finally nodded once in acknowledgment. The wolf rose, turned, and started off into the trees. He stopped once, glanced back over his shoulder at them, and raised his muzzle to lift the deep, bell-toned howl that summoned the other members of his pack to return to their interrupted hunt. Then, with a flicker he was gone, and only the echo of his howl remained.

CHAPTER FOUR

They rode east for the next several days, gradually descending into a broad, marshy valley where the undergrowth was denser and the air noticeably more humid. A brief summer shower rolled in one afternoon, accompanied by great, ripping crashes of thunder, a deluge of pounding rain, and winds that howled among the trees, bending and tossing them and tearing leaves and twigs from the underbrush to whirl and fly among the dark trunks. The storm soon passed, however, and the sun came out again. After that, the weather continued fair, and they made good time.

Garion felt a peculiar sense of incompleteness as he rode and he sometimes caught himself looking around for missing friends. The long journey in search of the Orb had established a sort of pattern in his mind, a sense of rightness and wrongness, and this trip felt wrong. Barak was not with them, for one thing, and the big, red-bearded Cherek's absence made Garion feel oddly insecure. He also missed the hawk-faced, silent Hettar and the armored form of Mandorallen riding always at the front, with the silver-and-blue pennon snapping from the tip of his lance. He was painfully lonely for Durnik the smith and he even missed Ce'Nedra's spiteful bickering. What had happened at Riva became less and less real to him, and all the elaborate ceremony that had attended his betrothal to the impossible little princess began to fade in his memory, like some half-forgotten dream.

It was one evening, however, after the horses had been picketed and supper was over and they had rolled themselves in their blankets to sleep, that Garion, staring into the dying embers of their fire, came at last to face the central vacancy that had entered his life. Aunt Pol was not with them, and he missed her terribly. Since childhood, he had felt that so long as Aunt Pol was nearby, nothing could really go wrong that she could not fix. Her calm, steady presence had been the one thing to which he had always clung. As clearly as if she stood before him, Garion could see her face, her glorious eyes, and the white lock at her brow; the sudden loneliness for her was as sharp as the edge of a knife.

Everything felt wrong without her. Belgarath was here, certainly, and Garion was fairly sure that his grandfather could deal with any purely physical dangers, but there were other, less obvious perils that the old man either did not consider or chose to ignore. To whom could Garion turn when he was afraid, for example? Being afraid was not the sort of thing that endangered life or limb, but it was still an injury of sorts—and sometimes a deeper and more serious kind of injury. Aunt Pol had always been able to banish his fears, but now she was not here, and Garion was afraid and he could not even admit it. He sighed and pulled his blankets more closely about him and slowly drifted into a troubled sleep.

It was about noon some days later when they reached the east fork of the River Cordu, a broad, dirty brown flow running through a brushy valley in a generally southerly direction toward the capital at Yar Nadrak. The pale green, waist-high brush extended back several hundred yards from either bank of the river and was silt-smeared by the high waters of the spring runoff. The sultry air above the brush was alive with clouds of gnats and mosquitoes.

A sullen boatman ferried them across to the village standing on the far bank. As they led their horses off onto the ferry landing, Belgarath spoke quietly. "I think we'll want to change direction here," he told them. "Let's split up. I'll go pick up supplies, and the two of you go find the town tavern. See if you can get some information about passes leading up through the north range into the lands of the Morindim. The sooner we get up there, the better. The Malloreans seem to be getting the upper hand here and they could clamp down without much warning. I don't want to have to start explaining my every move to Mallorean Grolims—not to mention the fact that there's a great deal of interest in Silk's whereabouts just now."

Silk rather glumly agreed. "I'd like to get that matter straightened out, but I don't suppose we really have the time, do we?"

"No, not really. The summer is very, very short up north, and the crossing to Mallorea is unpleasant, even in the best weather. When you get to the tavern, tell everybody that we want to try our luck in the gold fields of the north range. There's bound to be somebody around who'll want to show off his familiarity with trails and passes—particularly if you offer to buy him a few drinks."

"I thought you said you knew the way," Silk protested.

"I know *one* way—but it's a hundred leagues east of here. Let's see if there's something a little closer. I'll come by the tavern after I get the supplies." The old man mounted and went off up the dirt street, leading their packhorse behind him.

Silk and Garion had little trouble finding someone in the smelly tavern willing to talk about trails and passes. Quite to the contrary, their first question sparked a general debate.

"That's the long way around, Besher," one tipsy gold hunter interrupted another's detailed description of a mountain pass. "You go *left* at the falls of the stream. It saves you three days."

"I'm telling this, Varn," Besher retorted testily, banging his fist down on the scarred table. "You can tell them about the way you go when I'm finished."

"It'll take you all day—just like that trail you're so fond of. They want to go look for gold, not admire scenery." Varn's long, stubbled jaw thrust out belligerently.

"Which way do we go when we get to the long meadow up on top?" Silk asked quickly, trying to head off the hostilities.

"You go right," Besher declared, glaring at Varn.

Varn thought about that as if looking for an excuse to disagree. Finally he reluctantly nodded. "Of course that's the only way you *can* go," he added, "but once you get through the juniper grove, you turn left." He said it in the tone of a man anticipating contradiction.

"*Left?*" Besher objected loudly. "You're a blockhead, Varn. You go *right* again."

"Watch who you're calling a blockhead, you jackass!"

Without any further discussion, Besher punched Varn in the mouth, and the two of them began to pummel each other, reeling about and knocking over benches and tables.

"They're both wrong, of course," another miner sitting at a nearby table observed calmly, watching the fight with a clinical detachment. "You keep going straight after you get through the juniper grove."

Several burly men, wearing loose-fitting red tunics over their polished mail shirts, had entered the tavern unnoticed during the altercation, and they stepped forward, grinning, to separate Varn and Besher as the two rolled around on the dirty floor. Garion felt Silk stiffen beside him. "Malloreans!" the little man said softly.

"What do we do?" Garion whispered, looking around for a way of escape. But before Silk could answer, a black-robed Grolim stepped through the door.

"I like to see men who are so eager to fight," the Grolim purred in a peculiar accent. "The army needs such men."

"Recruiters!" Varn exclaimed, breaking away from the red-garbed Malloreans and dashing toward a side door. For a second it looked as if he might escape; but as he reached the doorway, someone outside rapped him sharply across the forehead with a stout cudgel. He reeled back, suddenly rubber-legged and vacant-eyed. The Mallorean who had hit him came inside, gave him a critical, appraising glance, and then judiciously clubbed him in the head again.

"Well?" the Grolim asked, looking around with amusement. "What's it to be? Would any more of you like to run, or would you all prefer to come along quietly?"

"Where are you taking us?" Besher demanded, trying to pull his arm out of the grip of one of the grinning recruiters.

"To Yar Nadrak first," the Grolim replied, "and then south to the plains of Mishrak ac Thull and the encampment of his Imperial Majesty 'Zakath, Emperor of all Mallorea. You've just joined the army, my friends. All of Angarak rejoices in your courage and patriotism, and Torak himself is pleased with you." As if to emphasize his words, the Grolim's hand strayed to the hilt of the sacrificial knife sheathed at his belt.

THE CHAIN CLINKED spitefully as Garion, fettered at the ankle, plodded along, one in a long line of disconsolate-looking conscripts, following a trail leading generally southward through the brush along the riverbank. The conscripts had all been roughly searched for weapons—all but Garion, who for some reason had been overlooked. He was painfully aware of the huge sword strapped to his back as he walked along; but, as always seemed to happen, no one else paid any attention to it.

Before they had left the village, while they were all being shackled, Garion and Silk had held a brief, urgent discussion in the minute finger movements of the Drasnian secret language.

*—I could pick this lock with my thumbnail—*Silk had asserted with a disdainful flip of his fingers.*—As soon as it gets dark tonight, I'll unhook us and we'll leave. I don't really think military life would agree with me, and it's wildly inappropriate for you to be joining an Angarak army just now—all things considered.—*

*—Where's Grandfather?—*Garion had asked.

—Oh, I imagine he's about.—

Garion, however, was worried, and a whole platoon of "what-ifs" immediately jumped into his mind. To avoid thinking about them, he covertly studied the

Malloreans who guarded them. The Grolim and the bulk of his detachment had moved on, once the captives had been shackled, seeking other villages and other recruits, leaving only five of their number behind to escort this group south. Malloreans were somewhat different from other Angaraks. Their eyes had that characteristic angularity, but their bodies seemed not to have the singleness of purpose which so dominated the western tribes. They were burly, but they did not have the broad-shouldered athleticism of the Murgos. They were tall, but did not have the lean, whippetlike frames of the Nadraks. They were obviously strong, but they did not have the thick-waisted brute power of the Thulls. There was about them, moreover, a kind of disdainful superiority when they looked at western Angaraks. They spoke to their prisoners in short, barking commands, and when they talked to each other, their dialect was so thick that it was nearly unintelligible. They wore mail shirts covered by coarse-woven red tunics. They did not ride their horses very well, Garion noted, and their curved swords and broad, round shields seemed to get in their way as they attempted to manage their reins.

Garion carefully kept his head down to hide the fact that his features—even more than Silk's—were distinctly non-Angarak. The guards, however, paid little attention to the conscripts as individuals, but seemed rather to be more interested in them as numbers. They rode continually up and down the sweating column, counting bodies and referring to a document they carried with concerned, even worried expressions. Garion surmised that unpleasant things would happen if the numbers did not match when they reached Yar Nadrak.

A faint, pale flicker in the underbrush some distance uphill from the trail caught Garion's eye, and he turned his head sharply in that direction. A large, silver-gray wolf was ghosting along just at the edge of the trees, his pace exactly matching theirs. Garion quickly lowered his head again, pretended to stumble, and fell heavily against Silk. "Grandfather's out there," he whispered.

"Did you only just notice him?" Silk sounded surprised. "I've been watching him for the last hour or more."

When the trail turned away from the river and entered the trees, Garion felt the tension building up in him. He could not be sure what Belgarath was going to do, but he knew that the concealment offered by the forest provided the opportunity for which his grandfather had doubtless been waiting. He tried to hide his growing nervousness as he walked along behind Silk, but the slightest sound in the woods around them made him start uncontrollably.

The trail dipped down into a fair-sized clearing, surrounded on all sides by tall ferns, and the Mallorean guards halted the column to allow their prisoners to rest. Garion sank gratefully to the springy turf beside Silk. The effort of walking with one leg shackled to the long chain which bound the conscripts together was considerable, and he found that he was sweating profusely. "What's he waiting for?" he whispered to Silk.

The rat-faced little man shrugged. "It's still a few hours until dark," he replied softly. "Maybe he wants to wait for that."

Then, some distance up the trail, they heard the sound of singing. The song was ribald and badly out of tune, but the singer was quite obviously enjoying himself, and the slurring of the words as he drew closer indicated that he was more than a little drunk.

The Malloreans grinned at each other. "Another patriot, perhaps," one of them smirked, "coming to enlist. Spread out, and we'll gather him up as soon as he comes into the clearing."

The singing Nadrak rode into view on a large roan horse. He wore the usual dark, stained leather clothing, and a fur cap perched precariously on one side of his head. He had a scraggly black beard, and he carried a wineskin in one hand. He seemed to be swaying in his saddle as he rode, but something about his eyes showed him not to be quite so drunk as he appeared. Garion stared at him openly as he rode into the clearing with a string of mules behind him. It was Yarblek, the Nadrak merchant they had encountered on the South Caravan Route in Cthol Murgos.

"Ho, there!" Yarblek greeted the Malloreans in a loud voice. "I see you've had good hunting. That's a healthy-looking bunch of recruits you've got there."

"The hunting just got easier." One of the Malloreans grinned at him, pulling his horse across the trail to block Yarblek's way.

"You mean me?" Yarblek laughed uproariously. "Don't be a fool. I'm too busy to play soldier."

"That's a shame," the Mallorean replied.

"I'm Yarblek, a merchant of Yar Turak and a friend of King Drosta himself. I'm acting on a commission that he personally put into my hands. If you interfere with me in any way, Drosta will have you flayed and roasted alive as soon as you get to Yar Nadrak."

The Mallorean looked a trifle less sure of himself. "We answer only to 'Zakath," he asserted a bit defensively. "King Drosta has no authority over us."

"You're in Gar og Nadrak, friend," Yarblek pointed out to him, "and Drosta does whatever he likes here. He might have to apologize to 'Zakath after it's all over, but by then the five of you will probably be peeled and cooked to a turn."

"I suppose you can prove that you're on official business?" the Mallorean guard hedged.

"Of course I can," Yarblek replied. He scratched at his head, his face taking on an expression of foolish perplexity. "Where did I put that parchment?" he muttered to himself. Then he snapped his fingers. "Oh, yes," he said, "now I remember. It's in the pack on that last mule. Here, have a drink, and I'll go get it." He tossed the wineskin to the Mallorean, turned his horse and rode back to the end of his pack string. He dismounted and began rummaging through a canvas pack.

"We'd better have a look at his documents before we decide," one of the others advised. "King Drosta's not the sort you want to cross."

"We might as well have a drink while we're waiting," another suggested, eyeing the wineskin.

"That's one thing we can agree on," the first replied, working loose the stopper of the leather bag. He raised the skin with both hands and lifted his chin to drink.

There was a solid-sounding thud, and the feathered shaft of an arrow was quite suddenly protruding from his throat, just at the top of his red tunic. The wine gushed from the skin to pour down over his astonished face. His companions gaped at him, then reached for their weapons with cries of alarm, but it was too late. Most of them tumbled from their saddles in the sudden storm of arrows that struck them from the concealment of the ferns. One, however, wheeled his mount to flee, clutching at the shaft buried deep in his side. The horse took no more than two leaps before three arrows sank into the Mallorean's back. He stiffened, then toppled over limply, his foot hanging up in his stirrup as he fell, and his frightened horse bolted, dragging him, bouncing and flopping, back down the trail.

"I can't seem to locate that document," Yarblek declared, walking back with a wicked grin on his face. He turned over the Mallorean he had been speaking to with his foot. "You didn't really want to see it anyway, did you?" he asked the dead man.

The Mallorean with the arrow in his throat stared blankly up at the sky, his mouth agape and a trickle of blood running out of his nose.

"I didn't think so." Yarblek laughed coarsely. He drew back his foot and kicked the dead man back over onto his face. Then he turned to smirk at Silk as his archers came out of the dark green ferns. "You certainly get around, Silk," he said. "I thought Taur Urgas had finished you back there in stinking Cthol Murgos."

"He miscalculated," Silk replied casually.

"How did you manage to get yourself conscripted into the Mallorean army?" Yarblek asked curiously, all traces of his feigned drunkenness gone now.

Silk shrugged. "I got careless."

"I've been following you for the last three days."

"I'm touched by your concern." Silk lifted his fettered ankle and jingled the chain. "Would it be too much trouble for you to unlock this?"

"You're not going to do anything foolish, are you?"

"Of course not."

"Find the key," Yarblek told one of his archers.

"What are you going to do with us?" Besher asked nervously, eyeing the dead guards with a certain apprehension.

Yarblek laughed. "What you do once that chain's off is up to you," he answered indifferently. "I wouldn't recommend staying in the vicinity of so many dead Malloreans, though. Somebody might come along and start asking questions."

"You're just going to let us go?" Besher demanded incredulously.

"I'm certainly not going to feed you," Yarblek told him.

The archers went down the chain, unlocking the shackles, and each Nadrak bolted into the bushes as soon as he was free.

"Well, then," Yarblek said, rubbing his palms together, "now that that's been taken care of, why don't we have a drink?"

"That guard spilled all your wine when he fell off his horse," Silk pointed out.

"That wasn't my wine," Yarblek snorted. "I stole it this morning. You should know I wouldn't offer my own drink to somebody I planned to kill."

"I wondered about that." Silk grinned at him. "I thought that maybe your manners had started to slip."

Yarblek's coarse face took on a faintly injured expression.

"Sorry," Silk apologized quickly. "I misjudged you."

"No harm done." Yarblek shrugged. "A lot of people misunderstand me." He sighed. "It's a burden I have to bear." He opened a pack on his lead mule and hefted out a small keg of ale. He set it on the ground and broached it with a practiced skill, bashing in its top with his fist. "Let's get drunk," he suggested.

"We'd really like to," Silk declined politely, "but we've got some rather urgent business to take care of."

"You have no idea how sorry I am about that," Yarblek replied, fishing several cups out of the pack.

"I knew you'd understand."

"Oh, I understand, all right, Silk." Yarblek bent and dipped two cups into the ale keg. "And I'm as sorry as I can be that your business is going to have to wait. Here." He gave Silk one cup and Garion the other. Then he turned and dipped out a cup for himself.

Silk looked at him with one raised eyebrow.

Yarblek sprawled on the ground beside the ale keg, comfortably resting his feet on the body of one of the dead Malloreans. "You see, Silk," he explained, "the whole point of all this is that Drosta wants you—very badly. He's offering a reward for you that's just *too* attractive to pass up. Friendship is one thing, but business is business, after all. Now, why don't you and your young friend make yourselves comfortable? This is a nice, shady clearing with soft moss to lie on. We'll all get drunk, and you can tell me how you managed to escape from Taur Urgas. Then you can tell me what happened to that handsome woman you had with you down in Cthol Murgos. Maybe I can make enough money from this to be able to afford to buy her. I'm not the marrying kind, but by Torak's teeth, that's a fine-looking woman. I'd almost be willing to give up my freedom for her."

"I'm sure she'd be flattered," Silk replied. "What then?"

"What when?"

"After we get drunk. What do we do then?"

"We'll probably get sick—that's what usually happens. After we get well, we'll run on down to Yar Nadrak. I'll collect the reward for you, and you'll be able to find out why King Drosta lek Thun wants to get his hands on you so badly." He looked at Silk with an amused expression. "You might as well sit down and have a drink, my friend. You aren't going anywhere just now."

CHAPTER FIVE

Yar Nadrak was a walled city, lying at the juncture of the east and west forks of the River Cordu. The forest had been cleared for a league or so in every direction from the capital by the simple expedient of setting fire to it, and the approach to the city passed through a wilderness of burned black snags and rank-growing bramble thickets. The city gates were stout and smeared with tar. Surmounting them was a stone replica of the mask of Torak. That beautiful, inhumanly cruel face gazed down at all who entered, and Garion suppressed a shudder as he rode under it.

The houses in the Nadrak capital were all very tall and had steeply sloping roofs. The windows of the second stories all had shutters, and most of the shutters were closed. Any exposed wood on the structures had been smeared with tar to preserve it, and the splotches of the black substance made all the buildings look somehow diseased.

There was a sullen, frightened air in the narrow, crooked streets of Yar Nadrak, and the inhabitants kept their eyes lowered as they hurried about their business. There appeared to be less leather involved in the clothing of the burghers of the capital than had been the case in the back country, but even here most garments were black, and only occasionally was there a splash of blue or yellow. The sole exception to this rule were the red tunics worn by the Mallorean soldiers. They seemed to be everywhere, roaming at will up and down the cobblestoned streets, accosting citizens rudely and talking loudly to each other in their heavily accented speech.

While the soldiers seemed for the most part to be merely swaggering bullies, young men who concealed their nervousness at being in a strange country with an outward show of bluster and braggadocio, the Mallorean Grolims were quite another matter. Unlike the western Grolims Garion had seen in Cthol Murgos, they rarely wore the polished steel mask, but rather assumed a set, grim expression, thin-lipped and narrow-eyed; as they went about the streets in their hooded black robes, everyone, Mallorean and Nadrak alike, gave way to them.

Garion and Silk, closely guarded and mounted on a pair of mules, followed the rangy Yarblek into the city. Yarblek and Silk had kept up their banter during the entire ride downriver, exchanging casual insults and reliving past indiscretions. Although he seemed friendly enough, Yarblek nonetheless remained watchful, and his men had guarded Silk and Garion every step of the way. Garion had covertly watched the forest almost continually during the three-day ride, but he had seen no sign of Belgarath and he entered the city in a state of jumpy apprehension. Silk, however, seemed relaxed and confident as always, and his behavior and attitude grated at Garion's nerves, for some reason.

After they had clattered along a crooked street for some distance, Yarblek turned down a narrow, dirty alleyway leading toward the river.

"I thought the palace was that way," Silk said to him, pointing toward the center of town.

"It is," Yarblek replied, "but we aren't going to the palace. Drosta's got company there, and he prefers to do business in private." The alleyway soon opened out into a seedy-looking street where the tall, narrow-looking houses had fallen somewhat into disrepair. The lanky Nadrak clamped his mouth shut as two Mallorean Grolims rounded a corner just ahead and came in their direction. Yarblek's expression was openly hostile as the two approached.

One of them stopped to return his gaze. "You seem to have a problem, friend," the Grolim suggested.

"That's my business, isn't it?" Yarblek retorted.

"Indeed it is," the Grolim replied coolly. "Don't let it get out of hand, though. Open disrespect for the priesthood is the sort of thing that could get you into serious trouble." The black-robed man's look was threatening.

On a sudden impulse, Garion carefully pushed out his mind toward the Grolim, probing very gently, but the thoughts he encountered showed no particular awareness and certainly none of the aura that always seemed to emanate from the mind of a sorcerer.

"Don't do that," the voice in his mind cautioned him. *"It's like ringing a bell or wearing a sign around your neck."*

Garion quickly pulled back his thoughts. *"I thought all Grolims were sorcerers,"* he replied silently. *"These two are just ordinary men."* But the other awareness was gone.

The two Grolims passed, and Yarblek spat contemptuously into the street. "Pigs," he muttered. "I'm starting to dislike Malloreans almost as much as Murgos."

"They seem to be taking over your country, Yarblek," Silk observed.

Yarblek grunted. "Let one Mallorean in, and before long they're underfoot everywhere."

"Why did you let them in to begin with?" Silk asked mildly.

"Silk," Yarblek said bluntly, "I know you're a spy, and I'm *not* going to discuss politics with you, so quit fishing for information."

"Just passing the time of day," Silk replied innocently.

"Why don't you mind your own business?"

"But this *is* my business, old friend."

Yarblek stared hard at him, then suddenly laughed.

"Where are we going?" Silk asked him, looking around at the shabby street. "This isn't the best part of town, as I recall."

"You'll find out," Yarblek told him.

They rode on down toward the river where the smell of floating garbage and open sewers was quite nearly overpowering. Garion saw rats feeding in the gutters, and the men in the street wore shabby clothing and had the furtive look of those who have reason to avoid the police.

Yarblek turned his horse abruptly and led them into another narrow, filthy alleyway. "We walk from here," he said, dismounting. "I want to go in the back way." Leaving their mounts with one of his men, they went on down the alley, stepping carefully over piles of rotting garbage.

"Down there," Yarblek told them, pointing at a short, rickety flight of wooden stairs leading down to a narrow doorway. "Once we get inside, keep your heads down. We don't want too many people noticing that you're not Nadraks."

They went down the creaking steps and slipped through the doorway into a dim, smoky tavern, reeking of sweat, spilled beer, and stale vomit. The fire pit in the center of the room was choked with ashes, and several large logs smoldered there, giving off a great deal of smoke and very little light. Two narrow, dirty windows at the front appeared only slightly less dark than the walls around them, and a single oil lamp hung on a chain nailed to one of the rafters.

"Sit here," Yarblek instructed them, nudging at a bench standing against the back wall. "I'll be right back." He went off toward the front part of the tavern. Garion looked around quickly, but saw immediately that a pair of Yarblek's men lounged unobtrusively beside the door.

"What are we going to do?" he whispered to Silk.

"We don't have much choice but to wait and see what happens," Silk replied.

"You don't seem very worried."

"I'm not, really."

"But we've been arrested, haven't we?"

Silk shook his head. "When you arrest somebody, you put shackles on him. King Drosta wants to talk to me, that's all."

"But the reward notice said—"

"I wouldn't pay too much attention to that, Garion. The reward notice was for the benefit of the Malloreans. Whatever Drosta's up to, he doesn't want them finding out about it."

Yarblek threaded his way back through the crowd in the tavern and thumped himself down on the grimy bench beside them. "Drosta should be here shortly," he said. "You want something to drink while we're waiting?"

Silk looked around with a faint expression of distaste. "I don't think so," he replied. "The ale barrels in places like this usually have a few drowned rats floating in them—not to mention the dead flies and roaches."

"Suit yourself," Yarblek said.

"Isn't this a peculiar sort of place to find a king?" Garion asked, looking around at the shabby interior of the tavern.

"You have to know King Drosta to understand," Silk told him. "He has some rather notorious appetites, and these riverfront dives suit him."

Yarblek laughed in agreement. "Our monarch's a lusty sort of fellow," he noted, "but don't ever make the mistake of thinking he's stupid—a little crude, perhaps, but not stupid. He can come to a place like this and no Mallorean will take the trouble to follow him. He's found that it's a good way to conduct business that he prefers not to have reported back to 'Zakath."

There was a stir near the front of the tavern, and two heavy-shouldered Nadraks in black leather tunics and pointed helmets pushed their way through the door. "Make way!" one of them barked. "And everybody rise!"

"Those who are *able* to rise," the other added dryly.

A wave of jeers and catcalls ran through the crowd as a thin man in a yellow satin doublet and a fur-trimmed green velvet cloak entered. His eyes were bulging and his face was deeply scarred with old pockmarks. His movements were quick and jerky, and his expression was a curious mixture of sardonic amusement and a kind of desperate, unsatisfied hunger.

"All hail his Majesty, Drosta lek Thun, King of the Nadraks!" one drunken man proclaimed in a loud voice, and the others in the tavern laughed coarsely, jeering and whistling and stamping their feet.

"My faithful subjects," the pockmarked man replied with a gross smirk. "Drunks, thieves, and procurers. I bask in the warm glow of your love for me." His contempt seemed directed almost as much at himself as at the ragged, unwashed crowd.

They whistled in unison and stamped their feet derisively.

"How many tonight, Drosta?" someone shouted.

"As many as I can." The king leered. "It's my duty to spread royal blessings wherever I go."

"Is that what you call it?" someone else demanded raucously.

"It's as good a name as any," Drosta replied with a shrug.

"The royal bedchamber awaits," the tavern owner declaimed with a mocking bow.

"Along with the royal bedbugs, I'm sure," Drosta added. "Ale for every man not too drunk to swill it down. Let my loyal subjects drink to my vitality."

The crowd cheered as the king pushed toward a stairway leading to the upper stories of the building. "My duty awaits me," he proclaimed, pointing with a grand gesture up the stairs. "Let all take note of how eagerly I go to embrace that stern responsibility." And he mounted the stairs to the derisive applause of the assembled riffraff.

"What now?" Silk asked.

"We'll wait a bit," Yarblek replied. "It'd be a little obvious if we went up immediately."

Garion shifted uncomfortably on the bench. A very faint, nervous kind of tingle had begun just behind his ears, a sort of prickling sensation that seemed to crawl over his skin. He had an unpleasant thought or two about the possibility of lice or fleas migrating from the scum in the tavern in search of fresh blood, but dismissed that idea. The tingling did not seem to be external.

At a table not far away, a shabbily dressed man, apparently far gone in drink, had been snoring with his head buried in his arms. In the middle of a snore he raised his face briefly and winked. It was Belgarath. He let his face drop back onto his arms as a wave of relief swept through Garion.

The drunken crowd in the tavern grew steadily more rowdy. A short, ugly fight broke out near the fire pit, and the revelers at first cheered, then joined in, kicking at the two who rolled about on the floor.

"Let's go up," Yarblek said shortly, rising to his feet. He pushed through the crowd and started upstairs.

"Grandfather's here," Garion whispered to Silk as they followed.

"I saw him," Silk replied shortly.

The stairs led to a dim upper hallway with dirty, threadbare carpeting on the floor. At the far end, King Drosta's two bored-looking guards leaned against the wall on either side of a solid door.

"My name's Yarblek," Silk's friend told them as he reached the door. "Drosta's expecting me."

The guards glanced at each other, then one tapped on the door. "That man you wanted to see is here, your Majesty."

"Send him in." Drosta's voice was muffled.

"He isn't alone," the guard advised.

"That's all right."

"Go ahead," the guard said to Yarblek, unlatching the door and pushing it open.

The king of the Nadraks was sprawled on a rumpled bed with his arms about the thin shoulders of a pair of dirty, scantily dressed young girls with tangled hair and hopeless-looking eyes. "Yarblek," the depraved monarch greeted the merchant, "what kept you?"

"I didn't want to attract attention by following you immediately, Drosta."

"I almost got sidetracked." Drosta leered at the two girls. "Aren't they luscious?"

"If you like the type." Yarblek shrugged. "I prefer a little more maturity."

"That's good, too," Drosta admitted, "but I love them all. I fall in love twenty times a day. Run along, my pretties," he told the girls. "I've got some business to take care of just now. I'll send for you later."

The two girls immediately left, closing the door quietly behind them.

Drosta sat up on the bed, scratching absently at one armpit. His stained and rumpled yellow doublet was unbuttoned, and his bony chest was covered with coarse black hair. He was thin, almost emaciated, and his scrawny arms looked like two sticks. His hair was lank and greasy, and his beard was so thin that it was little more than a few scraggly-looking black hairs sprouting from his chin. The pockmarks on his face were deep, angry red scars, and his neck and hands were covered with an unwholesome, scabby-looking rash. There was a distinctly unpleasant odor about him. "Are you sure this is the man I want?" he asked Yarblek. Garion looked at the Nadrak King sharply. The coarseness had gone out of his voice, and his tone was incisive, direct, the tone of a man who was all business. Garion made a few quick mental adjustments. Drosta lek Thun was not at all what he seemed.

"I've known him for years, Drosta," Yarblek replied. "This is Prince Kheldar of Drasnia. He's also known as Silk and sometimes Ambar of Kotu or Radek of Boktor. He's a thief, a swindler, and a spy. Aside from that, he's not too bad."

"We are delighted to meet so famous a man," King Drosta declared. "Welcome, Prince Kheldar."

"Your Majesty," Silk replied, bowing.

"I'd have invited you to the palace," Drosta continued, "but I've got some houseguests with the unfortunate habit of sticking their noses into my business." He laughed dryly. "Luckily, I found out very soon that Malloreans are a priggish race. They won't follow me into places like this, so we'll be able to talk freely." He looked around at the cheap, gaudy furnishings and red draperies with a sort of amused toleration. "Besides," he added, "I like it here."

Garion stood with his back against the wall near the door, trying to remain as unobtrusive as possible, but Drosta's nervous eyes picked him out. "Can he be trusted?" the king demanded of Silk.

"Completely," Silk assured him. "He's my apprentice. I'm teaching him the business."

"Which business? Stealing or spying?"

Silk shrugged. "It amounts to the same thing. Yarblek says you wanted to see me. I assume it has something to do with current matters rather than any past misunderstandings."

"You're quick, Kheldar," Drosta replied approvingly. "I need your help and I'm willing to pay for it."

Silk grinned. "I'm fond of the word pay."

"So I've heard. Do you know what's going on here in Gar og Nadrak?" Drosta's eyes were penetrating, and his veneer of gross self-indulgence had fallen completely away.

"I *am* in the intelligence service, your Majesty," Silk pointed out.

Drosta grunted, stood up, and went to a table where a decanter of wine and several glasses stood. "Drink?" he asked.

"Why not?"

Drosta filled four glasses, took one for himself and paced nervously about the room with an angry expression. "I don't *need* any of this, Kheldar," he burst out. "My family's spent generations—centuries—weaning Gar og Nadrak away from the domination of the Grolims. Now they're about to drag us back into howling barbarism again, and I don't have any choice but to go along with it. I've got a quarter of a million Malloreans roaming around at will inside my borders and an army I can't even count poised just to the south. If I raise so much as one word of protest, 'Zakath will crush my kingdom with one fist."

"Would he really do that?" Silk asked, taking a chair at the table.

"With just about as much emotion as you'd feel about swatting a fly," Drosta replied. "Have you ever met him?"

Silk shook his head.

"You're lucky," Drosta told him with a shudder. "Taur Urgas is a madman, but, much as I hate him, he's still human. 'Zakath is made out of ice. I've *got* to get in touch with Rhodar."

"Ah," Silk said. "*That's* what this is all about, then."

"You're a nice enough fellow, Kheldar," Drosta told him dryly, "but I wouldn't go to all this trouble just for the pleasure of your company. You've got to carry my message to Rhodar. I've tried to get word to him, but I can't catch up with him. He won't stay in one place long enough. How can a fat man move so cursed fast?"

"He's deceptive," Silk said shortly. "Exactly what have you got in mind?"

"An alliance," Drosta replied bluntly. "My back's against the wall. Either I ally myself with Rhodar, or I get swallowed up."

Silk carefully set down his glass. "That's a very large suggestion, your Majesty. In the present situation, it's going to take a great deal of fast-talking to arrange."

"That's why I sent for you, Kheldar. We're staring the end of the world right in the face. You've got to get to Rhodar and persuade him to pull his army back from the Thullish border. Make him stop this insanity before it goes too far."

"Making my uncle do things is a little beyond my abilities, King Drosta," Silk replied carefully. "I'm flattered that you think I've got that much influence with him, but things have usually been the other way around between us."

"Don't you understand what's going on, Kheldar?" King Drosta's voice was anguished, and he gesticulated almost wildly as he spoke. "Our only hope of survival lies in not giving the Murgos and the Malloreans any kind of reason to unite. We should work to stir up trouble between them, not to provide them with a common enemy. Taur Urgas and 'Zakath hate each other with a passion so intense that it's almost holy. There are more Murgos than grains of sand and more Malloreans than stars. The Grolims can babble their gibberish about the awakening of Torak until their tongues fall out, but Taur Urgas and 'Zakath have taken the field for just one reason—each of them wants to destroy the other and make himself overking of Angarak. They're headed directly toward a war of mutual extinction. We can be rid of both of them if we just don't interfere."

"I think I see what you mean," Silk murmured.

" 'Zakath's ferrying his Malloreans across the Sea of the East to his staging area near Thull Zelik, and Taur Urgas has the southern Murgos massed near Rak Goska. Inevitably, they're going to move on each other. We've *got* to stay out of the way and let them fight. Make Rhodar pull back before he spoils everything."

"Have you talked with the Thulls about this?" Silk asked.

Drosta snorted with contempt. "What's the point? I've tried to explain this to King Gethell, but talking to him is like talking to a pile of manure. The Thulls are so afraid of the Grolims that all you have to do is mention Torak's name and they go all to pieces. Gethell's a Thull through and through. There's nothing between his ears but sand."

"There's just one problem with all of this, Drosta," Silk told the agitated monarch. "I can't carry your message to King Rhodar."

"Can't?" Drosta exploded. "What do you mean, you *can't?"*

"My uncle and I aren't on the best of terms just now," Silk lied smoothly. "We had a little misunderstanding a few months ago, and about the first thing he'd do if he saw me coming is have me put in chains—and I'm almost certain things would go downhill from there."

Drosta groaned. "We're all doomed then," he declared, seeming to slump in on himself. "You were my last hope."

"Let me think a moment," Silk said. "We might be able to salvage something out of this yet." He stared at the floor, chewing absently on a fingernail as he turned the problem over in his mind. "*I* can't go," he concluded. "That's obvious. But that doesn't mean that somebody else couldn't."

"Who else would Rhodar trust?" Drosta demanded.

Silk turned to Yarblek, who had been listening to the conversation intently with a worried frown. "Are you in any kind of trouble in Drasnia at the moment?" he asked.

"Not that I know of."

"All right," Silk continued. "There's a fur dealer in Boktor—Geldahar's his name."

"Fat man? Sort of cross-eyed?" Yarblek asked.

"That's him. Why don't you take a shipment of furs and go to Boktor? While you're trying to sell Geldahar the furs, tell him that the salmon run is late this year."

"I'm sure he'll be fascinated to hear that."

"It's a code word," Silk explained with exaggerated patience. "As soon as you say that, he'll see to it that you get into the palace to see Queen Porenn."

"I've heard that she's a lovely woman," Yarblek said, "but that's a long trip just to see a pretty girl. I can probably find a pretty girl just down the hall."

"You're missing the point, Yarblek," Silk told him. "Porenn is Rhodar's queen, and he trusts her even more than he used to trust me. She'll know that I sent you, and she'll pass anything you tell her on to my uncle. Rhodar will be reading Drosta's message three days after you ride into Boktor. I guarantee it."

"You'd let a *woman* know about all this?" Drosta objected violently. "Kheldar, you're insane. The only woman safe with a secret is one who's had her tongue cut out."

Silk shook his head firmly. "Porenn's in control of Drasnian intelligence right now, Drosta. She already knows most of the secrets in the world. You're never going to get an emissary through an Alorn army to Rhodar, so forget that. There'll be Chereks with him, and they'll kill any Angarak on sight. If you want to communicate with Rhodar, you're going to have to use Drasnian intelligence as an intermediary, and that means going through Porenn."

Drosta looked dubious. "Maybe," he concluded after a moment's thought. "I'll try anything at this point—but why should Yarblek get involved? Why can't *you* carry my message to the Drasnian queen?"

Silk looked a trifle pained. "That wouldn't be a good idea at all, I'm afraid," he replied. "Porenn was rather central to my difficulties with my uncle. I'm definitely unwelcome at the palace just now."

One of King Drosta's shaggy eyebrows shot up. "So *that's* the way it is." He laughed. "Your reputation's well earned, I see." He turned to Yarblek. "It's up to you, then. Make the necessary arrangements for the trip to Boktor."

"You already owe me money, Drosta," Yarblek replied bluntly, "the reward for bringing in Kheldar, remember?"

Drosta shrugged. "Write it down someplace."

Yarblek shook his head stubbornly. "Not hardly. Let's keep your account current. You're known as a slow payer, once you've got what you want."

"Yarblek," Drosta said plaintively, "I'm your king."

Yarblek inclined his head somewhat mockingly. "I honor and respect your Majesty," he said, "but business is business, after all."

"I don't carry that much money with me," Drosta protested.

"That's all right, Drosta. I can wait." Yarblek crossed his arms and sat down in a large chair with the air of a man planning to stay for quite some time.

The king of the Nadraks stared at him helplessly.

Then the door opened and Belgarath stepped into the room, still dressed in the rags he had worn in the tavern downstairs. There was no furtiveness about his entrance, and he moved like a man on serious business.

"What *is* this?" Drosta exclaimed incredulously. "Guards!" he bawled. "Get this drunken old man out of here."

"They're asleep, Drosta," Belgarath replied calmly. "Don't be too harsh with them, though. It's not their fault." He closed the door.

"Who are you? What do you think you're doing?" Drosta demanded. "Get out of here!"

"I think you'd better take a closer look, Drosta," Silk advised with a dry little chuckle. "Appearances can be deceiving sometimes, and you shouldn't be so quick to try to throw somebody out. He might have something important to say to you."

"Do you know him, Kheldar?" Drosta asked.

"Just about everybody in the world knows him," Silk replied. "Or *of* him."

Drosta's face creased into a puzzled frown, but Yarblek had started from his chair, his lean face suddenly pale. "Drosta!" he gasped. "Look at him. Think a minute. You know who he is."

Drosta stared at the shabby-looking old man, and his bulging eyes slowly opened even wider. *"You!"* he blurted.

Yarblek was still gaping at Belgarath. "He's been involved in it from the very beginning. I should have put it together down in Cthol Murgos—him, the woman, all of it."

"What are you doing in Gar og Nadrak?" Drosta asked in an awed voice.

"Just passing through, Drosta," Belgarath replied. "If you're quite finished with your discussion here, I need these two Alorns. We have an appointment, and we're running a little behind schedule."

"I always thought you were a myth."

"I like to encourage that as much as I can," Belgarath told him. "It makes moving around a lot easier."

"Are you mixed up in what the Alorns are doing?"

"They're acting more or less on my suggestions, yes. Polgara's keeping an eye on them."

"Can *you* get word to them and tell them to disengage?"

"That won't really be necessary, Drosta. I wouldn't worry too much about 'Zakath and Taur Urgas, if I were you. There are more important things afoot than their squabbles."

"So *that's* what Rhodar's doing," Drosta said in sudden comprehension. "Is it really that late?"

"It's even later than you think," the old sorcerer answered. He crossed to the table and poured himself some of Drosta's wine. "Torak's already stirring, and the whole matter's likely to be settled before the snow flies."

"This is going too far, Belgarath," Drosta said. "I might try to maneuver my way around Taur Urgas and 'Zakath, but I'm *not* going to cross Torak." He turned decisively toward the door.

"Don't do anything rash, Drosta," Belgarath advised him calmly, sitting in a chair and taking a sip of his wine. "Grolims can be most unreasonable, and the fact that I'm here in Yar Nadrak could only be viewed as the result of some collusion on your part. They'd have you bent backward over an altar and your heart sizzling in the coals before you ever got the chance to explain—king or no king."

Drosta froze in his tracks, his pockmarked face going very pale. For a moment, he seemed to be struggling with himself. Then his shoulders slumped and his resolution seemed to wilt. "You've got me by the throat, haven't you, Belgarath?" he said with a short laugh. "You've managed to make me outsmart myself, and now you're going to use that to force me to betray the God of Angarak."

"Are you really all that fond of him?"

"Nobody's fond of Torak. I'm *afraid* of him, and that's a better reason to stay on the good side of him than any sentimental attachment. If he wakes up—" The king of the Nadraks shuddered.

"Have you ever given much thought to the kind of world we'd have if he didn't exist?" Belgarath suggested.

"That's too much to even wish for. He's a God. No one could hope to defeat him. He's too powerful for that."

"There are things more powerful than Gods, Drosta—two that I can think of offhand, and those two are rushing toward a final meeting. It probably wouldn't be a good idea to put yourself between them at this point."

But something else had occurred to Drosta. He turned slowly with a look of stunned incredulity and stared directly at Garion. He shook his head and wiped at his eyes, like a man trying to clear away a fog. Garion became painfully aware of the great sword strapped across his back. Drosta's bulging eyes widened even more as the realization of what he was seeing erased the Orb's suggestion that his brain not record what stood in plain sight before him. His expression became awed, and desperate hope dawned on his ugly face. "Your Majesty," he stammered, bowing with profound respect.

"Your Majesty," Garion replied, politely inclining his head.

"It looks as if I'm forced to wish you good luck," Drosta said in a quiet voice. "Despite what Belgarath says, I think you're going to need it."

"Thank you, King Drosta," Garion said.

CHAPTER SIX

 "Do you think we can trust Drosta?" Garion asked Silk as they followed Belgarath along the garbage-littered alley behind the tavern.

"Probably about as far as we could throw him," Silk replied. "He was honest about *one* thing though. His back's to the wall. That might make him bargain with Rhodar in good faith—initially at least."

When they reached the street at the end of the alley, Belgarath glanced up once at the evening sky. "We'd better hurry," he said. "I want to get out of the city before they close the gates. I left our horses in a thicket a mile or so outside the walls."

"You went back for them?" Silk sounded a little surprised.

"Of course I did. I don't plan to walk all the way to Morindland." He led them up the street away from the river.

They reached the city gates in fading light just as the guards were preparing to close them for the night. One of the Nadrak soldiers raised his hand as if to bar their way, then apparently changed his mind and motioned them through irritably, muttering curses under his breath. The huge, tar-smeared gate boomed shut behind them, and there was the clinking rattle of heavy chains from inside as the bolts were thrown and locked. Garion glanced up once at the carved face of Torak which brooded down at them from above the gate, then deliberately turned his back.

"Are we likely to be followed?" Silk asked Belgarath as they walked along the dirt highway leading away from the city.

"I wouldn't be very surprised," Belgarath replied. "Drosta knows—or suspects—a great deal about what we're doing. Mallorean Grolims are very subtle, and they can pick the thoughts out of his head without his knowing it. That's probably why they don't bother to follow him when he goes off on his little excursions."

"Shouldn't you take some steps?" Silk suggested as they moved through the gathering twilight.

"We're getting a bit too close to Mallorea to be making unnecessary noise," Belgarath told him. "Zedar can hear me moving around from a long way off, and Torak's only dozing now. I'd rather not take the chance of waking him up with any more loud clatter."

They walked along the highway toward the shadowy line of rank undergrowth at the edge of the open fields surrounding the city. The sound of frogs from the marshy ground near the river was very loud in the twilight.

"Torak isn't really asleep anymore then?" Garion asked finally. He had harbored somewhere at the back of his mind the vague hope that they might be able to creep up on the sleeping God and catch him unaware.

"No, not really," his grandfather replied. "The sound of your hand touching the Orb shook the whole world. Not even Torak could sleep through that. He isn't really awake yet, but he's not entirely asleep, either."

"Did it really make all that much noise?" Silk asked curiously.

"They probably heard it on the other side of the universe. I left the horses over there." The old man pointed toward a shadowy willow grove several hundred yards to the left of the road.

From behind them there was the rattle of a heavy chain, startling the frogs into momentary silence.

"They're opening the gate," Silk said. "They wouldn't do that unless somebody gave them an official reason to."

"Let's hurry," Belgarath said.

The horses stirred and nickered as the three of them pushed their way through the rustling willows in the rapidly descending darkness. They led the horses out of the grove, mounted, and rode back toward the highway.

"They know we're out here somewhere," Belgarath said. "There's not much point being coy about it."

"Just a second," Silk said. He dismounted and rummaged through one of the canvas bags tied to their packhorse. He pulled something out of the bag, then climbed back on his horse. "Let's go then."

They pushed into a gallop, thudding along the dirt road under a starry, moonless sky toward the denser shadows where the forest rose at the edge of the scrubby, burned-off expanse surrounding the Nadrak capital.

"Can you see them?" Belgarath called to Silk, who was bringing up the rear and looking back over his shoulder.

"I think so," Silk shouted back. "They're about a mile behind."

"That's too close."

"I'll take care of it as soon as we get into the woods," Silk replied confidently.

The dark forest loomed closer and closer as they galloped along the hard-packed road. Garion could smell the trees now.

They plunged into the black shadows under the trees and felt that slight extra warmth that always lies in a forest. Silk reined in sharply. "Keep going," he told them, swinging out of his saddle. "I'll catch up."

Belgarath and Garion rode on, slowing a bit in order to pick the road out of the darkness. After several minutes, Silk caught up with them. "Listen," the little man said, pulling his horse to a stop. His teeth flashed in the shadows as he grinned.

"They're coming," Garion warned urgently as he heard a rumble of hoofs. "Hadn't we better—"

"Listen," Silk whispered sharply.

From behind there were several startled exclamations and the heavy sound of men falling. A horse squealed and ran off somewhere.

Silk laughed wickedly. "I think we can press on," he said gaily. "They'll be delayed for a bit while they round up their horses."

"What did you do?" Garion asked him.

Silk shrugged. "I stretched a rope across the road, about chest-high on a mounted man. It's an old trick, but sometimes old tricks are the best. They'll have to be cautious now, so we should be able to lose them by morning."

"Let's go, then," Belgarath said.

"Where are we headed?" Silk asked as they moved into a canter.

"We'll make directly for the north range," the old man replied. "Too many people know we're here, so let's get to the land of the Morindim as soon as we can."

"If they're really after us, they'll follow us all the way, won't they?" Garion asked, looking back nervously.

"I don't think so," Belgarath told him. "They'll be a long way behind by the time we get there. I don't think they'll risk going into Morind territory just to follow a cold trail."

"Is it *that* dangerous, Grandfather?"

"The Morindim do nasty things to strangers if they catch them."

Garion thought about that. "Won't *we* be strangers too?" he asked. "To the Morindim, I mean?"

"I'll take care of that when we get there."

They galloped on through the remainder of the velvety night, leaving their now-cautious pursuers far behind. The blackness beneath the trees was dotted with the pale, winking glow of fireflies, and crickets chirped interminably. As the first light of morning began to filter through the forest, they reached the edge of another burned-off area, and Belgarath reined in to peer cautiously out at the rank scrub, dotted here and there with charred snags. "We'd better have something to eat," he suggested. "The horses need some rest, and we can catch a bit of sleep before we go on." He looked around in the gradually increasing light. "Let's get away from the road, though." He turned his horse and led them off along the edge of the burn. After several hundred yards, they reached a small clearing that jutted out into the coarse brush. A spring trickled water into a mossy pool at the very edge of the trees, and the grass in the clearing was intensely green. The outer edge of the opening was hemmed in by brambles and a tangle of charred limbs. "This looks like a good place," Belgarath decided.

"Not really," Silk disagreed. He was staring at a crudely squared-off block of stone standing in the center of the clearing. There were ugly black stains running down the sides of the stone.

"For our purposes it is," the old man replied. "The altars of Torak are generally avoided, and we don't particularly want company."

They dismounted at the edge of the trees, and Belgarath began rummaging through one of the packs for bread and dried meat. Garion was in a curiously abstracted mood. He was tired, and his weariness made him a bit light-headed. Quite deliberately, he walked across the springy turf to the bloodstained altar; he stared at it, his eyes meticulously recording details without considering their implication. The blackened stone sat solidly in the center of the clearing, casting no shadow in the pale dawn light. It was an old altar, and had not been used recently. The stains that had sunk into the pores of the rock were black with age, and the bones littering the ground around it were half-sunk in the earth and were covered with a greenish patina of moss. A scurrying spider darted into the vacant eye socket of a mossy skull, seeking refuge in the dark, vaulted emptiness. Many of the bones were broken and showed the marks of the small, sharp teeth of forest scavengers who would feed on anything that was dead. A cheap, tarnished silver brooch lay with its chain tangled about a lumpy vertebra, and not far away a brass buckle, green with verdigris, still clung to a bit of moldering leather.

"Come away from that thing, Garion," Silk told him with a note of revulsion in his voice.

"It sort of helps to look at it," Garion replied quite calmly, still staring at the altar and the bones. "It gives me something to think about beside being afraid." He squared his shoulders, and his great sword shifted on his back. "I don't really think the world needs this sort of thing. Maybe it's time somebody did something about it."

When he turned around, Belgarath was looking at him, his wise old eyes narrowed. "It's a start," the sorcerer observed. "Let's eat and get some sleep."

They took a quick breakfast, picketed their horses, and rolled themselves in their blankets under some bushes at the edge of the clearing. Not even the presence of the Grolim altar nor the peculiar resolve it had stirred in him was enough to keep Garion from falling asleep immediately.

It was almost noon when he awoke, pulled from sleep by a faint whispering sound in his mind. He sat up quickly, looking around to find the source of that disturbance, but neither the forest nor the brush-choked burn seemed to hold any threat. Belgarath stood not far away, looking up at the summer sky where a large, blue-banded hawk was circling.

"What are you doing here?" The old sorcerer did not speak aloud but rather cast the question at the sky with his mind. The hawk spiraled down to the clearing, flared his wings to avoid the altar, and landed on the turf. He looked directly at Belgarath with fierce yellow eyes, then shimmered and seemed to blur. When the shimmering was gone, the misshapen sorcerer Beldin stood in his place. He was still as ragged, dirty, and irritable as he had been the last time Garion had seen him.

"Is this all the farther you've managed to come?" he demanded harshly of Belgarath. "What have you been doing—stopping at every tavern along the way?"

"We ran into a small delay," Belgarath replied calmly.

Beldin grunted with a sour look. "If you keep dawdling along like this, it'll take you the rest of the year to get to Cthol Mishrak."

"We'll get there, Beldin. You worry too much."

"Somebody has to. You're being followed, you know."

"How far back are they?"

"Five leagues or so."

Belgarath shrugged. "That's far enough. They'll give up when we get to Morindland."

"What if they don't?"

"Have you been spending time with Polgara lately?" Belgarath asked dryly. "I thought I'd gotten away from all the 'what-ifs.' "

Beldin shrugged, a gesture made grotesque by the hump on his back. "I saw her last week," he reported. "She has some interesting plans for you, you know."

"She came to the Vale?" Belgarath sounded surprised.

"Passed through. She was with the red-haired girl's army."

Garion threw off his blanket. "With *whose* army?" he demanded.

"What's going on down there?" Belgarath asked sharply.

Beldin scratched at his tangled hair. "I never really got the straight of it," he admitted. "All I know is that the Alorns are following that little redheaded Tolnedran. She calls herself the Rivan Queen—whatever that means."

"Ce'Nedra?" Garion was incredulous, though, for some reason, he knew that he shouldn't be.

"I guess she went through Arendia like a pestilence," Beldin continued. "After she passed, there wasn't an able-bodied man left in the kingdom. Then she went on down into Tolnedra and goaded her father into convulsions—I didn't know that he was subject to fits."

"It crops up in the Borune line once in a while," Belgarath said. "It's nothing all that serious, but they try to keep it quiet."

"Anyway," the hunchback went on, "while Ran Borune was still frothing at the mouth, his daughter stole his legions. She's persuaded about half the world to take up arms and follow her." He gave Garion a quizzical look. "You're supposed to marry her, aren't you?"

Garion nodded, not trusting himself to speak.

Beldin grinned suddenly. "You might want to give some thought to running away."

"Ce'Nedra?" Garion blurted again.

"His wits seem a bit scrambled," Beldin observed.

"He's been under a strain, and his nerves aren't too good just now," Belgarath replied. "Are you going back to the Vale?"

Beldin nodded. "The twins and I are going to join Polgara when the campaign starts. She might need some help if the Grolims come at her in force."

"Campaign?" Belgarath exclaimed. "What campaign? I told them just to march up and down and make a lot of noise. I specifically told them *not* to invade."

"They ignored you, it seems. Alorns aren't noted for restraint in such matters. Apparently they got together and decided to take steps. The fat one seems fairly intelligent. He wants to get a Cherek fleet into the Sea of the East to commit a few constructive atrocities on Mallorean shipping. The rest of it seems to be pretty much diversionary."

Belgarath started to swear. "You can't let them out of your sight for a single instant," he raged. "How could Polgara lend herself to this idiocy?"

"The plan does have a certain merit, Belgarath. The more Malloreans they drown now, the fewer we have to fight later."

"We never planned to fight them, Beldin. The Angaraks won't unite unless Torak comes back to weld them together again—*or* unless they're faced with a common enemy. We just talked with Drosta lek Thun, the Nadrak King, and he's so sure that the Murgos and the Malloreans are about to go to war with each other that he wants to ally himself with the west just to get clear of it. When you get back, see if you can talk some sense into Rhodar and Anheg. I've got enough problems already."

"Your problems are only starting, Belgarath. The twins had a visitation a couple days ago."

"A what?"

Beldin shrugged. "What else would you call it? They were working on something—quite unrelated to all this—and the pair of them suddenly went into a trance and began to babble at me. At first they were just repeating that gibberish from the Mrin Codex—you know the place—where the Mrin Prophet's mind broke down and he degenerated into animal noises for a while. Anyway, they went back over that part—only this time it came out coherently."

"What did they say?" Belgarath demanded, his eyes burning.

"Are you sure you want to know?"

"Of course I want to know."

"All right. It went like this: 'Behold, the heart of the stone shall relent, and the beauty that was destroyed shall be restored, and the eye that is not shall be made whole again' "

Belgarath stared at him. "That's it?" he asked.

"That's it," Beldin told him.

"But what does it mean?" Garion asked.

"Just what it says, Belgarion," Beldin replied. "For some reason the Orb is going to restore Torak."

Garion began to tremble as the full impact of Beldin's words struck him. "Torak's going to win, then," he said numbly.

"It didn't say anything about winning or losing, Belgarion," Beldin corrected him. "All it said was that the Orb is going to undo what it did to Torak when he used it to crack the world. It doesn't say anything about *why*."

"That's always been the trouble with the Prophecy," Belgarath observed. "It can mean any one of a dozen different things."

"Or all of them," Beldin added. "That's what makes it so difficult to understand sometimes. We tend to concentrate on just one thing, but Prophecy includes everything at the same time. I'll work on it and see if I can wring some sense out of it. If I come up with anything, I'll let you know. I'd better be getting back." He leaned slightly forward and curled his arms out in a vaguely winglike gesture. "Watch out for the Morindim," he told Belgarath. "You're a fair sorcerer, but magic's altogether different, and sometimes it gets away from you."

"I think I can handle it if I have to," Belgarath replied tartly.

"Maybe," Beldin said. "If you can manage to stay sober." He shimmered back into the form of the hawk, beat his wings twice, and spiraled up out of the clearing and into the sky. Garion watched him until he was only a circling speck.

"That was a strange visit," Silk said, rolling out of his blankets. "It looks as if quite a bit's been going on since we left."

"And none of it very good," Belgarath added sourly. "Let's get moving. We're really going to have to hurry now. If Anheg gets his fleet into the Sea of the East and starts sinking Mallorean troop ships, 'Zakath might decide to march north and come across the land bridge. If we don't get there first, it could get very crowded up there." The old man scowled darkly. "I'd like to put my hands on your uncle just about now," he added. "I'd sweat a few pounds off him."

They quickly saddled their horses and rode back along the edge of the sunlit forest toward the road leading north.

Despite the rather lame assurances of the two sorcerers, Garion rode slumped in despair. They were going to lose, and Torak was going to kill him.

"Stop feeling so sorry for yourself," the inner voice told him finally.

"Why did you get me into this?" Garion demanded bitterly.

"We've discussed that before."

"He's going to kill me."

"What gives you that idea?"

"That's what the Prophecy said." Garion stopped abruptly as a thought occurred to him. *"You said it yourself. You're the Prophecy, aren't you?"*

"It's a misleading term—and I didn't say anything about winning or losing."

"Isn't that what it means?"

"No. It means exactly what it says."

"What else could it mean?"

"You're getting more stubborn every day. Stop worrying so much about meanings and just do what you have to do. You almost had it right, back there."

"If all you're going to do is talk in riddles, why bother with it at all? Why go to all the trouble of saying things that nobody's able to understand?"

"Because it's necessary to say it. The word determines the event. The word puts limits

on the event and shapes it. Without the word, the event is merely a random happening. That's the whole purpose of what you call prophecy—to separate the significant from the random."

"I don't understand."

"I didn't think you would, but you asked, after all. Now stop worrying about it. It has nothing to do with you."

Garion wanted to protest, but the voice was gone. The conversation, however, had made him feel a little better—not much, but a little. To take his mind off it, he pulled his horse in beside Belgarath's as they reentered the forest on the far side of the burn. "Exactly who are the Morindim, Grandfather?" he asked. "Everybody keeps talking about them as if they were terribly dangerous."

"They are," Belgarath replied, "but you can get through their country if you're careful."

"Are they on Torak's side?"

"The Morindim aren't on anybody's side. They don't even live in the same world with us."

"I don't follow that."

"The Morindum are like the Ulgos used to be—before UL accepted them. There were several groups of Godless Ones. They all wandered off in various directions. The Ulgos went to the west, the Morindim went north. Other groups went south or east and disappeared."

"Why didn't they just stay where they were?"

"They couldn't. There's a kind of compulsion involved in the decisions of the Gods. Anyway, the Ulgos finally found themselves a God. The Morindim didn't. The compulsion to remain separated from other people is still there. They live in that treeless emptiness up there beyond the north range—small nomadic bands, mostly."

"What did you mean when you said they don't live in the same world with us?"

"The world is a pretty terrible place for a Morind—a demon-haunted place. They worship devils and they live more in dreams than they do in reality. Their society is dominated by the dreamers and the magicians."

"There aren't really any devils, are there?" Garion asked skeptically.

"Oh, yes. The devils are very real."

"Where do they come from?"

Belgarath shrugged. "I haven't any idea. They do exist, though, and they're completely evil. The Morindim control them by the use of magic."

"Magic? Is that different from what we do?"

"Quite a bit. We're sorcerers—at least that's what we're called. What we do involves the Will and the Word, but that's not the only way to do things."

"I don't quite follow."

"It's not really all that complicated, Garion. There are several ways to tamper with the normal order of things. Vordai's a witch. What she does involves the use of spirits—usually benign, mischievous sometimes—but not actually wicked. A magician uses devils—evil spirits."

"Isn't that sort of dangerous?"

Belgarath nodded. "*Very* dangerous," he replied. "The magician tries to control the demon with spells—formulas, incantations, symbols, mystic diagrams—that sort of thing. As long as he doesn't make any mistakes, the demon is his absolute slave and has to do what he tells it to do. The demon doesn't want to be a slave, so it keeps looking for a way to break the spell."

"What happens if it does?"

"It generally devours the magician on the spot. That happens rather frequently. If you lose your concentration or summon a demon too strong for you, you're in trouble."

"What did Beldin mean when he said that you weren't very good at magic?" Silk asked.

"I've never spent that much time trying to learn about it," the old sorcerer replied. "I have alternatives, after all, and magic is dangerous and not very dependable."

"Don't use it then," Silk suggested.

"I hadn't really planned to. Usually the threat of magic is enough to keep the Morindim at a distance. Actual confrontations are rather rare."

"I can see why."

"After we get through the north range, we'll disguise ourselves. There are a number of markings and symbols that will make the Morindim avoid us."

"That sounds promising."

"Of course we have to get there first," the old man pointed out. "Let's pick up the pace a bit. We've still got a long way to go." And he pushed his horse into a gallop.

CHAPTER SEVEN

They rode hard for the better part of a week, moving steadily northward and avoiding the scattered settlements which dotted the Nadrak forest. Garion noticed that the nights grew steadily shorter; by the time they reached the foothills of the north range, darkness had virtually disappeared. Evening and morning merged into a few hours of luminous twilight as the sun dipped briefly below the horizon before bursting into view once more.

The north range marked the upper edge of the Nadrak forest. It was not so much a mountainous region as it was a string of peaks, a long finger of upthrusting terrain reaching out toward the east from the broad ranges that formed the spine of the continent. As they rode up a scarcely defined trail toward a saddle that stretched between two snowy peaks, the trees around them grew more stunted and finally disappeared entirely. Beyond that point, there would be no more trees. Belgarath stopped at the edge of one of these last groves and cut a half dozen long saplings.

The wind that came down off the peaks had a bitter chill to it and the arid smell of perpetual winter. When they reached the boulder-strewn summit, Garion looked out for the first time at the immense plain stretching below. The plain, unmarked by trees, was covered with tall grass that bent before the vagrant wind in long, undulating waves. Rivers wandered aimlessly across that emptiness, and a thousand shallow lakes and ponds scattered, blue and glistening under a northern sun, toward the horizon.

"How far does it reach?" Garion asked quietly.

"From here to the polar ice," Belgarath replied. "Several hundred leagues."

"And no one lives out there but the Morindim?"

"Nobody wants to. For most of the year, it's buried in snow and darkness. You can go for six months up here without ever seeing the sun."

They rode down the rocky slope toward the plain and found a low-roofed, shallow cave at the base of the granite cliff that seemed to be the demarcation line between the mountains and the foothills. "We'll stop here for a while," Belgarath told them, reining in his tired mount. "We've got some preparations to make, and the horses need some rest."

They were all kept quite busy for the next several days while Belgarath radically altered their appearances. Silk set crude traps among the maze of rabbit runs twisting through the tall grass, and Garion roamed the foothills in search of certain tuberous roots and a peculiar-smelling white flower. Belgarath sat at the mouth of the cave, fashioning various implements from his saplings. The roots Garion had gathered yielded a dark brown stain, and Belgarath carefully applied it to their skins. "The Morindim are dark-skinned," he explained as he sat painting Silk's arms and back with the stain. "Somewhat darker than Tolnedrans or Nyissans. This'll wear off after a few weeks, but it'll last long enough to get us through."

After he had stained all their skins into swarthiness, he crushed the odd-smelling flowers to produce a jet-black ink. "Silk's hair is the right color already," he said, "and mine'll get by, but Garion's just won't do." He diluted some of the ink with water and dyed Garion's sandy hair black. "That's better," he grunted when he had finished, "and there's enough left for the tattoos."

"Tattoos?" Garion asked, startled at the thought.

"The Morindim decorate themselves extensively."

"Will it hurt?"

"We're not really going to tattoo ourselves, Garion," Belgarath told him with a pained look. "They take too long to heal. Besides, I'm afraid your aunt would go into hysterics if I took you back to her with designs engraved all over you. This'll last long enough for us to get through Morindland. It'll wear off—eventually."

Silk was sitting cross-legged in front of the cave, looking for all the world like a tailor as he sewed fresh rabbit pelts to their clothing.

"Won't they start to smell after a few days?" Garion asked, wrinkling his nose.

"Probably," Silk admitted, "but I don't have time to cure the pelts."

Later, as Belgarath was carefully drawing the tattoos on their faces, he explained the guise they were going to assume. "Garion will be the quester," he said.

"What's that?" Garion asked.

"Don't move your face," Belgarath told him, frowning as he drew lines under Garion's eyes with a raven-feather quill. "The quest is a Morind ritual. It's customary for a young Morind of a certain rank to undertake a quest before he assumes a position of authority in his clan. You'll wear a white fur headband and carry that red spear I fixed up for you. It's ceremonial," he cautioned, "so don't try to stab anybody with it. That's very bad form."

"I'll remember that."

"We'll disguise your sword to look like some sort of relic or something. A magician *might* see past the Orb's suggestion that it's not there—depending on how good he is. One other thing—the quester is absolutely forbidden to speak under any circumstances, so keep your mouth shut. Silk will be your dreamer. He'll wear a white fur band on his left arm. Dreamers speak in riddles and gibberish for the most part, and they tend to fall into trances and have fits." He glanced over at Silk. "Do you think you can handle that?"

"Trust me," Silk replied, grinning.

"Not very likely," Belgarath grunted. "I'll be Garion's magician. I'll carry a staff with a horned skull on it that'll make most Morindim avoid us."

"Most?" Silk asked quickly.

"It's considered bad manners to interfere with a quest, but it happens now and then." The old man looked critically at Garion's tattoos. "Good enough," he said and turned to Silk with his quill.

When it was all done, the three of them were scarcely recognizable. The markings the old man had carefully drawn on their arms and faces were not pictures so much as they were designs. Their faces had been changed into hideous devil masks, and the exposed parts of their bodies were covered with symbols etched in black ink. They wore fur-covered trousers and vests and bone necklaces clattered about their necks. Their stained arms and shoulders were bared and intricately marked.

Then Belgarath went down into the valley lying just below the cave, seeking something. It did not take his probing mind long to find what he needed. As Garion watched with revulsion, the old man casually violated a grave. He dug up a grinning human skull and carefully tapped the dirt out of it. "I'll need some deer horns," he told Garion. "Not too large and fairly well matched." He squatted, fierce-looking in his furs and tattoos, and began to scrub at the skull with handfuls of dry sand.

There were weather-bleached horns lying here and there in the tall grass, since the deer of the region shed their antlers each winter. Garion gathered a dozen or so and returned to the cave to find his grandfather boring a pair of holes in the top of the skull. He critically examined the horns Garion had brought him, selected a pair of them and screwed them down into the holes. The grating sound of horn against bone set Garion's teeth on edge. "What do you think?" Belgarath asked, holding up the horned skull.

"It's grotesque," Garion shuddered.

"That was the general idea," the old man replied. He attached the skull firmly to the top of a long staff, decorated it with several feathers and then rose to his feet. "Let's pack up and leave," he said.

They rode down through the treeless foothills and out into the bending, waist-high grass as the sun swung down toward the southwestern horizon to dip briefly behind the peaks of the range they had just crossed. The smell of the uncured pelts

Silk had sewn to their clothing was not very pleasant, and Garion did his best not to look at the hideously altered skull surmounting Belgarath's staff as they rode.

"We're being watched," Silk mentioned rather casually after an hour or so of riding.

"I was sure we would be," Belgarath replied. "Just keep going."

Their first meeting with the Morindim came just as the sun rose. They had paused on the sloping gravel bank of a meandering stream to water their mounts, and a dozen or so fur-clad riders, their dark faces tattooed into devil masks, cantered up to the opposite bank and stopped. They did not speak, but looked hard at the identifying marks Belgarath had so painstakingly contrived. After a brief, whispered consultation, they turned their horses and rode back away from the stream. Several minutes later, one came galloping back, carrying a bundle wrapped in a fox skin. He paused, dropped the bundle on the bank of the stream, and then rode off again without looking back.

"What was that all about?" Garion asked.

"The bundle's a gift—of sorts," Belgarath answered. "It's an offering to any devils who might be accompanying us. Go pick it up."

"What's in it?"

"A bit of this, a bit of that. I wouldn't open it, if I were you. You're forgetting that you're not supposed to talk."

"There's nobody around," Garion replied, turning his head this way and that, looking for any sign of their being watched.

"Don't be too sure of that," the old man replied. "There could be a hundred of them hiding in the grass. Go pick up the gift and we'll move along. They're polite enough, but they'll be a lot happier when we take our devils out of their territory."

They rode on across the flat, featureless plain with a cloud of flies, drawn by the smell of their untanned fur garments, plaguing them.

Their next meeting, several days later, was less congenial. They had moved into a hilly region where huge, rounded, white boulders rose out of the grass and where shaggy-coated wild oxen with great, sweeping horns grazed. A high overcast had moved in, and the gray sky diffused the light, making the brief twilight that marked the passage of one day into the next an only slightly perceptible darkening. They were riding down a gentle slope toward a large lake, which lay like a sheet of lead under the cloudy sky, when there suddenly arose from the tall grass all around them tattooed and fur-clad warriors holding long spears and short bows that appeared to be made of bone.

Garion reined in sharply and looked at Belgarath for instruction.

"Just look straight at them," his grandfather told him quietly, "and remember that you're not permitted to speak."

"More of them coming," Silk said tersely, jerking his chin toward the crest of a nearby hill where perhaps a dozen Morindim, mounted on paint-decorated ponies, were approaching at a walk.

"Let me do the talking," Belgarath said.

"Gladly."

The man in the lead of the mounted group was burlier than most of his companions, and the black tattooing on his face had been outlined with red and blue, marking him as a man of some significance in his clan and making the devil mask of his features all the more hideous. He carried a large wooden club, painted with strange symbols and inlaid with rows of sharp teeth taken from various animals. The way he carried it indicated that it was more a badge of office than a weapon. He rode without a saddle and with a single bridle strap. He pulled his pony to a stop perhaps thirty yards away. "Why have you come into the lands of the Weasel Clan?" he demanded abruptly. His accent was strange and his eyes were flat with hostility.

Belgarath drew himself up indignantly. "Surely the Headman of the Weasel Clan has seen the quest-mark before," he replied coldly. "We have no interest in the lands of the Weasel Clan, but follow the commands of the Devil-Spirit of the Wolf Clan in the quest he has laid upon us."

"I have not heard of the Wolf Clan," the Headman replied. "Where are their lands?"

"To the west," Belgarath replied. "We have traveled for two waxings and wanings of the Moon-Spirit to reach this place."

The Headman seemed impressed by that.

A Morind with long white braids and with a thin, dirty-looking beard drew his pony in beside that of the Headman. In his right hand he carried a staff surmounted by the skull of a large bird. The gaping beak of the skull had been decorated with teeth, giving it a ferocious appearance. "What is the name of the Devil-Spirit of the Wolf Clan?" he demanded. "I may know him."

"That is doubtful, Magician of the Weasel Clan," Belgarath answered politely. "He seldom goes far from his people. In any case, I cannot speak his name, since he has forbidden it to any but the dreamers."

"Can you say what his aspect is and his attributes?" the white-braided magician asked.

Silk made a long-gurgling sound in the back of his throat, stiffened in his saddle and rolled his eyes gruesomely back in his head until only the whites showed. With a convulsive, jerking motion, he thrust both arms into the air. "Beware the Devil Agrinja, who stalks unseen behind us," he intoned in a hollow, oracular voice. "I have seen his three-eyed face and his hundred-fanged mouth in my dreams. The eye of mortal man may not behold him, but his seven-clawed hands reach out even now to rend apart all who would stand in the path of his chosen quester, the spear-bearer of the Wolf Clan. I have seen him feed in my nightmares. The ravener approaches and he hungers for man-meat. Flee his hunger." He shuddered, dropping his arms and slumping forward in his saddle as if suddenly exhausted.

"You've been here before, I see," Belgarath muttered under his breath. "Try to restrain your creativity, though. Remember that *I* might have to produce what you dream up."

Silk cast him a sidelong wink. His description of the Devil had made a distinct impression on the Morindim. The mounted men looked about nervously, and those standing in the waist-high grass moved involuntarily closer together, grasping their weapons in trembling hands.

Then a thin Morind with a white fur band around his left arm pushed through the cluster of frightened warriors. His right leg ended in a clubfoot, and he lurched grotesquely as he walked. He fixed Silk with a glare of pure hatred, then threw both hands wide, quivering and jerking. His back arched and he toppled over, threshing in the grass in the throes of an apparent seizure. He went completely stiff and then he started to speak. "The Devil-Spirit of the Weasel Clan, dread Horja, speaks to me. He demands to know why the Devil Agrinja sends his quester into the lands of the Weasel Clan. The Devil Horja is too awful to look upon. He has *four* eyes and a hundred and *ten* teeth, and each of his six hands has *eight* claws. He feeds on the bellies of men and he hungers."

"An imitator," Silk sniffed disdainfully, his head still down. "He can't even think up his own dream."

The magician of the Weasel Clan gave the dreamer lying supine in the grass a look of disgust, then turned back to Belgarath. "The Devil-Spirit Horja defies the Devil-Spirit Agrinja," he declared. "He bids him to begone or he will rip out the belly of the quester of Agrinja."

Belgarath swore under his breath.

"What now?" Silk muttered.

"I have to fight him," Belgarath replied sourly. "That's what this was leading up to from the beginning. White-braids there is trying to make a name for himself. He's probably been attacking every magician who crosses his path."

"Can you handle him?"

"We're about to find out." Belgarath slid out of his saddle. "I warn you to stand aside," he boomed, "lest I loose the hunger of our Devil-Spirit upon you." With the tip of his staff he drew a circle on the ground and a five-pointed star within the circle. Grimly, he stepped into the center of the design.

The white-braided magician of the Weasel Clan sneered and also slid off his pony. Quickly he drew a similar symbol on the ground and stepped into its protection.

"That's it," Silk muttered to Garion. "Once the symbols are drawn, neither one can back down."

Belgarath and the white-braided magician had each begun muttering incantations in a language Garion had never heard, brandishing their skull-surmounted staffs at each other. The dreamer of the Weasel Clan, suddenly realizing that he was in the middle of the impending battle, miraculously recovered from his seizure, scrambled to his feet, and lurched away with a terrified expression.

The Headman, trying to maintain his dignity, carefully backed his pony out of the immediate vicinity of the two muttering old men.

Atop a large, white boulder, twenty yards or so to the left of the two magicians, there was a shimmering disturbance in the air, somewhat like heat waves rising from a red tile roof on a hot day. The movement caught Garion's eye, and he stared in puzzlement at the strange phenomenon. As he watched, the shimmering became more pronounced, and it seemed that the shattered pieces of a rainbow infused it, flickering, shifting, undulating in waves almost like varihued flames rising from an invisible fire. As Garion watched, fascinated, a second shimmering became apparent, rising above the tall grass off to the right. The second disturbance also began to gather shards of color into itself. As he stared, first at one, then at the other, Garion saw—or imagined that he saw—a shape beginning to emerge in the center of each. The shapes at first were amorphous, shifting, changing, gathering form from the coruscating colors flashing about them in the shimmering air. Then it seemed that the shapes, having reached a certain point, flashed to completion, coalescing quite suddenly with a great rushing together, and two towering forms faced each other, snarling and slathering with mindless hatred. Each stood as high as a house, and their shoulders bulked wide. Their skins were multihued, with waves of color rippling through them.

The one standing in the grass had a third eye glaring balefully from between its other two, and his great arms ended in seven-clawed hands stretched out with a hideously hungry curving. His jutting, muzzlelike mouth gaped wide, filled with row upon row of needlelike teeth as he roared a thunderous howl of hatred and dreadful hunger.

Crouched upon the boulder stood the other. He had a great cluster of shoulders at the top of his trunk, and a nest of long, scaly arms that writhed out in all directions like snakes, each arm terminating in a widespread, many-clawed hand. Two sets of eyes, one atop the other, glared insanely from beneath heavy browridges, and his muzzle, like that of the other figure, sprouted a forest of teeth. He raised that awful face and bellowed, his jaws drooling foam.

But even as the two monsters glared at each other, there seemed to be a kind of writhing struggle going on inside them. Their skins rippled, and large moving lumps appeared in odd places on their chests and sides. Garion had the peculiar feeling that there was something else—something quite different and perhaps even worse—trapped inside each apparition. Growling, the two devils advanced upon each other, but despite their apparent eagerness to fight, they seemed almost driven, whipped toward the struggle. It was as if there was a dreadful reluctance in them, and their grotesque faces jerked this way and that, each snarling first at his opponent and then at the magician who controlled him. That reluctance, Garion perceived, stemmed from something deep inside the nature of each Devil. It was the enslavement, the compulsion to do the bidding of another, that they hated. The chains of spell and incantation in which Belgarath and the white-braided Morind had bound them were an intolerable agony, and there were whimpers of that agony mingled with their snarls.

Belgarath was sweating. Droplets of perspiration trickled down his dark-stained face. The incantations which held the Devil Agrinja locked within the apparition he had created to bind it rippled endlessly from his tongue. The slightest faltering of either the words or the image he had formed in his mind would break his power over the beast he had summoned, and it would turn upon him.

Writhing like things attempting to tear themselves apart from within, Agrinja and Horja closed on each other, grappling, clawing, tearing out chunks of scaly flesh with their awful jaws. The earth shuddered beneath them as they fought.

Too stunned to even be afraid, Garion watched the savage struggle. As he watched, he noted a peculiar difference between the two apparitions. Agrinja was bleeding from his wounds—a strange, dark blood, so deep red as to be almost black. Horja, however, did not bleed. Chunks ripped from his arms and shoulders were like bits of wood. The white-braided magician saw that difference as well, and his eyes grew suddenly afraid. His voice became shrill as he desperately cast incantations at Horja, struggling to keep the Devil under his control. The moving lumps beneath Horja's skin became larger, more agitated. The vast Devil broke free from Agrinja and stood, his chest heaving and a dreadful hope burning in his eyes.

White-braids was screaming now. The incantations tumbled from his mouth, faltering, stumbling. And then one unpronounceable formula tangled his tongue. Desperately he tried it again, and once again it stuck in his teeth.

With a bellow of triumph the Devil Horja straightened and seemed to explode. Bits and fragments of scaly hide flew in all directions as the monster shuddered free of the illusion which had bound him. He had two great arms and an almost human face surmounted by a pair of curving, needle-pointed horns. He had hoofs instead of feet, and his grayish skin dripped slime. He turned slowly and his burning eyes fixed on the gibbering magician.

"Horja!" the white-braided Morind shrieked, "I command you to—" The words faltered as he gaped in horror at the Devil which had suddenly escaped his control. "Horja! I am your master!" But Horja was already stalking toward him, his great hoofs crushing the grass as, step by step, he moved toward his former master.

In wild-eyed panic, the white-braided Morind flinched back, stepping unconsciously, and fatally, out of the protection of the circle and star drawn upon the ground.

Horja smiled then, a chilling smile, bent and caught the shrieking magician by each ankle, ignoring the blows rained on his head and shoulders by the skull-topped staff. Then the monster stood up, lifting the struggling man to hang upside down by the legs. The huge shoulders surged with an awful power, and, leering hideously, the Devil deliberately and with a cruel slowness tore the magician in two.

The Morindim fled.

Contemptuously the immense Devil hurled the chunks of his former master after them, spattering the grass with blood and worse. Then, with a savage hunting cry, he leaped in pursuit of them.

The three-eyed Agrinja had stood, still locked in a half-crouch, watching the destruction of the white-braided Morind almost with indifference. When it was over, he turned to cast eyes burning with hatred upon Belgarath.

The old sorcerer, drenched with sweat, raised his skull-staff in front of him, his face set with extreme concentration. The interior struggle rippled more intensely within the form of the monster, but gradually Belgarath's will mastered and solidified the shape. Agrinja howled in frustration, clawing at the air until all hint of shifting or changing was gone. Then the dreadful hands dropped, and the monster's head bowed in defeat.

"Begone," Belgarath commanded almost negligently, and Agrinja instantly vanished.

Garion suddenly began to tremble violently. His stomach heaved; he turned, tottered a few feet away, and fell to his knees and began to retch.

"What happened?" Silk demanded in a shaking voice.

"It got away from him," Belgarath replied calmly. "I think it was the blood that did it. When he saw that Agrinja was bleeding and that Horja wasn't, he realized that he'd forgotten something. That shook his confidence, and he lost his concentration. Garion, stop that."

"I can't," Garion groaned, his stomach heaving violently again.

"How long will Horja chase the others?" Silk asked.

"Until the sun goes down," Belgarath told him. "I imagine that the Weasel Clan is in for a bad afternoon."

"Is there any chance that he'll turn around and come after us?"

"He has no reason to. We didn't try to enslave him. As soon as Garion gets his stomach under control again, we can go on. We won't be bothered anymore."

Garion stumbled to his feet, weakly wiping his mouth.

"Are you all right?" Belgarath asked him.

"Not really," Garion replied, "but there's nothing left to come up."

"Get a drink of water and try not to think about it."

"Will you have to do that anymore?" Silk asked, his eyes a bit wild.

"No." Belgarath pointed. There were several riders along the crest of a hill perhaps a mile away. "The other Morindim in the area watched the whole thing. The word will spread, and nobody will come anywhere near us now. Let's mount up and get going. It's still a long way to the coast."

In bits and pieces, as they rode for the next several days, Garion picked up as much information as he really wanted about the dreadful contest he had witnessed.

"It's the *shape* that's the key to the whole thing," Belgarath concluded. "What the Morindim call Devil-Spirits don't look that much different from humans. You form an illusion drawn out of your imagination and force the spirit into it. As long as you can keep it locked up in that illusion, it has to do what you tell it to. If the illusion falters for any reason, the spirit breaks free and resumes its real form. After that, you have no control over it whatsoever. I have a certain advantage in these matters. Changing back and forth from a man to a wolf has sharpened my imagination a bit."

"Why did Beldin say you were a bad magician then?" Silk asked curiously.

"Beldin's a purist," the old man shrugged. "He feels that it's necessary to get everything into the shape—down to the last scale and toenail. It isn't, really, but he feels that way about it."

"Do you suppose we could talk about something else?" Garion asked.

They reached the coastline a day or so later. The sky had remained overcast, and the Sea of the East lay sullen and rolling under dirty gray clouds. The beach along which they rode was a broad shingle of black, round stones littered with chunks of white, bleached driftwood. Waves rolled foaming up the beach, only to slither back with an endless, mournful sigh. Sea birds hung in the stiff breeze, screaming.

"Which way?" Silk asked.

Belgarath looked around. "North," he replied.

"How far?"

"I'm not positive. It's been a long time, and I can't be sure exactly where we are."

"You're not the best guide in the world, old friend," Silk complained.

"You can't have everything."

They reached the land bridge two days later, and Garion stared at it in dismay. It was not at all what he had expected, but consisted of a series of round, wave-eroded white boulders sticking up out of the dark water and running in an irregular line off toward a dark smudge on the horizon. The wind was blowing out of the north, carrying with it a bitter chill and the smell of polar ice. Patches of white froth stretched from boulder to boulder as the swells ripped themselves to tatters on submerged reefs.

"How are we supposed to cross that?" Silk objected.

"We wait until low tide," Belgarath explained. "The reefs are mostly out of the water then."

"Mostly?"

"We might have to wade a bit from time to time. Let's strip these furs off our clothes before we start. It'll give us something to do while we're waiting for the tide to turn, and they're starting to get a bit fragrant."

They took shelter behind a pile of driftwood far up on the beach and removed the stiff, smelly furs from their clothing. Then they dug food out of their packs and ate. Garion noted that the stain that had darkened the skin on his hands had begun to wear thin and that the tattoo-drawings on the faces of his companions had grown noticeably fainter.

It grew darker, and the period of twilight that separated one day from the next seemed longer than it had no more than a week ago.

"Summer's nearly over up here," Belgarath noted, looking out at the boulders gradually emerging from the receding water in the murky twilight.

"How much longer before low tide?" Silk asked.

"Another hour or so."

They waited. The wind pushed at the pile of driftwood erratically and brushed the tall grass along the upper edge of the beach, bending and tossing it.

Finally Belgarath stood up. "Let's go," he said shortly. "We'll lead the horses. The reefs are slippery, so be careful how you set your feet down."

The passage along the reef between the first stepping-stones was not all that bad, but once they moved farther out, the wind became a definite factor. They were frequently drenched with stinging spray, and every so often a wave, larger than the others, broke over the top of the reef and swirled about their legs, tugging at them. The water was brutally cold.

"Do you think we'll be able to make it all the way across before the tide comes back in again?" Silk shouted over the noise.

"No," Belgarath shouted back. "We'll have to sit it out on top of one of the larger rocks."

That sounds unpleasant."

"Not nearly as unpleasant as swimming."

They were perhaps halfway across when it became evident that the tide had turned. Waves more and more frequently broke across the top of the reef, and one particularly large one pulled the legs of Garion's horse out from under him. Garion struggled to get the frightened animal up again, pulling at the reins as the horse's hoofs scrambled and slid on the slippery rocks of the reef. "We'd better find a place to stop, Grandfather," he yelled above the crash of the waves. "We'll be neck-deep in this before long."

"Two more islands," Belgarath told him. "There's a bigger one up ahead."

The last stretch of reef was completely submerged, and Garion flinched as he stepped down into the icy water. The breaking waves covered the surface with froth, making it impossible to see the bottom. He moved along blindly, probing the unseen path with numb feet. A large wave swelled and rose up as far as his armpits, and its powerful surge swept him off his feet. He clung to the reins of his horse, floundering and sputtering as he fought to get back up.

And then they were past the worst of it. They moved along the reef with the water only ankle-deep now; a few moments later, they climbed up onto the large, white boulder. Garion let out a long, explosive breath as he reached safety. The wind, blowing against his wet clothing, chilled him to the bone but at least they were out of the water.

Later, as they sat huddled together on the leeward side of the boulder, Garion looked out across the sullen black sea toward the low, forbidding coastline lying ahead. The beaches, like those of Morindland behind them, were black gravel, and the low hills behind them were dark under the scudding gray cloud. Nowhere was there any sign of life, but there was an implicit threat in the very shape of the land itself.

"Is that it?" he asked finally in a hushed voice.

Belgarath's face was unreadable as he gazed across the open water toward the coast ahead. "Yes," he replied. "That's Mallorea."

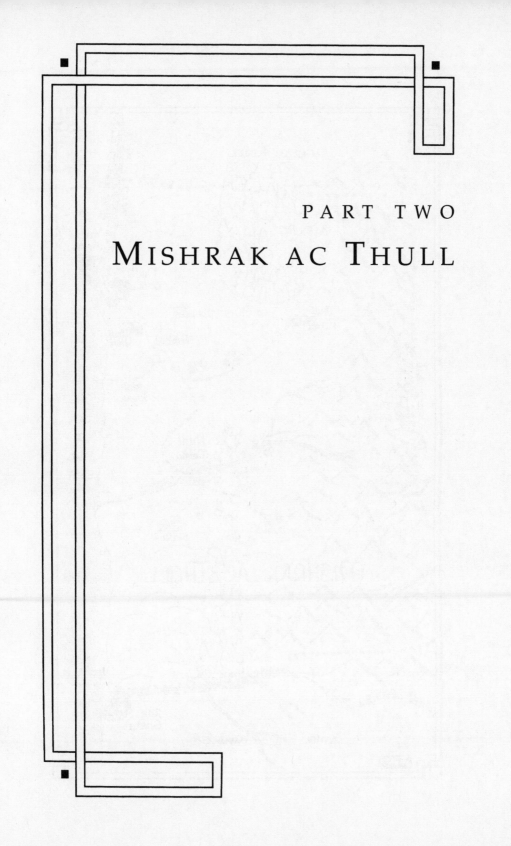

PART TWO

MISHRAK AC THULL

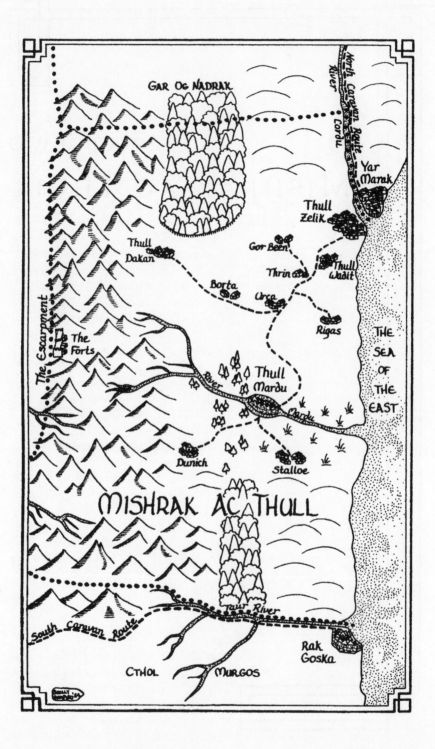

The crown had been Queen Islena's first mistake. It was heavy and it always gave her a headache. Her decision to wear it had come originally out of a sense of insecurity. The bearded warriors in Anheg's throne room intimidated her, and she felt the need of a visible symbol of her authority. Now she was afraid to appear without it. Each day she put it on with less pleasure and entered the main hall of Anheg's palace with less certainty.

The sad truth was that Queen Islena of Cherek was completely unprepared to rule. Until the day when, dressed in regal crimson velvet and with her gold crown firmly in place, she had marched into the vaulted throne room at Val Alorn to announce that she would rule the kingdom in her husband's absence, Islena's most momentous decisions had involved which gown she would wear and how her hair was to be arranged. Now it seemed that the fate of Cherek hung in the balance each time she was faced with a choice.

The warriors lounging indolently with their ale cups about the huge, open fire pit or wandering aimlessly about on the rush-strewn floor were no help whatsoever. Each time she entered the throne room, all conversation broke off and they rose to watch as she marched to the banner-hung throne, but their faces gave no hint of their true feelings toward her. Irrationally, she concluded that the whole problem had to do with the beards. How could she possibly know what a man was thinking when his face was sunk up to the ears in hair? Only the quick intervention of Lady Merel, the cool blond wife of the Earl of Trellheim, had stopped her from ordering a universal shave.

"You can't, Islena," Merel had told her flatly, removing the quill from the queen's hand, even as she had been in the act of signing the hastily drawn-up proclamation. "They're attached to their beards like little boys attached to a favorite toy. You can't make them cut off their whiskers."

"I'm the queen."

"Only as long as they permit you to be. They accept you out of respect for Anheg, and that's as far as it goes. If you tamper with their pride, they'll take you off the throne." And that dreadful threat had ended the matter then and there.

Islena found herself relying more and more on Barak's wife, and it was not long before the two of them, one in green and the other in royal crimson, were seldom apart. Even when Islena faltered, Merel's icy stare quelled the hints of disrespect which cropped up from time to time—usually when the ale had been distributed a bit too freely. It was Merel, ultimately, who made the day-to-day decisions which ran the kingdom. When Islena sat upon the throne, Merel, her blond braids coiled about her head to form her own crown, stood to one side in plain view of the hesitant queen. Cherek was ruled by the expressions on her face. A faint smile meant yes; a frown, no; a scarcely perceptible shrug, maybe. It worked out fairly well.

But there was one person who was not intimidated by Merel's cool gaze. Grodeg, the towering, white-bearded High Priest of Belar, inevitably requested private audience with the queen, and once Merel left the council room, Islena was lost.

Despite Anheg's call for a general mobilization, the members of the Bear-cult had not yet left to join the campaign. Their promises to join the fleet later all sounded sincere, but their excuses and delays grew more and more obvious as time went on. Islena knew that Grodeg was behind it all. Nearly every able-bodied man in the kingdom was off with the fleet, which was even now rowing up the broad expanse of the Aldur River to join Anheg in central Algaria. The household guard in the palace at Val Alorn had been reduced to grizzled old men and downy-cheeked boys. Only the Bear-cult remained, and Grodeg pushed his advantage to the limit.

He was polite enough, bowing to the queen when the occasion demanded, and never mentioning her past links with the cult, but his offers to help became more and more insistent; and when Islena faltered at his suggestions concerning this matter or that, he smoothly acted to implement them as if her hesitancy had been acceptance. Little by little, Islena was losing control, and Grodeg, with the armed might of the cult behind him, was taking charge. More and more the cult members infested the palace, giving orders, lounging about the throne room and openly grinning as they watched Islena's attempts to rule.

"You're going to have to do something, Islena," Merel said firmly one evening when the two were alone in the queen's private apartment. She was striding about the carpeted room, her hair gleaming like soft gold in the candlelight, but there was nothing soft in her expression.

"What can I do?" Islena pleaded, wringing her hands. "He's never openly disrespectful, and his decisions always *seem* to be in the best interests of Cherek."

"You need help, Islena," Merel told her.

"Whom can I turn to?" The Queen of Cherek was almost in tears.

The Lady Merel smoothed the front of her green velvet gown. "I think it's time that you wrote to Porenn," she declared.

"What do I say?" Islena begged of her.

Merel pointed at the small table in the corner where parchment and ink lay waiting. "Sit down," she instructed, "and write what I tell you to write."

COUNT BRADOR, THE Tolnedran ambassador, was definitely growing tiresome, Queen Layla decided. The plump little queen marched purposefully toward the chamber where she customarily gave audiences and where the ambassador awaited her with his satchel full of documents.

The courtiers in the halls bowed as she passed, her crown slightly askew and her heels clicking on the polished oak floors, but Queen Layla uncharacteristically ignored them. This was not the time for polite exchanges or idle chitchat. The Tolnedran had to be dealt with, and she had delayed too long already.

The ambassador was an olive-skinned man with receding hair and a hooked nose. He wore a brown mantle with the gold trim that indicated his relationship to the Borunes. He lounged rather indolently in a large, cushioned chair near the window of the sunny room where he and Queen Layla were to meet. He rose as she entered and bowed with exquisite grace. "Your Highness," he murmured politely.

"My dear Count Brador," Queen Layla gushed at him, putting on her most helpless and scatterbrained expression, "please do sit down. I'm sure we know each other well enough by now to skip all these tedious formalities." She sank into a chair fanning herself with one hand. "It's turned warm, hasn't it?"

"Summers are lovely here in Sendaria, your Highness," the count replied, settling back in his chair. "I wonder—have you had the chance to think over the proposals I gave you at our last meeting?"

Queen Layla stared at him blankly. "Which proposals were those, Count Brador?" She gave a helpless little giggle. "Please forgive me, but my mind seems to be absolutely gone these days. There are so many details. I wonder how my husband keeps them all straight."

"We were discussing the administration of the port at Camaar, your Highness," the count reminded her gently.

"We were?" The queen gave him a blank look of total incomprehension, secretly delighted at the flicker of annoyance that crossed his face. It was her best ploy. By pretending to have forgotten all previous conversations, she forced him to begin at the beginning every time they met. The count's strategy, she knew, depended upon a gradual build-up to his final proposal, and her pretended forgetfulness neatly defeated that. "Whatever led us into such a tedious subject as that?" she added

"Surely your Highness recalls," the count protested with just the slightest hint of annoyance. "The Tolnedran merchant vessel, *Star of Tol Horb,* was kept standing at anchor for a week and a half in the harbor before moorage could be found for her. Every day's delay in unloading her was costing a fortune."

"Things are so hectic these days," the queen of Sendaria sighed. "It's the manpower shortage, you understand. Everybody who hasn't gone off to war is busy freighting supplies to the army. I'll send a very stern note to the port authorities about it, though. Was there anything else, Count Brador?"

Brador coughed uncomfortably. "Uh—your Highness has already forwarded just such a note," he reminded her.

"I have?" Queen Layla feigned astonishment. "Wonderful. That takes care of everything then, doesn't it? And you've dropped by to thank me." She smiled girlishly. "How exquisitely courteous of you." She leaned forward to put one hand impulsively on his wrist, quite deliberately knocking the rolled parchment he was holding out of his hand. "How clumsy of me," she exclaimed, bending quickly to pick up the parchment before he could retrieve it. Then she sat back in her chair, tapping the rolled document absently against her cheek as if lost in thought.

"Uh—actually, your Highness, our discussions had moved somewhat beyond your note to the port authorities," Brador told her, nervously eyeing the parchment she had so deftly taken from him. "You may recall that I offered Tolnedran assistance in administering the port. I believe we agreed that such assistance might help to alleviate the manpower shortage your Highness just mentioned."

"What an absolutely marvelous idea," Layla exclaimed. She brought her plump little fist down on the arm of her chair as if in an outburst of enthusiasm. At that prearranged signal, two of her younger children burst into the room, arguing loudly.

"Mother!" Princess Gelda wailed in outrage, "Fernie stole my red ribbon!"

"I did not!" Princess Ferna denied the charge indignantly. "She gave it to me for my blue beads."

"Did not!" Gelda snapped.

"Did so!" Ferna replied.

"Children, children," Layla chided them. "Can't you see that Mother's busy? What will the dear count think of us?"

"But she stole it, Mother!" Gelda protested. "She stole my red ribbon."

"Did not!" Ferna said, spitefully sticking her tongue out at her sister.

Trailing behind them with a look of wide-eyed interest came little Prince Meldig, Queen Layla's youngest child. In one hand the prince held a jam pot, and his face was liberally smeared with the contents. "Oh, that's just impossible," Layla exclaimed, jumping to her feet. "You girls are supposed to be watching him." She bustled over to the jam-decorated prince, crumpled the parchment she was holding and began wiping his face with it. Abruptly she stopped. "Oh dear," she said as if suddenly realizing what she was doing. "Was this important, Count Brador?" she asked the Tolnedran, holding out the rumpled, sticky document.

Brador's shoulders, however, had slumped in defeat. "No, your Highness," he replied in a voice filled with resignation, "not really. The royal house of Sendaria has me quite outnumbered, it appears." He rose to his feet. "Perhaps another time," he murmured, bowing. "With you Highness's permission," he said, preparing to leave.

"You mustn't forget this, Count Brador," Layla said, pressing the parchment into his cringing hands.

The count's face had a faintly martyred expression as he withdrew. Queen Layla turned back to her children, who were grinning impishly at her. She began to scold them in a loud voice until she was certain the count was well out of earshot, then she knelt, embraced them all and began to laugh.

"Did we do it right, Mother?" Princess Gelda asked.

"You were absolutely perfect," Queen Layla replied, still laughing.

SADI THE EUNUCH had grown careless, lulled somewhat by the air of polite civility that had pervaded the palace at Sthiss Tor for the past year, and one of his associates, seizing upon his unwariness, had taken the opportunity to poison him. Sadi definitely did not appreciate being poisoned. The antidotes all tasted vile, and the aftereffects left him weak and light-headed. Thus it was that he viewed the appearance of the mail-shirted emissary of King Taur Urgas with thinly veiled irritation.

"Taur Urgas, King of the Murgos, greets Sadi, chief servant of Immortal Salmissra," the Murgo declaimed with a deep bow as he entered the cool, dimly lighted study from which Sadi conducted most of the nation's affairs.

"The servant of the Serpent Queen returns the greetings of the right arm of the Dragon-God of Angarak." Sadi mouthed the formula phrases almost indifferently. "Do you suppose we could get to the point? I'm feeling a bit indisposed at the moment."

"I was very pleased at your recovery," the ambassador lied, his scarred face carefully expressionless. "Has the poisoner been apprehended yet?" He drew up a chair and sat down at the polished table Sadi used for a desk.

"Naturally," Sadi replied, absently rubbing his hand over his shaved scalp.

"And executed?"

"Why would we want to do that? The man's a professional poisoner. He was only doing his job."

The Murgo looked a bit startled.

"We look upon a good poisoner as a national asset," Sadi told him. "If we start killing them every time they poison somebody, very soon there won't be any of them left, and you never know when *I* might want somebody poisoned."

The Murgo ambassador shook his head incredulously. "You people have an amazing amount of tolerance, Sadi," he said in his harshly accented voice. "What about his employer?"

"That's another matter," Sadi replied. "His employer is currently entertaining the leeches at the bottom of the river. Is your visit official, or did you merely stop by to inquire after my health?"

"A bit of each, Excellency."

"You Murgos are an economical race," Sadi observed dryly. "What does Taur Urgas want this time?"

"The Alorns are preparing to invade Mishrak ac Thull, your Excellency."

"So I've heard. What's that got to do with Nyissa?"

"Nyissans have no reason to be fond of Alorns."

"Nor any to be fond of Murgos, either," Sadi pointed out.

"It was Aloria that invaded Nyissa following the death of the Rivan King," the Murgo reminded him, "and it was Cthol Murgos that provided the market for Nyissa's primary export."

"My dear fellow, please get to the point," Sadi said, rubbing his scalp wearily. "I'm not going to operate on the basis of long-past insults or long-forgotten favors. The slave trade is no longer significant, and the scars left by the Alorn invasion disappeared centuries ago. What does Taur Urgas want?"

"My king wishes to avoid bloodshed," the Murgo stated. "The Tolnedran legions form a significant part of the armies massing in Algaria. If a threat—just a threat, mind you—of unfriendly activity suddenly appeared on his unprotected southern frontier, Ran Borune would recall those legions. Their loss would persuade the Alorns to abandon this adventure."

"You want *me* to invade Tolnedra?" Sadi demanded incredulously.

"Naturally not, Lord Sadi. His Majesty merely wishes your permission to move certain forces through your territory to pose the threat on Tolnedra's southern border. No blood need be shed at all."

"Except Nyissan blood, once the Murgo army withdraws. The legions would swarm down across the River of the Woods like angry hornets."

"Taur Urgas would be more than willing to leave garrisons behind to guarantee the integrity of Nyissan territory."

"I'm sure he would," Sadi observed dryly. "Advise your king that his proposal is quite unacceptable at this particular time."

"The King of Cthol Murgos is a powerful man," the Murgo said firmly, "and he remembers those who thwart him even more keenly than he remembers his friends."

"Taur Urgas is a madman," Sadi told him bluntly. "He wants to avoid trouble with the Alorns so that he can concentrate on 'Zakath. Despite his insanity, however, he's *not* so foolish as to send an army into Nyissa uninvited. An army must eat, and Nyissa's a bad place to forage for food—as history has demonstrated. The most tempting fruit has bitter juice."

"A Murgo army carries its own food," the ambassador replied stiffly.

"Good for them. But where do they plan to find drinking water? I don't believe we're getting anywhere with this. I'll convey your proposal to her Majesty. She, of course, will make the final decision. I suspect, however, that you'll need to offer something much more attractive than a permanent Murgo occupation to persuade her to consider the matter favorably. Was that all?"

The Murgo rose to his feet, his scarred face angry. He bowed coldly to Sadi and withdrew without further conversation.

Sadi thought about it for a while. He could gain a great deal of advantage at a minimal cost if he played this right. A few carefully worded dispatches to King Rhodar in Algaria would put Nyissa among the friends of the west. If Rhodar's army should happen to win, Nyissa would benefit. If, on the other hand, it appeared that the west were about to lose, the proposal of Taur Urgas could be accepted. In either case, Nyissa would be on the winning side. The whole notion appealed to Sadi enormously. He stood up, his iridescent silk robe rustling, and went to a nearby cabinet. He took out a crystal decanter containing a dark blue liquid and carefully measured some of the thick syrup into a small glass and drank it. Almost immediately a euphoric calm came over him as his favorite drug took effect. A moment or two later, he felt that he was ready to face his queen. He was even smiling as he walked from his study into the dim corridor leading to the throne room.

As always, Salmissra's chamber was dimly lighted by oil lamps hanging on long silver chains from the shadowy ceiling. The chorus of eunuchs still knelt adoringly in the queen's presence, but they no longer sang her praises. Noise of any kind irritated Salmissra now, and it was wise not to irritate her. The Serpent Queen still occupied the divanlike throne beneath the towering statue of Issa. She dozed interminably, stirring her mottled coils with the seething dry hiss of scale rubbing against scale. But even in restless doze, her tongue flickered nervously. Sadi approached the throne, perfunctorily prostrated himself on the polished stone floor, and waited. His scent on the air would announce him to the hooded serpent who was his queen.

"Yes, Sadi?" she whispered finally, her voice a dusty hiss.

"The Murgos wish an alliance, my Queen," Sadi informed her. "Taur Urgas wants to threaten the Tolnedrans from the south to force Ran Borune to withdraw his legions from the Thullish border."

"Interesting," she replied indifferently. Her dead eyes bored into him and her coils rustled. "What do you think?"

"Neutrality costs nothing, Divine Salmissra," Sadi replied. "Alliance with either side would be premature."

Salmissra turned, her mottled hood flaring as she regarded her reflection in the mirror beside her throne. The crown still rested on her head, as polished and glistening as her scales. Her tongue flickered, and her eyes, flat as glass, looked at the mirror. "Do what you think best, Sadi," she told him in an uncaring tone.

"I'll deal with the matter, my Queen," Sadi said, putting his face to the floor in preparation to leave.

"I have no need of Torak now," she mused, still staring at the mirror. "Polgara saw to that."

"Yes, my Queen," Sadi agreed in a neutral voice, beginning to rise.

She turned to look at him. "Stay a while, Sadi. I'm lonely."

Sadi sank immediately back to the polished floor.

"I have such strange dreams sometimes, Sadi," she hissed. "Such very strange dreams. I seem to remember things—things that happened when my blood was warm and I was a woman. Strange thoughts come to me in my dreams, and strange hungers." She looked directly at him, her hood flaring again as her pointed face stretched out toward him. "Was I really like that, Sadi? It all seems like something seen through smoke."

"It was a difficult time, my Queen." Sadi replied candidly. "For all of us."

"Polgara was right, you know," she continued in that expiring whisper. "The potions enflamed me. I think it's better this way—no passions, no hungers, no fears." She turned back to her mirror. "You may go now, Sadi."

He rose and started toward the door.

"Oh, Sadi."

"Yes, my Queen?"

"If I caused you trouble before, I'm sorry."

He stared at her.

"Not very much, of course—but just a little." Then she returned to her reflection.

Sadi was trembling as he closed the door behind him. Sometime later, he sent for Issus. The shabby, one-eyed hireling entered the chief eunuch's study with a certain hesitancy, and his face was a bit apprehensive.

"Come in, Issus," Sadi told him calmly.

"I hope you aren't holding any grudges, Sadi," Issus said nervously, looking about to be sure they were alone. "There was nothing personal in it, you know."

"It's all right, Issus," Sadi assured him. "You were only doing what you were paid to do."

"How did you manage to detect it?" Issus asked with a certain professional curiosity. "Most men are too far gone for the antidote to work before they realize they've been poisoned."

"Your concoction leaves just the faintest aftertaste of lemon," Sadi replied. "I've been trained to recognize it."

"Ah," Issus said. "I'll have to work on that. Otherwise it's a very good poison."

"An excellent poison, Issus," Sadi agreed. "That brings us to the reason I sent for you. There's a man I think I can dispense with."

Issus' single eye brightened, and he rubbed his hands together. "The usual fee?"

"Naturally."

"Who is he?"

"The Murgo ambassador."

Issus' face clouded for a moment. "He'll be difficult to get to." He scratched at his stubbled scalp.

"You'll find a way. I have the utmost confidence in you."

"I'm the best," Issus agreed with no trace of false modesty.

"The ambassador's pressing me in certain negotiations that I need to delay," Sadi continued. "His sudden demise should interrupt things a bit."

"You don't really have to explain, Sadi," Issus told him. "I don't need to know why you want him killed."

"But you do need to know *how*. For various reasons, I'd like for this to look very natural. Could you arrange for him—and perhaps a few others in his household—to come down with some kind of fever? Something suitably virulent?"

Issus frowned. "That's tricky. Something like that can get out of hand. You might end up infecting an entire neighborhood, and there'd be very few survivors."

Sadi shrugged. "One sometimes must make sacrifices. Can you do it?"

Issus nodded gravely.

"Do it then, and I'll compose a letter expressing my regrets to King Taur Urgas."

QUEEN SILAR SAT at her loom in the great hall of the Algar Stronghold, humming softly to herself as her fingers passed the shuttle back and forth with a drowsy, clicking sound. Sunlight streamed down from the narrow windows set high up in the wall, filling the huge, narrow room with a diffused golden light. King Cho-Hag and Hettar were away from the Stronghold, preparing a huge encampment some few leagues out from the base of the eastern escarpment for the army of Alorns, Arends, Sendars, and Tolnedrans approaching from the west. Although he was still within the borders of the kingdom, Cho-Hag had formally transferred authority to his wife, extracting a pledge of support from all of the assembled Clan-Chiefs.

The Queen of Algaria was a silent woman, and her calm face seldom betrayed her emotions. She had spent her entire life in the background, often so unobtrusively that people did not even realize that she was present. She had, however, kept her eyes and her ears open. Her crippled husband, moreover, had confided in her. His quiet, dark-haired queen knew exactly what was going on.

Elvar, Archpriest of Algaria, stood, white-robed and much puffed-up with his own importance, reading to her the set of carefully prepared proclamations which would effectively transfer all power to him. His tone was condescending as he explained them to her.

"Is that all?" she asked when he had finished.

"It's really for the best, your Highness," he told her loftily. "All the world knows that women are unsuited to rule. Shall I send for pen and ink?"

"Not just yet, Elvar," she replied calmly, her hands busy at her loom.

"But—"

"You know, I just had the oddest thought," she said, looking directly at him. "You're the Archpriest of Belar here in Algaria, but you never go out of the Stronghold. Isn't that a bit peculiar?"

"My duties, your Highness, compel me—"

"Isn't your first duty to the people—and to the children of Belar? We've been terribly selfish keeping you here when your heart must be yearning to be out among the clans, overseeing the religious instruction of the children."

He stared at her, his mouth suddenly agape.

"And all the other priests as well," she continued. "They all seem to be concentrated here at the Stronghold, pressed into administrative duties. A priest is too valuable a man for such tasks. This situation must be corrected immediately."

"But—"

"No, Elvar. My duty as queen is absolutely clear. The children of Algaria must come first. I release you from all your duties here at the Stronghold so that you may return to your chosen vocation." She smiled suddenly. "I'll even draw up an itinerary for you myself," she said brightly. She thought a moment. "The times are troubled," she added, "so perhaps I'd better provide you with an escort—several trustworthy men from my own clan who can be depended upon to make sure that you aren't interrupted in your travels or distracted from your preaching by any disturbing messages from abroad." She looked at him again. "That will be all, Elvar. You'd probably better go pack. It will be a number of seasons before you return, I imagine."

The Archpriest of Belar was making strangled noises.

"Oh, one other thing." The queen carefully chose another skein of yarn and held it up to the sunlight. "It's been years since anyone made a survey of the herds. As long as you're going to be out there anyway, I think I'd like an accurate count of all the calves and colts in Algaria. It'll give you something to occupy your mind. Send me a report from time to time, won't you?" She returned to her weaving. "You're dismissed, Elvar," she said placidly, not even bothering to look up as the Archpriest, shaking with rage, tottered away to make preparations for his roving imprisonment.

LORD MORIN, HIGH Chamberlain to his Imperial Majesty, Ran Borune XXIII, sighed as he entered the Emperor's private garden. Another tirade was undoubtedly in the offing, and Morin had already heard it all a dozen times at least. The Emperor had an extraordinary capacity for repeating himself sometimes.

Ran Borune, however, was in an odd mood. The bald, beak-nosed little Emperor sat pensively in his chair beneath a shady arbor, listening to the trilling of his canary. "He's never spoken again, did you know that, Morin?" the Emperor said as his chamberlain approached across the close-clipped grass. "Just that one time when Polgara was here." He looked at the little golden bird again, his eyes sad. Then he sighed. "I think I came out second best in that bargain. Polgara gave me a canary and took Ce'Nedra in exchange." He looked around at his sun-drenched garden and the cool marble walls surrounding it. "Is it just my imagination, Morin, or does the palace seem sort of cold and empty now?" He lapsed once more into moody silence, staring with unseeing eyes at a bed of crimson roses.

Then there was an odd sound, and Lord Morin looked sharply at the Emperor, half afraid that his ruler was about to go into another seizure. But there was no evidence of that. Instead, Morin perceived that Ran Borune was chuckling. "Did you see how she tricked me, Morin?" The Emperor laughed. "She deliberately goaded me into that fit. What a son she should have made! She could have been the greatest Emperor in Tolnedra's history." Ran Borune was laughing openly now, his secret delight at Ce'Nedra's cleverness suddenly emerging.

"She *is* your daughter after all, your Majesty," Lord Morin observed.

"To think that she could raise an army of that size when she's barely sixteen," the Emperor marveled. "What a splendid child!" He seemed quite suddenly to have recovered from the gloomy peevishness that had dogged him since his return to Tol Honeth. His laughter trailed away after several moments, and his bright little eyes narrowed shrewdly. "Those legions she stole from me are likely to become fractious without professional leadership," he mused.

"I'd say that's Ce'Nedra's problem, your Majesty," Morin replied. "Or Polgara's."

"Well—" The Emperor scratched one ear. "I don't know, Morin. The situation out there isn't too clear." He looked at his chamberlain. "Are you acquainted with General Varana?"

"The Duke of Anadile? Or course, your Majesty. A thoroughly professional sort of fellow—solid, unassuming, extremely intelligent."

"He's an old friend of the family," Ran Borune confided. "Ce'Nedra knows him and she'll listen to his advice. Why don't you go to him, Morin, and suggest that he might want to take a leave of absence—perhaps go to Algaria and have a look at things?"

"I'm certain that he'd be overjoyed at the idea of a vacation," Lord Morin agreed. "Garrison life in the summertime can be very tedious."

"It's just a suggestion," the Emperor stressed. "His presence in the war zone would have to be strictly unofficial."

"Naturally, your Majesty."

"And if he just *happened* to make a few suggestions—or even provide a bit of leadership, we certainly wouldn't have any knowledge of it, would we? After all, what a private citizen does with his own time is *his* business, right?"

"Absolutely, your Majesty."

The Emperor grinned broadly. "And we'll all stick to that story, won't we, Morin?"

"Like glue, your Majesty," Morin replied gravely.

THE CROWN PRINCE of Drasnia burped noisily in his mother's ear, sighed, and promptly fell asleep on her shoulder. Queen Porenn smiled at him, tucked him back in his cradle, and turned again to the stringy-appearing man in nonde-script clothing who sprawled in a nearby chair. The emaciated man was known only by the peculiar name "Javelin." Javelin was the chief of the Drasnian intelli-gence service and one of Porenn's closest advisers.

"Anyway," he continued his report, "the Tolnedran girl's army is about two days' march from the Stronghold. The engineers are moving along ahead of sched-ule with the hoists on top of the escarpment, and the Chereks are preparing to begin the portage from the east bank of the Aldur."

"Everything seems to be going according to plan, then," the queen said, re-suming her seat at the polished table near the window.

"There's a bit of trouble in Arendia," Javelin noted. "The usual ambushes and bickerings—nothing really serious. Queen Layla's got the Tolnedran, Bravor, so completely off balance that he might as well not even be in Sendaria." He scratched at his long, pointed jaw. "There's peculiar information coming out of Sthiss Tor. The Murgos are trying to negotiate something, but their emissaries keep dying. We'll try to get somebody closer to Sadi to find out exactly what's going on. Let's see—what else? Oh, the Honeths have finally united behind one candidate—a pompous, ar-rogant jackass who's offended just about everybody in Tol Honeth. They'll try to buy the crown for him, but he'd be hopelessly incompetent as emperor. Even with all their money, it's going to be difficult for them to put him on the throne. I guess that's about all, your Highness."

"I've had a letter from Islena in Val Alorn," Queen Porenn told him.

"Yes, your Highness," Javelin replied urbanely, "I know."

"Javelin, have you been reading my mail again?" she demanded with a sudden flash of irritation.

"Just trying to stay current with what's going on in the world, Porenn."

"I've told you to stop that."

"You didn't really expect me to do it, did you?" He seemed actually surprised. She laughed. "You're impossible."

"Of course I am. I'm supposed to be."

"Can we get any help to Islena?"

"I'll put some people on it," he assured her. "We can probably work through Merel, the wife of the Earl of Trellheim. She's starting to show some signs of matu-rity, and she's close to Islena."

"I think we'd better have a close look at our own intelligence service, too," Porenn suggested. "Let's pin down everyone who might have any connections with the Bear-cult. The time might come when we'll have to take steps."

Javelin nodded his agreement.

There was a light tapping at the door.

"Yes?" Porenn answered.

The door opened and a servant thrust his head into the room. "Excuse me, your Highness," he said, "but there's a Nadrak merchant here—a man named Yarblek. He says he wants to discuss the salmon run." The servant looked perplexed.

Queen Porenn straightened in her chair. "Send him in," she ordered, "at once."

CHAPTER NINE

The speeches were over. The orations that had caused Princess Ce'Nedra such agony had done their work, and she found herself less and less in the center of things. At first the days opened before her full of glorious freedom. The dreadful anxiety that had filled her at the prospect of addressing vast crowds of men two or three times a day was gone now. Her nervous exhaustion disappeared, and she no longer awoke in the middle of the night trembling and terrified. For almost an entire week she reveled in it, luxuriated in it. Then, of course, she became dreadfully bored.

The army she had gathered in Arendia and northern Tolnedra moved like a great sea in the foothills of Ulgoland. The Mimbrate knights, their armor glittering in the bright sunlight and their long, streaming, many-colored pennons snapping in the breeze, moved at the forefront of the host, and behind them, spreading out across the rolling green hills, marched the solid mass of Ce'Nedra's infantry, Sendars, Asturians, Rivans, and a few Chereks. And there, solidly in the center, forming the very core, marched the gleaming ranks of the legions of Imperial Tolnedra, their crimson standards aloft and the white plumes on their helmets waving in time to their measured steps. It was very stirring for the first few days to ride at the head of the enormous force, moving at her command toward the east, but the novelty of it all soon wore thin.

Princess Ce'Nedra's gradual drift away from the center of command was largely her own fault. The decisions now had to do more often than not with logistics—tedious little details concerning bivouac areas and field-kitchens—and Ce'Nedra found discussions of such matters tiresome. Those details, however, dictated the snail's pace of her army.

Quite suddenly, to everyone's astonishment, King Fulrach of Sendaria became the absolute commander of the host. It was he who decided how far they would march each day, when they would rest and where they would set up each night's encampment. His authority derived directly from the fact that the supply wagons were his. Quite early during the march down through northern Arendia, the dumpy-looking Sendarian monarch had taken one look at the rather sketchy plans the Alorn kings had drawn up for feeding the troops, had shaken his head in disapproval, and then had taken charge of that aspect of the campaign himself. Sendaria was a land of farms, and her storehouses bulged. Moreover, at certain seasons, every road and lane in Sendaria crawled with wagons. With an almost casual efficiency, King Fulrach issued a few orders, and soon whole caravans of heavily laden wagons moved down through Arendia to Tolnedra and then turned eastward to follow the army. The pace of the army was dictated by those creaking supply wagons.

They were only a few days into the Ulgo foothills when the full weight of King Fulrach's authority became clear.

"Fulrach," King Rhodar of Drasnia objected when the King of the Sendars called a halt for yet another rest period, "if we don't move any faster than this, it'll take us all summer to get to the eastern escarpment."

"You're exaggerating, Rhodar," King Fulrach replied mildly. "We're making pretty good time. The supply wagons are heavy, and the wagon horses have to be rested every hour."

"This is impossible," Rhodar declared. "I'm going to pick up the pace."

"That's up to you, of course." The brown-bearded Sendar shrugged, coolly eyeing Rhodar's vast paunch. "But if you exhaust my wagon horses today, you won't eat tomorrow."

And that ended that.

The going in the steep passes of Ulgoland was even slower. Ce'Nedra entered that land of thick forests and rocky crags with apprehension. She vividly remembered the flight with Grul the Eldrak and the attacks of the Algroths and the Hrulgin that had so terrified her that previous winter. There were few meetings with the monsters that lurked in the Ulgo mountains, however. The army was so large that even the fiercest creatures avoided it. Mandorallen, the Baron of Vo Mandor, rather regretfully reported only brief sightings.

"Mayhap if I were to ride a day's march in advance of our main force, I might find opportunity to engage some of the more frolicsome beasts," he mused aloud one evening, staring thoughtfully into the fire.

"You never get enough, do you?" Barak asked him pointedly.

"Never mind, Mandorallen," Polgara told the great knight. "The creatures aren't hurting us, and the Gorim of Ulgo would be happier if we didn't bother them."

Mandorallen sighed.

"Is he always like that?" King Anheg asked Barak curiously.

"You have absolutely no idea," Barak replied.

The slow march through Ulgoland, regardless of how much it chafed Rhodar, Brand, and Anheg, did, however, conserve the strength of the army, and they came down onto the plains of Algaria in surprisingly good shape.

"We'll go on to the Algarian Stronghold," King Rhodar decided as the army poured down out of the last pass and fanned out across the rolling grasslands. "We need to regroup a bit, and I don't see any point in moving to the base of the escarpment until the engineers are ready for us. Besides, I'd prefer not to announce the size of our army to any Thull who happens to glance down from the top of the cliff."

And so, in easy stages, the army marched across Algaria, trampling a mile-wide swath through the tall grass. Vast herds of cattle paused briefly in their grazing to watch with mild-eyed astonishment as the horde marched by, then returned to their feeding under the protective watch of mounted Algar clansmen.

The encampment that was set up around the towering Stronghold in south central Algaria stretched for miles, and the watch fires at night seemed almost a reflection of the stars. Once she was comfortably quartered in the Stronghold, Princess Ce'Nedra found herself even more removed from the day-to-day command of her troops. Her hours seemed filled with tedium. This is not to say that she did not receive reports. A rigorous schedule of training was instituted, in part because large portions of the army were not professional soldiers, but primarily to avoid the idleness that led to discipline problems. Each morning, Colonel Brendig, the sober-faced Sendarian baronet who seemed utterly devoid of humor, reported the progress of the previous day's training with excruciating thoroughness, along with all sorts of other tedious little details—most of which Ce'Nedra found extremely distasteful.

One morning after Brendig had respectfully withdrawn, Ce'Nedra finally exploded. "If he mentions the word 'sanitation' one more time, I think I'll scream," she declared to Adara and Polgara. The princess was pacing up and down, flinging her arms in the air in exasperation.

"It *is* fairly important in an army of this size, Ce'Nedra," Adara calmly pointed out.

"But does he have to *talk* about it all the time? It's a disgusting subject."

Polgara, who had been patiently teaching the little blond waif, Errand, how to lace up his boots, looked up, assessed Ce'Nedra's mood in a single glance, and then made a suggestion. "Why don't you young ladies take some horses and go for a ride? A bit of fresh air and exercise seems definitely to be in order."

It took only a short while for them to find the blond Mimbrate girl, Ariana. They knew exactly where to look. It took a bit longer, however, to wrench her away from her rapt contemplation of Lelldorin of Wildantor. Lelldorin, with the aid of his cousin Torasin, was struggling to teach a group of Arendish serfs the basics of archery. Torasin, a fiery young Asturian patriot, had joined the army late. There had been, Ce'Nedra gathered, some unpleasantness between two young men, but the prospect of war and glory had finally been too much for Torasin to resist. He had overtaken the army in the western foothills of Ulgoland, mounted on a horse half-dead from hard riding. His reconciliation with Lelldorin had been emotional, and now the two were closer than ever. Ariana, however, watched only Lelldorin. Her eyes glowed as she gazed at him with an adoration so totally mindless that it was frightening.

The three girls, dressed in soft leather Algar riding clothes, cantered out through the encampment in bright midmorning sunlight, followed inevitably by Olban, youngest son of the Rivan Warder, and a detachment of guards. Ce'Nedra did not know exactly what to make of Olban. Since a hidden Murgo had made an attempt on her life in the Arendish forest, the young Rivan had appointed himself the chief of her personal bodyguards, and absolutely nothing could move him to abandon that duty. For some reason, he seemed almost grateful for the opportunity to serve, and Ce'Nedra was glumly certain that only physical force could make him stop.

It was a warm, cloudless day, and the blue sky stretched over the incredible expanse of the Algarian plain, where tall grass bent before a vagrant breeze. Once they were out of sight of the encampment, Ce'Nedra's spirits rose enormously. She rode the white horse King Cho-Hag had given her, a patient, even-tempered animal she had named Noble. Noble was probably not a good name for him, since he was a lazy horse. A great part of his placidity arose from the fact that his new owner was so tiny that she had virtually no weight. Moreover, in an excess of affection, Ce'Nedra babied him outrageously, slipping apples and bits of sweets to him whenever possible. As a result of his light exercise and rich diet, Noble was developing a noticeable portliness.

In the company of her two friends, and trailed by the watchful young Olban, the princess, mounted on her stout white horse, rode out across the grassland, exulting in the sense of freedom their ride brought to her.

They reined in at the base of a long, sloping hill to rest their mounts. Noble, puffing like a bellows, cast a reproachful look over his shoulder at his tiny mistress, but she heartlessly ignored his unspoken complaint. "It's an absolutely wonderful day for a ride," she exclaimed enthusiastically.

Ariana sighed.

Ce'Nedra laughed at her. "Oh, come now, it's not as if Lelldorin were going someplace, Ariana, and it's good for men to miss us a little once in a while."

Ariana smiled rather wanly, then sighed again.

"Perhaps it's not as good for us to miss them, however," Adara murmured without any trace of a smile.

"What *is* that lovely fragrance?" Ce'Nedra asked suddenly.

Adara lifted her porcelain face to sniff at the light breeze, then suddenly looked around as if trying to pinpoint their exact location. "Come with me," she said with an uncharacteristic note of command in her voice, and she led them around the base of the hill to the far side. About halfway up the grassy slope there was a patch of low, dark green bushes covered with pale lavender flowers. There had been that morning a hatch of blue butterflies, and the winged creatures hovered in an ecstatic cloud over the flowers. Without pausing, Adara pressed her mount up the slope and swung down from her saddle. There with a low cry she knelt almost reverently, gathering the bushes in her arms as if embracing them.

When Ce'Nedra drew closer, she was amazed to see tears welling up in her gentle friend's gray eyes, although Adara was actually smiling. "Whatever is wrong, Adara?" she asked.

"They're *my* flowers," Adara replied in a vibrant voice. "I didn't realize that they'd grow and spread this way."

"What are you talking about?"

"Garion created this flower last winter—just for me. There was only one—just one. I saw it come into existence right there in his hand. I'd forgotten it until just now. Look how far it's spread in just one season."

Ce'Nedra felt a sudden pang of jealousy. Garion had never created a flower for *her*. She bent and pulled one of the lavender blooms from a bush, tugging perhaps just a bit harder than necessary. "It's lopsided," she sniffed, looking at the flower critically. Then she bit her lip, wishing she hadn't said that.

Adara gave her a quick look of protest.

"I'm only teasing, Adara," Ce'Nedra said quickly with a false little laugh. In spite of herself, still wanting to find something else wrong with the flower, she bent her face to the small, crooked blossom in her hand. Its fragrance seemed to erase all of her cares and to lift her spirits tremendously.

Ariana had also dismounted, and she too was breathing in the gentle odor of the flowers, although there was a slight frown on her face. "Might I gather some few of the blossoms, Lady Adara?" she inquired. "Methinks they have some strange property concealed within their blushing petals that may be of some interest to Lady Polgara—some healing agent too subtle for my limited familiarity with unguents and aromatic herbs to discern."

Rather predictably, Ce'Nedra, having gone one way, suddenly reversed herself. "Marvelous!" she exclaimed, clapping her hands with delight. "Wouldn't it be wonderful if your flower turned out to be a great medicine, Adara? Some miraculous cure? We could call it 'Adara's rose,' and sick men would bless your name forever."

"It doesn't exactly look like a rose, Ce'Nedra," Adara pointed out.

"Nonsense," Ce'Nedra brushed the distinction aside. "I'm supposed to be a queen, after all, so if I say it's a rose, then it's a rose, and that's that. We'll take the flowers back to Lady Polgara at once." She turned back to her tubby horse, who was lazily regarding the flowers as if wondering whether or not to eat a few of them. "Come, Noble," the princess said to him with extravagant overstatement. "We'll gallop back to the Stronghold."

Noble winced visibly at the word "gallop."

POLGARA EXAMINED THE flowers carefully, but, to the disappointment of the princess and her friends, she would not commit herself immediately concerning their medicinal value. A bit subdued, the little princess returned quietly to her quarters and her duties.

Colonel Brendig was awaiting her. Upon reflection, Ce'Nedra concluded that Colonel Brendig was by far the most practical man she had ever met. No detail was too small for him. In a lesser man, such concern with little things might have been passed off as mere fussiness, but the colonel's belief that big things were made up of little things gave his patient attention to detail a certain dignity. He seemed to be everywhere in the camp; in his wake, tent ropes were tightened, cluttered heaps of equipment were arranged into neat stacks, and casually open doublets were quickly buttoned up.

"I hope that her Majesty found her ride refreshing," the colonel said politely, bowing as Ce'Nedra entered the room.

"Thank you, Colonel Brendig," the princess replied. "My Majesty did." She was in a whimsical frame of mind, and it was always a delight to tease this sober-faced Sendar.

A brief smile touched Brendig's lips, and then he immediately got down to the business of the midday report. "I'm pleased to advise your Majesty that the Drasnian engineers have nearly completed the hoists atop the escarpment," he reported. "All that remains is the rigging of the counterweights which will help to lift the Cherek warships."

"That's nice," Ce'Nedra said with the vacant, empty-headed smile she knew drove him absolutely wild.

Brendig's jaw tightened slightly, but his face betrayed no other sign of his momentary flash of irritation. "The Chereks are beginning to remove the masts and rigging from their ships in preparation for the portage," he continued, "and the fortified positions up on top of the escarpment are several days ahead of schedule."

"How wonderful!" Ce'Nedra exclaimed, clapping her hands with a great show of girlish delight.

"Your Majesty, *please*," Brendig complained.

"I'm sorry, Colonel Brendig," Ce'Nedra apologized, affectionately patting his hand. "For some reason you bring out the very worst in me. Don't you *ever* smile?"

He looked at her with an absolutely straight face. "I am smiling, your Majesty," he said. "Oh—you have a visitor from Tolnedra."

"A visitor? Who?"

"A General Varana, the Duke of Anadile."

"Varana? Here? What on earth is he doing in Algaria? Is he alone?"

"There are a number of other Tolnedran gentlemen with him," Brendig replied. "They aren't in uniform, but they have the general bearing of military men. They *say* that they're here as private observers. General Varana expressed a desire to pay his respects whenever it might be convenient."

"Of course, Colonel Brendig," Ce'Nedra said with an enthusiasm that was no longer feigned. "Please send for him at once."

Ce'Nedra had known General Varana since her earliest childhood. He was a stocky man with graying, curly hair and a stiff left knee that gave him a noticeable limp. He was blessed with that wry, understated sense of humor so characteristic of the Anadilian family. Of all the noble houses of Tolnedra, the Borunes were most comfortable with the Anadiles. Both families were southern, for one thing, and the Anadiles usually sided with the Borunes in disputes with the powerful families of the north. Although Anadile was only a duchy, there had never been any hint of subservience in the family's alliances with the Grand Dukes of the House of Borune. Indeed, Anadilian dukes, more often than not, poked gentle fun at their more powerful neighbors. Serious historians and statesmen had long considered it a misfortune for the Empire that the talented House of Anadile had not enough wealth to make a serious bid for the Imperial Throne.

When General Varana politely limped into the room where Ce'Nedra impatiently awaited him, there was a faint smile hovering on his lips and a quizzical lift to one of his eyebrows. "Your Majesty," he greeted her with a bow.

"Uncle Varana," the princess exclaimed, flying to embrace him. Varana was not, in fact, her uncle, but she had always thought of him as such.

"What have you gone and done now, my little Ce'Nedra?" He laughed, enfolding her in his thick-muscled arms. "You're turning the world upside down, you know. What's a Borune doing in the middle of Algaria with an Alorn army at her back?"

"I'm going to invade Mishrak ac Thull," she declared impishly.

"Really? Whatever for? Did King Gethell of Thulldom insult the House of Borune in some way? I hadn't heard about it."

"It's an Alorn matter," Ce'Nedra replied airily.

"Oh, I see. That explains it, I suppose. Alorns don't need reasons for the things they do."

"You're laughing at me," she accused him.

"Of course I am, Ce'Nedra. The Anadiles have been laughing at the Borunes for thousands of years."

She pouted. "It's *very* serious, Uncle Varana."

"Naturally it is," he agreed, gently touching her out-thrust lower lip with one thick finger, "but that's no reason not to laugh about it."

"You're impossible," Ce'Nedra said helplessly, laughing in spite of herself. "What are you doing here?"

"Observing," he told her. "Generals do that a lot. You've got the only war that's going on just now, so several of us thought we'd drop by and have a look. Morin suggested it."

"My father's chamberlain?"

"I think that's his function, yes."

"Morin wouldn't do that—not on his own."

"Really? What astonishing news."

Ce'Nedra frowned, nibbling absently at a lock of her hair. Varana reached out and took the lock out from between her teeth. "Morin doesn't do anything unless my father tells him to," Ce'Nedra mused, once again lifting the curl to her lips.

Varana took the lock out of her fingers again.

"Don't do that," she told him.

"Why not? That's the way I broke you of sucking your thumb."

"This is different. I'm thinking."

"Think with your mouth closed."

"This was my father's idea, wasn't it?"

"I wouldn't presume to say I knew the Emperor's mind," he replied.

"Well, I would. What's that old fox up to?"

"That's hardly respectful, child."

"You say you're here to observe?"

He nodded.

"And perhaps make a few suggestions?"

He shrugged. "If anyone cares to listen. I'm not here officially, you understand. Imperial policy forbids that. Your claim to the Rivan throne is not formally recognized in Tol Honeth."

She cast a sidelong glance at him through her thick eyelashes. "These suggestions you might make—if you happened to be near a Tolnedran legion that seemed to need a bit of direction, is it at all possible that one of these suggestions might be 'forward march'?"

"That situation might arise, yes," he admitted gravely.

"And you have a number of other officers of the general staff with you?"

"I think several of them *do*, in fact, serve occasionally on that body." His eyes were twinkling with suppressed mirth.

Ce'Nedra lifted the lock again, and General Varana took it away from her once more.

"How would you like to meet King Rhodar of Drasnia?" she asked him.

"I'd be honored to meet his Majesty."

"Why don't we go see him, then?"

"Why don't we?"

"Oh, I love you, Uncle." She laughed, throwing her arms about him again.

They found King Rhodar in conference with the other leaders of the army in a large airy chamber King Cho-Hag had set aside for their use. There was no longer any pretense of formality among the leaders of the army, and most of them sprawled in comfortable horsehide chairs, watching as the crimson-robed Rhodar measured off distances with a piece of string on a large map that covered one entire wall. "It doesn't really seem all that far to me," he was saying to King Cho-Hag.

"That's because your map's flat, Rhodar," Cho-Hag replied. "The country's very hilly through there. Believe me, it'll take three days."

King Rhodar made an indelicate sound of disgust. "I guess we'll have to give up the idea, then. I'd like to burn out those forts, but I'm not going to start ordering suicide missions. Three days' ride is just too far."

"Your Majesty," Ce'Nedra said politely.

"Yes, child?" Rhodar was still frowning at the map.

"I'd like for you to meet someone."

King Rhodar turned.

"Your Majesty," Ce'Nedra said formally, "may I present his Grace, the Duke of Anadile? General Varana, his Majesty, King Rhodar of Drasnia."

The two men bowed politely to each other, their eyes probing, assessing.

"The general's reputation precedes him," King Rhodar noted.

"But his Majesty's skill as a military man has been kept a secret," Varana replied.

"Do you think that satisfies the demands of courtesy?" Rhodar asked.

"If not, we can both lie a little bit later on about how excruciatingly polite we were to each other," Varana suggested.

King Rhodar flashed him a quick grin. "All right, what's Tolnedra's leading tactician doing in Algaria?"

"Observing, your Majesty."

"You're going to stick to that story?"

"Naturally. For political reasons, Tolnedra must maintain a neutral posture in this affair. I'm certain that Drasnian intelligence has briefed your Majesty on the realities of the situation. The five spies you have in the Imperial palace are thoroughly professional."

"Six, actually," King Rhodar noted in passing.

General Varana raised one eyebrow. "I suppose we should have known," he said.

"It changes from time to time." Rhodar shrugged. "You know our strategic situation?"

"I've been filled in, yes."

"What's your assessment—as an observer?"

"You're in trouble."

"Thanks," Rhodar said dryly.

"The numbers dictate that you take a defensive posture."

Rhodar shook his head. "That might work if all we had to worry about was Taur Urgas and the Southern Murgos, but 'Zakath is landing more troops at Thull Zelik every day. If we fortify and try to sit tight, and he decides to move against us, he'll be able to bury us in Malloreans by autumn. The key to the whole situation is putting Anheg's fleet into the Sea of the East to stop those troop ships. We're going to have to gamble a bit in order to pull that off."

Varana studied the map. "If you're going to go down the River Mardu, you'll have to neutralize the Thullish capital," he said, pointing at Thull Mardu. "It's an island—like Tol Honeth—and it's right in the middle of the river. You'll never get a fleet past it as long as a hostile force holds it. You'll have to take the city."

"That had already occurred to us," King Anheg said from where he sprawled in his chair with his ever-present ale cup in his hand.

"You know Anheg?" Rhodar asked the general.

Varana nodded. "By reputation," he replied. He bowed to King Anheg. "Your Majesty," he said.

"General," Anheg responded, inclining his head.

"If Thull Mardu is heavily defended, it'll cost you a third of your army to take it," Varana continued.

"We're going to lure the garrison out," Rhodar told him.

"How?"

"That's going to be up to Korodullin and me," King Cho-Hag said quietly. "Once we get to the top of the escarpment, the Mimbrate knights are going to move out and crush every city and town in the uplands, and my clansmen will strike down into the farming regions to burn every standing crop."

"They'll realize that's only a diversion, your Majesty," Varana pointed out.

"Naturally," Brand agreed in his rumbling voice, "but a diversion from what? We don't think they'll fully realize that Thull Mardu is our main objective. We'll try our best to make our depredations as general as possible. The loss of those towns and crops might be acceptable at first, but it won't be long before they'll have to take steps to protect them."

"And you think they'll pull the garrison out of Thull Mardu to meet you?"

"That's the idea," King Rhodar replied.

Varana shook his head. "They'll bring Murgos up from Rak Goska and Malloreans from Thull Zelik. Then instead of a quick raid on Thull Mardu, you'll have a general war on your hands."

"That's what *you'd* do, General Varana," King Rhodar disagreed, "but you aren't 'Zakath or Taur Urgas. Our strategy's based on our assessment of those two men. Neither of them will commit his forces unless he's convinced that we pose a major threat. Each of them wants to save as much of his army as possible. In their view, we're only an incidental annoyance—and an excuse to put an army into the field. For them, the real war starts when they attack each other. Each of them will hold back, and King Gethell of the Thulls will have to meet us on his own with only token support from the Murgos and the Malloreans. If we move fast enough, we'll have Anheg's fleet into the Sea of the East and all our troops pulled back to the escarpment before they realize what we're up to."

"And then?"

"And then Taur Urgas will stay in Rak Goska as if his foot were nailed to the floor." King Anheg chuckled. "I'll be in the Sea of the East drowning Malloreans by the shipload, and he'll be cheering me on every step of the way."

"And 'Zakath won't dare risk those troops he already has at Thull Zelik by moving against us," Brand added. "If he loses too many men, Taur Urgas will have the upper hand."

General Varana considered that. "A three-way deadlock, then," he mused. "Three armies in the same region, and not one of them willing to move."

"The very best kind of war." King Rhodar grinned. "Nobody gets hurt."

"Tactically, your only problem is gauging the severity of your raids before you attack Thull Mandu," Varana noted. "They'll have to be serious enough to pull the garrison out of the city, but not so serious as to alarm 'Zakath or Taur Urgas. That's a very fine line to walk, gentlemen."

Rhodar nodded. "That's why we're so delighted to have Tolnedra's foremost tactician here to advise us," he said bowing floridly.

"Please, your Majesty," General Varana interposed, lifting one hand. "*Suggest*, not advise. An observer can only suggest. The term advice implies partisanship that is not in line with the Empire's position of strict neutrality."

"Ah," King Rhodar said. He turned to King Cho-Hag. "We must make arrangements for the comfort of the Imperial suggester and his staff," he declared with a broad grin.

Ce'Nedra watched with secret delight as these two brilliant men began what was obviously going to be a firm friendship. "I'll leave you gentlemen to your entertainments," she told them. "Military discussions give me a headache, so I'll rely on you not to get me in trouble." She curtsied to them with a winsome little smile and withdrew.

Two days later, Relg arrived from Ulgoland with the contingent of his leaf-mailed countrymen sent by the Gorim. Taiba, who had hovered silently in the background since the army had arrived at the Stronghold, joined Ce'Nedra and Lady Polgara to greet the Ulgos as the wagons which carried them creaked up the hill toward the main gate. The beautiful Marag woman wore a plain, even severe, linen dress, but her violet eyes were glowing. Relg, his cowled leaf-mail shirt covering his head and shoulders like lizard skin, climbed down from the lead wagon and only perfunctorily answered the greetings of Barak and Mandorallen. His large eyes searched the group gathered at the gate until they found Taiba, and then a kind of tension seemed to go out of him. Without speaking, he walked toward her. Their meeting was silent, and they did not touch, though Taiba's hand moved involuntarily toward him several times. They stood in the golden sunlight with their eyes lost in each other's faces, drawing about them a profound kind of privacy that absolutely ignored the presence of others. Taiba's eyes remained constantly on Relg's face, but there was in them nothing of that vacant, placid adoration that filled Ariana's eyes when she looked at Lelldorin. There was rather a question—even a challenge. Relg's answering look was the troubled gaze of a man torn between two overpowering compulsions. Ce'Nedra watched them for a few moments, but was finally forced to avert her eyes.

The Ulgos were quartered in dim, cavernous rooms built into the foundations of the Stronghold where Relg could lead his countrymen through the painful process of adjusting their eyes to the light of day and training them to ignore the unreasoning panic which assailed all Ulgos when they were exposed to the open sky.

That evening another smaller contingent arrived from the south. Three men, two in white robes and one in filthy rags, appeared at the gate demanding entrance. The Algars at the gate admitted them immediately, and one guard was sent to Lady Polgara's candlelit apartment to inform her of their arrival.

"You'd better bring them here," she advised the poor man, who was ashen-faced and trembling. "They haven't been in the company of other men for a very long time, and crowds might make them nervous."

"At once, Lady Polgara," the shaking Algar said, bowing. He hesitated for a moment. "Would he *really* do that to me?" he blurted.

"Would who do what to you?"

"The ugly one. He said that he was going to—" The man stopped, suddenly realizing to whom he was speaking. His face turned red. "I don't think I should re-peat what he said, Lady Polgara—but it was an awful thing to threaten a man with."

"Oh," she said. "I believe I know what you mean. It's one of his favorite ex-pressions. I think you're safe. He only says that to get people's attention. I'm not even sure you *can* do it to somebody and keep him alive at the same time."

"I'll bring them at once, Lady Polgara."

The sorceress turned to look at Ce'Nedra, Adara, and Ariana, who had joined her for supper. "Ladies," she said gravely, "we're about to have guests. Two of them are the sweetest men in the world, but the third is a bit uncontrolled in his use of language. If you're at all sensitive about such things, you'd better leave."

Ce'Nedra, remembering her encounter with the three in the Vale of Aldur, rose immediately.

"Not you, Ce'Nedra," Polgara told her. "You'll have to stay, I'm afraid."

Ce'Nedra swallowed hard. "I really would leave, if I were you," she advised her friends.

"Is he *that* bad?" Adara asked. "I've heard men swear before."

"Not like this one," Ce'Nedra warned.

"You've managed to make me very curious." Adara smiled. "I think I'll stay."

"Don't say I didn't warn you," Ce'Nedra murmured.

Beltira and Belkira were as saintly as Ce'Nedra remembered them, but the misshapen Beldin was even uglier and nastier. Ariana fled before he had even fin-ished greeting Lady Polagra. Adara turned deathly pale, but bravely kept her seat. Then the hideous little man turned to greet Ce'Nedra with a few raucous questions that made the princess blush to the roots of her hair. Adara prudently withdrew at that point.

"What's wrong with your wenches, Pol?" Beldin asked innocently, scratching at his matted hair. "They seemed a little vaporish."

"They're well-bred ladies, Uncle," Polgara replied. "Certain expressions are of-fensive to their ears."

"Is *that* all?" He laughed coarsely. "This redheaded one seems a bit less delicate."

"Your remarks offend me as much as they offend my companions, Master Beldin," Ce'Nedra retorted stiffly, "but I don't think I'll be routed by the foul mouthings of an ill-bred hunchback."

"Not bad," he complimented her, sprawling uncouthly in a chair, "but you've got to learn to relax. An insult's got a certain rhythm and flow to it that you haven't quite picked up yet."

"She's very young, Uncle," Polgara reminded him.

Beldin leered at the princess. "Isn't she, though?"

"Stop that," Polgara told him.

"We've come—"

"—to join your expedition," the twins said. "Beldin feels—"

"—that you might encounter Grolims, and—"

"—need our help."

"Isn't that pathetic?" Beldin demanded. "They still haven't learned to talk straight." He looked at Polgara. "Is this all the army you've got?"

"The Chereks will be joining us at the river," she replied.

"You should have talked faster," he told Ce'Nedra. "You haven't got nearly enough men. Southern Murgos proliferate like maggots in dead meat, and Malloreans spawn like blowflies."

"We'll explain our strategy to you in good time, Uncle," Polgara promised him. "We are *not* going to meet the armies of Angarak head-on. What we're doing here is only diversionary."

He grinned a hideous little grin. "I'd have given a lot to see your face when you found out that Belgarath had slipped away from you," he said.

"I wouldn't dwell on that, Master Beldin," Ce'Nedra advised. "Lady Polgara was not pleased by Belgarath's decision, and it might not be prudent to raise it again."

"I've seen Pol's little tantrums before." He shrugged. "Why don't you send somebody out for a pig or a sheep, Pol? I'm hungry."

"It's customary to cook it first, Uncle."

He looked puzzled. "What for?" he asked.

■ ┌─────────────────────────────────┐ ■
    │   CHAPTER TEN   │
    └─────────────────────────────────┘

Three days later the army began to move out from the Algar Stronghold toward the temporary encampment the Algars had erected on the east bank of the Aldur River. The troops of each nation moved in separate broad columns, trampling a vast track through the knee-high grass. In the center column the legions of Tolnedra, standards raised, marched with parade-ground perfection. The appearance of the legions had improved noticeably since the arrival of General Varana and his staff. The mutiny on the plains near Tol Vordue had given Ce'Nedra a large body of men, but no senior officers, and once the danger of surprise inspections was past, a certain laxity had set in. General Varana had not mentioned the rust spots on the breastplates nor the generally unshaven condition of the troops.

His expression of mild disapproval had seemed to be enough. The hard-bitten sergeants who now commanded the legions had taken one look at his face and had immediately taken steps. The rust spots vanished, and shaving regularly once again became popular. There were, to be sure, a few contusions here and there on some freshly shaved faces, mute evidence that the heavy-fisted sergeants had found it necessary to vigorously persuade their troops that the holiday was over.

To one side of the legions rode the glittering Mimbrate knights, their varicolored pennons snapping in the breeze from the upraised forest of their lances. Their faces shone with enthusiasm and little else. Ce'Nedra privately suspected that a large part of their fearsome reputation stemmed from that abysmal lack of anything remotely resembling thought. With only a little encouragement, a force of Mimbrates would cheerfully mount an assault on winter or a changing tide.

On the other flank of the marching legions came the green- and brown-clad bowmen of Asturia. The placement was quite deliberate. The Asturians were no more blessed with intelligence than their Mimbrate cousins, and it was generally considered prudent to interpose other troops between the two Arendish forces to avoid unpleasantness.

Beyond the Asturians marched the grim-faced Rivans, all in gray, and accompanying them were the few Chereks who were not with the fleet, which even now was in the process of being prepared for the portage to the base of the escarpment. Flanking the Mimbrates marched the Sendarian militiamen in their homemade uniforms, and at the rear of the host, the creaking lines of King Fulrach's supply wagons stretched back to the horizon. The Algar clans, however, did not ride in orderly columns, but rather in little groups and clusters as they drove herds of spare horses and half-wild cattle along on the extreme flanks of the host.

Ce'Nedra, in her armor and mounted on her white horse, rode in the company of General Varana. She was trying, without much success, to explain her cause to him.

"My dear child," the general said finally, "I'm a Tolnedran and a soldier. Neither of those conditions encourages me to accept any kind of mysticism. My primary concerns at this moment have to do with feeding this multitude. Your supply lines stretch all the way back across the mountains and then up through Arendia. That's a very long way, Ce'Nedra."

"King Fulrach's taken care of that, Uncle," she told him rather smugly. "All the time we've been marching, his Sendars have been freighting supplies along the Great North Road to Aldurford and then barging them upriver to the camp. There are whole acres of supply dumps waiting for us."

General Varana nodded approvingly. "It appears that Sendars make perfect quartermasters," he observed. "Is he bringing weapons as well?"

"I think they said something about that," Ce'Nedra replied. "Arrows, spare lances for the knights, that sort of thing. They seemed to know what they were doing, so I didn't ask too many questions."

"That's foolish, Ce'Nedra," Varana said bluntly. "When you're running an army, you should know every detail."

"I'm not running the army, Uncle," she pointed out. "I'm leading it. King Rhodar's running it."

"And what will you do if something happens to him?"

Ce'Nedra suddenly went cold.

"You *are* going to war, Ce'Nedra, and people *do* get killed and injured in wars. You'd better start taking an interest in what's going on around you, my little princess. Going off to war with your head wrapped in a pillow isn't going to improve your chances of success, you know." He gave her a very direct look. "Don't chew your fingernails, Ce'Nedra," he added. "It makes your hands unsightly."

The encampment at the river was vast, and in the very center stood King Fulrach's main supply dump, a virtual city of tents and neatly stacked equipment. A long string of flat-bottomed barges were moored to the riverbank, patiently waiting to be unloaded.

"Your people have been busy," King Rhodar observed to the dumpy-looking Sendarian monarch as they rode along a narrow alleyway between mountainous heaps of canvas-covered produce and stacks of stoutly boxed equipment. "How did you know what to have them bring?"

"I took notes while we were coming down through Arendia," King Fulrach replied. "It wasn't too hard to see what we were going to need—boots, arrows, spare swords, and the like. At present, about all we're bringing in is food. The Algar herds will provide fresh meat, but men get sick on a steady diet of nothing but meat."

"You've already got enough food here to feed the army for a year," King Anheg noted.

Fulrach shook his head. "Forty-five days," he corrected meticulously. "I want thirty days' worth here and two weeks' worth in the forts the Drasnians are building up on top of the escarpment. That's our margin of safety. As long as the barges replenish our food supplies daily, we'll always have that much on hand. Once you decide what your goals are, the rest is just simple mathematics."

"How do you know how much a man's going to eat in one day?" Rhodar asked, eyeing the high-piled foodstuffs. "Some days I'm hungrier than others."

Fulrach shrugged. "It averages out. Some eat more, some eat less; but in the end, it all comes out about the same."

"Fulrach, sometimes you're so practical, you almost make me sick," Anheg said.

"Somebody has to be."

"Don't you Sendars have any sense of adventure? Don't you *ever* do something without planning it all out in advance?"

"Not if we can help it," the King of Sendaria replied mildly.

Near the center of the supply dump a number of large pavilions had been erected for the use of the leaders of the army and their supporting staff. About midafternoon, after she had bathed and changed clothes, Princess Ce'Nedra went over to the main tent to see what was happening.

"They're anchored about a mile downriver," Barak was reporting to his cousin. "They've been here for about four days now. Greldik's more or less in charge."

"Greldik?" Anheg looked surprised. "He doesn't have any official position."

"He knows the river." Barak shrugged. "Over the years he's sailed just about any place where there's water and a chance to make some profit. He tells me that the sailors have been drinking pretty steadily since they anchored. They know what's coming."

Anheg chuckled. "We'd better not disappoint them, then. Rhodar, how much longer will it be before your engineers are ready to start lifting my ships up the escarpment?"

"A week or so," King Rhodar replied, looking up from his midafternoon snack.

"It'll be close enough," Anheg concluded. He turned back to Barak. "Tell Greldik that we'll start the portage tomorrow morning—before the sailors have time to sober up."

Ce'Nedra had not fully understood the meaning of the word "portage" until she arrived the following morning at the riverbank to find the sweating Chereks hauling their ships out of the water and manhandling them along by main strength on wooden rollers. She was appalled at the amount of effort required to move a ship even a few inches.

She was not alone in that. Durnik the smith took one shocked look at the procedure and immediately went looking for King Anheg. "Excuse me, your Honor," he said respectfully, "but isn't this bad for the boats—as well as the men?"

"Ships," Anheg corrected. "They're called ships. A boat is something else."

"Whatever you call them—won't banging them along over those logs spring their seams?"

Anheg shrugged. "They all leak quite a bit anyway," he replied. "And it's always been done this way."

Durnik quickly saw the futility of trying to talk to the King of Cherek. He went instead to Barak, who was rather glumly considering the huge ship his crew had rowed upriver to meet him. "She looks very impressive when she's afloat," the big red-bearded man was saying to his friend, Captain Greldik, "but I think she'll be even more impressive when we have to pick her up and carry her."

"You're the one who wanted the biggest warship afloat," Greldik reminded him with a broad smirk. "You'll have to buy enough ale to float that whale of yours before your crew's drunk enough to try to portage her—not to mention the fact that it's customary for a captain to join in when the time comes to portage."

"Stupid custom," Barak growled sourly.

"I'd say that you're in for a bad week, Barak." Greldik's grin grew broader.

Durnik took the two seamen aside and began talking earnestly with them, drawing diagrams on the sandy riverbank with a stick. The more he talked, the more interested they became.

What emerged from their discussions a day later were a pair of low-slung cradles with a dozen wheels on each side. As the rest of the Chereks jeered, the two ships were carefully slid out of the water onto the cradles and firmly lashed in place. The jeering faded noticeably, however, when the crews of the two ships began trundling their craft across the plain. Hettar, who happened to ride by, watched for a few moments with a puzzled frown. "Why are you pulling them by hand," he asked, "when you're in the middle of the largest herd of horses in the world?"

Barak's eyes went very wide, and then an almost reverent grin dawned on his face.

The jeers that had risen as Barak's and Greldik's ships had been maneuvered onto their wheeled carriages turned rather quickly into angry mutterings as the carriages, pulled by teams of Algar horses, rolled effortlessly toward the escarpment past men straining with every ounce of strength to move their ships a few inches at a time. To raise it all to artistry, Barak and Greldik ordered their men to lounge indolently on the decks of their ships, drinking ale and playing dice.

King Anheg stared very hard at his impudently grinning cousin as the big ship rolled past. His expression was profoundly offended. "That's going *too* far!" he exploded, jerking off his dented crown and throwing it down on the ground.

King Rhodar put on a perfectly straight face. "I'd be the first to admit that it's probably not nearly as good as moving them by hand, Anheg. I'm sure there are some rather profound philosophical reasons for all that sweating and grunting and cursing, but it *is* faster, wouldn't you say? And we really ought to move right along with this."

"It's unnatural," Anheg growled, still glaring at the two ships, which were already several hundred yards away.

Rhodar shrugged. "Anything's unnatural the first time you try it."

"I'll think about it," Anheg said darkly.

"I wouldn't think for too long," Rhodar suggested. "Your popularity as a monarch is going to go downhill with every mile—and Barak's the sort of man who'll parade that contraption of his back and forth in front of your sailors every step of the way to the escarpment."

"He *would* do that, wouldn't he?"

"I think you can count on it."

King Anheg sighed bitterly. "Go fetch that unwholesomely clever Sendarian blacksmith," he sourly instructed one of his men. "Let's get this over with."

Later that day the leaders of the army gathered again in the main tent for a strategy meeting. "Our biggest problem now is to conceal the size of our forces," King Rhodar told them all. "Instead of marching everybody to the escarpment all at once and then milling around at the base of the cliff, it might be better to move the troops in small contingents and have them go directly up to the forts on top as soon as they arrive."

"Will such a piecemeal approach not unduly delay our progress?" King Korodullin asked.

"Not that much," Rhodar replied. "We'll move your knights and Cho-Hag's clansmen up first so you can start burning cities and crops. That'll give the Thulls something to think about besides how many infantry regiments we're bringing up. We don't want them to start counting noses."

"Couldn't we build false campfires and so on to make it appear that we have more men?" Lelldorin suggested brightly.

"The whole idea is to make our army appear smaller, not bigger," Brand explained gently in his deep voice. "We don't want to alarm Taur Urgas or 'Zakath sufficiently to make them commit their forces. It'll be an easy campaign if all we have to deal with are King Gethell's Thulls. If the Murgos and the Malloreans intervene, we'll be in for a serious fight."

"And that's the one thing we definitely want to avoid," King Rhodar added.

"Oh," Lelldorin said, a bit abashed, "I didn't think of that." A slow flush rose in his cheeks.

"Lelldorin," Ce'Nedra said, hoping to help him cover his embarrassment. "I think I'd like to go out and visit with the troops for a bit. Would you accompany me?"

"Of course, your Majesty," the young Asturian agreed, quickly rising to his feet.

"That's not a bad idea," Rhodar agreed. "Encourage them a bit, Ce'Nedra. They've walked a long way, and their spirits may be sagging."

Lelldorin's cousin Torasin, dressed in his customary black doublet and hose, also rose to his feet. "I'll go along, if I may," he said. He grinned rather impudently at King Korodullin. "Asturians are good plotters, but rather poor strategists, so I probably wouldn't be able to add much to the discussions."

The King of Arendia smiled at the young man's remark. "Thou art pert, young Torasin, but methinks thou art not so fervent an enemy of the crown of Arendia as thou dost pretend."

Torasin bowed extravagantly, still grinning. Once they were outside the tent, he turned to Lelldorin. "I could almost learn to like that man—if it weren't for all those thees and thous," he declared.

"It's not so bad—once you get used to it," Lelldorin replied.

Torasin laughed. "If I had someone as pretty as Lady Ariana for a friend, she could thee me and thou me all she wanted," he said. He looked archly at Ce'Nedra. "Which troops did you wish to encourage, your Majesty?" he bantered.

"Let's visit your Asturian countrymen," she decided. "I don't think I'd care to take you two into the Mimbrate camp—unless your swords had been taken away from you and your mouths had been bricked up."

"Don't you trust us?" Lelldorin asked.

"I *know* you," she replied with a little toss of her head. "Where are the Asturians encamped?"

"That way," Torasin answered, pointing toward the south end of the supply dump.

Smells of cooking were carried by the breeze from the Sendarian field kitchens, and those smells reminded the princess of something. Instead of randomly circulating among the Asturian tents, she found herself quite deliberately searching for some specific people.

She found Lammer and Detton, the two serfs who had joined her army on the outskirts of Vo Wacune, finishing their afternoon meal in front of a patched tent. They both looked better fed than they had when she had first seen them, and they were no longer dressed in rags. When they saw her approaching, they scrambled awkwardly to their feet.

"Well, my friends," she asked, trying to put them at ease, "how do you find army life?"

"We don't have anything to complain about, your Ladyship," Detton replied respectfully.

"Except for all the walking," Lammer added. "I hadn't realized that the world was this big."

"They gave us boots," Detton told her, holding up one foot so that she could see his boot. "They were a bit stiff at first, but the blisters have all healed now."

"Are you getting enough to eat?" Ce'Nedra asked them.

"Plenty," Lammer said. "The Sendars even cook for us. Did you know that there aren't any serfs in the kingdom of the Sendars, my Lady? Isn't that astonishing? It gives a man something to think about."

"It does indeed," Detton agreed. "They grow all that food, and everybody always has plenty to eat and clothes to wear and a house to sleep in, and there's not a single serf in the whole kingdom."

"I see that they've given you equipment, too," the princess said, noting that the two now wore conical leather helmets and stiff leather vests.

Lammer nodded and pulled off his helmet. "It's got steel plates in it to keep a man from getting his brains knocked out," he told her. "They lined us all up as soon as we got here and gave every man a helmet and these hard leather tunics."

"They gave each of us a spear and a dagger, too," Detton said.

"Have they showed you how to use them?" Ce'Nedra asked.

"Not yet, your Ladyship," Detton replied. "We've been concentrating on learning how to shoot arrows."

Ce'Nedra turned to her two companions. "Could you see that somebody takes care of that?" she said. "I want to be sure that everybody knows how to defend himself, at least."

"We'll see to it, your Majesty," Lelldorin answered.

Not far away, a young serf was seated cross-legged in front of another tent. He lifted a handmade flute to his lips and began to play. Ce'Nedra had heard some of the finest musicians in the world performing at the palace in Tol Honeth, but the serf boy's flute caught at her heart and brought tears to her eyes. His melody soared toward the azure sky like an unfettered lark.

"How exquisite," she exclaimed.

Lammer nodded. "I don't know much about music," he said, "but the boy seems to play well. It's a shame he's not right in the head."

Ce'Nedra looked at him sharply. "What do you mean?"

"He comes from a village in the southern part of the forest of Arendia. I'm told it's a very poor village and that the lord of the region is very harsh with his serfs. The boy's an orphan, and he was put to watching the cows when he was young. One time one of the cows strayed, and the boy was beaten half to death. He can't talk anymore."

"Do you know his name?"

"Nobody seems to know it," Detton replied. "We take turns looking out for him—making sure he's fed and has a place to sleep. There's not much else you can do for him."

A small sound came from Lelldorin, and Ce'Nedra was startled to see tears streaming openly down the earnest young man's face.

The boy continued his playing, his melody heartbreakingly true, and his eyes sought out Ce'Nedra's and met them with a kind of grave recognition.

They did not stay much longer. The princess knew that her rank and position made the two serfs uncomfortable. She had made sure that they were all right and that her promise to them was being kept, and that was all that really mattered.

As Ce'Nedra, Lelldorin, and Torasin walked toward the camp of the Sendars, they suddenly heard the sound of squabbling on the other side of a large tent.

"I'll pile it anyplace I want to," one man was saying belligerently.

"You're blocking the street," another man replied.

"Street?" the first snorted. "What are you talking about? This isn't a town. There aren't any streets."

"Friend," the second man explained with exaggerated patience, "we have to bring the wagons through here to get to the main supply dump. Now please move your equipment so I can get through. I still have a lot to do today."

I'm not going to take orders from a Sendarian teamster who's found an easy way to avoid fighting. I'm a soldier."

"Really?" the Sendar replied dryly. "How much fighting have you seen?"

"I'll fight when the time comes."

"It may come quicker than you'd expected if you don't get your gear out of my way. If I have to get down off this wagon to move it myself, it's likely to make me irritable."

"I'm all weak with fright," the soldier retorted sarcastically.

"Are you going to move it?"

"No."

"I tried to warn you, friend," the teamster said in a resigned tone.

"If you touch my gear, I'll break your head."

"No. You'll *try* to break my head."

There was a sudden sound of scuffling and several heavy blows.

"Now get up and move your gear like I told you to," the teamster said. "I don't have all day to stand around and argue with you."

"You hit me when I wasn't looking," the soldier complained.

"Do you want to watch the next one coming?"

"All right, don't get excited. I'm moving it."

"I'm glad we understand each other."

"Does that sort of thing happen very often?" Ce'Nedra asked quietly.

Torasin, grinning broadly, nodded. "Some of your troops feel the need to bluster, your Majesty," he replied, "and the Sendarian wagoneers usually don't have the time to listen. Fistfights and street-brawling are second nature to those fellows, so their squabbles with the soldiers almost always end up the same way. It's very educational, really."

"Men!" Ce'Nedra said.

In the camp of the Sendars they met Durnik. With him there was an oddly matched pair of young men.

"A couple of old friends," Durnik said as he introduced them. "Just arrived on the supply barges. I think you've met Rundorig, Princess. He was at Faldor's farm when we visited there last winter."

Ce'Nedra did in fact remember Rundorig. The tall, hulking young man, she recalled, was the one who was going to marry Garion's childhood sweetheart, Zubrette. She greeted him warmly and gently reminded him that they had met before. Rundorig's Arendish background made his mind move rather slowly. His companion, however, was anything but slow. Durnik introduced him as Doroon, another of Garion's boyhood friends. Doroon was a small, wiry young man with a protruding Adam's apple and slightly bulging eyes. After a few moments of shyness, his tongue began to run away with him. It was a bit hard to follow Doroon. His mind flitted from idea to idea, and his mouth raced along breathlessly, trying to keep up.

"It was sort of rough going up in the mountains, your Ladyship," he replied in answer to her question about their trip from Sendaria, "what with how steep the road was and all. You'd think that as long as the Tolnedrans were building a highway, they'd have picked leveler ground—but they seem to be fascinated by straight lines—only that's not always the easiest way. I wonder why they're like that." The fact that Ce'Nedra herself was Tolnedran seemed not to have registered on Doroon.

"You came along the Great North Road?" she asked him.

"Yes—until we got to a place called Aldurford. That's a funny kind of name, isn't it? Although it makes sense if you stop and think about it. But that was after we got out of the mountains where the Murgos attacked us. You've never *seen* such a fight."

"Murgos?" Ce'Nedra asked him sharply, trying to pin down his skittering thoughts.

He nodded eagerly. "The man who was in charge of the wagons—he's a great big fellow from Muros, I think he said—wasn't it Muros he said he came from, Rundorig? Or maybe it was Camaar—for some reason I always get the two mixed up. What was I talking about?"

"The Murgos," Durnik supplied helpfully.

"Oh, yes. Anyway, the man in charge of the wagons said that there had been a lot of Murgos in Sendaria before the war. They pretended that they were merchants, but they weren't—they were spies. When the war started, they all went up into the mountains, and now they come out of the woods and try to ambush our supply wagons—but we were ready for them, weren't we Rundorig? Rundorig hit one of the Murgos with a big stick when the Murgo rode past our wagon—knocked him clear off his horse. Whack! Just like that! Knocked him clear off his horse. I'll bet *he* was surprised." Doroon laughed a short little laugh, and then his tongue raced off again, describing in jerky, helter-skelter detail the trip from Sendaria.

Princess Ce'Nedra was strangely touched by her meeting with Garion's two old friends. She felt, moreover, a tremendous burden of responsibility as she realized that she had reached into almost every life in the west with her campaign. She had separated husbands from their wives and fathers from their children; and she had carried simple men, who had never been farther than the next village, a thousand leagues and more to fight in a war they probably did not even begin to understand.

The next morning the leaders of the army rode the few remaining leagues to the installations at the base of the escarpment. As they topped a rise, Ce'Nedra reined Noble in sharply and gaped in openmouthed astonishment as she saw the eastern escarpment for the first time. It was impossible! Nothing could be so vast! The great black cliff reared itself above them like an enormous wave of rock, frozen and forever marking the boundary between east and west, and seemingly blocking any possibility of ever passing in either direction. It immediately stood as a kind of stark symbol of the division between the two parts of the world—a division that could no more be resolved than that enormous cliff could be leveled.

As they rode closer, Ce'Nedra noted a great deal of bustling activity both at the foot of the escarpment and along its upper rim. Great hawsers stretched down from overhead, and Ce'Nedra saw elaborately intertwined pulleys along the foot of the huge cliffs.

"Why are the pulleys at the bottom?" King Anheg demanded suspiciously.

King Rhodar shrugged. "How should I know? I'm not an engineer."

"All right, if you're going to be that way about it, I'm not going to let your people touch a single one of my ships until somebody tells me why the pulleys are down here instead of up there."

King Rhodar sighed and beckoned to an engineer who was meticulously greasing a huge pulley block. "Have you got a sketch of the rigging handy?" the portly monarch asked the grease-spattered workman.

The engineer nodded, pulled a rolled sheet of grimy parchment out from under his tunic, and handed it to his king. Rhodar glanced at it and handed it to Anheg.

Anheg stared at the complex drawing, struggling to trace out which line went where, and more important why it went there. "I can't read this," he complained.

"Neither can I," Rhodar told him pleasantly, "but you wanted to know why the pulleys are down here instead of up there. The drawing tells you why."

"But I can't read it."

"That's not my fault."

Not far away a cheer went up as a boulder half the size of a house and entwined in a nest of ropes rose majestically up the face of the cliff to the accompaniment of a vast creaking of hawsers.

"You'll have to admit that that's impressive, Anheg," Rhodar said. "Particularly when you note that the entire rock is being lifted by those eight horses over there—with the help of that counterweight, of course." He pointed at another block of stone which was just as majestically coming down from the top of the escarpment.

Anheg squinted at the two rocks. "Durnik," he said over his shoulder, "do you understand how all those work?"

"Yes, King Anheg," the smith replied. "You see, the counterweight off-balances the—"

"Don't explain it to me, please," Anheg said. "As long as somebody I know and trust understands, that's all that's really important."

Later that same day, the first Cherek ship was lifted to the top of the escarpment. King Anheg watched the procedure for a moment or two, then winced and turned his back. "It's unnatural," he muttered to Barak.

"You've taken to using that expression a great deal lately," Barak noted.

Anheg scowled at his cousin.

"I just mentioned it, that's all," Barak said innocently.

"I don't like changes, Barak. They make me nervous."

"The world moves on, Anheg. Things change every day."

"That doesn't necessarily mean that I have to like it," the King of Cherek growled. "I think I'll go to my tent for a drink or two."

"Want some company?" Barak offered.

"I thought you wanted to stand around and watch the world change."

"It can do that without my supervision."

"And probably will," Anheg added moodily. "All right, let's go. I don't want to watch this anymore." And the two of them went off in search of something to drink.

CHAPTER ELEVEN

Mayaserana, Queen of Arendia, was in a pensive mood. She sat at her embroidery in the large, sunny nursery high in the palace at Vo Mimbre. Her infant son, the crown prince of Arendia, cooed and gurgled in his cradle as he played with the string of brightly colored beads that had been the ostensible gift of the crown prince of Drasnia. Mayaserana had never met Queen Porenn, but the shared experience of motherhood made her feel very close to the reputedly exquisite little blonde on her far northern throne.

Seated in a chair not far from the queen sat Nerina, Baroness of Vo Ebor. Each lady wore velvet, the queen in deep purple, and the Baroness in pale blue, and each wore the high, conical white headdress so admired by the Mimbrate nobility. At the far end of the nursery, an elderly lutanist softly played a mournful air in a minor key.

The Baroness Nerina appeared to be even more melancholy than her queen. The circles beneath her eyes had grown deeper and deeper in the weeks since the departure of the Mimbrate knights, and she seldom smiled. Finally she sighed and laid aside her embroidery.

"The sadness of thy heart doth resound in thy sighing, Nerina," the queen said gently. "Think not so of dangers and separation, lest thy spirits fail thee utterly."

"Instruct me in the art of banishing care, Highness," Nerina replied, "for I am in sore need of such teaching. My heart is bowed beneath a burden of concern, and try though I might to control them, my thoughts, like unruly children, return ever to the dreadful peril of my absent lord and our dearest friend."

"Be comforted in the knowledge that thy burden is shared by every lady in all of Mimbre, Nerina."

Nerina sighed again. "My care, however, lies in more mournful certainty. Other ladies, their affections firm-fixed on one beloved, can dare to hope that he might return from dreadful war unscathed; but I, who love two, can find no reason for such optimism. I must needs lose one at the least, and the prospect doth crush my soul."

There was quiet dignity in Nerina's open acceptance of the implications of the two loves that had become so entwined in her heart that they could no longer be separated. Mayaserana, in one of those brief flashes of insight which so sharply illuminated understanding, perceived that Nerina's divided heart lay at the very core of the tragedy that had lifted her, her husband, and Sir Mandorallen into the realms of sad legend. If Nerina could but love one more than the other, the tragedy would end, but so perfectly balanced was her love for her husband with her love for Sir Mandorallen that she had reached a point of absolute stasis, forever frozen between the two of them.

The queen sighed. Nerina's divided heart seemed somehow a symbol of divided Arendia, but, though the gentle heart of the suffering baroness might never be made one, Mayaserana was resolved to make a last effort to heal the breach between Mimbre and Asturia. To that end, she had summoned to the palace a deputation of the more stable leaders of the rebellious north, and her summons had appeared over a title she rarely used, Duchess of Asturia. At her instruction, the Asturians were even now drawing up a list of their grievances for her consideration.

Later on that same sunny afternoon, Mayaserana sat alone on the double throne of Arendia, painfully aware of the vacancy beside her.

The leader and spokesman of the group of Asturian noblemen was a Count Reldegen, a tall, thin man with iron gray hair and beard, who walked with the aid of a stout cane. Reldegen wore a rich green doublet and black hose, and, like the rest of the deputation, his sword was belted at his side. The fact that the Asturians came armed into the queen's presence had stirred some angry muttering, but Mayaserana had refused to listen to urgings that their weapons be taken from them.

"My Lord Reldegen," the queen greeted the Asturian as he limped toward the throne.

"Your Grace," he replied with a bow.

"Your *Majesty*," a Mimbrate courtier corrected him in a shocked voice.

"Her Grace summoned us as the Duchess of Asturia," Reldegen informed the courtier coolly. "That title commands more respect from us than other, more recent embellishments."

"Gentlemen, please," the queen said firmly. "Prithee, let us not commence hostilities anew. Our purpose here is to examine the possibilities of peace. I entreat thee, my Lord Reldegen, speak to the purpose. Unburden thyself of the causes of that rancor which hath so hardened the heart of Asturia. Speak freely, my Lord, and with no fear of reprisal for thy words." She looked quite sternly at her advisers. "It is our command that no man be taken to task for what is spoken here."

The Mimbrates glowered at the Asturians, and the Asturians scowled back.

"Your Grace," Reldegen began, "our chief complaint lies, I think, in the simple fact that our Mimbrate overlords refuse to recognize our titles. A title's an empty thing, really, but it implies a responsibility which has been denied to us. Most of us here are indifferent to the privileges of rank, but we keenly feel the frustration of being refused the chance to discharge our obligations. Our most talented men are compelled to waste their lives in idleness, and might I point out, your Grace, that the loss of that talent injures Arendia even more than it injures us."

"Well spoken, my Lord," the queen murmured.

"Might I respond, your Majesty," the aged, white-bearded Baron of Vo Serin inquired.

"Certainly, my Lord," Mayaserana replied. "Let us all be free and open with one another."

"The titles of the Asturian gentlemen are theirs for the asking," the baron declared. "For five centuries the crown hath awaited but the required oath of fealty to bestow them. No title may be granted or recognized until its owner swears allegiance to the crown."

"Unfortunately, my Lord," Reldegen said, "we are unable to so swear. The oaths of our ancestors to the Duke of Asturia are still in force, and we are still bound by them."

"The Asturian Duke of whom thou speakest died five hundred years ago," the old baron reminded him.

"But his line did not die with him," Reldegen pointed out. "Her Grace is his direct descendant, and our pledges of loyalty are still in force."

The queen stared first at one and then at the other. "I pray thee," she said, "correct me if my perception is awry. Is the import of what hath been revealed here that Arendia hath been divided for half a millennium by an ancient *formality*?"

Reldegen pursed his lips thoughtfully. "There's a bit more to it than that, your Grace, but that does seem to be the core of the problem."

"Five hundred years of strife and bloodshed over a *technicality*?"

Count Reldegen struggled with it. He started to speak several times, but broke off each time with a look of helpless perplexity. In the end he began to laugh. "It *is* sort of Arendish, isn't it?" he asked rather whimsically.

The old Baron of Vo Serin gave him a quick look, then he too began to chuckle. "I pray thee, my Lord Reldegen, lock this discovery in thy heart lest we all become the subject of general mirth. Let us not confirm the suspicion that abject stupidity is our most prevailing trait."

"Why was this absurdity not discovered previously?" Mayaserana demanded.

Count Reldegen shrugged sadly. "I suppose because Asturians and Mimbrates don't talk to each other, your Grace. We were always too eager to get to the fighting."

"Very well," the queen said crisply, "what is required to rectify this sorry confusion?"

Count Reldegen looked at the Baron. "A proclamation perhaps?" he suggested.

The old man nodded thoughtfully. "Her Majesty could release thee from thy previous oath. It hath not been common practice, but there are precedents."

"And then we all swear fealty to her as Queen of Arendia?"

"That would seem to satisfy all the demands of honor and propriety, yes."

"But I'm the same person, am I not?" the queen objected.

"Technically thou art not, your Majesty," the baron explained. "The Duchess of Asturia and the Queen of Arendia are separate entities. Thou art indeed two persons in one body."

"This is most confusing, gentlemen," Mayaserana observed.

"That's probably why no one noticed it before, your Grace," Reldegen told her. "Both you and your husband have two titles and two separate formal identities."

He smiled briefly. "I'm surprised that there was room on the throne for such a crowd." His face grew serious. "It won't be a cure-all, your Grace," he added. "The divisions between Mimbre and Asturia are so deep-seated that they'll take generations to erase."

"And wilt thou also swear fealty to my husband?" the queen asked.

"As the King of Arendia, yes; as the Duke of Mimbre, never."

"That will do for a start, my Lord. Let us see then to this proclamation. Let us with ink and parchment bandage our poor Arendia's most gaping wound."

"Beautifully put, your Grace," Reldegen said admiringly.

RAN BORUNE XXIII had spent almost his entire life inside the Imperial compound at Tol Honeth. His infrequent trips to the major cities of Tolnedra had, for the most part been made inside closed carriages. It was entirely probable that Ran Borune had never walked a continuous mile in his life, and a man who has not walked a mile has no real conception of what a mile is. From the very outset, his advisers despaired of ever making him understand the concept of distance.

The suggestion that ultimately resolved the difficulty came from a rather surprising source. A sometime tutor named Jeebers—a man who had narrowly escaped imprisonment or worse the previous summer—put forth the suggestion diffidently. Master Jeebers now did everything diffidently. His near brush with Imperial displeasure had forever extinguished the pompous self-importance that had previously marred his character. A number of his acquaintances were surprised to discover that they even liked the balding, skinny man now.

Master Jeebers had pointed out that if the Emperor could only see things in exact scale, he might then understand. Like so many good ideas that had surfaced from time to time in Tolnedra, this one immediately got out of hand. An entire acre of the Imperial grounds was converted into a scale replica of the border region of eastern Algaria and the opposing stretches of Mishrak ac Thull. To give it all perspective, a number of inch-high human figures were cast in lead to aid the Emperor in conceptualizing the field of operations.

The Emperor immediately announced that he'd really like to have more of the lead figures to aid his understanding of the masses of men involved, and a new industry was born in Tol Honeth. Overnight lead became astonishingly scarce.

In order that he might better see the field, the Emperor mounted each morning to the top of a thirty-foot-high tower that had hastily been erected for that purpose. There, with the aid of a great-voiced sergeant of the Imperial guard, the Emperor deployed his leaden regiments of infantry and cavalry in precise accordance with the latest dispatches from Algaria.

The general staff very nearly resigned their commissions en masse. They were, for the most part, men of advanced middle age, and joining the Emperor atop his tower each morning involved some strenuous climbing. They all tried at various times to explain to the beak-nosed little man that they could see just as well from the ground, but Ran Borune would have none of it.

"Morin, he's killing us," one portly general complained bitterly to the Emperor's chamberlain. "I'd rather go off to war than climb that ladder four times a day."

"Move the Drasnian pikemen four paces to the left!" the sergeant bellowed from the top of the tower, and a dozen men on the ground began redeploying the tiny lead figures.

"We all must serve in the capacity our Emperor chooses for us," Lord Morin replied philosophically.

"I don't see *you* climbing the ladder," the general accused.

"Our Emperor has chosen another capacity for me," Morin said rather smugly.

That evening the weary little Emperor sought his bed. "It's very exciting, Morin," he murmured drowsily, holding the velvet-lined case that contained the solid-gold figures representing Ce'Nedra and Rhodar and the rest of the army's leaders close to his chest, "but it's very tiring, too."

"Yes, your Majesty."

"There always seems to be so much that I still have to do."

"That's the nature of command, your Majesty," Morin observed.

But the Emperor had already dropped off.

Lord Morin removed the case from the Emperor's hands and carefully pulled the covers up around the sleeping man's shoulders. "Sleep, Ran Borune," he said very gently. "You can play with your little toy soldiers again tomorrow."

SADI THE EUNUCH had quietly left the palace at Sthiss Tor by a secret doorway that opened behind the slaves' quarters onto a shabby back street that twisted and turned in the general direction of the harbor. He had quite deliberately waited for the cover of the afternoon rainstorm and had dressed himself in the shabby clothing of a dockworker. Accompanying him was the one-eyed assassin, Is-sus, who also wore nondescript clothing. Sadi's security precautions were routine, but his choice of Issus as his companion was not. Issus was not a member of the palace guard nor of Sadi's personal retinue, but Sadi was not concerned on this afternoon's outing with appearances or proprieties. Issus was by and large uncor-rupted by palace politics and had a reputation for unswerving loyalty to whomever was paying him at the moment.

The two passed down the rainswept street to a certain disreputable establish-ment frequented by lower-class workers, and went through a rather noisy taproom to the maze of cubicles at the back, where other entertainments were provided. At the end of a foul-smelling hallway, a lean, hard-eyed woman, whose arms were cov-ered from wrist to elbow with cheap, gaudy bracelets, pointed wordlessly at a scarred door, then turned abruptly and disappeared through another doorway.

Behind the door lay a filthy room with only a bed for furniture. On the bed were two sets of clothing that smelled of tar and salt water, and sitting on the floor were two large tankards of lukewarm ale. Wordlessly, Sadi and Issus changed clothes. From beneath the soiled pillow, Issus pulled a pair of wigs and two sets of false whiskers.

"How can they drink this?" Sadi demanded, sniffing at one of the tankards and wrinkling his nose.

Issus shrugged. "Alorns have peculiar tastes. You don't have to drink it all, Sadi. Splash most of it on your clothes. Drasnian sailors spill a lot of ale when they're out in search of amusement. How do I look?"

Sadi gave him a quick glance. "Ridiculous," he replied. "Hair and a beard don't really suit you, Issus."

Issus laughed. "And they look particularly out of place on *you*." He shrugged and carefully poured ale down the front of his tar-spattered tunic. "I suppose we look enough like Drasnians to get by, and we certainly smell like Drasnians. Hook your beard on a little tighter, and let's get moving before it stops raining."

"Are we going out the back?"

Issus shook his head. "If somebody's following us, he'll be watching the back. We'll leave the way ordinary Drasnian sailors leave."

"And how is that?"

"I've made arrangements to have us thrown out."

Sadi had never been thrown out of any place before, and he found the experience not particularly amusing. The two burly ruffians who unceremoniously pitched him into the street were a bit rough about it, and Sadi picked up several scrapes and abrasions in the process.

Issus staggered to his feet and stood bawling curses at the closed door, then lurched over and pulled Sadi up out of the mud. Together they reeled in apparent drunkenness down the street toward the Drasnian enclave. Sadi noted that there had been two men in a doorway across the street when he and Issus had been ejected and that the two did not move to follow.

Once they entered the Drasnian enclave, Issus led the way rather quickly to the house of Droblek, the Drasnian port authority. They were admitted immediately and conveyed at once to a dimly lighted but comfortable room where the enormously fat Droblek sat sweating. With him was Count Melgon, the aristocratic ambassador from Tolnedra.

"Novel attire for the chief eunuch of Salmissra's household," Count Melgon observed as Sadi pulled off his wig and false beard.

"Just a bit of deception, my Lord Ambassador," Sadi replied. "I didn't particularly want this meeting to become general knowledge."

"Can he be trusted?" Droblek asked bluntly, pointing at Issus.

Sadi's expression became whimsical. "*Can* you be trusted, Issus?" he asked.

"You've paid me for up to the end of the month." Issus shrugged. "After that, we'll see. I might get a better offer."

"You see?" Sadi said to the two seated men. "Issus can be trusted until the end of the month—at least as much as anybody in Sthiss Tor can be trusted. One thing I've noticed about Issus—he's a simple, uncomplicated man. Once you buy him, he stays bought. I think it's referred to as professional ethics."

Droblek grunted sourly. "Do you suppose we could get to the point? Why did you go to so much trouble to arrange this meeting? Why didn't you just summon us to the palace?"

"My dear Droblek," Sadi murmured, "you know the kind of intrigue that infests the palace. I'd prefer that what passes between us remain more or less confidential. The matter itself is rather uncomplicated. I've been approached by the emissary of Taur Urgas."

The two regarded him with no show of surprise.

"I gather that you two already knew."

"We're hardly children, Sadi," Count Melgon told him.

"I am at present in negotiations with the new ambassador from Rak Goska," Sadi mentioned.

"Isn't that the third one so far this summer?" Melgon asked.

Sadi nodded. "The Murgos seem to be particularly susceptible to certain fevers which abound in the swamps."

"We've noticed that," Droblek said dryly. "What is your prognosis for the present emissary's continued good health?"

"I don't imagine he's any more immune than his countrymen. He's already beginning to feel unwell."

"Maybe he'll be lucky and recover," Droblek suggested.

"Not very likely," Issus said with an ugly laugh.

"The tendency of Murgo ambassadors to die unexpectedly has succeeded in keeping the negotiations moving very slowly," Sadi continued. "I'd like for you gentlemen to inform King Rhodar and Ran Borune that these delays will probably continue."

"Why?" Droblek asked.

"I want them to understand and appreciate my efforts in their present campaign against the Angarak kingdoms."

"Tolnedra has no involvement in that campaign," Melgon asserted quickly.

"Of course not." Sadi smiled.

"Just how far are you willing to go, Sadi?" Droblek asked curiously.

"That depends almost entirely upon who's winning at any given moment," Sadi replied urbanely. "If the Rivan Queen's campaign in the east begins to run into difficulties, I suspect that the pestilence will subside and the Murgo emissaries will stop dying so conveniently. I'd almost have to make an accommodation with Taur Urgas at that point."

"Don't you find that just a bit contemptible, Sadi?" Droblek asked acidly.

Sadi shrugged. "We're a contemptible sort of people, Droblek," he admitted, "but we survive. That's no mean accomplishment for a weak nation lying between two major powers. Tell Rhodar and Ran Borune that I'll stall the Murgos off for as long as things continue to go in their favor. I want them both to be aware of their obligation to me."

"And will you advise them when your position is about to change?" Melgon asked.

"Of course not," Sadi replied. "I'm corrupt, Melgon. I'm not stupid."

"You're not much of an ally, Sadi," Droblek told him.

"I never pretended to be. I'm looking out for myself. At the moment, my interests and yours happen to coincide, that's all. I *do*, however, expect to be remembered for my assistance."

"You're trying to play it both ways, Sadi," Droblek accused him bluntly.

"I know." Sadi smiled. "Disgusting, isn't it?"

QUEEN ISLENA OF Cherek was in an absolute panic. This time Merel had gone too far. The advice they had received from Porenn had *seemed* quite sound—had indeed raised the possibility of a brilliant stroke which would disarm

Grodeg and the Bear-cult once and for all. The imagined prospect of the helpless rage into which this would plummet the towering ecclesiast was almost a satisfaction in itself. Like so many people, Queen Islena took such pleasure in an imagined triumph that the real thing became almost too much trouble. The victories of the imagination involved no risks, and a confrontation with an enemy always ended satisfactorily when both sides of the conversation came from one's own daydreams. Left to her own devices, Islena would probably have been content to let it go at that.

Merel, however, was less easily satisfied. The plan devised by the little queen of Drasnia had been quite sound, but it suffered from one flaw—they did not have enough men to bring it off. Merel, however, had located an ally with certain resources and had brought him into the queen's inner circle. A group of men in Cherek had not accompanied Anheg and the fleet to Algaria largely because they were not the sort of men who made good sailors. At Merel's stern-faced insistence, the Queen of Cherek suddenly developed an overpowering enthusiasm for hunting. It was in the forest, safe from prying ears, that the details of the coup were worked out.

"When you kill a snake, you cut off its head," Torvik the huntsman had pointed out as he, Merel, and Islena sat in a forest glade while Torvik's men roved through the woods harvesting enough game to make it appear that Islena had spent her day in a frenzy of slaughter. "You don't accomplish all that much by snipping pieces off its tail an inch or so at a time," the broad-shouldered huntsman continued. "The Bear-cult isn't really that concentrated in one place. With a little luck, we can gather up all the important members presently in Val Alorn in one sweep. That should irritate our snake enough to make him stick his neck out. Then we'll simply chop off his head."

Torvik's use of such terminology had made the queen wince. She had not been entirely sure that the blunt, grizzled forester had been speaking figuratively.

And now it had been done. Torvik and his huntsmen had moved quietly through the dark streets of Val Alorn for the entire night, gathering up the sleeping members of the Bear-cult, marching them in groups to the harbor and then locking them in the holds of waiting ships. Because of their years of experience, the hunters had been very thorough in rounding up their quarry. By morning, the only members of the Bear-cult left in the city were the High Priest of Belar and the dozen or so underpriests lodged in the temple.

Queen Islena sat, pale and trembling, on the throne of Cherek. She wore her purple gown and her gold crown. In her hand she held a scepter. The scepter had a comforting weight to it and could possibly be used as a weapon in an emergency. The queen was positive that an emergency was about to descend on her.

"This is all your fault, Merel," she bitterly accused her blond friend. "If you'd just left things alone, we wouldn't be in this mess."

"We'd be in a worse one," Merel replied coldly. "Pull yourself together, Islena. It's done now, and you can't undo it."

"Grodeg terrifies me," Islena blurted.

"He won't be armed. He won't be able to hurt you."

"I'm only a woman," Islena quailed. "He'll roar at me in that awful voice of his, and I'll go absolutely to pieces."

"Stop being such a coward, Islena," Merel snapped. "Your timidity's brought Cherek right to the edge of disaster. Every time Grodeg's raised his voice to you, you've given him anything he wanted—just because you're afraid of harsh talk. Are you a child? Does noise frighten you that much?"

"You forget yourself, Merel," Islena flared suddenly. "I *am* queen, after all."

"Then by all the Gods, *be* queen! Stop behaving like a silly, frightened serving girl. Sit up straight on your throne as if you had some iron in your backbone—and pinch your cheeks. You're as pale as a bedsheet." Merel's face hardened. "Listen to me, Islena," she said. "If you give even one hint that you're starting to weaken, I'll have Torvik run his spear into Grodeg right here in the throne room."

"You wouldn't!" Islena gasped. "You *can't* kill a priest."

"He's a man—just like any other man," Merel declared harshly. "If you stick a spear in his belly, he'll die."

"Not even Anheg would dare to do that."

"I'm not Anheg."

"You'll be cursed!"

"I'm not afraid of curses."

Torvik came into the throne room, a broad-bladed boarspear held negligently in one big hand. "He's coming," he announced laconically.

"Oh, dear," Islena quavered.

"Stop that!" Merel snapped.

Grodeg was livid with rage as he strode into the throne room. His white robe was rumpled as if he had thrown it on hastily, and his white hair and beard were uncombed. "I will speak with the queen alone!" he thundered as he approached across the rush-strewn floor.

"That is the queen's decision to make, not yours, my Lord High Priest," Merel advised him in a flinty voice.

"Does the wife of the Earl of Trellheim speak for the throne?" Grodeg demanded of Islena.

Islena faltered, then saw Torvik standing directly behind the tall priest. The boarspear in his hand was no longer so negligently grasped. "Calm yourself, revered Grodeg," the queen said, quite suddenly convinced that the life of the infuriated priest hinged not only on her words but even on her tone of voice. At the tiniest quaver, Merel would give the signal, and Torvik would sink that broad, sharp blade into Grodeg's back with about as much emotion as he showed about swatting a fly.

"I want to see you alone," Grodeg repeated stubbornly.

"No."

"No?" he roared incredulously.

"You heard me, Grodeg," she told him. "And stop shouting at me. My hearing is quite good."

He gaped at her, then quickly recovered. "Why have all my friends been arrested?" he demanded.

"They were not arrested, my Lord High Priest," the queen replied. "They have all volunteered to join my husband's fleet."

"Ridiculous!" he snorted.

"I think you'd better choose your words a bit more carefully, Grodeg," Merel told him. "The queen's patience with your impertinence is wearing thin."

"Impertinence?" he exclaimed. "How *dare* you speak that way to me?" He drew himself up and fixed a stern eye on the queen. "I insist upon a private audience," he told her in a thunderous voice.

The voice which had always cowed her before quite suddenly irritated Islena. She was trying to save this idiot's life, and he kept shouting at her. "My Lord Grodeg," she said with an unaccustomed hint of steel in her voice, "if you bellow at me one more time, I'll have you muzzled."

His eyes widened in amazement.

"We have nothing to discuss in private, my Lord," the queen continued. "All that remains is for you to receive your instructions—which you will follow to the letter. It is our decree that you will proceed directly to the harbor, where you will board the ship which is waiting to transport you to Algaria. There you will join the forces of Cherek in the campaign against the Angaraks."

"I refuse!" Grodeg retorted.

"Think carefully, my Lord Grodeg," Merel purred. "The queen has given you a royal command. Refusal could be considered treason."

"I am the High Priest of Belar," Grodeg ground out between clenched teeth, obviously having great difficulty in modulating his voice. "You wouldn't dare ship me off like some peasant conscript."

"I wonder if the High Priest of Belar might like to make a small wager on that," Torvik said with deceptive mildness. He set the butt of his spear on the floor, took a stone from the pouch at his belt and began to hone the already razor-sharp blade. The steely sound had an obviously chilling effect on Grodeg.

"You will go to the harbor now, Grodeg," Islena told him, "and you will get on that ship. If you do not, you will go to the dungeon, where you will keep the rats company until my husband returns. Those are your choices: join Anheg or join the rats. Decide quickly. You're starting to bore me, and quite frankly, I'm sick of the sight of you."

QUEEN PORENN OF Drasnia was in the nursery, ostensibly feeding her infant son. Out of respect for the queen's person, she was unspied upon while she was nursing. Porenn, however, was not alone. Javelin, the bone-thin chief of Drasnian intelligence, was with her. For the sake of appearance, Javelin was dressed in a serving maid's gown and cap, and he looked surprisingly feminine in the disguise he wore with no apparent trace of self-consciousness.

"Are there really that many cultists in the intelligence service?" the queen asked, a little dismayed.

Javelin sat with his back politely turned. "I'm afraid so, your Highness. We should have been more alert, but we had other things on our minds."

Porenn thought about it for a moment, unconsciously rocking her suckling baby. "Islena's moving already, isn't she?" she asked.

"That's the word I received this morning," Javelin replied, "Grodeg's on his way to the mouth of the Aldur River already, and the queen's men are moving out into the countryside, rounding up every member of the cult as they go."

"Will it in any way hamper our operations to jerk that many people out of Boktor?"

"We can manage, your Highness," Javelin assured her. "We might have to speed up the graduation of the current class at the academy and finish their training on the job, but we'll manage."

"Very well then, Javelin," Porenn decided. "Ship them all out. Get every cult member out of Boktor, and separate them. I want them sent to the most miserable duty posts you can devise, and I don't want any of them within fifty leagues of any other one. There will be no excuses, no sudden illnesses, and no resignations. Give each of them something to do, and then *make* him do it. I want every Bear-cultist who's crept into the intelligence service out of Boktor by nightfall."

"It'll be my pleasure, Porenn," Javelin said. "Oh, incidentally, that Nadrak merchant, Yarblek, is back from Yar Nadrak, and he wants to talk to you about the salmon runs again. He seems to have this obsessive interest in fish."

CHAPTER TWELVE

The raising of the Cherek fleet to the top of the eastern escarpment took a full two weeks, and King Rhodar chafed visibly at the pace of the operation.

"You knew this was going to take time, Rhodar," Ce'Nedra said to him as he fumed and sweated, pacing back and forth with frequent dark looks at the towering cliff face. "Why are you so upset?"

"Because the ships are right out in the open, Ce'Nedra," he replied testily. "There's no way to hide them or disguise them while they're being raised. Those ships are the key to our whole campaign, and if somebody on the other side starts putting a few things together, we might have to meet all of Angarak instead of just the Thulls."

"You worry too much," she told him. "Cho-Hag and Korodullin are burning everything in sight up there. 'Zakath and Taur Urgas have other things to think about beside what we're hauling up the cliff."

"It must be wonderful to be so unconcerned about things," he said sarcastically.

"Be nice, Rhodar," she said.

General Varana, still scrupulously dressed in his Tolnedran mantle, limped toward them with that studiously diffident expression that indicated he was about to make another suggestion.

"Varana," King Rhodar burst out irritably, "why don't you put on your uniform?"

"Because I'm not really officially here, your Majesty," the general replied calmly. "Tolnedra *is* neutral in this affair, you'll recall."

"That's a fiction, and we all know it."

"A necessary one, however. The Emperor is still holding diplomatic channels open to Taur Urgas and 'Zakath. Those discussions would deteriorate if someone saw a Tolnedran general swaggering around in full uniform." He paused briefly. "Would a small suggestion offend your Majesty?" he asked.

"That all depends on the suggestion," Rhodar retorted. Then he made a face and apologized. "I'm sorry, Varana. This delay's making me bad-tempered. What did you have in mind?"

"I think you might want to give some thought to moving your command operations up to the top about now. You'll want things running smoothly by the time the bulk of your infantry arrives, and it usually takes a couple of days to iron out the wrinkles when you set things up."

King Rhodar stared at a Cherek ship being hoisted ponderously up the cliff face. "I'm not going to ride up on one of those, Varana," he declared flatly.

"It's absolutely safe, your Majesty," Varana assured him. "I've made the trip myself several times. Even Lady Polgara went up that way just this morning."

"Polgara could fly down if something went wrong," Rhodar said. "I don't have her advantages. Can you imagine the size of the hole I'd make in the ground if I fell that far?"

"The alternative is extremely strenuous, your Majesty. There are several ravines running down from the top. They've been leveled out a bit so that the horses can go up, but they're still *very* steep."

"A little sweating won't hurt me."

Varana shrugged. "As your Majesty wishes."

"I'll keep you company, Rhodar," Ce'Nedra offered brightly.

He gave her a suspicious look.

"I don't really trust machines either," she confessed. "I'll go change clothes, and then we can start."

"You want to do it *today*?" His voice was plaintive.

"Why put it off?"

"I can think of a dozen reasons."

The term "very steep" turned out to be a gross understatement. "Precipitous" might have been more accurate. The incline made riding horses out of the question, but ropes had been strung along the steeper stretches to aid in the climb. Ce'Nedra, dressed in one of her short Dryad tunics, scampered hand over hand up the ropes with the agility of a squirrel. King Rhodar's pace, however, was much slower.

"Please stop groaning, Rhodar," she told him after they had climbed for an hour or so. "You sound like a sick cow."

"That's hardly fair, Ce'Nedra," he wheezed, stopping to mop his streaming face.

"I never promised to be fair," she retorted with an impish grin. "Come along, we still have a long way to go." And she flitted up another fifty yards or so.

"Don't you think you're a little underdressed?" he puffed disapprovingly, staring up at her. "Proper ladies don't show off so much leg."

"What's wrong with my legs?"

"They're bare—that's what's wrong with them."

"Don't be such a prig. I'm comfortable. That's all that matters. Are you coming or not?"

Rhodar groaned again. "Isn't it almost time for lunch?"

"We just had lunch."

"Did we? I'd forgotten already."

"You always seem to forget your last meal—usually before the crumbs have been brushed away."

"That's the nature of a fat man, Ce'Nedra." He sighed. "The last meal is history. It's the next one that's important." He stared mournfully up the brutal trail ahead and groaned again.

"This was all your idea," she heartlessly reminded him.

The sun was low in the west when they reached the top. As King Rhodar collapsed, Princess Ce'Nedra looked around curiously. The fortifications which had been erected along the top of the escarpment were extensive and quite imposing. The walls were of earth and stone and were perhaps thirty feet high. Through an open gate the princess saw a series of other, lower walls, each fronted by a ditch bristling with sharpened stakes and thorny brambles. At various points along the main wall rose imposing blockhouses, and within the walls were neat rows of huts for the soldiers.

The forts swarmed with men, and their various activities raised an almost perpetual cloud of dust. A party of Algar clansmen, smoke-stained and mounted on spent-looking horses, rode slowly in through the gate; and a few moments later, a contingent of gleaming Mimbrate knights, pennons snapping from their lances and the great hoofs of their chargers clattering on the stony ground, rode out in search of yet another town to destroy.

The huge hoists at the edge of the escarpment creaked and groaned under the weight of the Cherek ships being raised from the plain below; some distance away, within the fortified walls, the growing fleet sat awaiting the final portage to the headwaters of the upper River Mardu, some fifty leagues distant.

Polgara, accompanied by Durnik and the towering Barak, approached to greet the princess and the prostrate King of Drasnia.

"How was the climb?" Barak inquired.

"Ghastly," Rhodar wheezed. "Does anybody have anything to eat? I think I've melted off about ten pounds."

"It doesn't show," Barak told him.

"That sort of exertion isn't really good for you, Rhodar," Polgara told the gasping monarch. "Why were you so stubborn about it?"

"Because I have an absolute horror of heights," Rhodar replied. "I'd climb ten times as far to avoid being hauled up that cliff by those contraptions. The idea of all that empty air under me makes my flesh creep."

Barak grinned. "That's a lot of creeping."

"Will somebody *please* give me something to eat?" Rhodar asked in an anguished tone of voice.

"A bit of cold chicken?" Durnik offered solicitously, handing him a well-browned chicken leg.

"Where did you ever find a chicken?" Rhodar exclaimed, eagerly seizing the leg.

"The Thulls brought some with them," Durnik told him.

"Thulls?" Ce'Nedra gasped. "What are Thulls doing here?"

"Surrendering," Durnik replied. "Whole villages of them have been showing up for the past week or so. They walk up to the edge of the ditches along the front of the fortification and sit down and wait to be captured. They're very patient about it. Sometimes it's a day or so before anybody has the time to go out and capture them, but they don't seem to mind."

"Why do they want to be captured?" Ce'Nedra asked him.

"There aren't any Grolims here," Durnik explained. "No altars to Torak and no sacrificial knives. The Thulls seem to feel that getting away from that sort of thing is worth the inconvenience of being captured. We take them in and put them to work on the fortifications. They're good workers, if you give them the proper supervision."

"Is that entirely safe?" Rhodar asked around a mouthful of chicken. "There might be spies among them."

Durnik nodded. "We know," he said, "but the spies are usually Grolims. A Thull doesn't have the mental equipment to be a spy, so the Grolims have to do it themselves."

Rhodar lowered his chicken leg in astonishment. "You're letting Grolims inside the fortifications?" he demanded.

"It's nothing all that serious," Durnik told him. "The Thulls know who the Grolims are, and we let them deal with the problem. They usually take them a mile or so along the escarpment and then throw them off. At first they wanted to do it right here, but some of their elders pointed out that it might not be polite to drop Grolims down on top of the men working below, so they take them some place where they won't bother anybody when they fall. A very considerate people, the Thulls. One could almost get to like them."

"You've sunburned your nose, Ce'Nedra," Polgara told the little princess. "Didn't you think of wearing a hat?"

"Hats give me a headache." Ce'Nedra shrugged. "A little sunburn won't hurt me."

"You have an appearance to maintain, dear," Polgara pointed out. "You're not going to look very queenly with your nose peeling."

"It's nothing to worry about, Lady Polgara. You can fix it, can't you? You know—" Ce'Nedra made a little gesture with her hand that was meant to look magical.

Polgara gave her a long, chilly look.

King Anheg of Cherek, accompanied by the broad-shouldered Rivan Warder, approached them. "Did you have a nice climb?" he asked Rhodar pleasantly.

"How would you like a punch in the nose?" Rhodar asked him.

King Anheg laughed coarsely. "My," he said, "aren't we grumpy today? I've just had some news from home that ought to brighten your disposition a bit."

"Dispatches?" Rhodar groaned, hauling himself wearily to his feet.

Anheg nodded. "They sent them up from down below while you were getting your exercise. You're not going to believe what's been going on back there."

"Try me."

"You absolutely won't believe it."

"Anheg, spit it out."

"We're about to get some reinforcements. Islena and Porenn have been very busy these last few weeks."

Polgara looked at him sharply.

"Do you know something?" Anheg said, holding out a folded dispatch. "I wasn't even aware of the fact that Islena knew how to read and write, and now I get this."

"Don't be cryptic, Anheg," Polgara told him. "What have the ladies been up to?"

"I gather that after we left, the Bear-cult began to make itself a bit obnoxious. Grodeg apparently felt that with the men out of the way, he could take over. He started throwing his weight around in Val Alorn, and cult members began to surface in the headquarters of Drasnian intelligence in Boktor. It looks as if they've been making preparations for something for years. Anyway, Porenn and Islena began passing information back and forth, and when they realized how close Grodeg was to getting his hands on real power in the two kingdoms, they took steps. Porenn ordered all the cult members out of Boktor—sent them to the most miserable duty posts she could think of—and Islena rounded up the Bear-cult in Val Alorn—every last one of them—and shipped them out to join the army."

"They did *what*?" Rhodar gasped.

"Isn't it amazing?" A slow grin spread across Anheg's coarse face. "The beauty of the whole thing is that Islena could get away with it, while I couldn't. Women aren't supposed to be aware of the subtleties involved in arresting priests and noblemen—the need for evidence against them and so on—so what would be gross impropriety on my part will be laughed off as ignorance on hers. I'll have to apologize to Grodeg, of course, but it'll be after the fact. The cult will be here, and they'll have no honest reason to go back home."

Rhodar's answering grin was every bit as wicked as Anheg's. "How did Grodeg take it?"

"He was absolutely livid. I guess Islena faced him down personally. She gave him the choice of joining us or going to the dungeon."

"You can't put the High Priest of Belar in a dungeon," Rhodar exclaimed.

"Islena didn't know that, and Grodeg *knew* that she didn't. She'd have had him chained to the wall in the deepest hole she could find before anybody had gotten around to telling her that it was illegal. Can't you just see my Islena delivering that kind of ultimatum to the old windbag?" There was a note of fierce pride in Anheg's voice.

King Rhodar's face grew very sly. "There's bound to be some rather hot fighting in this campaign sooner or later," he noted.

Anheg nodded.

"The Bear-cult prides itself on its fighting ability, doesn't it?"

Anheg nodded again, grinning.

"They'd be perfect for spearheading any attacks, wouldn't they?"

Anheg's grin grew positively vicious.

"I imagine that their casualties will be heavy," the King of Drasnia suggested.

"It's in a good cause, after all," Anheg replied piously.

"If you two have quite finished gloating, I think it's time I got the princess in out of the sun," Polgara told the two grinning monarchs.

The fortified positions atop the escarpment bustled with activity for the next several days. Even as the last of the Cherek ships were raised up the cliffs, the Algars and Mimbrates extended their depredations out into the Thullish countryside. "There aren't any crops standing for fifty leagues in any direction," Hettar reported back. "We'll have to go out farther to find anything else to burn."

"You find many Murgos?" Barak asked the hawk-faced man.

"A few." Hettar shrugged. "Not enough to make it interesting, but we run across one every now and then."

"How's Mandorallen doing?"

"I haven't seen him for a few days," Hettar replied. "There's a lot of smoke coming from the direction he went, though, so I imagine he's keeping busy."

"What's the country like out there?" King Anheg asked.

"Not bad, once you get past the uplands. The part of Thulldom along the escarpment here is pretty forbidding."

"What do you mean by forbidding? I've got to haul ships through that country."

"Rock, sand, a few thornbushes and no water," Hettar replied. "And it's hotter than the back door of a furnace."

"Thanks," Anheg said.

"You wanted to know," Hettar told him. "Excuse me. I need a fresh horse and some more torches."

"You're going out again?" Barak asked him.

"It's something to do."

Once the last of the ships had been raised, the Drasnian hoists began lifting tons of food and equipment that soon swelled King Fulrach's supply dumps within the forts to overflowing. The Thullish prisoners proved to be an invaluable asset, carrying whatever burden they were told to carry without complaint or hesitation. Their coarse features shone with such simpleminded gratitude and eagerness to please that Ce'Nedra found it impossible to hate them, even though they were technically the enemy. Slowly, bit by bit, the princess discovered the facts that made the lives of the Thullish people such an unrelieved horror. There was not a family among them that had not lost several members to the knives of the Grolims—husbands, wives, children, and parents had all been selected for sacrifice, and the thought uppermost in every Thull's life was to avoid the same fate at any cost. The perpetual terror had erased every hint of human affection from the Thull's makeup. He lived in dreadful isolation, without love, without companionship, without any feeling but constant anxiety and dread. The reputedly insatiable appetite of Thullish women had nothing whatsoever to do with morals or lack of them. It was a simple matter of survival. To escape the knife, a Thullish woman was forced to remain perpetually pregnant. She was not driven by lust, but by fear, and her fear dehumanized her entirely.

"How can they live that way?" the princess burst out to Lady Polgara as the two of them returned to their makeshift quarters in the stout blockhouse which had been erected inside the walls for the use of the leaders of the army. "Why don't they rebel and drive the Grolims out?"

"And just who's supposed to lead a rebellion, Ce'Nedra?" Polgara asked her calmly. "The Thulls know that there are Grolims who can pick the thoughts from a man's mind as easily as you'd pick fruit in an orchard. If a Thull even considered organizing some kind of resistance, he'd be the next one dragged to the altar."

"But their lives are so *horrible*," Ce'Nedra objected.

"Perhaps we can change that," Polgara said. "In a way what we're trying to do is not only for the benefit of the west, but for the Angaraks as well. If we win, they'll be liberated from the Grolims. They might not thank us at first, but in time they might learn to appreciate it."

"Why shouldn't they thank us?"

"Because if we win, dear, it'll be because we've killed their God. That's a very hard thing to thank someone for."

"But Torak's a monster."

"He's still their God," Polgara replied. "The loss of one's God is a very subtle and terrible injury. Ask the Ulgos what it's like to live without one. It's been five thousand years since UL became their God, and they still remember what it was like before he accepted them."

"We *are* going to win, aren't we?" Ce'Nedra asked suddenly, all her fears flooding to the surface.

"I don't know, Ce'Nedra," Polgara answered quietly. "No one does—not me, not Beldin, not my father, not even Aldur. All we can do is try."

"What will happen if we lose?" the princess asked in a tiny, frightened voice.

"We'll be enslaved in exactly the same way the Thulls are," Polgara replied quietly. "Torak will become King and God over the entire world. The other Gods will be banished forever, and the Grolims will be unleashed upon us all."

"I won't live in that kind of world," Ce'Nedra declared.

"None of us would care to."

"Did you ever meet Torak?" the princess asked suddenly.

Polgara nodded. "Once or twice—the last time was at Vo Mimbre just before his duel with Brand."

"What's he really like?"

"He's a God. The force of his mind is overwhelming. When he speaks to you, you must listen to him—and when he commands, you *must* obey him."

"Not *you*, certainly."

"I don't think you understand, dear." Polgara's face was grave, and her glorious eyes were as distant as the moon. Without seeming to think about it, she reached out, picked up Errand and sat him on her lap. The child smiled at her and, as he so often did, he reached out and touched the white lock at her brow. "There's a compulsion in Torak's voice that's almost impossible to resist," she continued. "You *know* that he's twisted and evil, but when he speaks to you, your will to resist crumbles, and you're suddenly very weak and afraid."

"Surely *you* weren't afraid."

"You still don't understand. Of course I was afraid. We all were—even my father. Pray that you never meet Torak. He's not some petty Grolim like Chamdar or a scheming old wizard like Ctuchik. He's a God. He's hideously maimed, and at some point he was thwarted. Something he needed—something so profound that no human could even conceive of it—was denied to him, and that refusal or rejection drove him mad. His madness is not like the madness of Taur Urgas, who, in spite of everything is still human. Torak's madness is the madness of a God—a being who can *make* his diseased imaginings come to pass. Only the Orb can truly withstand him. I could perhaps resist him for a time, but if he lays the full force of his will upon me, ultimately I'll have to give him what he wants—and what he wants from me is too dreadful to think about."

"I don't exactly follow you, Lady Polgara."

Garion's aunt looked gravely at the tiny girl. "Perhaps you don't at that," she said. "It has to do with a part of the past that the Tolnedran Historical Society chooses to ignore. Sit down, Ce'Nedra, and I'll try to explain."

The princess sat on a rude bench in their rough chamber. Polgara's mood was unusual—very quiet, even pensive. She placed her arms about Errand and held him close, nestling her cheek against his blond curls as if taking comfort from the contact with this small boy. "There are two Prophecies, Ce'Nedra," she explained in her rich voice, "but the time's coming when there'll only be one. Everything that is or was or is yet to be will become a part of whichever Prophecy prevails. Every man, every woman, every child has two possible destinies. For some, the differences are not all that great, but in my case, they're rather profound."

"I don't quite understand."

"In the Prophecy which we serve—the one that has brought us here—I'm Polgara the sorceress, daughter to Belgarath and guardian to Belgarion."

"And in the other?"

"In the other, I am the bride of Torak."

Ce'Nedra gasped.

"And now you see why I was afraid," Polgara continued. "I've been terrified of Torak since my father first explained this to me when I was no older than you are now. I'm not so much afraid for myself, but more because I know that if I falter—if Torak's will overpowers mine—then the Prophecy we serve will fail. Torak will not only win me, but all of mankind as well. At Vo Mimbre, he called to me, and I felt—very briefly—the awful compulsion to run to him. But I defied him. I've never done anything in my life that was so hard to do. It was *my* defiance, however, that drove him into the duel with Brand, and only in that duel could the power of the Orb be released against him. My father gambled everything on the strength of my will. The old wolf is a great gambler sometimes."

"Then if—" Ce'Nedra could not say it.

"If Garion loses?" Polgara said it so calmly that it was quite obvious that she had considered the possibility many times before. "Then Torak will come to claim his bride, and there won't be any power on earth sufficient to stop him."

"I'd sooner die," the princess blurted.

"So would I, Ce'Nedra, but that option may not be open to me. Torak's will is so much stronger than mine that he may be able to take from me the ability or even the desire to will myself out of existence. If it should happen, it may very well be that I'll be deliriously happy to be his chosen and beloved—but deep inside, I think that a part of me will be screaming and will continue to scream in horror down through all the endless centuries to the very end of days."

It was too horrible to think about. Unable to restrain herself, the princess threw herself on her knees, clasped her arms about Polgara and Errand, and burst into tears.

"Now, now, there's no need to cry, Ce'Nedra," Polgara told her gently, smoothing the sobbing girl's hair with her hand. "Garion still hasn't reached the City of Endless Night, and Torak's still asleep. There's a little time left. And who knows? We might even win."

CHAPTER THIRTEEN

Once the Cherek fleet had been raised, the pace of activities within the fortifications began to quicken. King Rhodar's infantry units began to arrive from the encampment at the Aldur River to make the tortuous climb up the narrow ravines to the top of the escarpment; lines of wagons from the main supply dumps freighted food and equipment to the base of the cliff where the great hoists waited to lift the supplies up the mile-high basalt face; and the Mimbrate and Algar raiding parties moved out, usually before dawn, in their now far-flung search for as yet unravaged towns and crops. The depredations of the raiders, their short, savage sieges of poorly fortified Thullish towns and villages, and the mile-wide swaths of fire that they cut through fields of ripe grain had finally stung the sluggish Thulls into poorly organized attempts at resistance. The Thulls, however, inevitably raced to the last point of Mimbrate attack and arrived hours or even days too late, to discover only smoking ruins, dead soldiers, and terrified and dispossessed townsmen, or, when they attempted to intercept the swiftly moving Algars, they normally found only acre upon acre of blackened earth. The raiders had moved on, and the desperate attempts of the Thulls to catch up with them were entirely futile.

The notion of attacking the forts from which the raiders operated did not occur to the Thulls, or if it did, it was quickly dismissed. The Thulls were not emotionally suited to attacking heavily defended fortifications. They much preferred dashing about, chasing fires, and complaining bitterly to their Murgo and Mallorean allies about the lack of support they were receiving. The Malloreans of

Emperor 'Zakath steadfastly refused to emerge from their staging areas around Thull Zelik. The Murgos of Taur Urgas, however, did make a few sorties in southern Thulldom, in part as a gesture toward the notion of Angarak unity—but more, King Rhodar surmised, as a part of their overall maneuvering for position. Murgo scouts were even occasionally discovered in the vicinity of the forts themselves. In order to sweep the area clear of these prying Murgo eyes, patrols went out every day from the forts to range through the arid hills. The parched, rocky valleys near the forts were randomly searched by Drasnian pikemen and platoons of legionnaires. Algar clansmen, supposedly resting from their long-range raids, amused themselves with an impromptu game they called "Murgo hunting." They made a great show of their frequent excursions and piously insisted that they were sacrificing their rest time out of a sense of responsibility for the security of the forts. They did not, of course, fool anybody with their protestations.

"The area *does* need to be patrolled, Rhodar," King Cho-Hag insisted. "My children are performing a necessary duty, after all."

"Duty?" Rhodar snorted. "Put an Algar on a horse and show him a hill he hasn't seen the backside of yet, and he'll always find an excuse to go take a look."

"You wrong us," Cho-Hag replied with a look of hurt innocence.

"I *know* you."

Ce'Nedra and her two closest companions had watched the periodic departure of the lighthearted Algar horsemen with increasingly sour expressions. Though Ariana was perhaps more sedentary in her habits and was accustomed, as all Mimbrate ladies were, to waiting quite patiently while the men were out playing, Adara, Garion's Algar cousin, felt her confinement most keenly. Like all Algars, she felt a deepseated need to have the wind in her face and the thunder of hoofs in her ears. She grew petulant after a time and sighed often.

"And what shall we do today, ladies?" Ce'Nedra asked the two of them brightly one morning after breakfast. "How shall we amuse ourselves until lunchtime?" She said it rather extravagantly, since she already had plans for the day.

"There is always embroidery," Ariana suggested. "It doth pleasantly occupy the fingers and eyes while leaving the mind and lips free for conversation."

Adara sighed deeply.

"Or maybe we might go and observe my lord as he instructs his serfs in their warlike preparations." Ariana usually found some excuse to watch Lelldorin for at least half of each day.

"I'm not sure that I'm up to watching a group of men murder hay bales with arrows again today," Adara said a bit waspishly.

Ce'Nedra moved quickly to head off any incipient bickering. "We could make an inspection tour," she suggested archly.

"Ce'Nedra, we've looked at every blockhouse and every hut within the walls a dozen times already," Adara said with some asperity, "and if I have some polite old sergeant explain the workings of a catapult to me one more time, I think I'll scream."

"We have not, however, inspected the outer fortifications, have we?" the princess asked slyly. "Wouldn't you say that's part of our duty too?"

Adara looked at her quickly, and then a slow smile appeared on her face. "Absolutely," she agreed. "I'm surprised that we hadn't thought of that before. We've been most neglectful, haven't we?"

Ariana's face took on a worried frown. "King Rhodar, I fear, would be most strenuous in his objections to such a plan."

"Rhodar isn't here," Ce'Nedra pointed out. "He's off with King Fulrach taking an inventory of the supply dumps."

"Lady Polgara would most certainly not approve," Ariana suggested, though her tone indicated that she was weakening.

"Lady Polgara is conferring with Beldin the sorcerer," Adara mentioned, her eyes dancing mischievously.

Ce'Nedra smirked. "That rather leaves us to our own devices, doesn't it, ladies?"

"We shall be soundly scolded upon our return," Ariana said.

"And we'll all be very contrite, won't we?" Ce'Nedra giggled.

A quarter of an hour later, the princess and her two friends, dressed in soft black leather Algar riding clothes, passed at a canter out through the central gate of the vast fort. They were accompanied by Olban, the youngest son of the Rivan Warder. Olban had not liked the idea, but Ce'Nedra had given him no time to object and definitely no time to send a message to anyone who could step in and stop the whole excursion. Olban looked worried, but, as always, he accompanied the little Rivan Queen without question.

The stake-studded trenches in front of the walls were very interesting, but one trench looked much like another, and it took a rare mind indeed to find much pleasure in the finer points of excavation.

"Very nice," Ce'Nedra said brightly to a Drasnian pikeman standing guard atop a high mound of dirt. "Splendid ditches—and all those excellently sharp stakes." She looked out at the arid landscape before the fortifications. "Where did you ever find all the wood for them?"

"The Sendars brought it in, your Majesty," he replied, "from someplace up north, I think. We had the Thulls cut and sharpen the stakes for us. They're quite good stake-makers—if you tell them what you want."

"Didn't a mounted patrol go out this way about half an hour ago?" Ce'Nedra asked him.

"Yes, your Majesty. Lord Hettar of Algaria and some of his men. They went off that way." The guard pointed toward the south.

"Ah," Ce'Nedra said. "If anyone should ask, tell them that we're going out to join him. We should return in a few hours."

The guard looked a bit dubious about that, but Ce'Nedra moved quickly to head off any objections. "Lord Hettar promised to wait for us just beyond the south end of the fortifications," she told him. She turned to her companions. "We really mustn't keep him waiting too long. You ladies took absolutely *too* much time changing clothes." She smiled winsomely at the guard. "You know how it is," she said. "The riding habit must be just so, and the hair absolutely *has* to be brushed one last time. Sometimes it takes forever. Come along, ladies. We must hurry, or Lord Hettar will be vexed with us." With a brainless little giggle, the princess wheeled Noble and rode south at a gallop.

"Ce'*Nedra*," Ariana exclaimed in a shocked voice once they were out of earshot, "you *lied* to him."

"Of course."

"But that's dreadful."

"Not nearly as dreadful as spending another day embroidering daisies on a stupid petticoat," the princess replied.

They left the fortifications and crossed a low, burned-brown string of hills. The broad valley beyond was enormous. Dun-brown and treeless mountains reared up fully twenty miles away at the valley's far end. They cantered down into that vast emptiness, feeling dwarfed into insignificance by the colossal landscape. Their horses seemed no more than ants crawling toward the indifferent mountains.

"I hadn't realized it was so big," Ce'Nedra murmured, shading her eyes to gaze at the distant hilltops.

The floor of the valley was as flat as a tabletop, and it was only sparsely sprinkled with low, thorny bushes. The ground was scattered with round, fist-sized rocks, and the dust spurted, yellow and powdery, from each step of their horses' hoofs. Although it was scarcely midmorning, the sun was already a furnace, and shimmering heat waves rippled the valley floor ahead, making the dusty, gray-green bushes seem to dance in the windless air.

It grew hotter. There was no trace of moisture anywhere, and the sweat dried almost instantly on the flanks of their panting horses.

"I think we should give some thought to going back," Adara said, reining in her mount. "There's no way we can reach those hills at the end of the valley."

"She's right, your Majesty," Olban told the princess. "We've already come too far."

Ce'Nedra pulled Noble to a stop, and the white horse drooped his head as if on the verge of absolute exhaustion. "Oh, quit feeling sorry for yourself," she chided him irritably. This was not going at all as she had expected. She looked around. "I wonder if we could find some shade somewhere," she said. Her lips were dry, and the sun seemed to hammer down on her unprotected head.

"The terrain doth not suggest such comfort, Princess," Ariana said, looking around at the flat emptiness of the rock-strewn valley floor.

"Did anyone think to bring any water?" Ce'Nedra asked, dabbing at her forehead with a kerchief.

No one had.

"Maybe we *should* go back," she decided, looking about rather regretfully. "There's nothing to see out here, anyway."

"Riders coming," Adara said sharply, pointing toward a mounted group of men emerging from an indented gulley that lay like a fold on the flanks of a rounded hill a mile or so away.

"Murgos?" Olban demanded with a sharp intake of his breath. His hand went immediately to his sword.

Adara raised her hand to shade her eyes and stared at the approaching horsemen intently. "No," she replied. "They're Algars. I can tell by the way they ride."

"I hope they have some water with them," Ce'Nedra said.

The dozen or so Algar riders rode directly toward them with a great cloud of yellow dust rising behind them. Adara suddenly gasped, and her face went very pale.

"What is it?" Ce'Nedra asked her.

"Lord Hettar is with them," Adara said in a choked voice.

"How can you possibly recognize anybody at that distance?"

Adara bit her lip, but did not reply.

Hettar's face was fierce and unforgiving as he reined in his sweating horse. "What are you doing out here?" he demanded bluntly. His hawk face and black scalp lock gave him a wild, even frightening appearance.

"We thought we'd go riding, Lord Hettar," Ce'Nedra replied brightly, trying to outface him.

Hettar ignored that. "Have you lost your mind, Olban?" he harshly asked the young Rivan. "Why did you permit the ladies to leave the forts?"

"I do not tell her Majesty what to do," Olban answered stiffly, his face red.

"Oh, come now, Hettar," Ce'Nedra protested. "What's the harm in our taking a little ride?"

"We killed three Murgos not a mile from here just yesterday," Hettar told her. "If you want exercise, run around the inside of the forts for a few hours. Don't just ride out unprotected in hostile territory. You've acted very foolishly, Ce'Nedra. We'll go back now." His face was grim as a winter sea, and his tone left no room for discussion.

"We had just made the same decision, my Lord," Adara murmured, her eyes downcast.

Hettar looked sternly at the condition of their horses. "You're an Algar, Lady Adara," he said pointedly. "Didn't it occur to you to bring water for your mounts? Surely you know better than to take a horse out in this kind of heat without any precautions at all."

Adara's pale face grew stricken.

Hettar shook his head in disgust. "Water their horses," he curtly told one of his men, "and then we'll escort them back. Your excursion is over, ladies."

Adara's face was flaming with a look of almost unbearable shame. She twisted this way and that in her saddle, trying to avoid Hettar's stern, unforgiving stare. No sooner had her horse been watered than she jerked her reins and dug her heels into his flanks. Her startled mount scrambled his hoofs in the gravel and leaped away, running back the way they had come across the rock-littered valley floor.

Hettar swore and drove his mount after her.

"Whatever is she doing?" Ce'Nedra exclaimed.

"Lord Hettar's rebuke hath stung our gentle companion beyond her endurance," Ariana observed. "His good opinion is dearer to her than her life itself."

"Hettar?" Ce'Nedra was stunned.

"Hath not thine eye informed thee how it doth stand with our dear friend?" Ariana asked in mild surprise. "Thou art strangely unobservant, Princess."

"Hettar?" Ce'Nedra repeated. "I had no idea."

"Mayhap it is because I am Mimbrate," Ariana concluded. "The ladies of my people are most sensitive to the signs of gentle affection in others."

It took perhaps a hundred yards for Hettar to overtake Adara's plunging horse. He seized her reins in one fist and jerked her roughly to a stop, speaking sharply to her, demanding to know what she was doing. Adara twisted this way and that in her saddle, trying to keep him from seeing her face as he continued to chide her.

Then a flicker of movement no more than twenty feet from the two of them caught Ce'Nedra's eye. Astonishingly, a mail-shirted Murgo rose up out of the sand between two scrubby bushes, shaking off the sheet of brown-splotched canvas beneath which he had lain concealed. As he rose, his short bow was already drawn.

"Hettar!" Ce'Nedra screamed as the Murgo raised his bow.

Hettar's back was to the Murgo, but Adara saw the man aiming his arrow at the Algar's unprotected back. With a desperate move, she ripped her reins from Hettar's grip and drove her horse into his. His mount lurched back, stumbled and fell, throwing the unprepared man to the ground even as Adara, flailing her horse's flanks with the ends of her reins, plunged directly at the Murgo.

With only the faintest flicker of annoyance, the Murgo released his arrow at the charging girl.

Even at that distance, Ce'Nedra could hear the distinct sound the arrow made when it struck Adara. It was a sound she would remember with horror for the remainder of her life. Adara doubled sharply, her free hand clutching at the arrow buried low in her chest, but her plunging gallop did not falter nor change as she rode the Murgo down. He tumbled and rolled beneath the churning hoofs of her horse, then lurched again to his feet as soon as she had passed over him, his hand jerking at his sheathed sword. But Hettar was already upon him, saber flashing in the glaring sunlight. The Murgo screamed once as he fell.

Hettar, his dripping saber still in his hand, turned angrily to Adara. "What a stupid thing," he roared at her, but his shout cut off suddenly. Her horse had come to a stop a few yards beyond the Murgo, and she drooped in her saddle, her dark hair falling like a veil across her pale face and both of her hands pressed to her chest. Then, slowly, she toppled from her saddle.

With a strangled cry, Hettar dropped his saber and ran to her.

"Adara!" the princess wailed, her hands going to her face in horror even as Hettar gently turned the stricken girl over. The arrow, still standing out of her lower chest, throbbed with the rhythm of her faltering heartbeat.

When the rest of them reached the pair, Hettar was holding Adara in his arms, staring into her pale face with a stricken look. "You little fool," he was murmuring in a broken voice. "You little fool."

Ariana slid from her saddle even before her horse stopped moving and ran to Hettar's side. "Do not move her, my Lord," she told him sharply. "The arrow hath pierced her lung, and shouldst thou move her, its keen edge will gash out her life."

"Take it out," Hettar said from between clenched teeth.

"Nay, my Lord. To pull the arrow now will do more damage than to leave it."

"I can't bear to see it sticking out of her like that," he almost sobbed.

"Then don't look, my Lord," Ariana said bluntly, kneeling beside Adara and placing a cool, professional hand on the wounded girl's throat.

"She's not dead, is she?" Hettar almost begged.

Ariana shook her head. "Gravely wounded, but her life doth still pulse within her. Instruct thy men to improvise a litter at once, my Lord. We must convey our dear friend to the fortress and Lady Polgara's ministrations immediately, lest her life drain away."

"Can't *you* do something?" he croaked.

"Not here in this sun-blasted desolation, my Lord. I have neither instruments nor medications, and the wound may be past my skill. The Lady Polgara is her only hope. The litter, my Lord. Quickly!"

POLGARA'S FACE WAS somber, and her eyes as hard as flint when she emerged from Adara's sickroom late that afternoon.

"How is she?" Hettar demanded. He had been pacing up and down in the main corridor of the blockhouse for hours, stopping every so often to strike savagely at the crudely built stone walls with his impotent fists.

"Somewhat improved," Polgara replied. "The crisis is past, but she's still terribly weak. She's asking for you."

"She *will* recover, won't she?" Hettar's question had a note of fear in it.

"Probably—if there aren't any complications. She's young, and the wound looked more serious than it actually was. I gave her something that'll make her very talkative, but don't stay too long. She needs rest." Polgara's eyes moved to Ce'Nedra's tear-streaked face. "Come to my room after you've seen her, your Majesty," she said firmly. "You and I have something to discuss."

Adara's porcelain face was framed by the tumbled mass of her dark brown hair spreading across the pillow. She was very pale, but, though her eyes had a slightly unfocused look about them, they were very bright. Ariana sat quietly at the bedside.

"How do you feel, Adara?" Ce'Nedra asked in the quiet but cheerful voice one always assumes with the sick.

Adara gave her a wan little smile.

"Are you in any pain?"

"No," Adara's voice had a little dying fall to it. "No pain, but I feel very lightheaded and strange."

"Why did you do that, Adara?" Hettar asked very directly. "You didn't have to ride right at the Murgo like that."

"You spend too much time with horses, my Lord Sha-dar," Adara told him with a faint smile. "You've forgotten how to understand the feelings of your own kind."

"What's that supposed to mean?" He sounded puzzled.

"Exactly what it says, my Lord Hettar. If a mare looked admiringly at a stallion, you'd know how things stood immediately, wouldn't you? But when it comes to people, you simply can't see at all, can you?" She coughed weakly.

"Are you all right?" he asked sharply.

"I'm surprisingly well—considering the fact that I'm dying."

"What are you talking about? You're not dying."

She smiled slightly. "Please don't," she told him. "I know what an arrow in the chest means. That's why I wanted to see you. I wanted to look at your face once more. I've been watching your face for such a long time now."

"You're tired," he said brusquely. "You'll feel better after you've slept."

"I'll sleep, all right," she said ruefully, "but I doubt that I'll feel anything afterward. The sleep I'm going to is the sleep one doesn't wake up from."

"Nonsense."

"Of course it is, but it's true nonetheless." She sighed. "Well, dear Hettar, you've finally escaped me, haven't you? I gave you a good chase, though. I even asked Garion to see if he could use sorcery on you."

"Garion?"

She nodded slightly. "You see how desperate I was? He said he couldn't, though." She made a little face. "What good is sorcery if you can't use it to make someone fall in love?"

"Love?" he repeated in a startled voice.

"What did you think we were talking about, Lord Hettar? The weather?" She smiled fondly at him. "Sometimes you can be impossibly dense."

He stared at her in amazement.

"Don't be alarmed, my Lord. In a little while, I'll stop chasing you, and you'll be free."

"We'll talk about that when you're better," he told her gravely.

"I'm not going to get better. Haven't you been listening? I'm dying, Hettar."

"No," he said, "as a matter of fact, you're not dying. Polgara assured us that you're going to be all right."

Adara looked quickly at Ariana.

"Thine injury is not mortal, dear friend," Ariana confirmed gently. "Truly, thou art not dying."

Adara closed her eyes. "How inconvenient," she murmured, a faint blush coming to her cheeks. She opened her eyes again. "I apologize, Hettar. I wouldn't have said any of this if I'd known that my meddling physicians were going to save my life. As soon as I'm up and about, I'll return to my own clan. I won't bother you again with my foolish outbursts."

Hettar looked down at her, his hard-angled face expressionless. "I don't think I'd like that," he told her, gently taking her hand. "There are things you and I need to talk about. This isn't the time or the place, but don't go trying to make yourself unaccessible."

"You're just being kind." She sighed.

"No. Practical. You've given me something to think about beside killing Murgos. It's probably going to take me a while to get used to the idea, but after I've thought it over, we'll definitely need to talk."

She bit her lip and tried to hide her face. "What a stupid mess I've made of things," she said. "If I were somebody else, I'd laugh at me. It'd really be better if we didn't see each other again."

"No," he said firmly, still holding her hand, "it wouldn't. And don't try to hide from me, because I'll find you—even if I have to have every horse in Algaria go looking for you."

She gave him a startled look.

"I *am* a Sha-dar, remember? Horses do what I tell them to."

"That's not fair," she objected.

He gave her a quizzical little smile. "And trying to have Garion use sorcery on me *was*?" he asked her.

"Oh, dear!" She blushed.

"She must rest now," Ariana told them. "Thou canst speak with her further on the morrow."

When they were back out in the hallway, Ce'Nedra turned on the tall man. "You might have said something a bit more encouraging," she scolded him.

"It would have been premature," he replied. "We're a rather reserved people, Princess. We don't say things just to be talking. Adara understands the situation." Hettar seemed as fierce as ever, his sharp-angled face hard, and his manelike scalp lock flowing over one leather-armored shoulder. His eyes, however, had softened slightly, and there was a faintly puzzled crease between his brows. "Didn't Polgara want to see you?" he asked. It was polite, but it was a dismissal nonetheless.

Ce'Nedra stalked away, muttering to herself about the lack of consideration that seemed to infect the male half of the population.

Lady Polgara sat quietly in her room, waiting. "Well?" she said when the princess entered. "Would you care to explain?"

"Explain what?"

"The reason for the idiocy that almost cost Adara her life."

"Surely you don't think it was *my* fault," Ce'Nedra protested.

"Whose fault was it, then? What were you doing out there?"

"We just went for a little ride. It's so boring being cooped up all the time."

"Boring. What a fascinating reason to kill your friends."

Ce'Nedra gaped at her, her face suddenly very pale.

"Why do you think we built these fortifications to begin with, Ce'Nedra? It was to provide us with some measure of protection."

"I didn't know there were Murgos out there," the princess wailed.

"Did you bother to find out?"

The entire implication of what she had done quite suddenly came crashing in on Ce'Nedra. She began to tremble violently, and her shaking hand went to her mouth. It *was* her fault! No matter how she might twist and turn and try to evade the responsibility, her foolishness had nearly killed one of her dearest friends. Adara had almost paid with her life for a bit of childish thoughtlessness. Ce'Nedra buried her face in her hands in a sudden storm of weeping.

Polgara let her cry for several moments, giving her ample time to accept her guilt; and when she finally spoke, there was no hint of forgiveness in her voice. "Tears won't wash out blood, Ce'Nedra," she said. "I thought I could at least begin to trust your judgment, but it appears that I was wrong. You may leave now. I don't believe I have anything more to say to you this evening."

Sobbing, the princess fled.

"Is this place all like this?" King Anheg asked as the army trudged through one of the flat, gravel-strewn valleys with the bare, sun-baked mountains around it dancing in the shimmering heat. "I haven't seen a tree since we left the forts."

"The country changes about twenty leagues out, your Majesty," Hettar replied quietly, lounging in his saddle as they rode in the blazing sunlight. "We start to hit trees when we begin coming down out of the uplands. They're a kind of low, scraggly spruce, but they break up the monotony a bit."

The column behind them stretched out for miles, dwarfed into a thin line by the enormous emptiness and marked more by the cloud of yellow dust raised by thousands of feet than by the presence of men and horses. The Cherek ships, covered with canvas, jolted along over the rocky ground on their low, wheeled cradles, and the dust hung over them in the stifling heat like a gritty blanket.

"I'd pay a lot for a breeze right now," Anheg said wistfully, wiping his face.

"Just leave things the way they are, Anheg," Barak advised him. "It wouldn't take much to start a dust storm."

"How much farther is it to the river?" King Rhodar asked plaintively, looking at the unchanging landscape. The heat was having a brutal effect on the corpulent monarch. His face was beet red, and he was soaked and dripping with sweat.

"Still about forty leagues," Hettar replied.

General Varana, mounted on a roan stallion, cantered back from the vanguard of the column. The general wore a short leather kilt and a plain breastplate and helmet bearing no marks of his rank. "The Mimbrate knights just flushed out another pocket of Murgos," he reported.

"How many?" King Rhodar asked.

"Twenty or so. Three or four got away, but the Algars are chasing them."

"Shouldn't our patrols be farther out?" King Anheg fretted, mopping his face again. "Those ships don't look *that* much like wagons. I'd rather not have to fight my way down the River Mardu—if we ever get there."

"I've got people moving around out there, Anheg," King Cho-Hag assured him.

"Has anyone run across any Malloreans yet?" Anheg asked.

"Not so far," Cho-Hag replied. "All we've seen so far are Thulls and Murgos."

"It looks as if 'Zakath is holding firm at Thull Zelik," Varana added.

"I wish I knew more about him," Rhodar said.

"The Emperor's emissaries report that he's a very civilized man," Varana said. "Cultured, urbane, very polite."

"I'm sure there's another side to him," Rhodar disagreed. "The Nadraks are terrified of him, and it takes a lot to frighten a Nadrak."

"As long as he stays at Thull Zelik, I don't care what kind of man he is," Anheg declared.

Colonel Brendig rode forward from the toiling column of infantry and wagons stretched out behind them. "King Fulrach asks that we halt the column for a rest period," he reported.

"Again?" Anheg demanded irritably.

"We've marched for two hours, your Majesty," Brendig pointed out. "Marching in all this heat and dust is very exhausting for infantry. The men won't be much good in a fight if they're all wrung out from walking."

"Halt the column, Colonel," Polgara told the Sendarian baronet. "We can rely on Fulrach's judgment in these matters." She turned to the King of Cherek. "Stop being so peevish, Anheg," she chided him.

"I'm being broiled alive, Polgara," he complained.

"Try walking for a few miles," she told him sweetly. "That may give you some insight into how the infantry feels."

Anheg scowled, but remained silent.

Princess Ce'Nedra pulled in her sweating mount as the column halted. The princess had spoken very little since Adara had been wounded. The dreadful sense of her responsibility for her friend's nearly fatal injury had sobered her enormously, and she had retreated into a kind of shell that was totally unnatural for her. She removed the loose-woven straw hat that a captive Thull had made for her back at the fort and squinted at the blistering sky.

"Put the hat back on, Ce'Nedra," Lady Polgara told her. "I don't want you getting sunstroke."

Ce'Nedra obediently put her hat back on. "He's coming back," she reported, pointing at a speck in the sky high above them.

"Will you excuse me?" General Varana said, turning his horse to leave.

"You're being absurd, Varana," King Rhodar told the Tolnedran. "Why do you insist on refusing to admit he can do things you don't want to believe in?"

"It's a matter of principle, your Majesty," the general replied. "Tolnedrans do not believe in sorcery. I am a Tolnedran, therefore I do not admit that it exists." He hesitated. "I must concede, however, that his information is surprisingly accurate— however he gets it."

A large, blue-banded hawk fell suddenly out of the broiling air like a stone, flared his wings at the last moment, and settled on the ground directly in front of them.

General Varana resolutely turned his back and stared with apparently deep interest at a featureless hill some five miles distant.

The hawk began to shimmer and change even as he folded his wings. "Are you stopping *again*?" Beldin demanded irascibly.

"We have to rest the troops, Uncle," Polgara replied.

"This isn't a Sunday stroll, Pol," Beldin retorted. He began to scratch one armpit, befouling the air around him with a string of rancid curses.

"What's the matter?" Polgara asked mildly.

"Lice," he grunted.

"How did you get lice?"

"I visited some other birds to ask if they'd seen anything. I think I picked them up in a vulture's nest."

"What could possibly possess you to go consorting with vultures?"

"Vultures aren't that bad, Pol. They perform a necessary function, and the chicks do have a certain charm. The she-vulture had been picking at a dead horse about twenty leagues south of here. After she told me about it, I went down to take a look. There's a Murgo column coming this way."

"How many?" General Varana asked quickly, his back still turned to them.

"A thousand or so," Beldin shrugged. "They're pushing hard. They'll probably intercept you tomorrow morning."

"A thousand Murgos aren't that much to worry about," King Rhodar said, frowning. "Not to an army of this size. But what's the point of throwing a thousand men away? What does Taur Urgas hope to accomplish?" He turned to Hettar. "Do you suppose you could ride ahead and ask Korodullin and the Baron of Vo Mandor to join us. I think we ought to have a conference."

Hettar nodded and loped his horse ahead toward the gleaming ranks of the Mimbrate knights at the head of the column.

"Were there any Grolims with the Murgos, Uncle?" Polgara asked the filthy hunchback.

"Not unless they were well hidden," he replied. "I didn't probe too much, though. I didn't want to give myself away."

General Varana abruptly abandoned his careful study of the hills around them and turned his horse about to join them. "My first guess would be that the Murgo column is a token gesture from Taur Urgas. He probably wants to get on the good side of King Gethell; and since the Malloreans won't leave Thull Zelik, he can pick up some advantage by committing a few troops to aid in the defense of the Thullish towns and villages we've been destroying."

"That makes sense, Rhodar," Anheg agreed.

"Maybe," Rhodar said dubiously. "Taur Urgas doesn't think like a rational man, though."

King Korodullin, flanked by Mandorallen and the Baron of Vo Ebor, thundered back to join them. Their armor flashed in the sun, and all three were flushed and miserable-looking in their steel casings.

"How can you stand all that?" Rhodar asked.

"Custom, your Majesty," Korodullin replied. "The armor doth inflict some discomfort, but we have learned to endure it."

General Varana quickly sketched in the situation for them.

Mandorallen shrugged. "It is of no moment. I will take some few dozen men and smash this threat from the south."

Barak looked at King Anheg. "You see what I mean about him?" he said. "Now you can understand why I was so nervous all the time we were chasing across Cthol Murgos."

King Fulrach had ridden forward to join the conference, and he cleared his throat diffidently. "Might I make a suggestion?" he asked.

"We eagerly await the practical wisdom of the King of the Sendars," Korodullin replied with extravagant courtesy.

"The Murgo column doesn't really pose much of a threat, does it?" Fulrach inquired.

"Not really, your Majesty," Varana replied. "At least, now that we know that they're out there. We think that they're some kind of minor relief column sent to placate the Thulls. Their presence in our vicinity is probably entirely accidental."

"I don't want them getting close enough to recognize my ships, though," Anheg declared firmly.

"We'll take care of that, Anheg," Rhodar told him.

"Any one of the elements of our army might easily overcome so slight a threat," Fulrach continued, "but mightn't it be better—from a morale standpoint—to give the victory to the entire army?"

"I don't quite follow you, Fulrach," Anheg said.

"Instead of letting Sir Mandorallen annihilate these thousand Murgos all by himself, why not select a contingent from each part of the army to deal with them? Not only will that give us some experience in tactical coordination, but it'll give all the men a sense of pride. An easy victory now will stiffen their backs when we run into more difficult times later."

"Fulrach, sometimes you positively amaze me," Rhodar declared. "I think the whole trouble is that you don't *look* that clever."

The contingents that were to turn south to meet the approaching Murgos were selected by lot, once again at the suggestion of King Fulrach. "That way there'll be no suspicion in the army that this is some kind of elite force," he noted.

While the rest of the column pushed on toward the headwaters of the River Mardu, the miniature army under the command of Barak, Hettar, and Mandorallen veered to the south to intercept the enemy spearhead.

"They'll be all right, won't they?" Ce'Nedra nervously asked Polgara as she watched them growing smaller and smaller as they rode off across the arid valley toward the solid line of mountains to the south.

"I'm certain they will, dear," Polgara replied confidently.

The princess, however, did not sleep that night. For the first time, members of her army were committed to a real battle, and she tossed and turned the entire night, imagining all manner of disasters.

About midmorning of the following day, however, the special force returned. There were a few bandages here and there and perhaps a dozen empty saddles, but the look of victory shone on every face.

"Very nice little fight," Barak reported. The huge man was grinning broadly. "We caught them just before sundown. They never knew what hit them."

General Varana, who had accompanied the force to observe, was a bit more precise as he described the engagement to the assembled kings. "The general tactics did work pretty much as we'd planned," he said. "The Asturian archers swept the column with an arrow storm to begin with, and then the infantry units moved into position at the top of a long slope. We interspersed legionnaires, Drasnian pikemen, Sendars and the Arendish serf units evenly along the entire front with the archers behind them to continue harassing the enemy with arrows. As we expected, the Murgos charged. As soon as they'd committed themselves, the Chereks and Rivans moved into position behind them, and the Algars began slashing their flanks. When the Murgo assault began to falter, the Mimbrate knights made their charge."

"It was absolutely splendid!" Lelldorin exclaimed, his eyes very bright. There was a bandage around the young Asturian's upper arm, but he seemed to have forgotten that it was there as he gesticulated wildly. "Just at the point when the Murgos were completely confused, there was a sound like thunder, and the knights came curving around the side of a hill with their lances advanced and their pennons streaming. They bore down on the Murgos—a wave of solid steel—and the hoofs of their horses shook the earth. And then at the last moment, they all lowered their lances. It was like watching a wave break. And then they hit the Murgos with a great crash, and they didn't even slow down. They rode through them as if they weren't even there! They absolutely crushed them, and then we all ran in to finish up. It was glorious!"

"He's as bad as Mandorallen, isn't he?" Barak observed to Hettar.

"I think it's in their blood," Hettar replied sagely.

"Did any of them get away?" Anheg asked.

Barak gave his cousin an evil grin. "After it got dark, we could hear a few of them trying to crawl away. That's when Relg and his Ulgos went out to tidy up. Don't worry, Anheg. Nobody's going to report back to Taur Urgas."

"He *is* likely to be waiting for news, isn't he?" Anheg grinned.

"I hope he's patient, then," Barak replied, "because he'll be waiting for a long time."

Ariana, her face somber, took Lelldorin to task very firmly for his lack of discretion, even as she tended his wound. Her words far surpassed a simple scolding. She grew eloquent, and her lengthy, involuted sentences gave her remonstrance a depth and scope that reduced her young man very nearly to tears. His wound, admittedly minor, became a symbol of his careless lack of regard for her. Her expression grew martyred, and his grew anguished. Ce'Nedra observed how neatly Ariana twisted each of the young man's lame excuses into an even greater personal injury, and filed this excellent technique away in a compartment of her complex little mind for future use. True, Garion was somewhat brighter than Lelldorin, but the tactic would probably work on him too, if she practiced a little.

Taiba's meeting with Relg, on the other hand, involved no words. The beautiful Marag woman who had emerged from the slave pens beneath Rak Cthol only to enter a slavery even more profound, flew to the Ulgo fanatic's side upon his return. With a low cry, she unthinkingly embraced him. Relg flinched away from her, but the almost automatic, "Don't touch me," seemed to die on his lips, and his eyes went very wide as she clung to him. Then Taiba remembered his aversion and helplessly let her arms drop, but her violet eyes glowed as they drank in his pale, large-eyed face. Then slowly, almost as if he were putting his arm into a fire, Relg reached out and took her hand. A brief look of incredulity crossed her face, followed almost immediately by a slow blush. They looked into each other's eyes for a moment, then walked off together, hand in hand. Taiba's eyes were demurely downcast, but there hovered about her rich, sensual mouth a tiny little smile of triumph.

The victory over the Murgo column raised the spirits of the army tremendously. The heat and dust no longer seemed to sap their energy as it had during the first few days of the march, and a growing sense of camaraderie grew between the diversified units as they pushed steadily eastward.

It took them four more days of steady marching to reach the headwaters of the River Mardu and another day to push on down along the tumbling flow to a spot where the ships could safely be launched. Hettar and his Algar patrols ranged far ahead and reported that there remained only one more stretch of rapids about ten leagues ahead before the river settled into tranquillity on the Thullish plain.

"We can portage around the rapids," King Anheg declared. "Let's get these ships into the water. We've lost enough time already."

There was a rather high earthbank at that point, but the army attacked it vigorously with shovels and mattocks, and it was soon reduced to a sloping ramp. One by one the ships were rolled down the ramp into the water.

"We'll need a while to raise the masts," Anheg said.

"Leave that until later," Rhodar told him.

Anheg looked at him sharply.

"You're not going to be able to use your sails anyway, Anheg, and the masts stick up too high. The stupidest Thull in the world will know what's going on if he sees a forest of ship masts coming down the river toward him."

It was evening by the time the ships had all been launched and Polgara led the princess, Ariana and Taiba on board Barak's ship. A breeze coming upriver gently rippled the surface of the water and set the ship to rocking slowly. Beyond the watch fires, the Thullish grassland stretched as if forever beneath a purpling sky where, one by one, the stars were emerging.

"How far is it to Thull Mardu?" Ce'Nedra asked Barak.

The big man pulled at his beard, squinting downriver. "One day to the rapids," he replied, "then one day to make the portage around them. Then about two days after that."

"Four days," she said in a small voice.

He nodded.

"I wish it was over," she sighed.

"All in good time, Ce'Nedra," he told her. "All in good time."

CHAPTER FIFTEEN

The ships were horribly crowded, even though scarcely half the army could squeeze aboard them. The Algar clansmen and the Mimbrate knights patrolled the banks as the Chereks rowed downriver toward the rapids, and those infantry elements that could not be carried by the ships rode in close files on the spare horses of the cavalry.

The Thullish grasslands on either side of the river were gently rolling, long hillsides covered with deep, sun-browned grass. Just back from the river there were sparse clusters of the twisted, sprucelike trees that had dotted the lower foothills, and near the water itself rose thickets of willow and creeping brambles. The sky remained clear, and it was still hot, though the river added enough moisture to the air to alleviate the parched aridity that had plagued men and horses alike in the vast, stony uplands. It was an alien landscape for all of them, and the cavalry patrolling the banks rode warily with their hands close to their weapons.

And then they rounded a wide bend and saw the white, tumbling water of the rapids ahead. Barak swung the tiller of his big ship over and beached her. "Looks like it's time to get out and walk," he grunted.

A dispute had arisen near the bow of the ship. The brown-bearded King Fulrach was loudly protesting the decision to leave his supply wagons behind at the rapids. "I didn't bring them all this way just to leave them sitting here," he declared with uncharacteristic heat.

"They take too long to get anyplace," Anheg told him. "We're in a hurry, Fulrach. I've got to get my ships past Thull Mardu before the Murgos or the Malloreans wake up to what we're doing."

"You didn't object to having them along when you got hungry or thirsty in the uplands," Fulrach told him angrily.

"That was then. This is now. I've got to take care of my ships."

"And *I'm* going to take care of my wagons."

"They'll be all right, Fulrach," Rhodar said placatingly. "We *do* have to hurry, and your wagons can't move fast enough to keep up."

"If somebody comes along and burns them, you're going to get very hungry before we get back to the forts, Rhodar."

"We'll leave men to guard them, Fulrach. Be reasonable. You worry too much."

"Somebody's got to. You Alorns seem to forget that the fighting's only half of it."

"Stop acting like an old woman, Fulrach," Anheg said bluntly.

Fulrach's face grew very cold. "I don't know that I care for that last remark, Anheg," he said stiffly. Then he turned on his heel and stalked away.

"What's got into him?" the King of Cherek asked innocently.

"Anheg, if you don't learn how to keep your mouth shut, we might have to muzzle you," Rhodar told him.

"I thought we came here to fight Angaraks," Brand said mildly. "Have the rules been changed?"

The irritable bickering among her friends worried Ce'Nedra, and she went to Polgara with her concern.

"It's nothing all that important, dear," the lady replied as she scrubbed Errand's neck. "The upcoming battle's got them a bit edgy, that's all."

"But they're men," Ce'Nedra protested, "trained warriors."

"What does that have to do with it?" Polgara asked, reaching for a towel.

The princess couldn't think of an answer.

The portage at the rapids went smoothly, and the ships reentered the river below the tumbling stretch of seething white water by late afternoon. Ce'Nedra by now was virtually ill as a result of the almost unbearable tension. All the months she had spent in raising the army and marching eastward were about to come to a final culmination. Within two days, they would hurl themselves at the walls of Thull Mardu. Was it the right time? Was it, in fact, really necessary? Couldn't they just portage around the city and avoid the battle entirely? Although the Alorn kings had assured her that the city *had* to be neutralized, Ce'Nedra's doubts grew with each mile. What if this was a mistake? The princess worried and fretted and worried some more as she stood at the prow of Barak's ship, staring at the broad river winding through the Thullish grasslands.

Finally, just at evening of the second day after the portage, Hettar galloped back and reined in his horse on the north bank of the river. He motioned with his arm, and Barak swung his tiller over, angling the big ship in closer to the bank.

"The city's about two leagues ahead," the tall Algar called across the intervening space. "If you get too much closer, they'll see you from the walls."

"This is close enough, then," Rhodar decided. "Pass the word to anchor the ships. We'll wait here until dark."

Barak nodded and made a quick gesture to a waiting sailor. The man quickly raised a tall pole with a bit of bright red bunting nailed to its tip, and the fleet behind them slowed in answer to the signal. There was a creaking of windlasses as the anchors settled to the bottom, and the ships rocked and swung sluggishly in the current.

"I still don't like this part," Anheg growled morosely. "Too many things can go wrong in the dark."

"They'll go wrong for them, too," Brand told him.

"We've been over it a dozen times, Anheg," Rhodar said. "We all agreed that it's the best plan."

"It's never been done before," Anheg said.

"That's the whole point, isn't it?" Varana suggested. "The people inside the city won't expect it."

"Are you *sure* your men will be able to see where they're going?" Anheg demanded of Relg.

The zealot nodded. He was wearing his cowled leaf-mail shirt and was carefully testing the edge of his hook-pointed knife. "What you think of as darkness is normal light for us," he replied.

Anheg scowled at the purpling sky overhead. "I *hate* being the first one to try something new," he announced.

They waited as evening settled on the plain. From the thickets at the river's edge, birds clucked sleepily, and the frogs began their evening symphony. Slowly out of the gathering darkness, the cavalry units began to group up along the banks. The Mimbrate knights on their great chargers massed into ranks, and the Algar clansmen spread like a dark sea beyond them. Commanding the south bank were Cho-Hag and Korodullin. The north was led by Hettar and Mandorallen.

Slowly it grew darker.

A young Mimbrate knight who had been injured during the attack on the Murgo column stood leaning against the rail, looking pensively out into the twilight. The knight had dark, curly hair and the snowy complexion of a young girl. His shoulders were broad, his neck columnar, and his eyes had an open innocence in them. His expression, however, was faintly melancholy.

The waiting had become unbearable, and Ce'Nedra *had* to talk to someone. She leaned on the rail beside the young man. "Why so sad, Sir Knight?" she asked him quietly.

"Because I am forbidden to take part in this night's adventure by reason of this slight injury, your Majesty," he replied, touching his splinted arm. He seemed unsurprised by her presence or by the fact that she had spoken to him.

"Do you hate the Angaraks so much that missing the chance to kill them causes you pain?" Ce'Nedra's question was gently mocking.

"Nay, my Lady," he answered. "I have no malice in me for any man, whatever his race. What I lament is being denied the chance to try my skills in the contest."

"Contest? Is that how you think of it?"

"Assuredly, your Majesty. In what other light should it be considered? I hold no personal rancor toward the men of Angarak, and it is improper to hate thine opponent in a test of arms. Some few men have fallen beneath my lance or my sword at diverse tourneys, but I have never hated any of them. Much to the contrary, I have had some affection for them as we strove with one another."

"But you were trying to cripple them." Ce'Nedra was startled at the young man's casual attitude.

"It is a part of the contest, your Majesty. A true test of arms may not be decided save by the injury or death of one of the combatants."

"What's your name, Sir Knight?" she asked him.

"I am Sir Beridel," he replied, "son of Sir Andorig, Baron of Vo Enderig."

"The man with the apple tree?"

"The very same, your Majesty." The young man seemed pleased that she had heard of his father and the strange duty Belgarath had imposed on him. "My father now rides at the right hand of King Korodullin. I would ride with them this night but for this stroke of ill fortune." He looked sadly at his broken arm.

"There will be other nights, Sir Beridel," she assured him, "and other contests."

"Truly, your Majesty," he agreed. His face brightened momentarily, but then he sighed and went back to his somber brooding.

Ce'Nedra drifted away, leaving him to his thoughts.

"You can't really talk to them, you know," a rough voice said to her from the shadows. It was Beldin, the ugly hunchback.

"He doesn't seem to be afraid of anything," Ce'Nedra said a bit nervously. The foul-mouthed sorcerer always made her nervous.

"He's a Mimbrate Arend," Beldin snorted. "He doesn't have enough brains to be afraid."

"Are all the men in the army like him?"

"No. Most of them *are* afraid, but they'll go through with the attack anyway—for a variety of reasons."

"And you?" she could not help asking. "Are you afraid too?"

"My fears are a bit more exotic," he said dryly.

"Such as?"

"We've been at this for a very long time—Belgarath, Pol, the twins and I—and I'm more concerned about something going wrong than I am about my own personal safety."

"How do you mean, wrong?"

"The Prophecy is very complex—and it doesn't say everything. The two possible outcomes of all this are still absolutely balanced as far as I can tell. Something very, very slight could tip that balance one way or the other. It could be something that I've overlooked. That's what I'm afraid of."

"All we can do is the best we can."

"That might not be enough."

"What else can we do?"

"I don't know—and that's what worries me."

"Why worry about something if you can't do anything about it?"

"Now you're starting to sound like Belgarath. He tends to shrug things off and trust to his luck sometimes. I like things a little neater." He stared off into the darkness. "Stay close to Pol tonight, little girl," he said after a moment. "Don't get separated from her. It might take you someplace you hadn't planned to go, but you're supposed to stay with her, no matter what."

"What does that mean?"

"I don't *know* what it means," he retorted irritably. "All I know is that you and she and the blacksmith and that stray child you picked up are supposed to stay together. Something unexpected is going to happen."

"You mean a disaster? We must warn the others."

"We don't *know* that it's a disaster," he replied. "That's the whole problem. It might be necessary, and if it is, we don't want to tamper with it. I think we've about run this discussion into the ground. Go find Polgara and stay with her."

"Yes, Beldin," Ce'Nedra said meekly.

As the stars began to come out, the anchors were raised and the Cherek fleet began to slip quietly downriver toward Thull Mardu. Though they were still some miles above the city, commands were issued in hoarse whispers, and the men all took great care to avoid making noise as they shifted their weapons and equipment, tightening belts, giving their armor quick, last-minute checks and settling their helmets more firmly on their heads.

Amidships, Relg was leading his Ulgos in a quiet religious service, muttering the harsh gutturals of the Ulgo tongue in a scarcely audible murmur. Their pale faces had been smeared with soot, and they looked like so many shadows as they knelt in prayer to their strange God.

"They're the key to the whole thing," Rhodar observed quietly to Polgara as he watched the devotions of the Ulgos. "Are you sure that Relg is all right for this? Sometimes he seems a bit unstable."

"He'll be fine," Polgara replied. "The Ulgos have even more reason to hate Torak than you Alorns do."

The drifting ships slowly rounded a wide bend in the river, and there, a half mile downstream, stood the walled city of Thull Mardu, rising from its island in the middle of the river. There were a few torches atop the walls, and a faint glow rising from within. Barak turned and, shielding it with his body, he briefly uncovered a muffled lantern, letting out a single flicker of light. The anchors sank very slowly through the dark waters toward the river bottom; with a very faint creak of ropes, the ships slowed, then stopped.

Somewhere inside the city a dog began to bark excitedly. Then a door banged open, and the barking cut off suddenly with a yelp of pain.

"I don't have much use for a man who kicks his own dog," Barak muttered.

Relg and his men moved very quietly to the rail and began to clamber down ropes into the small boats waiting below.

Ce'Nedra watched breathlessly, straining with her eyes to see in the darkness. The very faint starlight briefly showed her several shadows drifting down toward the city. Then the shadows were gone. Behind them there was a faint splash of an oar, followed by an angrily hissed admonition. The princess turned and saw a moving tide of small boats coming downriver from the anchored fleet. The spearhead of the assault slid silently by, following Relg and his Ulgos toward the fortified island city of the Thulls.

"Are you sure there are enough of them?" Anheg whispered to Rhodar.

The rotund King of Drasnia nodded. "All they have to do is secure a landing place for us and hold the gate once the Ulgos get it open," he murmured. "There's enough of them for that."

A faint night breeze rippled the surface of the river, setting the ship to rocking. Unable to bear the suspense any longer, Ce'Nedra lifted her fingertips to the amulet Garion had given her so many months before. As always, a buzz of conversation filled her ears.

"*Yaga, tor gohek vilta.*" It was Relg's harsh voice, speaking in a whisper. "*Ka tak. Veed!*"

"Well?" Polgara asked, one eyebrow slightly raised.

"I can't tell what they're saying," Ce'Nedra replied helplessly. "They're talking in Ulgo."

A strangled groan quite suddenly seemed to come from the amulet itself and then was quickly and horribly cut off.

"I—I think they just killed somebody," Ce'Nedra said in a quavering voice.

"It's started then," Anheg said with a certain grim satisfaction.

Ce'Nedra pulled her fingertips from the amulet. She could no longer bear to listen to the sound of men dying in the dark.

They waited.

Then someone screamed, a scream filled with a terrible agony.

"That's it!" Barak declared. "That's the signal! Pull the anchor!" he shouted to his men.

Very suddenly beneath the high, dark walls of Thull Mardu, two separate fires flared up, and shadowy figures could be seen moving about them. At the same moment, there was a clanking rattle of heavy chains inside the city and a creaking groan as a broad gate swung ponderously down to form a bridge across the narrow north channel of the river.

"Man your oars!" Barak roared to his crew. He swung his tiller hard over, steering toward the rapidly lowering bridge.

More torches appeared along the tops of the walls, and there were shouts of alarm. Somewhere an iron bell began to clang a note of desperate urgency.

"It worked!" Anheg exclaimed, gleefully pounding Rhodar on the back. "It actually worked!"

"Of course it worked," Rhodar replied, his voice also jubilant. "Don't pound on me so hard, Anheg. I bruise easily."

All need for silence was gone now, and a great roar went up from the massed fleet following in Barak's wake. Torches flared, and the faces of the troops lining the rails were bathed in their ruddy glow.

A great splash suddenly erupted from the river twenty yards to the right of Barak's ship, showering everyone on deck with a deluge of water.

"Catapult!" Barak shouted, pointing at the walls looming ahead. Like a huge, preying insect, the heavy-beamed frame of the siege engine balanced atop the wall, its long throwing arm already cocking back to cast another boulder at the approaching fleet. Then the arm stopped as a storm of arrows swept the top of the wall clean. A crowd of Drasnians, easily identifiable by the long pikes they carried, overran the position.

"Watch out, down there," one of them roared into the confusion at the base of the wall, and the siege engine ponderously toppled outward and fell with a crash onto the rocks below.

There was a thunder of hoofs across the now-lowered bridge, and the Mimbrate knights crashed into the city.

"As soon as we tie up to the bridge, I want you and the princess and the other ladies to go to the north bank," King Rhodar said tersely to Polgara. "Get back out of harm's way. This'll probably take the rest of the night, and there's no point in exposing any of you to any accidents."

"Very well, Rhodar," Polgara agreed. "And don't *you* do anything foolish, either. You're a rather large target, you know."

"I'll be all right, Polgara—but I'm not going to miss this." He laughed then, a strangely boyish laugh. "I haven't had so much fun in years," he declared.

Polgara gave him a quick look. "Men!" she said in a tone that said everything.

A guard of Mimbrate knights escorted the ladies and Errand perhaps a thousand yards upstream to an indented cove on the north bank of the stream, well away from the press of the horsemen rushing toward the beleaguered city. The cove had a gently sloping sand beach and was protected on three sides by steep, grass-covered banks. Durnik the smith and Olban quickly raised a tent for them, built a small fire, and then climbed up the bank to watch the attack.

"It's going according to plan," Durnik reported from his vantage point. "The Cherek ships are lining up side by side across the south channel. As soon as they get the planking in place, the troops on the other side will be able to cross."

"Can you tell if the men inside have taken the south gate yet?" Olban demanded, peering toward the city.

"I can't tell for sure," Durnik replied. "There's fighting going on in that part of the city, though."

"I'd give anything to be there," Olban lamented.

"You stay right where you are, young man," Polgara told him firmly. "You appointed yourself bodyguard to the Rivan Queen, and you're not going to go running off just because things are more interesting someplace else."

"Yes, Lady Polgara," the young Rivan answered, suddenly abashed. "It's just—"

"Just what?"

"I wish I knew what was happening, that's all. My father and my brothers are in the middle of the fighting, and I have to stand here and watch."

A sudden great belch of flame shot up from inside the walls to illuminate the river with sooty red light.

Polgara sighed. "Why do they always have to burn things?" she asked sadly.

"It adds to the confusion, I suppose," Durnik replied.

"Perhaps," Polgara said, "but I've seen this happen too many times before. It's always the same. There always has to be a fire. I don't believe I care to watch any more of this." She turned her back on the burning city and walked slowly away from the riverbank.

The night was interminable. Toward dawn, as the stars began to fade from the paling sky, the Princess Ce'Nedra, drawn with fatigue, stood atop a grassy bank near the cove, watching with a kind of sick fascination as the city of Thull Mardu died. Entire districts seemed to be in flames, and great fountains of orange sparks belched toward the sky as roofs caved in and buildings collapsed. What had seemed so stirring, so glorious in her anticipation had turned out to be something quite different in reality, and she was sick at what she had done. She still, nonetheless, brought her fingertips up to touch the amulet at her throat. She *had* to know what was happening. No matter how horrible the events were in the city, not knowing what was happening was even worse.

"Sort of a nice little fight," she heard King Anheg say. The King of Cherek seemed to be someplace very high—atop the walls of the city perhaps.

"Pretty routine," Barak, Earl of Trellheim, replied. "The Murgo garrison fought pretty well, but the Thulls kept falling all over themselves trying to surrender."

"What did you do with all of them?" King Cho-Hag asked.

"We herded them into the central square," Barak answered. "They've been amusing themselves by killing the Grolims we flushed out of the temple."

Anheg suddenly chuckled, an evil sort of sound. "How's Grodeg?" he asked.

"It looks like he's going to live," Barak said.

"That's a shame. When I saw that axe sticking out of his back, I thought somebody's solved one of my problems for me."

"It was too low," Barak said rather mournfully. "It broke his spine, but it didn't hit anything else significant. He won't be walking anymore, but he's still breathing."

"You can't depend on a Murgo to do anything right," Anheg said in disgust.

"They *did* thin out the Bear-cult pretty thoroughly," Barak noted cheerfully. "I don't think there are more than two dozen of them left. They fought pretty well, though."

"That's what they were here for. How long do you think it'll be before daylight?"

"Half an hour, maybe."

"Where's Rhodar?"

"He and Fulrach are sacking the warehouses," King Cho-Hag replied. "The Murgos had some supply dumps here. Fulrach wants to confiscate them."

"He would," Anheg said. "Maybe we'd better send somebody for them. It's getting on toward the time when we'll want to think about pulling out of here. As soon as it gets light, all this smoke's going to announce what we've done to anyone within twenty leagues. It's about time to start the fleet moving, and it's a long march back to the forts on top of the escarpment."

"How long will it take you to get to the Sea of the East?" Cho-Hag asked.

"A couple days," Anheg told him. "You can move a ship pretty fast when you've got the current behind you. It'll take your army a week at least to get back to the forts, won't it?"

"Probably," Cho-Hag said. "The infantry can't move all that fast. There's Brendig! I'll send him to fetch Rhodar." He shouted down to the Sendar. "Colonel Brendig, see if you can find Rhodar. Ask him to join us."

"What's that?" Barak asked suddenly.

"What's what?" Anheg demanded.

"I thought I saw something out there—way to the south—where you can just start to make out that hilltop."

"I don't see anything."

"It was just a flicker—something moving."

"Probably a Murgo scout creeping in for a look." Anheg laughed shortly. "I don't imagine we'll be able to keep what happened here a secret for very long."

"There it is again," Barak said.

"I saw it that time, too," King Cho-Hag agreed.

There was a long silence as the sky imperceptibly grew lighter. Ce'Nedra held her breath.

"Belar!" Anheg swore in a stunned voice. "They stretch for miles!"

"Lelldorin!" Barak shouted down from the wall. "Brendig's gone to get Rhodar. Go find them and tell them to get up here at once. The plain to the south is covered with Murgos."

CHAPTER SIXTEEN

"Lady Polgara!" Ce'Nedra cried, jerking back the flap of the tent. "Lady Polgara!"

"What is it, Ce'Nedra?" Polgara's voice came from the darkness inside the tent.

"Barak and Anheg are up on the walls of the city," the princess said in a frightened voice. "They just saw a Murgo army coming up from the south."

Polgara came quickly out into the firelight holding the sleepy Errand by the hand. "Where's Beldin?" she demanded.

"I haven't seen him since early last night."

Polgara raised her face and closed her eyes. A moment or so later there was a rushing sound of wings, and the large hawk settled to the sand not far from their flickering fire.

Beldin was swearing sulfurously even as he shimmered and blurred back into his natural shape.

"How did they slip past you, Uncle?" Polgara asked him.

"There are Grolims with them," he growled, still sizzling the air around him with oaths. "The Grolims could feel me watching, so the troops moved only at night, and the Grolims shielded them."

"Where did they hide in the daytime?"

"In the Thullish villages, apparently. There are dozens of communities out there. It never occurred to me to pay all that much attention to them." He began to swear again, berating himself savagely for having missed the movement of the Murgo army.

"There's no point in swearing about it, Uncle," Polgara told him coolly. "It's done, now."

"Unfortunately there's a bit more, Pol," the sorcerer told her. "There's another army at least as big coming in from the north—Malloreans, Nadraks, and Thulls. We're caught right between them."

"How long have we got before they reach us?" Polgara asked.

Beldin shrugged. "Not long. The Murgos have some rough ground to cross—probably about an hour. The Malloreans will be here in quite a bit less."

Polgara began to curse fervently under her breath. "Go to Rhodar," she told the hunchback. "Tell him that we have to release Anheg's fleet immediately—before the Angaraks can bring up catapults and destroy the ships where they're anchored."

The deformed man nodded and stooped slightly, curving his arms out like wings even as he began to waver and change.

"Olban," Polgara called to the young Rivan, "go find Sir Mandorallen and Lord Hettar. Send them to me at once. Hurry."

Olban gave her one startled look, then ran for his horse.

Durnik the smith came sliding down the grassy bank onto their little beach. His face was grave. "You and the ladies must leave at once, Mistress Pol," he told her. "There's going to be fighting here, and the middle of a battle's no place for any of you."

"I'm not going anywhere, Durnik," she replied with a trace of irritation. "I started all this, and I'm going to see it through."

Ariana had gone back into the tent as soon as the situation became clear to her. She now emerged again, carrying the stout canvas bag in which she kept her medical supplies. "Have I thy permission to leave, Lady Polgara?" she asked with a certain cool professionalism. "In battle men are injured, and I must go make preparations for their care. This spot is somewhat too remote and confined to receive the wounded."

Polgara gave her a quick look. "All right," she agreed. "Just be careful not to get too close to the fighting."

Taiba pulled on her cloak. "I'll go with you," she told Ariana. "I don't know that much about it, but you can teach me as we go along."

"Go help them get set up, Durnik," Polgara told the smith. "Then come back here."

Durnik nodded gravely and helped the two women up the steep bank.

Mandorallen thundered up on his charger with Hettar at his side.

"You know what's happened?" Polgara demanded.

Mandorallen nodded.

"Is there any possibility of withdrawing before the enemy forces arrive?"

"Nay, my Lady Polgara," the great knight replied. "They are too close. Moreover, our purpose hath ever been to gain passage for the ships of Cherek into the Sea of the East. We must buy them time to sail beyond the reach of the siege engines of the Angaraks."

"I didn't want this," Polgara said angrily and she began to mutter curses again.

Brand, the gray-cloaked Rivan Warder, accompanied by General Varana, rode up to join Mandorallen and Hettar at the top of the steep bank. The four of them dismounted and slid down the bank to the sand. "We've begun evacuating the city," the big Rivan said in his deep voice, "and most of the fleet is pulling anchor. We're holding just enough ships to maintain the bridges across the south channel."

"Is there any possibility of putting the entire army on one bank or the other?" Polgara asked him.

He shook his head. "There isn't time, Polgara."

"We're going to be divided by the river," she pointed out, "and neither force is going to be strong enough to meet the Angaraks coming against it."

"A tactical necessity, my dear Lady Polgara," General Varana told her. "We have to hold both banks until the fleet is clear."

"I think Rhodar misjudged the Angarak intentions," Brand said. "He was so sure that Taur Urgas and 'Zakath would both want to avoid taking casualties that he didn't consider this possibility."

General Varana clasped his muscular hands behind his back and limped back and forth along the little beach, his face creased with thought. "I think I begin to understand the meaning of that Murgo column we destroyed in the uplands," he said.

"Your Grace?" Mandorallen asked, puzzled.

"It was a test of our commitment," Varana explained. "The Angaraks needed to know when we were making our major move. One of the basic rules of war is not to become involved in serious conflicts if what you're doing is merely diversionary. That column was bait. Unfortunately, we took it."

"You mean we shouldn't have attacked the column?" Hettar asked him.

Varana made a rueful face. "Apparently not. It gave away our intentions—let them know that *this* expedition was *not* a diversion. I underestimated Taur Urgas. He threw away a thousand men just to find out what we were up to."

"What now?" Hettar asked.

"We get ready to fight," Varana said. "I wish we had better terrain for it, but I suppose we'll have to make do with what we have."

Hettar looked out across the river, his hawk-face hungry. "I wonder if I've got time to make it over to the south bank," he mused.

"One side or the other," Brand said, looking puzzled. "What's the difference?"

"The Murgos are over there," Hettar replied. "I don't really have anything against Malloreans."

"This isn't a personal fight, Lord Hettar," Varana pointed out.

"It is with me," Hettar said grimly.

"We must needs see to the safety of Lady Polgara and the princess," Mandorallen said. "Mayhap an escort should be provided to convey them back to the forts atop the escarpment."

Brand shook his head. "The region's likely to be patrolled heavily," he disagreed. "It wouldn't be safe."

"He's right, Mandorallen," Polgara told the knight. "Besides, you need every man you've got right here." She looked off toward the northeast. "Then, too, there's that." She pointed toward a heavy cloudbank that had begun to stain the sky just above the horizon. The clouds were an inky black, seething and rolling and illuminated from within by fitful flickers of lightning.

"A storm?" General Varana asked, looking a bit surprised.

"Not at this time of year—and certainly not from that direction," Polgara replied. "The Grolims are up to something, and that's going to be *my* fight. Deploy your forces, gentlemen. If there's going to be a battle, let's be ready for it."

"The ships are moving," Durnik reported as he and Olban came back to the sheltered little cove, "and the troops are leaving the city."

King Rhodar rode up. His broad face was streaked with soot and perspiration. "Anheg's leaving," he said, swinging down from his saddle with a grunt.

"Where's Fulrach?" Brand asked.

"He's taking the bulk of the troops across to the south bank."

"Isn't that going to leave us a little undermanned on this side?" General Varana inquired politely.

"That bridge is too narrow," Rhodar told him. "It'd take hours to bring enough men across to make any difference. Brendig's already got a crew undermining the supports so that we can bring the bridge down before the Angaraks get here."

"What for?" Ce'Nedra asked him.

"Thull Mardu's too good a vantage point, your Highness," General Varana explained. "We don't want any Angaraks on the island if we can help it." He looked at King Rhodar. "Have you given any thought to tactics?" he asked.

"We want to give Anheg a half a day, if possible," Rhodar replied. "The ground along the river gets marshy about twenty leagues downstream, and the Angaraks won't be able to get close enough to pester him, once he gets that far. Let's form up a conventional infantry line—pikemen, the legions, Sendars, and so on. We'll put the archers in support and use the Algars to slash at the flanks. I want to hold the Mimbrate knights in reserve until the Malloreans mass up for their first charge."

"That's not a winning tactic, if your Majesty will forgive my saying so," General Varana said.

"We aren't here to win, Varana," Rhodar told him. "We're here to delay the Angaraks for about six hours and then withdraw. I'm not going to waste lives trying to win a battle I haven't any chance of winning." He turned to Hettar. "I want you to send a force of your clansmen on a sweep downriver. Tell them to uproot any Malloreans they find emplaced along the riverbank. The significance of the fleet still may have escaped 'Zakath and Taur Urgas. Angaraks aren't good sailors, so they probably don't realize what Anheg can do once he gets into the Seas of the East."

"Excuse me, your Majesty," Varana objected, "but all of your strategy—even the fleet—is merely a delaying action."

"That's the whole point, Varana," Rhodar told him bluntly. "All of this is really rather insignificant. What's really important is going to happen in Mallorea

when Belgarion reaches Cthol Mishrak. We'd better move, gentlemen. The Malloreans will be here before long, and we want to be ready for them."

The cloudbank Polgara had pointed out was sweeping toward them with an
alarming speed, a seething darkness of rolling purple, stalking forward on crooked
legs of lightning. A hot wind seemed to flee out ahead of it, flattening the grass and
whipping the manes and tails of the horses wildly. As King Rhodar and the others
moved out to meet the approaching Mallorean army, Polgara, her face pale and her
hair tossing behind her in the wind, climbed the grassy bank with Ce'Nedra and
Durnik behind her and stood watching the approach of the cloud. "Take the child,
Ce'Nedra," she said quite calmly. "Don't let go of him, no matter what happens."

"Yes, Lady Polgara," Ce'Nedra said, holding out her arms to Errand. The child
came to her immediately, his serious little face unafraid. She picked him up and
held him close, her cheek against his.

"Errand?" he said, pointing at the approaching storm.

Then, among the ranks of their army, shadowy figures rose up out of the
ground. The figures wore black robes and polished steel masks and carried cruel-
pointed short spears. Without pausing to even think, a mounted young Mimbrate
knight swept his broadsword from its scabbard and swung the whistling blade at
one of the steel-masked figures. His sword passed through the figure with no effect.
As he struck, however, a sizzling bolt of lightning struck him, seeming to attach itself to the point of his helmet. He stiffened convulsively as the lightning, like a
writhing snake of intense light, clung to the tip of his steel helm. Smoke boiled out
of the slits of his visor as he roasted inside his armor. His horse lurched forward
onto its knees while the ghastly, flickering light engulfed them both. Then the
lightning was gone, and horse and man collapsed, stone dead.

Polgara hissed and then raised her voice. She did not seem to be speaking that
loudly, but the effect of her words reached the farthest edges of the army. "Do not
touch the shadows," she warned. "They're Grolim illusions and can't hurt you unless you touch them. They're here to draw the lightning to you, so stay clear of
them."

"But, Mistress Pol," Durnik protested, "the troops won't be able to hold ranks
if they have to keep dodging the shadows."

"I'll take care of the shadows," she replied grimly. She raised both arms above
her head, her fists clenched. A look of dreadful concentration filled her face, and
then she spoke a single word, opening her hands as she did so. The grass, which
had been bending toward them in the hot wind preceding the storm, suddenly flat-
tened in the opposite direction as the force of Polgara's will rippled outward. As
that force passed over each shadowy Grolim illusion, the figures seemed to flinch,
then shrivel, and then with silent detonations, each shadow exploded into shards
and fragments of darkness.

Polgara was gasping as the last of the shadows on the farthest edge of the army
vanished, and she would have collapsed had Durnik not jumped to her side to support her. "Are you all right?" he asked worriedly.

"Just give me a moment," she said, wilting against him. "That took a great
deal of effort." She smiled at him, a wan little smile, and then her head drooped
wearily.

"Won't they come back?" Ce'Nedra demanded. "What I mean is, it didn't actually hurt the real Grolims, did it? Just their shadows."

Polgara laughed weakly. "Oh, it hurt them, all right," she replied. "Those Grolims don't *have* shadows anymore. Not one of them will ever cast a shadow again."

"Not ever?" the princess gasped.

"Not ever."

Then Beldin joined them, swooping in with the wind tearing at his feathers. "We've got work to do, Polgara," he growled even as he shimmered into his natural shape. "We're going to have to break up this storm they're bringing in from the west. I talked with the twins. They'll work on the southern side of it, and you and I'll take this side."

She looked at him inquiringly.

"Their army's going to be advancing right behind the storm," he explained. "There's no point in trying to hold it back now. It's got too much momentum. What we want to do is break open the rear edge of it and let it spill back over the Angaraks."

"How many Grolims are working on the storm, Uncle?" she asked him.

"Who knows?" He shrugged. "But it's taking every bit of effort they can muster just to keep it under control. If the four of us hit the back side all at once, the pressures in the storm itself will do the rest."

"Why not just let it pass over?" Durnik asked. "Our troops aren't children. They won't fall apart just because of a little squall."

"This isn't just a little squall, blacksmith," Beldin said acidly. Something large and white thudded to the ground a few feet away. "If you get four or five of those hailstones on top of the head, you won't care *how* the battle turns out."

"They're as big as hens' eggs," Durnik said in astonishment.

"And they'll probably get bigger." Beldin turned back to Polgara. "Give me your hand," he told her. "I'll pass the signal to Beltira, and we'll all strike at the same time. Get ready."

More of the hailstones thudded into the springy turf, and one particularly large one shattered into a thousand fragments as it crashed down on a large rock with stunning force. From the direction of the army came an intermittent banging as the hailstones bounced off the armor of the Mimbrate knights or clanged down on the hastily raised shields of the infantry.

And then, mixed with the hail, the rain squalls struck—seething sheets of water driven before the wind like raging waves. It was impossible to see, and almost impossible to breathe. Olban jumped forward with his shield raised to protect Ce'Nedra and Errand. He winced once as a large hailstone struck his shoulder, but his shield arm did not waver.

"It's breaking, Pol!" Beldin shouted. "Let's push it once more. Let them eat their own storm for a while."

Polgara's face twisted into an agony of concentration, and then she half slumped as she and Beldin unleashed their combined wills at the rolling sky. The sound of it was beyond belief as the vast forces collided. The sky ripped suddenly apart and lightning staggered and lurched through the smoking air. Great, incandescent bolts crashed into each other high above, showering the earth beneath with fireballs. Men fell, charred instantly into black, steaming husks in the driving downpour, but the casualties were not only among the men of the west.

The vast storm with its intolerable pressures recoiled as the combined wills of Polgara and Beldin on the north bank and the twins on the south bank ripped open the back edge of it, and the advancing Malloreans received that recoil full in the teeth. A curtain of lightning swept back across their close-packed ranks like an enormous, blinding broom, littering the earth with their smoking dead. As the fabric of Grolim sorcery which had driven the storm front toward the river ripped apart, the gale winds suddenly reversed and flowed back, shrieking and howling, confounding the advancing Angaraks with rain and hail.

From out of the center of the dreadful cloud overhead, swirling fingers of murky black twitched and reached down toward the earth with hideous roaring sounds. With a last, almost convulsive jerk, one of those huge, swirling funnels touched the earth in the midst of the red-clad Malloreans. Debris sprayed up and out from the point of the dreadful vortex as, with ponderous immensity, it cut an erratic course two hundred yards wide directly through the enemy ranks. Men and horses were ripped to pieces by the insane winds within the swirling column of cloud, and bits of armor and shreds of red tunics—and worse—showered down on the stunned and terrified Malloreans on either side of the swath of absolute destruction moving inexorably through their midst.

"Beautiful!" Beldin exulted, hopping up and down in a grotesque display of glee.

There was the sudden sound of a great horn, and the close-packed ranks of Drasnian pikemen and Tolnedran legionnaires facing the faltering ranks of the Malloreans opened. From behind them, his armor streaming water, Mandorallen led the charge of the Mimbrate knights. Full upon the confused and demoralized Malloreans they fell, and the sound of the impact as they struck was a terrible, rending crash, punctuated by screams. Rank upon rank were crushed beneath the charge, and the terrified Malloreans wavered and then broke and fled. Even as they ran, the clans of Algar swept in among them from the flanks, their sabers flashing in the rain.

At a second blast of Mandorallen's horn, the charging Mimbrates reined in, wheeled and galloped back, leaving a vast wreckage behind them.

The rain slackened fitfully, little more than errantly passing showers now, and patches of blue appeared among the racing clouds overhead. The Grolim storm had broken and dispersed back across the plains of Mishrak ac Thull.

Ce'Nedra looked toward the south bank and saw that the storm there had also dispersed and that the forces under the command of King Cho-Hag and King Korodullin were assaulting the front ranks of the demoralized Murgo army. Then the princess looked sharply at the south channel of the river. The last bridges of Cherek ships had broken loose during the violent storm, and there was now only open water on that side of the island. The last troops remaining in the city were streaming across the bridge over the north channel. A tall Sendarian lad was among the last to cross. As soon as he reached the bank, he came immediately upriver. As he drew nearer, Ce'Nedra recognized him. It was Rundorig, Garion's boyhood friend from Faldor's farm, and he was openly weeping.

"Goodman Durnik," he sobbed as he reached them, "Doroon's dead."

"What did you say?" Lady Polgara demanded, raising her tired face suddenly.

"Doroon, Mistress Pol," Rundorig wept. "He drowned. We were crossing over to the south bank when the storm broke the ropes holding the ships. Doroon fell into the river, and he didn't know how to swim. I tried to save him, but he went under before I could reach him." The tall young man buried his face in his hands.

Polgara's face went absolutely white, and her eyes filled with sudden tears. "Take care of him, Durnik," she told the smith, then turned and walked away, her head bowed in her grief.

"I tried, Durnik," Rundorig blurted, still sobbing. "I really tried to reach him—but there were too many people in my way. I couldn't get to him in time. I saw him go under, and there was nothing I could do."

Durnik's face was very grave as he put his arm about the weeping boy's shoulders. The smith's eyes were also filled, and he said nothing.

Ce'Nedra, however, could not weep. She had reached out her hand and plucked these unwarlike young men from their homes and dragged them halfway across the world, and now one of Garion's oldest friends had died in the chill waters of the River Mardu. His death was on her head, but she could not weep. A terrible fury suddenly filled her. She turned to Olban. "Kill them!" she hissed from between clenched teeth.

"My Queen?" Olban gaped at her.

"Go!" she commanded. "Take your sword and go. Kill as many Angaraks as you can—for me, Olban. Kill them for me!" And then she could weep.

Olban looked first at the sobbing little princess and then at the milling ranks of the Malloreans, still reeling from the savagery of the Mimbrate assault. His face grew exultant as he drew his sword. "As my Queen commands!" he shouted and ran to his horse.

Even as the decimated front ranks of the Malloreans fled, hurried by the saber-wielding Algars, greater and greater numbers of their countrymen reached the field, and soon the low hills to the north were covered with them. Their red tunics made it look almost as if the earth itself were bleeding. It was not the Malloreans, however, who mounted the next attack. Instead, thick-bodied Thulls in mud-colored smocks marched reluctantly into position. Directly behind the Thulls, mounted Malloreans urged them on with whips.

"Basic Mallorean strategy," Beldin growled. " 'Zakath wants to let the Thulls do most of the dying. He'll try to save his own troops for the campaign against Taur Urgas."

Ce'Nedra raised her tear-streaked face. "What do we do now?" she asked the misshapen sorcerer.

"We kill Thulls," he said bluntly. "A charge or two by the Mimbrates ought to break their spirits. Thulls don't make very good soldiers, and they'll run away as soon as we give them the chance."

Even as the sluggish forces of Mishrak ac Thull flowed like a mud slide downhill toward the solid line of pikemen and legionnaires, the Asturian archers just to the rear of the infantry raised their bows and filled the air with a solid, arching sheet of yard-long arrows. The Thulls quailed as rank after rank melted under the withering storm of arrows. The shouts of the Malloreans at the rear became more desperate, and the crack of their whips filled the air.

And then Mandorallen's horn sounded, the ranks of infantry opened, and the armored knights of Mimbre charged again. The Thulls took one look at the steel-clad men and horses crashing toward them and immediately bolted. The Mallorean whip-men were swarmed under and trampled in the panic-stricken flight of the Thull army.

"So much for the Thulls." Beldin grunted with satisfaction as he watched the rout. He grinned an evil grin. "I imagine that 'Zakath's going to speak firmly to King Gethell about this."

Mandorallen's knights thundered back to their positions behind the infantry, and the two armies glared at each other across a field littered with Angarak dead.

Ce'Nedra began to shiver as a sudden chill swept the battlefield. Although the sun had broken through the ragged clouds as the Grolim storm rapidly dispersed, there was no warmth to it. Even though all trace of wind had died, it grew colder. Then from the ground and from the dark surface of the river, tendrils of fog began to rise.

Beldin hissed. "Polgara," he snapped to the grieving sorceress, "I need you."

"Leave me alone, Uncle," she replied in a voice still choked with sorrow.

"You can cry later," he told her harshly. "The Grolims are drawing the heat out of the air. If we don't stir up a wind, the fog's going to get so thick you'll be able to walk on it."

She turned, and her face was very cold. "You don't respect anything, do you?" she said flatly.

"Not much," he admitted, "but that's beside the point. If the Grolims can build up a good fog bank, we'll have the whole stinking Mallorean army on top of us before we can even see them coming. Let's go, Pol. People get killed; it happens. You can get sentimental about it later." He held out his gnarled, lumpy hand to her.

The tendrils of fog had begun to thicken, lying in little pockets now. The littered battlefield in front of the infantry lines seemed to waver, and then disappeared entirely as the fog congealed into a solid wall of white.

"Wind, Pol," Beldin said, taking hold of her hand. "As much wind as you can raise."

The struggle which ensued then was a silent one. Polgara and Beldin, their hands joined together, gathered in their wills and then reached out with them, probing, searching for some weakness in the mass of dead-calm air that imprisoned the thickening fog along the banks of the river. Fitful little gusts of breeze swirled the eddying fog, then died as quickly as they had arisen.

"Harder, Pol," Beldin urged. His ugly face streamed with rivulets of sweat as he struggled with the vast inertness of unmoving air.

"It's not going to work this way, Uncle," she declared, pulling her hand free. Her face showed her own strain. "There's nothing to get hold of. What are the twins doing?"

"The Hierarchs of Rak Cthol are riding with Taur Urgas," the hunchback replied. "The twins have their hands full dealing with them. They won't be able to help."

Polgara straightened then, steeling herself. "We're trying to work too close," she said. "Every time we start a little local breeze, a dozen Grolims jump in and smother it."

"All right," Beldin agreed.

"We'll have to reach out farther," she continued. "Start the air moving somewhere out beyond their range so that by the time it gets here, it has so much momentum that they can't stop it."

Beldin's eyes narrowed. "That's dangerous, Pol," he told her. "Even if we *can* do it, it's going to exhaust the both of us. If they throw anything else at us, we won't have any strength left to fight them."

"It's a gamble, Uncle," she admitted, "but the Grolims are stubborn. They'll try to protect this fog bank even after all chance of maintaining it has gone. They'll get tired, too. Maybe too tired to try anything else."

"I don't like maybes."

"Have you got a better idea?"

"Not right now, no."

"All right, then."

They joined hands again.

It took, it seemed to the princess, an eternity. With her heart in her throat she stared at the two of them as they stood with their hands joined and their eyes closed—reaching out with their minds toward the hot, barren uplands to the west, trying with all their strength to pull that heated air down into the broad valley of the River Mardu. All around her, Ce'Nedra seemed to feel the oppressive chill of Grolim thought lying heavily on the stagnant air, holding it, resisting all effort to dissipate the choking fog.

Polgara was breathing in short gasps, her chest heaving and her face twisted with an inhuman striving. Beldin, his knotted shoulders hunched forward, struggled like a man attempting to lift a mountain.

And then Ce'Nedra caught the faintest scent of dust and dry, sun-parched grass. It was only momentary, and she thought at first that she had imagined it. Then it came again, stronger this time, and the fog eddied sluggishly. But once more that faint scent died, and with it the breath of air that had carried it.

Polgara groaned then, an almost strangled sound, and the fog began to swirl. The wet grass at Ce'Nedra's feet, drenched with droplets of mist, bent slightly, and the dusty smell of the Thullish uplands grew stronger.

It seemed that the blanket of concentration that had held the fog motionless became more desperate as the Grolims fought to stop the quickening breeze pouring down the valley from the arid stretches to the west. The blanket began to tatter and to fall apart as the weaker of the Grolims, pushed beyond their capacity, collapsed in exhaustion.

The breeze grew stronger, became a hot wind that rippled the surface of the river. The grass bent before it, and the fog began to seethe like some vast living thing, writhing at the touch of the arid wind.

Ce'Nedra could see the still-burning city of Thull Mardu now, and the infantry lines drawn up on the plain beside the river.

The hot, dusty wind blew stronger, and the fog, as insubstantial as the thought that had raised it from the earth, dissolved, and the morning sun broke through to bathe the field in golden light.

"Polgara!" Durnik cried in sudden alarm.

Ce'Nedra whirled in time to see her face drained deathly white, slowly toppling to the earth.

CHAPTER SEVENTEEN

L elldorin of Wildantor had been nervously pacing back and forth along the ranks of his bowmen, stopping often to listen for any sound coming out of the fog from the field lying in front of the massed infantry. "Can you hear anything?" he asked urgently of a Tolnedran legionnaire standing nearby.

The Tolnedran shook his head.

That same whisper came out of the fog from a dozen different places.

"Can you hear anything?"

"Can *you* hear anything?"

"What are they doing?"

Somewhere to the front, there was a faint click.

"There!" everyone cried almost in unison.

"Not yet!" Lelldorin snapped to one of his countrymen who was raising his bow. "It could be just a wounded Thull out there. Save your arrows."

"Is that a breeze?" a Drasnian pikeman asked. "Please, Belar, let it be a breeze."

Lelldorin stared into the fog, nervously fingering his bowstring.

Then he felt a faint touch of air on his cheek.

"A breeze," someone exulted.

"A breeze." The phrase raced through the massed army.

Then the faint breath of air died, and the fog settled again, seeming thicker than ever.

Someone groaned bitterly.

The fog stirred then and began to eddy sluggishly. It *was* a breeze!

Lelldorin held his breath.

The fog began to move, flowing gray over the ground like water.

"There's something moving out there!" a Tolnedran barked. "Get ready!"

The flowing fog moved faster, thinning, melting in the hot, dusty breeze blowing down the valley. Lelldorin strained his eyes to the front. There were moving shapes out there, no more than seventy paces from the infantry.

Then, as if all its stubborn resistance had broken at once, the fog shimmered and dissolved, and the sun broke through. The entire field before them was filled with Malloreans. Their stealthy forward pace froze momentarily as they flinched in the sudden light of the sun.

"Now!" Lelldorin shouted, raising his bow. Behind him, his archers with one universal motion followed his action, and the sudden release of a thousand bow-strings all at once was like some vast, thrumming note. A whistling sheet of arrows soared over the heads of the solidly standing infantry, seemed to hang motionless in the air for a moment, then hurtled into the close-packed Mallorean ranks.

The creeping attack of the Malloreans did not waver or falter; it simply dissolved. With a vast, sighing groan, entire regiments fell in their tracks under the Asturian arrow storm.

Lelldorin's hand flickered to the forest of arrows thrust point-first into the turf at his feet. He smoothly nocked another shaft, drew and released. And then again—and again. The sheet of arrows overhead was like some great slithering bridge arching over the infantry and riddling the Malloreans as it fell among them.

The storm of Asturian arrows crept inexorably across the field, and the Mallorean dead piled up in windrows as if some enormous scythe had passed through their ranks.

And then Sir Mandorallen's brazen horn sounded its mighty challenge, the ranks of archers and infantry opened, and the earth shook beneath the thunder of the charge of the Mimbrate knights.

Demoralized by the arrow storm and the sight of that inexorable charge descending upon them, the Malloreans broke and fled.

Laughing delightedly, Lelldorin's cousin Torasin lowered his bow to jeer at the backs of the routed Angaraks. "We did it, Lelldorin!" he shouted, still laughing. "We broke their backs!" He was half-turned now, not facing the littered field. His bow was in his hands; his dark hair was thrown back; and his face reflected his exultant delight. Lelldorin would always remember him so.

"Tor! Look out!" Lelldorin shouted, but it was too late. The Mallorean answer to the Asturian arrow storm was a storm of their own. From a hundred catapults concealed behind the low hills to the north, a great cloud of rocks hurtled into the air and crashed down into the close-packed ranks along the riverbank. A stone perhaps somewhat larger than a man's head struck Torasin full in the chest, smashing him to the ground.

"Tor!" Lelldorin's cry was anguished as he ran to his stricken cousin. Torasin's eyes were closed, and blood was flowing from his nose. His chest was crushed.

"Help me!" Lelldorin cried to a group of serfs standing nearby. The serfs obediently moved to assist him, but their eyes, speaking louder than any words, said that Torasin was already dead.

BARAK'S FACE WAS bleak as he stood at the tiller of his big ship. His oarsmen stroked to the beat of a muffled drum, and the ship raced downriver.

King Anheg of Cherek lounged against the rail. He had pulled off his helmet so that the cool river air could blow the stink of smoke out of his hair. His coarse-featured face was as grim as his cousin's. "What do you think their chances are?" he asked.

"Not very good," Barak replied bluntly. "We never counted on the Murgos and Malloreans hitting us at Thull Mardu. The army's split in two by the river, and both halves of it are outnumbered. They're going to have a bad time of it, I'm afraid." He glanced over his shoulder at the half dozen small, narrow-beamed boats trailing in the wake of his big ship. "Close it up!" he bellowed at the men in the smaller boats.

"Malloreans ahead! On the north bank!" the lookout at the mast shouted. "About a half mile!"

"Wet down the decks," Barak ordered.

The sailors tossed buckets on long ropes over the side, hauled up water, and soaked the wooden decks.

"Signal the ships behind us," Anheg told the bearded sailor standing in the very stern of the ship. The sailor nodded, turned and lifted a large flag attached to a long pole. He began to wave it vigorously at the ships strung out behind them.

"Be careful with that fire!" Barak shouted to the men clustered around a raised platform filled with gravel and covered with glowing coals. "If you set us ablaze, you'll all have to swim to the Sea of the East."

Just to the front of the platform stood three heavy-limbed catapults, cocked and ready.

King Anheg squinted ahead at the Malloreans gathered around a dozen or so siege engines standing solidly on the north bank. "Better send in your arrow-boats now," he suggested.

Barak grunted and waved his arm in a broad chopping motion to the six narrow boats in his wake. In answer, the lean little boats leaped ahead, cutting through the water. Mounted at the prow of each arrow-boat stood a long-armed catapult armed with a loosely packed bundle of arrows. Aided by the current, the narrow little boats sped past, their oars bending.

"Load the engines!" Barak roared to the men around the gravel-based fire. "And don't slop any of that tar on my decks."

With long iron hooks, the sailors lifted three large earthenware pots out of the coals. The pots contained a seething mixture of tar, pitch, and naptha. They were quickly dipped in tar barrels and then hastily wrapped in naptha-soaked rags. Then they were placed in the baskets of the waiting engines.

As the arrow-boats, speeding like greyhounds, swept in close to shore where the Malloreans struggled to aim their catapults, the arrow-bundles were suddenly hurled high into the air by the lashing arms of the Cherek engines. The arrows rose swiftly, then slowed at the top of their arching flight, separating and spreading out as they flew. Then, in a deadly rain, they fell upon the red-tunicked Malloreans.

Barak's ship, trailing just behind the arrow-boats, ran in close to the brush-covered riverbank, and the red-bearded man stood with both of his big hands on the tiller, staring intently at his catapult master, a gray-bearded old sailor with arms like oak stumps. The catapult master was squinting at a line of notches chipped into the railing in front of his engines. Over his head he held a long white baton and he indicated direction by pointing it either to the right or the left. Barak moved his tiller delicately in response to the movements of the baton. Then the baton cut sharply straight down, and Barak locked his tiller in an iron grip. The rags wrapped around the pots leaped into flame as they were touched by waiting torches.

"Shoot!" the catapult master barked. With a thudding crash, the beams lashed forward, hurling the flaming pots and their deadly contents in a high arch toward the struggling Malloreans and their siege engines. The pots burst open upon impact, spraying fire in front of them. The Mallorean catapults were engulfed in flame.

"Good shooting," Anheg noted professionally.

"Child's play," Barak shrugged. "A shoreline emplacement isn't much of a challenge, really." He glanced back. The arrow-boats of Greldik's ship were sweeping in to rake the Malloreans with more arrows, and the catapults on his bearded friend's decks were cocked and loaded. "Malloreans don't appear to be any brighter than Murgos. Didn't it ever occur to them that we might shoot back?"

"It's an Angarak failing," Anheg replied. "It shows up in all their writings. Torak never encouraged creative thinking."

Barak gave his cousin a speculative look. "You know what I think, Anheg? I think that all that fuss you raised back at Riva—about Ce'Nedra leading the army, I mean—I think that it wasn't entirely sincere. You're too intelligent to be so stubborn about something that wasn't that important."

Anheg winked broadly.

"No wonder they call you Anheg the sly," Barak chuckled. "What was it all about?"

"It pulled Brand's teeth." The King of Cherek grinned. "He's the one who could have stopped Ce'Nedra cold if I'd given him the chance. Rivans are very conservative, Barak. I sided with Brand and did all the talking. Then when I gave in, he didn't have any ground left to stand on."

"You were very convincing. I thought for a while that your reason had slipped."

"Thank you," the Cherek King replied with a mock bow. "When you've got a face like mine, it's easy for people to think the worst about you. I've found that useful from time to time. Here comes the Algars." He pointed at the hills just behind the burning Mallorean siege engines. A great crowd of horsemen came surging over the hilltops to sweep down like a wolfpack upon the confounded Malloreans.

Anheg sighed then. "I'd like to know what's happening to them back there at Thull Mardu," he said. "I don't suppose we'll ever find out, though."

"Not very likely," Barak agreed. "We'll all get sunk eventually, once we get out into the Sea of the East."

"We'll take a lot of Malloreans with us, though, won't we, Barak?"

Barak's reply was an evil grin.

"I don't really care much for the notion of drowning," Anheg said, making a face.

"Maybe you'll get lucky and catch an arrow in the belly."

"Thanks," Anheg said sourly.

An hour or so later, after three more Angarak positions on the riverbanks had been destroyed, the land along the River Mardu turned marshy, flattening out into a sea of reeds and bending cattails. At Anheg's orders, a raft piled high with fire-wood was moored to a dead snag and set afire. Once the blaze was going well, buckets of greenish crystals were hurled into the flames. A thick pillar of green smoke began to climb into the blue sky.

"I hope Rhodar can see that." The King of Cherek frowned.

"If he can't, the Algars will," Barak replied. "They'll get word back to him."

"I just hope he's got enough time left to make his retreat."

"Me too," Barak said. "But as you say, we'll probably never know."

KING CHO-HAG, CHIEF of the Clan-Chiefs of Algaria, sat his horse beside King Korodullin of Arendia. The fog was nearly gone now, and only a filmy haze remained. Not far away, the twin sorcerers, Beltira and Belkira, exhausted by their efforts, sat side by side on the ground, their heads bowed and their chests heaving. Cho-Hag shuddered inwardly at the thought of what might have happened if the two saintly old men had not been there. The hideous illusions of the Grolims that had risen from the earth just before the storm had struck terror in the hearts of the bravest warriors. Then the storm, its intensity deafening, had smashed down on the army, and after that had come the choking fog. The two sweet-faced sorcerers, however, had met and overcome each Grolim attack with calm determination. Now the Murgos were coming, and it was time for steel instead of sorcery.

"I'd let them get a little closer," Cho-Hag advised in his quiet voice as he and Korodullin watched the veritable sea of Murgos advancing against the emplaced ranks of Drasnian pikemen and Tolnedran legionnaires.

"Art thou sure of thy strategy, Cho-Hag?" the young Arendish King asked with a worried frown. "It hath ever been the custom of the knights of Mimbre to meet an attack head-on. Thy proposal to charge the flanks puzzles me."

"It'll kill more Murgos, Korodullin," Cho-Hag replied, shifting his weak legs in their stirrups. "When your knights charge in from either flank, you'll cut off whole regiments of the enemy. Then we can grind the ones who've been cut off up against the infantry."

"It is passing strange to me to work thus with foot troops," Korodullin confessed. "I have a vast ignorance of unmounted combat."

"You aren't alone, my friend," Cho-Hag told him. "It's as alien to me as it is to you. It'd be unfair of us, though, not to let the foot troops have a *few* Murgos, wouldn't it? They *did* walk a long way, after all."

The King of Arendia considered that gravely. He was quite obviously inca-pable of anything remotely resembling humor. "I had not considered that," he confessed. " 'Twould be selfish in the extreme of us to deny them *some* part in the battle, I must agree. How many Murgos dost thou think would be their fair portion?"

"Oh, I don't know," Cho-Hag replied with a straight face. "A few thousand or so, I imagine. We wouldn't want to appear stingy—but it doesn't do to be over-generous, either."

Korodullin sighed. "It is a difficult line to walk, King Cho-Hag—this fine di-vision between parsimony and foolish prodigality."

"One of the prices of kingship, Korodullin."

"Very true, Cho-Hag, very true." The young King of Arendia sighed again and bent all his concentration to the problem of how many of the advancing Murgos he could really afford to give away. "Thinkest thou that two Murgos apiece might content those who fight afoot?" he asked rather hesitantly.

"Sounds fair to me."

Korodullin smiled then with happy relief. "Then that is what we shall allot them," he declared. "I have not divided up Murgos before, but it is not nearly so difficult as I had imagined."

King Cho-Hag began to laugh.

LADY ARIANA PUT her arms about Lelldorin's shaking shoulders and drew him gently away from the pallet upon which his cousin's body lay.

"Can't you do *something*, Ariana?" he pleaded, tears streaming down his face. "Perhaps a bandage of some sort—and a poultice."

"He is beyond mine art, my Lord," Ariana replied gently, "and I share thy sorrow at his death."

"Don't say that word, Ariana. Torasin *can't* be dead."

"I'm sorry, my Lord," she said simply. "He is gone, and none of my remedies nor skill can bring him back."

"Polgara can do it," Lelldorin declared suddenly, an impossible hope leaping into his eyes. "Send for Polgara."

"I have no one to send, my Lord," Ariana told him, looking around the makeshift tent where she and Taiba and a few others were caring for the wounded. "The injured men here command all our attention and care."

"I'll go then," Lelldorin declared, his eyes still streaming tears. He spun and dashed from the tent.

Ariana sighed mournfully and drew a blanket over Torasin's pale face. Then she turned back to the wounded men who were being carried in a steady stream into her tent.

"Don't bother yourself with him, my Lady," a lean-faced Arendish serf told her as she bent over the body of the man's companion.

Ariana looked at the thin serf inquiringly.

"He's dead," the serf explained. "He took a Mallorean arrow right through the chest." He looked down at the dead man's face. "Poor Detton," he sighed. "He died in my arms. Do you know what his last words were?"

Ariana shook her head.

"He said, 'At least I had a good breakfast.' And then he died."

"Why didst thou bring him here, since thou didst know he was already dead?" Ariana asked him gently.

The lean, bitter-faced serf shrugged. "I didn't want to leave him just lying in a muddy ditch like a dead dog," he replied. "In his whole life, nobody ever treated him as if he mattered at all. He was my friend, and I didn't want to leave him there like a pile of garbage." He laughed a short, bitter laugh. "I don't suppose it matters very much to him, but at least there's a little bit of dignity here." He awkwardly patted the dead man's shoulder. "Sorry, Detton," he said, "but I guess I'd better go back to the fighting."

"What is thy name, friend?" Ariana asked.

"I'm called Lammer, my Lady."

"Is the need for thee in the battle urgent?"

"I doubt it, my Lady. I've been shooting arrows at the Malloreans. I'm not very good at it, but it's what I'm supposed to do."

"My need for thee is greater, then," she declared. "I have many wounded here and few hands to help with their care. Despite thy surly exterior, I sense a great compassion in thee. Wilt thou help me?"

He regarded her for a moment. "What do you want me to do?" he said.

"Taiba is boiling cloth for bandages over that fire there," she replied. "See to the fire first, then thou wilt find a cart just outside with blankets in it. Bring in the blankets, good Lammer. After that I will have other tasks for thee."

"All right," Lammer replied laconically, moving toward the fire.

"WHAT CAN WE do for her?" the Princess Ce'Nedra demanded of the misshapen Beldin. The princess was staring intently into Polgara's pale, unconscious face as the sorceress lay exhausted in the arms of Durnik the smith.

"Let her sleep," Beldin grunted. "She'll be all right in a day or so."

"What's the matter with her?" Durnik asked in a worried voice.

"She's exhausted," Beldin snapped. "Isn't that obvious?"

"Just from raising a breeze? I've seen her do things that looked a lot harder."

"You don't have the faintest idea of what you're talking about, blacksmith," Beldin growled. The hunchbacked sorcerer was himself pale and shaking. "When you start tampering with the weather, you're putting your hands on the most powerful forces in the world. I'd rather try to stop a tide or uproot a mountain than stir up a breeze in dead air."

"The Grolims brought in that storm," Durnik said.

"The air was already moving. Dead-calm air is altogether different. Do you have the remotest idea of how much air you've got to move to stir even the faintest breath of air? Do you know what kind of pressures are involved—how much all that air *weighs*?"

"Air doesn't weigh anything," Ce'Nedra protested.

"Really?" Beldin replied with heavy sarcasm. "I'm so glad you told me. Would the two of you shut up and let me get my breath?"

"But how is it that she collapsed and you didn't?" Ce'Nedra protested.

"I'm stronger than she is," Beldin replied, "and more vicious. Pol throws her whole heart into things when she gets excited. She always did. She pushed beyond her strength, and it exhausted her." The twisted little man straightened, shook himself like a dog coming out of water and looked around, his face bleak. "I've got work to do," he said. "I *think* we've pretty much worn out the Mallorean Grolims, but I'd better keep an eye on them, just to be safe. You two stay here with Pol—and keep an eye on that child." He pointed at Errand, who stood on the sandy beach with his small face very serious.

Then Beldin crouched, shimmering already into the form of a hawk, and launched himself into the air almost before his feathers were fully formed.

Ce'Nedra stared after him as he spiraled upward over the battlefield and then turned her attention back to the unconscious Polgara.

* * *

THE CHARGE OF Korodullin's Mimbrate knights came at the last possible moment. Like two great scythes, the armored men on their massive chargers sliced in at a thundering gallop from the flanks with their lances leveled and cut through the horde of Murgos rushing toward the waiting pikemen and legionnaires. The results were devastating. The air was filled with screams and the sounds of steel striking steel with stunning impact. In the wake of the charge lay a path of slaughtered Murgos, a trail of human wreckage a hundred yards wide.

King Cho-Hag, sitting on his horse on a hilltop some distance to the west, nodded his approval as he watched the carnage. "Good," he said finally. He looked around at the eager faces of the Algar clansmen clustered around him. "All right, my children," he said calmly, "let's go cut up the Murgo reserves." And he led them at a gallop as they poured down off the hill, smoothly swung around the outer flanks of the tightly packed assault forces and then slashed into the unprepared Murgo units bringing up the rear.

The slash-and-run tactics of the clans of the Algars left heaps of sabred dead in their wake as they darted in and out of the milling confusion of terrified Murgos. King Cho-Hag himself led several charges, and his skill with the sabre, which was legendary in Algaria, filled his followers with an awed pride as they watched his whiplike blows raining down on Murgo heads and shoulders. The whole thrust of Algar strategy was based on speed—a sudden dash on a fast horse and a series of lightninglike saber slashes, and then out before the enemy could gather his wits. King Cho-Hag's saber arm was the fastest in Algaria.

"My King!" one of his men shouted, pointing toward the center of several close-packed Murgo regiments milling about in a shallow valley a few hundred yards away. "There's the black banner!"

King Cho-Hag's eyes suddenly gleamed as a wild hope surged through him. "Bring my banner to the front!" he roared, and the clansman who carried the burgundy-and-white banner of the Chief of the Clan-Chiefs galloped forward with the standard streaming above his head. "Let's go, my children!" Cho-Hag shouted and drove his horse directly at the Murgos in the valley. With saber raised, the crippled King of the Algars led his men down into the Murgo horde. His warriors slashed to the right and to the left, but Cho-Hag plunged directly at the center, his eyes fixed on the black banner of Taur Urgas, King of the Murgos.

And then, in the midst of the household guard, Cho-Hag saw the bloodred mail of Taur Urgas himself. Cho-Hag raised his bloody saber and shouted a ringing challenge. "Stand and fight, you Murgo dog!" he roared.

Startled by that shout, Taur Urgas wheeled his horse to stare incredulously at the charging King of Algaria. His eyes suddenly bulged with the fervid light of insanity, and his lips, foam-flecked, drew back in a snarl of hatred. "Let him come!" he grated. "Clear the way for him!"

The startled members of his personal guard stared at him.

"Make way for the King of Algaria!" Taur Urgas shrieked. "He is mine!" And the Murgo troops melted out of Cho-Hag's path.

The Algar King reined in his horse. "And so it's finally come, Taur Urgas," he said coldly.

"It has indeed, Cho-Hag," Taur Urgas replied. "I've waited for this moment for years."

"If I'd known you were waiting, I'd have come sooner."

"Today is your last day, Cho-Hag." The Murgo King's eyes were completely mad now, and foam drooled from the corners of his mouth.

"Do you plan to fight with threats and hollow words, Taur Urgas? Or have you forgotten how to draw your sword?"

With an insane shriek, Taur Urgas ripped his broad-bladed sword from its scabbard and drove his black horse toward the Algar King. "Die!" he howled, slashing at the air even as he charged. "Die, Cho-Hag!"

It was not a duel, for there were proprieties in a duel. The two kings hacked at each other with an elemental brutality, thousands of years of pent-up hatred boiling in their blood. Taur Urgas, totally mad now, sobbed and gibbered as he swung his heavy sword at his enemy. Cho-Hag, cold as ice and with an arm as fast as the flickering tongue of a snake, slid the crushing Murgo blows aside, catching them on his sliding saber and flicking his blade like a whip, its edge biting again and again into the shoulders and face of the King of the Murgos.

The two armies, stunned by the savagery of the encounter, recoiled and gave the mounted kings room for their deadly struggle.

Frothing obscenities, Taur Urgas hacked insanely at the elusive form of his foe, but Cho-Hag, colder yet, feinted and parried and flicked his whistling sabre at the Murgo's bleeding face.

Finally, driven past even what few traces of reason were left to him, Taur Urgas hurled his horse directly at Cho-Hag with a wild animal scream. Standing in his stirrups, he grasped his sword hilt in both hands, raising it like an axe to smash his enemy forever. But Cho-Hag danced his horse to one side and thrust with all his strength, even as Taur Urgas began his massive blow. With a steely rasp, his saber ran through the Murgo's bloodred mail and through the tensed body, to emerge dripping from his back.

Unaware in his madness that he had just received a mortal wound, Taur Urgas raised his sword again, but the strength drained from his arms and the sword fell from his grasp. With stunned disbelief, he gaped at the saber emerging from his chest, and a bloody froth burst from his mouth. He lifted his hands like claws as if to tear away the face of his enemy, but Cho-Hag contemptuously slapped his hands away, even as he pulled his slender, curved blade out of the Murgo's body with a slithering whistle.

"And so it ends, Taur Urgas," he declared in an icy voice.

"No!" Taur Urgas croaked, trying to pull a heavy dagger from his belt.

Cho-Hag watched his feeble efforts coldly. Dark blood suddenly spurted from the open mouth of the Murgo King, and he toppled weakly from his saddle. Struggling, coughing blood, Taur Urgas lurched to his feet, gurgling curses at the man who had just killed him.

"Good fight, though," Cho-Hag told him with a bleak smile, and then he turned to ride away.

Taur Urgas fell, clawing at the turf in impotent rage. "Come back and fight," he sobbed. "Come back."

Cho-Hag glanced over his shoulder. "Sorry, your Majesty," he replied, "but I have pressing business elsewhere. I'm sure you understand." And with that he began to ride away.

"Come back!" Taur Urgas wailed, belching blood and curses and digging his fingers into the earth. "Come back!" Then he collapsed facedown in the bloody grass. "Come back and fight, Cho-Hag!" he gasped weakly.

The last that Cho-Hag saw of him, the dying King of Cthol Murgos was biting at the sod and clawing at the earth with trembling fingers.

A vast moan shuddered through the tight-packed regiments of the Murgos, and a sudden cheer rose from the ranks of the Algars as Cho-Hag, victorious, rode back to join the army.

"THEY'RE COMING AGAIN," General Varana announced with cool professionalism as he watched the waves of oncoming Malloreans.

"Where *is* that signal?" Rhodar demanded, staring intently downriver. "What's Anheg doing down there?"

The front ranks of the Mallorean assault struck with a resounding crash. The Drasnian pikemen began to thrust with their long, wide-bladed spears, wreaking havoc among the red-garbed attackers, and the legions raised their shields in the interlocked position that presented a solid wall against which the Malloreans beat futilely. Upon a sharp, barked command, the legionnaires turned their shields slightly and each man thrust his lance out through the opening between his shield and the next. The Tolnedran lances were not as long as the Drasnian pikes, but they were long enough. A huge, shuddering cry went through the front ranks of the Malloreans, and they fell in heaps beneath the feet of the men behind.

"Are they going to break through?" Rhodar puffed. Even though he was not directly involved in the fighting, the Drasnian King began to pant at each Mallorean charge.

Varana carefully assessed the strength of the assault. "No," he concluded, "not this time. Have you worked out how you're going to make your withdrawal? It's a little difficult to pull back when your troops are engaged."

"That's why I'm saving the Mimbrates," Rhodar replied. "They're resting their horses now for one last charge. As soon as we get the signal from Anheg, Mandorallen and his men will shove the Malloreans back, and the rest of us will run like rabbits."

"The charge will only hold them back for so long," Varana advised, "and then they'll come after you again."

"We'll form up again upriver a ways," Rhodar said.

"It's going to take a long time to get back to the escarpment if you're going to have to stop and fight every half mile or so," Varana told him.

"I know that," Rhodar snapped peevishly. "Have you got any better ideas?"

"No," Varana replied. "I was just pointing it out, that's all."

"Where *is* that signal?" Rhodar demanded again.

ON A QUIET hillside some distance from the struggle taking place on the north bank, the simpleminded serf boy from the Arendish forest was playing his flute. His melody was mournful, but even in its sadness, it soared to the sky. The boy did not understand the fighting and he had wandered away unnoticed. Now he sat alone on the grassy hillside in the warm, midmorning sunlight with his entire soul pouring out of his flute.

The Mallorean soldier who was creeping up behind him with drawn sword had no ear for music. He did not know—or care—that the song the boy played was the most beautiful song any man had ever heard.

The song ended very suddenly, never to begin again.

THE STREAM OF casualties being carried to Ariana's makeshift hospital grew heavier, and the overtaxed Mimbrate girl was soon forced into making some cruel decisions. Only those men with some chance of survival could be treated. The mortally hurt were quickly given a drink of a bitter-tasting potion of herbs that would ease their pain and then were left to die. Each such decision wrung Ariana's heart, and she worked with tears standing in her eyes.

And then Brand, the Rivan Warder, entered the tent with a stricken face. The big Rivan's mail shirt was blood-spattered, and there were savage sword cuts along the edge of his broad, round shield. Behind him, three of his sons bore the limp, bleeding form of their younger brother, Olban.

"Can you see to him?" Brand asked Ariana hoarsely.

A single glance, however, told the blond girl that the wound in Olban's chest was mortal. "I can make him comfortable," she replied a bit evasively. She quickly knelt beside the bleeding young man, lifted his head, and held a cup to his lips.

"Father," Olban said weakly after he had drunk, "I have something I have to tell you."

"Time enough for that later," Brand told him gruffly, "after you're better."

"I'm not going to get better, Father," Olban said in a voice scarcely more than a whisper.

"Nonsense," Brand told him, but there was no conviction in his voice.

"There's not much time, Father," Olban said, coughing weakly. "Please listen."

"Very well, Olban," the Warder said, leaning forward to catch his son's words.

"At Riva—after Belgarion came—I was humiliated because you had been deposed. I couldn't bear it, Father." Olban coughed again, and a bloody froth came to his lips.

"You should have known me better than that, Olban," Brand said gently.

"I do—now." Olban sighed. "But I was young and proud, and Belgarion—a nobody from Sendaria—had pushed you from your rightful place."

"It wasn't my place to begin with, Olban," Brand told him. "It was his. Belgarion's the Rivan King. That has nothing to do with position or place. It's a duty—and it's his, not mine."

"I hated him," Olban whispered. "I began to follow him everyplace. Wherever he went, I wasn't far behind him."

"What for?" Brand asked.

"At first I didn't know. Then one day he came out of the throne room wearing his robe and crown. He seemed so puffed-up with his own importance—as if he really *was* a king instead of just a common Sendarian scullion. Then I knew what I had to do. I took my dagger and I threw it at his back."

Brand's face suddenly froze.

"For a long time after that, I tried to avoid him," Olban continued. "I knew that what I had done was wrong—even as the dagger left my fingers. I thought that if I stayed away from him, he'd never find out that I was the one who'd tried to kill him. But he has powers, Father. He has ways of knowing things no man could possibly know. He sought me out one day and gave me back the dagger I'd thrown at him and he told me that I should never tell anyone what I'd done. He did that for you, Father—to keep my disgrace from you."

Grim-faced, Brand rose to his feet. "Come," he said to his other three sons. "We have fighting to do—and no time to waste on traitors." Quite deliberately he turned his back on his dying son.

"I tried to repay his mercy, Father," Olban pleaded. "I pledged my life to protecting his queen. Doesn't that count for anything?"

Brand's face was stony, and he kept his back turned in grim silence.

"Belgarion forgave me, Father. Can't you find it in your heart to forgive me too?"

"No," Brand said harshly, "I cannot."

"Please, Father," Olban begged. "Don't you have one tear for me?"

"Not one," Brand told him, but Ariana saw that his words were a lie. The grim, gray-clad man's eyes were full, but his face remained granitelike. Without another word, he strode from the tent.

Wordlessly, each of Olban's brothers clasped his hand in turn, and then they left to follow their father.

Olban wept quietly for a time, but then his growing weakness and the drug Ariana had given him drained away his grief. He lay, half dozing on his pallet for a time, then struggled to raise himself and beckoned to the Mimbrate girl. She knelt beside him, supporting him with one arm about his shoulders and her head bent to catch his faltering words. "Please," he whispered. "Please tell her Majesty what I said to my father—and tell her how sorry I was." And then his head fell forward against Ariana, and he quietly died in her arms.

Ariana had no time to mourn, for precisely then three Sendars carried Colonel Brendig into her tent. The colonel's left arm was mangled beyond all hope of repair.

"We were bringing down the bridge that crosses to the city," one of the Sendars reported tersely. "There was a support that wouldn't give way, so the colonel went down himself to chop it away. When it finally broke, the timbers of the bridge fell on him."

Ariana gravely examined Brendig's shattered arm. "I fear there is no recourse, my Lord," she told him. "The arm will have to come off, lest it mortify and carry thy life away with it."

Brendig nodded soberly. "That's about what I'd expected," he replied. "I suppose we'd better get on with it, then."

* * *

"THERE!" KING RHODAR shouted, pointing downriver. "The smoke—it's green! That's the signal. We can start the retreat now."

General Varana, however, was staring at the riverbank upstream. "It's too late, I'm afraid, your Majesty," he said quietly. "A column of Malloreans and Nadraks have just reached the river to the west of us. It very much looks as if we've been cut off."

CHAPTER EIGHTEEN

The news of the death of Taur Urgas spread through the Murgo army in a vast groan, and the heart went out of the black-robed troops. Taur Urgas had been feared by his men, but his savage madness had lent them all a peculiar sense that they were invincible. They had felt somehow that nothing could stand in his path, and that they, as the instruments of his brutal will, shared in some measure his apparent invulnerability. But with his death, each Murgo became aware with a sudden cold touch of fear that he also could die, and the assault on the armies of the west along the south bank faltered.

King Cho-Hag watched the crumbling of the Murgo resolve with a certain grim satisfaction, then rode down to the lines of infantry and the milling Mimbrate knights to confer with the other leaders. King Fulrach strode forward from the ranks of his Sendars. The dumpy, brown-bearded monarch looked almost comical in his burnished breastplate, but his sword showed signs of recent use, and his helmet was dented in a couple of places, mute evidence that the King of Sendaria had participated in the fight.

"Have you seen Anheg's signal yet?" Fulrach demanded as he approached.

Cho-Hag shook his head. "It should come any time now, though," he replied. "We'd better make some plans. Have you seen Korodullin?"

"The physicians are working on him," Fulrach said.

"Is he hurt?" Cho-Hag was startled.

"I don't think it's too serious. He went to help his friend, the Baron of Vo Ebor, and a Murgo hit him in the head with a mace. His helmet absorbed most of the blow. He's bleeding out of the ears a bit, but the physicians say he'll recover. The baron's in worse shape, though."

"Who's in charge of the Mimbrates, then?"

"Sir Andorig. He's a good man in a fight, but his understanding is a bit limited."

Cho-Hag laughed shortly. "You've just described most of Arendia, my friend. They're *all* good in a fight, and they *all* have limited understanding." Carefully he dismounted, holding on to his saddle as his weak legs nearly buckled. "We can make our decisions without Andorig's help, I think." He looked at the retreating Murgos. "As soon as we see Anheg's signal, I think we're going to want to get out of here in a hurry. The Murgos are demoralized right now, but they'll probably stiffen up again as soon as the shock wears off."

Fulrach nodded. "Did you really kill Taur Urgas in a duel?" he asked.

Cho-Hag nodded. "It wasn't really all that much of a duel. He was raving when he came at me and didn't even try to defend himself. When Anheg signals, we'll have the Mimbrates charge the Murgo front. The Murgos will probably break and run. I'll follow after them with my clansmen to hurry them along. That should give you and your foot troops time to start upriver. Andorig and I'll keep the Murgos off your back until you get clear. How does that sound?"

King Fulrach nodded. "It sounds workable," he agreed. "Do you think they'll try to follow us?"

Cho-Hag grinned. "I'll encourage them not to," he replied. "Have you got any idea of what's going on across the river?"

"It's hard to say, but things don't look very good."

"Can you think of any way we can send them help?"

"Not on short notice," Fulrach answered.

"Neither can I," Cho-Hag said. He began to pull himself back up into his saddle. "I'll go give Andorig his instructions. Keep your eyes open for Anheg's signal."

"BELGARATH!" CE'NEDRA CALLED out silently, her hand tightly clasped about the amulet at her throat. "Belgarath, can you hear me?" She was standing several yards away from where Durnik was trying to make the unconscious Polgara as comfortable as possible. The princess had her eyes tightly closed and she was putting every ounce of concentration into casting her thought to the sky, reaching out with all her heart toward the ancient sorcerer.

"Ce'Nedra?" The old man's voice was as clear as if he were standing beside her. "What are you doing? Where's Polgara?"

"Oh, Belgarath!" The princess almost sobbed with relief. "Help us. Lady Polgara's unconscious, and the Malloreans are attacking again. We're being slaughtered, Belgarath. Help us."

"Slow down," he commanded brusquely. "What happened to Pol? Where are you?"

"We're at Thull Mardu," Ce'Nedra replied. "We had to take the city so that the Cherek fleet could go on down the river. The Malloreans and the Murgos crept up on us. They've been attacking since early this morning."

Belgarath started to swear. "What's wrong with Pol?" he demanded harshly.

"The Grolims brought in an awful storm, and then there was fog. Lady Polgara and Beldin made the wind blow, and then she just collapsed. Beldin said that she exhausted herself and that we have to let her sleep."

"Where's Beldin?"

"He said that he had to keep an eye on the Grolims. Can you help us?"

"Ce'Nedra, I'm a thousand leagues away from you. Garion, Silk, and I are in Mallorea—practically on Torak's doorstep. If I so much as raise my hand, it'll wake him, and Garion's not ready to meet him yet."

"We're doomed, then," Ce'Nedra wailed.

"Stop that," he snapped. "This isn't the time for hysterics. You're going to have to wake Polgara."

"We've tried—and Beldin says that we've got to let her rest."

"She can rest later," Belgarath retorted. "Is that bag she always carries somewhere about—the one she keeps all those herbs in?"

"I—I think so. Durnik was carrying it a little while ago."

"Durnik's with you? Good. Now listen, and listen carefully. Get the bag and open it. What you want will be in a silk pouch. Don't open any jars or bottles. She keeps her poisons in those. In one of the silk bags you'll find a yellow-colored powder. It has a very acrid odor to it. Put a spoonful or so of that powder into a pot of boiling water. Put the pot beside Pol's head and cover her face with a cloak so she has to breathe the fumes."

"What will that do?"

"It'll wake her up."

"Are you sure?"

"Don't argue with me, Ce'Nedra. She'll wake up, believe me. Those fumes would wake up a dead stick. As soon as she's awake, she'll know what to do."

Ce'Nedra hesitated. "Is Garion there?" she blurted finally.

"He's asleep. We had a rough time last night."

"When he wakes up, tell him that I love him." She said it very fast, as if afraid that if she thought about it at all, she wouldn't be able to say it.

"Why confuse him?" the old man asked her.

"Belgarath!" Ce'Nedra's voice was stricken.

"I was teasing. I'll tell him. Now get to work—and don't do this any more. I'm trying to sneak up on Torak, and it's a little hard to sneak when you're shouting at somebody a thousand leagues away."

"We aren't shouting."

"Oh yes we are—it's a special kind of shouting, but it's shouting all the same. Now take your hand off that amulet and get to work." And then his voice was gone.

Durnik, of course, would never understand, so Ce'Nedra did what was necessary by herself. She rummaged around until she found a small pot. She filled it with water and set it on the small fire the smith had built the night before. Then she opened Polgara's herb bag. The blond child, Errand, stood at her side, watching her curiously.

"What are you doing, Princess?" Durnik asked, still hovering anxiously over the sleeping Polgara.

"I'm fixing something to make her rest easier," Ce'Nedra lied.

"Are you sure you know what you're doing? Some of those are very dangerous."

"I know which one I'm looking for," she replied. "Trust me, Durnik."

The powder she finally located was so acrid that it made her eyes water. She carefully measured out a bit of it and dumped it into the pot. The steaming fumes were awful, and the princess kept her face averted as she carried the pot to where Polgara lay. She set the pot beside the lady's pale, sleeping face and then laid a cloak across her. "Give me a stick," the princess said to the smith.

Durnik, his face dubious, handed her a broken-off arrow.

Ce'Nedra carefully propped up the cloak, making a small tent over the pot and Polgara's face.

"What now?" Durnik asked.

"Now we wait," Ce'Nedra told him.

Then, coming from the direction of the battle, a group of Sendarian soldiers, evidently wounded, appeared at the top of the grassy bank surrounding the secluded little beach. Their jerkins all had bloodstains on them, and several of the men wore bandages. Unlike most of the wounded who had already passed that morning, however, these men still carried their weapons.

Under the tented cloak, Polgara began to cough.

"What have you done?" Durnik cried, snatching the cloak away.

"It was necessary," Ce'Nedra replied. "I talked with Belgarath. He told me that I had to wake her up—and how to do it."

"You'll hurt her," Durnik accused. With sudden, uncharacteristic anger, he kicked the fuming pot, sending it rolling down the beach toward the water's edge.

Polgara's eyelids were fluttering as she continued to cough. When she opened her eyes, however, her look was blank, uncomprehending.

"Can you spare us some water?" one of the wounded Sendars asked as the group of men approached.

"There's a whole river right there," Ce'Nedra replied absently, pointing even as she intently stared into Polgara's eyes.

Durnik, however, gave the men a startled look, then suddenly reached for his sword.

But the men in Sendarian jerkins had jumped down from the bank and were already upon them. It took three of them to disarm the powerful smith and to hold his arms.

"You're not Sendars," Durnik exclaimed, struggling with his captors.

"How clever of you to notice," one of them replied in an accent so guttural that it was almost unintelligible. Another of them drew his sword and stood over the dazed Polgara. "Stop fighting, friend," he told Durnik with an ugly smirk, "or I'll kill this woman."

"Who are you?" Ce'Nedra demanded indignantly. "What do you think you're doing?"

"Actually, we're members of the Imperial Elite Guard," the man with the sword answered urbanely. "And we're here, your Highness, to extend to you the invitation of his Imperial Majesty 'Zakath, Emperor of Mallorea. His Majesty requests the honor of your presence in his pavilion." His face hardened, and he looked at his men. "Bring them," he ordered. "Let's get out of here before someone comes along and starts asking questions."

"They're digging in," Hettar reported to King Rhodar, gesturing toward the west and their now-blocked escape route. "They've already got a trench line running from the river for about a half a mile."

"Is there any chance of going around them?" Rhodar asked.

Hettar shook his head. "That whole flank's seething with Nadraks."

"We'll have to go through them, then," the King of Drasnia decided.

"I can't very well attack trenches with cavalry," Hettar pointed out.

"We'll storm them with the infantry units," Rhodar declared. "We'll have a certain advantage. The Asturian bows have a longer range than the short ones the Malloreans use. We'll move the archers to the front as we advance. They can rake the trenches and then harass the Mallorean archers behind the lines. The pikemen will go in first." The sweating fat man looked at General Varana. "Can your legionnaires clear the trenches once we open a hole for you?"

Varana nodded. "We train extensively for trench fighting," he replied confidently. "We'll clear the trenches."

"We'll bring the wounded with the main force," Rhodar said. "Somebody locate Polgara and the princess. It's time to leave."

"What task hast thou for Lord Hettar and me?" Mandorallen inquired. The great knight's armor showed a number of dents, but he spoke as calmly as if he had not spent the entire morning involved in heavy fighting.

"I want you and your knights to hold the rear," Rhodar told him. "Keep that army out there off my back." He turned to Hettar. "And I want you and your clansmen to go to work on the Nadraks. I don't want them to come swarming in while we're working in the trenches."

"It's a desperate move, King Rhodar," General Varana said seriously. "Attacking even hasty fortifications is always costly, and you're going to do it with another army coming at you from the rear. If your attack is beaten back, you'll be caught between two superior forces. They'll grind you to dog meat right on the spot."

"I know," Rhodar admitted glumly, "but our only hope of escape is breaking through those lines that have us blocked off. We've *got* to get back upriver. Tell your men that we *have* to take those trenches on the first charge. Otherwise, we're all going to die right here. All right, gentlemen, good luck."

Once again Mandorallen led his steel-clad knights in their fearsome charge, and once again the attacking Malloreans recoiled, driven back by the dreadful shock as the mounted men of Mimbre struck their front ranks. This time, however, the pikemen and legionnaires, as soon as they were disengaged from the enemy, turned sharply to the left and, at a jingling trot, abandoned their positions to follow the Sendars and Asturians who were already withdrawing from the field toward the west.

The delaying action of the Mimbrate knights was costly. Riderless horses galloped wildly about the battlefield, quite frequently adding to the havoc by trampling through the Mallorean ranks. Here and there among the red tunics that carpeted the field lay the single gleaming form of a fallen knight. Again and again the Mimbrates hurled themselves against the advancing red tide, slowing the Malloreans, but not quite able to stop them.

"It's going to be tight, your Majesty," General Varana advised as he and King Rhodar rode toward the hastily drawn lines blocking their escape. "Even if we break through, the bulk of the Mallorean forces are going to be hot on our heels."

"You've got a great talent for the obvious, General," Rhodar replied. "As soon as we get through, we'll put the archers at the rear and let the Malloreans march through a rain of arrows. That'll hold them back."

"Until the archers run out of arrows," Varana added.

"After we break through, I'll send the Algars on ahead. Fulrach's got whole wagonloads of arrows at the rapids."

"Which is two days march ahead."

"Do you always look at the dark side of things?"

"Just trying to anticipate, your Majesty."

"Would you mind anticipating someplace else?"

THE ALGARS HAD moved out to the right flank of the retreating army and were gathering in their characteristic small bands, preparing to charge the Nadraks drawn up on the hills above the river. Hettar, his scalp lock streaming, moved forward at a steady lope, his saber drawn and his eyes like flint. The Nadraks appeared at first to be awaiting his charge, but then, amazingly, they turned away and rode rapidly toward the river.

From the midst of that sudden surge, a half dozen men riding under the Nadrak banner swerved out toward the advancing Algars. One of the riders was waving a short stick with a white rag tied to it. The group reined in sharply about a hundred yards in front of Hettar's horse.

"I've got to talk to Rhodar," one of the Nadraks bellowed in a shrill voice. He was a tall, emaciated man with a pockmarked face and a scraggly beard, but on his head he wore a crown.

"Is this some trick?" Hettar shouted back.

"Of course it is, you jackass," the scrawny man replied. "But it's not on you this time. Get me to Rhodar at once."

"Keep an eye on them," Hettar told a nearby Clan-Chief, pointing at the Nadrak forces now streaming toward the Mallorean trenches lying in the path of the retreating army. "I'll take this maniac to see King Rhodar." He turned and led the group of Nadrak warriors toward the advancing infantry.

"Rhodar!" the thin man wearing the crown shrieked as they approached the Drasnian King. "Don't you ever answer your mail?"

"What are you doing, Drosta?" King Rhodar shouted back.

"I'm changing sides, Rhodar," King Drosta lek Thun replied with an almost hysterical laugh. "I'm joining forces with you. I've been in touch with your queen for weeks. Didn't you get her messages?"

"I thought you were playing games."

"Naturally I'm playing games." The Nadrak King giggled. "I've always got something up my sleeve. Right now my army's opening an escape route for you. You *do* want to escape, don't you?"

"Of course I do."

"So do I. My troops will butcher the Malloreans in those trenches, and then we can all make a run for it."

"I don't trust you, Drosta," Rhodar said bluntly.

"Rhodar," Drosta said in mock chagrin, "how can you say that to an old friend?" He giggled again, his voice shrill and nervous.

"I want to know why you're changing sides in the middle of a battle— particularly when your side's winning."

"Rhodar, my kingdom's awash with Malloreans. If I don't help you to defeat them, 'Zakath will simply absorb Gar og Nadrak. It's much too long and involved to talk about now. Will you accept my aid?"

"I'll take all the help I can get."

"Good. Maybe later we can get drunk together and talk things over, but for right now, let's get out of here before 'Zakath hears about this and comes after me personally." The King of Gar og Nadrak laughed again, the same shrill, almost hysterical laugh as before. "I did it, Rhodar," he exulted. "I actually betrayed 'Zakath of Mallorea and got away with it."

"You haven't gotten away with it yet, Drosta," Rhodar told him dryly.

"I will if we run fast enough, Rhodar, and right now I *really* feel like running."

'ZAKATH, DREAD EMPEROR of boundless Mallorea, was a man of medium height with glossy black hair and a pale, olive-tinged complexion. His features were regular, even handsome, but his eyes were haunted by a profound melancholy. He appeared to be about thirty-five years old, and he wore a plain linen robe with no ornament or decoration upon it to indicate his exalted rank.

His pavilion stood in the center of the camp of the Malloreans, a vast sea of tents standing on the plains of Mishrak ac Thull. The earthen floor of the pavilion was covered with priceless Mallorean carpets, and the polished tables and chairs were inlaid with gold and with mother-of-pearl. Candles filled the pavilion with glowing light. Somewhere nearby, a small group of musicians played subdued melodies set in a minor key.

The Emperor's only companion was a half-grown cat, a common, mackeral-striped tabby with that gangling, long-legged awkwardness of the adolescent feline. While 'Zakath watched with a sort of sad-eyed amusement, the young cat stalked a scrap of balled-up parchment, her feet noiseless on the carpet and her face set in a look of intent concentration.

As Princess Ce'Nedra and her companions were escorted into the pavilion, 'Zakath, seated on a low, cushioned divan, held up his hand for silence, his eyes still fixed on the cat. "She hunts," the Emperor murmured in a dead voice.

The cat crept nearer to her intended prey, crouched and shifted her hind feet nervously, her bottom twitching from side to side and her tail lashing. Then she leaped at the parchment. The ball crackled as she pounced on it, and, startled, she jumped high into the air. She batted the ball experimentally with one paw; suddenly finding a new game, she bounded it across the floor with a series of soft-pawed jabs, scampering after it with awkward enthusiasm.

'Zakath smiled sadly. "A young cat," he said, "with much yet to learn." He rose gracefully to his feet and bowed to Ce'Nedra. "Your Imperial Highness," he greeted her formally. His voice was resonant, but there was that peculiar deadness in it.

"Your Imperial Majesty," Ce'Nedra replied, inclining her head in response.

"Please, Goodman," 'Zakath said to Durnik, who was supporting the still-dazed Polgara, "let the lady rest here." He indicated the divan. "I'll send for my physicians, and they will see to her indisposition."

"Your Majesty is too kind." Ce'Nedra mouthed the ritual phrase, but her eyes were searching 'Zakath's face for some hint of his real intentions. "One is surprised to meet such courtesy—under the circumstances."

He smiled again, rather whimsically. "And, of course, all Malloreans are supposed to be raving fanatics—like Murgos. Courtesy is out of character, right?"

"We have very little information about Mallorea and its people," the princess responded. "I was not certain what to expect."

"That's surprising," the Emperor observed. "I have a great deal of information about your father and your Alorn friends."

"Your Majesty has the aid of Grolims in gathering intelligence," Ce'Nedra said, "while we must rely on ordinary men."

"The Grolims are overrated, Princess. Their first loyalty is to Torak; their second to their own hierarchy. They tell me only what they want to tell me—although periodically I manage to have a bit of additional information extracted from one of them. It helps to keep the rest of them honest."

An attendant entered the pavilion, fell to his knees, and pressed his face to the carpet.

"Yes?" 'Zakath inquired.

"Your Imperial Majesty asked that the King of Thulldom be brought here," the attendant replied.

"Ah, yes. I'd nearly forgotten. Please excuse me for a moment, Princess Ce'Nedra—a small matter requiring my attention. Please, you and your friends make yourselves comfortable." He looked critically at Ce'Nedra's armor. "After we've dined, I'll have the women of my household see to more suitable clothing for you and for Lady Polgara. Does the child require anything?" He looked curiously at Errand, who was intently watching the cat.

"He'll be all right, your Majesty," Ce'Nedra replied. Her mind was working very rapidly. This urbane, polished gentleman might be easier to deal with than she had anticipated.

"Bring in the King of the Thulls," 'Zakath ordered, his hand wearily shading his eyes.

"At once, your Imperial Majesty," the attendant said, scrambling to his feet and backing out of the pavilion, bent in a deep bow.

Gethell, the King of Mishrak ac Thull, was a thick-bodied man with lank, mud-colored hair. His face was a pasty white as he was led in, and he was trembling violently. "Y-your Imperial Majesty," he stammered in a croaking voice.

"You forgot to bow, Gethell," 'Zakath reminded him gently. One of the Mallorean guards doubled his fist and drove it into Gethell's stomach. The Thullish monarch doubled over.

"Much better," 'Zakath said approvingly. "I've asked you here in regard to some distressing news I received from the battlefield, Gethell. My commanders report that your troops did not behave well during the engagement at Thull Mardu. I am no soldier, but it seems to me that your men might have stood at least *one* charge by the Mimbrate knights before they ran away. I'm informed, however, that they did not. Have you any explanation for that?"

Gethell began to babble incoherently.

"I thought not," 'Zakath told him. "It's been my experience that the failure of people to do what's expected of them is the result of poor leadership. It appears that you've not taken the trouble to encourage your men to be brave. That was a serious oversight on your part, Gethell."

"Forgive me, dread 'Zakath," the King of the Thulls wailed, falling to his knees in terror.

"But of course I forgive you, my dear fellow," 'Zakath told him. "How absurd of you to think that I wouldn't. A reprimand of some sort *is* in order, though, don't you think?"

"I freely accept full responsibility," Gethell declared, still on his knees.

"Splendid, Gethell. Absolutely splendid. I'm so glad that this interview is going so well. We've managed to avoid all kinds of unpleasantness." He turned to the attendant. "Would you be so good as to take King Gethell out and have him flogged?" he asked.

"At once, your Imperial Majesty."

Gethell's eyes started from his head as the two soldiers dragged him to his feet.

"Now," 'Zakath mused. "What do we do with him after we've flogged him?" He thought a moment. "Ah, I know. Is there any stout timber in the vicinity?"

"It's all open grassland, your Imperial Majesty."

"What a pity." 'Zakath sighed. "I was going to have you crucified, Gethell, but I suppose I'll have to forgo that. Perhaps an extra fifty lashes will serve as well."

Gethell began to blubber.

"Oh, come now, my dear fellow, that just won't do. You *are* a king, after all, and you absolutely *must* provide a good example for your men. Run along now. I have guests. One hopes that the sight of your public flogging will give your troops greater incentive to do better. They'll reason that if I'd do that to *you*, then what I'll do to *them* will be infinitely worse. When you recover, encourage them in that belief, because the next time this happens, I'll have made arrangements to have the necessary timber on hand. Take him away," he said to his men without so much as a glance over his shoulder.

"Forgive me for the interruption, your Highness," he apologized. "These little administrative details consume so much of one's time."

The King of the Thulls was dragged sobbing from the pavilion.

"I've ordered a small supper for you and your friends, Princess Ce'Nedra," 'Zakath continued. "All the finest delicacies. Then I'll make arrangements for the absolute comfort of you and your companions."

"I hope that this won't offend your Imperial Majesty," Ce'Nedra began bravely, "but one is curious about your plans in regard to our future."

"Please set your mind at rest, your Highness," 'Zakath replied in his dead-sounding voice. "Word has reached me that the madman, Taur Urgas, is dead. I will never be able to repay you for that service, and I bear you absolutely no ill will whatsoever." He glanced toward one corner of his tent where his cat, purring ecstatically, was lying on her back in Errand's lap with all four paws in the air. The smiling child was gently stroking her furry belly. "How charming," 'Zakath murmured in an oddly melancholy voice.

Then the Emperor of boundless Mallorea rose and approached the divan where Durnik supported Lady Polgara. "My Queen," he said, bowing to her with profound respect. "Your beauty quite transcends all reports."

Polgara opened her eyes and gave him a level gaze. A wild hope leaped in Ce'Nedra's heart. Polgara was conscious.

"You are courteous, my Lord," Polgara told him in a weak voice.

"You *are* my queen, Polgara," 'Zakath told her, "and I can now understand my God's ages-old longing for you." He sighed then as his apparently habitual melancholy descended upon him once again.

"What are you going to do with us?" Durnik asked, his arms still holding Polgara protectively.

'Zakath sighed again. "The God of my people is not a good or kindly God," he told the smith. "If the arranging of things had been left to me, all might have been different. I was not consulted, however. I am Angarak, and I must bow to the will of Torak. The sleep of the Dragon-God grows fitful, and I must obey his commands. Though it wounds me deeply, I must turn you and your companions over to the Grolims. They will deliver you up to Zedar, disciple of Torak in Cthol Mishrak, City of Night, where *he* will decide your fate."

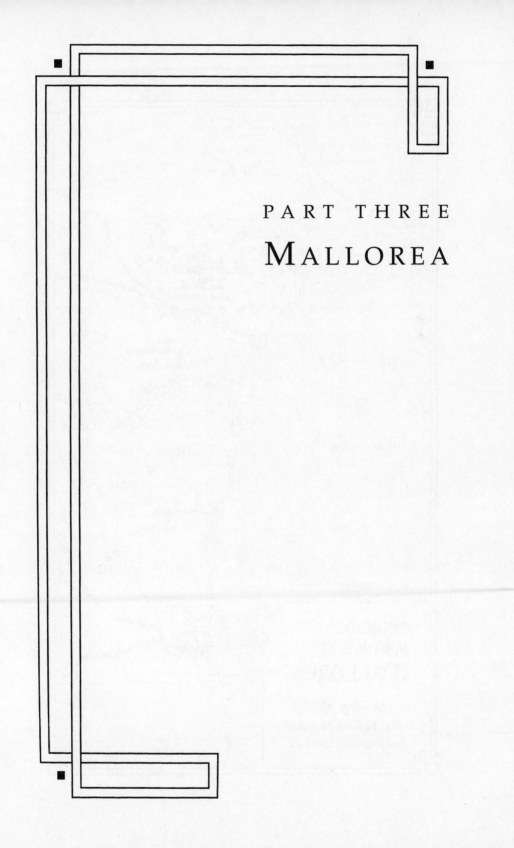

PART THREE

MALLOREA

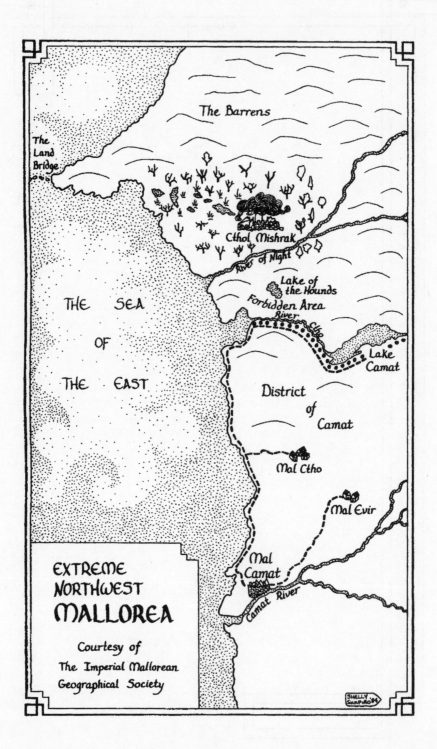

The Barrens

The Land Bridge

Cthol Mishrak

River of Night

Lake of the Hounds

Forbidden Area

River

THE SEA

OF

THE EAST

Lake Camat

District

of

Camat

Mal Ctho

Mal Evir

Mal Camat

Camat River

EXTREME
NORTHWEST
MALLOREA

Courtesy of
The Imperial Mallorean
Geographical Society

SHELLY
SHAPIRO 84

They remained for nearly a week in the Imperial compound as the personal guests of the Emperor 'Zakath, who for some strange reason seemed to take a melancholy pleasure in their company. Quarters were provided for them within the labyrinth of silken tents and pavilions that sheltered 'Zakath's household staff, and their every comfort received the personal attention of the Emperor himself.

The strange, sad-eyed man puzzled Princess Ce'Nedra. Although he was the absolute soul of courtesy, the memory of his interview with King Gethell frightened her. His ruthlessness was all the more chilling because he never lost his temper. He never seemed to sleep either, and when, often in the middle of the night, he felt some obscure need for conversation, he would send for Ce'Nedra. He never apologized for having interrupted her rest. It apparently did not even occur to him that his summons might in some way inconvenience her.

"Where did King Rhodar receive his military training?" 'Zakath asked her during one of these midnight interviews. "None of my information about him even hints about any such talent." The Emperor was seated deep in the purple cushions of a soft chair with golden candlelight playing over his face and his cat dozing in his lap.

"I really couldn't say, your Majesty," Ce'Nedra replied, toying absently with the sleeve of the pale silk gown that had been provided for her soon after her arrival. "I only met Rhodar last winter."

"Very peculiar," 'Zakath mused. "We had always assumed that he was just a foolish old man doting on his young wife. We had never even considered him a possible threat. We concentrated our attentions on Brand and Anheg. Brand is too self-effacing to be a good leader, and Anheg seemed too erratic to give us much concern. Then Rhodar appeared out of nowhere to take charge of things. The Alorns are an enigma, aren't they? How can a sensible Tolnedran girl stand them?"

She smiled briefly. "They have a certain charm, your Majesty," she told him rather pertly.

"Where is Belgarion?" The question came without any warning.

"We don't know, your Majesty," Ce'Nedra answered evasively. "Lady Polgara was furious when he slipped away."

"In the company of Belgarath and Kheldar," the Emperor added. "We heard of the search for them. Tell me, Princess, does he by any chance have Cthrag Yaska with him?"

"Cthrag Yaska?"

"The burning stone—what you in the west call the Orb of Aldur."

"I'm not at liberty to discuss that, your Majesty," she told him rather primly, "and I'm sure you're too courteous to try to wring the information out of me."

"Princess," he said reprovingly.

"I'm sorry, your Majesty," she apologized and gave him that quick, little-girl smile that was always her weapon of last resort.

'Zakath smiled gently. "You're a devious young woman, Ce'Nedra," he said.

"Yes, your Majesty," she acknowledged. "What prompted you and Taur Urgas to bury your enmity and unite against us?" Ce'Nedra wanted to demonstrate that she too could ask surprise questions.

"There was no unity in our attack, Princess," he replied. "I was merely responding to Taur Urgas."

"I don't understand."

"So long as he remained at Rak Goska, I was perfectly content to stay at Thull Zelik; but as soon as he began to march north, I had to respond. The land of the Thulls is of too much strategic importance to allow it to be occupied by a hostile force."

"And what now, 'Zakath?" Ce'Nedra asked him impudently. "Taur Urgas is dead. Where will you turn now in search of an enemy?"

He smiled a wintry smile. "How little you understand us, Ce'Nedra. Taur Urgas was only the symbol of Murgo fanaticism. Ctuchik is dead, and Taur Urgas is dead, but Murgodom lives on—even as Mallorea will live on when I am gone. Our enmity goes back for eons. At last, however, a Mallorean Emperor is in a position to crush Cthol Murgos once and for all and make himself undisputed overking of Angarak."

"It's all for power, then?"

"What else is there?" he asked sadly. "When I was very young, I thought that there might be something else—but events proved that I was wrong." A brief look of pain crossed his face, and he sighed. "In time you will discover that same truth. Your Belgarion will grow colder as the years pass and the chill satisfaction of power comes more and more to possess him. When it is complete, and only his love of power remains, then he and I will move against each other as inevitably as two great tides. I will not attack him until his education is complete. There is no satisfaction in destroying a man who does not fully comprehend reality. When all of his illusions are gone and only his love of power remains, then he will be a fit opponent." His face had grown bleak. He looked at her, his eyes as dead and cold as ice. "I think I've kept you from your rest too long, Princess," he said. "Go to bed and dream of love and other absurdities. The dreams will die all too soon, so enjoy them while you can."

Early the next morning, Ce'Nedra entered the pavilion where Polgara rested, recuperating from the struggle with the Grolims at Thull Mardu. She was alert, but still dreadfully weak.

"He's ever bit as insane as Taur Urgas was," Ce'Nedra reported. "He's so obsessed with the idea of becoming overking of Angarak that he isn't even paying any attention to what we've been doing."

"That may change once Anheg starts sinking his troop ships," Polgara replied.

"There's nothing we can do at the moment, so just keep listening to him and be polite."

"Do you think we should try to escape?"

"No."

Ce'Nedra looked at her, a bit startled.

"What's happening is supposed to happen. There's some reason that the four of us—you, Durnik, Errand, and I—are supposed to go to Mallorea. Let's not tamper with it."

"You knew this was going to happen?"

Polgara gave her a weary smile. "I knew that's where we were going. I didn't know how, exactly. 'Zakath isn't interfering in any way, so don't aggravate him."

Ce'Nedra sighed in resignation. "Whatever you say, Lady Polgara," she said.

It was early afternoon of that same day when the first reports of King Anheg's activities in the Sea of the East reached the Emperor 'Zakath. Ce'Nedra, who was present when the dispatches were delivered, felt a secret sense of satisfaction as the icy man showed the first hint of irritation she had seen in him.

"Are you certain of this?" he demanded of the trembling messenger, holding up the parchment.

"I only carried the dispatch, dread Lord." The messenger quailed, cringing back from his Emperor's anger.

"Were you at Thull Zelik when the ships arrived?"

"There was only one ship, dread Lord."

"One ship out of fifty?" 'Zakath's tone was incredulous. "Weren't there others—perhaps coming along the coast?"

"The sailors said there weren't, your Imperial Majesty."

"What kind of barbarian is this Anheg of Cherek?" 'Zakath exclaimed to Ce'Nedra. "Each of those ships carried two hundred men."

"King Anheg is an Alorn, your Majesty," Ce'Nedra replied coolly. "They're an unpredictable people."

With a great deal of effort, 'Zakath regained his composure. "I see," he said after a moment's reflection. "This was your plan from the beginning, wasn't it, Princess? The entire attack on Thull Mardu was a subterfuge."

"Not entirely, your Majesty. I was assured that the city had to be neutralized to permit the passage of the fleet."

"But why is he drowning *my* soldiers? I bear the Alorns no malice."

"Torak does—or so I'm told—and it's Torak who'll command the combined armies of Angarak. We can't allow your forces to land on this continent, your Majesty. We can't give Torak that advantage."

"Torak's asleep—and he's likely to remain so for a number of years yet."

"Our information indicates that it won't be nearly so long. Belgarath himself is convinced that the time is near at hand."

His eyes narrowed slightly. "I must hand you all over to the Grolims, then," he said. "I'd hoped to wait until Polgara had regained her strength before subjecting her to the journey; but if what you say is true, there's little time to waste. Advise your friends to make their preparations, Princess. You will depart for Thull Zelik tomorrow morning."

"As your Majesty wishes," Ce'Nedra replied, a chill going down her spine as she bowed her head in acquiescence.

"I'm a secular man, Princess," he said by way of explanation. "I bow to the altar of Torak when the occasion demands it, but I make no pretense at excessive piety. I won't involve myself in a religious dispute between Belgarath and Zedar, and I most certainly won't stand between Torak and Aldur when they confront each other. I'd strongly advise you to follow the same course."

"That decision isn't mine to make, your Majesty. My part in this was decided for me long before I was born."

He looked amused. "The Prophecy, you mean? We Angaraks have one also, Princess, and I don't imagine yours is any more reliable than ours. Prophecy is no more than a trick of the priesthood to maintain its grip on the gullible."

"Then you believe in nothing, my Lord?"

"I believe in my own power. Nothing else makes any sense."

The Grolims who escorted them in easy stages northward across the summer-browned plains of Mishrak ac Thull toward Thull Zelik were coldly proper. Ce'Nedra could not be sure if their behavior was the result of warnings from the Emperor of Mallorea or their fear of Polgara. The stifling heat was past now, and the air smelled faintly of the dusty end of summer. The Thullish plain was dotted with villages, random collections of thatch-roofed cottages and dirt streets. The villagers watched, sullen and afraid, as the priests of Torak rode through the little towns, their faces cold and aloof.

The plain to the west of Thull Zelik was covered with the red tents of the vast staging area that had been erected for the Mallorean army. With the exception of caretaker detachments, however, the huge camp was empty. The troops already in Mishrak ac Thull were with 'Zakath near Thull Mardu, and the steady stream of new arrivals had been quite suddenly cut off.

Thull Zelik itself was like any port town in the world, smelling of salt water, fish, tar, and rotting seaweed. The gray stone buildings were low and squat, almost like the Thulls themselves, and the cobblestoned streets all sloped down to the harbor, which lay in the curve of a broad estuary and faced a somewhat similar harbor on the other side.

"What city is that?" Ce'Nedra curiously asked one of the Grolims as she looked across the dirty water toward the far shore.

"Yar Marak," the black-robed priest answered curtly.

"Ah," she said, remembering now her tedious geography lessons. The two cities, one Thullish, the other Nadrak, faced each other across the estuary at the mouth of the River Cordu, and the boundary between Mishrak ac Thull and Gar og Nadrak ran down the precise center of the river.

"When the Emperor returns from Thull Mardu, I imagine he'll take steps to eradicate that place over there," one of the other Grolims added. "He was not pleased with the behavior of King Drosta on the battlefield, and, some chastisement seems in order."

They proceeded directly down a cobbled avenue to the harbor, where but a few ships were moored to the wharves.

"My crew absolutely refuses to put to sea," the Mallorean captain of the ship upon which they were to embark reported to the Grolims. "The Chereks out there are like a pack of wolves, burning and sinking everything afloat."

"The Cherek fleet is farther south," the priest in charge of the detachment of Grolims declared.

"The Cherek fleet is everywhere, revered priest," the captain disagreed. "Two days ago they burned four coastal towns two hundred leagues to the south of here, and yesterday they sank a dozen ships a hundred leagues to the north. You wouldn't believe how fast they can move. They don't even take the time to loot the towns they burn." He shuddered. "They're not men! They're a natural disaster."

"We will set sail within the hour," the Grolim insisted.

"Not unless your priests know how to man oars and handle the rigging," the captain told him. "My men are terrified. They won't sail."

"We'll convince them," the Grolim said darkly. He gave a few orders to his underpriests. An altar was quickly erected on the high stern deck, and a brazier filled with glowing coals was placed to one side of it.

The leader of the Grolims took his place at the altar and began chanting in a deep, hollow voice, his arms raised to the sky. In his right hand he held a gleaming knife. At random, his cohorts selected a sailor and dragged him, screaming and struggling, to the stern deck. As Ce'Nedra watched with horror, he was bent backward across the altar and butchered with an almost casual efficiency. The Grolim who had wielded the knife lifted the dead man's dripping heart. "Behold our offering, Dragon-God of Angarak!" he cried in a great voice, then turned and deposited the heart in the smoking brazier. The heart steamed and sizzled horribly for a moment, then began to blacken and shrivel as the fire consumed it. From the bow of the ship a gong clanged in iron celebration of the sacrifice.

The Grolim at the altar, his bloody hands dripping, turned to confront the ashen-faced sailors crowded amidships. "Our ceremonies will continue until the ship sails," he told them. "Who will be the next to give his heart to our beloved God?"

The ship set sail immediately.

Ce'Nedra, sick with revulsion, turned her face away. She looked at Polgara, whose eyes burned with hatred and who seemed in the grip of an overpowering interior struggle. Ce'Nedra knew her, and she knew that it was only by a tremendous effort of her will that Polgara was able to keep herself from unleashing a terrible retribution on the bloodstained Grolim at the altar. Beside her, protected in the clasp of one of her arms, stood Errand. On the child's face was an expression Ce'Nedra had never seen there before. His look was sad, compassionate, and at the same time filled with a kind of iron-hard resolution, as if, had he but the power, he would destroy every altar to Torak in all the world.

"You will go belowdecks now," one of their Grolim captors told them. "It will be a matter of some days before we reach the shores of boundless Mallorea."

They sailed north, hugging the Nadrak coastline, fearfully ready to run for any beach that offered itself, should Cherek ships appear on the horizon. At a certain point, the Mallorean captain peered about at the empty sea, swallowed hard, and swung his tiller over for the quick, terrified dash across open water to the east.

Once, a day or more out from the Nadrak coast, they saw a dreadful column of thick black smoke rising far to the south, and a day or so farther on they sailed through a sea littered with charred debris where bodies, pale and bloated, bobbed in the dark waves of the eastern sea. The frightened sailors pulled their oars with all their strength, not even needing the encouragement of whips to row faster.

Then, one murky morning when the sky behind them threatened rain squalls and the air was oppressively heavy with the advancing storm, a low, dark smudge appeared on the horizon ahead of them, and the sailors doubled their efforts, rushing desperately toward the safety of the Mallorean coast ahead.

The beach upon which the small boats from their ship landed them was a sloping shingle of dark, salt-crusted gravel where the waves made a strange, mournful sighing as they receded. Awaiting them some distance up from the water's edge sat a mounted party of Grolims, their black robes belted at the waist with crimson sashes.

"Archpriests," Polgara noted coldly. "We're to be escorted with some ceremony, I take it."

The Grolim who had commanded their escort went quickly up the gravel stand toward the waiting group and prostrated himself before them, speaking with a hushed reverence. One of the Archpriests, an aged man with a deeply lined face and sunken eyes, dismounted rather stiffly and came down to where Ce'Nedra and her friends had just stepped from the small boat.

"My Queen," he said to Polgara, bowing respectfully. "I am Urtag, Archpriest of the district of Camat. I am here with my brethren to escort you to the City of Night."

"I'm disappointed not to find Zedar waiting," the sorceress replied coldly. "I trust he's not indisposed."

Urtag gave her a quick look of irritation. "Do not rail against your fore-ordained fate, Queen of Angarak," he advised her.

"I have two fates awaiting me, Urtag," she said. "Which one I will follow has not yet been decided."

"I do not have any doubts about the matter," he declared.

"That's probably because you've never dared to look at the alternatives," she replied. "Shall we go, Urtag? A windy beach is hardly the place for philosophical discussion."

The Grolim Archpriests had brought horses with them, and the party was soon mounted and riding away from the sea across a line of low, wooded hills in a generally northeasterly direction. The trees bordering the upper edge of the gravel beach had been dark-boughed spruces, but once they topped the first rise they entered a vast forest of white-barked aspens. To Ce'Nedra's eyes, the stark, white trunks looked almost corpselike, and the entire forest had a gloomy, unhealthy quality about it.

"Mistress Pol," Durnik said in a voice that was scarcely more than a whisper, "shouldn't we be working on some kind of plan?"

"For what, Durnik?" she asked him.

"For our escape, of course."

"But we don't want to escape, Durnik."

"We don't?"

"The Grolims are taking us to the place we want to go."

"Why do we want to go to this Cthol Mishrak of theirs?"

"We have something to do there."

"From everything I've heard it's a bad sort of place," he told her. "Are you sure you haven't made some mistake?"

She reached out and laid her hand on his arm. "Dear Durnik," she said, "you'll just have to trust me."

"Of course, Mistress Pol," he replied immediately. "But shouldn't I know what to expect? If I should have to take steps to protect you, I ought to be prepared."

"I'd tell you if I knew, Durnik," she said, "but I don't know what we should expect. All I know is that the four of us are supposed to go to Cthol Mishrak. What's going to happen there needs us in order for it to be complete. Each of us has something to do there."

"Even me?"

"Especially you, Durnik. At first I didn't understand who you really are. That's why I tried to keep you from coming along. But now I *do* understand. You have to be there because you're going to do the one thing that's going to turn the entire outcome one way or the other."

"What is it?"

"We don't know."

His eyes grew wide. "What if I do it wrong?" he asked in a worried voice.

"I don't think you can," she assured him. "From everything I understand, what you're going to do will flow very naturally out of who and what you are." She gave him a brief, wry little smile. "You won't be able to do it wrong, Durnik—any more than you'd be able to lie or cheat or steal. It's built into you to do it right, so don't worry about it."

"That's all very well for you to say, Mistress Pol," he replied, "but if you don't mind, I *will* worry about it just a bit—privately, of course."

She laughed then, a light, fond little laugh. "You dear, dear man," she said impulsively taking his hand. "Whatever would we do without you?"

Durnik blushed and tried to look away, but her glorious eyes held his, and he blushed even more.

After they had passed through the forest of aspen, they entered a strangely desolate landscape. White boulders stuck up out of tangled weeds like tombstones in a long-abandoned graveyard, and dead trees thrust their crooked limbs at the overcast sky like pleading fingers. The horizon ahead was covered with a bank of darker cloud, a cloud so intensely black that it seemed almost purple. Oddly, Ce'Nedra noted, the cloudbank did not seem to be moving at all. There was no sign anywhere of any human habitation, and the route they followed was not even marked by a trail.

"Does no one live there?" the princess asked Polgara.

"Cthol Mishrak is deserted except for a few Grolims," the sorceress replied. "Torak smashed the city and drove its people out the day my father and King Cherek and his sons stole the Orb back from the iron tower."

"When was that?"

"A very long time ago, Ce'Nedra. As nearly as we've been able to determine, it was precisely on the same day that Beldaran and I were born—and the day our mother died. It's a bit hard to say for sure. We were a bit casual about keeping track of time in those days."

"If your mother had died and Belgarath was here, who took care of you?"

"Beldin, of course." Polgara smiled. "He wasn't a very good mother, but he did the best he could until Father returned."

"Is that why you're so fond of him?"

"One of the reasons, yes."

The ominous cloudbank still did not move. It stretched across the sky as stationary as a range of mountains; as they rode toward it, it loomed higher and higher.

"That's a very strange cloud," Durnik noted, looking speculatively at the thick curtain of purple ahead. "The storm's coming in behind us, but that cloud doesn't seem to be moving at all."

"It doesn't move, Durnik," Polgara told him. "It never has moved. When the Angaraks built Cthol Mishrak, Torak put that cloud there to hide the city. It's been there ever since."

"How long is that?"

"About five thousand years."

"The sun never shines there?"

"Never."

The Grolim Archpriests had begun to look about with a certain apprehension, and finally Urtag called a halt. "We must make ourselves known," he declared. "We don't want the watchers to mistake us for intruders."

The other Archpriests nodded nervously, and then all removed polished steel masks from beneath their robes and carefully covered their faces with them. Then each of them untied a thick torch from his saddle and ignited it with a brief, mumbled incantation. The torches burned with a peculiarly green-tinged flame and gave off a reeking, sulfurous smoke.

"I wonder what would happen if I were to blow out your torches," Polgara suggested with a hint of mischievous smile. "I could, you know."

Urtag gave her a worried look. "This is no time for foolishness, my Lady," he warned her. "The watchers are very savage with intruders. Our lives depend on those torches. Please don't do anything to bring down a disaster on us all."

She laughed lightly and let it go at that.

As they rode in beneath the cloud, it grew steadily darker. It was not precisely the clean darkness of night, but was rather a kind of dirty murkiness, a deep shade hovering in the air. They crested a rise and saw before them a cloud-enshrouded basin, and in its center, half-obscured by the pervasive gloom, stood the ravaged City of Night. The vegetation around them had shrunk to a few sparse weeds and an unhealthy-looking, stunted grass, pale and sick for want of sun. The boulders thrusting up out of the earth were splotched with a sort of leprous lichen that ate into the rock itself, and nodules of a white fungus lumped in grotesque profusion, spreading out across the dank soil as if the ground itself were diseased.

With a slow, careful pace, their sputtering torches held above their heads, the

Grolim Archpriests led the way down into the gloomy basin and across the unwholesome plain toward the shattered walls of Cthol Mishrak.

As they entered the city, the princess saw furtive hints of movement among the tumbled stones. Shadowy forms scurried from place to place among the ruins, and the sound of their movements was the clicking scrape made by creatures whose feet were clawed. Some of the shapes were upright, others were not. Ce'Nedra grew cold and afraid. The watchers of Cthol Mishrak were neither beast nor human, and they seemed to exude a kind of indiscriminate malice toward all other living things. More than anything, she was afraid that one of them might suddenly turn and confront her with a face that might rip away her sanity by its hideousness.

As they passed down a broken street, Urtag began to intone an ancient prayer to Torak, his voice hollow and shaking. The dank air grew colder, and the disease-like lichen ate at the tumbled stones of the ruined houses. Mold seemed to cling to everything, and the pale fungus grew in grotesque lumps in corners and crannies. The smell of decay was everywhere, a damp, rotten stench, and slimy pools of stagnant water lay among the ruins.

In the center of the city stood the rusted stump of a vast iron tower, the broken-off girders which had supported it thicker than a man's waist. Just to the south of the stump lay a broad, rusted trail of total destruction where the tower had fallen, crushing everything beneath it. Over the eons, the iron had rusted down into a sort of damp red mud that outlined the enormous dimensions of the fallen structure.

The stump had eroded down, the years rounding off the broken edges. The rust mingled in places with a kind of thick black ooze that ran down the faces of the iron plates like gobbets of clotted blood.

Urtag, trembling visibly now, dismounted before a vast, arched portal and led them through a half-open iron door. The echoing chamber they entered was as large as the Imperial throne room in Tol Honeth. Wordlessly, his torch held high over his head, Urtag led them across the pitted floor to another iron-arched doorway and then down a flight of clanging iron steps that reached into the darkness beneath. At the bottom of the stairs, perhaps fifty feet below the wreckage above, stood another door of black iron, studded with great, round rivet heads. Hesitantly, Urtag rapped his knuckles on the door, and the sound of his rapping echoed hollowly in the chamber beyond.

"Who comes to disturb the slumber of the Dragon-God of Angarak?" a muffled voice demanded from behind the door.

"I am Urtag, the Archpriest of Camat." The Grolim's voice was frightened. "As commanded, I bring the prisoners to the Disciple of Torak."

There was a moment of silence, and then the rattling sound of an immense chain, followed by the grating of an enormous bolt. Then slowly, creakingly, the door opened.

Ce'Nedra gasped. Standing in the doorway was Belgarath! It was a moment before her startled eyes began to sort out the subtle differences that informed her that the white-haired man before her was not indeed the old sorcerer, but rather someone who looked so much like him that they could easily pass for brothers. Subtle though the differences were, they were nonetheless profound. In the eyes of the man in the doorway there was a haunted look—a look compounded of grief and horror and a dreadful self-loathing, all overlaid with the helpless adoration of a man who has given himself utterly to a dreadful master.

"Welcome to the tomb of the one-eyed God, Polgara," he greeted the sorceress.

"It's been a long time, Belzedar," she replied in an oddly neutral voice.

"I've given up the right to that name," he told her, and his tone was faintly regretful.

"It was your decision, Zedar."

He shrugged. "Perhaps," he said. "Perhaps not. Maybe what I'm doing is also necessary." He pushed the door open wider. "Come inside, if you will. This crypt is habitable—if only barely." He looked directly at Urtag then. "You have performed a service, Urtag, Archpriest of Torak, and a service should not be unrewarded. Come." And he turned and led them back into the vaulted chamber beyond. The walls were of stone, massive blocks set without mortar, and bolted to the topmost tier were great iron arches supporting the ceiling and the immense ruin above. The great chill of masses of cold stone and iron was held off by large, glowing braziers set in each corner. In the center of the room stood a table and several chairs, and along one wall lay a cluster of loosely rolled pallets and a neat stack of gray woolen blankets. On the table stood a pair of large candles, their flame unwinking and steady in the dead air of the tomb.

Zedar paused briefly at the table to pick up one of the candles, then led them across the flagstone floor to an arched alcove set in the far wall. "Your reward, Urtag," he said to the Grolim. "Come and behold the face of your God." He lifted the candle.

Lying upon its back on a stone bier within the alcove lay a huge figure, robed and cowled in black. The face was concealed by a polished steel mask. The eyes of the mask were closed.

Urtag took one terrified look, then prostrated himself on the floor.

There was a deep, rasping sigh, and the recumbent figure in the alcove moved slightly. As Ce'Nedra stared in horrified fascination, the vast, steel-covered face turned restlessly toward them. For a moment the polished left eyelid opened. Behind that eyelid burned the dreadful fire of the eye that was not. The steel face moved as if it were flesh, twisting into an expression of contempt at the priest groveling on the flagstones, and a hollow murmuring came from behind the polished lips.

Urtag started violently and raised his suddenly stricken face, listening to the hollow muttering which he alone in the dim crypt could hear clearly. The hollow voice continued, murmuring in Urtag's ears. The Archpriest's face drained as he listened, and a look of unspeakable horror slowly twisted his features. The hollow muttering droned on. The words were indistinct, but the inflections were not. Desperately, Ce'Nedra covered her ears.

Finally Urtag screamed and scrambled to his feet. His face had gone absolutely white, and his eyes were starting from their sockets. Gibbering insanely, Urtag fled, and the sound of his screams echoed back down the iron stairway as he ran in terror from the ruined tower.

CHAPTER TWENTY

The whispering had begun almost as soon Belgarath, Silk, and Garion reached the coast of Mallorea. It was indistinct at first, little more than a sibilant breath sounding perpetually in Garion's ears, but in the days that followed as they moved steadily south, occasional words began to emerge. The words were the sort to be reckoned with—home, mother, love, and death—words upon which attention immediately fastened.

Unlike the land of the Morindim which they had left behind, northernmost Mallorea was a land of rolling hills covered with a tough-stemmed, dark green grass. Occasional nameless rivers wound among those hills, roiling and turbulent beneath a lead-gray sky. They had not seen the sun for what seemed weeks. A sort of dry overcast had moved in off the Sea of the East, and a stiff breeze, chill and smelling of the polar ice, pressed continually at their backs as they moved south.

Belgarath now rode with extreme caution. There was no sign of that half-doze that was his custom in more civilized parts of the world, and Garion could feel the subtle push of the old man's mind as he probed ahead for any hidden dangers. So delicate was the sorcerer's searching that it seemed only a slowly expiring breath, light, tentative, concealed artfully in the sound of the breeze passing through the tall grass.

Silk also rode warily, pausing frequently to listen, and seeming on occasion to sniff at the air. Often he would even go so far as to dismount and put his ear to the turf, to see if he might pick up the muffled tread of unseen horses approaching.

"Nervous work," the little man said as he remounted after one such pause.

"Better to be a little overcautious than to blunder into something," Belgarath replied. "Did you hear anything?"

"I think I heard a worm crawling around down there," Silk answered brightly. "He didn't say anything, though. You know how worms are."

"Do you mind?"

"You did ask, Belgarath."

"Oh, shut up!"

"You heard him ask, didn't you, Garion?"

"That is probably the most offensive habit I've ever encountered in anyone," Belgarath told the little thief.

"I know," Silk answered. "That's why I do it. Infuriating, isn't it? How far do we have to go before we come to woods again?"

"Several more days. We're still a goodly distance north of the tree line. Winter's too long and summer too short for trees to grow up here."

"Boring sort of place, isn't it?" Silk observed, looking around at the endless grass and the rounded hills that all looked the same.

"Under the circumstances, I can stand a little boredom. The alternatives aren't all that pleasant."

"I can accept that."

They rode on, their horses wading through the knee-high, gray-green grass.

The whispering inside Garion's head began again. "Hear me, Child of Light." That sentence emerged quite clearly from the rest of the unintelligible sibilance. There was a dreadfully compelling quality in that single statement. Garion concentrated, trying to hear more.

"I wouldn't do that," the familiar dry voice told him.

"What?"

"Don't do what he tells you to do."

"Who is it?"

"Torak, of course. Who did you think it was?"

"He's awake?"

"Not yet. Not fully at any rate—but then he's never been entirely asleep either."

"What's he trying to do?"

"He's trying to talk you out of killing him."

"He's not afraid of me, is he?"

"Of course he's afraid. He doesn't know what's going to happen any more than you do, and he's just as frightened of you as you are of him."

That immediately made Garion feel better. *"What should I do about the way he keeps whispering to me?"*

"There's not much you can do. Just don't get into the habit of obeying his orders, that's all."

They camped that evening as they usually did in a well-sheltered hollow between two hills and, as usual, they built no fire to give away their location.

"I'm getting a bit tired of cold suppers," Silk complained, biting down hard on a piece of dried meat. "This beef's like a strip of old leather."

"The exercise is good for your jaws," Belgarath told him.

"You can be a very unpleasant old man when you set your mind to it, do you know that?"

"The nights are getting longer, aren't they?" Garion said to head off any further wrangling.

"The summer's winding down," Belgarath told him. "It'll be autumn up here in another few weeks, and winter's going to be right on its heels."

"I wonder where we'll be when winter comes," Garion said rather plaintively.

"I wouldn't do that," Silk advised. "Thinking about it isn't going to help, and it's only going to make you nervous."

"Nervouser," Garion corrected. "I'm already nervous."

"Is there such a word as 'nervouser'?" Silk asked Belgarath curiously.

"There is now," Belgarath replied. "Garion just invented it."

"I wish I could invent a word," Silk said admiringly to Garion, his ferretlike little eyes gleaming mischievously.

"Please don't poke fun at me, Silk. I'm having enough trouble as it is."

"Let's get some sleep," Belgarath suggested. "This conversation isn't going anywhere, and we've got a long way to ride tomorrow."

That night the whispering invaded Garion's sleep, and it seemed to convey its meaning in images rather than words. There was an offer of friendship—of a hand outstretched in love. The loneliness that had haunted his boyhood from the moment he had discovered that he was an orphan seemed to fade, to pass somehow behind him with that offer, and he found himself rather desperately wanting to run toward that hand reaching toward him.

Then, very clearly, he saw two figures standing side by side. The figure of the man was very tall and very powerful, and the figure of the woman was so familiar that the very sight of her caught at Garion's heart. The tall, powerful man seemed to be a stranger, and yet was not. His face went far beyond mere human handsomeness. It was quite the most beautiful face Garion had ever seen. The woman, of course, was not a stranger. The white lock at the brow and the glorious eyes were the most familiar things in Garion's life. Side by side, the beautiful stranger and Aunt Pol reached out their arms to him.

"You will be our son," the whispering voice told him. "Our beloved son. I will be your father, and Polgara your mother. This will be no imaginary thing, Child of Light, for I can make all things happen. Polgara will really be your mother, and all of her love will be yours alone; and I, your father, will love and cherish you both. Will you turn away from us and face again the bitter loneliness of the orphan child? Does that chill emptiness compare with the warmth of loving parents? Come to us, Belgarion, and accept our love."

Garion jerked himself out of sleep, sitting bolt upright, trembling and sweating. *"I need help,"* he cried out silently, reaching into the vaults of his mind to find that other, nameless presence.

"What's your problem now?" the dry voice asked him.

"He's cheating," Garion declared, outraged.

"Cheating? Did somebody come along and make up a set of rules while I wasn't watching?"

"You know what I mean. He's offering to make Aunt Pol my mother if I'll do what he says."

"He's lying. He can't alter the past. Ignore him."

"How can I? He keeps reaching into my mind and putting his hand on the most sensitive spots."

"Think about Ce'Nedra. That'll confuse him."

"Ce'Nedra?"

"Every time he tries to tempt you with Polgara, think about your flighty little princess. Remember exactly how she looked when you peeked at her while she was bathing that time back in the Wood of the Dryads."

"I did not peek!"

"Really? How is it that you remember every single detail so vividly, then?"

Garion blushed. He had forgotten that his daydreams were not entirely private.

"Just concentrate on Ce'Nedra. It'll probably irritate Torak almost as much as it does me." The voice paused. *"Is that all you can really think about?"* it asked then.

Garion did not try to answer that.

They pushed on southward under the dirty overcast and two days later they reached the first trees, scattered sparsely at the edge of the grassland where great herds of antlered creatures grazed as placidly and unafraid as cattle. As the three of them rode south, the scattered clumps of trees became thicker, and soon spread into a forest of dark-boughed evergreens.

The whispering blandishments of Torak continued, but Garion countered them with thoughts of his red-haired little princess. He could sense the irritation of his enemy each time he intruded these daydreams upon the carefully orchestrated images Torak kept trying to instill in his imagination. Torak wanted him to think of his loneliness and fear and of the possibility of becoming a part of a loving family, but the intrusion of Ce'Nedra into the picture confused and baffled the God. Garion soon perceived that Torak's understanding of men was severely limited. Concerned more with elementals, with those towering compulsions and ambitions which had inflamed him for the endless eons, Torak could not cope with the scattered complexities and conflicting desires that motivated most men. Garion seized on his advantage to thwart the insidious and compelling whispers with which Torak tried to lure him from his purpose.

The whole business was somehow peculiarly familiar. This had happened before—not perhaps in exactly the same way, but very similarly. He sorted through his memories, trying to pin down this strange sense of repetition. It was the sight of a twisted tree stump, lightning-blasted and charred, that suddenly brought it all flooding back in on him. The stump, when seen from a certain angle, bore a vague resemblance to a man on horseback, a dark rider who seemed to watch them as they rode by. Because the sky was overcast, the stump cast no shadow, and the image clicked into place. Throughout his childhood, hovering always on the edge of his vision, Garion had seen the strange, menacing shape of a dark-cloaked rider on a black horse, shadowless even in the brightest sunlight. That had been Asharak the Murgo, of course, the Grolim whom Garion had destroyed in his first open act as a sorcerer. But had it? There had existed between Garion and that dark figure which had so haunted his childhood a strange bond. They had been enemies; Garion had always known that; but in their enmity there had always been a curious closeness, something that seemed to pull them together. Garion quite deliberately began to examine a startling possibility. Suppose that the dark rider had *not* in fact been Asharak—or if it had been, suppose that Asharak had somehow been suffused by another, more powerful awareness.

The more he thought about it, the more convinced Garion became that he had stumbled inadvertently across the truth of the matter. Torak had demonstrated that even though his body slept his awareness could still move about the world, twisting events to his own purposes. Asharak had been involved, certainly, but the dominating force had always been the consciousness of Torak. The Dark God had stood watch over him since infancy. The fear he had sensed in that dark shape that had hovered always on the edge of his boyhood had not been Asharak's fear, but Torak's. Torak had known who he was from the beginning, had known that one day Garion would take up the sword of the Rivan King and come to the meeting that had been ordained since before the world was made.

Acting upon a sudden impulse, Garion put his left hand inside his tunic and took hold of his amulet. Twisting slightly, he reached up and laid the marked palm of his right hand on the Orb, which stood on the pommel of the great sword strapped across his back.

"I know you now," he declared silently, hurling the thought at the murky sky. *"You might as well give up trying to win me over to your side, because I'm not going to change my mind. Aunt Pol is not your wife, and I'm not your son. You'd better stop trying to play games with my thoughts and get ready, because I'm coming to kill you."*

The Orb beneath his hand flared with a sudden exultation as Garion threw his challenge into the Dark God's teeth, and the sword at Garion's back suddenly burst into a blue flame that flickered through the sheath enclosing it.

There was a moment of deadly silence, and then what had been a whisper suddenly became a vast roar. *"Come, then, Belgarion, Child of Light,"* Torak hurled back the challenge. *"I await thee in the City of Night. Bring all thy will and all thy courage with thee, for I am ready for our meeting."*

"What in the name of the seven Gods do you think you're doing?" Belgarath almost screamed at Garion, his face mottled with angry astonishment.

"Torak's been whispering at me for almost a week now," Garion explained calmly, taking his hand from the Orb. "He's been offering me all kinds of things if I'd give up this whole idea. I got tired of it, so I told him to stop."

Belgarath spluttered indignantly, waving his hands at Garion.

"He knows I'm coming, Grandfather," Garion said, trying to placate the infuriated old man. "He's known who I was since the day I was born. He's been watching me all this time. We're not going to be able to take him by surprise, so why try? I wanted to let him know that I was on to him. Maybe it's time for *him* to start worrying and being afraid just a little bit, too."

Silk was staring at Garion. "He's an Alorn, all right," he observed finally.

"He's an idiot!" Belgarath snapped angrily. He turned back to Garion. "Did it ever occur to you that there might be something out here to worry about besides Torak?" he demanded.

Garion blinked.

"Cthol Mishrak is *not* unguarded, you young blockhead. You've just succeeded in announcing our presence to every Grolim within a hundred leagues."

"I didn't think of that," Garion mumbled.

"I didn't think you'd thought. Sometimes I don't think you know *how* to think."

Silk looked around apprehensively. "Now what do we do?" he asked.

"We'd better get out of here—as fast as our horses can carry us," Belgarath said. He glared at Garion. "Are you sure you don't have a trumpet somewhere under your clothes?" he asked with heavy sarcasm. "Maybe you'd like to blow a few fanfares as we go along." He shook his head in disgust and then gathered up his reins. "Let's ride," he said.

CHAPTER TWENTY-ONE

The Aspens were stark white and motionless under the dead sky, and they rose, straight and slender, like the bars of an interminable cage. Belgarath led them at a walk, carefully weaving his way through the endless stretches of this vast, silent forest.

"How much farther?" Silk asked the old man tensely.

"Not much more than a day, now," Belgarath replied. "The clouds ahead are getting thicker."

"You say the cloudbank never moves?"

"Never. It's been stationary since Torak put it there."

"What if a wind came along? Wouldn't that move it?"

Belgarath shook his head. "The normal rules have been suspended in that region. For all I know, the cloud might not actually be cloud. It might be something else."

"Like what?"

"An illusion of some kind, perhaps. The Gods are very good at illusions."

"Are they looking for us? The Grolims, I mean."

Belgarath nodded.

"Are you taking steps to keep them from finding us?"

"Naturally." The old man looked at him. "Why this sudden urge for conversation? You've been talking steadily for the last hour."

"I'm a little edgy," Silk admitted. "This is unfamiliar territory, and that always makes me nervous. I'm much more comfortable when I've got my escape routes worked out in advance."

"Are you always ready to run?"

"In my profession you have to be. What was that?"

Garion heard it too. Faintly, somewhere far off behind them, there was a deep-toned baying—one animal at first, but soon joined by several others. "Wolves?" he suggested.

Belgarath's face had grown bleak. "No," he replied, "not wolves." He shook his reins, and his nervous horse began to trot, the sound of its hoofs muffled by the rotting loam lying thick beneath the aspens.

"What is it then, Grandfather?" Garion asked, also pushing his horse into a trot.

"Torak's Hounds," Belgarath replied tersely.

"Dogs?"

"Not really. They're Grolims—rather specialized ones. When the Angaraks built the city, Torak decided that he needed something to guard the surrounding countryside. Certain Grolims volunteered to take on nonhuman shapes. The change was permanent."

"I've dealt with watchdogs before," Silk said confidently.

"Not like these. Let's see if we can outrun them." Belgarath didn't sound very hopeful.

They pushed their horses into a gallop, weaving in and out among the tree trunks. The limbs slapped against their faces as they rode, and Garion raised his arm to ward them off as the three of them plunged on.

They crested a low ridge and galloped down the far side. The baying behind them seemed to be closer now.

Then Silk's horse stumbled, and the little man was almost thrown from his saddle. "This isn't working, Belgarath," he said as the old man and Garion reined in. "This ground's too treacherous for us to keep this pace."

Belgarath held up his hand and listened for a moment. The deep-toned baying was definitely closer. "They're outrunning us anyway," the old man agreed.

"You'd better think of something," Silk said, looking back nervously.

"I'm working on it." Belgarath raised his face to sniff at the air. "Let's keep going. I just got a whiff of stagnant water. The area's dotted with swampy places. We might be able to hide our scent if we can get into a big enough patch of water."

They moved on down the slope toward the bottom of the valley. The odor of standing water grew steadily stronger as they rode.

"Just ahead." Garion pointed toward a patch of brown water intermittently visible among the white tree trunks.

The swamp was quite extensive, a broad patch of reeking, oily water trapped in the bottom of a thickly grown basin. Dead trees thrust up out of the water, their leafless branches seeming almost like clawed hands reaching up in mute supplication to the indifferent sky.

Silk wrinkled his nose. "It stinks bad enough to hide our scent from almost anything," he said.

"We'll see," Belgarath replied. "This might throw off an ordinary dog, but don't forget that the Hounds are really Grolims. They have the ability to reason, so they won't be relying on scent alone."

They pushed their reluctant horses into the murky water and began to splash along, changing direction frequently, weaving in and out among the dead tree trunks. Their horses' hooves stirred up rotting vegetation from the bottom, filling the air with an even more powerful stench.

The sound of the baying Hounds drew closer, filled now with an excitement and a terrible hunger.

"I think they've hit the edge of the swamp," Silk said, cocking his head to listen.

There was a momentary bafflement in the baying behind them.

"Grandfather!" Garion cried, reining in sharply.

Directly before them, knee-deep in the brown water stood a slavering black dog-shape. It was enormous—fully as large as a horse, and its eyes actually burned with a malevolent green fire. Its front shoulders and chest were massive, and the fangs protruding from its mouth were at least a foot long, curving down cruelly and dripping foam.

"We have you now," it growled, seeming almost to chew on the words as it twisted its muzzle into speech. The voice issuing from its mouth was a rasping, tearing sound.

Silk's hand instantly flashed toward one of his hidden daggers.

"Never mind," Belgarath told him. "It's only a projection—a shadow."

"It can do that?" Silk's tone was startled.

"I told you that they're Grolims."

"We hunger," the fiery-eyed Hound rumbled. "I will return soon with my packmates, and we will feed on man-meat." Then the shape flickered and vanished.

"They know where we are now." Silk's voice was alarmed. "You'd better do something, Belgarath. Can't you use sorcery?"

"That'd just pinpoint our location. There are other things out there as well as the Hounds."

"I'd say we'll have to chance it. Let's worry about one thing at a time. Did you see those teeth?"

"They're coming," Garion said tensely. From far back in the swamp, he could clearly hear the sound of splashing.

"Do something, Belgarath!"

The sky overhead had grown darker, and the air seemed suddenly oppressively heavy. From far off there was an angry mutter of thunder. A vast sigh seemed to pass through the forest.

"Keep going," Belgarath said, and they splashed off through the slimy brown water toward the far side of the swamp. The aspen trees on the solid ground ahead of them quite suddenly turned the silvery undersides of their leaves upward, and it was almost as if a great, pale wave had shuddered through the forest.

The Hounds were very close now, and their baying was triumphant as they plunged through the oily, reeking swamp.

And then there was a brilliant blue-white flash, and a shattering clap of thunder. The sky ripped open above them. With a sound nearly as loud as the thunder, they were engulfed in a sudden deluge. The wind howled, ripping away the aspen leaves in great sheets and whirling them through the air. The rain drove horizontally before the sudden gale, churning the swamp to froth and obliterating everything more than a few feet away.

"Did you do this?" Silk shouted at Belgarath.

But Belgarath's stunned face clearly said that the storm was as much a surprise to him as to Silk. They both turned to look at Garion. "Did you do it?" Belgarath demanded.

"He didn't. I did." The voice which came from Garion's mouth was not his. "I've labored too long at this to be thwarted by a pack of dogs."

"I didn't hear a thing," Belgarath marveled, wiping at his streaming face. "Not even a whisper."

"You were listening at the wrong time," the voice of Garion's inner companion replied. "I set it in motion early last spring. It's just now getting here."

"You knew we'd need it?"

"Obviously. Turn east. The Hounds won't be able to track you in all this. Swing around and come at the city from the east side. There are fewer watchers on that flank."

The downpour continued, punctuated by ripping claps of thunder and flashes of lightning.

"How long will the rain last?" Belgarath shouted over the noise.

"Long enough. It's been building in the Sea of the East for a week. It hit the coast this morning. Turn east."

"Can we talk as we ride?" Belgarath asked. "I have a great many questions."

"This is hardly the time for discussion, Belgarath. You have to hurry. The others arrived at Cthol Mishrak this morning, just ahead of the storm. Everything's ready there, so move."

"It's going to be *tonight*?"

"Yes, if you get there in time. Torak's almost awake now. I think you'd better be there when he opens his eyes."

Belgarath wiped his streaming face again, and his eyes had a worried look. "Let's go," he said sharply and he led them splashing off through the driving rain to solid ground.

The rain continued for several hours, driven before a screaming wind. Sodden, miserable, and half-blinded by flying leaves and twigs, the three of them cantered toward the east. The baying of the Hounds trapped in the swamp faded behind them, taking on a baffled, frustrated note as the thunderous deluge obliterated all scents from the swamp and the forest.

When night fell, they had reached a low range of hills far to the east, and the rain had subsided into a steady, unpleasant drizzle, punctuated by periodic squalls of chilly, gusting wind and erratic downpours that swept in randomly off the Sea of the East.

"Are you sure you know the way?" Silk asked Belgarath.

"I can find it," Belgarath said grimly. "Cthol Mishrak's got a peculiar smell to it."

The rain slackened into a few scattered droplets pattering on the leaves overhead and died out entirely by the time they reached the edge of the wood. The smell of which Belgarath had spoken was not a sharp reek, but rather was a muted, dank compound of odors. Damp rust seemed to be a major part of it, although the reek of stagnant water was also present, and the musty scent of fungus. The overall effect was one of decay. When they reached the last of the trees, Belgarath reined in. "Well, there it is," he said in a quiet voice.

The basin before them was faintly illuminated by a kind of pale, sickly radiance that seemed to emanate from the ground itself, and in the center of that large depression reared the jagged, broken remains of the city.

"What's that strange light?" Garion whispered tensely.

Belgarath grunted. "Phosphorescence. It comes from the fungus that grows everywhere out there. The sun never shines on Cthol Mishrak, so it's a natural breeding ground for unwholesome things that grow in the dark. We'll leave the horses here." He dismounted.

"Is that a very good idea?" Silk asked him as he too swung down from his saddle. "We might want to leave in a hurry." The little man was still wet and shivering.

"No," Belgarath said calmly. "If things go well, nothing in the city's going to

be interested in giving us any trouble. If things don't go well, it's not going to matter anyway."

"I don't like unalterable commitments," Silk muttered sourly.

"You picked the wrong journey, then," Belgarath replied. "What we're about
to do is just about as unalterable as things ever get. Once we start, there won't be
any possible way to turn back."

"I still don't have to like it, do I? What now?"

"Garion and I are going to change into something a bit less conspicuous.
You're an expert at moving about in the dark without being seen or heard, but we
aren't that skilled at it."

"You're going to use sorcery—*this* close to Torak?" Silk asked him incredulously.

"We're going to be very quiet about it," Belgarath assured him. "A shape-
change is directed almost entirely inward, so there isn't much noise involved anyway." He turned to Garion. "We're going to do it slowly," he said. "That spreads
out what little sound there is and makes it even fainter. Do you understand?"

"I think so, Grandfather."

"I'll go first. Watch me." The old man glanced at their horses. "Let's move
away a bit. Horses are afraid of wolves. We don't want them to get hysterical and
start crashing around."

They crept along the edge of the trees until they were some distance from the
horses.

"This ought to be far enough," Belgarath said. "Now watch." He concentrated for a moment, and then his form began to shimmer and blur. The change-
over was very gradual, and for several moments his face and the wolf's face seemed
to coexist in the same place. The sound it made was only the faintest of whispers.
Then it was done, and the great silver wolf sat on his haunches.

"Now you do it," he told Garion with the slight change of expression that is so
much a part of the speech of wolves.

Garion concentrated very hard, holding the shape firmly in his mind. He did
it so slowly that it seemed that he could actually feel the fur growing on his body.

Silk had been rubbing dirt on his face and hands to reduce the visibility of his
skin. He looked at the two wolves, his eyes questioning.

Belgarath nodded once and led the way out onto the bare earth of the basin
that sloped down toward the rotting ruins of Cthol Mishrak.

There were other shapes moving in the faint light, prowling, snuffling. Some
of the shapes had a dog smell to them; others smelled faintly reptilian. Grolims,
robed and cowled, stood watch on various hummocks and rocks, searching the
darkness with their eyes and their minds for intruders.

The earth beneath Garion's paws felt dead. There was no growth, no life on
this wasted heath. With Silk crouched low between them, the two wolves crept,
belly low, toward the ruin, taking full advantage of rocky outcrops and eroded gul-
lies. Their pace seemed excruciatingly slow to Garion, but Belgarath paid little attention to the passage of time. Occasionally, when they passed near one of the
watching Grolims, they moved but one paw at a time. The minutes dragged by as
they crept closer and closer to the broken City of Night.

Near the shattered wall, two of the hooded priests of Torak stood in quiet conversation. Their muted voices fell clearly upon Garion's intensely sharpened ears.

"The Hounds seem nervous tonight," one of them said.

"The storm," the other replied. "Bad weather always makes them edgy."

"I wonder what it's like to be a Hound," the first Grolim mused.

"If you like, perhaps they'll let you join them."

"I don't think I'm *that* curious."

Silk and the two wolves, moving as silently as smoke, passed no more than ten yards from the two idly chatting guards, and crept over the fallen stones into the dead City of Night. Once among the ruins, they were able to move faster. The shadows concealed their movements, and they flitted among the blasted stones in Belgarath's wake, moving steadily toward the center of the city where the stump of the iron tower now reared stark and black toward the murky sky.

The reek of rust, stagnation, and decay was much stronger, coming to Garion's wolf-sharp nose in almost overpowering waves. It was a gagging smell, and he clamped his muzzle shut and tried not to think about it.

"Who's there?" a voice came sharply from just ahead of them. A Grolim with a drawn sword stepped out into the rubble-strewn street, peering intently into the deep shadows where the three crouched, frozen into immobility. Garion sensed rather than heard or saw Silk's slow, deliberate reach toward the dagger sheathed at the back of his neck. Then the little man's arm swung sharply down, and his knife made a fluttering whistle as it sped with deadly accuracy, turning end for end as it flew.

The Grolim grunted, doubling over sharply, then he sighed and toppled forward, his sword clanging as it fell.

"Let's move!" Silk ran past the huddled form of the dead Grolim sprawled on the stones.

Garion smelled fresh blood as he loped past, and the smell brought a sudden, hot taste to his mouth.

They reached the massive tangle of twisted girders and crumpled plates that had been the iron tower and crept silently through the open doorway into the total blackness of the chamber within. The smell of rust was everywhere now; coupled with it was a smell of ancient, brooding evil. Garion stopped, sniffing nervously at the tainted air, feeling his hackles rising on his ruffed neck. With an effort, he suppressed the low growl that rose involuntarily in his throat.

He felt Belgarath's shoulder brush him and he followed the old wolf, guided now by scent alone in the utter blackness. At the far end of the huge, empty, iron room there was another doorway.

Belgarath stopped, and Garion felt again that faint brushing whisper as the old man slowly shifted back into the shape of a man. Garion clenched in his own will and let himself gradually flow back into his own form.

Silk was breathing a string of colorful curses, fervent but almost inaudible.

"What's the matter?" Belgarath whispered.

"I forgot to stop for my knife," Silk replied, grating his teeth together. "It's one of my favorites."

"What now, Grandfather?" Garion asked, his whisper hoarse.

"Just beyond this door, there's a flight of stairs leading down."

"What's at the bottom?"

"A cellar. It's a sort of tomb where Zedar's got Torak's body. Shall we go down?"

Garion sighed, then squared his shoulders. "I guess that's what we came for," he replied.

CHAPTER TWENTY-TWO

"Y ou don't actually believe I'll accept that, do you, Zedar?"

Garion froze in the act of putting his hand on the iron door at the foot of the stairs.

"You can't evade your responsibility with the pretense of necessity," the voice beyond the door continued.

"Aren't we all driven by necessity, Polgara?" a stranger's voice replied with a kind of weary sadness. "I won't say that I was blameless, but wasn't my apostasy predestined? The universe has been divided against itself since the beginning of time, and now the two Prophecies rush toward each other for their final meeting when all will be resolved. Who can say that what I have done was not essential to that meeting?"

"That's an evasion, Zedar," Aunt Pol told him.

"What's *she* doing here?" Garion whispered to Belgarath.

"She's supposed to be here," Belgarath whispered back with an odd note of satisfaction. "Listen."

"I don't think we'll gain anything by wrangling with each other, Polgara," Zedar the Apostate was saying. "We each believe that what we did was right. Neither of us could ever persuade the other to change sides at this point. Why don't we just let it go at that?"

"Very well, Zedar," Aunt Pol replied coolly.

"What now?" Silk breathed.

"There should be others in there, too," Belgarath answered softly. "Let's make sure before we go bursting in."

The iron door in front of them did not fit tightly, and faint light seeped through the cracks around the frame. Garion could make out Belgarath's intent face in that dim light.

"How's your father?" Zedar asked in a neutral tone.

"About the same as always. He's very angry with you, you know."

"That was to be expected, I suppose."

"He's finished eating, Lady Polgara," Garion heard Ce'Nedra say. He looked sharply at Belgarath, but the old man put one finger to his lips.

"Spread one of those pallets out for him, dear," Aunt Pol instructed, "and cover him with some blankets. It's very late, and he's sleepy."

"I'll do that," Durnik offered.

"Good," Belgarath breathed. "They're all here."

"How did they get here?" Silk whispered.

"I haven't the faintest idea, and I'm not going to worry about it. The important thing is that they're here."

"I'm glad you were able to rescue him from Ctuchik," Zedar said. "I grew rather fond of him during the years we spent together."

"Where did you find him?" Aunt Pol asked. "We've never been able to pin down what country he's from."

"I forgot precisely," Zedar answered, and his voice was faintly troubled. "Perhaps it was Camaar or Tol Honeth—or maybe some city on the other side of Mallorea. The details keep slipping away from me—almost as if I weren't supposed to examine them too closely."

"Try to remember," she said. "It might be important."

Zedar sighed. "If it amuses you," he said. He paused as if thinking. "I'd grown restless for some reason," he began. "It was—oh, fifty or sixty years ago. My studies no longer interested me, and the bickering of the various Grolim factions began to irritate me. I took to wandering about—not really paying much attention to where I was. I must have crossed and crisscrossed the Kingdoms of the West and the Angarak Kingdoms a half dozen times in those years.

"Anyway, I was passing through some city somewhere when the idea struck me all at once. We all know that the Orb will destroy anyone who touches it with the slightest trace of evil in his heart, but what would it do to someone who touched it in total innocence? I was stunned by the simplicity of the idea. The street I was on was full of people, and I needed quiet to consider this remarkable idea, so I turned a corner into some forgotten alley, and there the child was—almost as if he'd been waiting for me. He seemed to be about two years old at the time—old enough to walk and not much more. I held out my hand to him and said, 'I have a little errand for you, my boy.' He came to me and repeated the word, 'Errand.' It's the only word I've ever heard him say."

"What did the Orb do when he first touched it?" Aunt Pol asked him.

"It flickered. In some peculiar way it seemed to recognize him, and something seemed to pass between them when he laid his hand on it." He sighed. "No, Polgara, I don't know who the child is—or even what he is. For all I know, he may even be an illusion. The idea to use him in the first place came to me so suddenly that I sometimes wonder if perhaps it was placed in my mind. It's entirely possible, I suppose, that I didn't find *him*, but that he found *me*." He fell silent again.

There was a long pause on the other side of the iron door.

"Why, Zedar?" Aunt Pol asked him very quietly. "Why did you betray our Master?" Her voice was strangely compassionate.

"To save the Orb," he replied sadly. "That was the idea at first, at least. From the moment I first saw it, it owned me. After Torak took it from our Master, Belgarath and the others began making their plans to regain it by force, but I knew that if Aldur himself did not join his hand with theirs to strike directly at Torak, they'd fail—and Aldur would not do that. I reasoned that if force must fail, then guile might succeed. I thought that by pretending allegiance to Torak, I might gain his confidence and steal it back from him."

"What happened, Zedar?" Her question was very direct.

There was another long, painful pause.

"Oh, Polgara!" Zedar's voice came in a strangled sob. "You cannot know! I was so sure of myself—so certain that I could keep a part of my mind free from Torak's domination—but I was wrong—wrong! His mind and will overwhelm me. He took me in his hand and he crushed out all of my resistance. The touch of his hand, Polgara!" There was horror in Zedar's voice. "It reaches down into the very depths of your soul. I know Torak for what he is—loathesome, twisted, evil beyond your understanding of the word—but when he calls me, I must go; and what he bids me do, I must do—even though my soul shrieks within me against it. Even now, as he sleeps, his fist is around my heart." There was another hoarse sob.

"Didn't you know that it's impossible to resist a God?" Aunt Pol asked in that same compassionate voice. "Was it pride, Zedar? Were you so sure of your power that you thought you could trick him—that you could conceal your intention from him?"

Zedar sighed. "Perhaps," he admitted. "Aldur was a gentle Master. He never brought his mind down on me, so I wasn't prepared for what Torak did to me. Torak is not gentle. What he wants, he takes—and if he must rip out your soul in the taking, it doesn't matter to him in the slightest. You'll discover his power, Polgara. Soon he'll awaken and he'll destroy Belgarion. Not even the Rivan King is a match for that awful mind. And then Torak will take you as his bride—as he's always said he would. Don't resist him, Polgara. Save yourself that agony. In the end, you'll go to him anyway. You'll go willingly—even eagerly."

There was a sudden scraping sound in the room beyond the iron door, and a quick rush of feet.

"Durnik!" Aunt Pol cried sharply. "No!"

"What's happening?" Garion demanded of Belgarath.

"*That's* what it means!" Belgarath gasped. "Get that door open!"

"Get back, you fool!" Zedar was shouting.

There was a sudden crash, the sound of bodies locked in struggle smashing into furniture.

"I warn you," Zedar cried again. "Get back!"

There was the sharp sound of a blow, of a fist striking solid bone.

"Zedar!" Belgarath roared, yanking at the iron door.

Then within the room there was a thunderous detonation.

"Durnik!" Aunt Pol shrieked.

In a sudden burst of fury, Belgarath raised his clenched hand, joined his flaming will with his arm and drove his fist at the locked door. The massive force of his blow ripped the iron door from its hinges as if it had been no more than paper.

The room beyond had a vaulted, curved ceiling supported by great iron girders, black with age. Garion seemed to see everything in the room at once with a curious kind of detachment, as if all emotion had been drained from him. He saw Ce'Nedra and Errand clinging to each other in fright beside one wall. Aunt Pol was standing as if locked in place, her eyes wide as she stared in stunned disbelief at the still form of Durnik the smith, who lay crumpled on the floor, and whose face had that deadly pale cast to it that could only mean one thing. A terrible flood of realization suddenly swept her face—a realization of an irrevocable loss. "No!" she cried out. "My Durnik—No!" She rushed to the fallen man, fell on her knees beside him and gathered his still form into her arms with a heartbroken wail of grief and despair.

And then Garion saw Zedar the Apostate for the first time. The sorcerer was also staring at Durnik's body. There was a desperate regret on his face—a knowledge that he had finally committed the one act that forever put him past all hope of redemption. "You fool," he muttered. "Why? Why did you make me kill you? That's the one thing above all others I didn't want to do."

Then Belgarath, as inexorable as death itself, lunged through the shattered remains of the door and rushed upon the man he had once called brother.

Zedar flinched back from the old sorcerer's awful rage. "I didn't mean to do it, Belgarath," he quavered, his hands raised to ward off Belgarath's rush. "The fool tried to attack me. He was—"

"You—" Belgarath grated at him from between teeth clenched with hate. "You—you—" But he was past speech. No word could contain his rage. He raised both arms and struck at Zedar's face with his fists. Zedar reeled back, but Belgarath was upon him, grappling, pounding at him with his hands.

Garion could feel flickers of will from one or the other of them; but caught up in emotions so powerful that they erased thought, neither was coherent enough to focus the force within him. And so, like two tavern brawlers, they rolled on the floor, kicking, gouging, pounding at each other, Belgarath consumed with fury and Zedar with fear and chagrin.

Desperately, the Apostate jerked a dagger from the sheath at his waist, and Belgarath seized his wrist in both hands and pounded it on the floor until the knife went skittering away. Then each struggled to reach the dagger, clawing and jerking at each other, their faces frozen into intense grimaces as each strove to reach the dagger first.

At some point during the frenzied seconds when they had burst into the room, Garion had, unthinking, drawn the great sword from its sheath across his back, but the Orb and the blade were cold and unresponsive in his hand as he stood watching the deadly struggle between the two sorcerers.

Belgarath's hands were locked about Zedar's throat, and Zedar, strangling, clawed desperately at the old man's arms. Belgarath's face was contorted into an animal snarl, his lips drawn back from clenched teeth as he throttled his ancient enemy. As if finally driven past all hope of sanity, he struggled to his feet, dragging Zedar up with him. Holding the Apostate by the throat with one hand, he began to rain blows on him with the other. Then, between one blow and the next, he swung his arm down and pointed at the stones beneath their feet. With a dreadful grinding, a great crack appeared, zigzagging across the floor. The rocks shrieked in protest as the crack widened. Still struggling, the two men toppled and fell into the yawning fissure. The earth seemed to shudder. With a terrible sound, the crack ground shut.

Incredulously, his mouth suddenly agape, Garion stared in stunned disbelief at the scarcely discernible crack through which the two men had fallen.

Ce'Nedra screamed, her hands going to her face in horror.

"Do something!" Silk shouted at Garion, but Garion could only stare at him in blank incomprehension.

"Polgara!" Silk said desperately, turning to Aunt Pol. Still incapacitated by her sudden, overwhelming grief, she could not respond, but knelt with Durnik's lifeless body in her arms, weeping uncontrollably as she rocked back and forth, holding him tightly against her.

From infinitely far beneath there was a sullen detonation, and then another. Even in the bowels of the earth, the deadly struggle continued.

As if compelled, Garion's eyes sought out the embrasure in the far wall; there in the dim light he could make out the recumbent form of Kal Torak. Strangely emotionless, Garion stared at the form of his enemy, meticulously noting every detail. He saw the black robe and the polished mask. And he saw Cthrek Goru, Torak's great black sword.

Although he did not—could not—move or even feel, a struggle, nonetheless, raged inside him—a struggle perhaps even more dreadful than that which had just plunged Belgarath and Zedar into the depths of the earth. The two forces which had first diverged and then turned and rushed at each other down the endless corridors of time had finally met within him. The EVENT which was the ultimate conclusion of the two Prophecies, had begun, and its first skirmishes were taking place within Garion's mind. Minute and very subtle adjustments were shifting some of his most deeply ingrained attitudes and perceptions.

Torak moved, stirring restlessly, as those same two forces met within *him*.

Dreadful flashes of the sleeping God's mind assailed Garion, and he saw clearly the terrible subterfuge that lay behind Torak's offer of friendship and love. Had his fear of their duel drawn him into yielding, fully half of creation would have shimmered and vanished. More than that, what Torak had offered was not love but an enslavement so vile that it was beyond imagining.

But he had not yielded. He had somehow evaded the overwhelming force of Torak's mind and had placed himself utterly in the hands of the Prophecy that had drawn him here. With an absolute denial of self, he had become the instrument of the Prophecy. He was no longer afraid. Sword in hand, the Child of Light awaited the moment when the Prophecy would release him to join in deadly struggle with the Dark God.

Then, even as Silk desperately tried to arouse either Garion or Polgara to action, the stones of the floor buckled upward, and Belgarath rose from the earth.

Garion, still abstracted and bemused, saw that all traces of the sometimes foolish old man he had known before were gone. The thieving old storyteller had vanished. Even the irritable old man who had led the quest for the Orb no longer existed. In their place stood the form of Belgarath the sorcerer, the Eternal Man, shimmering in the aura of his full power.

CHAPTER TWENTY-THREE

"Where is Zedar?" Aunt Pol asked, raising her tear-streaked face from Durnik's lifeless body to stare with a dreadful intensity at her father.

"I left him down there," Belgarath replied bleakly.

"Dead?"

"No."

"Bring him back."

"Why?"

"To face me." Her eyes burned.

The old man shook his head. "No, Pol," he said to her. "You've never killed anyone. Let's leave it that way."

She gently lowered Durnik's body to the floor and rose to her feet, her pale face twisted with grief and an awful need. "Then *I* will go to him," she declared, raising both arms as if to strike at the earth beneath her feet.

"No," Belgarath told her, extending his own hand, "you will *not*."

They stood facing each other, locked in a dreadful, silent struggle. Aunt Pol's look at first was one of annoyance at her father's interference. She raised one arm again to bring the force of her will crashing down at the earth, but once again Belgarath put forth his hand.

"Let me go, Father."

"No."

She redoubled her efforts, twisting as if trying to free herself from his unseen restraint. "Let me go, old man," she cried.

"No. Don't do this, Pol. I don't want to hurt you."

She tried again, more desperately this time, but once again Belgarath smothered her will with his. His face hardened, and he set his jaw.

In a last effort, she flung the whole force of her mind against the barrier he had erected. Like some great rock, however, the old man remained firm. Finally her shoulders slumped, and she turned, knelt beside Durnik's body, and began to weep again.

"I'm sorry, Pol," he said gently. "I never wanted to have to do that. Are you all right?"

"How can you ask that?" she demanded brokenly, wringing her hands over Durnik's silent body.

"That's not what I meant."

She turned her back on him and buried her face in her hands.

"I don't think you could have reached him anyway, Pol," the old man told her. "You know as well as I that what one of us does, another cannot undo."

Silk, his ferretlike face shocked, spoke in a hushed voice. "What did you do to him?"

"I took him down until we came to solid rock. And then I sealed him up in it."

"Can't he just come up out of the earth the way you did?"

"No. That's impossible for him now. Sorcery is thought, and no man can exactly duplicate the thought of another. Zedar's imprisoned inside the rock forever—or until I choose to free him." The old man looked mournfully at Durnik's body. "And I don't think I'll choose to do that."

"He'll die, won't he?" Silk asked.

Belgarath shook his head. "No. That was part of what I did to him. He'll lie inside the rock until the end of days."

"That's monstrous, Belgarath," Silk said in a sick voice.

"So was that," Belgarath replied grimly, pointing to Durnik.

Garion could hear what they were saying and could see them all quite clearly, but it seemed somehow that they were actually someplace else. The others in the underground crypt seemed to be on the periphery of his attention. For him there was only one other in the vaulted chamber, and that other was Kal Torak, his enemy.

The restless stirring of the drowsing God became more evident. Garion's peculiarly multiple awareness—in part his own, in part derived from the Orb, and as ever overlaid by the consciousness which he had always called the dry voice in his mind—perceived in that stirring the pain that lay beneath the maimed God's movements. Torak was actually writhing as he half slept. An injured man would heal in time, and his pain would gradually diminish and ultimately disappear, because injury was a part of the human condition. A man was born to be hurt from time to time, and the mechanism for recovery was born with him. A God, on the other hand, was invulnerable, and he had no need for the ability to heal. Thus it was with Torak. The fire which the Orb had loosed upon him when he had used it to crack the world still seared his flesh, and his pain had not diminished in the slightest down through all the endless centuries since his maiming. Behind that steel mask, the flesh of the Dragon-God's face still smoked, and his burned eye still boiled endlessly in its socket. Garion shuddered, almost pitying that perpetual agony.

The child, Errand, pulled himself free from Ce'Nedra's trembling arms and crossed the flagstone floor of the tomb, his small face intent. He stopped, bent and put his hand on Durnik's shoulder. Gently he shook the dead man as if trying to wake him. His little face became puzzled when the smith did not respond. He shook again, a bit harder, his eyes uncomprehending.

"Errand," Ce'Nedra called to him, her voice breaking, "come back. There's nothing we can do."

Errand looked at her, then back at Durnik. Then he gently patted the smith's shoulder with a peculiar little gesture, sighed, and went back to the princess. She caught him suddenly in her arms and began to weep, burying her face against his small body. Once again with that same curious little gesture, he patted her flaming hair.

Then from the alcove in the far wall there came a long, rasping sigh, a shuddering expiration of breath. Garion looked sharply toward the alcove, his hand tightening on the hilt of his cold sword. Torak had turned his head, and his eyes were open. The hideous fire burned in the eye that was not as the God came awake.

Belgarath drew in his breath in a sharp hiss as Torak raised the charred stump of his left hand as if to brush away the last of his sleep, even as his right hand groped for the massive hilt of Cthrek Goru, his black sword. "Garion!" Belgarath said sharply.

But Garion, still locked in stasis by the forces focusing upon him, could only stare at the awakening God. A part of him struggled to shake free, and his hand trembled as he fought to lift his sword.

"Not yet," the voice whispered.

"Garion!" Belgarath actually shouted this time. Then, in a move seemingly born of desperation, the old sorcerer lunged past the bemused young man to fling himself upon the still recumbent form of the Dark God.

Torak's hand released the hilt of his sword and almost contemptuously grasped the front of Belgarath's tunic, lifting the struggling old man from him as one might lift a child. The steel mask twisted into an ugly sneer as the God held the helpless sorcerer out from him. Then, like a great wind, the force of Torak's mind struck, hurling Belgarath across the room, ripping away the front of his tunic. Something glittered across Torak's knuckles, and Garion realized that it was the silver chain of Belgarath's amulet—the polished medallion of the standing wolf. In a very peculiar way the medallion had always been the center of Belgarath's power, and now it lay in the grip of his ancient enemy.

With a dreadfully slow deliberation, the Dark God rose from his bier, towering over all of them, Cthrek Goru in his hand.

"Garion!" Ce'Nedra screamed. "Do something!"

With deadly pace Torak strode toward the dazed Belgarath, raising his sword. But Aunt Pol sprang to her feet and threw herself between them.

Slowly Torak lowered his sword, and then he smiled a loathsome smile. "My bride," he rasped in a horrid voice.

"Never, Torak," she declared.

He ignored her defiance. "Thou hast come to me at last, Polgara," he gloated.

"I have come to watch you die."

"Die, Polgara? Me? No, my bride, that is not why thou hast come. My will hast drawn thee to me as was foretold. And now thou art mine. Come to me, my beloved."

"Never!"

"Never, Polgara?" There was a dreadful insinuation in the God's rasping voice. "Thou wilt submit to me, my bride. I will bend thee to my will. Thy struggles shall but make my victory over thee the sweeter. In the end, I will have thee. Come here."

So overwhelming was the force of his mind that she swayed almost as a tree sways in the grip of a great wind. "No," she gasped, closing her eyes and turning her face away sharply.

"Look at me, Polgara," he commanded, his voice almost purring. "I am thy fate. All that thou didst think to love before me shall fall away, and thou shalt love only me. Look at me."

Helplessly she turned her head and opened her eyes to stare at him. The hatred and defiance seemed to melt out of her, and a terrible fear came into her face.

"Thy will crumbles, my beloved," he told her. "Now come to me."

She *must* resist! All the confusion was gone now, and Garion understood at last. *This* was the real battle. If Aunt Pol succumbed, they were all lost. It had all been for this.

"Help her," the voice within him said.

"Aunt Pol!" Garion threw the thought at her. *"Remember Durnik!"* He knew without knowing how he knew that this was the one thing that could sustain her in her deadly struggle. He ranged through his memory, throwing images of Durnik at her—of the smith's strong hands at work at his forge—of his serious eyes—of the quiet sound of his voice—and most of all of the good man's unspoken love for her, the love that had been the center of Durnik's entire life.

She had begun involuntarily to move, no more than a slight shifting of her weight in preparation for that first fatal step in response to Torak's overpowering command. Once she had made that step, she would be lost. But Garion's memories of Durnik struck her like a blow. Her shoulders, which had already begun to droop in defeat, suddenly straightened, and her eyes flashed with renewed defiance. "Never!" she told the expectantly waiting God. "I *will* not!"

Torak's face slowly stiffened. His eyes blazed as he brought the full, crushing force of his will to bear upon her, but she stood firmly against all that he could do, clinging to the memory of Durnik as if to something so solid that not even the will of the Dark God could tear her from it.

A look of baffled frustration contorted Torak's face as he perceived that she would never yield—that her love would be forever denied to him. She had won, and her victory was like a knife twisting slowly inside him. Thwarted, enraged, maddened by her now-unalterable will to resist, Torak raised his face and suddenly howled—a shocking, animal-like sound of overwhelming frustration.

"Then perish both!" he raged. "Die with thy father!" And with that, he once more raised his deadly sword.

Unflinching, Aunt Pol faced the raging God.

"Now, Belgarion!" The voice cracked in Garion's mind.

The Orb, which had remained cold and dead throughout all the dreadful confrontation between Aunt Pol and the maimed God, suddenly flared into life, and the sword of the Rivan King exploded into fire, filling the crypt with an intense blue light. Garion leaped forward, extending his sword to catch the deadly blow which was already descending upon Aunt Pol's unprotected face.

The steel sound of blade against blade was like the striking of a great bell, and it rang within the crypt, shimmering and echoing from the walls. Torak's sword, deflected by the flaming blade, plowed a shower of sparks from the flagstone floor. The God's single eye widened as he recognized all in one glance the Rivan King, the flaming sword and the blazing Orb of Aldur. Garion saw in the look that Torak had already forgotten Aunt Pol and that now the maimed God's full attention was focused on *him*.

"And so thou hast come at last, Belgarion," the God greeted him gravely. "I have awaited thy coming since the beginning of days. Thy fate awaits thee here.

Hail, Belgarion, and farewell." His arm lashed back, and he swung a vast blow, but Garion, without even thinking, raised his own sword and once again the crypt rang with the bell note of blade against blade.

"Thou art but a boy, Belgarion," Torak said. "Wilt thou pit thyself against the might and invincible will of a God? Submit to me, and I will spare thy life."

The will of the God of Angarak was now directed at *him*, and in that instant, Garion fully understood how hard Aunt Pol's struggle had been. He felt the terrible compulsion to obey draining the strength from him. But suddenly a vast chorus of voices rang down through all the centuries to him, crying out the single word, "No!" All the lives of all who preceded him had been directed at this one moment, and those lives infused him now. Though he alone held Iron-grip's sword, Belgarion of Riva was *not* alone, and Torak's will could not sway him.

In a move of absolute defiance, Garion again raised his flaming sword.

"So be it, then," Torak roared. "To the death, Belgarion!"

At first it seemed but some trick of the flickering light that filled the tomb, but almost as soon as that thought occurred, Garion saw that Torak *was* growing larger, swelling upward, towering, expanding. With an awful wrenching sound, he shouldered aside the rusted iron roof of the tomb, bursting upward.

Once again without thinking, without even stopping to consider *how* to do it, Garion also began to expand, and he too exploded through the confining ceiling, shuddering away the rusty debris as he rose.

In open air among the decaying ruins of the City of Night the two titanic adversaries faced each other beneath the perpetual cloud that blotted out the sky.

"The conditions are met," the dry voice spoke through Garion's lips.

"So it would seem," another, equally unemotional voice came from Torak's steel-encased mouth.

"Do you wish to involve others?" Garion's voice asked.

"It hardly seems necessary. These two have sufficient capacity for what must be brought to bear upon them."

"Then let it be decided here."

"Agreed."

And with that Garion felt a sudden release as all constraint was removed from him. Torak, also released, raised Cthrek Goru, his lips drawn back in a snarl of hate.

Their struggle was immense. Rocks shattered beneath the colossal force of deflected blows. The sword of the Rivan King danced in blue flames, and Cthrek Goru, Torak's blade of shadows, swept a visible darkness with it at every blow. Beyond thought, beyond any emotion but blind hatred, the two swung and parried and lurched through the broken ruins, crushing all beneath them. The elements themselves erupted as the fight continued. The wind shrieked through the rotting city, tearing at the trembling stones. Lightning seethed about them, glaring and flickering. The earth rumbled and shook beneath their massive feet. The featureless cloud that had concealed the City of Night beneath its dark mantle for five millennia began to boil and race above them. Great patches of stars appeared and disappeared in the roiling middle of the surging cloud. The Grolims, both human and nonhuman, aghast at the towering struggle that had suddenly erupted in their very midst, fled, shrieking in terror.

Garion's blows were directed at Torak's blind side, and the Dark God flinched from the fire of the Orb each time the flaming sword struck, but the shadow of Cthrek Goru put a deathly chill into Garion's blood each time it passed over him.

They were more evenly matched than Garion had imagined possible. Torak's advantage of size had been erased when they had both swelled into immensity, and Garion's inexperience was offset by Torak's maiming.

It was the uneven ground that betrayed Garion. Retreating before a sudden flurry of massive blows, he felt one heel catch on a heap of tumbled rock, and the rotten stones crumbled and rolled beneath his feet. Despite his scrambling attempt to keep his balance, he fell.

Torak's single eye blazed in triumph as he raised the dark sword. But, seizing his sword hilt in both hands, Garion raised his burning blade to meet that vast blow. When the swords struck, edge to edge, a huge shower of sparks cascaded down over Garion.

Again Torak raised Cthrek Goru, but a strange hunger flickered across his steel-encased face. "Yield!" he roared.

Garion stared up at the huge form towering over him, his mind racing.

"I have no wish to kill thee, boy," Torak said, almost pleading. "Yield and I will spare thy life."

And then Garion understood. His enemy was not trying to kill him, but was striving instead to force him to submit. Torak's driving need was for domination! *This* was where the real struggle between them lay!

"Throw down thy sword, Child of Light, and bow before me," the God commanded, and the force of his mind was like a crushing weight.

"I *will* not," Garion gasped, wrenching away from that awful compulsion. "You may kill me, but I will *not* yield."

Torak's face twisted as if his perpetual agony had been doubled by Garion's refusal. "Thou *must*," he almost sobbed. "Thou art helpless before me. Submit to me."

"No!" Garion shouted, and, taking advantage of Torak's chagrin at that violent rejection, he rolled out from under the shadow of Cthrek Goru and sprang to his feet. Everything was clear now, and he knew at last how he could win.

"Hear me, maimed and despised God," he grated from between clenched teeth. "You are nothing. Your people fear you, but they do not love you. You tried to deceive me into loving you; you tried to force Aunt Pol to love you; but I refuse you—even as she did. You're a God, but you are nothing. In all the universe there is not one person—not one thing—that loves you. You are alone and empty, and even if you kill me, I'll still win. Unloved and despised, you'll howl out your miserable life to the end of days."

Garion's words struck the maimed God like blows, and the Orb, as if echoing those words, blazed anew, lashing at the Dragon-God with its consuming hatred. *This* was the EVENT for which the Universe had waited since the beginning of time. *This* was why Garion had come to this decaying ruin—not to fight Torak, but to reject him.

With an animal howl of anguish and rage, the Child of Dark raised Cthrek Goru above his head and ran at the Rivan King. Garion made no attempt to ward off the blow, but gripped the hilt of his flaming sword in both hands and, extending his blade before him, he lunged at his charging enemy.

It was so easy. The sword of the Rivan King slid into Torak's chest like a stick into water, and as it ran into the God's suddenly stiffening body, the power of the Orb surged up the flaring blade.

Torak's vast hand opened convulsively, and Cthrek Goru tumbled harmlessly from his grip. He opened his mouth to cry out, and blue flame gushed like blood from his mouth. He clawed at his face, ripping away the polished steel mask to reveal the hideously maimed features that had lain beneath. Tears started from his eyes, both the eye that was and the eye that was not, but the tears were also fire, for the sword of the Rivan King buried in his chest filled him with its flame.

He lurched backward. With a steely slither, the sword slid out of his body. But the fire the blade had ignited within him did not go out. He clutched the gaping wound, and blue flame spurted out between his fingers, spattering in little burning pools among the rotting stones about him.

His maimed face, still streaked with fiery tears, contorted in agony. He lifted that burning face to the heaving sky and raised his vast arms. In mortal anguish, the stricken God cried to heaven, "Mother!" and the sound of his voice echoed from the farthest star.

He stood so for a frozen moment, his arms upraised in supplication, and then he tottered, and then he fell dead at Garion's feet.

For an instant there was absolute silence. Then a howling cry started at Torak's dead lips, fading into unimaginable distance as the dark Prophecy fled, taking the inky shadow of Cthrek Goru with it.

Again there was silence. The racing clouds overhead stopped at once in their maddest plunge, and the stars that had appeared among the tatters of that cloud went out. The entire universe shuddered—and stopped. There was a moment of absolute darkness as all light everywhere went out and all motion ceased. In that dreadful instant all that existed—all that had been, all that was, all that was yet to be was wrenched suddenly into the course of one Prophecy. Where there had always been two, there was now but one.

And then, faint at first, the wind began to blow, purging away the rotten stink of the City of Night, and the stars came on again like suddenly reilluminated jewels on the velvety throat of night. As the light returned, Garion stood wearily over the body of the God he had just killed. His sword still flickered blue in his hand, and the Orb exulted in the vaults of his mind. Vaguely he was aware that in that shuddering moment when all light had died, both he and Torak had returned to their normal size, but he was too tired to wonder about it.

From the shattered tomb not far away, Belgarath emerged, shaken and drawn. The broken chain of his medallion dangled from his tightly clenched hand, and he stopped to stare for a moment at Garion and the fallen God.

The wind moaned in the shattered ruins, and somewhere, far off in the night, the Hounds of Torak howled a mournful dirge for their fallen master.

Belgarath straightened his shoulders; then, in a gesture peculiarly like that which Torak had made in the moment of his death, he raised his arms to the sky.

"Master!" he cried out in a huge voice. "It is finished!"

CHAPTER TWENTY-FOUR

It was over, but there was a bitterness in the taste of Garion's victory. A man did not lightly kill a God, no matter how twisted or evil the God might be. And so Belgarion of Riva stood sadly over the body of his fallen enemy as the wind, smelling faintly of the approaching dawn, washed over the decaying ruins of the City of Night.

"Regrets, Garion?" Belgarath asked quietly, putting his hand on his grandson's shoulder.

Garion sighed. "No, Grandfather," he said. "I suppose not—not really. It had to be done, didn't it?"

Belgarath nodded gravely.

"It's just that he was so alone at the end. I took everything away from him before I killed him. I'm not very proud of that."

"As you say, it had to be done. It was the only way you could beat him."

"I just wish I could have left him something, that's all."

From the ruins of the shattered iron tower, a sad little procession emerged. Aunt Pol, Silk, and Ce'Nedra were bringing out the body of Durnik the smith, and walking gravely beside them came Errand.

A pang of almost unbearable grief ran through Garion. Durnik, his oldest friend, was pale and dead, and in that vast internal upheaval that had preceded the duel with Torak, Garion had not even been able to mourn.

"It was necessary, you understand," Belgarath said sadly.

"Why? Why did Durnik have to die, Grandfather?" Garion's voice was anguished, and tears stood openly in his eyes.

"Because his death gave your Aunt the will to resist Torak. That's always been the one flaw in the Prophecy—the possibility that Pol might yield. All Torak needed was one person to love him. It would have made him invincible."

"What would have happened if she'd gone to him?"

"You'd have lost the fight. That's why Durnik had to die." The old man sighed regretfully. "I wish it could have been otherwise, but it was inevitable."

The three who had borne Durnik from the broken tomb gently laid his still form on the ground, and Ce'Nedra sadly joined Belgarath and Garion. Wordlessly, the tiny girl slipped her hand into Garion's, and the three of them stood, silently watching as Aunt Pol, past tears now, gently straightened Durnik's arms at his sides and then covered him with her cloak. She sat then upon the earth, took his head into her lap and almost absently stroked his hair, her head bowed over his in her grief.

"I can't bear it," Ce'Nedra suddenly sobbed, and she buried her face in Garion's shoulder and began to weep.

Then then there was a light where there had been only darkness before. As Garion stared, a single beam of brilliant blue light descended from the broken and tattered cloud rolling overhead. The entire ruin seemed bathed in its intense radiance as the light touched the earth. Like a great, glowing column, the beam of light reached down to the earth from the night sky, was joined by other beams, red and yellow and green and shades Garion could not even name. Like the colors at the foot of a sudden rainbow, the great columns of light stood side by side on the other side of Torak's fallen body. Then, indistinctly, Garion perceived that a glowing, incandescent figure stood within the center of each column of light. The Gods had returned to mourn the passing of their brother. Garion recognized Aldur, and he could easily identify each of the others. Mara still wept, and dead-eyed Issa seemed to undulate, serpentlike, as he stood within his glowing column of pale green light. Nedra's face was shrewd, and Chaldan's proud. Belar, the blond-haired, boyish God of the Alorns had a roguish, impudent look about him, though his face, like those of his brothers, was sad at the death of Torak. The Gods had returned to earth in glowing light and with sound as well. The reeking air of Cthol Mishrak was suddenly alive with that sound as each colored beam of light gave off a different note, the notes joining in a harmony so profound that it seemed the answer to every question that had ever been asked.

And finally, joining the other columns of light, a single, blindingly white beam slowly descended, and within the center of that radiance stood the white-robed form of UL, that strange God whom Garion had seen once in Prolgu.

The figure of Aldur, still embraced in its glowing blue nimbus, approached the ancient God of Ulgo. "Father," Aldur said sadly, "our brother, thy son Torak, is slain."

Shimmering and incandescent, the form of UL, father of the other Gods, moved across the rubble-strewn ground to stand over the silent body of Torak. "I tried to turn thee from this path, my son," he said softly, and a single tear coursed its way down his eternal cheek. Then he turned back to Aldur. "Take up the form of thy brother, my son, and place it upon some more suitable resting place. It grieves me to see him lie so low upon the earth."

Aldur, joined by his brethren, took up the body of Torak and placed it upon a large block of stone lying amid the ancient ruins, and then, standing in a quiet gleaming circle about the bier, they mourned the passing of the God of Angarak.

Unafraid as always, seemingly not even aware that the glowing figures which had descended from the sky were not human, Errand walked quite confidently to the shining form of UL. He reached out his small hand and tugged insistently at the God's robe. "Father," he said.

UL looked down at the small face.

"Father," Errand repeated, perhaps echoing Aldur, who had in his use of that name, revealed at last the true identity of the God of Ulgo. "Father," the little boy said again. Then he turned and pointed at the silent form of Durnik. "Errand!" It was in some strange way more a command than a request.

The face of UL became troubled. "It is not possible, child," he replied.

"Father," the little boy insisted. "Errand."

UL looked inquiringly at Garion, his eyes profoundly unsettled. "The child's request is serious," he said gravely, speaking not to Garion but to that other awareness, "and it places an obligation upon me—but it crosses the uncrossable boundary."

"The boundary must remain intact," the dry voice replied through Garion's lips. "Thy sons are passionate, Holy UL, and having once crossed this line, they may be tempted to do so again, and perhaps in one such crossing they may change that which must not be changed. Let us not provide the instrumentality whereby Destiny must once more follow two divergent paths."

UL sighed.

"Wilt thou and thy sons, however, lend of your power to *my* instrument so that *he* may cross the boundary?"

UL looked startled at that.

"Thus will the boundary be protected, and thine obligation shall be met. It can happen in no other way."

"Let it be as thou wilt," UL agreed. He turned then and a peculiar look passed between the father of the Gods and his eldest son, Aldur.

Aldur, still bathed in blue light, turned from his sad contemplation of his dead brother toward Aunt Pol, who was still bowed over Durnik's body.

"Be comforted, my daughter," he told her. "His sacrifice was for thee and for all mankind."

"That is slight comfort, Master," she replied, her eyes full of tears. "This was the best of men."

"All men die, my daughter, the best as well as the worst. In thy life thou hast seen this many times."

"Yes, Master, but this is different."

"In what way, beloved Polgara?" Aldur seemed to be pressing her for some reason.

Aunt Pol bit her lip. "Because I loved him, Master," she replied finally.

The faintest touch of a smile appeared on Aldur's lips. "Is that so difficult to say, my daughter?"

She could not answer, but bowed again over Durnik's lifeless form.

"Wouldst thou have us restore this man to thee, my daughter?" Aldur asked then.

Her face came up sharply. "That isn't possible, Master," she said. "Please don't toy with my grief like this."

"Let us, however, consider that it *may* be possible," he told her. "Wouldst thou have us restore him?"

"With all my heart, Master."

"To what end? What task hast thou for this man that demands his restoration?"

She bit her lip again. "To be my husband, Master," she blurted finally with a trace of defiance in her voice.

"And was that also so very difficult to say? Art thou sure, however, that this love of thine derives not from thy grief, and that once this good man is restored, thy mind might not turn away from him? He *is*, thou must admit, most ordinary."

"Durnik has never been ordinary," she flared with sudden heat. "He is the best and bravest man in the world."

"I meant him no disrespect, Polgara, but no power doth infuse him. The force of the Will and the Word is not in him."

"Is that so important, Master?"

"Marriage must be a joining of equals, my daughter. How could this good, brave man be husband to thee, so long as *thy* power remains?"

She looked at him helplessly.

"Couldst thou, Polgara, limit thyself? Wouldst thou become his equal? With power no more than his?"

She stared at him, hesitated, then blurted the one word, "Yes."

Garion was shocked—not so much by Aunt Pol's acceptance but rather by Aldur's request. Aunt Pol's power was central to her very being. To remove it from her would leave her with nothing. What would she be without it? How could she even live without it? It was a cruel price to demand, and Garion had believed that Aldur was a kindly God.

"I will accept thy sacrifice, Polgara," Aldur was saying. "I will speak with my father and my brothers. For good and proper reasons, we have denied ourselves this power, and we must all agree to it before any of us might attempt this violation of the natural order of things." And he returned to the sorrowful gathering about Torak's bier.

"How could he do that?" Garion, his arm still about Ce'Nedra, demanded of his grandfather.

"Do what?"

"Ask her to give up her power like that? Won't it destroy her?"

"She's much stronger than you think, Garion," Belgarath assured him, "and Aldur's reasoning is sound. No marriage could survive that kind of inequality."

Among the glowing Gods, however, one angry voice was raised. "No!" It was Mara, the weeping God of the Marags, who were no more. "Why should one man be restored when all my slaughtered children still lie cold and dead? Did Aldur hear *my* pleas? Did he come to *my* aid when my children died? I will not consent."

"I hadn't counted on that," Belgarath muttered. "I'd better take steps before this goes any further." He crossed the littered ground and bowed respectfully. "Forgive my intrusion," he said, "but would my Master's brother accept a woman of the Marags as a gift in exchange for his aid in restoring Durnik?"

Mara's tears, which had been perpetual, suddenly stopped, and his face became incredulous. "A Marag woman?" he demanded sharply. "None such exist. I would have known in my heart if one of my children had survived in Maragor."

"Of a certainty, Lord Mara," Belgarath agreed quickly. "But what of those few who were carried *out* of Maragor to dwell in perpetual slavery?"

"Knowest thou of such a one, Belgarath?" Mara asked with a desperate eagerness.

The old man nodded. "We discovered her in the slave pens beneath Rak Cthol, Lord Mara. Her name is Taiba. She is but one, but a race may be restored by such a one as she—particularly if she be watched over by a loving God."

"Where is Taiba, my daughter?"

"In the care of Relg, the Ulgo," Belgarath replied. "They seem quite attached to each other," he added blandly.

Mara looked at him thoughtfully. "A race may not be restored by one," he said, "even in the care of the most loving God. It requires two." He turned to UL.

"Wilt thou give me this Ulgo, Father?" he asked. "He shall become the sire of my people."

UL gave Belgarath a rather penetrating look. "Thou knowest that Relg hath another duty to perform," he said pointedly.

Belgarath's expression was almost impish. "I'm certain that the Gorim and I can work out the details, Most Holy," he declared with utmost self-confidence.

"Aren't you forgetting something, Belgarath?" Silk asked diffidently, as if not wanting to intrude. "Relg has this little problem, remember?"

Belgarath gave the little man a hard look.

"I just thought I ought to mention it," Silk said innocently.

Mara looked sharply at them. "What is this?"

"A minor difficulty, Lord Mara," Belgarath said quickly. "One I'm certain Taiba can overcome. I have the utmost confidence in her in that particular area."

"I will have the truth of this," Mara said firmly.

Belgarath sighed and gave Silk another grim look. "Relg is a zealot, Lord Mara," he explained. "For religious reasons, he avoids certain—ah—forms of human contact."

"Fatherhood is his destiny," UL said. "From him will issue a special child. I will explain this to him. He is an obedient man, and he will put aside his aversions for my sake."

"Then thou wilt give him to me, Father?" Mara asked eagerly.

"He is thine—with but one restriction—of which we will speak later."

"Let us see to this brave Sendar, then," Mara said, and all traces of his weeping were now gone.

"*Belgarion,*" the voice in Garion's mind said.

"*What?*"

"*The restoration of your friend is in your hands now.*"

"*Me? Why me?*"

"*Must you always say that? Do you want Durnik's life restored?*"

"*Of course, but I can't do it. I wouldn't even know where to begin.*"

"*You did it before. Remember the colt in the cave of the Gods?*"

Garion had almost forgotten that.

"*You are my instrument, Belgarion. I can keep you from making mistakes—most of the time anyway. Just relax; I'll show you what to do.*"

Garion was already moving without conscious volition. He let his arm fall from about Ce'Nedra's shoulders, and, his sword still in his hand, he walked slowly toward Aunt Pol and Durnik's body. He looked once into her eyes as she sat with the dead man's head in her lap, and then he knelt beside the body.

"For me, Garion," she murmured to him.

"If I can, Aunt Pol," he said. Then, without knowing why, he laid the sword of the Rivan King upon the ground and took hold of the Orb at its pommel. With a faint click, the Orb came free in his hand. Errand, smiling now, approached from the other side and also knelt, taking up Durnik's lifeless hand in his. Holding the Orb in both hands, Garion reached out and put it against the dead man's chest. He was faintly conscious of the fact that the Gods had gathered about in a circle and that they had reached out their arms, palm to palm, forming an unbroken ring.

Within that circle, a great light began to pulsate, and the Orb, as if in answer, glowed between his hands.

The blank wall he had seen once before was there again, still black, impenetrable, and silent. As he had before in the cave of the Gods, Garion pushed tentatively against the substance of death itself, striving to reach through and pull his friend back into the world of the living.

It was different this time. The colt he had brought to life in the cave had never lived except within its mother's body. Its death had been as tenuous as its life, and it lay but a short distance beyond the barrier. Durnik, however, had been a man full grown, and his death, like his life, was far more profound. With all his strength, Garion pushed. He could feel the enormous force of the combined wills of the Gods joining with his in the silent struggle, but the barrier would not yield.

"Use the Orb!" the voice commanded.

This time Garion focused all the power, his own and that of the Gods, upon the round stone between his hands. It flickered, then glowed, then flickered again.

"Help me!" Garion commanded it.

As if suddenly understanding, the Orb flared into a coruscating eruption of colored light. The barrier was weakening.

With an encouraging little smile, Errand reached out and laid one hand upon the blazing Orb.

The barrier broke. Durnik's chest heaved, and he coughed once.

With profoundly respectful expression upon their eternal faces, the Gods stepped back. Aunt Pol cried out in sudden relief and clasped her arms about Durnik, cradling him against her.

"Errand," the child said to Garion with a peculiar note of satisfaction. Garion stumbled to his feet, exhausted by the struggle and nearly staggering as he moved away.

"Are you all right?" Ce'Nedra demanded of him, even as she ducked her head beneath his arm and firmly pulled it about her tiny shoulders.

He nodded, though his knees almost buckled.

"Lean on me," she told him.

He was about to protest, but she put her hand firmly to his lips. "Don't argue, Garion," she told him. "You know that I love you and that you're going to be leaning on me for the rest of your life anyway, so you might as well get used to the idea."

"I think my life's going to be different now, Master," Belgarath was saying to Aldur. "Pol's always been there, ready to come when I called her—not always willingly, perhaps—but she always came. Now she'll have other concerns." He sighed. "I suppose our children all grow up and get married sometime."

"This particular pose doth not become thee, my son," Aldur told him.

Belgarath grinned. "I've never been able to slip anything past you, Master," he said. Then his face grew serious again. "Polgara's been almost like a son to me," he told Aldur, "but perhaps it's time that I let her be a woman. I've denied her that for too long."

"As it seemeth best to thee, my son," Aldur said. "And now, I pray thee, go apart a little way and permit us our family grief." He looked at Torak's body lying on the bier and then at Garion. "I have but one more task for thee, Belgarion," he said. "Take the Orb and place it upon my brother's breast."

"Yes, Master," Garion replied immediately. He removed his arm from around Ce'Nedra's shoulders and walked to the bier, trying not to look at the dead God's seared and twisted face. He reached out and laid the round blue stone upon the motionless chest of Kal Torak. Then he stepped back. Once again his little princess wormed her way beneath his arm and clasped him about the waist. It was not unpleasant, but he had the brief, irrational thought that things would be awkward if she was going to insist on this close embrace for the rest of their lives.

Once again the Gods formed their circle, and once again the Orb began to glow. Gradually, the seared face started to change, its maiming slowly disappearing. The light surrounding the Gods and the bier grew stronger, and the glow of the Orb became incandescent. The last Garion saw of the face of Torak, it was calm, composed and unmarked. It was a beautiful face, but it was nonetheless still a dead face.

And then the light grew so intense that Garion could no longer look at it. When it subsided, and when Garion looked back at the bier, the Gods and the body of Torak were gone. Only the Orb remained, glowing slightly as it lay on the rough stone.

Errand, once again with that confident look, went to the bier. Standing on his tiptoes, he reached across the block to retrieve the glowing stone. Then he carried it to Garion. "Errand, Belgarion," he said firmly, handing the Orb back, and in their touch as the Orb exchanged hands, Garion felt something profoundly different.

Drawn together by what had happened, the little group silently gathered about Aunt Pol and Durnik. To the east, the sky had begun to lighten, and the rosy blush of dawn touched the few last remaining tatters of the cloud that had covered Cthol Mishrak. The events of the dreadful night had been titanic, but now the night was nearly over, and they stood together, not speaking as they watched the dawn.

The storm that had raged through the long night had passed. For years beyond counting, the universe had been divided against itself, but now it was one again. If there were such things as beginnings, this was a beginning. And so it was, through broken cloud, that the sun rose on the morning of the first day.

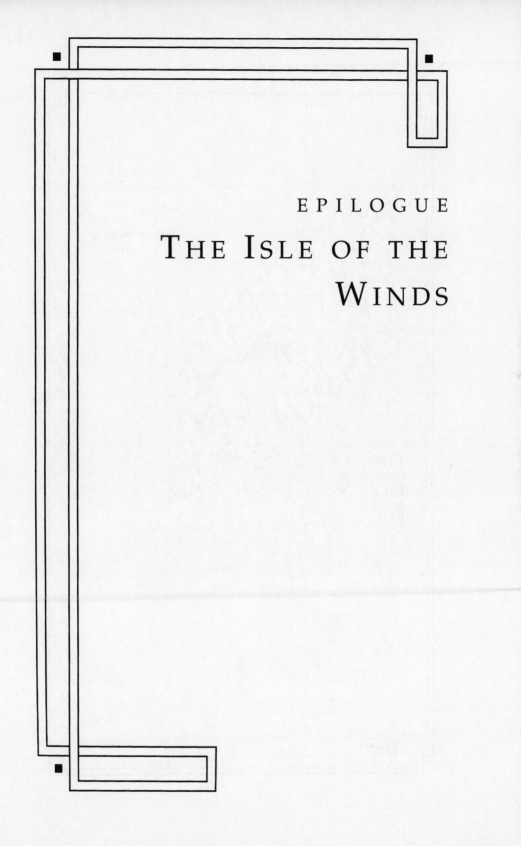

EPILOGUE

THE ISLE OF THE WINDS

Belgarion of Riva slept very fitfully the night before his wedding. Had he and Ce'Nedra been married in some simple, private little ceremony shortly after his meeting with Torak, things might have gone more smoothly. At that time both he and his flighty little princess had been too tired and too overwhelmed by the events which had taken place to be anything but absolutely honest with each other. During those few short days he had found her to be almost a different person. She had watched his every move with a kind of patient adoration, and she was forever touching him—his hair, his face, his arms—her fingers gentle and curious. The peculiar way she had of coming up to him, no matter who was present or what was going on, and worming her way into the circle of his arm had been, on the whole, rather nice.

Those days had not, however, lasted. Once she had reassured herself that he was all right and that he was really there and not some figment of her imagination which might be snatched away at any moment, Ce'Nedra had gradually changed. He felt somehow like a possession; following her initial delight in ownership, his princess had rather deliberately embarked upon some grand plan of alteration.

And now the day upon which her possession of him was to be formalized was only hours away. His sleep came in fits and starts with dreams mingling peculiarly with memories as he dipped in and out of sleep like a sea bird skimming across the waves.

He was at Faldor's farm again. Even in his sleep he could hear the ringing of Durnik's hammer and smell the odors coming from Aunt Pol's kitchen. Rundorig was there—and Zubrette—and Doroon—and there was Brill, creeping around a corner. He half woke and turned restlessly in the royal bed. That wasn't possible. Doroon was dead, drowned in the River Mardu, and Brill had vanished forever over the parapet of mile-high Rak Cthol.

And then he was in the palace at Sthiss Tor, and Salmissra, her blatant nudity glowing through her filmy gown, was touching his face with her cold fingers.

But Salmissra was no longer a woman. He had watched her himself as she had changed into a serpent.

Grul the Eldrak hammered at the frozen ground with his iron-shod club, bellowing, "Come 'Grat, fight!" and Ce'Nedra was screaming.

In the chaotic world of dreams half mixed with memories he saw Ctuchik, his face contorted with horror, exploding once more into nothingness in the hanging turret at Rak Cthol.

And then he stood once again in the decaying ruin of Cthol Mishrak, his sword ablaze, and watched as Torak raised his arms to the rolling cloud, weeping tears of fire, and once again he heard the stricken God's final cry, "Mother!"

He stirred, half rousing and shuddering as he always did when that dream recurred, but dipped almost immediately into sleep again.

He was standing on the deck of Barak's ship just off the Mallorean coast, listening as King Anheg explained why Barak was chained to the mast.

"We had to do it, Belgarath," the coarse-faced monarch said mournfully. "Right during the middle of that storm, he turned into a *bear!* He drove the crew to row toward Mallorea all night long, and then, just before daybreak, he turned back into a man again."

"Unchain him, Anheg," Belgarath said disgustedly. "He's not going to turn into a bear again—not as long as Garion's safe and well."

Garion rolled over and sat up. *That* had been a startling revelation. There had been a purpose behind Barak's periodic alterations.

"You're Garion's defender," Belgarath had explained to the big man. "That's why you were born. Any time Garion was in mortal danger, you changed into a bear in order to protect him."

"You mean to say that I'm a sorcerer?" Barak had demanded incredulously.

"Hardly. The shape-change isn't all that difficult, and you didn't do it consciously. The Prophecy did the work, not you."

Barak had spent the rest of the voyage back to Mishrak ac Thull trying to come up with a tastefully understated way to add that concept to his coat of arms.

Garion climbed out of his high, canopied bed and went to the window. The stars in the spring sky looked down at the sleeping city of Rivan and at the dark waters of the Sea of the Winds beyond the harbor. There was no sign that dawn was anywhere near yet. Garion sighed, poured himself a drink of water from the pitcher on the table, and went back to bed and his troubled sleep.

He was at Thull Zelik, and Hettar and Mandorallen were reporting on the activities of 'Zakath, the Mallorean Emperor. "He's laying siege to Rak Goska right now," hawk-faced Hettar was saying. There had been a peculiar softening in Hettar's face since Garion had last seen him, as if something very significant had happened. The tall Algar turned to Garion. "Eventually you're going to have to do something about 'Zakath," he said. "I don't think you want him roaming around at will in this part of the world."

"Why me?" Garion asked without thinking.

"You're Overlord of the West, remember?"

Once again Garion awoke. Sooner or later he *would* have to deal with 'Zakath; there was no question about that. Maybe after the wedding, he'd have time to consider the matter. That thought, however, stopped him. Strangely, he had no conception of anything that might happen after the wedding. It stood before him like some huge door that led into a place he had never been. 'Zakath would have to wait. Garion had to get through the wedding first.

Half asleep, somewhere between dreaming and remembering, Garion relived a significant little exchange between himself and her Imperial Highness.

"It's stupid, Ce'Nedra," he was protesting. "I'm not going to fight anybody, so why should I ride in waving my sword?"

"They deserve to see you, Garion," she explained as if talking to a child. "They left their homes and rode into battle at your summons."

"I didn't summon anybody."

"I did it in your behalf. They're a very good army, really, and I raised them all by myself. Aren't you proud of me?"

"I didn't ask you to do that."

"You were too proud to ask. That's one of your failings, Garion. You must never be too proud to ask the people who love you for help. Every man in the army loves you. They followed me because of you. Is it too much trouble for the great Overlord of the West to reward his faithful soldiers with just a little bit of a display of appreciation? Or have you become too grand and lofty for simple gratitude?"

"You're twisting things, Ce'Nedra. You do that a lot, you know."

But Ce'Nedra had already moved on as if the entire matter were settled. "And of course you *will* wear your crown—and some nice armor. I think a mail shirt would be appropriate."

"I'm not going to make a clown of myself just to satisfy your urges toward cheap theatricality."

Her eyes filled. Her lower lip trembled. "You don't love me anymore," she accused him in a quavering little voice.

Garion groaned even in his sleep. It *always* came down to that. She won every single argument with that artful bit of deception. He *knew* it was not genuine. He *knew* that she only did it to get her own way, but he was absolutely defenseless against it. It might have nothing whatsoever to do with the matter under discussion, but she always managed to twist things around until she could unleash that devastating accusation, and all hope of his winning even the smallest point was immediately lost. Where had she learned to be so heartlessly dishonest?

And so it was that Garion, dressed in mail, wearing his crown and self-consciously holding his flaming sword aloft, had ridden into the forts atop the eastern escarpment to the thunderous cheers of Ce'Nedra's army.

So much had happened since Garion and Silk and Belgarath had crept from the citadel at Riva the previous spring. The young king lay musing in his high, canopied bed, having almost given up on sleep. Ce'Nedra *had* in fact raised an army. As he had heard more of the details, he had been more and more astonished—not only by her audacity but also by the enormous amount of energy and sheer will she had expended in the process. She had been guided and assisted, certainly, but the initial concept had been hers. His admiration for her was tinged slightly with apprehension. He was going to marry a very strong-minded young woman—and one who was not overly troubled by scruples.

He rolled over and punched at his pillow, hoping somehow by that familiar act to bring on more normal sleep, but once again he slipped into restless dreaming. Relg and Taiba were walking toward him, and they were holding hands!

And then he was at the Stronghold, sitting at Adara's bedside. His beautiful cousin was even paler than he remembered, and she had a persistent, racking cough. Even as the two of them talked, Aunt Pol was taking steps to remedy the last complications of the wound which had so nearly claimed the girl's life.

"I was mortified, of course," Adara was saying. "I'd taken so much care to conceal it from him, and now I'd gone and blurted it out to him, and I wasn't even dying."

"Hettar?" Garion said again. He'd already said it three times.

"If you don't stop that, Garion, I'm going to be cross with you," Adara said quite firmly.

"I'm sorry," he apologized quickly. "It's just that I've never considered him in that light. He's a good friend, but I never thought of him as particularly lovable. He's so—I don't know—implacable, I suppose."

"I have certain reasons to believe that may change," Adara said with a faint blush. Then she began to cough again.

"Drink this, dear," Aunt Pol ordered, coming to the bedside with a fuming cup.

"It's going to taste awful," Garion warned his cousin.

"That'll do, Garion," Aunt Pol told him. "I can manage this without the helpful comments."

And then he was in the caves beneath Prolgu, standing beside Relg as the Gorim performed the simple ceremony uniting the zealot and the Marag woman who had so totally changed Relg's life. Garion sensed another presence in the underground chamber, and he wondered if anyone had yet told Relg about the bargain that had been struck in Cthol Mishrak. He'd thought about saying something himself, but had decided against it. All things considered, it might be best to let Relg adjust to one thing at a time. Marriage to Taiba was probably going to be enough of a shock to the fanatic's system for now. Garion could feel Mara's gloating exultation as the ceremony concluded. The weeping God no longer wept.

It was useless, Garion decided. He was not going to be able to sleep—at least not the kind of sleep that would do him any good. He threw off the covers and pulled on his robe. The fire in his fireplace had been banked for the night, and he stirred it up again. Then he sat in the chair in front of it, staring pensively into the dancing flames.

Even if his wedding to Ce'Nedra had taken place immediately upon their arrival back at Riva, things might still have turned out all right, but the arrangements for a royal wedding of this magnitude were far too complex to be made overnight, and many of those who were to be honored guests were still recuperating from wounds received during the battle of Thull Mardu.

The interim had given Ce'Nedra time to embark upon a full-blown plan of modification. She had, it appeared, a certain concept of him—some ideal which only she could perceive—and she was absolutely determined to cram him into that mold despite all his objections and protests. Nothing could make her relent in her single-minded drive to make him over. It was so unfair. He was quite content to accept her exactly as she was. She had her flaws—many of them—but he was willing to take the good with the bad. Why couldn't she extend him the same courtesy? But each time he tried to put his foot down and absolutely refuse one of her whims, her eyes would fill with tears, her lip would tremble, and the fatal, "You don't love me anymore," would drop quaveringly upon him. Belgarion of Riva had considered flight several times during that long winter.

Now it was spring again, and the storms which isolated the Isle of the Winds during the winter months were past. The day which Garion felt would never come had suddenly rushed upon him. Today was the day in which he would take the Imperial Princess Ce'Nedra to wife, and it was too late to run.

He knew that if he brooded about it much longer, he'd push himself over the edge into total panic, and so he stood up and quickly dressed himself in plain tunic and hose, ignoring the more ostentatious garments which his valet—at Ce'Nedra's explicit instructions—had laid out for him.

It was about an hour before daylight as the young king of Riva opened the door to the royal apartment and slipped into the silent corridor outside.

He wandered for a time through the dim, empty halls of the Citadel, and then, inevitably, his undirected steps led him to Aunt Pol's door. She was already awake and seated by her fire with a cup of fragrant tea in her hands. She wore a deep blue dressing gown, and her dark hair flowed down across her shoulders in a lustrous wave.

"You're up early," she noted.

"I couldn't sleep."

"You should have. You have a very full day ahead of you."

"I know. That's why I couldn't sleep."

"Tea?"

"No, thanks." He sat in the carved chair on the other side of the fireplace. "Everything's changing, Aunt Pol," he said after a moment of thoughtful silence. "After today, nothing will ever be the same again, will it?"

"Probably not," she said, "but that doesn't necessarily mean that it'll be a change for the worse."

"How do *you* feel about the idea of getting married?"

"A bit nervous," she admitted calmly.

"You?"

"I've never been married before either, Garion."

Something had been bothering him about that. "Was it really such a good idea, Aunt Pol?" he asked her. "I mean, arranging to have you and Durnik get married on the same day as Ce'Nedra and I? What I'm trying to say is that you're the most important woman in the world. Shouldn't your wedding be a special occasion?"

"That was what we were trying to avoid, Garion," she replied. "Durnik and I decided that we wanted our wedding to be private, and we hope that it'll be lost in all the confusion and ceremony that's going to surround yours."

"How is he? I haven't seen him for several days now."

"He's still a bit strange. I don't think he'll ever be the same man we all knew."

"He's all right, isn't he?" Garion's question was concerned.

"He's fine, Garion. He's just a bit different, that's all. Something happened to him that's never happened to any other man, and it changed him. He's as practical as ever, but now he looks at the other side of things as well. I think I rather like that."

"Do you *really* have to leave Riva?" he asked suddenly. "You and Durnik could stay here in the Citadel."

"We want our own place, Garion," she told him. "We need to be alone with each other. Besides, if I were here, every time you and Ce'Nedra had a squabble, I'd have one or both of you hammering on my door. I've done my best to raise you two. Now you're going to have to work things out on your own."

"Where will you go?"

"To the Vale. My mother's cottage is still there. It's a very solid house. All it needs is new thatching on the roof and new doors and windows. Durnik knows how to take care of that, and it'll be a good place for Errand to grow up."

"Errand? You're taking him with you?"

"Someone has to care for him, and I've grown used to having a small boy around. Besides, Father and I've decided that we'd like for him to be some distance from the Orb. He's still the only one beside you who can touch it. Someone at some time might seize upon that and try to use him in the same way Zedar did."

"What'd be the point? I mean, Torak's gone now. What good would the Orb do anybody else?"

She looked at him very gravely, and the white lock of her brow seemed to glow in the soft light. "I don't believe that was the only reason for the Orb's existence, Garion," she told him seriously. "Something hasn't been completed yet."

"What? What else is there left to do?"

"We don't know. The Mrin Codex doesn't end with the meeting between the Child of Light and the Child of Dark. You're the Guardian of the Orb now, and it's still as important as ever, so don't just put it on the back shelf of a closet somewhere and forget about it. Be watchful, and don't let ordinary affairs dull your mind. Keeping the Orb is still your first duty—and I'm not going to be here to remind you about it every day."

He didn't want to think about that. "What'll you do if somebody comes to the Vale and tries to take Errand away? You won't be able to protect him, now that—" He faltered to a stop. He had not spoken to her about that.

"Go ahead and say it, Garion," she said directly. "Let's look it right in the face. You were going to say now that I no longer have any power."

"What's it like, Aunt Pol? Is it like losing something—a sort of emptiness, maybe?"

"I feel the same as always, dear. Of course I haven't tried to *do* anything since I agreed to give it up. It might be painful if I tried to make something happen and failed. I don't think I'd care for the experience, so I simply haven't tried." She shrugged. "That part of my life is over, so I'll just have to put it behind me. Errand will be safe, though. Beldin's in the Vale—and the twins. That's enough power in one place to keep away anything that might want to harm him."

"Why's Durnik spending so much time with Grandfather?" Garion asked suddenly. "Ever since we got back to Riva, they've been together just about every minute of the day."

She gave him a knowing smile. "I imagine they're preparing some surprise for me," she replied. "Some suitable wedding present. They both tend to be a trifle transparent."

"What is it?" Garion asked curiously.

"I haven't the slightest idea—and I wouldn't dream of trying to find out. Whatever it is, they've both worked too hard at it for me to spoil it for them by snooping around." She glanced at the window where the first light of dawn was appearing. "Perhaps you'd better run along now, dear," she suggested. "I have to start getting ready. This is a very special day for me, too, and I really want to look my best."

"You could never look anything less than beautiful, Aunt Pol," he told her sincerely.

"Why thank you, Garion." She smiled at him, looking somehow almost girlish. "But I'd rather not take the chance." She gave him an appraising glance and touched his cheek. "Why don't you visit the baths, dear," she suggested, "and wash your hair and get somebody to shave you."

"I can do that myself, Aunt Pol."

"That's not a good idea, Garion. You're a little nervous today, and you don't want to put a razor to your face when your hands are trembling."

He laughed a bit ruefully, kissed her, and started toward the door. Then he stopped and turned back toward her. "I love you, Aunt Pol," he said simply.

"Yes, dear, I know. I love you, too."

After he had visited the baths, Garion went looking for Lelldorin. Among the matters that had finally been settled was the marital status of the young Asturian and his semi-official bride. Ariana had finally despaired of Lelldorin's ever making the first move on his own and had solved the entire problem by simply moving in with him. She had been quite firm about it. Garion gathered that Lelldorin's resistance had faded rather quickly. His expression of late had been somewhat more foolish than usual, and Ariana's had been, although radiant, just a trifle smug. In a peculiar way, they closely resembled Relg and Taiba in that respect. Since his wedding, Relg's expression had been one of almost perpetual astonishment, while Taiba's had that same smugness that marked Ariana's. Garion wondered if he might not awaken tomorrow morning to see that same self-satisfied little smirk on Ce'Nedra's lips.

There was a purpose to Garion's search for his Asturian friend. As a result of one of Ce'Nedra's whims, their wedding was going to be followed by a grand ball, and Lelldorin had been teaching Garion how to dance.

The idea of the ball had been greeted with enthusiasm by all the ladies; the men, however, had not been universal in their approval. Barak had been particularly vehement in his objections. "You want *me* to get in the middle of the floor and dance?" he had demanded of the princess in an outraged tone of voice. "What's wrong with all of us just getting drunk? That's the normal way to celebrate a wedding."

"You'll be just fine," Ce'Nedra had told him, patting his cheek in that infuriating way of hers. "And you will do it, won't you, Barak—for me?" And she had insincerely fluttered her eyelashes at him.

Barak had stamped away, muttering curses under his breath.

Garion found Lelldorin and Ariana doting on each other across the breakfast table in their rooms.

"Wilt thou take breakfast with us, your Majesty?" Ariana inquired politely.

"Thanks all the same, my Lady," Garion declined, "but I don't seem to have much appetite today."

"Nerves," Lelldorin observed sagely.

"I think I've got most of it," Garion rushed to the core of his problem, "but that crossover baffles me. My feet keep getting all tangled up."

Lelldorin immediately fetched a lute, and with Ariana's help, walked Garion through the complex procedure.

"Thou art becoming most skilled, your Majesty," Ariana complimented him at the end of the lesson.

"All I want to do is get through it without tripping and falling on my face in public."

"The princess would surely support thee, shouldst thou stumble."

"I'm not sure about that. She might enjoy watching me make a fool of myself."

"How little thou knowest of women." Ariana gave Lelldorin an adoring look—a look he fatuously returned.

"Will you two stop that?" Garion demanded irritably. "Can't you wait until you're alone to carry on that way?"

"My heart is too full of love for me to hide it, Garion," Lelldorin said extravagantly.

"So I've noticed," Garion said dryly. "I've got to go see Silk, so I'll leave you two to your amusements."

Ariana blushed, then smiled. "Might we take that as a royal command, your Majesty?" she asked archly.

Garion fled.

Silk had arrived from the east late the previous evening, and Garion was anxious for news. He found the little Drasnian lingering over a breakfast of partridge and hot, spiced wine.

"Isn't that a little heavy for breakfast?" Garion asked him.

"I've never been that partial to gruel first thing in the morning," Silk replied. "Gruel's the sort of thing a man has to work himself up to."

Garion went directly to the point. "What's happening in Cthol Murgos?"

" 'Zakath is still laying siege to Rak Goska," Silk reported. "He's transporting in more troops, though. It's pretty obvious that he's going to strike into southern Cthol Murgos as soon as the ground's firm enough to move an army."

"Are the Thulls with him?"

"Only a few. Most of them are concentrating on finding the few Grolims left in their kingdom. I always thought Thulls were a stupid people, but you'd be amazed at how creative they can be when it comes to finding new and interesting ways for Grolims to die."

"We're going to have to keep an eye on 'Zakath," Garion said. "I wouldn't want him to come creeping up on me from the south."

"I think you can count on him not to creep," Silk said. "He sent you a message of congratulations, incidentally."

"He did *what*?"

"He's a civilized man, Garion—*and* a politician. He was badly shaken by the fact that you killed Torak. I think he's actually afraid of you, so he wants to stay on your good side—at least until he finishes up in southern Cthol Murgos."

"Who's in command of the Murgos, now that Taur Urgas is dead?"

"Urgit, his third son by his second wife. There was the usual squabble over the succession by the various sons of Taur Urgas' assorted wives. The fatalities were numerous, I understand."

"What kind of man is Urgit?"

"He's a schemer. I don't think he's any match for 'Zakath, but he'll keep the Malloreans busy for ten or twenty years. By then, 'Zakath may be too old and tired of war to give you any problems."

"Let's hope so."

"Oh, I almost forgot. Hettar married your cousin last week."

"Adara? I thought she was ill."

"Not that much, apparently. They're coming to your wedding—along with Cho-Hag and Silar."

"Is *everybody* getting married?"

Silk laughed. "Not *me*, my young friend. In spite of this universal plunge toward matrimony, *I* still haven't lost my senses. If worse comes to worse, I still know how to run. The Algars should arrive sometime this morning. They met Korodullin's entourage, and they're all coming together. Their ship was right behind mine when we left Camaar."

"Was Mandorallen with them?"

Silk nodded. "Along with the Baroness of Vo Ebor. The Baron's still much too ill to travel. I think he's hoping that he'll die, to leave the way clear for his wife and Mandorallen."

Garion sighed.

"Don't let it make you unhappy, Garion," Silk advised. "Arends actually enjoy that kind of misery. Mandorallen's perfectly content to suffer nobly."

"That's a rotten thing to say," Garion accused the little man.

Silk shrugged. "I'm a rotten sort of person," he admitted.

"Where are you going after—" Garion left it hanging.

"After I see you safely married?" Silk suggested pleasantly. "As soon as I recover from all the drinking I'll do tonight, I'll be off for Gar og Nadrak. There's a great deal of opportunity in the new situation there. I've been in contact with Yarblek. He and I are going to form a partnership."

"With Yarblek?"

"He's not so bad—if you keep an eye on him—and he's very shrewd. We'll probably do rather well together."

"I can imagine." Garion laughed. "One of you is bad enough all by himself, but with the two of you acting together, no honest merchant's going to escape with his skin."

Silk grinned wickedly. "That was sort of what we had in mind."

"I imagine that you'll get very rich."

"I suppose I could learn to live with that." Silk's eyes took on a distant look. "That's not really what it's all about, though," he noted. "It's a game. The money's just a way of keeping score. It's the game that's important."

"It seems to me that you told me that once before."

"Nothing's changed since then, Garion," Silk told him with a laugh.

Aunt Pol's wedding to Durnik took place later that morning in a small, private chapel in the west wing of the Citadel. There were but few guests. Belgarath and the twins, Beltira and Belkira, were there of course, and Silk and Barak. Aunt Pol, beautiful in a deep blue velvet gown, was attended by Queen Layla, and Garion stood with Durnik. The ceremony was performed by the hunchbacked Beldin, dressed for once in decent clothing and with a strangely gentle expression on his ugly face.

Garion's emotions were very complex during the ceremony. He realized with a sharp little pang that Aunt Pol would no longer be exclusively his. An elemental, childish part of him resented that. He was, however, pleased that it was Durnik whom she was marrying. If anyone deserved her, it was Durnik. The good, plain man's eyes were filled with absolute love, and he obviously could not take them from her face. Aunt Pol herself was gravely radiant as she stood at Durnik's side.

As Garion stepped back while the two exchanged vows, he heard a faint rustle. Just inside the door of the chapel, in a hooded cloak that covered her from head to foot and wearing a heavy veil that covered her face, stood Princess Ce'Nedra. She had made a large issue of the fact that by an ancient Tolnedran custom, Garion was not supposed to see her before their wedding on this day, and the cloak and veil provided her with the illusion of invisibility. He could imagine her wrestling with the problem until she had come up with this solution. Nothing could have kept her from Polgara's wedding, but all the niceties and formalities had to be observed. Garion smiled slightly as he turned back to the ceremony.

It was the expression on Beldin's face that made him turn again to look sharply toward the back of the chapel—an expression of surprise that turned to calm recognition. At first Garion saw nothing, but then a faint movement up among the rafters caught his eye. The pale, ghostly shape of a snowy owl perched on one of the dark beams, watching as Aunt Pol and Durnik were married.

When the ceremony was concluded and after Durnik had respectfully and rather nervously kissed his bride, the white owl spread her pinions to circle the chapel in ghostly silence. She hovered briefly as if in silent benediction over the happy couple; then with two soft beats of her wings, she moved through the breathless air to Belgarath. The old sorcerer resolutely averted his eyes.

"You may as well look at her, Father," Aunt Pol told him. "She won't leave until you recognize her."

Belgarath sighed then, and looked directly at the oddly luminous bird hovering in the air before him. "I still miss you," he said very simply. "Even after all this time."

The owl regarded him with her golden, unblinking eyes for a moment, then flickered and vanished.

"What an absolutely astonishing thing," Queen Layla gasped.

"We're astonishing people, Layla," Aunt Pol replied, "and we have a number of peculiar friends—and relatives." She smiled then, her arm closely linked in Durnik's. "Besides," she added with a twinkle in her eye, "you wouldn't really expect a girl to get married without her mother in attendance, would you?"

Following the wedding, they all walked through the corridors of the Citadel back to the central fortress and stopped outside the door of Aunt Pol's private

apartment. Garion was about to follow Silk and Barak as, after a few brief congratulations, they moved on down the hallway, but Belgarath put his hand on his
grandson's arm. "Stay a moment," the old man said.

"I don't think we should intrude, Grandfather," Garion said nervously.

"We'll only stay for a few minutes," Belgarath assured him. The old man's lips
were actually quivering with a suppressed mirth. "There's something I want you to
see."

One of Aunt Pol's eyebrows raised questioningly as her father and Garion followed into the apartment. "Are we responding to some ancient and obscure custom,
Father?" she asked.

"No, Pol," he replied innocently. "Garion and I only want to toast your happiness, that's all."

"What exactly are you up to, Old Wolf?" she asked him, but her eyes had an
amused look in them.

"Do I have to be up to something?"

"You usually are, Father." She did, however, fetch four crystal goblets and a
decanter of fine old Tolnedran wine.

"The four of us started all this together quite a long time ago," Belgarath recalled. "Perhaps, before we all separate, we should take a moment to remember
that we've come a long way since then, and some rather strange things have happened to us. We've all changed in one way or another, I think."

"You haven't changed all that much, Father," Aunt Pol said meaningfully.
"Would you get to the point?"

Belgarath's eyes were twinkling openly now with some huge, suppressed
mirth. "Durnik has something for you," he said.

Durnik swallowed hard. "Now?" he asked Belgarath apprehensively.

Belgarath nodded.

"I know how much you love beautiful things—like that bird over there,"
Durnik said to Aunt Pol, looking at the crystal wren Garion had given her the previous year. "I wanted to give you something like that, too—only I can't work in
glass or in gemstones. I'm a metalsmith, so I have to work in steel." He had been
unwrapping something covered in plain cloth. What he produced finally was an intricately wrought steel rose, just beginning to open. The details were exquisite, and
the flower glowed with a burnished life of its own.

"Why, Durnik," Aunt Pol said, genuinely pleased. "How very lovely."

Durnik, however, did not give her the rose yet. "It has no color, though," he
noted a bit critically, "and no fragrance." He glanced nervously at Belgarath.

"Do it," the old man told him. "The way I showed you."

Durnik turned back to Aunt Pol, still holding the burnished rose in his hand.
"I really have nothing to give you, my Pol," he told her humbly, "except an honest
heart—and this." He held out the rose in his hand, and his face took on an expression of intense concentration.

Garion heard it very clearly. It was a familiar, rushing surge of whispered
sound, filled with a peculiarly bell-like shimmer. The polished rose in Durnik's outstretched hand seemed to pulsate slightly, and then gradually it began to change.

The outsides of the petals were as white as new snow, but the insides, where the flower was just opening, were a deep, blushing red. When Durnik finished, he held a living flower out to Aunt Pol, its petals beaded with dew.

Aunt Pol gasped as she stared incredulously at the rose. It was unlike any flower that had ever existed. With a trembling hand she took it from him, her eyes filled with sudden tears. "How is it possible?" she asked in an awed voice.

"Durnik's a very special man now," Belgarath told her. "So far as I know, he's the only man who ever died and then lived again. That couldn't help changing him—at least a little. But then, I suspect that there's always been a poet lurking under the surface of our good, practical friend. Maybe the only real difference is that now he has a way of letting that poet out."

Durnik, looking just a bit embarrassed, touched the rose with a tentative finger. "It does have one advantage, my Pol," he noted. "The steel is still in it, so it won't ever fade or wilt. It'll stay just as it is now. Even in the middle of winter, you'll have at least one flower."

"Oh, Durnik!" she cried, embracing him.

Durnik looked a bit abashed as he awkwardly returned her embrace. "If you really like it, I could make you some others," he told her. "A whole garden of them, I suppose. It's not really all that hard, once you get the hang of it."

Aunt Pol's eyes, however, had suddenly widened. With one arm still about Durnik, she turned slightly to look at the crystal wren perched upon its glass twig. "Fly," she said, and the glowing bird spread its wings and flew to her outstretched hand. Curiously it inspected the rose, dipped its beak into a dewdrop, and then it lifted its head and began to sing a trilling little song. Gently Aunt Pol raised her hand aloft, and the crystal bird soared back to its glass twig. The echo of its song still hung in the silent air.

"I expect it's time for Garion and me to be going," Belgarath said, his face rather sentimental and misty.

Aunt Pol, however, had quite obviously realized something. Her eyes narrowed slightly, then went very wide. "Just a moment, Old Wolf," she said to Belgarath with a faint hint of steel in her voice. "You knew about this from the very beginning, didn't you?"

"About what, Pol?" he asked innocently.

"That Durnik—that I—" For the first time in his life Garion saw her at a loss for words. "You knew!" she flared.

"Naturally. As soon as Durnik woke up, I could feel something different in him. I'm surprised you didn't feel it yourself. I had to work with him a bit to bring it out, though."

"Why didn't you tell me?"

"You didn't ask, Pol."

"You—I—" With an enormous effort she gained control of herself. "All of these months you let me go on thinking that my power was gone, and it was there all the time! It was still there, and you put me through all of that?"

"Oh, really, Pol. If you'd just stopped to think, you'd have realized that you can't give it up like that. Once it's there, it's there."

"But our Master said—"

Belgarath raised one hand. "If you'll just stop and remember, Pol, all he really asked was if you'd be willing to limit your independence in marriage and go through life with no more power than Durnik has. Since there's no way he could remove *your* power, he obviously had something else in mind."

"You let me believe—"

"I have no control over what you believe, Pol," he replied in his most reasonable tone of voice.

"You tricked me!"

"No, Pol," he corrected, "you tricked yourself." Then he smiled fondly at her. "Now, before you go off into a tirade, think about it for a moment. All things considered, it didn't really hurt you, did it? And isn't it really nicer to find out about it this way?" His smile became a grin. "You can even consider it my wedding present to you, if you'd like," he added.

She stared at him for a moment, obviously wanting to be cross about the whole thing, but the look he returned her was impish. The confrontation between them had been obscure, but he had quite obviously won this time. Finally, no longer able to maintain even the fiction of anger, she laughed helplessly and put her hand affectionately on his arm. "You're a dreadful old man, Father," she told him.

"I know," he admitted. "Coming, Garion?"

Once they were in the hall outside, Belgarath began to chuckle.

"What's so funny?" Garion asked him.

"I've been waiting for that moment for months," his grandfather said, still chortling. "Did you see her face when she finally realized what had happened? She's been moping around with that look of noble self-sacrifice for all this time, and then she suddenly finds out that it was absolutely unnecessary." His face took on a wicked little smirk. "Your aunt's always been just a little too sure of herself, you know. Maybe it was good for her to go for a little while thinking that she was just an ordinary person. It might give her some perspective."

"She was right." Garion laughed. "You *are* a dreadful old man."

Belgarath grinned. "One does one's best."

They went along the hallway to the royal apartment where the clothes Garion was to wear for his wedding were already laid out.

"Grandfather," Garion said, sitting down to pull off his boots, "there's something I've been meaning to ask you. Just before Torak died, he called out to his mother."

Belgarath, tankard in hand, nodded.

"Who is his mother?"

"The universe," the old man replied.

"I don't understand."

Belgarath scratched thoughtfully at his short, white beard. "As I understand it, each of the Gods began as an idea in the mind of UL, the father of the Gods, but it was the universe that brought them forth. It's very complicated. I don't understand it entirely myself. Anyway, as he was dying, Torak cried out to the one thing that he felt still loved him. He was wrong, of course. UL and the other Gods *did* still love him, even though they knew that he had become twisted and totally evil. And the universe grieved for him."

"The universe?"

"Didn't you feel it? That instant when everything stopped and all the lights went out?"

"I thought that was just me."

"No, Garion. For that single instant all the light in the universe went out, and everything stopped moving—everything—everywhere. A part of that was the grief of the universe for her dead son."

Garion thought about that. "He had to die, though, didn't he?"

Belgarath nodded. "It was the only way that things could get back on the right course. Torak had to die so that things could go toward what they're supposed to. Otherwise, everything would have ultimately wound up in chaos."

A sudden strange thought struck Garion. "Grandfather," he said, "who is Errand?"

"I don't know," Belgarath replied. "Perhaps he's just a strange little boy. Perhaps he's something else. You'd probably better start changing clothes."

"I was trying not to think about that."

"Oh, come now. This is the happiest day of your life."

"Really?"

"It might help if you keep saying that to yourself."

By general consent, the Gorim of Ulgo had been selected to perform the ceremony uniting Garion and Ce'Nedra in marriage. The frail, saintly old man had made the journey from Prolgu in short, easy stages, carried by litter through the caves to Sendaria, then conveyed in King Fulrach's royal carriage to the city of Sendar and thence by ship to Riva. The revelation of the fact that the God of the Ulgos was the father of the other Gods had struck theological circles like a thunderclap. Entire libraries of turgid philosophical speculation had instantly become obsolete, and priests everywhere now stumbled about in a state of shock. Grodeg, the High Priest of Belar, fainted dead away at the news. The towering ecclesiastic, already crippled for life by the wounds he had received during the battle of Thull Mardu, did not take this final blow well. When he recovered from his swoon, his attendants found that his mind had reverted to childhood, and he spent his days now surrounded by toys and brightly colored bits of string.

The royal wedding, of course, took place in the Hall of the Rivan King, and everyone was there. King Rhodar was in crimson, King Anheg in blue. King Fulrach wore brown, and King Cho-Hag the customary Algar black. Brand, the Rivan Warder, his face made even more somber by the death of his youngest son, was dressed in Rivan gray. There were other royal visitors as well. Ran Borune XXIII in his gold-colored mantle was strangely jovial as he bantered with the shaven-headed Sadi. Oddly enough, the two of them got on well together. The possibilities of the new situation in the west appealed to them both, and they were obviously moving toward an accommodation of some sort. King Korodullin wore royal purple and stood about with the other kings—although he spoke but little. The blow to his head during the battle of Thull Mardu had affected his hearing, and the young king of Arendia was obviously uncomfortable in company.

In the very center of the gathered monarchs stood King Drosta lek Thun of Gar og Nadrak, wearing a curiously unattractive yellow doublet. The nervous, emaciated king of the Nadraks spoke in short little bursts, and when he laughed, there was a shrill quality in his voice. King Drosta made many arrangements that afternoon—some of which he even intended to honor.

Belgarion of Riva, of course, did not participate in those discussions—which was probably just as well. The Rivan King's mind was a trifle distracted at that moment. Dressed all in blue, he paced nervously in a nearby antechamber where he and Lelldorin awaited the fanfare which was to summon them into the great hall. "I wish this was all over," he said for the sixth time.

"Just be patient, Garion," Lelldorin advised him again.

"What are they *doing* out there?"

"Probably waiting for word that her Highness is ready. At this particular time, she's far more important than you are. That's the way weddings are, you know."

"You're the lucky one. You and Ariana just ran off and got married without all this fuss."

Lelldorin laughed ruefully. "I didn't really escape it, Garion," he said, "just postponed it for a while. All the preparations here have inflamed my Ariana. As soon as we return to Arendia, she wants us to have a proper wedding."

"What is it about weddings that does such strange things to the female mind?"

"Who can say?" Lelldorin shrugged. "A woman's mind is a mystery—as you'll soon discover."

Garion gave him a sour look and adjusted his crown once again. "I wish it were all over," he said again.

In time the fanfare echoed through the Hall of the Rivan King, the door opened, and, trembling visibly, Garion adjusted his crown one last time and marched out to meet his fate. Although he knew most of the people in the hall, the faces around him were all a blur as he and Lelldorin walked past the peat fires glowing in the pits in the floor toward the throne where his great sword once more hung in its proper place with the Orb of Aldur glowing on its pommel.

The hall was hung with buntings and banners, and there was a vast profusion of spring flowers. The wedding guests, in silks, satins, and brightly colored brocades, seemed themselves almost like some flower garden as they twisted and strained to watch the entrance of the royal bridegroom.

Awaiting him before the throne stood the white-robed old Gorim of Ulgo, a smile on his gentle face. "Greetings, Belgarion," the Gorim murmured as Garion mounted the steps.

"Holy Gorim," Garion replied with a nervous bow.

"Be tranquil, my son," the Gorim advised, noting Garion's shaking hands.

"I'm trying, Holy One."

The brazen horns sounded yet another fanfare, and the door at the back of the hall swung wide. The Imperial Princess Ce'Nedra, dressed in her creamy, pearl-studded wedding gown, stood in the doorway with her cousin Xera at her side. She was stunning. Her flaming hair streamed down across one shoulder of her gown, and she wore the varicolored golden circlet of which she had always been so fond. Her face was demure, and a delicate little blush colored her cheeks. She kept her eyes downcast, although once she flickered a quick glance at Garion, and he saw the little twinkle that lurked behind her thick lashes. He knew then with absolute certainty that all that demure modesty was a pose. She stood long enough to allow all to look their fill at her perfection before, accompanied by the sound of gently cascading harps, she came down the aisle to meet her quivering bridegroom. In a ceremony Garion thought just a trifle overdone, Barak's two little daughters preceded the bride, strewing her path with flowers.

When she reached the dais, Ce'Nedra rather impulsively kissed the kindly old Gorim's cheek and then took her place at Garion's side. There was a fragrance about her that was strangely flowerlike—a fragrance that for some reason made Garion's knees tremble.

The Gorim looked out at the assemblage and began to speak. "We are gathered today," he began, "to witness the last unraveling of the Prophecy which has guided all our lives through the deadliest of peril and brought us safely to this happy moment. As foretold, the Rivan King has returned. He has met our ancient foe and he has prevailed. His reward stands radiant at his side."

Reward? Garion had not considered it in precisely that light before. He thought about it a bit as the Gorim continued, but it didn't really help all that much. He felt a sharp little nudge in his ribs.

"Pay attention," Ce'Nedra whispered.

It got down to the questions and answers shortly after that. Garion's voice cracked slightly, but that was only to be expected. Ce'Nedra's voice, however, was clear and firm. Couldn't she at least *pretend* to be nervous—just a little?

The rings which they exchanged were carried on a small velvet cushion by Errand. The child took his duties quite seriously, but even on *his* small face there was that slightly amused look. Garion resented that. Was *everyone* secretly laughing at him?

The ceremony concluded with the Gorim's benediction, which Garion did not hear. The Orb of Aldur, glowing with an insufferable smugness, filled his ears with its song of jubilation during the Gorim's blessing, adding its own peculiar congratulations.

Ce'Nedra had turned to him. "Well?" she whispered.

"Well what?" he whispered back.

"Aren't you going to kiss me?"

"Here? In front of everybody?"

"It's customary."

"It's a stupid custom."

"Just do it, Garion," she said with a warm little smile of encouragement. "We can discuss it later."

Garion tried for a certain dignity in the kiss—a kind of chaste formality in keeping with the general tone of the occasion. Ce'Nedra, however, would have none of that. She threw herself into the business with an enthusiasm which Garion found slightly alarming. Her arms locked about his neck and her lips were glued to his. He irrationally wondered just how far she intended to go with this. His knees were already beginning to buckle.

The cheer which resounded through the hall saved him. The trouble with kissing in public was that one was never sure just how long one should keep it up. If it were too short, people might suspect a lack of regard; it it were too long, they might begin to snicker. Grinning rather foolishly, Belgarion of Riva turned to face the wedding guests.

The wedding ball and the supper which was part of it immediately followed the ceremony. Chatting gaily, the wedding guests trooped through a long corridor to a brightly decorated hall which had been converted into a grand ballroom ablaze with candles. The orchestra was composed of Rivan musicians under the direction of a fussy Arendish concertmaster, who strove mightily to keep the independent Rivans from improvising on those melodies which pleased them.

This was the part Garion had dreaded the most. The first dance was to be a solo affair featuring the royal couple. He was expected to march Ce'Nedra to the center of the floor and perform in public. With a sudden horror, he realized—even as he and his radiant bride went to the center of the room—that he had forgotten everything Lelldorin had taught him.

The dance which was popular at that particular season in the courts of the south was graceful and quite intricate. The partners were to face in the same direction, the man behind and slightly to one side of the woman. Their arms were supposed to be extended and their hands joined. Garion managed that part without too much trouble. It was all those quick, tiny little steps in time to the music that had him worried.

In spite of everything, though, he did quite well. The fragrance of Ce'Nedra's hair, however, continued to work on him, and he noted that his hands trembled visibly as the two of them danced. At the end of the first melody, the wedding guests applauded enthusiastically; as the orchestra took up the second tune, they all joined in, and the floor was filled with whirling colors as the dance became general.

"I guess we didn't do too badly," Garion murmured.

"We were just fine," Ce'Nedra assured him.

They continued to dance.

"Garion," she said after a few moments.

"Yes?"

"Do you really love me?"

"Of course I do. What a silly thing to ask."

"Silly?"

"Wrong word," he amended quickly. "Sorry."

"Garion," she said after a few more measures.

"Yes?"

"I love you too, you know."

"Of course I know."

"Of course? Aren't you taking a bit much for granted?"

"Why are we arguing?" he asked rather plaintively.

"We aren't arguing, Garion," she told him loftily. "We're discussing."

"Oh," he said. "That's all right then."

As was expected, the royal couple danced with everyone. Ce'Nedra was passed from king to king like some royal prize, and Garion escorted queens and ladies alike to the center of the floor for the obligatory few measures. Tiny blond Queen Porenn of Drasnia gave him excellent advice, as did the stately Queen Islena of Cherek. Plump little Queen Layla was motherly—even a bit giddy. Queen Silar gravely congratulated him, and Mayaserana of Arendia suggested that he'd dance better if he weren't quite so stiff. Barak's wife, Merel, dressed in rich green brocade, gave him the best advice of all. "You'll fight with each other, of course," she told him as they danced, "but never go to sleep angry. That was always *my* mistake."

And finally Garion danced with his cousin Adara.

"Are you happy?" he asked her.

"More than you could ever imagine," she replied with a gentle smile.

"Then everything worked out for the best, didn't it?"

"Yes, Garion. It's as if it had all been fated to happen. Everything feels so right, somehow."

"It's possible that it *was* fated," Garion mused. "I sometimes think we have very little control over our own lives—I know I don't."

She smiled. "Very deep thoughts for a bridegroom on his wedding day." Then her face grew gravely serious. "Don't let Ce'Nedra drive you to distraction," she advised. "And don't always give in to her."

"You've heard about what's been happening?"

She nodded. "Don't take it too seriously, Garion. She's been testing you, that's all."

"Are you trying to say that I *still* have to prove something?"

"With Ce'Nedra—probably every day. I know your little princess, Garion. All she really wants is for you to prove that you love her—and don't be afraid to say it to her. I think you'll be surprised at how agreeable she'll be if you just take the trouble to tell her that you love her—frequently."

"She knows that already."

"But you have to tell her."

"How often do you think I ought to say it?"

"Oh, probably every hour or so."

He was almost certain that she was joking.

"I've noticed that Sendars are a reserved sort of people," she told him. "That isn't going to work with Ce'Nedra. You're going to have to put your upbringing aside and come right out and say it. It'll be worth the trouble, believe me."

"I'll try," he promised her.

She laughed and lightly kissed his cheek. "Poor Garion," she said.

"Why poor Garion?"

"You still have so much to learn."

The dance continued.

Exhausted finally and famished by their efforts, Garion and his bride made their way to the groaning table and sat down to take their wedding supper. The supper was quite special. Two days before the wedding, Aunt Pol had calmly marched into the royal kitchen and had taken charge. As a result, everything was perfect. The smells from the heavily laden table were overwhelming. King Rhodar absolutely could not pass by without just one more nibble.

The music and the dance continued, and Garion watched, relieved that he had escaped the floor. His eyes sought out old friends in the crowd. Barak, huge but strangely gentle, danced with Merel, his wife. They looked very good together. Lelldorin danced with Ariana, and their eyes were lost in each other's faces. Relg and Taiba did not dance, but sat together in a secluded corner. They were, Garion noted, holding hands. Relg's expression was still slightly startled, but he did not look unhappy.

Near the center of the floor, Hettar and Adara danced with the innate grace of those who spend their lives on horseback. Hettar's hawklike face was different somehow, and Adara was flushed with happiness. Garion decided that it might be a good time to try Adara's advice. He leaned toward Ce'Nedra's pink little ear and cleared his throat. "I love you," he whispered. It was difficult the first time, so he tried it again—just to get the feel of it. "I love you," he whispered again. It was easier the second time.

The effect on his princess was electrifying. She blushed a sudden rosy red, and her eyes went very wide and somehow defenseless. Her entire heart seemed to be in those eyes. She appeared unable to speak, but reached out instead gently to touch his face. As he returned her gaze, he was quite amazed at the change that the simple phrase had made in her. Adara, it appeared, had been right. He stored that bit of information away rather carefully, feeling more confident than he had in months.

The hall was filled with colors as the guests danced in celebration of the royal wedding. There were, however, a few faces that did not reflect the general happiness. Near the center of the floor, Mandorallen danced with the Lady Nerina, Baroness of Vo Ebor, and their faces mirrored that tragedy which was still central to their lives. Not far from them, Silk danced with Queen Porenn. The little man's face bore once again that same bitter, self-mocking expression Garion had first seen in King Anheg's palace in Val Alorn.

Garion sighed.

"Melancholy already, my husband?" Ce'Nedra asked him with a little twinkle. Once again, even as they sat, she ducked her head beneath his arm and drew it about her in that peculiar way of hers. She smelled very good, and he noted that she was very soft and warm.

"I was just remembering a few things," he replied to her question.

"Good. Try to get that all out of the way now. I wouldn't want it interfering later."

Garion's face turned bright red, and Ce'Nedra laughed a wicked little laugh. "I think that perhaps later is not much further off," she said then. "You must dance with Lady Polgara, and I'll dance with your grandfather. And then I think it'll be time for us to retire. It's been a very full day."

"I am a bit tired," Garion agreed.

"Your day isn't over yet, Belgarion of Riva," she told him pointedly.

Feeling a bit peculiar about it, Garion approached Aunt Pol where she and Durnik sat watching the dance. "Will you dance with me, Aunt Polgara?" he asked with a formal little bow.

She looked at him a bit quizzically. "So you've finally admitted it," she said.

"Admitted what?"

"Who I really am."

"I've known."

"But you've never called me by my full name before, Garion," she pointed out, rising and gently smoothing back his hair. "I think it might be a rather significant step."

They danced together in the glowing candlelight to the music of lutes and pipes. Polgara's steps were more measured and slow than the dance Lelldorin had so painstakingly taught to Garion. She had reached back, Garion realized, into the dim past, and she led him through the stately measures of a dance she had learned centuries before, during her sojourn with the Wacite Arends. Together they moved through the slow, graceful, and somehow melancholy measures of a dance which had vanished forever some twenty-five centuries before, to live on only in Polgara's memory.

Ce'Nedra was blushing furiously when Belgarath returned her to Garion for their last dance. The old man grinned impishly, bowed to his daughter and took her hands to lead her as well. The four of them danced not far from each other, and Garion clearly heard his aunt's question. "Have we done well, Father?"

Belgarath's smile was quite genuine. "Why yes, Polgara," he replied. "As a matter of fact, I think we've done very well indeed."

"Then it was all worth it, wasn't it, Father?"

"Yes, Pol, it really was."

They danced on.

"What did he say to you?" Garion whispered to Ce'Nedra.

She blushed. "Never mind. Maybe I'll tell you—later."

There was that word again.

The dance ended, and an expectant hush fell over the crowd. Ce'Nedra went to her father, kissed him lightly, and then returned. "Well?" she said to Garion.

"Well what?"

She laughed. "Oh, you're impossible." Then she took his hand and very firmly led him from the hall.

IT WAS QUITE LATE—perhaps two hours past midnight. Belgarath the Sorcerer was in a whimsical mood as he wandered about the deserted halls of the Rivan Citadel with a tankard in his hand. Belgarath had done a bit of celebrating, and he was feeling decidedly mellow—though not nearly as much as many of the other wedding guests, who had already mellowed themselves into insensibility.

The old man stopped once to examine a guard who was snoring in a doorway, sprawled in a puddle of spilled ale. Then, humming rather tunelessly and adding a couple of skipping little dance steps as he proceeded down the hall, the white-bearded old sorcerer made his way in the general direction of the ballroom, where he was certain there was a bit of ale left.

As he passed the Hall of the Rivan King, he noted that the door was ajar and that there was a light inside. Curious, he stuck his head through the doorway to see if anyone might be about. The Hall was deserted, and the light infusing it came from the Orb of Aldur, resting on the pommel of the sword of the Rivan King.

"Oh," Belgarath said to the stone, "it's you." Then the old man walked a trifle unsteadily down the aisle to the foot of the dais. "Well, old friend," he said, squinting up at the Orb, "I see they've all gone off and left you alone too."

The Orb flickered its recognition of him.

Belgarath sat down heavily on the edge of the dais and took a drink of ale. "We've come a long way together, haven't we?" he said to the Orb in a conversational tone.

The Orb ignored him.

"I wish you weren't so serious about things all the time. You're a very stodgy companion." The old man took another drink.

They were silent for a while, and Belgarath pulled off one of his boots, sighed and wriggled his toes contentedly.

"You really don't understand any of this, do you, my friend?" he asked the Orb finally. "In spite of everything, you still have the soul of a stone. You understand hate and loyalty and unswerving commitment, but you can't comprehend the more human feelings—compassion, friendship, love—love most of all, I think. It's sort of a shame that you don't understand, really, because those were the things that finally decided all this. They've been mixed up in it from the very beginning—but then you wouldn't know about that, would you?"

The Orb continued to ignore him, its attention obviously elsewhere.

"What *are* you concentrating on so hard?" the old man asked curiously.

The Orb, which had glowed with a bright blue radiance flickered again, and its blue became suddenly infused with a pale pink which steadily grew more and more pronounced until the stone was actually blushing.

Belgarath cast one twinkling glance in the general direction of the royal apartment. "Oh," he said, understanding. Then he began to chuckle.

The Orb blushed even brighter.

Belgarath laughed, pulled his boot back on and rose unsteadily to his feet. "Perhaps you understand more than I thought you did," he said to the stone. He drained the last few drops from his tankard. "I'd really like to stay and discuss it," he said, "but I've run out of ale. I'm sure you'll excuse me." Then he went back up the broad aisle.

When he reached the doorway, he stopped and cast one amused glance back at the still furiously blushing Orb. Then he chuckled again and went out, quietly closing the door behind him.

ABOUT THE AUTHOR

David Eddings published his first novel, *High Hunt*, in 1973, before turning to the field of fantasy with The Belgariad, soon followed by The Malloreon. Born in Spokane, Washington, in 1931, and raised in the Puget Sound area north of Seattle, he received his bachelor of arts degree from Reed College in Portland, Oregon, in 1954, and a master of arts degree from the University of Washington in 1961. He has served in the United States Army, has worked as a buyer for the Boeing Company, and has been a grocery clerk and a college English teacher. He now lives with Leigh, his wife and collaborator, in Nevada.